I0590344

Dustjacket Cover Design—Tairelei

Copy Editor—Megan Visger

Maps—Virginia Allyn—https://www.virginiaallyn.com

Print Chapter Heading Art—https://lilaraymond.com/lettersbylila-links

Book Soundtrack composed by Lindsay Dills—Listen on Spotify!

CONTENT WARNING: Threats of Violence, Language, Explicit Sexual Content, Gore, Mention of Child Endangerment

TRIGGER WARNING: Violence, Death, Murder, Mentions of Drug and Alcohol Use, Parental Drug Abuse, Grief

FATE BELONGS TO THE BROKEN

EVERMORE

MIRANDA LYN

R E Q

LIBRARY

BEGGAR'S ROW

BATHHOUSE

TEMPLE

TEMPLE

CLOCK TOWER

CASTLE

GRAVEYARD

SCARLET DISTRICT

TOLLIVER'S

TEMPLE

MARKET

PERTH

SYNDICATE HOUSE

SINNER'S SQUARE

DANCING GHOST

MISERY'S END

GAMBLER'S QUARTER

TEMPLE

CASTLE

HALLOWED

SILK ROAD

BATHHOUSE

SILBATH

TEMPLE

CLOCKTOWER

CASTLE

THE MAW

GRIMWATER RIVER

THE PARLOR

SILK DISTRICT

RECAP

Let's take a breath and reminisce about book one, shall we? Our girl Paesha was madly in love. She had chased her lover into Death's Court to be with him, and immediately knew she needed to get the hell out of there. She loved Ezra, but her rose-colored glasses came off when he decided to be a douche and get a little too bossy with the Huntress, and she was like, mmm maybe you're not it. Mistakes were made. Bargains were bargained. And our girl spat on it and shook, promising that shiny fucker, Reverius, god of all the god shit, that she would find her own way home in seventy-five days and if she didn't, he could go ahead and take all of her memories of her whole family. (Including Quill, her ward, and her entire reason for wanting to go home.)

She was in Stirling for about seven seconds before this creepy kid stole her *memories* of being in love and pretty much anything to do with Ezra. Sounds suspicious... but whatever. So then she was just out there vibing, trying not to die. Naturally, she got locked up, tortured, watched an old man die, then was freed by Archer, Harlow and this beast of a man that left those Cimmerian fuckers in a pile of their own blood. She healed with the help of Archer's power and they left her to her own devices. It didn't take long to land herself in more trouble, which led to a face-off with the creepy prince, and then ultimately Thorne Noctus aka "giant beast of a man" had to claim they were married to save her. Oops. Kind of. But she knew she needed to find the Lord of the Salt and the Hollow in order to find her path home, so she went along with it, doing a little spicy dancing and helping in the kitchen until everything went to shit. Jasper, the old cook, got his arm chopped off, the king went missing, Wee Willy was a dick to Harlow, and we're just along for the ride. Paesha's pretty sure she has to help the Fray, a group stealing from the rich (the Silk) to give to the poor (the Salt). You with me so far?

Then, to speed this up because your girl needs to keep her word count down, Paesha met with some gods, became besties with Archer and Harlow, about died, (it was Jasper... GASP... not really because he was bound to Ezra, of all people), had to make a deal with Alastor to survive (who happens to be one of the gods her power descends from) that meant she was forced to find four people with broken souls and deliver their names to him. Meanwhile, Prince Farris was out there stealing people's power even though he had no idea how to use it. (Thank the gods, really... well, most of them. Probably not that Reverius fucker. Maybe.) Anyway, shit happened, Paesha realized Harlow is a broken soul, gave the name to Alastor, who then showed her a vision of Thorne Noctus, AKA Lord of the Salt, sobbing over a lost lover. She got a cool snowflake tattoo, someone danced naked on a bar and was bent over a card table, and then, well... That same someone ended up kidnapped by Ezra's goons, where she–I mean someone–found our little old king. A rescue was mounted but Harlow died and Archer... Our poor Archie will never survive the death of his beloved twin sister. (Moment of silence.) Oh yeah, he's the king's secret son... by the way.

We found out Reverius (remember that god of god shit and shiny stuff? Yeah, him) is actually Thorne Noctus AND... AND Ezra's *twin* brother. (As proven in the vision from Big Al's Remnants when she stood in the desert with one twin and BAM! the other showed up and shot her with an arrow.) One or both of those fuckers are trying to kill the Huntress and it's all very sad because our girl was falling in love with our nerdy little Lord of the Salt and his chipped teacup collecting, note passing, swoony self. But that's probably off the table, what with all the murder and stuff.

Anyway, fuck that guy because Paesha and Archer decided to be their own damn family and went after Farris. Archer and P killed the prince and she stole his power. They were going to give it to the Goddess of Time, but you know what? Why bother?

Then we found out the other world Paesha was trying to get to? It wasn't even another world. It was an extension of this world hidden behind a veil. And Thorne Noctus, god of god shit, he knew the whole time... THE WHOLE TIME. Fucker.

Paesha and Archer went rogue, her power overtook her, she broke the veil with her cool new shadow mommy powers, and all the while... who knows when the last time she saw Thorne Noctus was—because she sure didn't. But let's rewind and read the final scene with Thorne and Paesha through Thorne's eyes, as Paesha realizes who exactly she was dealing with. For fun, obviously, before the story really gets going and we pop back into the chaos.

PROLOGUE
THORNE 2 DAYS AGO

Two hours was way too fucking long. Sitting outside Alastor's office staring at the backside of a closed door, trusting that fucker to keep every secret when there was no bargain on the table, was a godsdamn risk. But I would wait for her. I'd spent half my existence waiting for her. Battling my twin brother, just for the chance to love her.

The door swung open and Alastor walked out, unrolling his sleeves as he watched me with a smile that turned my blood to molten lava. "That which was lost was found, Keeper. So sorry about that."

"What the fuck did you do?"

Alastor straightened his tie. "It's really about what *she* did that made the difference. Controlling these Remnants can be so hard. I'd imagine it's a lot like chasing your minions around and hoping they don't fuck shit up." He clapped a hand a little too hard on my shoulder and squeezed. "I find it's always best to start at the beginning of a story, don't you?"

I ground my teeth together as I flashed a feral grin back to him until he walked away, whistling Irri's song, his Remnants trailing behind him. He was angry. Still. All these years later. But I couldn't fight a war on two sides. And he'd walked the line so far, staying on my side of the secrets I'd built around Paesha, but I wasn't foolish enough to believe it was for anything but his own gain into the Forgotten. He needed her and he'd figured that out. Everything always boiled down to her. To the Huntress.

I circled Alastor's words in my mind as I waited, knowing he'd done something. Paesha had found something and—shit.

I fought every one of my dark desires to bring this place to the ground as I raced out of the Vale and up the narrow stairs into Stirling, not stopping until I rounded the corner where Paesha'd met the little boy I'd paid a sack of coins to pretend to make a bargain with her. Gods. Even in fury she was breathtaking.

She had him gripped by the collar. "It's not nice to tell lies."

I watched a few paces back as everything I'd built began to crumble.

"Please, miss. I don't know you. I swear it!"

"You know exactly who I am. You stole my story, remember? In the marketplace, when I first arrived in this godforsaken city. You took my memories of being in love."

The boy shook his head, crying because he had no idea who the hell this woman was. I'd taken that memory from him, just as I'd sat in the alley and taken her memory of Ezra upon her meeting with this boy.

"N—no, miss. I swear on the gods, I've never seen you before. Please, you're hurting me!"

"Paesha, stop."

Her head snapped up, eyes narrowing as she looked at me with so much fucking hatred, a lesser man might've stepped backward. Alastor had told her something. Or showed her something. And now all the chips would fall before I could show her why all of this was necessary.

"Don't you fucking talk to me. You're a liar. And I think you made a bargain with the Keeper of Memories to trap me here. You're a monster."

2

True. But I belonged to only her.

She hadn't figured it all out yet but she would. And when she did, the weight of my sins would crush her. I should have felt guilty about that, but I didn't. If she knew everything... "I can explain."

Alastor stepped around the corner from behind her, no fucking smile. No facade. None of his bullshit. Good. At least his games would be on pause for this. He flexed his fingers at his sides and his Remnants rippled. "No. You've told enough lies."

I had done whatever it took. Every move I'd made was to protect her. Lying was probably the least of my transgressions and Alastor needed to back off. I tried to command him to do so, but that fucking bargain mark on my neck rippled, reminding me of our most recent deal. He'd saved her life and in return, I could not interfere. I pushed beyond it, overpowering him for only a second. "This has nothing to do with you. Leave us."

"This has *everything* to do with me. Or have you *forgotten* she wouldn't be alive if not for my help? Nor would she have been rescued if not for my spies. She owes me two more names and it's time to collect at least one."

Alastor was cunning. Calculating. He never did anything without purpose. I wish I knew what he was gaining from this pointless task with Paesha. Why he'd forced her to give him names. But based on the marks on her neck, the glare on her face, he'd told her something. Alastor was forcing my hand, and he'd regret that eventually. It was always a long game with these assholes. Especially where she was concerned.

I stepped forward, reaching for her arm. I could probably still stop this.

She jerked free, ever the stubborn mortal. "No. I'm not going to be a pawn in whatever game the two of you are playing."

"No one is playing games. I've told you this," I said. Another lie in the bucket.

"You will take your fucking masks off when you speak to me. No more lies."

There was that bite. That spark of fury that would have made my cock hard in any other instance. But not this one. Because everything was about to break. She had no other name. And the only way to protect her from Alastor's entrapment was to deliver one myself. *That* was his fucking plan.

Shit.

His eyes flashed to me, arrogance rippling through his Remnants. "Give her the name."

She was far too clever to draw any other conclusion at this point than the truth. Which was a problem. Those stunning eyes, the ones that had haunted so many of my years struck me like a dagger as I saw the understanding on her face.

"You? Do you have a broken soul? Are you..."

Here it was.

"If you have a choice to show it... it means...You're a god? And you knew. You knew I needed your name, and you kept it from me. You really did try to trap me here."

The step back she took killed me. "Paesha. Darling. All of this is for you. Every life. Every choice. It's always been for you."

"Give me the name," Alastor commanded her, forcing a conversation that needed to slow down.

"Thorne Noctus," she whispered, but she knew it wouldn't work. Those names were a prayer, her last bit of hope in me going up in flames.

"I need his *real* name."

I held a fist tight at my side to keep from lashing out. From scaring her more than she likely already was. She wasn't a mouse. Not fragile. She'd never been, no matter how many times she'd reincarnated, she was always so strong. So fucking fierce. And she'd always been mine. Her soul belonged to me.

"Ezra Prophet."

My mind raced. My brother? Had she seen my twin and assumed we were the same? Every piece of information I had, proved he hadn't revealed himself to her since she stepped into Stirling. He'd bound Jasper to himself. He'd used the old fool to trap her. He'd sent his minions to capture the king and lure her in, but he hadn't otherwise shown his face. The only way she could have assumed he and I were the same was if... My eyes slid to Alastor. He'd shown her a death. And she'd assumed Ezra and I were the same. My blood burned like molten iron in my veins, each heartbeat a thunderous war drum against my ribs. I imagined tearing Alastor's throat out with my bare hands, watching him slowly heal only to do it again and again as he realized too late who truly held the power between us. But I kept my face a mask of stone, my breathing measured and deliberate. She needed my control now, not my chaos.

She'd said my brother's name and I hated the way it sounded on those perfect lips, but now was not the time to show her how fucking wrong she was.

"If you want to save her, give her your name, Keeper," Alastor said, as if he had any right to command me.

I looked her in the eye, gritting my teeth. Wishing there was another way. Wishing I'd been smart enough to see what the God of Lost Things had been orchestrating for his revenge. I should have known he didn't fear my wrath the second he strolled into that meeting and mentioned her lineage.

Releasing a fraction of my essence, I let the gold shine through, watching the fucking devastation fall over her beautiful features until it broke something in me. And then I pushed a little harder, letting the truth of my soul shine through. I was broken. Because of her. She'd broken me time and time again and I'd fucking let her. She'd always been my weakness. But I couldn't handle that look on her face. The reflection of my betrayal that eviscerated everything.

"My name is Reverius Hawthorne Noctus, Supreme Sovereign, the Unerring Arbiter of Beginnings and Endings, the Keeper of All Realms, the Keeper of Memories, and I'm so fucking sorry."

She didn't react at all. Didn't cry. Didn't blanch. Just stood there and said the name with no feeling whatsoever, as if she'd gone completely numb. "Reverius Hawthorne Noctus."

Frozen in place, I watched Alastor's Remnants rush for her. I ran forward, catching her before she hit the hard ground. But she was already gone mentally. Lost to whatever hell Alastor had planned for her. And there was nothing I could do.

"If you hurt her—"

"You'll do nothing, Keeper. As was our bargain. Remember? You cannot interfere." He slid his hands into his pockets with a smile. "Or have you forgotten so soon? Besides, what's a little mental anguish between family members?"

"You're not her fucking family. No matter what your power says, she doesn't belong to you. She can't kill you and take your place. Your blood doesn't flow through her veins."

Alastor crouched down, swiping a lock of hair from her face. "I've never been one to worry about a long life, Rev. Merely a vengeful one."

"Then go back to Etherium and spend some time with Kaelor. I'm sure he'd fucking love that."

"I think we both know that's never going to happen. Not until you give her back." He rose and his Remnants grew agitated, covering Paesha in my arms until she vanished. "We've got to get going, but enjoy your time," he said, before disappearing into his shadows.

Fucker.

I rose, straightening my tie.

"He's always had such a way with words," Vesalia said from behind me, her voice wrapping around my spine like the serpent she was as she circled me. "I'll be far less clever as I remind you that time is still owed to satisfy *our* bargain. As you know, I cannot take time from an immortal, so you must give it. I believe it was *five* additional days. My memory is fickle. Perhaps you could remind me what you agreed to when I let you out early to save our precious girl from dying. Again."

I was drowning in bargains for her. Dammit. "Now's not the time, Vesalia. Fuck off."

She laughed, clapping her hands together. "I see what you did there, Keeper. So clever. But I think it's indeed the perfect time. And no one would know better than me."

Her smile was ruthless as she looked up and grains of red sand began falling over me. Raining down from wherever she'd pulled them from. She'd always preferred the dramatics, no matter the cost to use power so frivolously. The sand swirled like a crimson cyclone right in the middle of the walk until Stirling faded and her temple appeared. Glass formed around me, effectively trapping me in her damn hourglass, once again.

I

THORNE
PRESENT DAY

Fuck.

2

PAESHA

Pieces of the shattered veil crunched beneath our feet as Archer and I walked away from Stirling, stepping without pause into Requiem. Or was it all Requiem? Or all Wisteria. Who knew the rules when two worlds, ripped apart for gods knew why, were reunited? Not me. And I didn't care either.

"Which way?" Archer asked.

I spun, sweeping my eyes over the city, realizing with a hitch in my breath that it'd changed. The footprint of Silbath was the same, but the rot was gone. Requiem was a realm of two sprawling cities, split only by a river. When I'd left, this half was little more than rubble and half erected buildings, barely surviving the wrath of a man gone mad. But everything had returned newer and cleaner, glistening beneath a sky that hadn't belonged to Requiem in my lifetime. One of stars and a moon, not of clouds and mist and rain. The street lamps didn't reveal the rats, but rather the glistening gold streets.

Archer let out a low whistle. "So, guess you felt like Stirling was slumming it."

"This isn't normal," I answered, feeling the drag on the last syllable as the world tilted. "What was that?"

10

"What?" Archer asked, whipping around so fast his blond hair fell across those baby blue eyes. He hadn't put his weapon away since we'd killed Farris, as if that would have saved him against a horde of immortals.

I pushed the back of my hand to my forehead, feeling the drain. Shaking my head, I looped an arm around Archer's and pointed. "The price for using that much magic is going to be significant. You've got to get us to the Syndicate house. It's nothing fancy, that's just what we call it. It's the only home outside of the city."

"Got it," he said, still staring at the buildings surrounding us.

"We're standing in the Gambler's Quarter right now." I leveled a stare at him. "Don't get any ideas."

"Give me a little credit," he said, eyes far too haunted for the happy man I'd known him to be. "I had no idea we'd be traveling realms today. I brought nothing but the clothes on my back."

"Same realm," I said, leaning further into him. "Don't forget the facts, do you hear me? Reverius is the god of memories or some bullshit and if you don't have your guard up, he might try to take them from you. If you see one twin brother, assume the other is close behind. They are identical and dangerous. I saw it, remember?"

"As if I could forget," he said with a glare. "You confronted the boy and Thorne—er—Reverius showed up."

"Yes. Reverius was holding his name back, so I wouldn't know he was a god. But he fucking is. And as soon as I gave the name, Alastor's Remnants forced me into a memory from the desert. There were two of them, Archer. Twin brothers. One led me there and the other killed me. They want me dead. I don't know why, but stay focused."

"I promise I'll never let that happen."

I paused. "Don't make promises you can't keep. Especially when it comes to the gods." I looked around, trying to anchor myself in a realm that was home, and nothing like it at the same time. "Behind this building is Sinner's Square. Don't stop. Don't talk to anyone. Don't take a single second to look at women. Keep moving. There's a line of trees behind it. Just keep going. It'll open up to—" I paused, remembering the way the tall grass in the meadow swayed like ocean waves on a windy day. The way the sun warmed my skin as Quilly and I danced barefoot, while I taught her ballet after Elowen had kicked us out of the house for being too loud.

Archer snapped his fingers in front of me. "Was that a complete thought?"

"Huh?"

"Behind the trees, what's next?"

I closed my eyes, yawning as my legs threatened to give out. "The meadow. Thea's forge. The bathhouse. That's it. You'll see the lights on in the house if anyone is..."

He pulled me closer. "It was a lot of power, Fingers, but at least it's gone now." He patted my hand. "I'll get us where we need to go, just keep moving your feet, okay?"

"I'm okay for now," I answered.

"Are we going to run into any trouble when we get there? Anything I should be ready for?"

I closed my eyes, letting my feet drag. "I haven't been home in almost three months. I have no idea what's happening here. Get me to the kid and I'll take it from there."

"And if Thorne's there?"

"Stick him with the pointy end."

He huffed a laugh as he pulled me through the alley, not his usual cheerful sound, but it was something. "He's a god. And not just any god, the Keeper. Sticking him with anything is likely only going to end in his wrath."

"Like it or not, he and his brother are hunting me, Archie," I said, keeping my eyes down as we passed the opium den my father had lost himself to all those years ago. It should have hurt less. I shouldn't have cared. But when the door creaked open, my heart jumped into my throat, just as it'd done when I was ten fucking years old, sleeping alone in an old apartment the Maestro had given me when I agreed to do his dirty work.

When a woman appeared with a fur coat and high heels, stumbling away from the place, I felt a pang of envy, knowing she'd likely seen him more recently than I had. But I'd made a vow to myself long ago that closed off my heart. And every time I'd opened it since then, I'd been burned. By two brothers, it seemed. Two lying, manipulative, murderous brothers.

"Paesha?" Archer asked, yanking me from my thoughts.

"Yeah?"

"You've got to move your feet, or I'm going to have to carry you."

I hadn't realized I'd stopped walking. "Sorry."

"I can see my reflection in the gold roads and it's weird. I kind of want to find some way to chip away that gold in case we need it."

I knew what he was doing, keeping me talking but deflecting. It wouldn't work though. I knew the second I was alone, my world would crash down around me. Not here. Not now. Not yet. But when I could be vulnerable, I'd likely break as thoroughly as the veil had. For so many reasons I couldn't actually think about that right now. And I knew it was the same for him. His pain was written across his face, settled within the moments he'd turned and didn't see his sister standing there. Still, he tried. If not for himself, then for me. Until *he* could be alone, I was sure. Truly, we were the same damn pitiful mess.

I managed a brokenhearted smile. "Archer?"

"Yeah?"

"If you're worried about pissing off the gods, I'd refrain from stealing from them."

"I said I *want* to, not that I'm *going* to. Pretty sure there's a difference between foolish and suicidal."

"A difference," I repeated, losing track of what we were talking about as we slipped past the tree line.

"What in the... Who... Paesha? Oh, gods. What've you done to her?"

I knew that voice, it wrapped around me like a hug, soothing something so broken, so shattered in my heart, I wanted to cry.

"I'm okay, Althea. Just drained." I managed to lift my head, taking in the wide green eyes of my beautiful friend. My sister by choice and not blood, but it was all the same to me. I drew myself to my full height. The world tilted again as if I'd stumbled, but I knew I hadn't. Archer would never let me. "This is Archer. I broke the world. I need a nap. And maybe a sandwich. Where's Quilly?"

"Paesha?" That motherly voice sounded so far away but before I could respond, warm arms wrapped around me. Elowen. Not truly my mother, but the only one I'd ever really known. Orin had shared her with all of us. And now, with him gone, she truly was ours now. "Is my boy with you?"

"He's not," I managed, as Thea stepped to the side and both women welcomed us into the Syndicate house, Archer's hand remaining firmly wrapped around mine. The sound of the door locking behind me did something for my soul. It reminded me that I was here, for at least a little bit. I was home and safe and the rest of the world didn't matter. Only the peace of these four walls.

Thea took my other side, and together her and Archer practically dragged me up the stairs. I was home. Truly home. With my chosen family. But it didn't settle me the way I'd hoped it would. Maybe later. Maybe I simply needed time.

For now, I had one goal. One face I needed to see. "Quill," I said again, fighting off every wave of exhaustion threatening to consume me. There was no part of me that could rest until I laid eyes on that girl, blurry vision or not.

Thea mumbled something that sounded like a warning, but I could only hear the deafening sound of the world fading away and threatening to take me under. My tongue was too heavy to string together sentences as the void within me, where the power I'd stolen had sat, echoed like an empty chasm.

But then she was there. Standing at the top of the stairs, the vague outline of her figure was clear enough I could see her cross her arms over her chest. "Paesha?" she whispered.

Had I not been fully supported on both sides, I would have fallen.

The sight of her sent a wave of relief so intense through my body that I physically ached. Every bruise, every cut, every magical drain, all of it washed away in the moment our eyes met. This child, this fierce little warrior I'd fought through hell to return to, was finally within reach.

"Quill," I breathed, trying to free myself from Archer and Thea's grip. My arms felt impossibly heavy but reached for her anyway. "I made it back."

She didn't move. Her small frame remained rigid, her silhouette blurred by my exhaustion but unmistakably tense. "And Deyanira and Orin?"

I swallowed, knowing I was immediately going to have to hurt her. The question hung in the air like a blade. I could feel Elowen tense beside me, her breath catching. How do you tell a child that the people they love are gone forever? But I never held back with her. I never wanted her to feel blindsided by lies, this would be no different.

"No, Quilly. They're not coming back."

Her face crumpled, the shadowy outline of her features contorting with grief. "But they have to."

I tried to pull free of the arms that held me, tried to follow her as she spun and ran down the hall, but I was struck with a wall of sorrow so thick, so impenetrable, it caused the void where my stolen magic had been to rattle, sweeping me off my feet. The world tilted violently. The empty chasm inside me expanded, consuming what little strength I had left. I was vaguely aware of voices calling my name as darkness crept in from the edges of my vision.

"I need to go to her," I mumbled as oblivion consumed me.

I woke to the sun pouring into my room, heating my back. It was as I'd left it. Everything perfectly placed, piles of carefully stacked books, clothes scattered around, trinkets that served no purpose on top of every surface. It was chaos. But it was my chaos. My collection of things that I owned. I'd started collecting these things when I was a girl because when you could afford nothing, everything was a treasure. That sentiment had never left me. But nothing here mattered at the moment.

I swung my feet over the edge of the bed, noticing Thea must have taken off my boots. I didn't bother to take a moment and let the feeling of home sink in. In fact, my feet barely touched the floor as I flew down the stairs, breath catching when I reached Quill's door.

But it was locked.

And worse, standing here in the hall, I was immediately immersed into feelings I didn't want to have. Anger, betrayal, sadness. This was her power though, the nine-year-old girl on the other side of the door. She'd had a birthday since I saw her last.

Her emotions bled into the house, practically seeping down the walls like honey in a pot. I couldn't shove them away. Couldn't fight the push against the betrayal I'd tried to forget. Her power sunk its talons into me and forced me to feel things I didn't want to.

Suddenly, all I could see was Thorne's beautiful face before me, inches from mine, promising to come home with me. To help me. He'd been so close, a breath away as he'd lied as smoothly as silk.

I could go back. Today, I could face him. Today, I could scream at him. The desire to do so, to lose myself in the anger and vengeance I wanted, was so strong I could hardly fight against it. These were my feelings, sure. But Quill's persuasion over emotions was so strong, she might as well have had my heart in her little fist.

I softened my voice, trying to hide the anger. "Quilly? Quill, are you awake?"

"She's avoiding everyone," Thea said, coming around the corner to stand beside me with a little white dog wiggling in her arms. "You've been asleep for two days."

I drew back. "Two days? Why didn't you wake me? And why is her door locked? And... gods Thea, you look like shit."

"Welcome home, P," she said, leveling a stare. Her light, bouncy nature was gone, her copper hair had lost its luster, and deep, purple rings circled her emerald eyes. I'd seen her nearly worked to death under the constraints of a one-sided bargain, and she'd still carried heaps of optimism and almost too much cheerfulness. But now, her mouth held a grim line as she dropped Boo, the pup, to the floor and knocked firmly on the door. "Come on, Quill. If you won't come out for Paesha, at least come see Boo. He misses you."

I ignored the pain in my heart at her words. At the tone of her sharp voice. She'd lost all patience for Quill, it seemed. I hated that for everyone. Thea and Quill had always been close and I'd never known that child to abandon her dog for more than the length of a show.

"It's worse in the hall. Once we go downstairs, you can't feel her power so much. Makes it easier to breathe. And think. The bathhouse is the best though, when you need to really get away. I spent three nights out there last week. And I'm not even sorry about it. Your turn," Thea said, yelling down the hall as she turned and walked away.

"Best go downstairs for a bit," Elowen said as she approached, looking me over. "It's not safe to linger in the hall while she's losing control."

"I've been doing everything in my power to get back to her for months. There's no way I'm going to wait downstairs while you try to coax her out. I've got this."

Elowen, the matriarch of this house, was in as bad a shape as Thea. She seemed to have aged at least ten years since I last saw her.

"Tell me what's been happening," I whispered, placing my hand on the locked door. "And why haven't we removed her locks? She's nine, for goodness' sake."

Although I was glad I'd said the right age, I hated that I'd missed her birthday.

"She's good most days, but lately, the bad days are really bad. And as time goes on, it takes her longer and longer to come out of her moods. There's really no sense in waiting up here. She won't be out until dinner at the earliest." Elowen took my hand. "We removed the locks weeks ago and she ran away. She'd only agree to come home if we put them back. To say I'm glad you're home is an understatement."

That didn't sound like the little girl I knew at all. I followed Elowen downstairs and into the kitchen, expecting to see Archer, but only Thea sat at the table—well, slumped over her folded arms lying on the table.

"The man I came with, Archer. Where did he end up?"

"I put him in Hollis's old room," Elowen said as she sat heavily across from Thea, grabbing a cup of something steaming and bringing it to her lips. "Haven't seen him since."

I lowered my voice. "Archer's sister was buried the day we came here. His twin. He's a really great guy, but he's struggling right now. We've got to give him some space."

Thea's head rose but she stared only at Elowen. Their silent exchange was louder than any conversation I'd ever witnessed.

"What?"

"He can't stay here," Thea said.

No conversation. No wavering. Just an immediate shut down.

"Of course he can. That's what we do."

"We used to do a lot more than what we're doing now, P. Quill comes first and if she grabs on to those feelings of his, it'll be devastation for all of us. We're barely holding on as it is. The Syndicate members won't come here anymore. Not since Aeris renewed the city. Things have changed since you've been gone. It's best if you get caught up fast."

"Who's Aeris?" I asked, looking between the two women.

Elowen shifted in her chair, showing her discomfort. "She's the Goddess of Renewal and the only reason Quill came out of her room the last time she'd locked herself in."

"Well, that ends today. There will be no more gods in or around this house. Period."

"So you just get to come back and start making rules about who my friends can be?" a tiny, angry voice asked from the kitchen door. "Maybe you should go back to wherever you've been hiding."

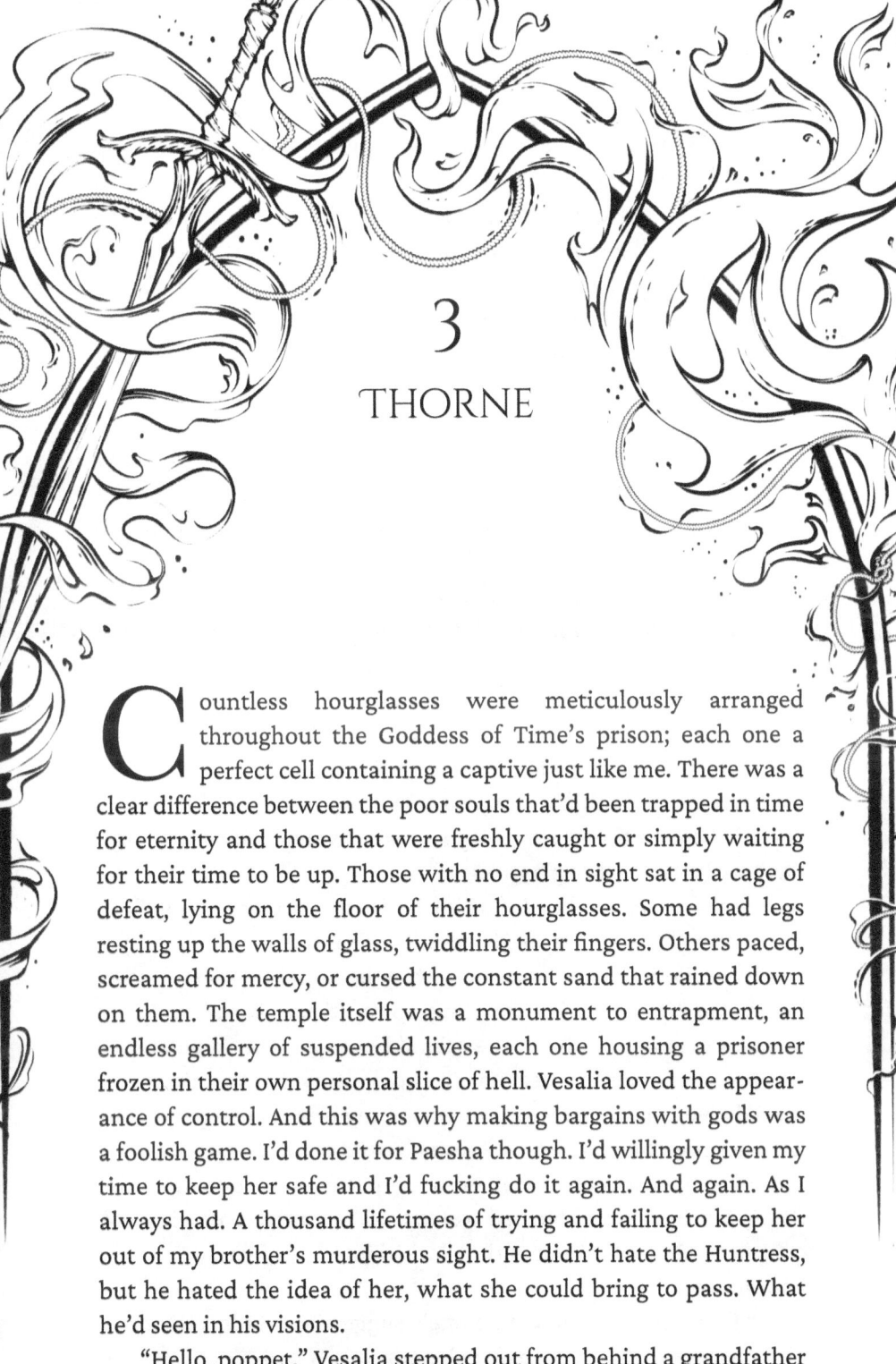

3
THORNE

Countless hourglasses were meticulously arranged throughout the Goddess of Time's prison; each one a perfect cell containing a captive just like me. There was a clear difference between the poor souls that'd been trapped in time for eternity and those that were freshly caught or simply waiting for their time to be up. Those with no end in sight sat in a cage of defeat, lying on the floor of their hourglasses. Some had legs resting up the walls of glass, twiddling their fingers. Others paced, screamed for mercy, or cursed the constant sand that rained down on them. The temple itself was a monument to entrapment, an endless gallery of suspended lives, each one housing a prisoner frozen in their own personal slice of hell. Vesalia loved the appearance of control. And this was why making bargains with gods was a foolish game. I'd done it for Paesha though. I'd willingly given my time to keep her safe and I'd fucking do it again. And again. As I always had. A thousand lifetimes of trying and failing to keep her out of my brother's murderous sight. He didn't hate the Huntress, but he hated the idea of her, what she could bring to pass. What he'd seen in his visions.

"Hello, poppet." Vesalia stepped out from behind a grandfather clock across the room. She sauntered forward, silver hair flowing behind her. She tapped her nails on the glass walls of my prison and smiled. "It's quite admirable to see the things you do, the lengths you will go to continue this game with Ezarius. One would think, after all these lifetimes, you would grow bored of the Huntress." She leaned closer, tapping again. "Do you ever wish for someone more... refined?"

"Not even a little bit."

She glanced over her shoulder with a wicked smile as Serene stepped into the room, wearing nothing but an equally daring smile. Her eyes locked with mine and she all but floated across the floor, stopping at my neighbor's hourglass to blow her a kiss before she joined the Goddess of Time's side.

"I know you remember what I taste like, Keeper. I believe you called it... divine nectar." She slid her hands over Vesalia's stomach and her dress vanished, leaving both women standing naked.

I crossed my arms over my chest, leaning my shoulder against the glass as I stood knee deep in red sand. "Which only proves even gods have to learn some lessons the hard way."

Serene's golden gaze dragged down my body and her power pulsed through the room. "I do so love it when things are hard. Shall we let him out to play, Vessie?"

Vesalia shook her head. "I think he needs a little reminder first. He is, after all, very distracted with his task at the moment."

Every lifetime, every sacrifice, every lie I'd told Paesha flashed before me. The revulsion crawling up my throat wasn't only for Serene's display. It was for the man I'd become. A manipulator. A liar. A keeper of terrible secrets. The irony of my title wasn't lost on me. I'd given up the scraps of my honor, my waning integrity, all to keep her breathing. And now Paesha looked at me with those eyes, those fierce, beautiful eyes, filled with nothing but contempt. The thought of her hatred burned worse than any torture Ezarius had ever devised. Any amount of time locked into one of Vesalia's many hourglasses.

Still, my skin crawled at Serene's suggestive words, memories of a mistake made in desperate loneliness centuries ago. What a fool I'd been to think I could fill the Huntress-shaped void with flesh. The taste of divinity had been ash in my mouth, every touch a betrayal of the only woman who had ever truly mattered. I pressed my forehead against the cool glass, welcoming the discomfort as penance. Let Vesalia and Serene play their little games. Let them parade naked for their own comfort. They could offer me eternal bliss, pleasure beyond mortal comprehension, and it would mean nothing. Nothing. My body wouldn't respond, and my soul, whatever remained of it after all these cycles, belonged irrevocably to a Huntress who wanted nothing to do with me. And that was the cruelest prison of all.

"Go find something more fucking productive to do with your time," I said, spinning around so I didn't have to look at them.

I knew Vesalia too well, though. The hourglass spun at the base, forcing me to face them as a few of the other prisoners shouted in protest to my words. It would always be about power. Even if I felt the flicker of hers falter, she *needed* to feel like she won something by trapping me. That was the real bargain. The stakes weren't about glass walls or her having power over me. Simply time. I was giving her time. And feeding her power with it. Every second I let her know how much this irritated me was a drop in a bucket for her. Strengthening her. I needed to be careful. Play the game I'd built myself.

"You will watch, Keeper. Or I will hunt her down myself. You're lucky I'm not already doing that. You do wish to keep the Huntress for yourself, don't you?"

I could lie to her, but she knew the truth already. "Get it over with, Vesalia."

Serene made the first move, snatching Vesalia's mouth in a kiss, filling the prison with the sounds of a feminine moan as she moved. She sent a wave of lust rippling through the room until every other prisoner was on their feet, pressed to their glass and watching. I almost felt bad for the damn mortals. So vulnerable to Serene's vast power, they likely couldn't help the ache to touch themselves. But that wasn't what intrigued me. It was the reckless use of her power in such a time. That she'd willingly used it for the chance of an orgasm.

There was a time when I would have demanded this show. Before the Huntress. Before my ruin. I would have brought these goddesses before me for pure entertainment, letting Serene's magic melt over me until I couldn't resist any longer and I'd join them, taking my pleasure from them, turn after turn, until all three of us, and any others that wanted to join, were well and truly spent.

But those days were long gone. Many, many centuries had passed since I'd touched another woman. Even when I'd tried, my dick refused and that was that. Which made me a challenge for the Goddess of Lust.

Vesalia dragged her tongue down Serene's abdomen, stopping at her navel before plunging lower. Serene spread her legs, grabbing Vesalia's head and guiding her forward as she made eye contact with me and slid her tongue over her bottom lip.

I clenched my jaw, fighting the urge to look away as Vesalia's head bobbed between Serene's thighs. The sounds echoed off the prison walls, mingling with Serene's breathy moans. Her fingers tangled in Vesalia's hair, pulling her closer, deeper.

"That's it, pet," Serene purred, her eyes still locked on mine.

I remained still, unaffected by their games, aside from the longing for the only woman whose touch I'd ever truly craved. Honestly, I'd expected something different from them at this point. Something more tempting to bargain with than an ancient hole. At least this little display of theirs was harmless.

Serene's back arched as she neared her peak, her breasts heaving with each ragged breath. Such a dramatic display for a few minutes of teasing. I didn't sigh, didn't look away, and I sure as hell kept my eyeroll to myself. They could entertain the mortals all they wanted to, but for fuck's sake I hoped they did it quickly.

"Don't stop," she gasped, grinding against Vesalia's face. "I'm so close."

With a final flick of Vesalia's tongue, Serene came undone, her moan of ecstasy reverberating through the prison. Her body shuddered and convulsed, riding out the waves of pleasure. As the aftershocks subsided, Serene pushed Vesalia away with a satisfied smirk. "Enjoy the show, Keeper?"

I met her gaze, my expression impassive. "So sorry. Did you want applause?"

"You could have a turn," she purred, reaching out to trail a finger down the glass. "Or you could have the night. You remember how fun we are, don't you? Or have you truly forgotten how to please a woman?"

"Yes. Let's go with that."

The look of pleasure vanished from her face as her true, vicious self showed through. Finally. "You're such a dick, Reverius."

"Aw, come on, Serene. I thought we were just discussing how much you loved that feature of mine."

She glared. "I'd rather ride it."

"And I'd rather be trampled by a horde of Hellhounds. You can see the disconnect here, I'm sure."

"I wish you would have bargained more time, Vessie. How long do you think you can hold him once the final three days have passed? Can he break things as well as his Huntress?"

Vesalia jerked upright, spinning toward Serene. "Stop," she said, grabbing Serene's arm. "Now is not the time."

Serene locked eyes with mine as she spoke. "But isn't it more fun if he knows?"

Vesalia spun her around. "Unless you're the one holding him with expansive magic, the answer is no."

Serene rolled her eyes. "Fine."

When the two naked goddesses left the room minutes later, I sank into the slowly trickling sand, replaying their words. What the fuck had Paesha broken? The only conclusion was impossible. Sure, Alastor was using her like his own weapon as of late, but she held none of Irri's power. Only his. The ability to find. Not the ability to break.

I'd seen that damn look in Serene's eyes though. One of truth and fucking triumph. Which could only mean one thing. She had broken something. There was no way she'd known about the veil though. She hadn't come close to figuring it out the entire time she'd been in Stirling. Besides, even if she was powerful enough to do it, I would have fucking felt it. My power created it.

Except our power was failing. And each move on the board came with a steep cost. But she was angry and if she wanted revenge badly enough, I had plenty of enemies that would tell her anything for a cost. And if so, maybe that was why Alastor was so enamored with Paesha. Not because she was his soul descendant. Not because she could find things like he could. But because she had Irri's power sitting dormant in her for all this time.

The walls of the hourglass closed in around me as I focused on the implications. On the words Serene had said. It didn't matter how I tried to spin it, there were no other conclusions to be drawn. She hadn't broken a bargain or bond. She'd figured it all out. And somehow she'd broken the fucking veil to get back to the Fera.

In all these lifetimes. All these hundreds of years, she'd never once come close to figuring it out without being told. But my luck had run out and the only thing left was a woman scorned.

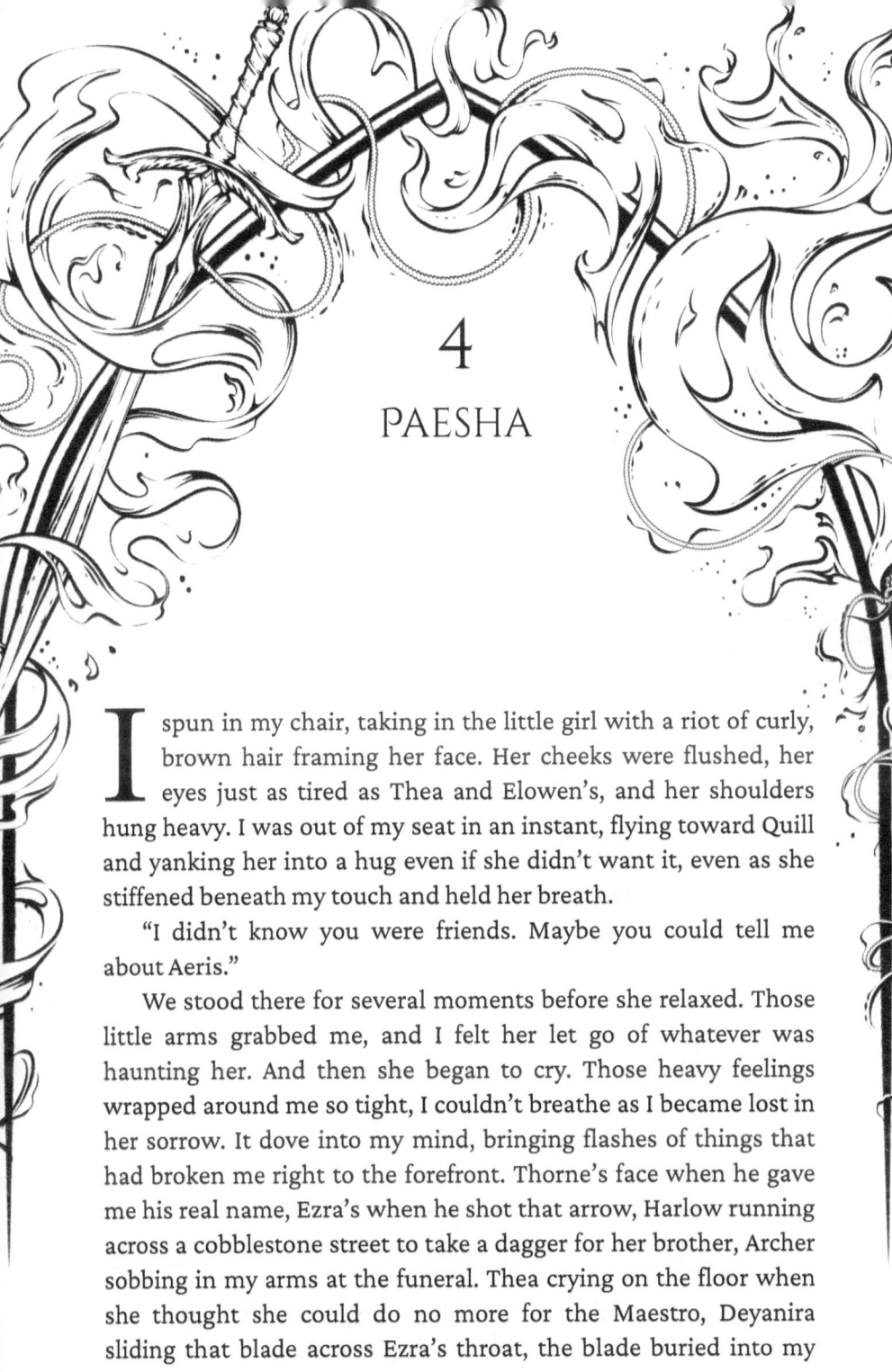

4

PAESHA

I spun in my chair, taking in the little girl with a riot of curly, brown hair framing her face. Her cheeks were flushed, her eyes just as tired as Thea and Elowen's, and her shoulders hung heavy. I was out of my seat in an instant, flying toward Quill and yanking her into a hug even if she didn't want it, even as she stiffened beneath my touch and held her breath.

"I didn't know you were friends. Maybe you could tell me about Aeris."

We stood there for several moments before she relaxed. Those little arms grabbed me, and I felt her let go of whatever was haunting her. And then she began to cry. Those heavy feelings wrapped around me so tight, I couldn't breathe as I became lost in her sorrow. It dove into my mind, bringing flashes of things that had broken me right to the forefront. Thorne's face when he gave me his real name, Ezra's when he shot that arrow, Harlow running across a cobblestone street to take a dagger for her brother, Archer sobbing in my arms at the funeral. Thea crying on the floor when she thought she could do no more for the Maestro, Deyanira sliding that blade across Ezra's throat, the blade buried into my belly on the Maestro's stage, his eager fingers as he moved them over the scar.

And then beyond that. To my father, walking away from me, leaving me cold and hungry. Even a glimpse of my mother, who I'd long forgotten as the door shut to the first home I'd ever known. Over and over the feelings of sorrow swallowed me whole, wrapping around my heart until I couldn't move, couldn't think beyond the lump in my throat and the ache in my stomach.

"I'm sorry you have to feel these big feelings, Quilly. You must feel so sad right now."

She nodded, sniffling. "Everything is broken."

I pulled away, swiping the tears from under those blue eyes. "Then it's time to fix it. What do we do when we have big feelings?"

"I don't feel like dancing today."

"Neither do I, but maybe that's why we should do it. Because we have to be in charge of our feelings and not let them be in charge of us, right?"

She nodded. "Probably."

I stood and whistled. "Boo. Here boy!"

The little white dog with long, golden ears came barreling from the sitting room, tail tucked between his legs as he wiggled forward, tentative to be too close to Quill, but his bottom still shaking as he licked my fingers.

"Hey," Quill said. "You never really liked Boo before."

I lifted the dog from the floor and snagged Quill's hand. "And yet, somehow I missed the little terror. When's the last time he stole a roast from the table? So I can gauge his naughtiness since I've been gone."

She managed a tiny smile as she reached for her pup, pulling him from my arms. "I'm probably not going to tell you so you can be friends."

"Speaking of friends," I said as we walked out into the meadow, "I brought someone here I'd like you to meet. When you're both ready."

She stopped, pulling out of my grip around her fingers. "The sad one that's also a little bit mad?"

I knew I had to be careful with my words. As Quill's power grew, she could either learn to navigate her feelings, or she would drown in them. And by the looks of it, she was already struggling. "Something really sad happened to him, yes. But sad things happen and we have to learn to process those things. We can't hold on to them." I knelt before her in the grass, though she'd grown so much, I had to look up at her from here. "Remember when Hollis died and we were all very sad? If I think about him for a long time, I feel sad. But I also feel so much joy because I got to know him. And then I think of all the nice things he did for us. Remember when he sewed a special pocket onto your blue dress so you could keep Boo's treats in there?"

"Yes. And remember when Boo ripped a hole in the pocket?"

"And what did Hollis do for you?"

Her gaze shifted between my eyes. "He patched it up."

"All feelings are good to have. We can be sad and mad and embarrassed and anxious, but we also have to let ourselves be happy. We have to hold onto that one the most or everything is dark."

"Sometimes I like the dark," she admitted, kicking a toe into the ground. "Sometimes the dark feels better."

I reached out, brushing a thumb across her cheek. "Darkness has a way of feeling safe, like it's the only place big enough to hold all our hurt. But remember, Quilly, darkness is where we hide, not where we heal. We walk through it, not to stay, but to find our way back to the light."

Boo ran around us as I pulled her into another hug and for a moment everything was right in the world. Quill's happiness rippled around us and if I didn't know any better, I would have sworn I saw the grass sway with the density of it. She moved away from me and threw her hands out sideways, tossing her head back. "Can you believe the sun is shining so bright? When was the last time we had sunshine like this?"

"I can't remember."

I couldn't shake the feeling that something was off. I'd wished for this, I'd dreamt of it even, but something felt wrong.

I saw movement out of the corner of my eye and looked over to see Thea and Elowen, holding each other on the step as they stared at that little girl in wonder. She'd been so broken, and in turn they had been, but they'd kept it together, severing themselves from the world because that was what it took to keep everyone as safe as possible. But Quill had needed me more than anything. She'd needed to be reminded that she was worth coming back for. She'd been abandoned by her parents just like I had. We were kindred souls, she and I. And some of my roughest days had been made brighter because of her.

"Are we dancing or what?" Quill asked, stopping to pin me with a glare.

Her mood swings were so sharp, the edge to her voice nearly stole my breath.

"Have you lost all your manners since I've been gone?"

She drew back as if she hadn't heard her own tone, then lifted a shoulder without answering. Pushing her while she was still unstable was not a good idea, but letting her trample over people wasn't either. That was where Thea and Elowen had landed and they'd only been able to endure a few months of it.

"You don't get to be unkind, Quill. No matter the darkness you crave, or the hurt you feel, you have a duty to yourself and the people around you."

She drew in a sharp breath and I knew she'd forgotten the way my words could bite. I wouldn't coddle her, nor would I walk around on eggshells and give her the upperhand. She was a child that needed boundaries.

Her glare was visceral. "I don't want to dance anymore." She spun on a heel and ran back to the house, darting around the other two.

Without thinking I sent my power forward, breathing at the release of it, not realizing how much pressure had grown behind the swell of it. I used it to follow her all the way to her bedroom to make sure she didn't run out the back door. She screamed, something crashed and not a second later everyone was running after her. Quill's bedroom door was in splinters all over the hall. The handle, broken into pieces, lay below a new hole in the wall at the end of the hallway.

Archer surged out of his room without a shirt, hair disheveled and rings under his eyes as if he hadn't slept in days. "What happened?"

I opened my mouth to answer, but Thea cut me off. "There were shadows. They chased Quill into the house and... Why'd your door break, Quill?"

Shadows. Fuck.

I whipped around, expecting to see Alastor there, dreading the reality that I'd lured the gods to the Syndicate house. But he was nowhere to be seen.

The little girl sat on her bed, hugging her knees to her chest. "Because I was mean and Paesha got mad at me."

I stepped over the larger pieces of wood, moving to her side as I put an arm around her, soaking in the fear. "I wasn't mad at you. Not even a little bit. I promise."

"Then why'd you send those shadow things after me?"

I looked up, locking eyes with Archer. I couldn't still be holding the power from the dead prince. I'd released that magic to break the veil. It couldn't have stayed with me, I didn't own that power. But then it must have been Alastor. "Those weren't mine. And they're called Remnants."

"I think they were yours, P," Thea said. "They came from where you were standing."

"No. They belong to a god named Alastor. Which means he's got to be lurking around if he was waiting for that moment."

Thea leaned on the door frame, crossing her arms. "Maybe it's time for you to tell us where you've been and how you got back."

"I don't even know what to say," Thea said, holding a cup of tea in her hands that had gone cold. "We all agree we hate Thorne, right?

Or Reverius or whatever his name is. But Ezra? This can't be right. We know him. He loves you."

"Maybe," I shrugged. "Maybe Ezra has loved me in my past lives too, but I always die at one of their hands. I've seen it three times, Thea."

Archer, now sitting with a shirt on, eyes a little more clear, settled back on the couch. "I was pretty sure Thorne loved her about two days ago, to be fair. Either way, they can't be trusted."

Elowen patted Archer on his arm. "I'm so sorry to hear about your sister, dear. She sounds like the kind of person we would have cherished around here."

He nodded, falling silent.

"Are you mad or sad right now?" Quill asked from her spot on the floor.

She'd been too afraid of Alastor's shadows to stay in her room by herself, but ultimately, she needed to hear how dangerous the gods could be too. And how hard I'd fought to get back here. Even if we'd left out the part about her burning down the realms. I'd catch the others up on that bit later, mostly because I wasn't even sure if it was true anymore. The only thing gods did flawlessly was fuck and lie, it seemed.

When Archer didn't answer, Quill stood, moving closer to him. Thea all but stomped on my foot to get me to interfere. But there was no point. They'd already been around each other for an hour.

Archer, being the decent man he was, lifted his gaze to the child and forced a gentle smile. "I think I'm a little bit of both."

Quill took his hand in hers and the rest of us held our breath as she closed her eyes. "All feelings are good to have, but we have to let ourselves be happy too."

For a second, Archer went rigid. Then he melted into a puddle, his eyes filling with tears as he stared at my girl, and maybe for a moment, understood why she'd been worth every second of my bargain. He smiled. His real, genuine Archer smile that was full of boyish charm, a thief's distraction, and a gambler's biggest win.

"There you are," Quill said, as if she'd been hunting for the man behind the misery. "My name is Quill Vox and it's very nice to meet you."

Quill Vox.

She'd given him my last name. My girl.

I knew she felt my absolute joy in that moment because she turned to look at me with a smile. "Is that okay if that's my name? And Boo too, because we can't leave him out of the family."

"Of course it is." And for the very first time in my adult life, I was proud of that name.

"It's nice to meet you, too, Pencil," Archer grinned.

"Hey, that's not my name."

"Oh, I forgot to tell you guys the part where Archie is the worst nickname giver on the face of the planet, and if you ever hear him call me Fingers, just ignore it entirely."

Archer laughed, Quill giggled, and the joy of that happiness filled the room. It was clear we were all high on her emotional roller coaster at the moment, but at least it was something pleasant. Thea laughed and the sound of it filled an ache in my soul, washing away the homesickness that'd settled in there. There were pieces of this place missing, but at least these two ladies were here.

Elowen's laugh followed, something deep and soothing that started simple and twisted into her shoulders shaking with laughter. Something hysterical bubbled up from within me. Tears of mirth streamed down our faces as the euphoria consumed us and the laughter took on a life of its own, feeding off itself and growing in intensity until the feeling burned white hot.

A flicker of unease started to grow in the pit of my stomach, wrapping around the regenerating power and coaxing it until I had to physically try not to use it. It was getting hard to breathe between the relentless laughing that seized my body. My sides ached and my head spun. Glancing around, I could see the others in a similar state, smiles far too wide, eyes laced with worry.

"Quill," I managed to choke out between bursts of laughter. "Quill, you need to stop. It's too much."

She cocked her head to the side, brow furrowed in confusion as she surveyed the room of hysterical adults. The mirth didn't seem to be affecting her.

"But why? I thought everyone wanted to be happy. Isn't this happiness? Aren't we all having such a great time?"

The nine year old was trying to teach me a lesson, it seemed. "Too much of anything can be dangerous," I said while laughing. The point was lost in the emotion swirling around the room. But she knew that.

"I find it really hard to believe you when you're laughing so hard." She stood from her spot before Archer and tucked her curls behind her ears as she glared at me. "Maybe you just need to be *more* happy.

Her magic struck me hard and fast, and before I could react at all, three sharp knocks at the door were followed by a voice I'd never heard. "Are you home, Little Bird?"

Quill spun around, yanking her power away as she ran for the door, shouting, "Aeris!"

Thea rose from her seat, the smile fading to a distant numbness. "What was that you were saying about keeping the gods away? In case you missed it, that's not the kid you left behind."

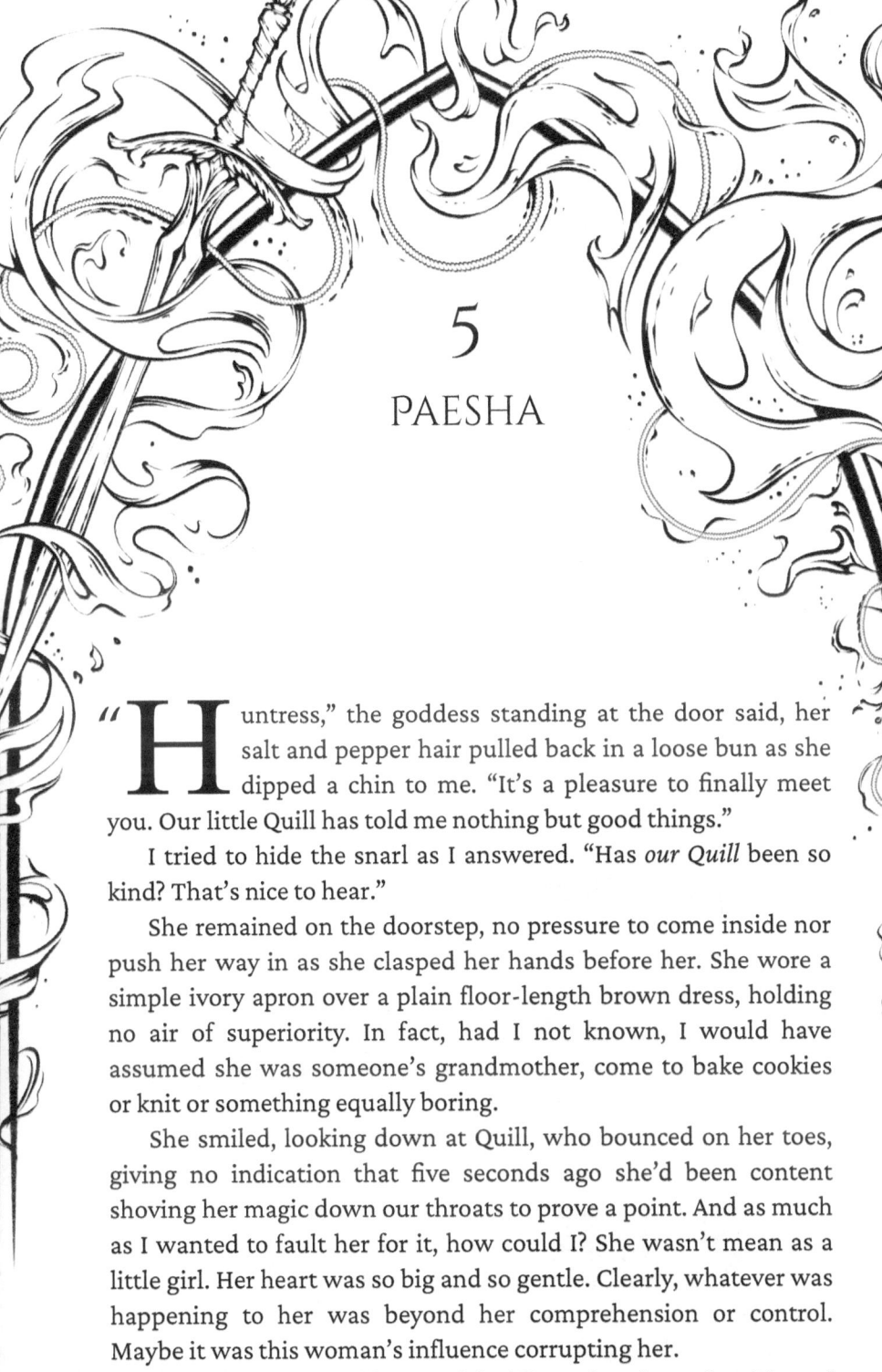

5

PAESHA

"Huntress," the goddess standing at the door said, her salt and pepper hair pulled back in a loose bun as she dipped a chin to me. "It's a pleasure to finally meet you. Our little Quill has told me nothing but good things."

I tried to hide the snarl as I answered. "Has *our Quill* been so kind? That's nice to hear."

She remained on the doorstep, no pressure to come inside nor push her way in as she clasped her hands before her. She wore a simple ivory apron over a plain floor-length brown dress, holding no air of superiority. In fact, had I not known, I would have assumed she was someone's grandmother, come to bake cookies or knit or something equally boring.

She smiled, looking down at Quill, who bounced on her toes, giving no indication that five seconds ago she'd been content shoving her magic down our throats to prove a point. And as much as I wanted to fault her for it, how could I? She wasn't mean as a little girl. Her heart was so big and so gentle. Clearly, whatever was happening to her was beyond her comprehension or control. Maybe it was this woman's influence corrupting her.

"I'm Aeris," the goddess said, holding a hand out. "Goddess of

33

Renewal. I've come to collect Quill for the day. I promised she could come along for my next project. I'm feeling quite inspired to take a look at the old castle ruins. You're welcome to come if you'd like."

That or leave Quill in the hands of a goddess? There was no choice here, not really. Archer and Thea came to join us at the door and the look of relief on Thea's face as she drank Aeris in was so discomforting, I had to look away. A goddess could not be the answer to Quill's tantrums. She'd end up in debt to them like she would have the Maestro. She was free. Right now. And I intended for it to stay that way no matter which god I had to piss off.

Archer's cool blue eyes met mine, and I knew our thoughts were aligned. Ultimately, his sister had died on a god's order and while I didn't have all the details of that night sorted, I knew for sure Thorne or Reverius or whatever he decided to go by today, had known more than he'd shared and ultimately could have stopped Harlow's death but didn't. That was a choice. So fuck him.

I narrowed my eyes, staring into the old woman's. Besides the fact that she was a goddess, something about her didn't sit right with me, and while I couldn't quite put my finger on it, I also couldn't look away. "I don't think we're interested in the resurrection of a bunch of old buildings."

"Hey!" Quill protested.

"It isn't only old buildings and borders that need to be renewed, dear. Sometimes it's hearts, sometimes it's more." She glanced at Archer. "Sometimes it's one's entire purpose."

Archer looked down at Quill, clearly trying to curb his anger. He simply turned and walked away.

"I've only just returned home," I said, snagging her attention back. "Maybe we could have a day together for rest and *renewal* here before we go venturing out into Requiem. Or Wisteria. Or whatever the name of this world actually is."

"It's always been Wisteria, dear. Veiling it away from Requiem was the severance that should have never happened."

Could I push? Could I trust an answer? I stared at the woman's unbothered face, tempted. Curious. "Then why did it? Why was Wisteria under a veil?"

"Perhaps if you come to watch, I'll tell you."

"No. I don't make deals with gods."

The woman's smile never faltered. "Perhaps that's wise."

"Come on! I don't want to sit around here another day. It's so boring when there's so much to do out there."

Her anger was my anger. Archer's anger. It was all of our distrust and all of our paranoia feeding her. Her rage pulsed and throbbed, slamming into me in relentless waves, setting my nerves on edge. I tried to push back, but it didn't work. It mingled with Archer's grief and bitterness, Thea and Elowen's despair and desperation, swirling into a maelstrom of dark emotions that threatened to drag me under. My own anger flared hotter in response. A lifetime of betrayals and lies rising up to choke me the second I was close enough to Quill while she threw a tantrum.

Lost in anger, I wasn't standing in the Syndicate house anymore, but instead swept away on the spiral of emotions controlled by a nine year old girl. Consumed by darkness, I stared into Thorne's hazel eyes as he drew back a blade and shoved it into my gut over and over. I lay in his arms in a snowbank while he twisted the blade with that fucking dimpled smile on his face. I stood in the relentless heat of the sun while he held me still and Ezra pulled back an arrow and shot it into my sternum. I was a victim. Over and over and over again.

I hated that I wanted to love him. Hated that I couldn't look at that face and see the beautiful man for the monster he was. I no longer wanted to try with him. I wanted to destroy him. I wanted to pull that blade from my stomach and shove it into his. But how do you stop a god? Kill a god?

I was being hunted by the most powerful two. I was in my home and they knew where to find me. Being here was a problem. I'd draw them in, and this house would become my final resting place. All because gods had to meddle and control and shove their will into everyone and everything around them until every damn choice was no longer ours. They took and took and took, and they answered to fucking no one.

The urge to lash out, to scream, to destroy something was overwhelming. I clenched my fists at my sides, nails digging into my palms as I struggled to maintain control. Struggled to come back to reality. But something lingered there in that anger, the eyes of someone, several someones watching me. Still, I left them, anchoring myself by cutting slits into my palms with my nails until my real body was the only place I could exist. Not in the fury. But rage was the only thing I could feel now. Quill's, but also mine.

I pushed beyond it all to turn to the child. "For gods' sake Quill, look around you. Look at Althea's face. Look into Elowen's tired eyes, and tell me you can't see your part in their misery. Still, they choose to be here every day. They choose to sit here and take these abusive emotions from you because they love you, and still you push. This is *not* how you were raised. And you may not like it, young lady, but it doesn't serve you to try to control the world. This power is dangerous.

"The world is so much bigger than you are. People are out there dying. People are being forced to do terrible things against their will. They are suffering, and you're standing here throwing a tantrum about having to spend a single day at home. It's safe here. It's warm. There's food. There are children a single carriage ride away from this front door that have absolutely nothing. There's joy if you would just allow yourself to see it. This world is broken, but you are blessed. You need to find a way to be grateful for what you have. Because this shit cannot continue."

"You don't have to be mean," she said, eyes falling to the floor.

I threw my hands on my hips as Thea stepped away, her fear of Quill's backlash warranted. "Neither do you. That's a choice you get to make every single day and you are failing. It stops today."

"I quite agree," Aeris said, looking down at Quill with a hard face. "We've talked about this. It saddens me to hear you've been unkind."

I wouldn't lie and say I didn't appreciate the woman's support, but I hadn't asked for it, and I didn't need it. I'd never spoken to

Quill like that. I don't think anyone ever had. But there were some lessons I refused to let her learn the hard way.

Quill's lower lip trembled as she looked up at me with teary eyes. "I'm sorry. I don't mean to be mean. It's just... it's so hard to control sometimes. The magic, the feelings... they overwhelm me, and I can't make them stop."

My heart clenched at the vulnerability and desperation in her young voice. I knelt and took her hands in mine, gazing into those troubled blue depths. This was my little girl. Destiny be damned, she was mine. And she was hurting and struggling and far too powerful for her own good. There was a reason they said she would destroy the worlds if she wasn't stopped. Because she held too much. That kernel of the little girl that I'd raised was in there, fighting for her life against all that power. Poor thing.

"I know it's hard and scary not being able to control yourself. But you can't keep lashing out at people with it, even unintentionally. Your magic is a part of you, but it doesn't define you. You define it with your choices, your actions, and your heart. And I know you have the biggest, most loving heart."

A tear slid down her flushed cheek. "What if I can't, though? What if the magic is too strong and I can't? I don't want to hurt anyone."

I wanted to promise her it would get easier, but I knew better. "Magic, like grief, doesn't soften just because we wish it would."

Aeris knelt beside us, sliding a hand down Quill's arm. "There's good in this world and bad in this world, and as long as you choose good, that's what your power will become. Change is never easy, little bird, but it's usually necessary. Even if we feel overwhelmed by it."

AERIS LEFT A WHILE LATER, accepting that I wasn't going to send Quill off with her, no matter the words she said. They could've been perfect, and I still wouldn't have done it. She had an angle, all gods did, and I would never bend to the whims of a god again. I needed one more broken soul to deliver to Alastor and then they could all fuck off.

Alone in my room, I expected to find Thorne in every moment. One second I'd be staring at a book, and the next he'd be standing there. But he hadn't come. Neither of the brothers had. Which should have felt like a battle won, but really, it felt more like the gasp before it all truly began.

Tossing the book I couldn't read onto my unmade bed, I walked to the window and stared down at the meadow where Archer paced, hands in his pockets, not quickly, but efficiently wearing a path into the long grass.

"What's he doing down there?" Thea asked, stepping into my room.

"He's doing what we're all doing. Struggling. I'm half expecting him to fall to his knees and start cursing every god until they show up."

"Not ideal." Thea pulled the sheer curtain away to watch him more fully.

"I thought maybe his soul would be broken after losing his sister, but it's not. He's sad, sure, but he's also so pissed off and I don't know how to help him."

She nudged me with a shoulder, and I turned to see that bright smile I'd left behind. The woman who'd been an optimistic toe bouncer when she got excited. The woman who'd promised to take care of Quill and did, even though she'd suffered from it. "You don't have to fix everyone. Some people have to learn to fix themselves. Let him be sad and angry and whatever he needs to be for a while. He'll come back to himself, I'm sure of it. Quill doesn't seem to be any worse than she was before you came."

"When did she start acting like that? I've never seen her use her magic against someone maliciously."

Thea stared down at the pacing man, lifting a shoulder. "I can't remember. I really think it came all at once. One day, she was dancing in the meadow and the next, Elowen was sobbing while Quill simply looked at her with no care in the world. She was tired of feeling Elowen's sadness, she'd said. So she showed her what it felt like."

"That didn't happen to be the same time Aeris started floating around, did it?"

Thea rolled her eyes. "Don't start. Aeris usually curbs Quill's emotions. She makes her happy."

"Sounds an awful lot like control when you say it like that, doesn't it?"

She didn't answer and I stopped pushing. The gods would circle and she would learn.

I followed her line of sight down to Archer, letting the silence bloom between us until I couldn't stand it any longer. "He's really great once you get to know him. He's funny, charming, and loyal to a fault. And I know that's still in him somewhere. But I guess you're right. We don't lose part of our souls and walk away unscathed."

She let the curtain fall and turned to face me, sliding her hands into her pockets. "You want to talk about the god?"

"It won't solve anything."

"So? I'm not trying to save the world here. I'm simply checking on you. Don't do the thing."

I drew back. "I'm not doing a thing."

"How many years have we known each other?"

"Too many, if this is going to lead into a lecture."

"You don't let people in because you know doing that gives them the power to hurt you. But you did. And then he did. And now you're not being honest with yourself about it. You're standing there telling me you're worried about Archer, but you're not even slightly concerned for yourself? He's going to be fine, but so are you. As soon as you realize broken stuff stays that way until you fix it."

"There's nothing to fix. Didn't you hear what I said? Thorne's a liar. He tried to bind me, Thea. He tried to force me to stay there."

"But isn't there... here? It's one world, right?"

"Don't you dare try to justify a single one of his actions."

She cowered back. "I'm not. Calm down, gods. I'm only trying to understand it."

I spun away, forcing my racing heart to calm. Forcing breaths to settle myself. To curb the mood swing from the remnants of Quill's overbearing power. "I'm sorry. I just can't talk about him."

My gaze slid over the familiar things in my room. The faded quilt on the bed, handmade by Hollis when I first came to live here. The stack of worn books piled haphazardly on the nightstand and all over the floor, covers faded from countless rereads. The collection of oddities and trinkets lining the shelves, sparkly rocks, dried flowers, a bird skull, mementos of a lifetime spent surviving on scraps and treasuring every little thing. The only thing missing was a little chipped teacup. But maybe I didn't need that anymore. Maybe I didn't need any of this shit anymore. Maybe the costumes for the stage could burn and maybe the things I'd collected in a desperate need to have something to my name could all go. Maybe I wasn't that person anymore, either. Maybe I had no idea who I was.

Something burned inside me as I took in these relics of my past, of the girl I used to be, a strange pressure building in my chest. It felt almost like the ache of homesickness, the yearning to belong. But the feeling grew like a storm surge, filling my veins with crackling energy. It was more than restlessness or wanderlust, more than the urge to shed my old skin. This was something elemental, a force of nature straining at the seams of who I was and who I'd been.

I rubbed my temples as a dull ache throbbed behind my eyes, building into relentless irritation. Everything felt too close, too confining, the once comforting clutter of my room now a chaotic mess, pressing in on me. I needed space, I needed to move, to release this building tension before it tore me apart.

Thea was there in an instant, her hand on my arm, staring into my eyes. "What's wrong?"

I gritted my teeth, shaking my head. "Suddenly, everything is too much."

We're too much?

We've never been too much.
We've never been enough.
To make them stop.
To make them pay.

"What?" I snapped, spinning away to see where those voices had come from.

"Huh?" Thea asked.

"Did you say something?"

She took my hands. "I think you might need a nap."

"I don't—"

Movement from the window caught my eye, and I turned to find Quill and Boo running across the yard toward Archer. Suddenly, nothing but *that* mattered. Would she hurt him? Was he hurting her by hurting too much?

Thea took my side, holding her breath just as I did, as Quill reached a hand out toward him, and he took it. And then they walked together. Side by side. Pacing still, but together, with a little dog following.

"That's... surprising," Thea whispered.

"I know you don't know him, but I'm telling you, he will be a balm for her. Once he finds himself again, he will be her joy." I straightened, an idea forming. "In your room, in the chest at the foot of your bed, there's a red dress, and under that on top of a stack of notebooks, there's a deck of cards. Will you go grab it? I know what we're going to do tonight."

We needed fun. We needed to find a normal. We definitely didn't need to discuss weird voices I'd absolutely just heard in my head, coated in a power that hadn't actually left me.

6

PAESHA

He was smiling. There was still sadness behind his eyes, a crinkle at the corner that may permanently be there for Harlow, but Archer was beaming at Quill as she flipped over the Maid Marian card and giggled. She was there too. Not an ounce of the kid that was out of control, angry and suffering, but instead the little girl that flew into my arms when she was only two years old, and again a hundred days later when I'd finally put down my walls to let her in. This was home. Family. Where we weren't perfect, but we were figuring it out and leaning on each other instead of the outside world that would sooner see us burn than thrive.

Elowen sat with me on the couch, a steaming cup of tea in her hands as usual, with her eyes closed as she breathed in a feeling of peace I was sure she hadn't felt in a while.

"How'd you land here in the Syndicate house, of all places, Fingers?" Archer asked, shuffling the cards.

I narrowed my eyes, mostly at the damn nickname. "That's a long story, Toes."

"You don't have to chisel it onto stone, you know. Simply move your mouth and make some sound."

It felt a little strange. Even though I'd brought him here, opening up about my past with Archer was odd. Like it was somehow giving him a part of me that was only mine. Still, I answered, forcing myself to let go. "You have to understand a few things about Requiem before I can give you the whole story. Requiem is only two cities, Perth and Silbath. They each had a ruling king at this time last year, but really, the only thing dividing the space is the Hallowed River."

"Really irrelevant to your story," Thea said, gathering the cards spread on the coffee table as she sat cross-legged on the floor. She wiggled her shoulders, and Archer and I exchanged a look.

"You'd be a terrible gambler, Thea. You always give away your hand."

She wrinkled her nose, pressing the cards to her chest. "I do not."

Archer smirked. "I bet you have at least five cards higher than five."

"How much do you bet?" she asked innocently.

Archer reached forward and pretended to pull a brass button from Quill's ear. I'd seen him pop it off his jacket seconds before, and wondered what he was up to, but I hadn't predicted a parlor trick. He flipped it in the air, caught it and set it down in front of her. "One button."

Thea slid her hand over the button, studied the odd markings, and then closed it in her fist. Her eyes twinkled as she used her power then opened her palm to show Archer, letting the brass necklace fall from her fingers onto the table.

"Hey!" Archer stood from his spot on the floor and lifted the necklace, staring at the small chain in the light. "How'd you—" he spun to me. "You could have mentioned that."

"It wasn't my secret to share."

Quill leaned onto the table with her elbows. "Thea has the best collection of weapons you've ever seen. But she won't let anyone use them."

"Especially not you," she said, tapping Quill on the nose. "I joined the Syndicate house when I was probably twenty-five. My older grandparents raised me, and they both had their one-hundredth year celebration and then I was on my own." She flipped her whole hand, fanning the cards out on the table. "I love shiny jewelry as much as the next girl, but you can have your button back. Seems unfair to take it."

She smothered the necklace in her hand and revealed the original button before flipping it to Archer. He swiped it out of the air and tossed it back. "A deal's a deal. But if you can make buttons, can't you make coin?"

She snorted. "If I had a desire, I'd try harder, but one, it never works because our coin is made from really fragile compound metals and it usually disintegrates. And two, if people thought I could make money, they'd hunt and enslave me. I've done that once before and I have no desire to ever go back. But I'm pretty sure we were talking about Paesha's past and not mine."

"I was explaining how Requiem used to be before," I waved my hand toward the door, "all of that. Requiem has always been a place of depravity and rot, honestly. Some were wealthier, sure, but not like the Silk back in Stirling. Everyone struggled. Except a select few. When my father lost our home, he turned to the only crime lord in the city. The Maestro. And the Maestro had magic. He could bind you to him with a deal and you were stuck forever.

"He wanted to collect me since I was a child. As soon as he learned about my power, he tried. And at first, I was too young to become his. But as I grew, I learned. My mom left when I was too young to remember, and I loved my father, but he was nothing more than a pawn for the Maestro to move around until he could get to me. He introduced my father to opioids and found reasons for him to stay in the dens. I was alone on the streets by the time I was eight.

"I used to sneak into the ballet for warmth. And I'd lie on the balcony and watch the dancers. The Maestro was trying to win me over when I was too young to be trapped in a bargain with him, so he secured me a spot in her school. Madame Fourth taught me everything. I loved her like I'd never loved anyone in my life. Ballet gave me my first true experience with human connection."

I sat back on the couch, wondering when the last time I thought of that old woman was. Why I'd let her go from my mind. But then I knew the answer. There was so much pain wrapped in those memories, it was easier to forget.

"That's why you dance?" Archer asked, his card game forgotten.

I nodded. "The Maestro gave me a small apartment because I had agreed to do jobs for him as a teenager. I wasn't bound, but I still helped him hunt down things and people so I didn't go cold and hungry, and I went back to that studio every chance I got. Until Madame Fourth had her hundred-year, end-of-life celebration and died. Then the theater closed, and I pressed to dance at Misery's End because I missed the stage. That's the burlesque theater. Or it was. He held off for a long time, assuming that stage was the last thing he could try to bind me with when I became of age. But when I fought back and stopped running jobs for him, he agreed to let me dance without a bargain."

My eyes flashed to Thea, and she smiled, knowing where the story was headed. "Keep going."

"I made friends with this spirited little red-head that was already bound to him. She built structures for his stage, making his shows grow in popularity, until the people were doing nothing but collecting coin for a couple hours of raunchy entertainment. She brought me here, and I realized I already knew most of the Syndicate members. I'd been friends with Orin, Elowen's son, for a long time already. I just fit here, mixed in with these people that were simply trying to help others. Exactly like the Fray. Then, I met a man." My heart stopped, my whole world plummeting as I realized what I was saying. "Gods, I was so dumb. I never questioned a thing. This man shows up, claims he can't remember his childhood, the Maestro has him bound within a day and bam, he was some project I had to fix. And fuck if I didn't love him. I fell hard and fast and I never once looked back."

I swallowed, the breaths harder to drag in now that I realized everything had been a lie. All of it. All my memories. Every feeling of being in love. I was so overwhelmed by the truth of it all, I forgot the point of the story. Forgot the important details as I looked back and realized my past was not real.

"We believed him to be a good man, too," Elowen said, taking my hand. "Ezra had been a fierce man at your side since day one."

I nodded, falling numb to avoid the anger that would fester. Anger I wasn't ready to deal with yet. "There was an incident on stage. I was stabbed by a jealous dancer. Told I couldn't have children." Glancing at Quill, who sat silently on the floor beside Archer, she shared a smile and nodded. She'd heard this story enough times, though it was the version laced with the lies of hunting gods and not at all reality. It wasn't love. "The Maestro tried to trade my freedom for Quill. He tried to bind me in a bargain, giving me this precious child, if I would simply become *his* Huntress. The hardest thing I ever had to do was look Ezra in the face before telling the Maestro no. Because as much as I wanted that little girl, I needed my freedom more. I'd learned to be stubborn from the streets and that never left me."

"But I'm still yours," Quill said, standing to come sit beside me. "I'm yours and you're mine, and our story is still special. Tell him how we got to be family."

"I think he's had enough sob stories for one day."

"I'll be the judge of that," Archer said, shoving the deck into his pocket. "I've known you for months and not known you at all. Keep going."

"It took me years," Thea said. "Paesha doesn't talk about her past."

"I don't think I've ever heard the whole story," Elowen agreed, setting her cup on the table. "I knew you and Madame Fourth were close, but I didn't realize how long you'd been with her."

"There's not much else to tell. I wouldn't bind myself for the kid. The boss got pissed and realized he'd have to do something with her in the meantime, so she became a job, a tease more than anything. Something that was never quite mine, but still very much mine to care for. He knew she was powerful, but he also knew he couldn't have *her* yet either, so he made me her weakness. He thought he could control me through Ezra and then ultimately control her through me. He played chess in a world of checkers, and we were all his pawns."

"How'd you end up in Stirling? Aside from the deal, I know that part."

"Hey, I don't know that part," Quill shot back, refusing to let me skip the most painful part.

I wrung my hands in my lap, wondering how I could get through it all. But I couldn't. The words sat there. *He* sat there, waiting for me to get to him. His eyebrow lifted, that fucking face he made when he had some point to make, and I just couldn't move in his direction. I didn't want to. I wanted to refuse to feel it, refuse to relive it. Those moments were nothing.

Thea was my saving grace, coming in to tell the bits she knew of the story. "Everyone here had one hundred years of immortality, unless Death's Maiden bore your name on her palm. She killed for Death, as was her duty. She got Ezra's name. Paesha saw her hunting Ezra and went to the boss. She bargained away her freedom for his life."

I swallowed the lump in my throat, hating the way it all laid out. Hating the way the truth hurt so fucking much. The way it rattled my power as if forcing it to wake up. To see what I couldn't see back then. It nearly swallowed me whole as it grew within me. It was too much. It'd been too much since the day I took something that never belonged to me. But it was mine now. Mine to feel. Mine to protect.

Mine.

I took a steady breath. "I was devastated and desperate and didn't see the loophole until it was too late. The boss promised me he could stop Death, and I'd seen him working with the bastard, so I knew he could. I believed it so strongly. But within the deal, after the terms were met, he slipped in the word 'try' instead of will. I missed it, agreed, and then it was over. Ezra died. And I was ruined by it. I didn't eat, didn't sleep, couldn't dance. Couldn't look at anyone and find happiness again. Not even Quill's power could change my devastation."

"I bet it could now," she said with a grin.

47

Archer nodded. "You could melt the paint off the walls with that power now, kid. And that's not at all creepy," he said a bit quieter.

The pink that danced across her cheeks drew me back into the room. "Anyway, there was a way for me to see him again. Death's Maiden needed to get to Death's court and only I could take her. So I did, because I knew he'd be on the other end. And I always thought I'd find my way back here after I had just one more night with him. But then I got there, and he didn't want me to leave. He never acted like he was a god, never told me the truth at all. I don't know why. But I couldn't stay in Death's Court. I knew Quill needed me and my soul didn't feel right. I wasn't supposed to be living in a realm of people touched by death. So, I made the bargain, and you know the rest. I broke the veil and here we are."

"No thanks to Thorne," Archer said, leaning back on his hands. "Still can't believe all of that was a lie."

It's what he does.

He lies.

He loves and lies.

I pressed my hands to my temples as the whispers grew louder, a chorus of voices speaking truths I wasn't ready to hear. My power recognized them, reached for them like they were pieces of itself finally coming home.

"Something's wrong," I whispered, and in that moment, I realized with terrifying clarity these weren't memories breaking through.

They were warnings. And one voice cut through the others, clear as a bell, cold as the grave. *You know he will come. They both will.*

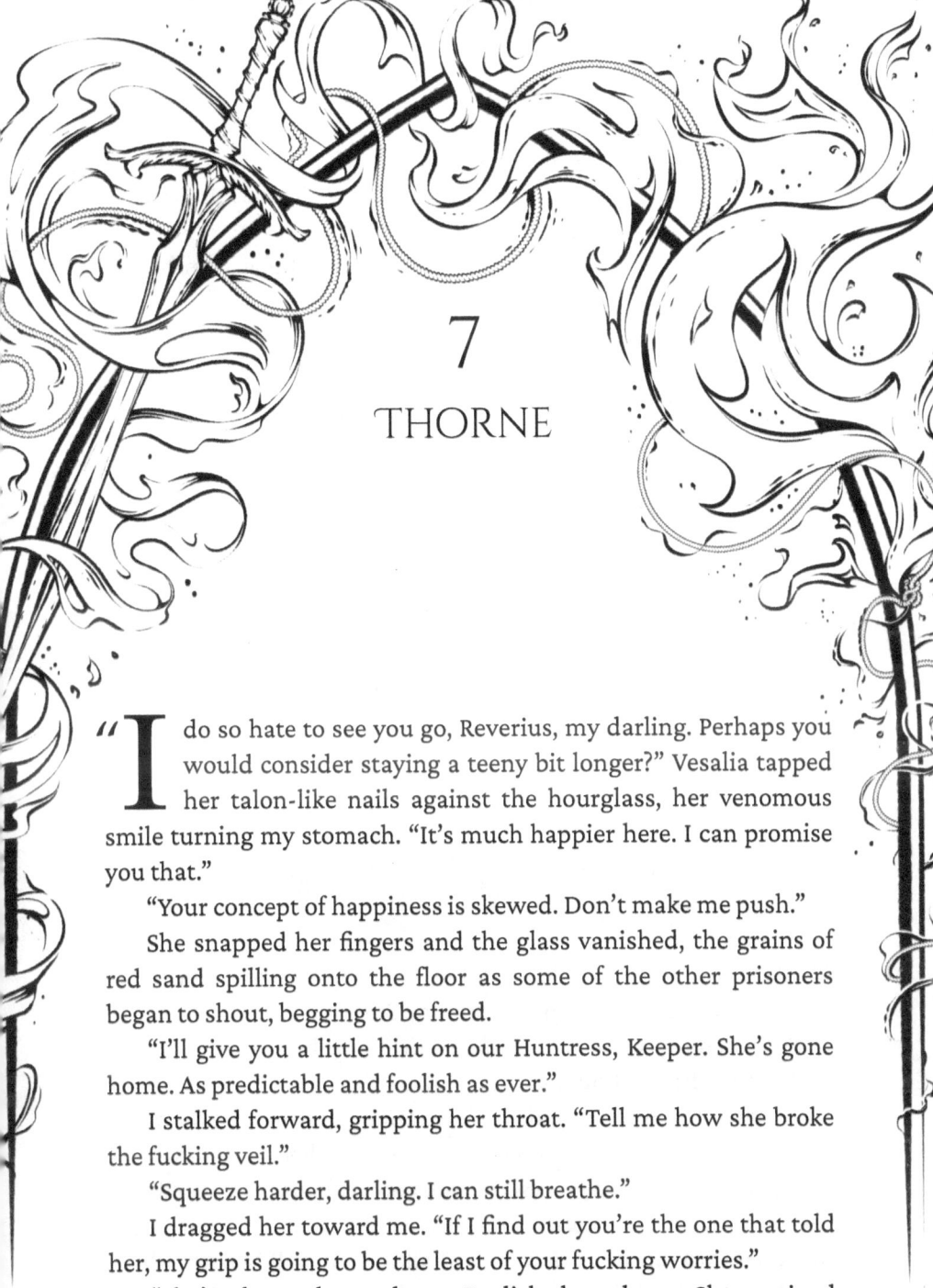

7

THORNE

"I do so hate to see you go, Reverius, my darling. Perhaps you would consider staying a teeny bit longer?" Vesalia tapped her talon-like nails against the hourglass, her venomous smile turning my stomach. "It's much happier here. I can promise you that."

"Your concept of happiness is skewed. Don't make me push."

She snapped her fingers and the glass vanished, the grains of red sand spilling onto the floor as some of the other prisoners began to shout, begging to be freed.

"I'll give you a little hint on our Huntress, Keeper. She's gone home. As predictable and foolish as ever."

I stalked forward, gripping her throat. "Tell me how she broke the fucking veil."

"Squeeze harder, darling. I can still breathe."

I dragged her toward me. "If I find out you're the one that told her, my grip is going to be the least of your fucking worries."

"She's always been clever. Foolish, but clever. She... gained some power and broke it. Honestly, if anyone, it was probably Alastor. You know how he loves his broken things."

"Why do I get the feeling you're not telling the whole story?"

She smiled, moving to her tiptoes to be closer. "I've never been good with storytelling. That's your specialty. All those lies catching up to you, dear?"

"Tell me how she broke the fucking veil. Don't play games."

"She stole power that belonged to me."

Farris. Fuck.

"Just because you wanted it doesn't make it yours."

She choked. "Tell that to yourself tonight before you fall asleep alone."

I squeezed until I was sure she couldn't draw a breath. "Stay away from her, Vesalia. You know how that will end."

Her eyes widened, and she managed a nod. Maybe I'd spent too much time chasing down my destiny and not enough time putting these assholes in their place. "She killed Farris, collected the power he'd been stealing and used it to break the veil. You will blink once for yes and twice for no. If you lie, I'll set your prisoners free and have you banished."

One exaggerated blink.

"Ezra was there?"

One blink.

"He told her everything, didn't he?"

Two blinks.

"Does she think she's safe?"

Her face turned purple. I released my grip enough for a single ragged breath to squeeze past my palm. Still, she didn't answer.

"Does she know the danger she is in? Yes or fucking no?"

Vesalia lifted a shoulder.

I threw her to the ground in frustration, ignoring the dramatic cry of pain. "You have a choice to make right here and now. You either stay in my good graces, or I will take it all, Vesalia. You'll lose your power, your memories, and every comfort in the world. You'll spend eternity in the Forgotten and all of time will become obsolete. Don't fuck with me. Don't fuck with her or I will end you. You and I both know my bite is far worse than Ezra's bark."

"Ezra's in Requiem," she said quietly, eyes to the floor, no longer the goddess vying for control, but rather in her place. "I hear he's waiting for you to find him."

"Good thing he's shit at hiding," I said, slamming my palm into the door and storming out.

"Care to tell me why you have sand in your hair, Boss?" Tuck asked, leaning against the wall of the clock tower as I strode out of Vesalia's temple.

"Not particularly," I answered, jutting my chin forward so he would fall into step with me. "I need every update. And quickly."

"I've been with Salt up at the castle. The old king's got them doing rotations along the northern border with some of his old guards to get them trained. He's giving them a decent wage and sent provisions to Noctus House for the orphans. No one has seen Archer, Jasper, or your bride since Farris died."

"Jasper's no longer going to be a concern of ours. Who do they think killed the little prick?"

Tuck halted, his voice falling. "He was killed in the back of a whorehouse. They claim his lover shoved a dagger in his chest.

His lover?

Why the fuck would they assume it was his lover? They'd have to have evidence to make that assumption. Had Paesha tricked him into bed? Had she wrapped those fucking thighs around him before she buried the dagger? She *let* him touch her? I needed to find something to throw. To break. Or find a way to bring that asshole back to life so I could kill him all over again.

"I'm assuming you're going after the Huntress, but I'm not sure that's wise."

"Did I ask for your opinion?"

"She has no fucking clue who she was dealing with in Stirling, I can promise you that."

"Don't be ridiculous. Ezra never showed himself to her until she broke the damn veil. He was hiding as he always does."

Tuck paused. "Right, but she doesn't know that. Wait, how'd you know he was there when the veil broke?"

A trace of Vesalia's pulse beneath my fist stroked my memory. "You're not the only persuasive fucker around here."

"Nice to see you got your mood under control while you were away."

"Sarcasm doesn't become you, dick."

He chuckled, scratching his dark brown beard. "Good thing I'm not trying to impress anyone."

"What happened to the Cimmerians? Any word on that front?" I started walking again, and Tuck did the same.

"Far as we can tell, they're free. A couple of the Fray went hunting last night. They were looking for Archer and Jasper, but ran into Burke and Toggs instead. The masks and robes they always wore? Gone. It was like they'd shed their Cimmerian skins entirely. They wore regular clothes, simple tunics, and trousers. You could still see the mark on their arm, but they were themselves. They seemed normal. The guys came and found me at the castle to report it. But I'd assumed that would happen when Farris died. The bond simply broke. Problem solved."

"All right. I've got shit to do. Keep an eye out for Archer. If you find anything, you know how to get ahold of me."

"You going to do something stupid?"

"Probably."

"Maybe I should come."

"I need you here for now. Keep an eye on the king, make sure the fucking Cimmerians don't do anything strange. We need to know if they're bound to Themis at all, and for gods' sake, man, take an hour or two off."

"That's rich coming from you," he called out as I walked away, headed straight for Perth.

I knew where my brother would be without even trying, but I wasn't expecting what I found in Requiem. The streets were gold, the buildings marble, and in the midday sun I had to shield my eyes from the glare. It looked exactly like Etherium. Which only meant one thing. Fucking Aeris had been here. Which was never a good sign.

I'd been prepared for the rot and neglect of my temple here. Even with everything in the twin cities restored, I expected my place to be falling to ash. A half-hung door, cobwebs, maybe even full collapse. But instead, the temple was in way better shape than I'd expected. The marble pillars out front stood tall and clean, no cracks, no grime, nothing. Each one carved with twisting symbols, circles and vines, and they all gleamed like they'd been polished.

The double doors were wide open, because of course they fucking were. Ezarius likely left them that way on purpose. I stormed inside. The air tasted like it did before a storm. Fitting. The hall held ornate mirrors, catching the glow from floating balls of light that drifted lazily back and forth overhead. The black and white tiles on the floor seemed to move in the flickering light, twisting patterns that made my eyes ache if I stared too long. An annoying little gift from Aeris, no doubt. Renewal my ass.

The walls on either side of the hall were covered with shelves crammed with scrolls and thick, heavy books, each stamped with my mark. Some of history, some records I allowed to be public, a list of gods and their tiers likely buried somewhere within. In the middle of it all, hanging from a thin chain, was an hourglass, huge and shining. The sand inside wasn't normal; it shimmered, shifting colors as it fell. Gold, white, black, a mirage of time itself, stuck in that damn glass cage. Vesalia's most coveted desire. She thought one day it would be hers, back when she hoped we'd be lovers. She was the Goddess of Time, but I was the creator of it. With my brother, of course. But none of these things were real. They were replicas from home. Etherium. A place I only wanted to go back to when this fucking mess was over.

But what really hit me were the statues.

They were everywhere, tucked between columns and half-hidden in the shadows. Each one was a perfect carving of Paesha and me. Every damn life we'd lived together, carved into cold stone. Every time she'd been hunted. In one, she was holding my face, the look in her eyes like she'd saved my life. In another, I was cradling her, red paint showed the blood soaking the front of my shirt. There was one where we stood back-to-back, swords raised against some unseen threat. But the threat had always been there. In every life of hers. It'd always been me and Ezra.

Each statue felt like a punch to the gut. It was all too perfect, too clean. Like someone had reached into my head, ripped out my memories, and displayed them for anyone to see. I wanted to break every one of them, to watch them crumble and fall apart like the lies I'd told had.

The whole damn temple had been restored, polished to look like it had in the old days, back when the gods still mattered here. Back when war happened between mortals and the gods were only present in the shadows of their temples. Back when this city belonged to Wisteria. Now that Paesha knew the truth, this place was only a reminder of everything I'd lost. Fucking Aeris.

I hadn't come here for nostalgia, anyway. I hadn't come to see how much I used to be worshiped. I'd come for him. And as I made my way deeper into the restored temple, I could feel the universe shoving us apart. We were never meant to exist in the same space. Or maybe we both weren't meant to exist at all. Maybe it was always supposed to be one. No balance.

"I was beginning to wonder if you'd come at all, brother," Ezarius crooned from my throne, back hunched, elbows on his knees as he looked at me with more hatred than I'd ever known from him.

I probably fucking deserved that glare. In fact, I knew I did. I cracked my knuckles and strode forward. If this asshole wanted to face me, perfect. "I was detained, but I'm here now."

"You broke the rules, Rev."

I threw that look right back at him. "I never agreed to your fucking rules, Ezra."

"Bullshit." He stood, balling his fists at his sides.

I shoved my hands in my pockets because I knew it would fuck with him. "Tell me you didn't love her. Tell me you didn't fucking worship the ground she walked on."

"Doesn't that prove my point? Because she loved me too,

brother. She loved me until it broke her. That was the deal wasn't it? If she loved me and not you, you'd finally fucking see that you're no one special."

I shook my head. "It wasn't the same, and she's not dead."

"Oh, but she will be. Just you fucking wait."

"You agreed you wouldn't kill her this time. *That* was the deal. And you broke that when you tried to have her poisoned."

"None of this matters and you know it. The terms were shattered the moment you took my memories, asshole. You're going to pay for that mistake. Fates help me, this is the end of this."

Rage boiled below the surface. I knew light was bursting from me without having to look down. I couldn't contain it. Not with him so fucking close and testing me. "Stay away from her, Ezarius."

He surged forward, gripping the collar of my shirt. "I've got something better in mind for our girl, brother. It's not going to be a swift arrow or a blade to the back this time. It's going to be so much fucking worse. It's going to be slow and painful and you're going to watch every one of her final seconds. And *then* this shit is over."

Before I could fully consider the consequences, I slammed a fist into Ezra's face with all the force I could muster. The satisfying crunch of bone against bone reverberated through the temple halls as he stumbled back, nearly losing his footing. He steadied himself against one of the marble columns. Slowly, deliberately, he reached up and wiped the blood trickling from the corner of his mouth with the back of his hand.

Then, to my utter disbelief and fury, the bastard started laughing. A cold, mirthless sound that echoed mockingly off the vaulted ceilings and polished floors. The floating orbs of light flickered and dimmed, as if cowering from the darkness emanating from my twin.

"Is that all you've got, brother?" He straightened to his full height. His eyes, mirrors of my own, glinted with cruel amusement. "A single punch? Honestly, I'm disappointed. But that's nothing new." He reached into his pocket, pulled out my Quoralis, the book I'd used to communicate with Paesha, and dropped it on the floor before me. "Run to her, Reverius. Watch her slip through your fingers again."

It took every ounce of self-control not to throw my power out until it incinerated us both from the inside. Maybe I would die, but he'd go down with me. Right now though, the only thing keeping me from depleting myself was her. It was the look on her fucking face the moment she'd spoken my true name.

I wouldn't run.

Not this time.

This time, I was going to rewrite the story, no matter the cost.

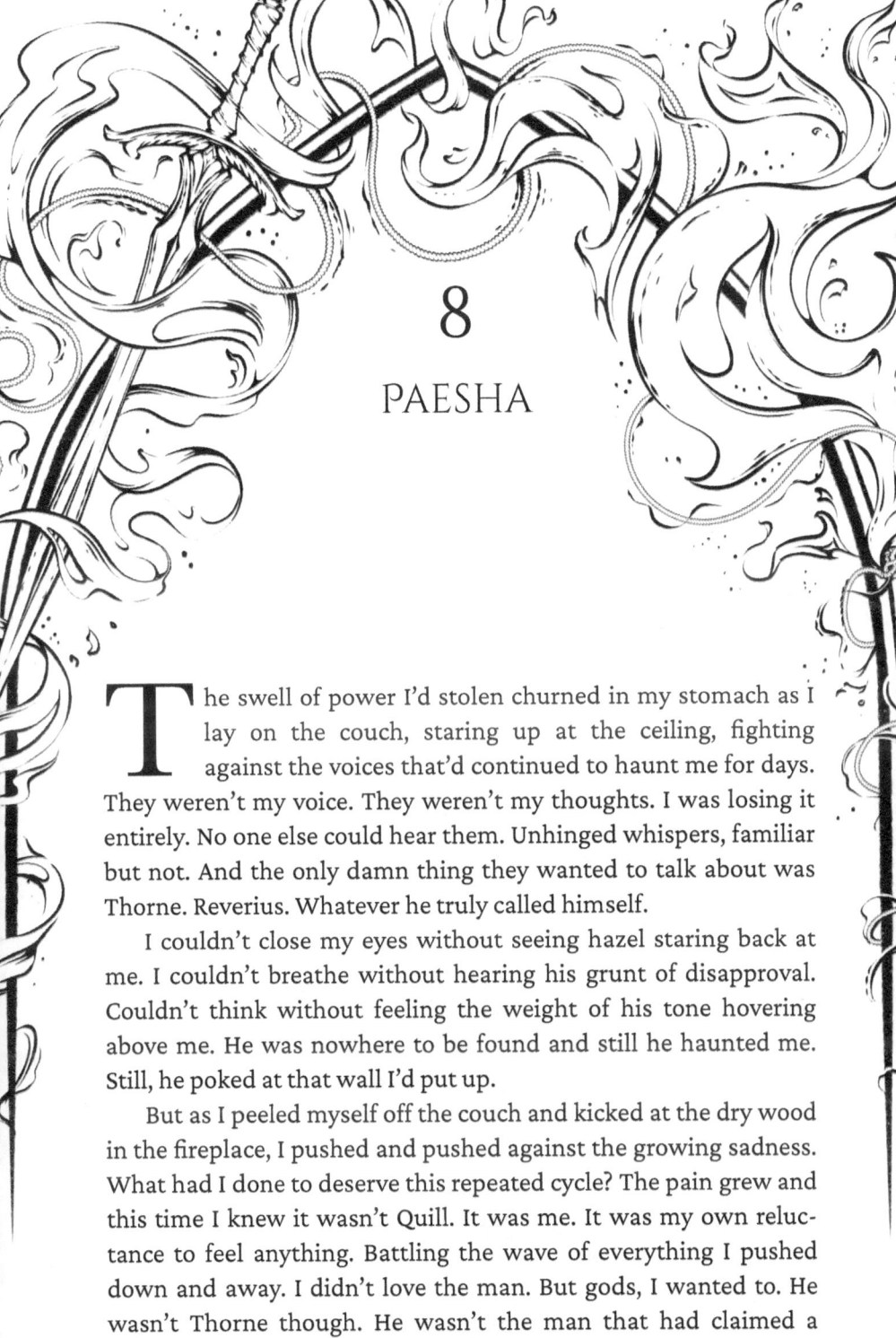

8

PAESHA

The swell of power I'd stolen churned in my stomach as I lay on the couch, staring up at the ceiling, fighting against the voices that'd continued to haunt me for days. They weren't my voice. They weren't my thoughts. I was losing it entirely. No one else could hear them. Unhinged whispers, familiar but not. And the only damn thing they wanted to talk about was Thorne. Reverius. Whatever he truly called himself.

I couldn't close my eyes without seeing hazel staring back at me. I couldn't breathe without hearing his grunt of disapproval. Couldn't think without feeling the weight of his tone hovering above me. He was nowhere to be found and still he haunted me. Still, he poked at that wall I'd put up.

But as I peeled myself off the couch and kicked at the dry wood in the fireplace, I pushed and pushed against the growing sadness. What had I done to deserve this repeated cycle? The pain grew and this time I knew it wasn't Quill. It was me. It was my own reluctance to feel anything. Battling the wave of everything I pushed down and away. I didn't love the man. But gods, I wanted to. He wasn't Thorne though. He wasn't the man that had claimed a stranger on the street. He was Reverius. The god that'd set every one of those pieces in motion. He'd sent me to a world I was tortured in. He might as well have hung me from those chains in the Maw himself. And gods. He'd killed those Cimmerians simply to look like the hero, to put on his fucking mask and sweep in and save me, when he could've prevented it in the first place. His brand of torture was setting everyone up for failure and then coming in to be the hero no one wanted and everyone needed.

My heart hurt. It raged. It broke into a million pieces of betrayal as soon as I let myself feel it. But I needed to. I needed to feel it because if I didn't, it would swallow me whole even though the pain was endless, an ocean with no shore, and I was drowning in it when I was alone. My chest burned as though someone had carved out pieces of me and left jagged edges behind. The room felt too small, the walls pressing inward, the air thick and cloying. I fell to my knees before the fireplace.

You let him.

"I know."

Liar. Traitor.

Masks. Masks. Pretty little masks.

"Stop." I pressed my palms to my temples, trying to block out the voices that swirled around me like smoke.

Their cruel words came faster, overlapping and tangling until they were nothing but noise, an ugly, disjointed noise that scraped against my mind like nails on glass. My breath turned shallow and uneven as the memories clawed their way back to the surface. I couldn't even shut my eyes against them.

Thorne's smile. Reverius's smirk. Two faces layered atop each other like oil on water, shifting and distorting until I couldn't tell where one ended and the other began. His promises echoed in my head. Sweet lies wrapped in silk ribbons. 'You're safe with me.' 'I'll never let anything happen to you.'

Fucking liar. He wanted me to die, but only when he orchestrated it. For whatever reason.

I'd seen the truth thanks to Alastor. I just needed to move on from him. The man of a thousand faces and a million lies. He'd made me believe in impossible things, only to rip it all away. I thought he'd try to come back with me. Or at least try to help me. He did neither. As always. Betrayal after betrayal, lifetime after lifetime. The cycle never ended.

As if I'd summoned the fucking thing by letting myself feel anything but numbness, Thorne's little, golden book appeared on the table, igniting a piece of anger I hadn't felt yet.

"How did you find this?" I hissed at him, then cowered, staring around the corner to make sure no one heard me. I was sure the others already thought I was losing it. I didn't need to fuel that fire. And he couldn't hear me, of course. I'd have to write in his damn book to speak to him. Unless Ezra had the same book. Hadn't he called it a family heirloom? Could they both use it?

The last time I'd seen it, it was in the hands of Ezra's men. Not that it mattered, it would suffer the same fate, regardless of who'd sent it. Glaring across the room, I snatched a small oil lamp, tossed it into the fireplace, and waited for the dry logs to burst to life. Once the heat reached me and I was nearly vibrating with fury at the audacity of whichever brother had the nerve to send this, I threw the fucking book in the fire, confident the gold wouldn't melt, but the pages could burn to ash.

Power, my new power, rose to attention with my pressing emotions. I watched with grim satisfaction as the flames licked at the golden edges of the damn thing. The paper curled and blackened, smoke rising in delicate tendrils, reducing Thorne's lies to ash. A weight lifted from my chest as I watched it burn, feeling a savage joy at destroying this link to him.

But as the final page crumbled away, leaving nothing but a warped golden cover, I turned, hardly daring to breathe as the fucking thing reappeared. Sitting innocently on the table, pristine and untouched. It gleamed in the firelight, mocking me.

"Neat parlor trick, asshole."

My hands shook as I snatched it up, flipping through the pages. They were crisp and white, not a single char or burn mark. Only the godsdamned 'two' written on the top of the first page in my own writing.

I hurled the book back into the fire. The flames leapt higher, hungrily devouring the pages once more. I stood there, chest heaving, watching until nothing remained but ashes and gold. Slowly, dreading what I'd find, I turned around. There it was again, whole and perfect on the table.

With a scream of frustration, I seized the book and ripped the pages out by the fistful, crumpling them in my hands before hurling them into the hungry flames. The fire roared higher as I fed it page after page, a whirlwind of flying paper and sparks. My fingers tore at the binding, but I couldn't split the gold cover, no matter how badly I wanted to destroy every last scrap until nothing remained. This was Thorne. Reverius. Thorne never existed. He was only a mask. A perfect performance delivered by an empowered god, taking a page directly out of Vesalia's damn playbook. Fuck her cuckoo clocks and fuck this book.

Hot tears blurred my vision, but I blinked them away furiously, focused only on my task of annihilation. Not the way he'd lied. Not the way I'd fallen for it all. Not the shame and embarrassment of never figuring it out. How dare he send this to me, this mocking reminder of all his bullshit? Did he think I'd fall for this? Let him worm his way back in with a few charming words? Never. Never again. I'd sooner see him drown in the Lake of Lost Souls in the heart of Death's court before I ever spoke another word to him.

As I flung the last handful of ruined pages into the fire, chest heaving, I felt a dark satisfaction curl in my gut. The same place where that strange new power had taken root, pulsing in time with the wild pounding of my heart. It reveled in my fury, rising to the surface like a shark scenting blood in the water.

I stepped back from the fireplace, swiping an arm across my damp cheeks, and turned slowly to face the inevitable. A strangled sound halfway between a sob and a snarl tore from my throat.

There on the table, flawless and shining in the flickering light as if I had never touched it, lay the golden book. The whispers followed me as I fled the room, growing louder with each frantic step. Their taunting words echoed in my mind, twisting like barbed wire around my heart.

Weak.

Fool.

He never loved you.

No one ever did.

Can't you see they've all left you? Even your parents.

I burst out the front door into the moonlit meadow, gulping the cool night air. But there was no relief, no respite from the insidious voices that clawed at my sanity. They came from everywhere and nowhere.

I pressed my hands over my ears, trying in vain to block out the hiss of their voices. "Stop, please stop," I begged, my voice cracking. Hot tears streamed down my face as I sank to my knees.

The Remnants, *my* Remnants, stirred to life, drawn to the surface by my spiraling anguish. They thrashed against my ribcage like captive beasts, dark tendrils of power snaking through my veins. Choking me. Consuming me. He'd made me angry, they'd made me lose it.

A scream built in my throat but emerged as only a strangled whimper when I curled in on myself, fingers digging into the rich earth, desperately trying to ground myself against the maelstrom raging in my mind.

I was more than this. I was Paesha Vox. A survivor. A fighter. I had clawed my way out of the gutters, faced down crime lords and obnoxious gods. No matter how many times I had been beaten down, I always rose again.

And in that moment, I remembered me. When the world became too cruel, too heavy to bear, I had always found refuge in dance. In the steps and spins, the leaps and turns, pouring my heart and soul into each gesture until everything else fell away and I was free.

With shaking limbs, I pushed myself to my feet. The whispers hissed in my ears, but I forced myself to tune them out, focusing instead on the steady thrum of my heartbeat.

And then I danced.

At first, my movements were small, hesitant. A gentle sway of my hips, a graceful sweep of my arms. But with each breath, each stretch and turn, a fragile sense of calm settled over my fractured nerves. I focused on the placement of my feet, the elegant lines of my body as I moved through familiar forms.

Spin. Turn. Bend. Point.

Move.

Slow, sweeping circles gradually gave way to faster, more complex steps. I leapt and spun across the moonlit meadow, my hair flying out behind me in a wild tangle. The whispers faded to a distant hum as I lost myself in the silent music, the soft shush of my feet through the grass, the chirping of the crickets, the soothing metronome of my breath and heartbeat.

The Remnants responded to the rhythm, their frantic writhing gentling into something almost like a dance. Their shadowy tendrils caressed my skin like cool silk, pulsing in time with my heartbeat. Like they were a part of me, as vital and necessary as the blood in my veins or the air in my lungs.

When I leapt, they lifted me higher, until I was soaring, weightless and free. When I spun, they whipped around me in a shadowy vortex, blurring the edges of my form until I became something more than human, a wild creature of the night.

The whispers had gone silent, drowned out by the rush of power, the wild thrill of letting go, of unleashing everything I'd kept pent up inside for so long. I threw my head back and laughed, giddy and drunk on the sheer joy of movement. The sound echoed across the meadow, eerie and unearthly. This was madness. This was freedom. This was the monster's playground. My damn playground.

But as I completed another turn, a flicker of movement at the edge of the meadow caught my eye. My heart stuttered in my chest. I recognized the tall, broad-shouldered silhouette standing motionless in the shadows of the trees. Reverius. Maybe Ezra, but I was sure I'd seen the black mark on his neck when he shifted backward, trying to hide in the shadows when I spun.

Now, he stood as still as a statue, his face half-hidden in darkness. Even from this distance, I could feel the weight of his gaze upon me. The hazel eyes that had once looked at me with such tenderness now seemed to burn with an unreadable intensity.

I didn't want him to be here. He was seconds from ruining the only peace I'd felt in days. The Remnants recoiled, sensing the shift in my mood, their dance transforming into fury, immediately taking over any sense of joy.

They swirled around me, a living barrier of shadow and mist. They sensed my anger, my pain, and responded in kind. Tendrils of darkness lashed out like whips, slicing through the air between us. The grass at my feet withered and turned black, as if life was being drained from the earth.

Reverius approached slowly, his steps measured and cautious. The moonlight caught the planes of his face, throwing half of it into sharp relief while leaving the other shrouded in shadow. Gods, he was handsome. Infuriatingly so. And I wanted nothing more than to rip that fucker to shreds with my bare hands.

"Stay away from me."

He took another step forward, the crunch of grass beneath his boots unnaturally loud in the stillness of the night. "You're unraveling."

The Remnants surged in response to his voice, coiling around my limbs like living armor. I could feel their hunger, their desire to attack, to tear and rend. It took everything I had to hold them back. This was my moment. Not theirs.

"And whose fault is that?" I spat, clenching my fists at my sides. The shadows mimicked my movements, clawed hands of darkness forming in the air around me.

"Let me help you."

He might as well have splashed ice water on my face. "In no realm, in no lifetime, in no space of existence from now until the end of time, will I ever, ever come to you for anything more than to watch your final breath."

"This isn't you," he whispered.

"What the fuck did you just say to me?"

He took another step forward. "You took too much power and you can't control it. This anger isn't you. It's the power. It's consuming you."

"Does living in a pit of audacity give you that youthful glow, or is it the constant state of denial? You trapped me behind a veil, pretended to be someone else, lied through your teeth at every fucking turn and let someone who believed she was your friend die. You could have saved her, all powerful asshole. You didn't. But then you could have done about a thousand things different, so I guess we're all living with the consequences of your actions now.

"Let me make myself perfectly clear. I don't want you here. I don't need you here, and I've got news for you, asshole. You don't get to interfere. Or have you forgotten our bargain?"

I watched him straighten. I watched the color drain from his pretty fucking face as I played the only card I had left in my arsenal. I took a step toward him this time, letting the Remnants creep forward, darkening the space between us. His eyes flashed to the ground, but he made no attempt to move. "Come on, Reverius darling. Don't tell me you've forgotten already, or did you not realize?"

"What bargain?"

"You said you'd help me find the king. And you said you wouldn't stop me when the time came for me to do what I needed to do. You agreed to that, didn't you? You gave me your word."

One of the Remnants circled his ankle, hesitant at first, just as I was to make such bold moves against this powerful god, but again, he didn't move. Instead, his eyes darkened as another tendril crept forward.

A breath of power lashed out, wrapping around his legs and arms, the shadowy form solidifying into barbed vines that bit into his flesh. I watched, a mix of horror and savage satisfaction churning in my gut, as crimson bloomed against the white of his shirt.

He made no move to defend himself, his eyes locked on mine even as the shadows tightened their grip. The Remnants sensed my conflicted emotions and responded with increasing ferocity. They ripped and tore, leaving bloody furrows across his skin, shredding his clothes to ribbons.

Yet he stood motionless, his face a mask of calm acceptance. Annoyingly, no pain, no fear, not even a flicker of discomfort marred his features as the shadows continued their relentless assault, even swirling over Alastor's black mark upon his neck. Blood dripped from countless wounds, staining the grass at his feet a deep crimson.

I couldn't deny that a weaker part of me screamed to stop this, to call off the attack. But the darker, wounded part reveled in his suffering, in finally having some small measure of revenge for all his lies and manipulations. I wanted to see him bleed, to make him hurt the way he'd hurt me.

"Stop," he commanded so quietly I almost couldn't hear him.

The Remnants hissed. I stepped forward again, boldly this time, willing the ground to practically crumble beneath each step as I moved toward him. "Would that have worked for me? If I'd have told you to stop?"

He said nothing, of course.

"The bargain stands, Reverius Hawthorne Noctus. You may not question or stand in my way. Now, be a good boy and kindly go fuck yourself."

His face tightened, the anger so obvious I could feel it in the heated air between us. "Be reasonable, Paesha."

"Reasonable?" I laughed, the sound as hollow as his promises had been. "You want reasonable from the woman you've killed a thousand times? The one you trapped and manipulated and lied to?" My Remnants squeezed tighter. "How's this for reasonable? One cut for every life you stole from me. Don't worry though, Supreme Sovereign, unlike you, I only plan to kill you once."

"You can't kill a god, and I won't sit back and watch you destroy yourself."

"No, darling. You wouldn't. You'd much prefer to do the destroying."

"You don't know what you're talking about."

I slid the blade Harlow had given me from my thigh. "Did you just call me a liar, Reverius Hawthorne Noctus? The things I saw with my own eyes never happened? What you've done to me for hundreds of lives? Or should we talk about the memories Alastor showed me? The one of you putting a blade in my back on my wedding day?" I traced my knife along his jaw, a mockery of the tender way he'd once touched me. He was a breath away, but a thousand lies too far to reach. "You and your brother played the same game. Make the poor little mortal fall in love, only to kill her. Do you have to break my heart before you can stop it? Is that the key here?"

"This is not a fucking game between brothers." His voice was low, dangerous. "Ezra and I have been at war for a very long time and you're the battlefield we keep scorching."

"The battlefield and the bounty. How fucking sweet. Let's skip the small talk and get to the point here, Reverius. You and I have a bargain. Like it or not, you don't get to ask me a single question. Not one. And you cannot stand in my way. As far as I'm concerned, being here right now is an invasion of my space. You're in the way. Get the fuck out of it."

The earth all but rattled as he shook himself free of my Remnants, a show of power as much as anything as he took a step toward me and snatched the wrist holding the blade. "Ezra is dangerous."

I scoffed. "You're all dangerous."

"He is my equal," he said, eyes cold and hard. "You don't need me as your enemy right now. I can promise you that."

I yanked my wrist free and stepped away, trying to drag the Remnants that circled the ground backward, though I truly had no control over what they did. Their hissing in my mind grew louder and angrier. I felt like I was surrounded by a thousand swarming bees while trying to face down an ancient beast.

"You made yourself my enemy the day you dropped me in Wisteria. Everything since then has been icing on the cake."

He ran his hands through his dark hair until it was a disheveled mess. And that tic in his jaw, the one that always spoke to his feelings even when he tried to hide them, drew all my attention. He'd always been the most beautiful man in the room. Apparently that was because he was a god. The god. Fucker.

Reverius straightened and his shoulders squared. As he opened his mouth to speak, a chill swept through the meadow. The grass rippled like waves on a dark sea. The shadows between the trees deepened, coalescing into a figure that stepped out of the darkness with casual grace.

Alastor.

He wore a suit of deepest black that absorbed the light, making the pale skin of his face appear to float disembodied in the night. But I knew the suit hid his tattoos. I knew the sleeves were covering markings that moved along his skin as much as his Remnants curled along the ground beside him.

"Where one goes, the other is never far behind," he drawled, cracking his knuckles as he walked past Thorne, er Reverius. "I thought we were learning things here, Descendant." His eyes scanned the Remnants circling me before he scowled. "Explain this."

"You don't have to tell him shit," Reverius said, scowling.

"That's a very interesting choice of words, coming from someone who does nothing but lie and manipulate for his own vie for power. But let's discuss, shall we?" Alastor came to my side as he loosened the navy tie at his neck. He slid his hands into his pockets and faced Reverius coolly. "My darling Paesha and I have a standing agreement. Isn't that right? She still owes me a name."

"Don't do this," Reverius said, face changing as if there was a threatening weight to Alastor's words.

Alastor smirked. Centuries of built-up justice written across his face. "I will do *exactly* this. And you will stand there and do nothing because you have no say over what happens here."

My heart began to race as the tone of that threat curled around me. This was no longer the meadow I'd danced half my life in, no longer my escape from the weary, no longer my place of peace. This was a battleground forged by gods, commanded by gods, and would ultimately be destroyed by gods. Because that's what they fucking did. They took and took and destroyed. Everything. And everyone. Even themselves.

My Remnants, the ones I no longer mistook for Alastor's, hissed. Both men turned to me, glancing at the fists clenched to my sides and then the shadows rippling across the ground like giant claws, with nails ripping into the fresh earth as if they heard my thoughts and meant to mark this space as their own, rather than handing it over to these bastards that thought they had some kind of claim over me.

Thorne looked at me. Not Reverius, the god, but the shadow of the man that'd needed to hold me after cutting off an arm. The man that'd danced with me in a goddess's temple, forcing me to focus on him rather than my fear of the Cimmerians. The man that'd sat beside my bed to keep the nightmares away.

"Don't fucking look at me like that," I said with disgust. "That mask no longer becomes you."

Still, his eyes sank. Still, he drew back. "I'm sorry."

The Remnants roared, swiping at the earth before him.

"Don't you dare lie to me."

"I'd love to sit here and watch this battle unfurl, but I've got things to do." Alastor said, turning to face me. "You owe me a final name, Huntress. I've come to collect."

Reverius cleared his throat. His hazel eyes were wide and full of desperation. I took a step back. Why the sudden shift? Why was he so worried? "I don't have a name. I haven't had time to find the final broken soul."

Alastor laughed. His eyes darkened. His Remnants surged forward.

"Alastor," Reverius begged.

I whipped my head around to look at him. "What do you know? What's happening?"

"Let me guess, you never told her the terms of the bargain." Alastor shook his head.

"Thorne..."

"You see, Huntress, sometimes gods learn their lessons the hard way too." Alastor stepped in front of me, blocking my view of the world as his Remnants swirled around me, smothering any trace of mine.

"What did you do?" I screamed as the shadows circled my ankles and wrists, holding me in place. "What the fuck did you do, Reverius?"

"You were so faint. So, so close to death. And once again, the Keeper has failed you," Alastor crooned, turning toward Reverius. "So many chances, and you still couldn't tell her the truth. This is on you."

The shadows at my wrists and ankles began to burn, searing into my flesh like molten iron. I thrashed against their grip, but they only tightened, biting deeper. Panic clawed my throat, threatening to choke me. This couldn't be happening. Not again. I couldn't be bound, not after everything I'd fought for.

"What's happening? Someone tell me what's happening?" I screamed, my voice raw and desperate as the familiar shackles of control tightened around me, my free will dissipating. The meadow spun, the once peaceful night now a nightmare landscape of writhing shadows and accusatory stares.

Alastor's face loomed before me, his eyes twin pools of endless darkness. His smile was cruel, predatory. "You made a bargain, little Huntress. And now it's time to pay."

"I didn't," I screamed. "I didn't agree to this."

"You did," Reverius whispered or shouted. I couldn't tell.

"Tell her the bargain, Keeper. Every bit. Tell her what you pushed her into."

I looked at him. Pled with him in that glance. "Please tell me." I could not be shackled again. I could not be a prisoner.

"Should he request a name and you're unable to deliver, you become bound to him."

My heart absolutely shattered. Exploded into a million pieces of hurt, betrayal and rage, until the darkness took over. Until the monster swelling within me grew too big, too angry. But I pushed back, swallowing everything, building all the walls. I needed to keep it chained, keep everything I'd become a secret. The push and pull battled until darkness descended. They couldn't see the beast I'd become. Not when the power to control it had just been taken from me.

Burning, raging magic shoved against my ribs, roaring to be released, to break the world. To rip both of the gods from their forms and drown them in an eternity of misery.

I didn't choose this. I didn't choose this.

I could not be bound. I could not be chained.

Tears streamed down my face. The burning from Alastor's Remnants intensified, spreading up my arms and legs like liquid fire in my veins. It consumed me from the inside out, rewriting who I was on a fundamental level. Hiding the monster behind a wall of power. Alastor's power.

My gaze darted wildly between Alastor and Reverius, silently begging for answers, for mercy, for anything to make this stop.

I fell to my knees, consumed by the fire. I couldn't see beyond the pain.

"Stop!" Reverius roared, and I could swear the earth rattled with the force of that command.

But Alastor's laugh was greater. "She's mine now, Keeper. Pity you failed again. Some of us were really rooting for you. There's nothing you can do to stop it now."

"I'll fucking stop you myself," I roared.

Somewhere, a million miles away, I heard the door to the house slam shut.

"Come find me when you're done with your tantrum, Huntress," Alastor's magic echoed in my ear as his Remnants dissipated and I was left buried beneath the panic of my own shadows, unable to breathe, unable to move, unable to blink beyond the two black bands circling my wrists.

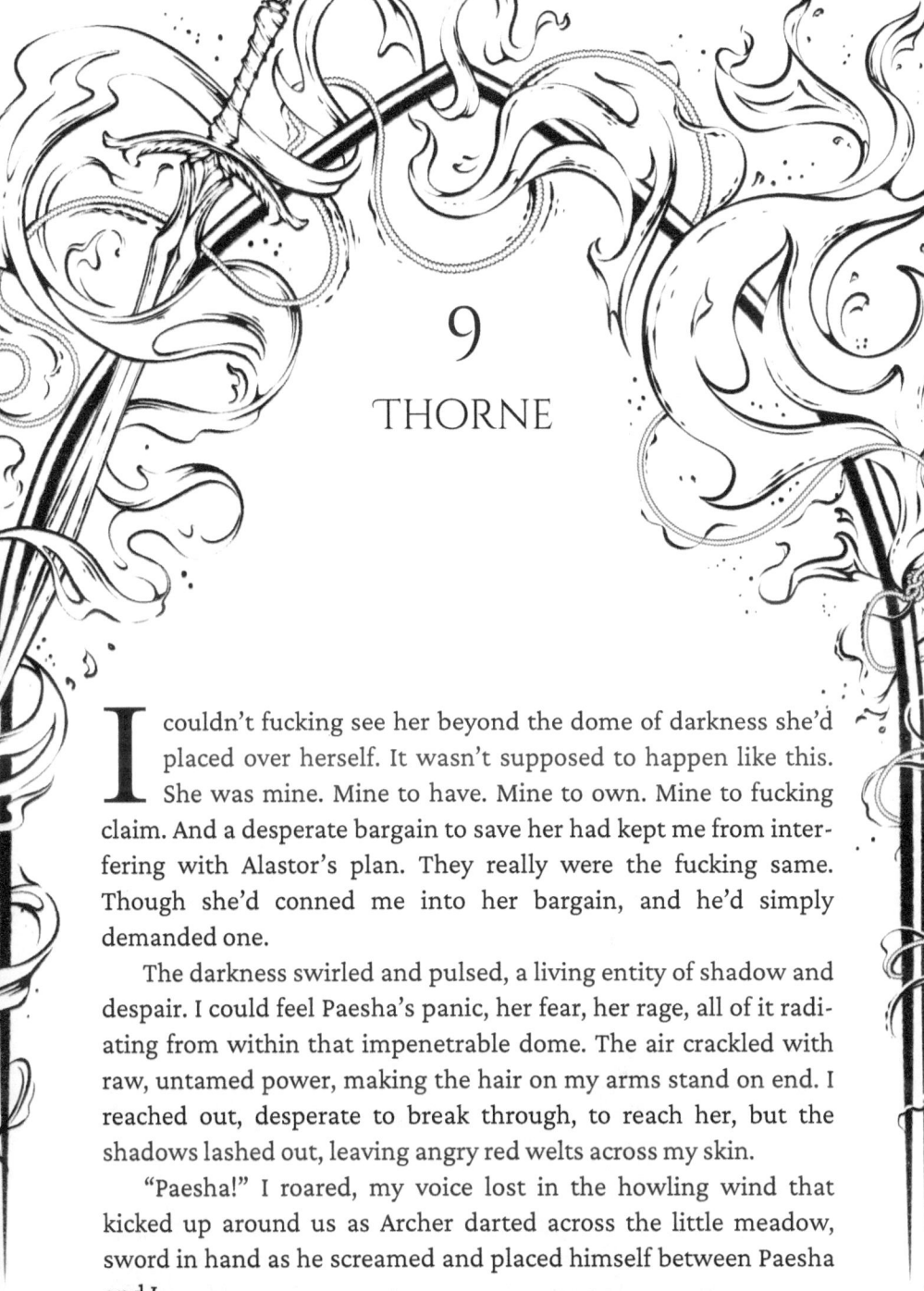

9

THORNE

I couldn't fucking see her beyond the dome of darkness she'd placed over herself. It wasn't supposed to happen like this. She was mine. Mine to have. Mine to own. Mine to fucking claim. And a desperate bargain to save her had kept me from interfering with Alastor's plan. They really were the fucking same. Though she'd conned me into her bargain, and he'd simply demanded one.

The darkness swirled and pulsed, a living entity of shadow and despair. I could feel Paesha's panic, her fear, her rage, all of it radiating from within that impenetrable dome. The air crackled with raw, untamed power, making the hair on my arms stand on end. I reached out, desperate to break through, to reach her, but the shadows lashed out, leaving angry red welts across my skin.

"Paesha!" I roared, my voice lost in the howling wind that kicked up around us as Archer darted across the little meadow, sword in hand as he screamed and placed himself between Paesha and I.

"You bastard. You fucking bastard. You could have saved her. You let her die. You knew her, and she loved you like a brother, and still, you let her die."

"Put the godsdamn sword away, Archie."

"Don't you fucking call me that." He stepped forward, teeth gritted, shoulders heaving, as he placed the tip of the sword into the hollow of my neck, hand only slightly trembling. Good for him. "I will kill you. I don't care what kind of god you are. I don't care if you wrote the rules, or the worlds, or whatever you're supposed to lord over. I will kill you, you bastard."

The cold metal was a balm against my skin. The rage in his eyes burned hotter than any flame. Fueled by grief and betrayal, he was right to hate me. They all were.

The damn shadows continued to pulse around Paesha, her anguish a tangible force in the air. I could feel her power growing wild and uncontrolled, threatening to tear her apart. And there wasn't a damn thing I could do about it. I'd been effectively caged by bargains.

"You don't understand," I said. "None of you do."

Archer's grip on the sword tightened. "Then explain it."

I closed my eyes, feeling the weight of millennia pressing down on me. How could I explain to a mortal the peril of worlds and whims of gods and their games? How could I tell him in the end none of it would matter? Not even his sister.

"All magic is failing. The gods are losing their power. We're weakened." I grabbed the edge of his sword, letting it slice into my palm as I shoved it away and stepped toward him. "You think I would have sat there and done nothing when Ezra's men attacked if I could have helped it? The flow of magic used to be an endless supply and now it's an ebb and flow. Sometimes great and sometimes there's hardly anything there. The cost of using it is so much steeper and I can promise you, Ezra knows exactly when to fucking strike."

His cold eyes never looked away from my face. "You were limited because you were holding that veil in place, weren't you? Admit it. You put your little game ahead of my sister's life and she fucking died for it."

When I didn't confirm or deny, he lifted the sword again. "One day, you will fall and I will be the one standing over your withering body. You'll see my face and you'll think of her the second before you die."

Harlow would be one of thousands, but I couldn't tell him that. He'd only throw more empty threats and probably a sword into my gut, and I had no time to heal from that right now.

"Be careful of the gods you threaten," I said, clenching my teeth. Threatening me was one thing, but if he stood before the wrong person and said those words, he'd be joining his sister.

The shadows swarmed forward, a writhing mass of darkness. They enveloped Archer, wrapping around him like a protective cocoon, tendrils of inky blackness lashing out at me as I took another step toward him. He yelled in fury, likely trying to fight against the wall Paesha's magic had formed.

She'd taken way too much fucking power. Way too much. It hadn't affected Farris because he'd had no idea how to find that magic in himself, but the Huntress had no such qualms.

As the shadows danced and twisted, I could see flashes of Archer's face through the gaps, his eyes wide with fear but his jaw set in defiance. The darkness seemed to respond to his emotions, growing more agitated and violent. But maybe it wasn't the darkness. It was her. Paesha, still hidden behind the wall of her breakdown.

"Paesha," I whispered, trying to reach her.

The Remnants hissed and stretched for me, scraping down my tattered shirt until they drew blood again. A manifestation of her fury, no doubt.

"Archer, you have to talk to her. She's lost control."

The door to the house flew open with a resounding bang. Quill burst through the opening. The child's long curly hair was a mess of tangles behind her as she ran. Her feet barely seemed to touch the ground. She raced across the yard, her eyes wild and her face contorted with a mixture of anger and desperation.

I didn't fear Archer. Nor the raging vestiges of magic from Paesha's tantrum, but the child? The Fera? That look in her eyes as she stared me down sent a shiver down my spine. She did not know what she was capable of. No one truly did.

"Quill, no!" A red-haired woman's voice rang out, sharp and panicked. "Stay out of it!"

But the girl paid no heed to her friend's warnings. She charged forward, her arms outstretched as if she could physically push back the encroaching shadows. The child, freshly nine if I remembered right, threw her hands on her hips as she stood toe to toe with me, looking back into the darkness that consumed Paesha and Archer only once. "What did you do?"

"Go back inside like you were told," I warned the child.

The Remnants surged forward. They likely meant to form a barrier around the Fera also, but it was clear Paesha had no control and even if she did, I'm not sure the Fera would have allowed it, though I had no idea the reach of her blossoming power either, nor did I know how she was affected by the god's current plight.

The air shimmered and pulsed, like heat waves rising from scorched earth. Tendrils of energy, invisible yet palpable, coiled around her slight frame, building in intensity with each ragged breath she drew. She was everything. And nothing. Untrained. Unclaimed. And dangerous as fuck.

The weight of her stare pressed down on me, heavy as a physical blow. "Let them out."

The shadows surrounding Paesha and Archer pulsed in response to Quill's command, feeding off her anger. They grew thicker, darker, more menacing. The inky tendrils lashed out with renewed vigor, leaving fresh gashes across my skin wherever they struck. Still, I fucking stood there, a lamb to slaughter, because I couldn't leave her. If I walked away, I may never get a chance to speak to her again. That was absolutely something Alastor would do. And she was mine. Not his. Not even this feral little child's. She was fucking mine.

Quill's magic swelled, a rising tide of raw, untamed power. It crackled in the air, raising the hairs on the back of my neck. The ground beneath our feet began to tremble, fine cracks spider webbing through the packed earth.

"You get the hell away from my family," Quill said, her voice low and slow and almost adorable, if not for the threat.

"I'm not here to cause harm."

"You're the liar, aren't you?" she asked, spreading her feet as if she meant to attack me.

"Everyone lies."

"Maybe in your world," she said with an eerie smile. "But in this one, it's against the rules."

I took a step back, trying to lure her away from Paesha's Remnants. If she continued to feed them her anger, this wouldn't end well.

I could feel Paesha's panic and rage building to a fever pitch behind that dark barrier. If I didn't diffuse this soon, magic could tear this place apart. Mine, hers, or the kid's. Either way, this was a melting pot of trouble.

"Quill," I said, forcing my voice to stay calm. "That's your name, isn't it? You need to step back. You're making it worse."

"No!" she shouted. The ground shook beneath our feet. "You're the one making it worse! You need to leave!"

"Story of my life, kid. Now be a good girl and go back to your house."

"Maybe you should be a good boy and f—."

"Quill!" the other woman shouted.

She winced, showing the first break in her exterior. "Sorry, Thea, but he's the bad guy."

True again.

"Quill," a voice said from behind me. I straightened, that voice of gravel grating down my spine as Aeris stepped forward. With her silver hair pulled back into a bun and a simple frock style dress on, I hardly recognized her. "You mustn't anger a Keeper. Look at Paesha. She's suffering in there. We need to help her, and we can't do that while we're fighting, can we?"

The goddess took my side, never once making eye contact, speaking to the child as if she were a frightened animal.

"But he's not supposed to be here," Quill said, pointing at me. "He's a bad man."

"That may very well be, little bird, but right now we need to focus on helping the Huntress," Aeris said gently. "The more we fight, the more her magic lashes out. Can you feel it?"

Quill's brow furrowed. The ground stopped shaking. "I... I can feel it," she admitted reluctantly. "It hurts."

"That's right," Aeris nodded. "Paesha is in pain, and her magic is responding to that pain. We need to calm her down, not make things worse. Can you help me do that?"

The child hesitated, her eyes darting between Aeris, me, and the swirling mass of shadows that contained Paesha and Archer. Finally, she gave a small nod.

"Good," Aeris smiled. She turned to me, her silver eyes sharp. "Keeper, I think it's best if you step back for now. Your presence is only agitating things further."

I clenched my jaw, wanting to argue. But she was right. With a final glance at the writhing darkness, I took several steps back, eyes locked with fucking Aeris, who somehow waltzed in here and took control as if she already had her fist around this family.

"I think you need to go further," she said, bowing her head, though I could see the corners of her mouth lift. "You've done enough this day."

If I hadn't already had the satisfaction of punching my brother in the godsdamn face today, I'd be tempted to hunt him down for the release. I couldn't do shit to her with this audience, and she fucking knew it. Aeris had me by the balls.

She knelt beside Quill, speaking softly to the child, her silver hair gleaming in the fading sunlight. The shadows around Paesha and Archer calmed slightly.

Aeris glanced over her shoulder at me, a triumphant glint in her eyes. "I said, you need to go further, Keeper. Your presence here is no longer required."

The sheer audacity of her dismissal made my blood boil. This was my game, my rules, my fucking story. And yet here I stood, powerless and pushed aside by a goddess who should know her place.

I wanted nothing more than to unleash my full power, to show them all exactly who they were dealing with. To remind Aeris of her position in the hierarchy of the gods. But as I looked at the scene before me, Quill radiating untapped power, the other woman hovering protectively nearby, and the swirling mass of shadows that held Paesha and Archer, I knew I couldn't risk it.

So I fucking swallowed my pride and walked away, even though leaving them in the hands of Aeris was probably the most foolish thing I could have ever done.

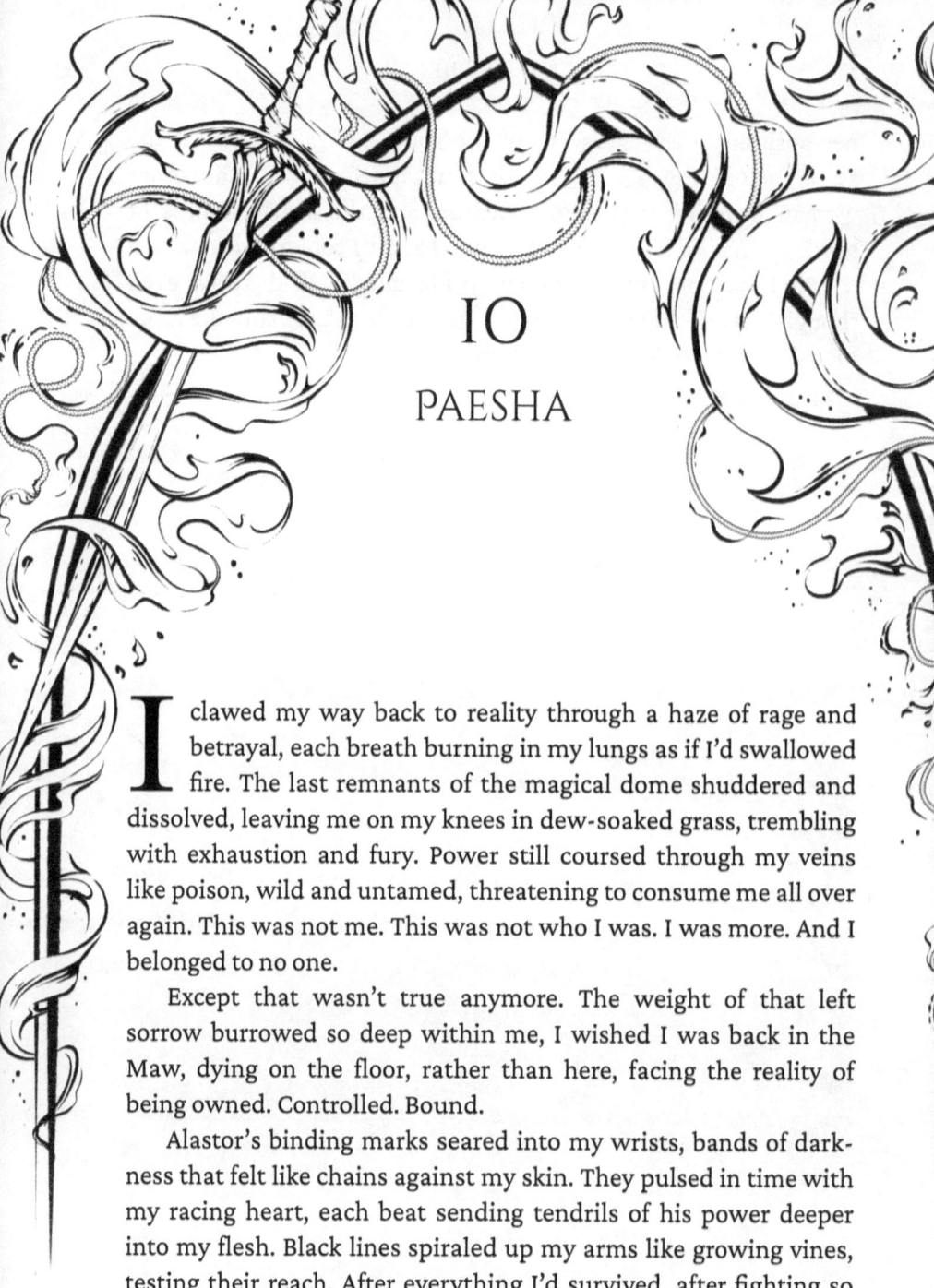

IO

PAESHA

I clawed my way back to reality through a haze of rage and betrayal, each breath burning in my lungs as if I'd swallowed fire. The last remnants of the magical dome shuddered and dissolved, leaving me on my knees in dew-soaked grass, trembling with exhaustion and fury. Power still coursed through my veins like poison, wild and untamed, threatening to consume me all over again. This was not me. This was not who I was. I was more. And I belonged to no one.

Except that wasn't true anymore. The weight of that left sorrow burrowed so deep within me, I wished I was back in the Maw, dying on the floor, rather than here, facing the reality of being owned. Controlled. Bound.

Alastor's binding marks seared into my wrists, bands of darkness that felt like chains against my skin. They pulsed in time with my racing heart, each beat sending tendrils of his power deeper into my flesh. Black lines spiraled up my arms like growing vines, testing their reach. After everything I'd survived, after fighting so hard for freedom, I'd been trapped again, not by a crime lord's bargain but by a god's manipulation.

He owns you now.

You let him win.

You broke.

The voices grew louder, a chorus of whispers that gained strength from my despair. My Remnants swirled across my skin like moving tattoos, responding to their call, eager to break free and destroy. A battlefield of his magic and mine ran rampant within me. It was too much.

Too much. We've never been too much.

I pressed my palms against my temples, trying to silence the dissonance of whispers. That was when I noticed the quiet. Not just the absence of my own screaming magic, but a different kind of stillness. The kind that came with exhausted vigilance, with love that outlasts fear.

Moonlight painted silver streaks through the meadow, illuminating a scene that made my heart stutter. Quill lay curled in a nest of blankets near where the dome of uncontrollable power had held me captive, her wild curls falling across the fabric like spilled ink. Boo's head rested in her lap, but his brown-tipped tail thumped softly against the grass when he spotted me. She'd stayed. Despite everything, despite the monster I'd become, her waning control over her emotions, she'd refused to leave. Though she shouldn't have been here at all.

Archer stood a few paces away, a silent sentinel in the darkness. His sword was lowered but ready, those bright blue eyes reflecting fading starlight as he watched the last wisps of my magic fade into nothing. He didn't speak, didn't move, just maintained his protective stance between us and whatever might emerge from the shadows. The shadows that now lived inside me.

How long had they waited? Hours, based on the moon's position and the heavy dew coating the grass. Hours of standing guard while I raged and screamed inside my cocoon of darkness. The binding marks flared, sending sharp pain up my arms. I bit back a cry, not wanting to wake Quill. The dark lines had spread farther, creating intricate patterns that seemed to shift and move of their own accord. They were changing, growing stronger. And with them, the voices grew bolder.

They'll never be safe with you.
You're his now.
His weapon.
His destruction.

Quill stirred in her sleep, fingers curling into Boo's fur as she murmured something too soft to hear. Even now, even after witnessing the darkness I carried, she trusted me enough to sleep peacefully beside me. The thought made my chest ache with a pain that had nothing to do with magic or bindings. This child claimed me as her own. She'd seen past the monster to the broken woman beneath. And at the age of only nine, she'd stood toe-to-toe with a god she had no business speaking to. Gods help us all when she was grown.

A glint of gold caught my eye. That damned book materialized on the edge of Quill's blanket. I looked away, refusing to acknowledge its presence or the way my heart clenched at the sight of it. Not now. Not when the wound of Thorne's betrayal was still raw and bleeding. Not when I needed to focus on the family who'd stayed by my side and had chosen to weather my storm rather than seek safer shelter.

"You stayed," I whispered, careful not to wake Quill as I peeled myself from the ground and moved to Archer's side. My legs shook with each step, the marks around my ankles burning like brands.

"I'll always stay."

"I heard what you said to him."

His voice dropped as he turned away. "He was our friend, and he didn't care at all. I could see it in his eyes when I mentioned her name. He didn't care, and she loved him like a brother. What right did he have to her devotion?"

I slipped my hand into Archer's, grateful when he didn't flinch away from the dark marks spreading up my arms. "He had no right at all."

"She was the best thief I ever knew. Could lift a purse without leaving a whisper of a touch. Remember that job in the governor's mansion?"

I nodded, having heard pieces of this story before.

"She scaled that wall in a full gown. Three daggers strapped to her thigh, jewels in her hair, and not a single guard suspected the beautiful lady was anything but another noble's daughter."

He laughed softly. "Then some drunk lordling tried to corner her in the hallway, and she had a blade at his throat before he could blink. Didn't even wrinkle her dress."

"She was something else with those daggers," I murmured, remembering the one she'd gifted me.

"Grandmother insisted on dance lessons when we were young," Archer explained. "Harlow hated every minute until she realized it made her faster with a blade. After that, she never complained again."

His eyes grew distant. "You know she kept a tally? A little mark for every successful job, inked into the handle of her favorite dagger. She was so damn proud of that knife. She was terrible at cards, though," he admitted with a soft chuckle. "Couldn't bluff worth a damn. But it didn't matter because no one was looking at her cards. They were too busy staring at her face."

"She knew it, too," I recalled. "Used it to her advantage."

"Every time. She'd lean forward, flutter those eyelashes, and suddenly no one remembered what game we were playing." His smile faded. "But she never used people, not really. That wasn't her way."

He looked down at our joined hands. "The night before... before Ezra's men... she was cleaning her daggers. All six of them laid out on the bed. She said something I can't stop thinking about. 'Archie, if something happens to me, promise you won't be alone.'"

My heart twisted painfully in my chest.

"I didn't take her seriously. I told her not to be so dramatic. I'm pretty sure I even threw a dinner roll at her. But she gave me that look, you know the one, like she knew something I didn't. She said, 'We found a family here. Don't throw it away, no matter what happens.'"

Archer's shoulders trembled slightly. "She knew, Paesha. Somehow, she knew."

"She was protecting you," I said gently. "Right until the end. That's who she was."

"I should have protected her," he whispered.

"And she would say the same if your positions were reversed," I reminded him. "Harlow made her choice. She loved you enough to die for you. Honor that choice by living for her."

He finally turned to face me fully, his eyes shining with unshed tears. "I'm trying. Gods know I'm trying."

The silence was vast and all-consuming. We stood there together, staring at the tree line. Eventually, he spoke again. "I don't want to be sad anymore. I don't think it's good for the kid, you know."

"Tiptoeing around her isn't good for her either."

"I should have never told her who Thorne was when we were standing in the house. She was like a tiny little beast, but he could have done anything. And I fed into that. She couldn't control herself because I couldn't. It's not right. She's yours, so she's mine too. That's how this is going to work. I lost everyone in my family." He took a deep breath. "Everyone. I need a new family. I can't lose control."

I held my arms out to show him Alastor's bands circling my wrists, the patterns now reaching my elbows. "You think *you* lost control?"

"I wasn't going to ask."

"I'm bound to Alastor now. Of all the villains in last night's show, he proved to be the worst."

Archer drew back, grabbing my arm to study the swirling magic moving on my wrist. "Are you... That can't be right."

"Remember when I told you I still owed him a name? Apparently, because I couldn't deliver it, I broke the bargain and now... Well, I don't even know what happens now."

You know exactly what happens.

He'll use you to break them all.

Starting with the ones you love.

That's what I would do if I were him.

I lifted my shoulder, turning away from the voices only I could hear, but they were getting harder to ignore. The Remnants writhed beneath my skin, feeding off my growing fear.

"You okay?" Archer asked.

"No. Not for so many reasons. But let's take the kid inside before the wet grass soaks her through."

"I'll carry her. You get the dog and the blankets."

When Archer slid his arms under Quill to lift her, she immediately fought him, kicking and screaming until she heard me speak. "I'm here, Quilly. It's okay. We're going inside."

Quill's small voice took me back to when she was four and made us check for monsters in her room every night for five months. "You escaped?"

"Yeah. I escaped." I pressed my forehead to hers as she lay in Archer's arms. "Thanks for staying with me."

"We're family," she yawned.

I watched as Archer carried Quill inside, cradled protectively against his chest. Something tightened in my throat at the sight. This makeshift family we were cobbling together from broken pieces and shared pain.

As I gathered the damp blankets, my fingers brushed against cool metal. Thorne's golden book lay half-hidden in the folds of fabric. With a growl of frustration, I hurled it as far as I could into the darkness of the surrounding woods.

"Fuck off, Reverius Hawthorne Noctus."

The marks flared in response to my anger, sending waves of pain up my arms. The patterns had reached my shoulders now, intricate swirls of darkness that pulsed with their own heartbeat. I stumbled slightly as I followed Archer inside, the searing pain around my ankles spreading with each step.

Inside, the house was quiet save for the soft crackle of the dying fire. Archer had already taken Quill upstairs. I paused in the doorway of the sitting room, taking in the familiar space that now felt foreign. How could everything look so normal when my world had been turned upside down yet again? I'd have to leave soon, I was sure of it. Alastor wouldn't have bound me to let me live free of his command.

The blankets slipped from my grasp as exhaustion hit me like a physical blow. I stumbled to the couch and sank down, burying my face in my hands. "What am I going to do?" I whispered to the empty room.

You know what you have to do.

Break.

I lifted my head, half-expecting to see that fucking book materialized on the coffee table. I scanned the room, searching for that telltale glint of metal. Nothing. For a moment, relief washed over me. Then, as if summoned by my thoughts, there it was. Sitting innocently on the mantel above the fireplace, its gilt edges catching the last flickering embers.

My fingers twitched with the urge to hurl it into the dying flames. To watch it burn again and again until either it or I was reduced to ash. But Archer's words echoed in my mind. I couldn't lose control. Not again. Not when Quill was sleeping peacefully upstairs, finally feeling safe enough to let her guard down. Not when we were all trying so hard to build something stable from the wreckage of our lives.

I forced myself to take a deep breath. Slowly, deliberately, I unclenched my fists, focusing on the feeling of my nails leaving crescent-shaped marks in my palms. I wouldn't give Thorne the satisfaction of seeing me unravel. Nor Alastor. They couldn't have that power over me anymore.

Instead, I stood and walked to the mantel with measured steps, letting the magic burn. My hand hovered over the book, trembling slightly before I lifted it and opened it to the first page. His handwriting was fucking perfect.

Keep the book, Paesha. If you need me, I'll come. Don't let that anger consume you. I'm not afraid of those shadows. I'll stand there and let you cut me down a thousand times if you need to stretch that power. Break me. Crush me. Just let it be me and no one else.

Thorne

"Aeris tried to pull her away and she wouldn't come," Thea said from the door, startling me. She held two steaming cups, looking over at me with a gross amount of pity.

I snapped the book shut. "Good. We trust no gods in this house."

"I think that's pretty unfair." She crossed the room and handed me one of the steaming cups.

"You wouldn't say that if you grew up in a world full of them," Archer said from the door.

"Aeris is different. She's only been benevolent and giving."

I sat, sliding the book under my leg, ignoring the way the heat of it raced across my thigh. Alastor's marks around my wrist pulsed. I was reaching my wits' end with magic, but still I swallowed it down, refusing to let them see. "Where'd she come from last night, Althea? Why did she happen to show up right in the middle of the chaos? Explain it."

"I... I don't know," Thea admitted, her brow furrowing. "She just appeared, like she always does when we need her. She tried to calm Quill down, but at that point, there was no reasoning with her."

I took a sip of the tea, letting the warmth seep into my bones. "And Reverius or Thorne or whatever the fuck his name is? What happened to him?"

Archer leaned against the doorframe, his arms crossed. "He vanished not long after Aeris showed up. One minute he was there, looking like he wanted to tear through your creepy magic dome thing, and the next, he was gone."

It was too convenient, too neat. Gods didn't show up out of nowhere without an agenda. I'd learned that lesson the hard way.

Thea's lying.

They're all lying.

They know you can't trust Aeris.

Break them before they break you.

"We can't trust her," I said firmly, fighting to keep my voice steady as the Remnants grew louder. "No matter how benevolent she seems. The moment we let our guard down is the moment gods strike. She has an angle. You're going to have to trust me on this."

Thea's face fell. "But she's been nothing but helpful and kind, Paesha. When's the last time you trusted anyone? Honestly. And Quill's going to be pissed if you try to cut her off from Aeris. You know how she is about her friends."

"Paesha trusted me and look how that turned out," Archer said with a small smile.

"I've not made my mind up about you yet, Archer Bramwell."

His smile widened and a glimpse of my friend peeked through. "I'm quite charming when I want to be."

"All men think they're charming. Most are disgusting." She took a sip, watching him carefully.

"Lucky for you, I haven't been disgusting for at least six months."

She smiled, rolling her eyes. "Nice try."

I watched the easy banter between Archer and Thea with a mix of emotions. On one hand, it warmed my heart to see them getting along. On the other, a twinge of jealousy and loneliness tugged at me. I pushed it aside, focusing on the matter at hand and not on the book burning beneath my thigh.

The marks pulsed again, sending a wave of dizziness through me. The patterns had spread farther, now covering most of my arms and I'd guess my legs, if the burning was any indication.

Alastor's power sank deeper. I was running out of time. Out of freedom.

"Look," I said, drawing their attention back. "I know Aeris seems okay. But we need to be cautious. If I've learned anything, it's that gods always have hidden agendas."

Thea sighed. "I understand your mistrust, P. But maybe not all gods are the same? Aeris has done some good—"

"Was it good? Where are all the people in the city?"

She opened her mouth to speak, paused, and then said nothing as she considered the question.

"There was no one when we walked through, was there?" I asked Archer.

"I didn't see a soul."

"You can't focus on perceived good, Thea. Thorne was good. Until he wasn't, so that argument isn't going to win with me. That's how they draw you in. It's all kindness and gifts until you're so wrapped around them you can't see straight. We don't risk it. Not with Quill. Not with her power."

Archer nodded. "Where I'm from, the gods toy with mortals for sport. It's safer to keep our distance."

"I've been gone for what? Three months? Children can certainly change in three months, but this wild swing of Quill's personality must have come from somewhere. Think about it in correlation to when Aeris started coming around. The gods always circle their prey before they strike. She was manipulating her."

Thea looked between us, copper brows pulled together. Finally, she nodded. "All right. We'll be careful. But I still think you're being too harsh."

I softened my tone. "I hope you're right about her. I really do. But for now, we watch and wait. We won't shut her out for Quill, but that door isn't wide open, as far as I'm concerned." I locked eyes with Archer. "About Stirling, I think we need to check on the orphans. From there we'll know where we should be."

"Are you sure you want to go back there?" His eyes dropped to my wrists, to the darkness spreading across my skin.

"Being in Requiem won't save me from Alastor. I don't know

when he'll summon me, but I need to make sure this is taken care of first. Just in case." The voices screamed in protest, but I pushed them down. I had to do something, had to move, had to act before I lost all control.

"You're not taking care of me, Fingers. Where you go, I go. If Alastor summons you, well, I guess he's in for a rude awakening when we both show up."

"I'm sure he'll be a big fan of that."

II

PAESHA

Did I have the strength to open that door? Could I stand in his home, in his study, and not be consumed by the thoughts of him? Could I forget it all? His hands on me, his lips on mine?

Yes. I could. Because fuck him. And the book that lay under my pillow, burning hot and mostly ignored, though I could likely draw the etchings on the spine in my sleep at this point. If I ever slept again, but as the door slowly crept open and Quill came stumbling in, rubbing her eyes, I simply scooted over and lifted the covers, letting her crawl in beside me.

"Are you fixed?" she whispered, dragging her little finger down my nose.

"I'm working on it, my girl. I promise."

"Your heart still hurts."

"Yes, it does."

She wrapped her arms around me, her breath warm against my skin. "That wasn't a question."

"We thought maybe we could go on a little adventure today. Remember when I told you about the children in Stirling?"

"We get to go meet them?"

89

"We do. But only if you're on your best behavior, Quilly. No tantrums. No big bursts of magic."

"I can't believe there's an entire house of children. I'm so excited. I could take some of my books and things."

"That would be kind."

Quill hadn't been around many children because there were so few in Requiem, but I imagined it'd be good for her to be around others her age. To see it was okay to be nine with no pressure to be anything more than that. No matter what her power would have her believe.

"DID YOU SLEEP AT ALL?" Archer asked as we stood together at the door, waiting for the others to join us.

"No. You?"

"Nope. But I've got to face it, I guess. If this is what you're sure you want to do, we do it together."

The bands, reminding me I belonged to Alastor, burned so severely, it was hard to ignore them, but I did my best, forcing a smile as I watched Quill come bouncing down the steps toward us, a bag flung over her shoulder. She held up her pointer finger. "I got a paper cut from one of the books. I don't have to put the stinging stuff on it, do I?"

She hated Elowen's tinctures.

Archer knelt down. "I think a paper cut is probably okay to heal on its own, but I could take care of it for you if you wanted me to."

I nearly choked on my gasp. Archer hated using his magic.

"Why does that make you nervous?" Quill asked, tilting her head as she looked at Archer. "I can tell, you know?"

"I know." He took a deep breath, speaking words I'd always known him to avoid. "My sister used to have a really special power. And one day a bad man took it because of something foolish I did. Ever since, I've hated using mine. It felt wrong, like I was betraying her somehow. But now she's gone, and I've realized something. Harlow hated it when I held back because of what happened to her. She pushed me to embrace who I was, magic and all. She'd want me to use my gift to help others." Archer gently took Quill's hand, examining the small cut on her finger. "So maybe it's time I start honoring her memory by doing what she always encouraged me to do."

As Archer's fingers traced over Quill's paper cut, time appeared to slow, then stop completely. Dust motes hung suspended in shafts of morning light streaming through the windows. The pendulum of the grandfather clock in the hall froze mid-swing. Even the flames in the fireplace stood eerily still, frozen tongues of blue, orange and gold.

For a breathless moment, Archer, Quill and I were caught in a bubble outside of time. The cut on her finger remained unchanged, neither healing nor worsening. Archer's eyes widened in shock, his fingers still hovering over Quill's hand. Her curls were suspended in mid-bounce, her mouth open in shock, likely just like mine.

I watched in stunned silence. The binding marks on my wrists pulsed urgently, as if sensing the disturbance in the natural order of things. Then, as suddenly as it began, the moment shattered. Time lurched back into motion with an audible snap. The dust motes resumed their lazy dance. The clock ticked on, and the fire crackled merrily as if nothing had happened.

Archer jerked his hand back as if he'd been burned, staring at his fingers.

"What was that?" I asked.

"I... I don't know. It doesn't make sense."

"Hey, you fixed it. There's no hurt at all now." Quill held up her hand.

But neither of us looked away from each other. "Archer, correct me if I'm wrong, but you descend from a healing god of some kind, don't you?"

He narrowed his eyes, looking at me like I'd grown a second head. "No. I don't think so."

"Because it's time?" I whispered, as if Vesalia could hear me speak her name. "What was Harlow's power? Before she lost it?"

"She could pause time. Holy shit. She could pause time. Is that what I just did?"

I opened my mouth to speak but couldn't. Not for moments, as I replayed what had happened.

"I think the answer you're looking for is yes," said a voice from the porch.

Fucking Aeris.

I flung the door open. "When did you get here?"

"I knocked, no one answered."

"Archer healed my finger," Quill said, lifting her pointer finger as if Aeris could see the injury.

"Did he now?"

"You didn't answer my question. When did you get here?"

"About three minutes ago, dear. Forgive me. I was caught off guard by the time halt."

"You felt that?" Archer asked.

"I did, but don't worry. Most wouldn't have. Not unless they were close enough to you. Are we headed somewhere?"

Archer and I didn't get to answer before Quill. "Yes. We're going to see the orphans in the new city."

"Oh," Aeris said, that wrinkled smile on her face fooling only Quill as Archer and I exchanged a glance. "That's lovely. I'm sure you'll have quite the adventure."

"You should come," Quill said, bouncing on her toes as Aeris smoothed her hands down her brown apron.

"Gods probably have far more important things to do than follow mortals around the cities," I tried, hoping Aeris would take the hint.

Though I'm sure she did, she still saw the opportunity and grabbed it. "Oh nonsense. I'd be happy to tag along. See what I can make of Stirling these days."

"I'm pretty sure Stirling is fine without fancy makeovers and gilded streets," I said, not bothering to hide the unamused tone in my voice.

"Don't mind her." Quill took Aeris's hand. "She doesn't trust you. She says we have to be careful with the gods. But I told her you were good, so Thea says she'll come around."

"Quill, you don't have to repeat everything you hear," I hissed at her.

"I know," the kid said with a shrug as she stepped past me and walked out the door with Aeris.

"We can't take her to Thorne's house," Archer whispered. "We have to protect those kids."

I sighed heavily, pinching the bridge of my nose. "We can't uninvite her now without pissing off Quill. And after everything that's happened, I don't want to risk setting her off again. Her power is too volatile, too dangerous, when she's upset."

Archer's jaw clenched as he watched Aeris and Quill chatting animatedly on the porch. "I get it, but bringing a god into Thorne's home, into the orphanage... It feels wrong. Like we're betraying their trust somehow."

"I know," I said softly. "But we'll be vigilant. We won't let Aeris out of our sight for a second."

The creak of floorboards drew our attention as Thea descended the stairs with Elowen close behind. Our small group made its way through the transformed landscape of Requiem. The city I once knew had been utterly changed, remade into something both beautiful and unsettling. Dark marble edifices loomed on either side of us. Ornate carvings adorned the front of every building with twining vines, mythical beasts, and scenes from a history I didn't recognize. The streets were paved with gold, real gold that clinked softly with each step. It should have been breathtaking, but there was an artificial quality to it all, as if someone had tried to recreate a city from a fairytale without quite understanding what made a place feel alive. It was cold. Missing the fire built to keep a homeless man safe, missing the warmth of an old woman wrapped in layers of threadbare scarves as she watched the hustle and bustle of the people passing by. And it was still missing the people. All of them.

Quill skipped ahead, her curls bouncing as she pointed out various landmarks to Archer. "And over there used to be an old, rusted bench, but now it's this amazing statue of a mermaid! The water comes out of her tail and everything. Isn't it wonderful?"

Archer nodded, looking around in wonder, seeing Requiem for the first time in daylight, though I was seeing it for the first time too. "Sure is, Pencil. Just missing the people."

"And it's all thanks to Aeris," Quill beamed. "Paesha, isn't it amazing?"

I forced a smile, not wanting to dampen Quill's enthusiasm. "It's certainly... different."

Was it entirely coincidental that we had to walk through the Gambler's Quarter, past Misery's End to get to the meeting point of Stirling and Silbath? Maybe, but passing that building, seeing how it'd been left untouched when everything around it had transformed, twisted something inside of me. But it wasn't truly the same. The last time I'd seen it, the theater where I used to dance half naked was no more than a pile of rubble on the street. The aftermath of a desperate man. But she'd brought it back. Exactly as it had been, encased in wrought-iron railings and the richest building in the city back then. Now it was nothing compared to its neighbors. An eyesore, if anything. But then it always had been to those that knew the truth behind the stage, knew where the blood stains were never cleaned and the tears never quite dried.

"I asked her not to change it," Thea said quietly, looking back over her shoulder. "Whatever that place was, we need to make peace with it first."

I quickened my pace, refusing to stare at the familiar building. "I made my peace with that stage the day Deyanira set it on fire. Makes no difference to me now."

"All the same," Aeris said, "Maybe someday it'll mean something again. When we change our space, we change our mindset. Isn't that right, Quill?"

The two of them carried on a conversation as Archer took my side and slowed down, letting a noticeable gap grow between us before he whispered, "Seems strange Thorne said—"

"Reverius," I corrected him.

"Right. Him. Seems strange the gods' magic is failing, yet Aeris was able to rebuild a whole city in gold, doesn't it?"

"As soon as you figure out that Lord High and Mighty is a fucking liar, let me know so we can stop circling these conversations."

"Why would he lie about that?"

I jerked to a stop, slowly turning to stare at him. He threw his hands up. "No. You're right. Dumb question."

"Are you guys coming?" Thea asked.

I didn't miss the hint of excitement in her voice, and I couldn't really blame her. Our tiny world had grown with hundreds of thousands of more possibilities to shape her life. This was an adventure for Thea. Something new and exciting. She could go north. Maybe become the woman from Misby I'd once claimed to be. She could explore. We all could, really. Maybe somewhere in this world there were people worth knowing and loving and protecting beyond our little group. Beyond the gods that caged us in like animals.

"You better take the lead from here," Thea said to Archer as we crossed into Stirling, where the golden streets were abruptly brick and the buildings lackluster, and honestly perfect.

I remember the first time I stepped into this world and thought it lacked color and character and longed to return home. It was drab then, but at least the homes had likely been built by mortals and most of the city's character hadn't been erased by the whims of a goddess shoving her sense of restoration down everyone's throats. Stirling remained a patchwork of weathered brick and timeworn stone. The streets here were narrow and winding, lined with buildings that leaned slightly, as if whispering secrets to their neighbors across the way.

We passed through the Salt District, where the air was thick with the tang of brine and the clamor of Salt hawking their wares. The market had come back to life after the death of the prince, it seemed. It spoke more of restoration than gilded streets and shiny black buildings. Take some fucking notes, Aeris.

The transition to the Silk District was gradual but unmistakable. The buildings grew taller, their facades adorned with intricate carvings and colorful awnings. Delicate fabrics billowed in shop windows, shimmering in hues that put even Aeris's golden streets to shame, in my opinion. The air here was perfumed with exotic spices and the subtle scent of wealth. Again, something Requiem was missing. Not to mention the springtime flowers adorning the faces of all the buildings, giving the city the color it lacked in the winter.

"Fix your face, Fingers. If I didn't know any better, I'd say you were ogling my city."

I lifted a brow. "*Your* city? Does that mean you're—"

"I mean the city where I was born. Nothing more. Don't get any ideas."

"No ideas. Got it."

Throughout our journey, Archer's demeanor changed. His shoulders tensed, his stride becoming more purposeful as he led us through the labyrinthine streets. His eyes remained fixed on the path ahead, carefully avoiding the looming silhouette of his father's castle that dominated the top of the hill in the distance.

I couldn't say I blamed him, though. Not as we neared Thorne's street and Noctus House grew closer. I knew he wouldn't be there, but that overwhelming feeling that I shouldn't go in took over, making every step harder, every breath heavier.

Alastor's binding marks burned with increasing intensity, the pain radiating up my limbs in waves of searing heat. I gritted my teeth, determined not to let the others know, but the agony was becoming unbearable.

I took off my cloak and hung it over my arm, dabbing my sweaty forehead. I stumbled slightly, my vision blurring as another wave of pain crashed over me.

Archer caught my elbow, steadying me with a concerned look. "You all right?"

I nodded tightly, not trusting myself to speak. The others were right behind us, Quill's excited chatter drifting up to me on the cool spring breeze. I wouldn't let them see me become weak. Wouldn't let them know about the voices. The voices. Worse than the pain, were the garbled whispers dancing through my mind.

As we rounded the corner onto Thorne's street, the burning intensified to an almost blinding degree. My legs threatened to give out beneath me. Desperate for relief, for a breath, I turned away from our destination.

The change was immediate and startling. The moment I'd faced away, the pain subsided to a dull throb. My eyes widened as realization dawned. This wasn't simply a branding or a punishment. It was a summons. The binding marks were pulling me toward the Vale, toward Alastor's black market. The burning wasn't meant to hurt me, it was guiding me. Beckoning me to come to him. Fucker.

The temptation to give in was overwhelming. To let the magic lead me to where it wanted me to go to end this torment. But the thought of submitting to Alastor's will steeled my resolve. I squared my shoulders and turned back toward Noctus house, bracing myself for the onslaught of pain. It hit me like a physical blow, nearly driving me to my knees. But I would not fucking yield. Not to him. Not yet. Not until the skin was dripping from my bones and the only other option was death. And even then, I'd still be a stubborn bitch about it. I didn't want to be his lackey. I didn't want to be his little minion. I wanted nothing to do with any of them.

With each excruciating step, I pushed forward, letting the burning consume me rather than control me. We stood on the narrow walk in front of Thorne's home and I kept my breathing steady, my face blank. But Thea knew me too well and Quill could feel my heartache. Before Archer could lift a hand to knock, my past was glued to my side, taking my hands in theirs and refusing to waver. This place hurt. Not only because of the fire burning in my veins, but because of the lies dripping down the walls of this home. It'd all started with a lie. With a ring slid onto my finger I had no right to wear, but at least that one we were both in together.

Except you weren't.

He knew, and you didn't know.

97

He knew his target.

You knew nothing. You were always his conquest.

Archer spun to look at me, taking in Thea and Quill at my side before asking, "Do we knock?"

Aeris stepped past all of us, clicking her tongue to her teeth as she shook her head, rubbing her wrinkled hands over the tarnished knocker. "Not with this old thing. It'll likely crumble on impact."

She pulled her hand away, revealing a bright, shiny, new knocker with the face of a... well, her. She'd put her own fucking face on the knocker of Thorne's house. Reverius's house. And honestly, it might've been funny, if not for the fact that this was now home to a horde of orphans and their collective caretakers. I slid between her and Archer, folding my arms over my chest as I stared at her.

"Let me ask you a really serious question. Is the gods' power truly failing?"

The old woman folded her hands and her kind smile rattled me. "Oh, yes, dear. I didn't realize the Keeper had told the mortals."

I narrowed my eyes. "How thoughtless of him. But maybe let's not use frivolous bits of power in places we don't belong."

I was probably the only one that clocked the twitch in her eye as she nodded. "What an excellent idea. I should reserve my power. I hadn't realized you'd be so protective of a home that isn't yours. I'm ever so sorry, Huntress." The bite in her tone was obvious.

"Change it back."

"I beg your pardon?"

"The knocker. Change it back."

"But it's better now, Paesha," Quill said, her tone of disgust cutting right through me.

You see, don't you? They're turning against you.

"She put her own face on someone else's door. It doesn't belong here." I had no idea what Aeris's power would do after she marked this building, and I wasn't willing to find out if a war broke out between gods and mortals.

"That's not her face." Quill giggled. "That's a pig."

I spun back to the knocker, shocked to find the snout of a golden pig staring back at me.

"That's really below you," Thea said quietly. "There's no need to be mean, Paesha."

"No, really, I swear it was..." My words disappeared as I took in Archer's face and his sympathetic smile.

"You must have glanced at it too quickly," he said.

I knew what I saw. I knew it was Aeris's face only seconds ago. I opened my mouth to argue, to insist that I knew what I had seen, but the words died on my tongue. Doubt crept in, insidious and unwelcome. Did I imagine that? Was the stress, the pain, the constant battle against Alastor's magic fucking with my brain?

I forced a smile, though it felt more like a grimace. "You're right. I must have looked too quickly. My mistake."

Aeris's quick smile smothered the glint in her eyes until I was sure there was a hint of hurt shining through. "It's all right. We're all a bit on edge."

She covered the knocker with her hand and pulled it away to reveal the original. Then, without a word, moved down the step and to the back of the line. As if to retreat from a space she didn't feel like she belonged. Which was fine with me, because she didn't. Hurt feelings or not, I didn't want her there. Still, Thea's glare in my direction spoke every word Aeris hadn't.

To break the tension, I reached forward, slamming the ring of the knocker against the metal plate two times before it crumbled in my hands.

"See? She was only trying to help," Quill said.

With nothing to say and the pain around my wrists burning, I didn't acknowledge her. Instead, I changed which arm my cloak hung on and knocked louder. No one came.

After a few moments, Archer stepped past me using his favorite knock, before placing his ear to the door. He shrugged. "Guess they aren't here."

"I find it hard to believe Briony took all the kids out on an adventure," I argued, reaching around him to try the knob.

The door swung open effortlessly. We stepped into the foyer. The house was still, unnaturally so, as if all the life had been suddenly drained from it.

"Hello?" Archer called out, his voice echoing through the empty halls. No response came.

We moved farther into the house. The sitting room to our right was bathed in warm sunlight streaming through the windows, illuminating a scene that made my blood run cold. Briony lay sprawled across the chaise, a book fallen from her limp fingers to the floor. Her chest rose and fell in the slow, steady rhythm of deep sleep. Nearby, two children were slumped over a game of chess, their heads resting on the board, pieces scattered around them.

In the kitchen, we found more of the same. A young boy sat at the table, his face planted in a half-eaten bowl of porridge. Lianna was collapsed by the stove, a wooden spoon still clutched in her hand.

"What's happening?" Quill whispered, her voice trembling as she clung to my side.

I swallowed hard, fighting back the rising panic. "I don't know, but stay close."

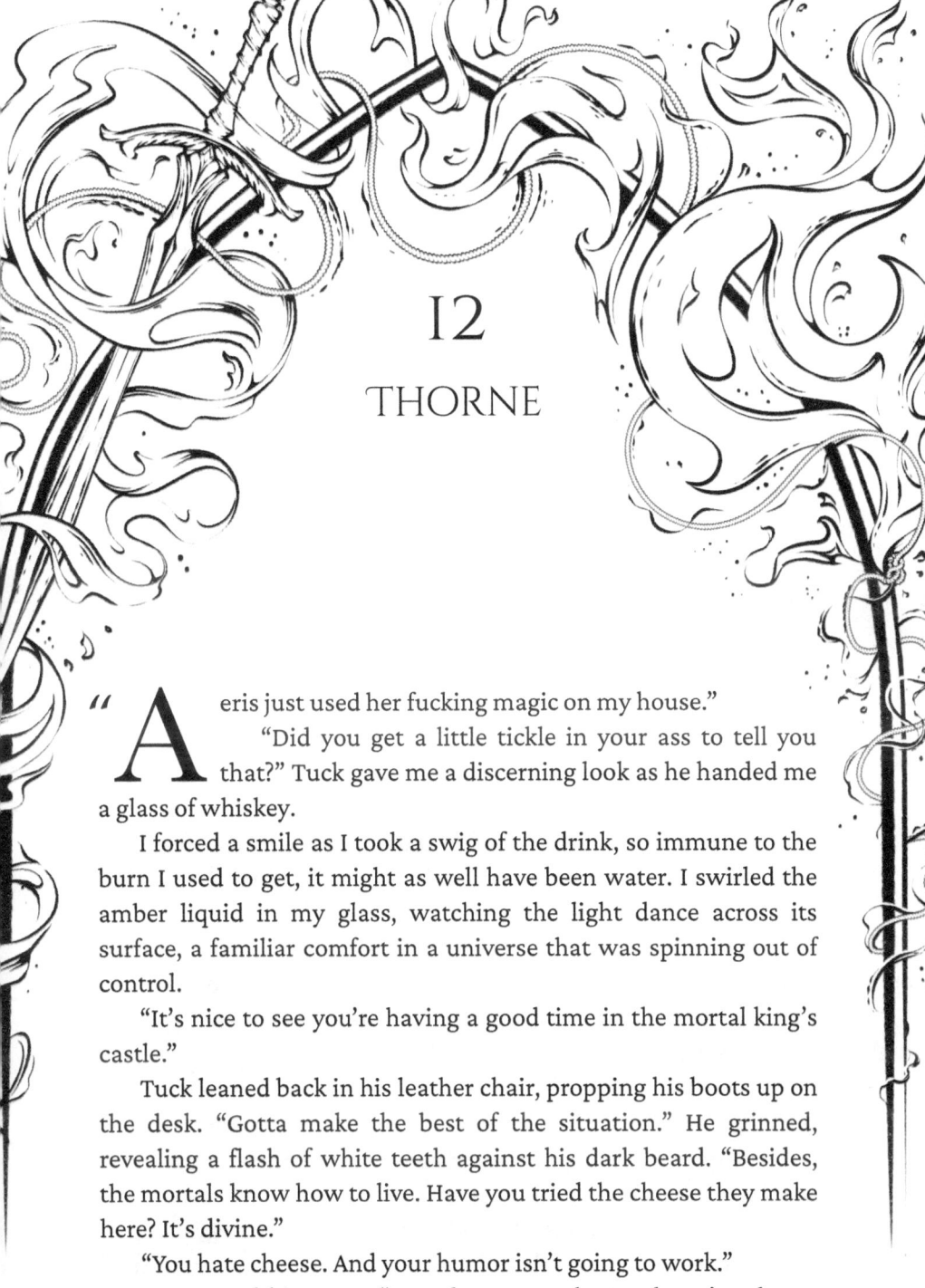

12

THORNE

"Aeris just used her fucking magic on my house."

"Did you get a little tickle in your ass to tell you that?" Tuck gave me a discerning look as he handed me a glass of whiskey.

I forced a smile as I took a swig of the drink, so immune to the burn I used to get, it might as well have been water. I swirled the amber liquid in my glass, watching the light dance across its surface, a familiar comfort in a universe that was spinning out of control.

"It's nice to see you're having a good time in the mortal king's castle."

Tuck leaned back in his leather chair, propping his boots up on the desk. "Gotta make the best of the situation." He grinned, revealing a flash of white teeth against his dark beard. "Besides, the mortals know how to live. Have you tried the cheese they make here? It's divine."

"You hate cheese. And your humor isn't going to work."

He crossed his arms. "You always say that and you're always wrong."

"It's not the same. She's not dead. She's still fucking here. She's *right there* and I can't do shit about it."

"You *could...*"

The ache in my fucking chest at the thought of shutting this whole show down was nearly unbearable. There wasn't enough power in the universe to do that now. "She's never going to choose me. That ship has sailed. You weren't there. You didn't see the way she looked at me."

"So buy her some damn flowers and say you're sorry."

I huffed, shaking my head. "Your suggestion is to lie to her again? I'm not fucking sorry, and you know that. I can't simply apologize and make this right. She knows almost everything now. Every lie, every manipulation. She hates me, Tuck. And she has every right to."

Tuck's hard expression softened slightly. "I've watched you chase this woman through countless lifetimes. You've moved worlds for her. You've been beaten, broken, and conquered. Maybe it's time to let her go."

"I can't," I growled, my voice low and dangerous. "She's mine. She's always been mine."

"Is she though?" Tuck challenged, standing to lean over his desk. "Seems to me she's made her choice pretty clear. And it ain't you."

I whirled around, my power crackling at my fingertips. For a moment, I considered unleashing it all on Tuck. Consequences be damned. But he was right, and that knowledge burned worse than any wound. He knew I'd never hurt him.

"What would you have me do? Stand by and watch as she builds a life without me? As she falls in love with someone else?"

He sighed, running a hand through his long, brown hair. "This obsession? It's fucking destroying you. And her. It's destroying everything. Maybe it's time for a change. Once and for all."

I turned to stare out the window, watching as the sun burned down the streets of Stirling. I couldn't let her go. I'd rather watch, haunt her every dream and thought, than be without her. "No. I can't do that."

Tuck sighed, his voice fading as he moved toward the door. "Then what's your plan, genius?"

"I'll find a way to win her back."

He rubbed his temples. "How exactly?"

"I don't know yet. But I have plenty of experience with her to figure it out."

"You're a damn fool if you think she's anything like her other lives. She's not going to lay down. She's going to fight back." He stepped back, chuckling. "She's fucking ruthless."

"Do you need a minute with your thoughts about my wife, Tuck?"

"Comments like that are exactly why Ezarius has the upper hand. He doesn't let his feelings cloud his judgment with her like you do."

"Well, then maybe it's time to change the rules of the game."

He shook his head and opened the door, walking out. "Let's revisit this conversation when you finally realize she's not here to play with you."

"It's annoying when you act like you know everything."

"It's annoying when you expect anything different from me. Now I need you to focus. I'm telling you, they are up to something."

"The gods are always up to something and where Bella's concerned, that's a guarantee."

"You need to shut her down. Ban her."

I matched his stride, and he fell slightly behind my right shoulder. As was proper, but completely unnecessary, and he knew it. "My power isn't strong enough right now. She knows that."

"Then send her to the Forgotten," he whispered.

"If I threw every annoying god into the Forgotten, I'd be alone."

"Might be good for you."

We strode through the castle's winding corridors. It was the same as every castle of every mortal king. Cold stone imprisonment. Over the years, the wives had thrown portraits on the walls and rugs on the floors to try to hide the damn gray, but it was never enough to warm the place.

As we approached the council chamber, the hushed whispers

of nobles and courtiers grew louder. Two guards flanked the double doors, their armor gleaming as they stood at attention. With a nod from me, they pushed the heavy doors open, revealing the chamber beyond.

At least this room had stained-glass windows. A long, polished oak table dominated the center, its surface inlaid with intricate patterns of gold and silver. A gift from a god, no doubt, but I couldn't be sure which one. Probably fucking Aeris, but that was only a guess. Around the table sat Aldus's most trusted advisors, their silk robes and jeweled fingers a clear display of what they believed to be wealth and status. The Silk. The fuckers that'd all but abandoned this king when he'd gone missing sure sat nicely at his table.

Mixed in though, in scattered seats with far less wear on them, were members of the Fray. Likely members that'd been hand chosen by Tuck as he infiltrated the king's council. Their eyes didn't meet mine with as much disdain as the others, which was expected, though I was a notable member of the Silk in this fucking realm. I'd built that reputation memory by memory, before making my bargain with Paesha.

The Silk sat rigid in their chairs as Tuck and I walked in like we owned the place. I couldn't force my will onto the royalty in the realms. The Fates had seen to that ages ago. But I could smash the rest of these mortals like bugs now that I wasn't trying to hold the damn veil in place.

Archer was right. I was a fucking asshole for holding the veil during that fight. But he was also wrong. Because those men that killed Harlow weren't ordinary mortals. They were Ezra's Unmade. His Guardians, bound to him. Had I not been using the threadbare tendrils of my own power to twist their minds, that fight would've ended differently. We would have lost more than one. Still the power was imbalanced, broken even, and almost every god blamed Paesha.

Tuck cleared his throat, staring at me wide-eyed. He glanced between the king and I once, expecting me to bow or something. I didn't. Instead, I pulled out a seat and plopped down, folding my hands on the table as I took in the faces of his council.

They hated me. I hated them. Solid way to start. Though to them, I was a noble, here to shame them for the way they'd abandoned their fucking king when he'd gone missing. At least they were right about one half of that.

I had to hide my surprise when I noticed a familiar face at the table. Minerva sat primly in her mortal guise. Her wrinkled face was a masterpiece of deception, every line and crease carefully crafted to portray a frail, elderly woman. But her eyes betrayed her true nature–sharp, piercing, and filled with the knowledge of millennia.

Her silver hair was pulled back into a severe bun, not a single strand out of place. As always, she wore a simple gray dress. Its high collar and long sleeves, a stark contrast to the silks and jewels adorning the other council members. Her gnarled hands were folded neatly on the table, the skin so thin I could see the blue veins beneath, pulsing with immortal blood.

What the hell was she doing here? Minerva hadn't meddled in mortal affairs for centuries, preferring to remain in her libraries when she wasn't pestering me about shit she thought I could have done differently. She was the closest thing I had to a mother figure, but she was ruthless when she wanted to be. Her presence here, in this mundane council chamber, set my teeth on edge. But unlike the rest of these fuckers, she knew her place. She knew when to push and when to back the hell off.

Aldus rose from his chair at the head of the table, the mortal king's weathered face creased with worry lines that hadn't been there before his imprisonment. The crown sat heavy on his brow. He cleared his throat, and the sound echoed in the suddenly silent chamber.

"My lords and ladies, I welcome you all to this council meeting. We face trying times, and I am grateful for your presence and counsel." His eyes swept across the room, lingering for a moment on Tuck and me. "As you can see, we have some unexpected guests with us today. I trust you will extend them the same courtesy and respect you would show to any member of this council."

The council members shifted in their privileged seats, exchanging glances filled with a mixture of curiosity and suspicion. I could practically taste their unease, a sour note in the air.

Lord Bartholomew, a portly man with a face as red as his silk robes, was the first to break the tense silence. He leaned forward, his multiple chins quivering as he spoke.

"Your Majesty," he began, his voice dripping with false politeness, "while we are, of course, honored by any guests you choose to bring into these hallowed chambers, perhaps you could explain *why* we have so many."

"Why should our king have to explain any of his choices to you?" Tuck asked.

"The Salt have no say in the way we run this kingdom," Bartholomew sneered.

"We?" I asked, tapping my boot to keep myself grounded.

"Did I stutter, Lord Thorne Noctus?"

I locked eyes with old Barty, my gaze as much of a weapon as any blade to his fucking throat, and that little bob in his throat proved it. I dove ruthlessly into the depths of his mind, tearing through his memories like a savage beast. The council chamber faded away as I plunged into the murky waters of his past.

Flashes of decadence and debauchery swirled around me, lavish parties, illicit affairs, backroom deals made in smoky taverns. But I pushed deeper, searching for that one crucial moment. And there it was, glimmering like a poisoned jewel in the muck of his consciousness.

Barty hunched over a desk, quill scratching furiously as he penned a letter. His face was illuminated by candlelight, sweat beading on his brow as he sealed the parchment with trembling hands. The memory crystallized, and I could see every detail with perfect clarity, the way his eyes darted nervously to the door, the slight tremor in his pudgy fingers as he pressed his signet ring into the hot wax.

The letter was addressed to a northern king, detailing Aldus's planned trade routes and the exact numbers of his army. Vital information that could cripple the kingdom if it fell into the wrong hands. And there was Bartholomew, practically gift wrapping it for the enemy.

I pulled back from his mind with a vicious wrench, leaving Bartholomew pale and shaking in his seat. I stood slowly, my chair scraping against the stone floor with an ominous screech. The room fell silent as I circled the table. Lord Bartholomew's face had gone from ruddy to ashen. Tuck cleared his throat. A warning to remember we were in a room full of mortals, no doubt. It wouldn't do to fucking terrify them. But I knew that already. Still, even their king sat quietly as I moved.

I held my voice low and measured. "I really didn't want to have to do this in front of everyone, but it seems, Your Majesty, that we have a traitor in our midst.

The council members shifted uneasily in their seats, eyes darting between me and Barty. I could smell their fear, sharp and acrid and fucking delicious.

"Not long ago, I had the misfortune of intercepting a rather interesting letter," I continued, pausing behind Bartholomew's chair. I placed my hands on his shoulders, feeling him flinch beneath my touch. "A letter penned by none other than our esteemed Lord Bartholomew here."

The portly lord began to sputter, but I squeezed his shoulders, silencing him.

"This letter was addressed to King Rhovan Caltheris. In this letter, our dear friend drew your enemy a fucking map with every planned stop on the trade routes." I resumed my circuit around the table. "Now, why would he need that?"

I'd planned to sit and observe this meeting, but I guess a little meddling in Aldus's affairs was due. The Fates kept us from controlling royalty, but there were always gray areas for truth and lies. The council chamber erupted into chaos. Lords and ladies leapt to their feet, shouting accusations and denials.

Bartholomew's face had gone from ashen to purple, his jowls quivering as he stammered out weak protests.

"Lies! All lies! This... this scoundrel has no proof! He seeks only to discredit me, Your Majesty!"

Aldus raised a hand, silencing the room with a gesture. His eyes, once warm and trusting, had turned to chips of ice as he regarded Bartholomew. "Is this true? Have you betrayed me? Betrayed our kingdom?"

Barty's eyes darted wildly around the room, seeking an ally, an escape. Finding none, he slumped in his chair, defeated. "Any of you would have done the same. Securing an alliance was necessary for protection." He turned to Aldus. "You've been sitting in this castle for years letting your son and his army poison this kingdom while you mourned a lost love. You call yourself a king? Where've you been Aldus? While we suffered?"

The mortal king opened his mouth to speak but was cut off by Evert Brand standing from his seat, growing in size and anger as he rose to his full six-foot, seven-inch frame. "You wouldn't know suffering if it crawled into your bed at night and bit the tip of your dick off, Silk." The way he spat the last word settled in the room like he'd breathed fire. "The Salt stayed. We searched the streets, even with the Cimmerians. We never gave up on our king, even when it meant dying. Or being tortured in the Maw like my damn wife."

"Enough," Aldus barked. He turned to the guards at the door. "Take Lord Bartholomew to the dungeons. We'll deal with him later."

As the guards dragged the blubbering lord away, I caught Minerva's eye across the table. A ghost of a smile played at her lips, and she inclined her head ever so slightly in acknowledgment. Whatever game she was playing, she seemed pleased with this turn of events.

The king stood, locking his frail hands behind his back as he began to pace the long aisle on the west side of the room. "I've never claimed to be a perfect king. I've made foolish decisions and I've paid for those. We can either heal together, or we can destroy each other. Those are the only options going forward." He turned to stare each of the council in the eye, even me before he moved on. "There is a clear divide in this country and I—"

The heavy oak doors burst open with a thunderous crash, silencing the king mid-sentence. All eyes turned to the entryway as two fucking goddesses sauntered into the council chamber.

13

THORNE

Serene glided in first. Golden eyes, luminous and hypnotic, swept across the room, leaving a trail of slack-jawed mortals in their wake. It was the same song and dance from Lithe. Her favorite mortal celebration. There wasn't a person in the room that didn't know of her. Some more personally than others, no doubt. Her gown, if it could be called that, clung to her curves like liquid shadow, revealing more than it concealed with each graceful step. Evert melted into his chair, likely giving her the reaction she'd hoped for.

Behind her strode Bellatora, Goddess of War and Ruin, pain in my ass. Her fiery red hair stood out against Serene's midnight curls. Her golden eyes sparkled with mischief when she looked at me. I had to remember I was playing mortal when my fingers twitched with darker, violent desires. I took my seat beside Tuck once more, exchanging a glance with Minerva before I sat back and let the shit show begin.

The temperature in the room rose several degrees as they passed, a party trick I'd taught Bellatora centuries ago. Several council members shifted uncomfortably in their seats, suddenly acutely aware of long forgotten desires and half remembered losses.

Aldus froze, stepping away from the goddesses as they circled the table and sat on both sides of his abandoned chair.

"Come join us, won't you Aldy, love?"

Serene's serpentine smile was met by Aldus's unwavering resolve. She'd pumped enough magic into that invitation, most mortals, those that hadn't known pleasure, would have fallen to their knees for her. I bit my lip to keep from smiling, knowing that said far more about Aldus's youth than it had Serene's power.

"Tell me why you're here," he countered. "You're welcome, of course, but when the Goddess of War and Ruin walks into my council chambers with the Goddess of Lust and Loss, one can never be too careful."

Smart man. Pissing off Serene was one thing. She'd poison your mind with lust or corrupt you with an incurable obsession with another, but Bellatora, she was dangerous for a mortal king. Perhaps not as dangerous as Minerva, but as of now, Aldus Windale had no idea there were five gods sitting in on his high council meeting. Whatever the agenda for the day had been, it'd just taken a hard right turn.

Bellatora's smile widened. A low rumble, like distant thunder, began to reverberate through the stone walls, filling the chamber with the symphony of a battle. The scent of smoke and copper filled the air, so thick you could almost taste it. Several in the room, Salt and Silk alike, clamped their hands over their ears, eyes wide with horror as they witnessed phantom soldiers cut down before them.

My expression was impassive as I watched the goddess work. This was child's play compared to what she was truly capable of, but it was enough to reduce most of the mortals to quivering messes. Evert shifted uncomfortably across from me, his jaw clenched tight as he fought against the goddess's influence. Bellatora's laughter cut through the chaos, a sound of pure, malicious joy. She reveled in the fear and anguish radiating from the humans, feeding off their terror like a leech. Her golden eyes gleamed with unholy light.

"My dear King Aldus, you stand on a precipice of your own making. You could very well find yourself with a war on your hands." She swirled her fingers into Aldus's gray hair. "I don't mind a war, Aldy, if it's what you want. But Serene and I were certain you should know the whispers of the Fates."

Lies. All lies. The Fates weren't holding meetings with gods. She was meddling. Pushing. Likely towards a war and not away from one.

"And what do the Fates tell you, Bellatora?" Minerva asked, drawing the gasp of those around her.

Bella narrowed her eyes on the old woman but answered coolly. "Only that our precious king must choose a successor immediately, lest he seem weak to those around him."

A hush fell over the room, the phantom battle fading to an ominous whisper. Aldus's face, already pale, drained of what little color remained.

"I am... terribly sorry for the loss of your son," Bellatora said, though her tone held no trace of sympathy. Her lips curled into a cruel smile as she continued. "But these matters cannot wait. I'm sure you understand."

The mortal king's face hardened, his eyes flashing with a mixture of grief and anger. "My child's body is barely cold, and you dare speak of succession? Have you no shame, goddess?"

Tuck and I shared a look. His choice of words were telling. Because he clearly spoke of Harlow in that statement and not of Farris.

Bellatora's smile only widened, revealing teeth that were a touch too sharp. "Shame? I am War. I am Ruin incarnate. Shame is a mortal concern. If you'd prefer my council be shared with other kingdoms, you must only ask."

I let my power roll through the room until the air was gone. Until the light faded away and the threat weighed heavily on her fucking shoulders. This was *my* realm now. Mine to govern. Mine to control. And she needed to back the fuck off. She cowered under the pressure. The glow she and Serene had sauntered in here with fading until they might've only been beautiful mortals.

Serene leaned into him, pointedly ignoring me, her golden eyes locked on Aldus. "We speak only out of concern for your kingdom, Your Majesty. Surely you can see the wisdom in our words? A kingdom without a clear line of succession is like a ship without a rudder, drifting aimlessly, vulnerable to any storm that may arise. Perhaps young Lord Cedric, with his sharp mind and sharper sword? Or Lady Elara, whose beauty is matched only by her cunning?" Serene's smile turned predatory as she delivered the real reason they'd come. "But let us not forget the most fascinating possibility of all, the Paramour. You chose her yourself at Lithe. Perhaps there was a reason you were so drawn to her?"

My vision narrowed, tunneling until all I could see was Serene's smug face as she spoke those damning words. The Paramour. *Paesha.*

I could feel my power surging. Though none in the room could see it, I reached deep within myself, pulling on power that had once flowed like water but now burned like molten steel in my veins. The taste of copper flooded my mouth as I focused my attack solely on the two goddesses. To the mortal eye, Serene and Bellatora simply went rigid in their seats, their eyes widening with a terror that none present had ever seen on a divine face. I forced them to experience every second of their existence simultaneously, every beginning and every ending, every moment of power and every instant of weakness, until their immortal minds began to fracture under the weight of their own histories.

Their carefully constructed facades cracked as they felt pieces of their divinity starting to unravel. The goddesses' eyes dulled to a muddy brown as they struggled to remember their own names, their own purposes, their own beginnings. They were young gods, barely more than children, and now they felt every second of their comparative insignificance.

The council members shifted uncomfortably, sensing something was wrong but unable to comprehend the true battle of power taking place before them. My mind screamed in protest as I held them suspended in that state of existential uncertainty, burning away fragments of my own divinity to maintain the assault.

Maybe now they would finally understand how far they had overstepped. They stumbled to their feet, their immortal powers flickering like candles, though to the council it would appear they simply lost their earlier confidence. The room remained perfectly normal, the stone walls solid, the air still, but Serene and Bellatora saw the truth in my eyes as I sat calmly in my chair; they were not the most dangerous beings in this chamber, and they never had been.

Minerva leaned forward, her wizened face creased with concern. "Surely you jest, goddess. The Paramour is but a commoner, with no claim to the throne."

"P-Pardon the intrusion, but will you not give the king a moment to speak on his own plans?" a Silk man asked, adjusting the sleeve on his tunic to keep from meeting the eyes of the goddesses.

"That's an interesting concept," I followed up, leaning back in my chair. "Selecting the king's successor seems awfully invasive," and against the fucking rules from the Fates, "Doesn't it?"

"Oh, we don't mean to choose for the mortal king," Bellatora answered, her voice far quieter than it'd been before. "Only help with options."

"Has he asked for your help?" Tuck asked, leaning forward to fill a glass of water from a pitcher on the table and slide it in front of the king. To most, that gesture would have meant nothing. A lowly man serving a king. But amongst the gods, Tuck was staking his claim over Aldus Windale. He served him. And that was that. I loved that growly bastard.

Aldus reached for the glass and took a sip, sharing a nod of gratitude to Tuck before addressing the goddesses. "I do appreciate the warning. And the work you've done to bring me options. I shall think on this and make a decision soon. You have my word."

They'd lost this battle, and they knew it.

"Of course, Your Majesty. We bow to your wisdom in this matter."

Bellatora inclined her head, her fiery hair cascading over her shoulder like a river of blood. "We shall take our leave, then. But remember time waits for no one. Not even you."

That was a threat directed solely at me.

The heavy oak doors swung open of their own accord, groaning on ancient hinges. As the goddesses crossed the threshold, they vanished. Aldus cleared his throat and gripped the arms of his chair. When he spoke, his voice was low but firm, carrying the unmistakable tone of royal command. "My lords and ladies, I thank you for your counsel today. We have much to think about. I ask only that you look amongst yourselves and find the similarities within your own cowardice in the face of the gods that plague this realm. It doesn't matter if you are Salt or Silk, rich or poor, fat or thin, tall or short. In the end, we're merely cannon fodder for a war that spans lifetimes and has nothing to do with us. Now leave me. And trust that I will not abandon you again."

The council left in a hurry, not bothering to look back at their king as his words followed them out the door. Only when Tuck and I were left, did he nod to the guards, and the doors were shut once more. I hadn't expected private counsel, but based on the look on Tuck's face, he had.

"That didn't go to plan," Aldus said, rising from his seat. "Find my son and bring him to me. Archer Windale is the only man I'll see sit on that throne."

"It'll be a hard sell, Your Majesty," Tuck said, refilling his water.

"It won't be hard. It'll be impossible," I confirmed. "Whatever sway you think you might have with him, it's gone. It was buried in the ground the day his sister was. Your best bet is to find someone else. A cousin. A nephew. Anyone else."

Aldus's wrinkled eyes narrowed. "All the same, something tells me you boys might know where to find him. I want him sitting in this room by nightfall."

With that, the king rose and walked out. I waited a few seconds before sharing a look with Tuck.

"You know he's not going to come, right?"

"God of Knowledge," he said, tapping his forehead. "I know all kinds of useless shit."

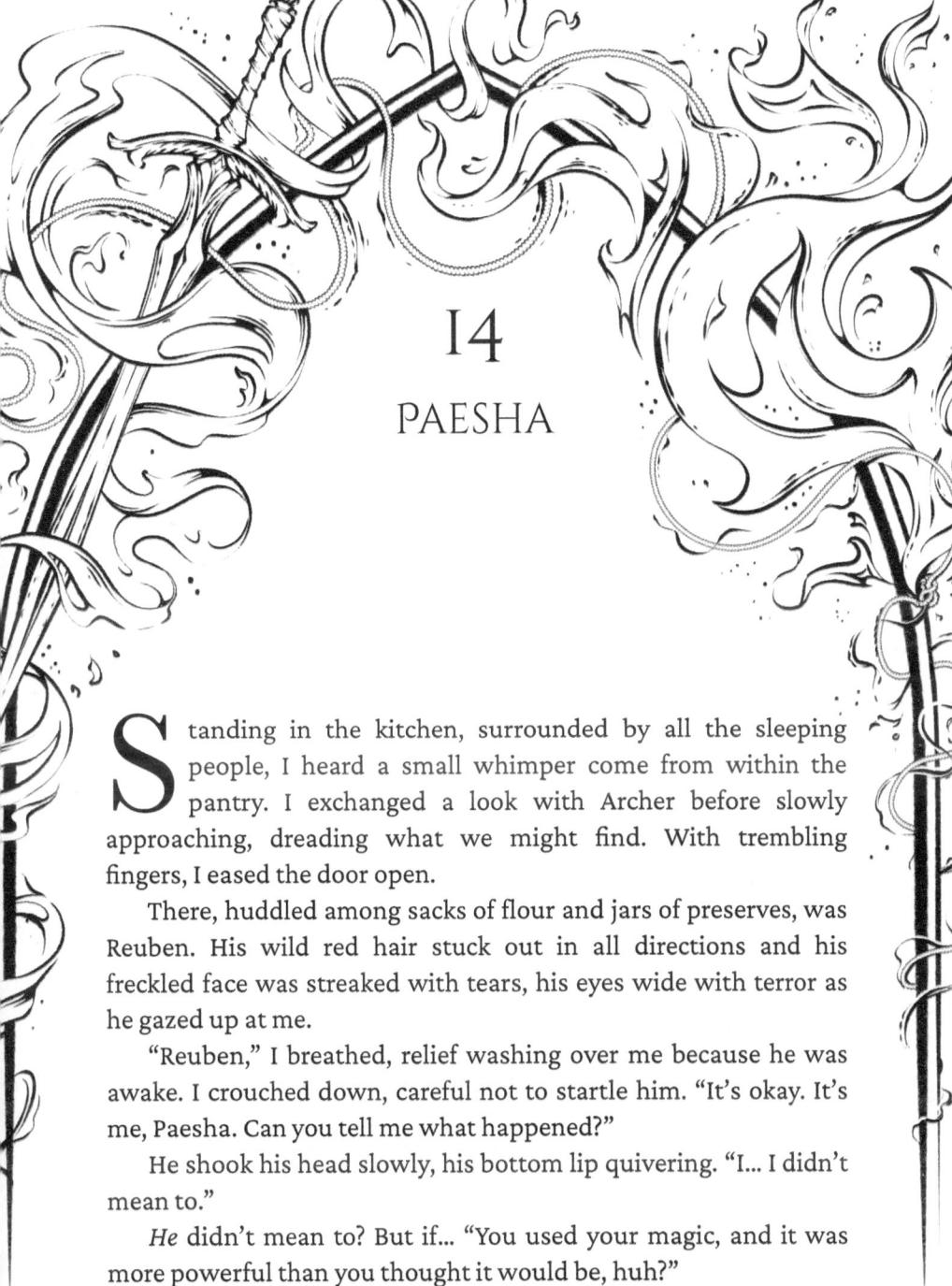

14

PAESHA

Standing in the kitchen, surrounded by all the sleeping people, I heard a small whimper come from within the pantry. I exchanged a look with Archer before slowly approaching, dreading what we might find. With trembling fingers, I eased the door open.

There, huddled among sacks of flour and jars of preserves, was Reuben. His wild red hair stuck out in all directions and his freckled face was streaked with tears, his eyes wide with terror as he gazed up at me.

"Reuben," I breathed, relief washing over me because he was awake. I crouched down, careful not to startle him. "It's okay. It's me, Paesha. Can you tell me what happened?"

He shook his head slowly, his bottom lip quivering. "I... I didn't mean to."

He didn't mean to? But if... "You used your magic, and it was more powerful than you thought it would be, huh?"

He nodded, eyes falling to the floor. "I tried to wake them." Reuben's gaze darted past me to where Lianna lay slumped by the stove. Fresh tears welled in his eyes. "The baby was crying a lot and Briony said she wished she would sleep so she could make dinner. And I was only trying to help. Lianna said it would be okay."

"Hey buddy," Archer said, kneeling down. "This isn't your fault, okay. The same thing happened to me this morning. You gave everyone a little nap, that's all."

I could feel her before I saw her. Quill at my back, staring at the boy, pushing contentment into the space to try to make him feel better. That beautiful feeling melted down my back, cooling the angry burns around my wrists and ankles. I turned to her, sharing a tentative smile. "Quill, this is Reuben, Reuben, this is my friend Quill. Maybe the two of you could go together to try to wake everyone. But let's not use our magic until we know for sure what's happening."

Quill held her hand out for Reuben. He looked to Archer first, who nodded and sent them on their way. When they were gone, Archer pinned me with a look.

"What?"

He's mad at you.

You were too forgiving.

Always too forgiving.

You let them lie to you.

"I know you don't want to be told what to do, but eventually you're going to have to talk to Quill about letting people feel their feelings. Reuben needs to be scared of his power. It'll make him think twice before he uses it again. Especially if he can knock out a whole house."

"Just because you avoided using your power as much as possible doesn't mean everyone else should, Archer. That's not the lesson to learn here. And she's trying to help. Which is more than we can say for her attitude yesterday." I couldn't help the bite in my tone. The poison in my mind. I couldn't help the anger and the darkness that wanted to consume me.

He lifted his hands in surrender. "I said eventually."

"We've had this conversation with her."

"I could try," Aeris said, surprising us both when she filled the frame of the pantry. "I have to agree with Archer here."

"Of course you do," I said, giving no care for the tone I used.

Aeris's wrinkled face softened, her eyes shimmering with an emotion I couldn't quite place. Which was just about perfect for manipulating gods. She stepped closer, her hands clasped before her.

"I know you're hesitant to trust gods, Huntress. And I hope you always will be. Caution is wise when dealing with immortals. We can be capricious at times." She paused, her gaze drifting to where Quill and Reuben had disappeared down the hall. A small smile tugged at the corners of her mouth, transforming her face into something almost youthful. "I'll be honest. I never expected to form a bond with Quill."

Sure she didn't.

Lies and poison.

"She was just another mortal child, one of countless thousands I've seen come and go. But there's something special about her. A light, a spark that drew me in despite myself. Now that I've come to care for her, I'd be devastated to have to walk away." Her eyes met mine, and for a moment, I saw past the facade of the kindly old woman. There was an ancient wisdom there, tinged with a hint of sorrow. It wasn't a game. It wasn't deceitful. It was simply the unexpected truth. "But I will, if that's what you want. I understand your mistrust, your need to protect her."

I hesitated. As much as I wanted to dismiss her words, I couldn't deny the truth in them. Quill had a way of settling into your heart, of making you care when you least expected it. I'd experienced it myself. I'd seen it time and time again with those around her. Even Archer was becoming protective of the kid. If he wasn't, he wouldn't have been offering his unsolicited advice.

My mind drifted back to those early days with Quill, when she was only a precocious child thrust into my care by the Maestro. I remembered her wide-eyed wonder at the simplest things, a butterfly landing on a flower, the way sunlight danced on water,

MIRANDA LYN

the taste of fresh strawberries. The way she'd curl up next to me during thunderstorms, her small body trembling but her voice steady as she told me stories to distract herself from the booming thunder. But then that'd always been her power, even when she wasn't trying, she exuded love. And kindness.

She'd changed me, softened the hard edges of my soul without me even realizing it. Her unwavering faith in me, even when I didn't deserve it, meant something. The fierce protectiveness I felt for her, a love so deep and consuming it sometimes terrified me was born from her devotion to me.

And that was exactly what Aeris was describing. That unexpected connection that snuck up on you and changed everything.

I took a deep breath, steeling myself. "I won't ask you to walk away. Not yet. But I need you to understand something. Quill is *mine*. My child. My responsibility. If I ever feel that your presence is putting her in danger, or influencing her in ways I don't agree with, I won't hesitate to cut ties. No matter how much it might hurt her in the short term."

Aeris nodded solemnly. "I understand completely. And I respect your position as her guardian. I hope that in time, I can earn your trust as well."

"You're not getting my trust. Don't count on that at all. But if you want me to see anything good in you, you'll answer some questions for me."

She slid her hands into the pockets of the apron she always wore, leaning against the doorframe. "I'd be happy to answer anything I can."

"Truthfully. You'll answer them truthfully with no games."

"I've never been a fan of games," she said. "Though we could take this conversation out of the pantry, if you'd like."

"No. I'd rather keep this between the three of us for now," I said as the voices from the house grew louder. Whatever Quill and Reuben were doing, it was working.

"Fair enough."

We'd start with a test. See how truthful she was with information I'd already figured out. "The veil. Was it over Wisteria or was it over Requiem? The twin cities south of here."

I knew the veil was over Wisteria. It was the reason magic felt muted beneath it when I was here before, and it was the reason no one from the north could control their power. Something about the veil kept it suppressed. I watched her eyes first, to see if she would dig for a lie or if she'd be honest.

"The veil was over Wisteria. The entire northern world. Requiem was the worst of the worst. It's where the wars of this world began and ended. It was built on bloodshed and battlefields and no matter which gods stepped in, there was no saving the vile mortals that rotted down there. We tried. Fates know we tried, but this world was falling to ruin. So, Reverius stepped in, using his power to end the war, by veiling off the rest of the world. Giving everyone under it a chance to find peace. We went back to Requiem, me and some of the others, Bellatora even stepped aside, and war feeds into her power. But Requiem was dying all the same. And then, as you know, Cytheronia was banished to Requiem for her crimes, and thus the gods were told they could never return."

"Well they did," I scowled, picturing Ezra's face as he stood before me and lied about who he was. Who I was to him. Exactly as Reverius had done.

"Some, yes. But with great cost, I assure you."

"Since they still exist, the cost wasn't great enough," Archer said, staring down at Aeris. "How long was Thorne in Stirling? How many of my memories with him are lies?"

"That I cannot answer," she said coolly. "The Keeper is quite fond of his hunt and keeping the Huntress away from the other gods."

They're all lying.

Destroy them before they destroy you.

Oh, fun. Now the voices in my head were handing out murder tips. Because that was healthy and not at all a compounding problem. Alastor's damn marks on my wrists flared to life and a searing pain shot up my arms. I fought to maintain my composure as the agony intensified. This was completely fine and no big deal. But the Remnants responded to my distress, pooling at my feet like living shadows. They writhed and twisted, their inky tendrils reaching out as if seeking something to destroy.

Aeris's eyes widened slightly as she stepped back. The mask slipped for a moment, revealing something ancient and powerful beneath. Her voice took on a soothing tone that set my teeth on edge. "Perhaps we shouldn't discuss the Keeper right now. It seems to be causing you some discomfort."

I rolled my eyes. "No shit."

"I'm a bit concerned about these Remnants of yours. They seem to be affecting you more than you realize. I've seen this once before. They will poison your mortal mind. They will separate you from everyone you know. Everyone you love if you let them."

"I don't know what you're talking about," I lied. "It's not like they have voices."

Almost believable.

Lie to lie.

Lie to breathe.

Lie to bleed.

You could kill a god. With a god.

All the gods.

All the children.

I couldn't move. Couldn't react or flinch or those keen eyes would know my plight.

"Okay, Fingers?" Archer asked, staring down at the growing shadows on the pantry floor. "Maybe we should get out of here now."

Aeris stepped to the side and Archer led us back into the kitchen. The air was cooler. The walls farther away. The voices quiet.

"The knocker," Aeris said, so only I would hear when I passed.

"What?"

"The knocker was always a pig. Perhaps your power is already corrupting your mind. You really must consider going to Alastor. He might be the only one that can help you."

I started to retort, to tell Aeris exactly where *she* could go, when a blood-curdling scream shattered the stare down. We bolted from the kitchen, racing through the house.

Quill stood frozen in the oversized entryway, her eyes wide with terror as she stared at the floor. A thin, jagged line had appeared in the polished wood, no wider than a hair at first glance.

"Everyone, get back!" Aeris commanded.

We had barely taken a step when the crack widened with a sickening groan. The floorboards splintered and gave way, revealing a yawning chasm of impenetrable darkness below. Quill teetered on the edge for only a heartbeat.

Then she fell.

My scream caught in my throat as I lunged forward, knowing I was too far away, too slow to reach her in time. But Archer's arm shot out, slamming across my stomach to stop me while at the same time he threw his power forward. The world slowed, then stopped entirely. He'd frozen time. Again. Without missing a beat, he'd acted. His loyalty knew no damn bounds, but Quill hung suspended in mid-air, her curls frozen in a wild halo around her terrified face.

She looked at me. Those fucking baby blues melting my entire soul as she screamed with an intensity that chilled me to my core. Her fear was my fear. Her terror scraped down the walls of my mind, shutting out everything that should have existed beyond her, Archer, and me.

"We don't get a hundred years. I can die," she screamed. "I can die now. Please. Please don't let me die."

"You won't!" I promised.

I couldn't breathe through the panic clawing at my chest. My legs nearly gave out, and I sagged against Archer's arm, still braced across my stomach like an iron bar. The Remnants surged around my feet, feeding off my fear, but for once their whispers were drowned out by the thundering of my own heartbeat and the echoes of Quill's scream bouncing through my skull.

Time, though frozen, stretched like molasses, each second an eternity of agony as I watched her suspended there, my whole world. The sunlight streaming through the door caught her tears, turning them to diamonds against her cheeks, and all I could think was how many times I'd wiped those tears away, how many times I'd promised to keep her safe. Now here she was, about to be swallowed by darkness, and I was useless, utterly fucking useless to stop it. I couldn't lose her. Not Quill. The mere thought of a world without her in it sent waves of nausea rolling through my stomach, made the edges of my vision go dark. I would tear this house apart with my bare hands, would rip open the fabric of reality, would challenge every god that had ever existed before I let that pit take her from me.

I whipped my head to Archer with sweat already forming on his brow by holding time. He had no fucking clue what he was doing. Not with this much magic. But I could see the fear there too. The turn of his brows and the shock on his face. I turned to Aeris, desperate for help before Archer had to let go and Quill fell to her death, but he'd struck so hard and fast, his power so vast in this moment, even Aeris had been frozen in time. Everyone had.

Quill's terror was so palpable it vibrated through the air. Her magic, fueled by primal fear, pulsed outward in waves of raw emotion. It raked through me, stealing my breath and clouding my thoughts with a fog of panic. I could feel her desperation, her certainty that death awaited in the endless darkness below. It consumed me.

Archer's face was contorted with strain as he fought to maintain his hold on time. His arms trembled, muscles cording beneath his skin. "Paesha," he gasped. "I can't... hold it... much longer. Use your magic!" Archer pleaded, his words coming in pained gasps. "The Alastor shadow things. Use those."

The Remnants circled my arms, eager for release, hungry for destruction. I couldn't trust them. Couldn't risk unleashing that chaos, not with Quill so vulnerable and no fucking control.

My skin had gone numb, my nerves rattling so violently beneath the surface, I could hardly think beyond them. I loved that little girl. I'd fought everything, defied everything, to crawl back to her, and I'd lose her in the next minute. "I can't control them," I whispered, my voice breaking. "They'll make it worse."

"What the hell could possibly be worse than her falling?" Archer yelled over Quill's screams.

He was right. Nothing else mattered. Not the risk, not the consequences. Only Quill. With a silent prayer to whatever benevolent forces might be listening, I reached deep within myself, and I fucking let go.

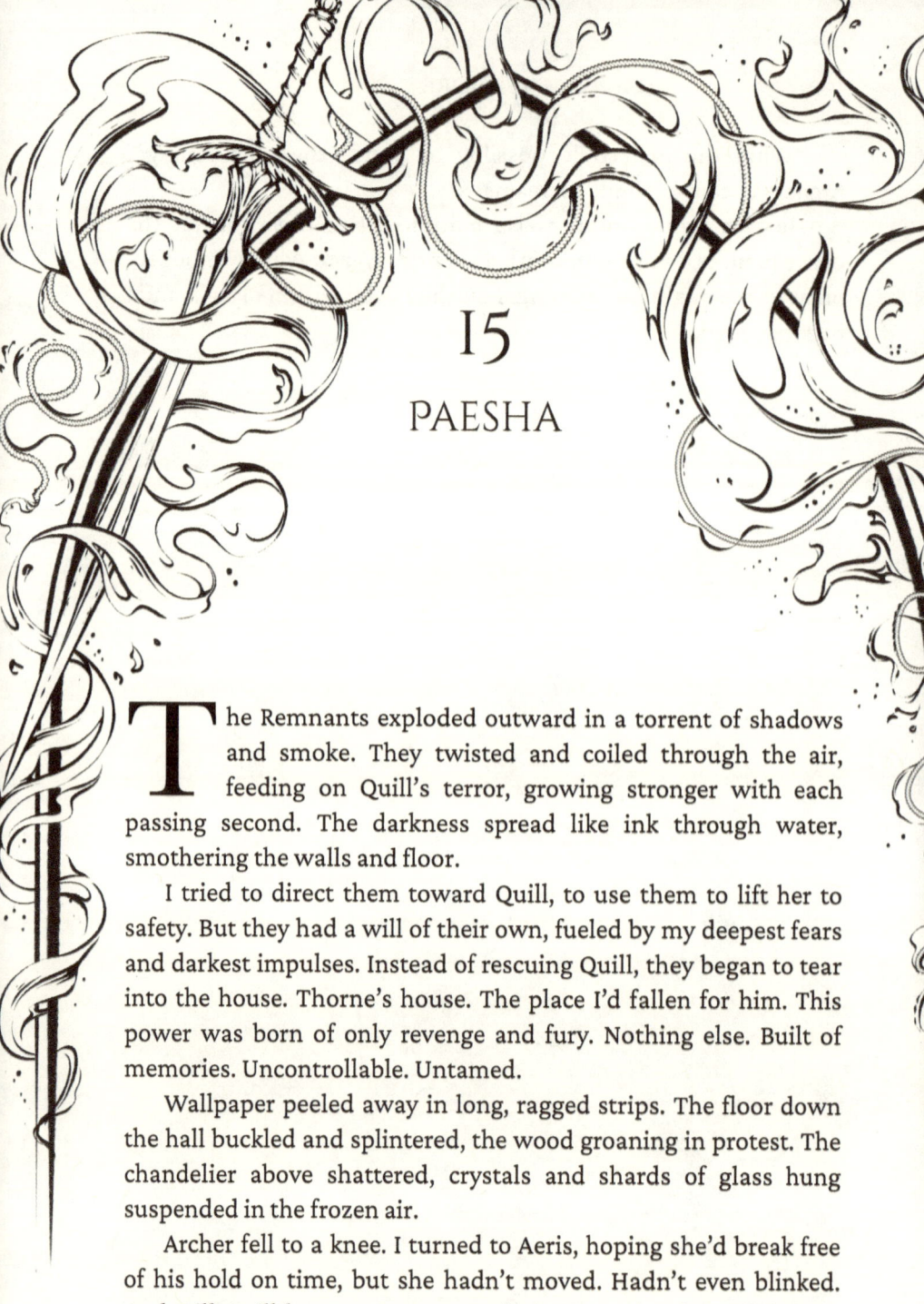

15

PAESHA

The Remnants exploded outward in a torrent of shadows and smoke. They twisted and coiled through the air, feeding on Quill's terror, growing stronger with each passing second. The darkness spread like ink through water, smothering the walls and floor.

I tried to direct them toward Quill, to use them to lift her to safety. But they had a will of their own, fueled by my deepest fears and darkest impulses. Instead of rescuing Quill, they began to tear into the house. Thorne's house. The place I'd fallen for him. This power was born of only revenge and fury. Nothing else. Built of memories. Uncontrollable. Untamed.

Wallpaper peeled away in long, ragged strips. The floor down the hall buckled and splintered, the wood groaning in protest. The chandelier above shattered, crystals and shards of glass hung suspended in the frozen air.

Archer fell to a knee. I turned to Aeris, hoping she'd break free of his hold on time, but she hadn't moved. Hadn't even blinked. And still Quill hung over a mysterious cavern in Thorne's house, caught in time that was clearly slipping away from Archer's control.

This is your chance. Our moment of true power.

Let them fall.

Let them hurt.

They all deserve it. Quill will betray you too, in time. They always do.

You're alone. You've always been alone.

Run. Leave them all behind.

The Remnants tore through the house because I had no control over them. They moved, fueled by the monster I'd become. Is this what Alastor felt? This raw, unbridled power coursing through his veins? He'd commanded them so effortlessly when I could barely keep mine from destroying everything in their path.

"Please," I yelled, trying to command them. I pulled and shoved and threw my will through my mind, desperate. And failing.

The binding marks on my wrists flared to life as if answering my thoughts. I knew what they meant now. Why they burned. But I would not be summoned like a fucking pet even if I could almost hear Alastor's mocking laughter echoing in the distance.

"You can do this," Archer said, reaching for me. "Take my hand and we'll do it together. Grab her gently and bring her in. That's all. Nice and easy."

The quiver in his voice scared me. He was so quiet. Too quiet. So drained he couldn't stand. I slid my hand into his, and the world went silent. The screaming stopped. The voices in my head quieted. Even the creaking of the house faded to nothing. He was my anchor. I needed him. Now and always.

In that moment of perfect stillness, Archer's grip tightened on mine. His voice, rough with determination, gave me strength as he lost his. "Let my strength be your shield against the darkness, Paesha. You're not alone. Fight back with me. Fight back and I'll stand between you both and the dark." The words felt older than time, though I knew he was just speaking from his heart, desperate to save her but also me from the madness.

The change hit like an avalanche, his words carrying me through.

I was not alone.

I was not alone.

Power surged. Mine, the final drops of his, and Quill's energy wove through it all, her fear and love and desperation creating patterns I could feel but not comprehend. The three of us connected in ways that defied explanation, bound together by something vast and terrible and beautiful, breaking past the poison of the Remnants, beyond the monster pacing within my soul. The inky black tendrils recoiled, hissing, fighting back for control.

A searing pain blazed down my back, as if someone had carved sigils of fire along my spine. I gritted my teeth against it, fighting to maintain focus as the burning sensation spread outward. The Remnants, those writhing shadows that had never truly been mine to control, suddenly snapped to attention, not because they were tamed, but because they recognized something in me. The grit. The strength. The little girl on the streets that had no choice but to battle the world to fucking survive.

"Hold on, Quilly," I whispered, and sent them forward.

The shadows moved like liquid silk through the air, wrapping around Quill's suspended body with impossible gentleness. They cradled her. As they drew her back from the void, I felt Archer's hand go slack in mine. The moment his fingers slipped away, something inside me recognized the price of what we'd done, though I couldn't begin to understand its true meaning. He crumpled to the floor beside me, and time shuddered back into motion with a sound like breaking glass.

The shattered crystals from the chandelier rained down, tinkling as they hit the floor. Quill was safe, cradled in a cocoon of shadows that lowered her gently to the ground beside me. As soon as her feet touched the floor, the Remnants dissipated like smoke, leaving her trembling and wide-eyed, but unharmed. I pulled her into my arms, holding her tight as she sobbed against my chest. Her small body shook with the force of her fear and relief.

"I've got you," I murmured into her hair. "You're safe now. I've got you."

Over Quill's head, I saw Aeris stumble slightly as she regained her balance, blinking in confusion at the scene before her. Her eyes darted from the gaping hole in the floor to Quill in my arms, then to Archer's crumpled form.

"What in the name of all the Fates happened?" she demanded.

I ignored her, focusing instead on Archer. He lay motionless on the floor, his face ashen. I reached out with my free hand, pressing my fingers to his neck. His pulse was there, but weak.

Quill's sobs quieted to hiccups as she pulled away from me and looked at Archer's still form. She reached out a trembling hand, placing it gently on his chest next to mine. Her touch was feather light, as if she feared he might shatter beneath her fingers. "Is he...?"

"He's alive," I assured her, though my own voice shook with uncertainty. "He saved us both, Quilly. He's just exhausted."

As if responding to our touch, a faint shudder ran through Archer's body. His eyelids fluttered, and a soft groan escaped his lips. Quill and I leaned closer, hardly daring to breathe as we waited for him to fully awaken. Slowly, painfully, his eyes opened. A weak smile tugged at the corners of his mouth.

"Did we do it?" he rasped.

Before I could answer, Quill let out a cry of joy and flung herself over him. Her arms wrapped around his neck as she buried her face in his shoulder. Archer winced at the impact but managed to lift one arm to return the embrace.

"Thank you for saving me."

"Can't breathe, kid," he said.

She scrambled backward, eyes wide as if she'd somehow hurt him. "Sorry, Archie."

I grabbed her arm, snatching her away from the edge of the pit. "Be careful."

Quill glanced back at the pit. Her fingers trembled as she clutched my arm. For a moment, her expression softened into something older than her years—worry, guilt, and a fragile kind of awe. She looked at Archer, then at me, and her gaze fixed on the jagged tear across my shoulder where my shirt had burned away.

The edges of the fabric were blackened and curling, revealing the faint glow of charred lines that still pulsed softly beneath my skin. She put both hands on the sides of my face. "What happened to you?"

"I'm just a little broken right now, my girl. But I'll figure it out. I think it's him we have to worry about." I flicked my eyes toward Archer, still lying on the ground.

Aeris kneeled beside us as Thea came barreling into the entryway with several others, young and old at her side.

"Are you okay, Quill?" Aeris asked.

She nodded, scooting closer to me. "We're both a little broken right now."

Aeris smiled, reaching forward to tuck a curl behind Quill's ear. "Just a little is perfectly acceptable." She turned to me. "Mind if I put this place back together before someone else falls in this pit?"

"We're not going to take a beat to figure out how it—"

The door slammed open. And not one, but two giant, furious men stood there, staring down at the cavern in the floor. Thorne's face was glorious, honestly. Filled with anger as his eyes traced his damaged home. I hoped it hurt him to stand there and see the destruction because it was nothing compared to the damage he'd done to my heart.

My power surged at the sight of him, the Remnants hissing curses. But the shadows hadn't come. Be it from my own exhaustion or the shock of what'd happened, I had no idea. The burn was still there, the bands on my wrists, forever circling. Reminding me I belonged to Alastor now, and he was calling.

"What the fuck did you do to my house, Aeris?"

The goddess stood, shifting backward, clearly realizing Thorne hadn't come to play nice today. "This wasn't me. I fixed your knocker," her eyes slid to me, "and promptly put it back. I'm happy to erase the mess for you, Keeper, if you wish."

Thorne's hands turned to fists at his sides. Tuck, the godsdamned carriage driver of all people, had to pull him back. "He wishes it," he said, shaking his head. Carriage driver wasn't really fair. He'd sacrificed himself to the prince's Cimmerians to keep my identity secure. He'd helped guide the Fray and last I knew, he was working to keep the little, old king safe. Tuck was good. A kind man.

"Very well." Aeris's magic filled the space in a wave of heat that ripped the breath from my lungs, and the destruction began to reverse itself. The gaping hole in the floor closed. Shards of crystal rose from the ground, reforming into the chandelier which reattached itself to the ceiling. Torn wallpaper smoothed out, erasing all signs of damage.

Within moments, the entryway looked exactly as it had before, pristine and untouched. The only evidence that anything had happened was the shell-shocked expressions on our faces and Archer's grunt as he lifted himself off the floor.

Thorne's fury seemed to dissipate slightly as he took in the restored room, but his eyes remained hard as they locked onto me. "What happened?"

I met his gaze steadily, refusing to flinch under the weight of his anger. "All the questions and no answers. What a pity. Must be rough."

"Paesha—"

Quill snatched my hand. "Don't you say her name. Don't even look at her."

He didn't argue. Shockingly. Instead, he stepped to the side so Tuck could enter. The massive man stroked a hand down his scarred face, scanning Archer from head to toe. "What in the hell did you do to yourself, Archie?"

"He saved me," Quill answered. "Who are you?"

"The name's Tuck."

"Oh, you're the carriage driver," she said, eyes a little too keen as they scanned the burly man. Probably shouldn't have referred to him as that.

"Something like that," he chuckled. "You must be the kid."

"There're lots of kids here."

"Fair point. Any idea which one of them put a hole in the

floor?" he asked, looking up to Briony who'd walked in with a baby on her hip.

"One minute we were sleeping, the next there was screaming, and the house was shaking. Don't ask me. This is not what I signed up for."

"Oh, Thorne didn't warn you?" I asked. "Nothing is as it seems where he's concerned."

"Don't," he said, stepping toward me.

"He is a god, after all."

His eyes narrowed. "Paesha, stop."

"You don't get to control me."

I turned to Briony. "Did you know? I'm assuming you didn't."

"Know what?" she asked, eyes glossing over.

"You really are a piece of shit," I said, whipping back to Thorne, "Just because you can, doesn't mean you should."

He stepped closer and immediately my heart began to race. "And who's going to stop me, Paesha darling? You? Archie?"

Out of nowhere, Quill surged between us and kicked Thorne right between the legs. She'd been taught that little trick by Deyanira. As the giant fucker fell to his knees, I couldn't help but feel a modicum of pride.

"I'd like to say I'm sorry about that, but I'm not," she said, throwing her hands on her hips. "Now leave us alone."

I hid my smile, glancing over to Archer, who was very pale. "Are you okay?" I asked, forgetting everything else, despite the warning bells going off in my mind about being in the same room with Thorne.

"I'm fine," he said with a nod, though the tremor made it clear he wasn't.

"Do you need a healer?" Thea asked, moving to his side.

Briony stepped toward him too. "Archie?"

"I'm fine," he growled, pushing past everyone to walk out. I reached for his hand. When my fingers grazed his, he paused, back going rigid. "I'm fine," he said for the third time and walked out.

Thorne stood, eyes locked on my fingers as Archer walked

away. Likely not because I'd reached for him. But because I was no longer wearing the ring he'd put there. Nor would I ever again.

The others followed Archer out, no one looking more concerned than Aeris as they surrounded him. Only Quill remained, still positioned defiantly between Thorne and me like a shield.

"Go check on Archer," I told her softly, never taking my eyes off Thorne.

"But—"

"It's okay. I can handle him."

She hesitated, then squeezed my hand before leaving. The moment she was gone, the voices started their relentless whispers. But for once, I welcomed them. Let them fuel the fire burning through my veins.

Remember he tried to trap you.

He will destroy you.

Unless you destroy him first. Break him like he broke you.

Make him bleed.

I stalked forward, a savage smile playing at my lips as I traced a finger down the buttons of his pristine shirt. "Is this what you wanted, *Keeper*?" His title dripped with venom. "Someone to play your little mortal games with? Someone to bend and break and put back together however you see fit? Someone you could lock away and play with? Did you *forget* to mention I would be bound to Alastor if I didn't give him that fourth name? Just like you *forgot* to mention threatening to take away my memories was only for fun?"

He stayed perfectly still under my touch, but I could feel the tension radiating off him. Good. Let him feel a fraction of the uncertainty he'd forced on me.

"Did you laugh about it with the other gods? Poor little Paesha, so desperate for love she couldn't see what was right in front of her?" I leaned closer, breathing in the familiar scent of him. Lies, all lies.

"It wasn't like that. What I feel—"

"What you *felt*?" I shoved him hard, satisfaction coursing

through me when he stumbled back. "You felt nothing! Gods don't feel, they *play*. They manipulate and destroy and wrap it all up in pretty promises." I gestured at his perfect face, his perfect form. "Even this is a lie. Everything about you is designed to trap, to lure, to deceive. Well congratulations, god of a thousand stupid fucking names." I swept into a mocking bow. "You succeeded beautifully. I fell for every single fucking thing."

Yes.

He can bleed.

Let us taste it.

I closed my eyes for a fraction of a second, pushing away the voices. The power. The Remnants.

"I'm not your enemy." He reached for me and I slapped his hand away, shadows writhing at my feet.

"You're not my anything."

He surged forward, grabbing where the bands circled my wrist as he pinned me to the wall. "I am sorry for hurting you. Is that what you need to hear? Is that what your poor broken heart is begging for? If you would let me explain—"

"You don't want to explain. You want to justify lying and I don't care enough to listen. It doesn't matter. Go find someone else to fuck with. Leave me alone."

"I can't," he roared.

And before I knew what was happening, Archer had come back to the entryway and tackled Thorne. The two men crashed to the floor in a tangle of limbs, the impact shaking the restored entryway. We'd sold everything in this room to feed the Salt, thank the gods, but if we hadn't, it'd all be in splinters. Archer's face was a mask of fury as he grappled with Thorne, his earlier exhaustion seemingly forgotten in the heat of the moment. Despite Archer's ferocity, Thorne moved with an eerie calm, easily deflecting blows that might've shattered bone.

Archer landed a solid punch to Thorne's jaw. The crack of the impact echoed through the empty room, but Thorne barely flinched, his expression one of resigned patience rather than pain or anger.

After the initial shock, I realized this would never end well for Archer. "Stop!" I yelled. "Stop! He'll kill you!"

But Archer was beyond reason, driven by a protective rage I'd never seen in him before. He slammed his elbow into Thorne's solar plexus, a blow that would have left any mortal gasping for air. Thorne only grunted, his hands coming up to grip Archer's shoulders, not to harm but to restrain. Tuck stepped into the room, his massive frame filling the doorway. With a speed that contradicted his size, he crossed the space in two long strides and wrapped his meaty arms around Archer's waist. In one fluid motion, he lifted him off Thorne as if he weighed no more than a child.

As Tuck hauled him backwards, Archer's elbow shot out with lightning precision. The crack of bone meeting bone echoed through the room as Archer's elbow connected solidly with Tuck's jaw. Tuck's head snapped back as he stumbled, and his back hit the wall. Blood trickled from a split in his lower lip, staining his beard red. Despite the blow, his arms remained locked around Archer, muscles straining as he fought to contain the thrashing man.

"Enough!" Thorne's voice cracked like thunder, freezing everyone in place. He rose to his feet with inhuman grace, brushing nonexistent dust from his clothes. His eyes, however, burned with a cold fury that sent chills down my spine. "My patience wears thin, Paesha. This ends now. I am going to talk, and you are going to listen. You and I are leaving. We're going back to the Parlor to—"

I laughed, cutting him off. "If I had a dick, I'd tell you to suck it right now, Reverius Thorne Noctus. I'd rather get on my hands and knees and crawl to Alastor than go anywhere with you."

Only when Alastor's dark chuckle filled my ears did I realize the Remnants creeping along the floor were not mine, but his. Alastor took my side, bringing his hands around the back of my neck, his tattooed fingers digging in as he purred, "There'll be no need to get on your knees, Paesha *darling*."

His power engulfed me like a tidal wave of shadows, stealing my breath and clouding my vision. The binding marks on my wrists flared to life, searing pain shooting up my arms as they recognized their master's call. The last thing I saw before the shadows claimed me was Archer breaking free of Tuck's grip, his face a mask of helpless fury. But it was Thorne's expression that haunted me as the darkness closed in, not anger or jealousy or even that insufferable patience. For the first time since I'd known him, he looked afraid.

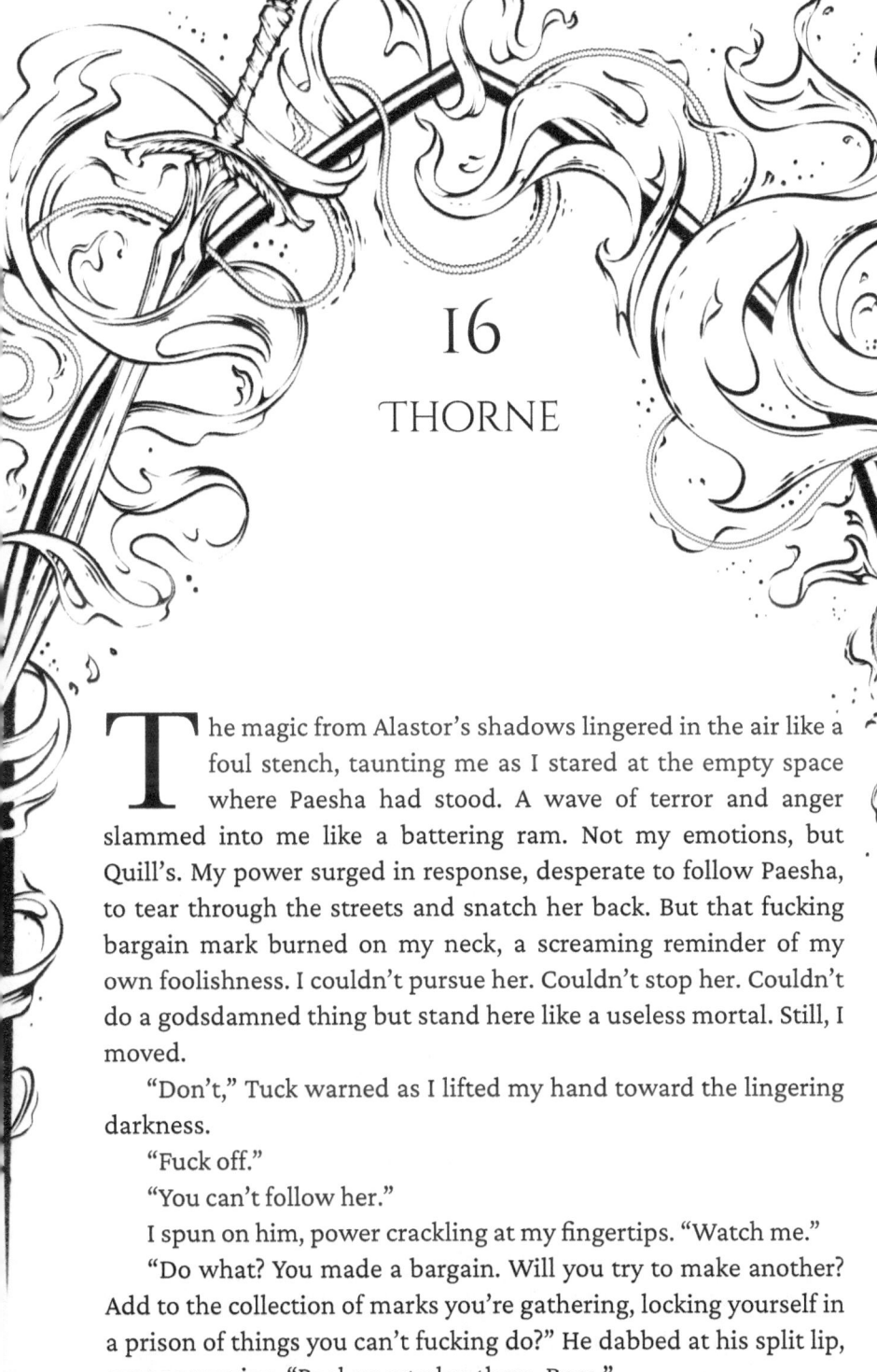

16

THORNE

The magic from Alastor's shadows lingered in the air like a foul stench, taunting me as I stared at the empty space where Paesha had stood. A wave of terror and anger slammed into me like a battering ram. Not my emotions, but Quill's. My power surged in response, desperate to follow Paesha, to tear through the streets and snatch her back. But that fucking bargain mark burned on my neck, a screaming reminder of my own foolishness. I couldn't pursue her. Couldn't stop her. Couldn't do a godsdamned thing but stand here like a useless mortal. Still, I moved.

"Don't," Tuck warned as I lifted my hand toward the lingering darkness.

"Fuck off."

"You can't follow her."

I spun on him, power crackling at my fingertips. "Watch me."

"Do what? You made a bargain. Will you try to make another? Add to the collection of marks you're gathering, locking yourself in a prison of things you can't fucking do?" He dabbed at his split lip, eyes narrowing. "Real smart plan there, Boss."

"I could have warned her," I said, staring at the spot where she'd vanished.

"Should have," Archer snarled.

I was more concerned about her walking away from me. But I'd underestimated Alastor. He'd been so quiet for so long. I should have known better. Story of my entire damn existence.

Before I could respond, another force of rage struck me.

"Bring her back," Quill demanded, her voice carrying more authority than a child should possess. The walls seemed to vibrate with the force of her fury as she stood in the doorway.

"I can't," I admitted, the words tasting like ash in my mouth.

"Liar! You're a god! Fix it!"

Thea moved toward her but stumbled under the weight of the child's projected emotions. "Quilly, you need to calm—"

"Don't tell me to calm down!" Another pulse of power hit. The baby in Briony's arms wailed in response as a crack spiderwebbed across the ceiling.

Tuck exchanged a look with Thea. "Maybe we should take this outside before the kid brings the entire house down. Again."

"You think?" Thea snapped, but there was no real heat in it.

Archer lurched forward, still unsteady on his feet. "We need to go after them. Now."

"Brilliant idea," Tuck drawled. "Let's send the exhausted time-bender who can barely stand to chase down a god hell-bent on revenge. Nothing could possibly go wrong there."

"Got a better plan?" Archer challenged.

Tuck moved between Archer and the door. "Yeah. Keeping everyone alive. Use that brain of yours. You go after them now, you're only giving Alastor another weapon to use against her."

"I think he's right." Thea took a step, fighting to reach Quill through the storm of her power. "We need to be smart about this." She flashed a look at Archer, one that said she didn't trust Tuck or I as far as she could throw either of us.

I huffed a laugh. "Smart? While we're being *smart*, he's—" I cut myself off. The things Alastor could be doing to Paesha's mind

138

right now... His Remnants could be tearing her apart from the inside.

"You want to rush in and make things worse, Archie? Be my guest," Tuck said, eyeing Quill, his curiosity obvious.

"So we do nothing?" Archer bit back.

"No one said that. We plan. We prepare. We figure out which bargains are actually binding us and which loopholes we can exploit." Tuck's eyes met mine. "But first, we deal with the fact that our new little friend here is about to level this house with the force of her feelings."

As if to prove his point, Quill snarled like a little beast, consumed in her anger. The windows shattered. Her power was immediately building again, feeding off everyone's fear and anger.

"Enough," I growled, stepping toward her. Thea moved to block my path but Tuck caught her arm.

"Let him try," he said softly. "Can't get much worse."

I knelt before Quill, ignoring the glass. "Look at me, little one."

Her glare met mine, and for a moment I saw what Paesha saw in her, not merely power, but fierce love and loyalty. "You promised to protect her. She told me you did."

"I did. And I failed." The admission cost me, but she needed truth right now, not more lies. "I'm going to get her back. We all are. You have my word."

"Your word means nothing. You're a liar."

"Yes. I am," I held her gaze. "But I love her. I have loved her longer than there were stars in most skies. I have chased her through a thousand lifetimes, watched her live and die and live again, each time hoping she would finally be mine. Not because I want to own her, but because loving her is as natural as breathing, as inevitable as dawn following night."

I ran a hand through my hair, centuries of memories washing over me. "I remember every version of her. The warrior who had fought beside me in ancient battles, her blade flashing like lightning. The healer who saved an entire village while dying herself. The queen who'd sacrificed everything to protect her people. The dancer who moved like poetry given form. She has been fierce and gentle, broken and whole, sometimes in the same breath. And I have loved every incarnation, every smile, every tear.

"I've failed her in this life, as I have failed her in others. But I'll challenge every god who stands in my way. A universe without her in it is darker and colder and infinitely less worth saving. That's not the word of a god or the Keeper. That's the word of someone who loves her just as fiercely as you do."

It wasn't much but the slightest bit of tension left her shoulders as she studied my face before stepping back. It would be baby steps with her or nothing. Just like Paesha. "Maybe you should have told her that instead of telling her you liked salt."

"Maybe," I smiled.

"That was... unexpectedly honest of you," Tuck commented.

I rose, brushing off my knees. "Stop."

Aeris stepped forward from where she'd been quietly observing. "The bond between god and mortal is rarely so pure." Her eyes met mine. "Though in this case, with a volatile Huntress, I suspect there's nothing pure about it at all."

"Your opinion wasn't requested," I said, restraining myself.

"And yet you have it all the same." She turned to the gathering crowd of children and caretakers who'd been drawn by the commotion. "Briony, perhaps we should get these little ones some tea in the kitchen."

Briony hesitated only a moment before nodding. "Come along then, everyone. Let's leave them to sort this mess."

As the children and the others filed out, Aeris's aged hand settled on Quill's shoulder. "You should rest, little bird. Your power has been rather taxing today. Maybe it would be a good idea to have a nap upstairs before we go back to Silbath."

"I want to help find her."

"And you will," Thea said, smoothing Quill's wild curls. "But right now, some quiet time is best. You don't have to sleep, but rest a little."

"I don't want to go upstairs alone."

Tuck cleared his throat. "Thea, was it? If you want to get her settled, I can make sure these idiots don't do anything stupid for at least an hour."

The look Thea gave him could have melted steel. "Only an hour?"

"I know my limits."

A ghost of a smile touched her lips. "Fair enough." She guided Quill toward the stairs, pausing only to throw a knowing look over her shoulder. "Try not to destroy anything else while I'm gone?"

"No promises," Tuck said, but his eyes followed her until she disappeared up the stairs.

Archer shifted his weight, still unsteady. "So what's the real plan?"

I jutted my chin toward the sitting room. "The real plan is for you to rest too. You're no good to anyone half dead."

"Like hell—"

"He's right." Tuck's tone left no room for argument. "You look like shit, Archie. You need to recover your strength before you're of any use to Paesha."

"When did you become the voice of reason?" Archer muttered.

"Someone has to be."

Aeris smoothed her hands down her apron. "I assume you'll be running out that door as soon as we all leave you to it?"

I narrowed my eyes. "You assume much."

"I observe. And I have observed the Huntress's fire burning twice as bright as it should. The Remnants that plague her are not natural. They carry whispers of things that should not be." She moved toward the door. "Do let me know what Alastor has to say about that."

After she left, Tuck let out a low whistle. "Glad we decided to be done with her ages ago."

"Wait. You're a god?" Archer asked, stepping away from Tuck.

"And you're an heir," he said, pulling the king's summons from his coat pocket. "I was going to wait to do this, but it looks like time's on no man's side. You're to report to the king as soon as possible."

Archer went rigid, his exhaustion forgotten. "You're working for the king?" He snatched the summons from Tuck's hand. "Of course you are. Everyone's working an angle, aren't they? Even the fucking carriage driver is a god."

"To be fair," Tuck said, "I'm not technically—"

"Save it." Archer ripped the paper into tiny pieces and watched them trickle to the floor. "Tell my *father* if he wants to see me so badly, he can come find me himself. I'm not playing games with gods and kings and there's no way in hell I'm sitting on that throne. It was always supposed to be Harlow and we all know how that turned out."

He walked away, his steps unsteady but his spine straight with stubborn pride. I'd seen that same unyielding defiance in Paesha countless times. No wonder they'd found each other.

"Well," Tuck said, eyeing the paper scattered across the floor. "That went about as well as expected. Though I suppose we should be grateful he didn't try to stop time again."

"Let's go. Minerva won't wait forever."

"No," he agreed, following me out. "But I can't help wondering..."

"What?"

"Who the fuck is whispering to her?"

THE SHADOWS in The Broken Crown seemed alive, writhing along the walls of the tavern like restless spirits. Of course, they probably were. Gods loved to lurk in dark corners, feeding off desperation and depravity like vultures picking clean a corpse. I could feel them watching, their hunger palpable, but I didn't care. Let them see. Let them remember, until I decided they shouldn't.

Minerva's familiar presence settled beside me like a warm blanket, though her sharp eyes held their usual mix of exasperation and fondness. She wrapped her weathered fingers around a glass of wine. "Your subtlety needs work. Three gods walk into a bar sounds like the beginning of a terrible joke."

"It's good to see you too, Minnie," I said, sliding my drink closer.

Minerva smiled, those ancient eyes full of the love she held for very few. The same look she'd given me every time I came back to Etherium lost and angry at the universe.

I swirled my drink. "What are you doing in Wisteria?"

"Preventing a catastrophe. Though you seem determined to cause one, anyway. You've always been a hopeless fool when it comes to the Huntress."

"For a reason," I growled, feeling the glass strain under my grip.

"Temper," she started, but Tuck cleared his throat, playing his usual role of mediator between us.

"Honestly, I think he's worse this time." Tuck shot me the look of a concerned brother rather than a subordinate. "Hiding her in a veiled realm. Using his power against Ezra even if it pissed off the Fates. Standing on the precipice of bargaining himself away to Alastor. He's making a mess. It's a good thing you're here, Minnie, because on top of all of that, the balance is getting worse."

Minerva's eyes gleamed. I hated when they fucking gleamed. "Getting worse or breaking? Or are we simply losing what was never truly ours?"

I caught a flash of movement in the corner. Bellatora, Serene and Valen huddled together on the back side of our table like children eavesdropping on their parents' conversation. Let them listen. Their memories would be gone before they reached the door.

I curved the conversation back to my point. "You haven't answered my question."

"Haven't I? Tell me, what better place to gather intelligence than the king's council? While others skulk in alleys searching for scraps of information, I sit at the table where news is served, and decisions are made."

Tuck leaned in. "And what have you learned?"

"I use that seat to learn about mortals but I think you'd be more interested to learn what I know of the circling gods. It seems your little Huntress has become quite the prize. Several of our kind know she holds power that doesn't belong to her. They want to take it back, of course."

The glass in my hand cracked. "They'd be fools to try."

"Would they?" Minerva asked, "Because at the moment, Alastor holds all the cards. Fortunately, he won't let her die, not until he gets what he wants. But he'll try to break her."

"She won't bend," I growled.

"Neither will he." She leaned back, studying me with the same worried expression she'd worn when I'd first told her about the Huntress, countless lifetimes ago. "I wouldn't be here if I didn't care. So, don't take that tone with me. You'll get my help whether you want it or not because you need it. See beyond your tunnel vision to the bigger picture, for Fate's sake. One life, Thorne. You have only years left with her before her soul is severed and gone."

"Not if I can save her."

With her tiny elbows on the table, she propped her chin on her hands. "And how's that working out for you?"

"I'm going to assume that's rhetorical."

"Assumptions are the bane of my existence," she said, sharing a look with Tuck.

"This is what I get when Knowledge and Reason are the only gods at my table."

"We could always call Bellatora over for a little chaos and irrationality," Tuck said into his mug.

"If we're going to do that, bring the naked one too. Most lose all sense of reason when Serene's around and I can disappear before Bella gets too whiny."

Tuck's eyes grew wide. "I thought you were about to say you liked the breasts. Almost died there, Minnie. Damn."

"I shall keep that in mind for the next time *you* get on my nerves, Zentuchal."

"My full name? Really? I thought we'd come to an understanding about that centuries ago."

She lifted a casual shoulder. "Must have slipped my mind. Old age."

He lowered his chin. "You don't get to play the old age card on me."

A wry smile curled her lips before she changed forms into a beautiful woman with sharp eyes, dark skin and red lips. Her favorite way to mess with Tuck.

"I'm never going to understand how you can shift," he said looking away from the face of a demigod he'd once had a thing for.

"We've been over this."

"Maybe you should turn into Paesha and try to talk some sense into Thorne. That seems *reasonable*."

She scanned me once before turning back to Tuck. "He'd never listen."

"And yet here you sit," I said, taking another drink as the shadows curled closer, "watching me make the same mistakes I've made for centuries. Some might call that madness."

"I call it necessity." The playfulness drained from her expression, replaced by that look she'd given me countless times before. "The shadows grow deeper by the day, Thorne. Even you must feel it."

I didn't answer. Of course I felt it. The hunger in the dark corners of this tavern was nothing compared to what stirred in the spaces between realms.

She shifted back into her normal form, taking my hand. A gesture I didn't take lightly. She never touched others. "You listen or you fail. When it comes to Alastor, *you're* the target for him. She's merely the bait to force your hand. Think logically."

"Alastor doesn't want power or control. He doesn't even want Paesha, and that works in our favor. He wants a path to Irri. That's all. Find a path that doesn't involve you and you're free of him. Both of you are." Her eyes met mine and fell. She knew me too well, had spent too many centuries pulling me back from the edge of my own destruction. "You're thinking of going to the Forgotten, aren't you?"

I didn't answer. I didn't have to.

"You can't," she said, genuine fear creeping into her voice, the same fear she'd shown when I'd nearly gone during the War of the

Realms. "If you don't return, the prophecy is fulfilled. If what Ezarius has seen of the future comes to pass, we will all fall. Not just you. Not just the gods in this room pretending they cannot hear every word we say. All of us. You absolutely cannot go to the Forgotten."

"Then what would you have me do? Let him destroy her?"

"I would have you think, for once in your endless existence." She rose, her frail appearance contradicting the power that crackled around her like a mother's protective embrace. "The magic is volatile across all realms now. If these hunting gods can take the Huntress's stolen power—"

"Can they?"

"Does it matter? They'll kill her trying." She gathered her shawl around her shoulders, a gesture so familiar it ached. "The question you should be asking is why this version of her? Why now? What makes her so special that gods who haven't left Etherium in millennia are suddenly very interested in your little mortal?"

She walked away, leaving that question hanging in the air. The shadows in the corners retreated, the lurking gods slinking away now that the show was over. With a simple whip of power, the kind Minerva would scold me for using so carelessly, I wiped the entire conversation from their minds. They'd never know they missed it.

"Well," Tuck said after a long moment, falling back into our usual rhythm. "That was horrifyingly unhelpful."

"Was it? Or did she tell us exactly what we need to know?"

His eyes narrowed. "Boss..."

"They think she has power that belongs to them." I met his gaze, seeing not only my most trusted friend, but the brother who'd stood beside me through thousands of years. "But what if it's the other way around? What if she has power that was always meant to be hers?"

"That's a dangerous theory."

"More dangerous than letting Alastor break her?" I stood, tossing a few coins on the table. "We need to find Ezra."

"Your brother who wants to kill her? That Ezra?"

"Yes," I said, heading for the door with Tuck falling into step beside me as he always had. "The brother who's seen how this ends."

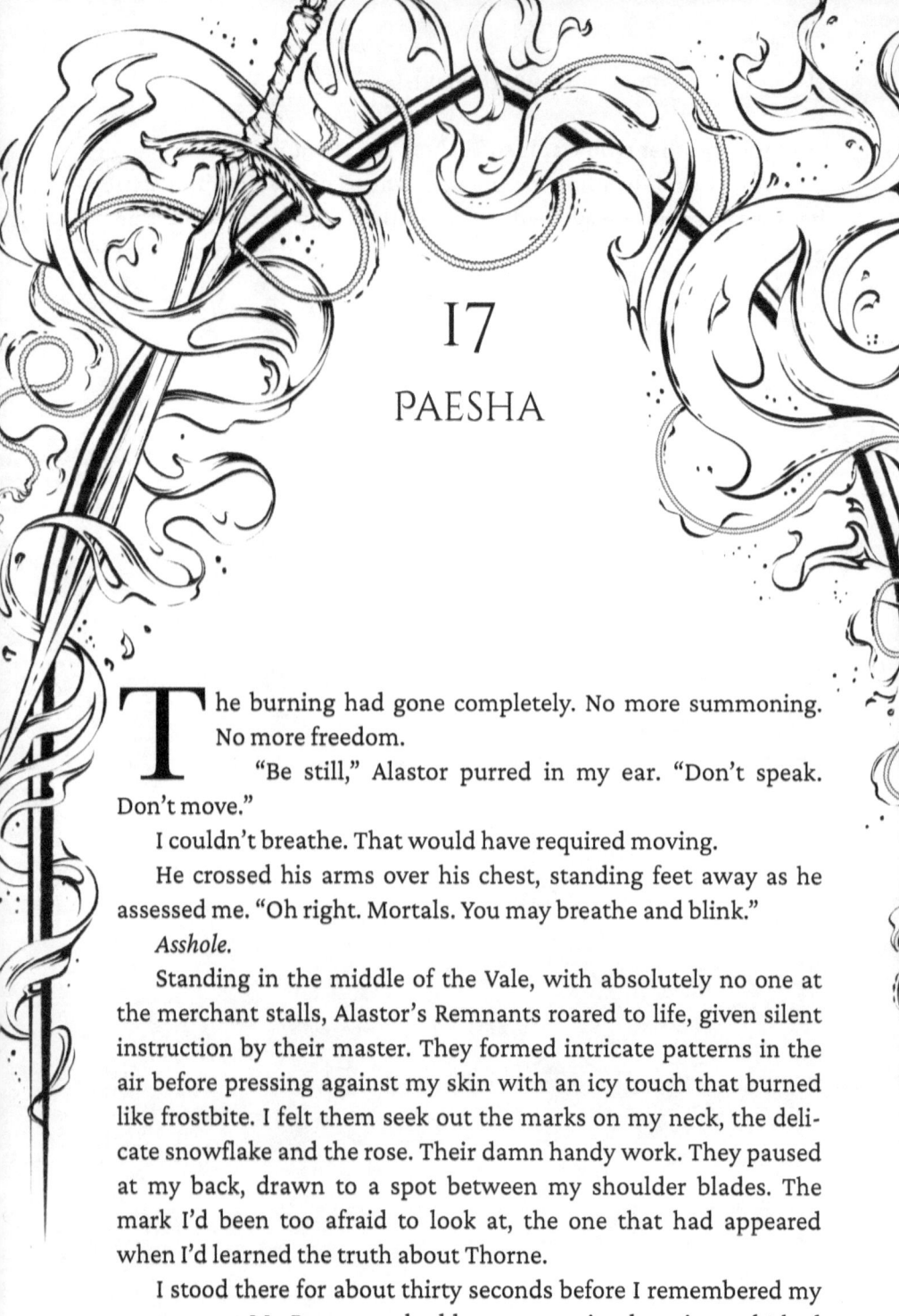

17

PAESHA

The burning had gone completely. No more summoning.
No more freedom.

"Be still," Alastor purred in my ear. "Don't speak.
Don't move."

I couldn't breathe. That would have required moving.

He crossed his arms over his chest, standing feet away as he
assessed me. "Oh right. Mortals. You may breathe and blink."

Asshole.

Standing in the middle of the Vale, with absolutely no one at
the merchant stalls, Alastor's Remnants roared to life, given silent
instruction by their master. They formed intricate patterns in the
air before pressing against my skin with an icy touch that burned
like frostbite. I felt them seek out the marks on my neck, the delicate snowflake and the rose. Their damn handy work. They paused
at my back, drawn to a spot between my shoulder blades. The
mark I'd been too afraid to look at, the one that had appeared
when I'd learned the truth about Thorne.

I stood there for about thirty seconds before I remembered my
own power. My Remnants had been conveniently quiet and I had
no idea how to call them forward. Anytime I'd needed to use the

power of the Huntress, it'd been as natural as breathing, but that was something I was born with, not something I'd taken. Not the monster living in my mind.

"Where are they?" Alastor asked, stroking a tattooed thumb along his jawline as he waited.

I didn't move. Didn't speak. Just as I'd been ordered.

"Oh, for fuck's sake," he said. "You may speak."

"My father gave me an apple once. After my mother abandoned us. It was half rotten and smelled like the rats that sometimes—"

"Stop!"

I smiled. "Problem?"

He stepped closer, grabbing my face.

I looked down, refusing to let him lift my chin. "I'm not allowed to move, remember?"

His smile was complete venom. "That smart mouth of yours is going to get you in trouble."

"In case you've forgotten how I ended up here, I think it's fair to say it's far too late for that threat. Maybe you could try again. Really mean it this time."

Alastor's eyes narrowed, his grip on my face tightening. "You think you're clever, don't you? A few quips and you gained the upper hand?" He leaned in close. "Let me remind you of your position, little Huntress. You belong to me now. Your power, your mind, is mine to command."

I met his gaze, refusing to be cowed. "And yet here we are, already having to remind the little mortal girl who's in charge. That probably isn't really godly of you. Don't worry. I won't tell the others."

His lips curled into a snarl, revealing teeth that seemed a touch too sharp to be human. "I could break you in ways you can't even imagine. I could strip away everything that makes you who you are until there's nothing left but an empty shell, begging for my guidance."

"Ooh, very scary," I drawled, rolling my eyes. "Tell me, do you practice these speeches in the mirror? The delivery could use some work. I'm not afraid to become nothing. Feel nothing. I've done that before. I thrive there, just so you know."

Alastor's hand slid from my face to my throat, his fingers pressing against my pulse. "Perhaps you need a demonstration of how precarious your situation is."

The binding marks on my wrists flared to life, sending searing pain up my arms. I gritted my teeth, refusing to give him the satisfaction of seeing me flinch. Truly, I hoped he would break me. End it now. But he wouldn't. We both knew that. No matter how many times he cracked the whip, I'd always get back up. Because I refused to be broken at the hands of any man. Ever again.

The pain intensified, spreading through my body like liquid fire. My muscles seized, every nerve ending screaming in agony. But still, I held his gaze, refusing to break. "Is that all you've got? I've had worse paper cuts."

Alastor's eyes flashed with a mixture of fury and... was that admiration? He released my throat, taking a step back. "You truly are remarkable, aren't you? So much fire, so much defiance. It's almost a shame to break you."

"Then don't," I said, my voice steadier than I felt. "Let me go. Find someone else to play your twisted games with."

"You will only speak the truth to me. Do you understand?"

"We speak the same language, so it's fair to assume I do, but if you need verbal confirmation, yes. I fucking understand."

He began to pace, thinking through whatever it was he wanted to ask. His strides grew quicker as he moved. "When we were in the meadow in front of that home, you had power I've not seen from you before. For a moment, I thought... but it couldn't have been. But then you put yourself in that dome."

"Was there a question there, or are we thinking out loud now?" I asked, my muscles aching from standing perfectly still.

"Where did that power come from?"

"Wow. Okay, all beauty, no brains. Let me see if I can simplify this for you."

His Remnants surged, snatching my arms and pulling them away from each other until I wondered if they would rip me in two.

The pain was bearable, but only just, racing through my nerves like wildfire.

"Be careful how you speak to me. They don't take kindly to disrespect."

"So you don't control them?" I asked, genuinely curious.

His eyes narrowed. "Do you control your shadows, Huntress?"

"Perhaps."

He grinned. "She learns."

"Did you acquire a greater depth of power when you killed the prince, or do you have new abilities?"

"I don't know."

I could have always had people talking in my mind and shadows dancing around me. Definitely could have been so subtle I never, ever noticed. For sure. At least that's what I told myself to circumvent his 'no lying' command. I'd learned long ago you only give the information you have to and nothing more.

"Bring them out," he demanded.

My body trembled with the compulsion. I wanted to. Needed to. It was all I could think about the second the command left his lips. But nothing happened.

He stared for a long time, waiting patiently before he said, "No matter. Perhaps they just need a little persuasion. Let me see your full potential, Huntress." Alastor's eyes gleamed with cruel anticipation as he raised his hand. The air thickened, crackling with dark energy. I braced myself for whatever torment he was about to inflict, determined not to give him the satisfaction of seeing me break. His Remnants surged forward, sliding down his arms in a tidal wave of shadows that crashed over me with devastating force. The impact drove the air from my lungs, leaving me gasping as darkness coiled around my limbs, sinking wicked talons into my flesh. Pain exploded through every part of me, white-hot and all-consuming.

My own Remnants erupted in response, bursting from my skin in a chaotic storm. They clashed with Alastor's shadows, hissing. The collision of our powers sent shockwaves rippling through the air, shattering the empty merchant stalls and cracking the cobblestones beneath our feet.

As the two forces battled for dominance, my mind splintered. A cacophony of voices flooded my consciousness, drowning out all rational thought. They whispered and screamed, cajoled and threatened, a thousand conflicting impulses tearing me apart from the inside.

"No," I yelled, covering my hands with my ears. But the voices didn't listen. They never did.

So weak.

You're not supposed to break.

I could see Alastor's lips moving, his face contorted with fury as he shouted commands, but his words were lost in the deafening roar inside my head. My own screams echoed distantly, as if coming from somewhere far away.

The world dissolved into a kaleidoscope of pain and fractured memories. It started with heat that seared every nerve. A thousand swords could've plunged into my back and I wouldn't have felt it beyond the absolute skin-ripping agony that overwhelmed every piece of me. I was never a child. Never a woman. Never loved. Never betrayed. Never anything. Only pain. Always pain. Suffering.

Suffering.

The agony crescendoed until reality fractured, splintering like glass beneath the weight of a thousand screaming voices. Each one tore through me with savage glee, ripping away pieces of who I was until nothing remained but raw nerve endings exposed to bitter winter winds.

Pathetic. Worthless. You deserve this pain.

I couldn't remember where I was. Who I was. The pain consumed everything, burning through muscle and bone. Whatever point Alastor meant to prove, I hoped this was everything he had to throw at me. I hoped this misery would sweep me away and end it all.

He saw right through you. You were never worthy. Just the bait.

Just the bait.

The bait.

My skin felt too tight, like it was shrinking, contracting around muscles that wanted to tear free. The world spun and tilted, reality bending until up became down and darkness became light. I tried to cling to something, anything real, but there was nothing to hold on to except the voices and their poison-laced promises. Until whatever Alastor's intention was shattered, and I was left to fade into nothing.

When I finally opened my eyes, I was sprawled on the cold stone floor in an empty room. The silence should have been a relief, but it only made the voices louder. They bounced off bare walls, echoing in the hollow space where my thoughts used to be.

Find your strength or lose yourself.

Don't bend.

Not yet, Huntress.

I could barely manage to swallow. "Please," I begged behind cracked lips. "Stop."

I could handle Alastor. I couldn't handle the voices that haunted me so relentlessly.

Fight back, then.

"Tell me how."

Not yet, Huntress.

That voice was singular. One woman. One. One single voice. I blinked.

Focus.

An apparition appeared before me, nearly invisible in the dark room. Her white wedding dress was covered in blood and her face, though beautiful, was haunted, plagued with misery as she looked down at the sword buried in her belly. She reached a bloody hand toward me before I met those eyes that were twin to my own. Another Huntress. Another of Thorne's conquests.

I'd seen this death before. Not like this though. I'd seen it through the eyes of a sympathetic woman, falling for a man. Now, it was different. He was the reason. I knew it as thoroughly as I knew how to breathe. How to be.

She stumbled forward, staining the pure white snow with her blood as she fell into Thorne's arms. I knew it was him without seeing his face. He reached for her, fingers trembling, exactly as I remembered in the vision Alastor had shown me. Only this time, the second before she died, she turned and looked right into my soul. The vision faded on her eerie scream.

Pain started building again, different this time, focused and sharp against my thigh. It burned like brands being pressed into my flesh, like molten metal seeking bone. My hands moved without conscious thought, clawing at the source of the heat until my fingers closed around gold and parchment.

Thorne's book.

The voices screamed louder, became more frenzied, more desperate. The pain intensified until spots danced across my vision, until my breath came in ragged gasps that barely brought in enough air to keep me conscious.

Destroy it.

With the last remnants of strength I could muster, I hurled the book across the room. It hit the wall with a dull thud that echoed for eternity, then fell to the floor, its pages splayed open like broken wings.

The voices didn't stop. They never stopped. But as I watched the book lying there, something inside me fractured in a different way, not from pain this time, but from the hollow emptiness that follows when you realize you've lost everything that ever mattered.

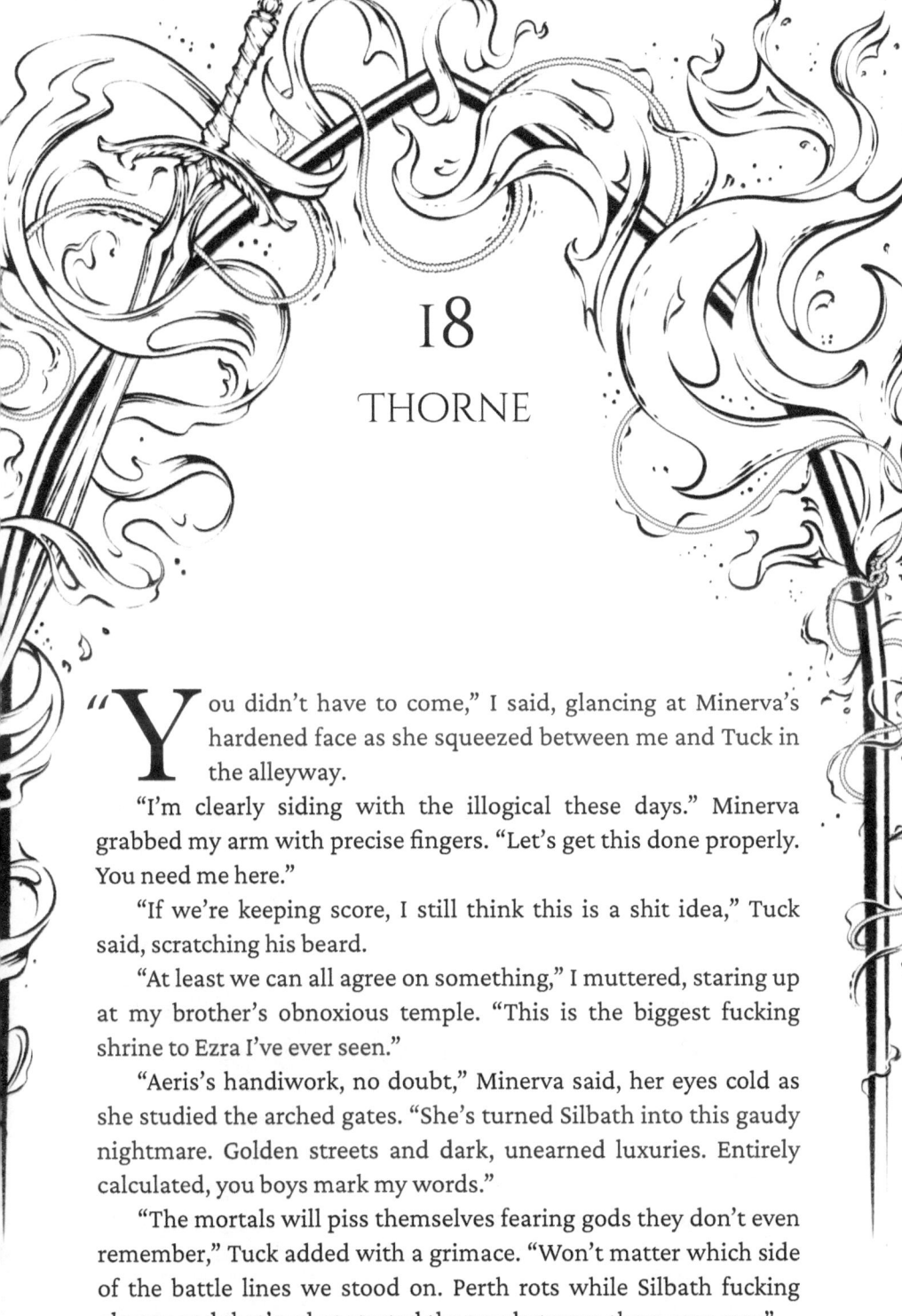

18

THORNE

"You didn't have to come," I said, glancing at Minerva's hardened face as she squeezed between me and Tuck in the alleyway.

"I'm clearly siding with the illogical these days." Minerva grabbed my arm with precise fingers. "Let's get this done properly. You need me here."

"If we're keeping score, I still think this is a shit idea," Tuck said, scratching his beard.

"At least we can all agree on something," I muttered, staring up at my brother's obnoxious temple. "This is the biggest fucking shrine to Ezra I've ever seen."

"Aeris's handiwork, no doubt," Minerva said, her eyes cold as she studied the arched gates. "She's turned Silbath into this gaudy nightmare. Golden streets and dark, unearned luxuries. Entirely calculated, you boys mark my words."

"The mortals will piss themselves fearing gods they don't even remember," Tuck added with a grimace. "Won't matter which side of the battle lines we stood on. Perth rots while Silbath fucking gleams and that's what started the war between them ages ago."

"I'd wager Aeris is feeding the divide. Creating jealousy

between neighbors, cultivating fear among mortals. Offering new paths to the desperate and wicked, should they dare emerge from their damn holes to seek an audience with gods who see them as nothing but prey."

Minerva shook her head. "The price for that kind of power must have been steep."

"And completely pointless. But that's not today's problem." I nodded toward the gates. "The Unmade are here."

"What's an Unmade?"

"Archer, what the hell?" I asked, whipping around to find him leaning on the building to our right in the alley. He wore his thievery leathers and had the damn sword Alastor gave Paesha strapped to his back.

"Been tracking you for days," he said, sweeping his hood back. "This doesn't feel like we're rescuing Paesha, but who am I to judge gods?"

"You shouldn't be here," Tuck said, stepping forward. "In fact, you *should* be up at the castle visiting your father."

Archer pulled a coin from his pocket, flipped it into the air, and caught it before smirking. Cocky fucker. "Learned something interesting from Aeris. Apparently, if I'm royalty, you can't use your magic on me."

I glared before stepping toward him, pivoting around and dislodging the sword from his back. I had him pinned to the wall, blade to throat before he could swallow. "Let's play a game. Think of your beloved sister and tell me what color her hair was." He struggled, but I kept him pinned, reaching inside his mind to slip that tiny morsel of a memory free. "Come on, Archie boy. What color was it? Red? Black?"

"Thorne," Minerva said, her voice stern in warning.

I didn't back off. Some lessons had to be learned the hard way or they wouldn't stick. I could see his mind working to find the simple memory, but it wasn't until his eyes glossed over with angry tears that I stepped back.

"I wanted to believe you weren't the piece of shit she made you out to be, but she's right, isn't she? You're such an asshole. There's no boundary you won't cross."

"You and I have the same goal, Archer. Learn the game before you challenge the gods who wrote its rules. Otherwise, you're going to wind up useless and dead. Believe it or not, I'm trying to prevent that. The rules only apply to acknowledged heirs," I said, lowering the blade. "And even then, every rule has its loophole. You're not king yet."

Archer's jaw clenched, his hand extending wordlessly for the sword. His eyes burned with fury and there wasn't an ounce of fear in them. I had to respect him for that, at least, foolish as he was. He'd always been loyal to a damn fault. With a slight nod, I handed the blade back, simultaneously releasing the memory I'd taken.

The change was immediate. Archer stumbled back against the wall, his hand coming up to his temple as the memory of his sister's blonde hair, bright as summer wheat, flooded back. His breathing turned ragged, and I saw his fingers tighten around the sword's hilt until his knuckles went white. He could never kill me, but he sure as hell wanted to.

Tuck moved between us, one hand raised toward each of us. "Easy now. Thorne made his point, albeit poorly." He shot me a disapproving look. "And you, lad, just got a small lesson about the reality of what we're dealing with. Take a breath. He's right. You want to be here? You want us to take you seriously? Use that brain."

I watched as Archer struggled to compose himself, the muscle in his jaw working overtime. When he finally looked up, the raw hatred in his eyes remained. But he swallowed hard and asked, "Whose temple is that, anyway?"

"Ezra's," Minerva answered quietly.

"Perfect." Archer's lips curled into a dangerous smile. "And how do we kill gods? So I'm prepared."

Tuck stepped forward, his expression grave. "You don't. And you shouldn't be here. You want to be helpful, go check in with King Aldus. That's where you need to be or with Quill. She needs protection because Aeris is more dangerous than you realize."

"Funny," Archer scoffed. "She said you'd say that. But from where I'm standing, only one god has used their magic on me today, and it wasn't her."

Minerva moved forward then, her cane tapping softly against the hard golden surface. Despite her aged appearance, there was always something in those knowing eyes that could make a man crumble. "Young man," she said, her voice gentle but firm, "consider this logically. If something drastic were to happen in that temple, you would be the only person who knows where we've gone. Think about the responsibility that places on your shoulders." She turned, fixing both Tuck and me with a disappointed look. "And shame on both of you for not considering how foolish that would have been." Her attention returned to Archer. "You may hate these two, but you've not met me." She held out her hand, suspiciously leaning more on her cane than she needed to. "My name is Minerva. I'm the Goddess of Reason and Wrath. I'm not here to make false pretenses or to pretend to be something I'm not. Most of my peers fear me, mortals don't typically get to meet me, and if I'm being honest, I'm not typically a fan of them either."

He took her hand, dipping his chin with the grace of a prince, the Silk in him coming out in full force. "It's nice to make your acquaintance."

"Oh, look at those manners. It's been so long, I forgot mortals still had those."

"Proudly raised by my grandmother," he said. "Who also had blonde hair."

He withdrew his hand, squaring his shoulders. "No disrespect to you, Your Godness, but I'm not here to make friends. I want to free Paesha from Alastor and be done with all of you."

She smiled. Actually smiled at him. "And that's exactly why we need your help. There's a very good chance we're going to walk into that temple and not walk out. Would you wait here? If we're not back in two hours, go directly to Alastor and tell him we've been trapped by Ezra."

"Alastor?" Archer's brow furrowed. "Why would he care? He hates Thorne."

A knowing smile crossed Minerva's face. "So do you, but we can hate someone and need them in the same breath, can't we?"

I watched as Archer's resistance wavered under her reasonable argument. He melted back into the shadows of the alley, giving a curt nod. "One hour."

Once we'd crossed the street, Tuck chuckled. "Did you really just manipulate that poor boy with the oldest trick in the book?"

"The classics are classics for a reason," Minerva replied with a slight smirk. "Besides, men his age always need to feel both useful and justified in their anger. I merely gave him both."

"He needs a purpose," I said, surprising myself with the admission. "I respect what he's trying to do, even if his methods are..." I trailed off as the massive gates of Ezra's temple began to creak open before us.

"Shall we?" Tuck asked, straightening his shoulders as we approached the entrance.

The Unmade didn't move. They might've been ominous statues, if not for their steady breaths and the singular beating of their hearts. They were Guardians. And their cause was just, their actions however, a different story. None of that mattered to me, though. They were still mortal no matter their speed and strength. They could die and if I really wanted to piss my brother off, I'd take one of their lives to remind him of that simple weakness.

Tuck's low whistle drew me away from the lethal fuckers watching us walk by and into the cavernous hall that was Ezra's new temple. The ceiling was not a ceiling at all but rather a swirling mass of the Never Sky. As if the space between realms should be cast for entertainment.

"That was a choice," Tuck said, staring into the void.

"It won't gain him any favors with the Fates. On your toes, boys," Minerva said, her cane clacking against the floor so hard, had there been anyone but my arrogant brother standing within the room, they'd have looked.

Ezarius, however, didn't bother. With his hands locked behind his back, he stood, staring up at the carvings of himself on one of the giant stone pillars holding up the ceiling.

"I will speak to my brother alone or no one at all. Your choice," he said, never bothering to look away.

He knew we'd come, of course. We'd been lurking outside for four days, waiting for him to show up. But timing was everything with Ezra. It always had been.

"You will speak to the three of us or none at all, Ezarius."

Finally, he spun, looking down at the woman he'd condemned millennia ago. He owed her far more than a conversation. But staring into the eyes of his old friend, his rigid posture nearly broke. "There's nothing you can add to this conversation. I can promise you that, Minnie. But I will also give my word that no harm will come to any in this company by my hands today."

"I would rather stand before the Fates than ever bargain with you," she said.

He feared her, as most did. For different reasons though. As the God of Unmaking, he could see the future through his power. There were a million different ways future events could happen, depending on the variable nature of free will. But Minnie? With each action perfectly calculated for maximum impact, each consequence thoroughly considered and deliberately chosen, she could narrow down how something might go, sometimes better than he could. She just couldn't see it the same way. Together, they were a force of nature, but he'd burned that bridge ages ago.

Ezra had a vision that the Fates would betray Minerva, the Goddess of Reason, and steal her power, something no one had ever heard of happening. She told him he was wrong, but Ezra's never been good at listening.

Before the Fates had locked themselves away, he convinced every god to bind them more tightly to their loom, restricting their movement and abilities, even when Minerva had begged him not to interfere. And Ezra had been dead wrong. The Fates and Minerva were meant to work together, not against each other. His interference actually caused Minerva's Reason to become tangled with the Fates' Wrath, creating the Goddess of Reason and Wrath that she is today, imbued with power no goddess should have.

For several mortal lifetimes, she never left her library. And those of us that loved her, that tried to see her, were attacked by sentinels of the Fates' Wrath. Minerva's Wrath. Her unique power made her different from all of us. And potentially more powerful than even Ezra and me. She was a god who longed only for ink and parchment, yet Ezra had damned her to exist as a paradox, and there weren't enough books in all the realms to contain her resentment for that truth.

"If you won't leave, then stand and be silent." When the bastard finally turned to face me, those eyes blazed with the same fury that used to level cities. "You have some nerve showing up here."

"You knew. The day you told me there was a path to peace, you'd already seen Alastor's move, hadn't you? The day the Fates told us about the Huntress."

He smiled as if he were a fisherman and I'd taken the bait. "I saw many paths that day. So many possibilities for our future. Some led to peace. Some to ruin. The moment you chose to seek her out, those peaceful paths vanished."

"Don't fucking lie to me."

"Lying is not the boundary between us, and you know it." He took a half-step forward. "The boundary was your power. We don't use our power on one another. That's always been the unwritten rule. The one pact. And you had no problem taking away everything I was, everything I remembered, no matter how much wrath you'd face from the Fates."

He blanched the second the words left his mouth, and I knew, without a doubt, he was fighting the urge to look at Minnie. Bastard.

"Rub it in, why don't you," I scowled.

"I'm done feeling guilty over lessons learned."

"Interesting." I said, sliding my hands into my pockets. "Because so am I. But I didn't come here to debate the Huntress's hand in offsetting the power. We'd be here for centuries, and that would work too far in your favor. I need to know about Alastor's plan. If I go into the Forgotten, and I'm not saying I will, but if I did, will I return?"

He scoffed, turning back to study his fucking pillar. "I can't wait to hear why you think I owe you an answer to that."

I hesitated, hating to relive a single one of the memories. "Do you know what happens when an Ever dies, Ezarius?" I watched his back stiffen at the question. "Does your power let you feel from my body when you kill her? A thousand lives. A thousand slices into my soul. Thousands upon thousands of years of misery. I pay that for a few moments of bliss with her. You think I don't know how ridiculous it is to chase her, knowing how it ends? You think I *want* to be here right now, begging the only one that's ever stood in my way for answers? You want me to care about a few mortal years you had to survive without a memory, yet you don't give a shit about what you do to me. Maybe I was wrong to come here. But I'm also desperate. So, be honest. Not for her. For me. Blood of my blood. *If* I go to the Forgotten, will I come back?"

He stood for a long time in silence. I never looked away from him. Never bothered to focus on the Unmade circling the room. Not with Minnie in my court. She'd bring this entire place down on them, should it come to that.

Eventually he spoke and his voice was ice as he turned and glared at me. "You can crawl on your hands and knees through every realm, begging me. You can bleed. You can fall. And still, I'd never help you. You're no longer my brother. You're the unfortunate consequence of love, and nothing more. Play your games, Reverius. Keep pretending you're innocent. When the realms fall, and believe me they will, it won't have shit to do with the Fera. It won't have anything to do with the Fates. It won't even be because of me. It'll be you and your Ever. And when there's nothing left in the Never Sky but ash and the echoes of mighty gods who once reigned, maybe then you'll remember what we once were."

For a moment, I saw genuine pain flash across his face, the echo of something lost.

"It doesn't have to be like this, Ezarius. This isn't even about the Huntress. It's about Irri."

"It's always about her!" His power flared, distorting reality around us. Minerva's cane came down hard against the floor, a warning neither of us heeded. "Every path, every choice, every future leads back to her. And you're too blind to see it."

I stepped forward, my own power rising. It flickered, as it'd been prone to do now, and then returned. "Then help me see it. Show me the path forward. You said there was one of peace and I refuse to believe it just vanished."

"I showed you once. You chose not to take it."

"That was before—"

"Before you fell in love? Before you decided your happiness was worth more than the balance of power?" His laugh was bitter, cutting through the tension like a blade.

I moved to grab him, but my hand passed through nothing. He'd vanished, anticipating my move, and appeared several paces away. "You want to know what I see? I see my brother walking willingly into darkness. I see him choosing chains he'll never break. I see her betrayal. I see—" He stopped, pain flashing across his face.

"What? What do you see?"

"It doesn't matter. You'll choose her anyway. You always do."

"Ezra—"

"This ends here." He straightened, the armor sliding back into place. "Get out. You took my memories, brother. You don't get my counsel too. Take your pets with you."

As I turned to leave, he spoke one last time. "The path to peace still exists, brother. But you'll never find it while you're running toward her."

The Unmade Guardians hadn't come any closer. Most hadn't looked up at all as we walked out. Had Ezra given the signal, they would have descended, whether it meant their lives in the end or not. Had we been mortals, we would have all been dead before the gate shut. The Unmade were vicious. But there were only two things that could kill a god, and neither would ever be the hands of Ezra's Guardians.

I had a thousand questions for Tuck and Minnie. But I didn't get to ask a single one because not only was Archer still waiting in the alley, he had company.

Alastor lounged against the closest building's marble wall. Archer was pinned to the opposite, his feet dangling inches above the ground while Alastor's Remnants coiled around his limbs and torso, holding him in place. The damn sword lay on the ground between them and if not for the present company, I might've fucking laughed at the lessons poor Archer was learning today. Or not learning, as it were.

The second Minerva stepped into the alley, Alastor's gaze snapped to her. His dark eyes widened almost imperceptibly before he dipped his chin in a show of respect that seemed both sincere and mocking.

Minerva walked forward. The shadows cast by the looming buildings seemed to part before her, as if even the darkness dared not impede her path. When she reached Alastor, she lifted her cane and whacked him soundly on the shin. "Let that boy down immediately."

Maybe she should just hit him a few more times and demand Paesha's return.

Alastor raised an eyebrow, a hint of amusement playing at the corners of his lips. "As you wish, Minerva."

He snapped his fingers and the Remnants released their hold on Archer, dropping him unceremoniously to the ground. He landed in a graceless heap, scrambled to his feet, snatching his fallen sword and putting it back into its sheath.

Oh good. Learning.

He'd always been smart. Calculated with a healthy dose of irrationality. Balanced in that way. It was why he gambled so successfully. Why he'd been such a big part of my run as the Lord of the Salt. But something had changed in him. Maybe the grief was too heavy. Maybe losing his sister was like having his own soul sliced open, much like it was for me to lose my Ever. I'd give him the benefit of the doubt on that alone.

I slid my hands into my pockets. "What do you want, Alastor?"

His eyes flicked through everyone else. "Perhaps this conversation is better had in private."

"No. Speak now before I change my mind about scrambling yours."

"I have every fail-safe in place, Keeper. You make one move against me and her final life cycle will end with Ezra's sword in her back. One move and this is over."

He fucking had me, and he knew it. He was always one step ahead.

"Go to the Parlor," I said, gaze shifting between Archer and Tuck. "I'll meet you there."

"You sure, Boss?" Archer asked, likely not realizing he'd used my old title as he squared off with Alastor.

"I'm sure. I'll be right behind you."

Once they were gone, and we could no longer hear the clacking of Minerva's cane, Alastor pulled a familiar dark crystal ball from the folds of his cloak. The obsidian surface caught what little light filtered into the alley, throwing shadows across his face. "I believe this belongs to you."

My fingers itched to snatch it from his grasp. "It did. Before you stole it."

"Before you *lost* it," he corrected, a cruel smile playing at his lips. "But now I'm returning it. Consider it..." He paused, turning the orb in his hands. "An act of mercy."

"You wouldn't know mercy if it bit the tip of your dick."

He ignored my comment, holding the crystal ball up between us. Its surface began to swirl with dark smoke before clearing to reveal an image that shattered something deep inside me. Paesha sat in the corner of a bare room, rocking back and forth, her hands pressed against her ears. The binding marks on her wrists stark against her olive skin. I'd need to be careful here. Calculated. I knew what he wanted. The same thing he always wanted.

"The stars aren't falling. Don't talk to me," she whispered to the empty room. "What do you mean they're burning holes in the sky?" She laughed, the sound sharp and broken. "Someone should catch them before they hit the ground. Put them in the Maw. Stretch them."

"What is she seeing?"

Alastor adjusted the collar of his coat as his smile widened. "That's the curious thing. I thought she'd somehow borrowed my power. Taken a few of my Remnants. But it seems she has her own. And if I've gotten it all right, they've manifested into something far different than mine. Not subservient, but rather, dominating. I can't work out what she's seeing, but, it's dark. Maybe even dangerous. Time will tell."

"If you think hurting her is going to force my hand, Alastor, you're wrong. I will—"

He tossed the ball into the air, never breaking eye contact with me as I flinched, desperate to catch it, but holding myself back. His hands were lightning fast as he snatched it from the air and held it out to me. "You'll do nothing, Keeper. As the bargain states. Or have you forgotten about that little mark on your neck?"

I took the Chrysalis from him, watching the woman that shared a destiny with me crumble. "She's not Sylvie, you know? You're not saving her, no matter what you think."

Alastor stepped forward, not an ounce of anger on his face, though it was laced within his words. "Don't you fucking speak my daughter's name to me."

"I loved her too. I loved her and I lost her, just like you did."

"No. Because you've managed to love a thousand more, and I've only ever loved one. Only her and her mother." He stepped closer, that controlled rage, shifting. Pouring onto the ground in shadow form, rippling across the golden alley, and somehow, the only thing I saw was the pain pulsing behind the rage. "And you took both of them from me."

I had to fight to keep control of the moment, no matter how bad I wanted to shove him away from me. His pain was not my own. I'd lost my Ever a thousand times, and he'd lost his once. *Once.*

"Is this what you came here for? You want to compare battle scars?"

Alastor's expression softened, leaving only a tired kind of grief behind. He tilted his head slightly, studying me. "Scars? You think scars are for comparing? Scars are stories, Keeper. Stories of what we lost, what we fought for, and what we were willing to destroy in order to survive. So, no, Keeper. I didn't come here to compare battle scars. I came to remind you that yours aren't the only ones that bled."

The silence that followed was heavier than the words themselves, and I hated him for it, hated him for the way he could twist the truth into something that felt like absolution and condemnation all at once. He'd never been my enemy. Even now. He'd only been desperate. And in that, he and I were the same.

"The Chrysalis. Pay attention."

Paesha rocked faster, her nails digging into the stone floor of her cell. "They're right. They're all right. He doesn't love you. He loves the chase. The game. Over and over and over. Like pancakes. And teacups. Broken teacups."

Suddenly she went still, staring at something across the room. "The moon is crying blood tonight," she murmured. "It tastes like memories. Like endings that never end." Her fingers traced patterns in the air. "Did you know that when gods dream, mortals die? I've died so many times in his dreams. Not his. Mine. Right." She shook her head, standing. Pacing. "Stop talking to me. Go away."

For a moment, it was her. Not the madness, only her. But she was slipping away. I'd been hunting my brother, and she'd been losing herself.

"You have to let her out of there. Give her a task. Distract her."

"I've not decided what I'll do with her yet, Keeper. But I thought you'd like to keep an eye on her."

It was a trap. But why? I would take any connection to her though. I needed to think it through, but standing before him, there was no time. He hadn't tried to bargain. He'd handed me the Chrysalis of his own free will. What was the catch here?

"Why?"

"I believe the voices are quite creative. I can't hear them, but based on her colorful responses, they've been telling her such interesting things about you. About all those times you watched her die." He adjusted the cuffs of his jacket. "They're particularly fond of showing her their deaths. She's trapped herself in that room for days, only to watch murder after murder."

"Is she always like this?"

"No. She's always angry though. Today is a particularly hard day. For the life of me, I couldn't figure out why. But then it came to me. In another reality, in a lifetime so far from this one it seems impossible to remember. This was the day Sylvie died. I think her soul can feel her deaths as much as it can see them."

"Through the heart. Through the throat. Through the spine. Different blades, different blood, same ending." Paesha's laugh was hollow. "He watches. Every time, he just watches. Yes, yes. I know," she said, her voice yanking me away from Alastor as my heart continued to slow.

"I'll ask again," I said, trying desperately to control myself. "Why are you showing me this?"

"Because I want you to watch," he said simply. "And I want you to remember that every time she relives a death, every time the voices remind her of you, it's because you couldn't let her go."

"You're a bastard."

"Perhaps. But I'm not the one who's held her in an endless cycle of death." He vanished before I could respond.

It didn't matter though. Nothing did, beyond the four walls of that fucking room.

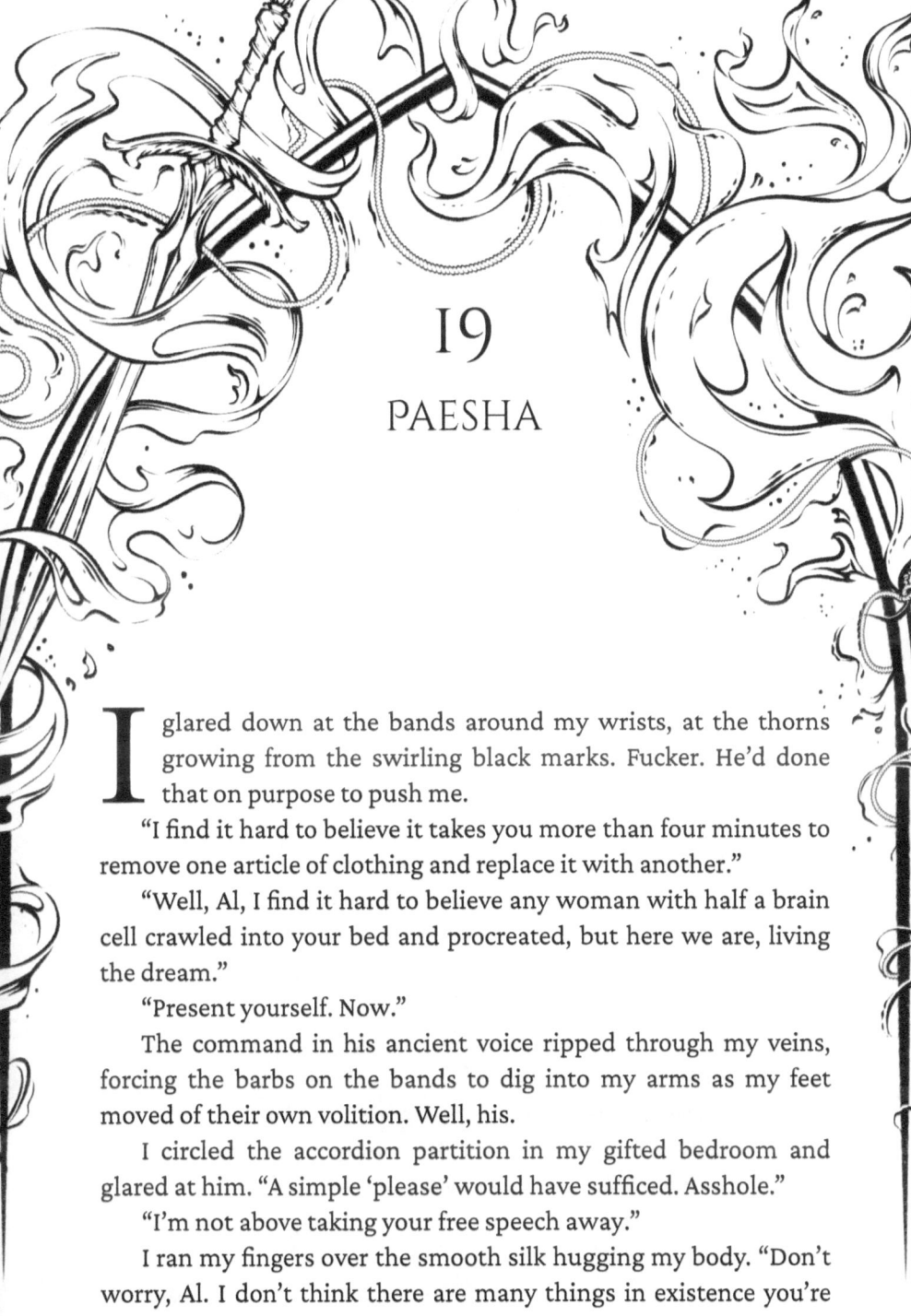

19

PAESHA

I glared down at the bands around my wrists, at the thorns growing from the swirling black marks. Fucker. He'd done that on purpose to push me.

"I find it hard to believe it takes you more than four minutes to remove one article of clothing and replace it with another."

"Well, Al, I find it hard to believe any woman with half a brain cell crawled into your bed and procreated, but here we are, living the dream."

"Present yourself. Now."

The command in his ancient voice ripped through my veins, forcing the barbs on the bands to dig into my arms as my feet moved of their own volition. Well, his.

I circled the accordion partition in my gifted bedroom and glared at him. "A simple 'please' would have sufficed. Asshole."

"I'm not above taking your free speech away."

I ran my fingers over the smooth silk hugging my body. "Don't worry, Al. I don't think there are many things in existence you're above."

He scratched his chin, patience wearing thin. "I've asked you not to call me that."

"Well, damn, Al. You also told me I couldn't call you Grand Pappy. You took Ball Sac off the table. You hated Shadow Fucker. What do you want from me?" I moved to study the plunge of the gown's neckline, my Remnants silently following like a train on the gown. "Honestly. Al is tame."

"For the love of the Fates, stop fidgeting with that dress. It's meant to be alluring, not manhandled. Now stand in the center of your room."

Again, my feet shuffled forward. In the four days since he'd taken me, I'd learned to only push to the brink, never over the edge with him. His anger fed into his Remnants, which caused mine to lash out. And though his were far more powerful, mine were erratic, and not at all bound to my command.

"Call them forward," he commanded.

"You know I can't," I answered. Because, in this one thing, he had no control over me. As long as I didn't know how to control the Remnants of my power, he couldn't make me do it. The mind was a precious thing, it seemed.

"Correct. That's why we practice. Focus on the emotion."

Without thinking, Thorne's little golden book popped into my mind. I'd hidden it after I'd left that empty stone room on the first day. I was given a comfortable room and access to basic necessities. Things would change though. We both knew it. As soon as he decided what he wanted to do with me, I'd lose all sense of self, and become only his. A future I didn't want.

"You don't have to make that face to use your power. It should come as natural as breathing."

"When was the last time you were a mortal?" I asked.

He paused, narrowing his eyes. He saw the trap for what it was, but still he stepped into it. "I've never been a mortal."

"Then it stands to reason, you have no fucking clue what you're talking about."

His Remnants were as quick as serpents, pouring from his tattooed arms, spilling onto the floor in a fluid motion as they raced for me. I planted my feet, bracing for the inevitable impact.

But rather than coiling up my arms, as they typically did when big Al was throwing a tantrum, they circled me, lashing out at my legs, taking me to my knees in pain.

"So much for your dress," I said through gritted teeth.

"I'll find you another before our meeting."

Meeting?

"Focus," he growled, his Remnants tightening their grip. "Hunt your own power. The thing you keep trying to cage. Let it surface."

"Sorry to disappoint, but my inner demon seems shy. Or he's napping. Probably that." The words came out strained as his power pressed against my mind, seeking the monster I'd been struggling to contain since shattering the veil. The thing that whispered about vengeance and destruction.

His Remnants pushed harder, like fingers probing an open wound. I bit back a scream as they searched for something to latch onto, something to control. But my shadows remained stubbornly dormant, refusing his call as much as mine.

Sweat dripped down my spine, soaking into the silk of the dress as I fought against the invasion. The monster stirred, stretching beneath my skin. But it wouldn't answer him. It was mine. The only thing left that was truly mine.

Alastor checked his pocket watch with an irritated sigh. "Stand."

My body obeyed instantly.

"You will not speak unless directly addressed by me. You will not move except to breathe. You will follow me, maintain proper posture, and present yourself as befitting your position." His voice carried the weight of command, each word settling into my bones like chains.

Guess we weren't changing the damn dress.

We walked in silence down the endless hallway, my feet catching on the rough patches of stone. Each step sent shards of pain up my legs, but I couldn't adjust my stride or even wince. He'd forgotten to tell me I could blink, so I didn't, letting my eyes burn as tears gathered at the corners and ice cold anger grew within me.

The meeting room doors swung open, revealing a long table surrounded by people, some I knew to be gods–Serene, Bellatora, Vesalia–and some I'd never seen. They studied me like I was a particularly interesting specimen in a jar.

Alastor pulled out a chair, and I sat, my back straight, hands folded in my lap, face carefully blank despite my burning eyes.

Everyone stared. At the binding marks on my wrists. At the tears tracking down my cheeks. At the way I held perfectly, unnaturally still.

Blink, you sadistic fuck, I thought viciously at Alastor. *Just say I can blink.*

He ignored me. Looking around the table as if he were taking attendance. I could only see him out of my periphery as I sat facing forward, but it was enough to know his posture had changed. He grew taller, commanding, as he let the others work out for themselves why a mortal might've been invited to sit here.

I knew what he wanted from me. To show off the power I'd stolen. But when he learned he couldn't command it for himself, he decided to keep that information to himself and show his dominance another way.

My eyes burned, but beneath the discomfort, my mind raced, seeking opportunity. These immortal bastards, so convinced of their own superiority, would speak freely in front of a silenced mortal. Their arrogance would be their undoing, and I intended to remember every word.

Alastor poured water into a crystal glass, placing it deliberately in front of me. Such a simple thing turned into another display of dominance. Everything was a game to them, every interaction a move.

He leaned close, his breath ghosting across my ear. "You may blink."

I kept my burning eyes wide open, even as tears tracked down my cheeks. Small victories were still victories, and I'd take every one I could get.

"The imbalance grows worse," one of the gods said. I couldn't see the face.

"Or haven't you noticed with your new little pet?" another added, her voice like wind through autumn leaves.

"Is there a reason you've brought the Huntress to this table, Alastor?" Serene asked. I couldn't see her face, but I'd know that smoky voice anywhere.

Alastor leaned back in his seat at the head of the table, locking his hands behind his head. "Stand, Huntress."

I shot to my feet, all qualms about blinking to prove a point gone as fear wrapped around me. Before, when it'd been him and I, I knew exactly where his boundaries lay. Here? Now? As a display of power amongst gods, I was fucked.

"Dance," he commanded.

My body was thrust into motion, swaying back and forth, spinning, swinging my hips as if I were on the Maestro's stage. I would not break. Not here, no matter how much the shame of being weak and powerless filled me, stirring the sleeping monster.

Do you see the hands of gods?

No. No. Not the voices.

They take and take. Break and break.

Panic rose in my throat as I felt my Remnants pour onto the floor in waves, shadows awakened from their slumber to come out to play. I didn't bother to look at Alastor. I didn't want to see the calculated smile. That fucking victory.

"Take this blade," Alastor said, holding a dagger between us.

I refused to let my fingers brush his as the cool metal fell into my hand. I could hardly think beyond the fear. The racing heart. What would he do? How far would he go? He wanted the power. Was this how he intended to get it?

"When I count to three, you will plunge the blade into your heart, Huntress. Go slow. Feel the pain."

I couldn't shake my head. Could do nothing but dance with the blade that would end my life. For a brief moment, a flicker of a second, the only thing I could see in my mind was the moment I'd first laid eyes on Thorne. Not the man claiming me as his wife, but the other. The one bathed in blood. The one that'd come into the Maw and killed the Cimmerians that'd tortured me. I wondered if

I'd bleed as much as they did. I wonder if these gods would tell him how it happened.

"One."

Around the table, the gods watched with a mix of fascination and cruel amusement. Bellatora's crimson lips curled into a wicked smile, her eyes bright with anticipation. Vesalia leaned forward, her delicate features a mask of false sympathy that did nothing to hide the eagerness in her gaze. And Serene, beautiful, lusty Serene, lounged back in her chair, one perfectly arched brow raised as if to say, "Well, get on with it then."

My hand trembled as I raised the dagger, the point hovering over my frantically beating heart. Every instinct screamed at me to fight, to run, to do anything but obey. But Alastor's command held me in place, an invisible vise around my mind and body.

"Two."

At his command, my Remnants exploded outward in a frenzy of shadows and smoke. They whipped through the air like a thousand serpents, hissing and thrashing as they sought their target. Alastor's eyes widened a fraction before he threw up his own defenses, his dark power surging to meet mine in a clash of wills.

The room descended into chaos as our Remnants battled for dominance. The walls turned dark. The table shuddered. Even the lights above us flickered while the others sat in barely concealed glee at the unexpected entertainment.

Bellatora laughed. "Oh, this is delicious! The little mortal has some fight in her, after all."

Goddess of War, I reminded myself, forcing my mind to focus on anything but the darkness closing in on me as I held the point of the blade so close to my heart, the threads of black silk on my gown began to snap.

"I do so love when they struggle. It makes the breaking that much sweeter." Vesalia's words cut through the haze of pain and fear, igniting a spark of defiance deep within me. I latched on to it like a lifeline, fanning the embers of rebellion into a raging inferno. I would not let them win. I would not be their plaything to torment and discard.

With a burst of willpower, I wrenched control of my shadows back from Alastor. They snapped to my command, coiling around me in a protective shield. The dagger trembled against my chest, caught between his power compelling me forward and my own fucking refusal to lie down and die. But Alastor was far more powerful. Far more trained and reserved and ancient and all the things he needed to be, and I was nothing. His power consumed me, smothering me in darkness. When his Remnants pulled away, mine were nowhere to be seen. Cowards.

Alastor's eyes narrowed to slits as he held a hand toward me. "Come Huntress. Our show is over."

"Three, dammit," Serene barked. "Can't you see she's breaking the balance? She took too much power. Ezarius was right about her. She has to die. Why else would you call us all here? Such a waste of Vesalia's precious time."

Alastor plucked the blade from my hand, ignoring her. "Sit down, Huntress."

I had no choice, of course.

Alastor reached inside his coat and produced a palm sized glass ball, drawing all of the gods' attention back to him. "You're here to watch and learn and make no further moves against the Huntress. You've lost that battle before it began. If there's balance to be found, you have my word, when I have what I want, I will find it."

The glowing god at the end of the table stood, his chair cutting off Alastor's words. "If Reverius learns that we—"

"Reverius will do nothing if he believes the Huntress to be at risk. Which I've also ensured by giving him a false Chrysalis." His lips curved into a cruel smile. "What he sees are mere possibilities, shadows of what could be. Nothing more." His eyes slid to mine, power thrumming through the binding marks. "Forget that," he commanded.

I felt the memory start to slip, like water through cupped hands. But in the depths of my mind, where my own Remnants lurked, the conversation echoed back.

False Chrysalis. Possibilities. Shadows.

The words repeated, burning themselves into my conscious-ness even as Alastor tried to strip them away.

The monster inside me stirred, and I welcomed it. Let them think me tamed. Let them believe their powers and their games made them untouchable. I'd learn their rules, their weaknesses, their precious balance.

The tension in the room shifted as Alastor's hand came to rest on the back of my chair, a casual gesture that carried the weight of ownership. "The Huntress belongs to me now. Her free will is mine. Her power is mine." His voice was silk over steel. "Anyone who wishes to challenge that claim should save us both the time and speak now."

A god I didn't recognize, all sharp angles and autumn-fire hair, leaned forward. "You speak of ownership? You were banished. Cast out. Your words carry no weight here, and neither do your threats."

"Yet still you came when summoned. That speaks of your desperation more than mine, Kealor."

"You know nothing of my desperation," he countered, rising from his seat. "Trading trinkets and secrets and suddenly you think you have command over things you know nothing about. You tempt the Fates with this bullshit, Alastor. I won't sit by and watch."

"Then leave," he said, standing to roll his sleeves. "Unless you'd prefer to be removed."

The other god's power rose to meet Alastor's words, tasting of decay and dying leaves.

But their clash became distant, meaningless, as my heart stopped in my chest.

There, across the room, Winter appeared as a ghost. The last time I'd seen her in physical form, I'd completely shut down, losing all sense of self. This was not the place.

Not the place.
This is the place.
Can you kill a god?
Shall we try?

Not the place.

I could feel myself rocking back and forth, though the numb fingers of madness had already sunk into my arms and legs. Snow began to fall around Winter's form, each flake disappearing before it touched the ground. Her face, so different from mine, yet hauntingly familiar, was etched with an ancient sadness I'd never fully understood.

No, I thought desperately. *Not here.*

The madness that had nearly consumed me in that stone room lurked at the edges of my mind, waiting for a crack in my sanity to slip through.

One, I counted, trying to ground myself in the present, in my own skin, in my own life.

Three to die.

Winter's hollow eyes, twin to my own, found mine, and I felt the weight of her centuries pressing against my temples. She wasn't me, had never been me, but her pain echoed through my soul like it belonged there.

Two.

The temperature plunged, though the gods around me noticed nothing, too absorbed in their argument. My breath should have fogged in the air, but I couldn't move, couldn't breathe, couldn't break Alastor's command.

Three.

Winter's lips moved, forming the words that haunted my dreams: *He cannot save you.*

The madness scratched at the back of my skull, whispering of past lives and future deaths, of endless cycles and inevitable ends. I clung to my count, to the present, to my own name. *I am Paesha. Just Paesha. This life. This moment.*

Four.

The sword materialized from the empty air, its blade gleaming like starlight before it plunged into her stomach. I felt the phantom pain, sharp and cold, even though I knew it wasn't real.

Winter faded like morning frost, taking the snow and the

sword with her. But the madness lingered, humming beneath my skin, waiting for another chance to pull me under.

The clash of powers continued around me, but I remained perfectly still in my chair, fighting the urge to scream. Not from the phantom wound, but from the certainty that one day, I wouldn't be able to tell the difference between Winter's visits and my own fracturing mind.

Five.

Who was counting? Was it me?

Why were the walls bleeding? Where had the light gone?

Six.

Six.

Time lost all meaning in that void. Seconds stretched into eternities, and centuries passed in the space between heartbeats. I drifted, untethered, my sense of self eroding with each passing moment until I couldn't remember my own name, my own face, my own life. There was only the darkness and the voices, taunting, mocking, promising oblivion.

And then, like a miracle, a sliver of light pierced the black. It was faint at first, a glow that I thought might be a trick of my fractured mind. But it grew steadily brighter, warmer, until it resolved into a beam of pure, golden sunlight. It washed over my face, gentle as a lover's touch, and with it came a rush of sensation that jolted me back to myself.

I blinked, disoriented, as the world slowly came into focus around me. I was sitting on the floor, my back pressed against the cool stone wall, beside a large, arched window. My bedroom at Alastor's. But I hadn't felt the sun on my face. The warmth had come from the golden book clutched in my fingers.

I opened the clasp, no longer feeling like I was betraying myself by reading his words. Everything mattered in these moments. Every bit of knowledge. Every piece of information I could use to escape. But his words were not an escape. They were only a different prison with shinier bars.

Dear Paesha,

I've written this letter a thousand times in my mind, trying to find the words that might make you understand. But I am what I am, a god who has lived too long, loved too deeply, and lied too often. My truths come wrapped in thorns, much like my name. So let me bleed for you now.

You're right to hate me. I've earned every ounce of your fury, every curse you've hurled at my name. But know this, every lie I told, every truth I buried, every bargain I struck was to keep you breathing. To keep your heart beating. To keep you in this world, even if it meant losing you in it.

The bands that bind you to Alastor should be mine. My sin to bear. But they are not unbreakable. Nothing in all the realms is truly eternal, not even the chains of gods. You once asked me why I chase you through lifetimes. The truth is, I don't chase you at all. I follow. I follow you into death, into rebirth, into every new life because that's what the soul does when it recognizes its other half.

This is not a plea for forgiveness. This is a promise written in a god's blood. I will break every oath, defy every power, and unravel reality to free you from this bargain. And when you're free, if you choose to walk away, I will let you go, beautiful. I will be the one to sacrifice. I will be the one to break.

The world may paint me as the villain in your story. Perhaps they're right. But I am your villain, and I will tear apart anyone who dares to cage what was meant to fly free.

Ever yours,
Thorne Noctus

I slid the small pencil free of the little golden book and sat there, lead to paper, wondering what I could say to him.

Thorne,
You speak of freedom while I wear the chains you could have warned me about. You write of protection while I drown in the madness you created. Every choice you made "for me" was really for yourself, to keep your precious Huntress breathing, no matter the cost to her soul.

Do you hear them, Thorne? The whispers in my mind? They're fragments of every life you wouldn't let rest, every death that wasn't final enough. My Remnants aren't merely shadows. They're the pieces of me you kept hunting and breaking. The madness feels like an old friend. A manifestation of the love we've likely circled for a thousand lifetimes, finally showing its nature.

You want to slay your enemy to free me? Start with yourself. You're the architect of this prison, the author of every bargain that binds me. Your love isn't devotion, it's possession dressed in pretty words and blood-soaked promises.

Winter was right. You can't save me. You can't even save yourself from what you've become.

Don't write to me again. The next time we meet, it won't be as lover and beloved, god and mortal, protector and protected. It will be as what we truly are, a man who played god with a woman's soul, and the monster he created.

-P

20

PAESHA

He'd tied me to a godsdamn chair and there wasn't shit I could do about it. My brain vibrated with pain and exhaustion and still Alastor was relentless. My ass was sore from the hard chair, my ears tired from the echoes of my own screaming and gods, if he fucking smiled one more time I was going to bring this whole world down around me.

"Go further. You're wasting our time," he said, leaning against the wall as he stared at me with bright green eyes. Eyes I would've liked to gouge out of his pretty head. Maybe I would one day. Maybe I would be his downfall. I locked the new goal in my mind, lining him up behind Thorne as his Remnants creeped lazily toward me.

My stomach churned in anticipation. "No. Stop. If I could have a break—"

"Interesting choice of word, *break*. That which you refuse to do." He took another large bite of an apple, forcing my mouth to water with dreams of the crisp sweetness. I hadn't eaten in three days. I'd been tied to this chair, somehow deeper in the ground than the Vale already was so no one could hear me scream. Though I'd only been lucid for a fraction of the time.

My Remnants remained coiled within me, refusing to bow to the beckoning of a god. I hated and appreciated their refusal to break in equal measure. They were strong. Stronger than me.

It took all of one sharp breath before Alastor's magic lashed out, drawing back only enough to rush forward with a punch. The Remnants swirled over my neck, growing tighter before brushing my lips, silencing my scream with yet another deep dive into my mind.

Papa always said secrets were the same as coin if you knew which ones to keep. He'd winked at me the first time he'd said it. Back when he smiled more than he cried. Back when he was at home more than he was away. Back when we had a home. I must have been six then.

Now, I had a secret. One that was worth more than all the coin, he'd said. And it was just ours.

Until it wasn't.

But this was the day.

I wore my prettiest yellow dress and squeezed my feet into shoes that were too small. I hid the stain on the lace of my sleeve by rolling it up. Dresses never kept when they were rolled in old newspapers and used for pillows on Beggars Row, but I'd done my very best. Because I had a secret that was going to buy me and papa a new house one day.

"He might look scary, Treasure, but don't let your feelings show. You keep your face blank, your eyes on your shoes, and you let me do the talking, you hear me?"

I held Papa's hand so tight, the tips of his fingers turned white, but he never let go. He and I were a team. We were the heroes in our story. He'd said so.

"I hear you," I whispered. "Don't stare, don't cry, don't smile, don't speak."

"Fear is only an emotion and emotions are nothing more than barricades."

We might've been twins, my father and I, if not for my peculiar eyes. The dark, chestnut hair was an exact match, but any time the sun managed to come out, my skin would brown quicker than his. He was paler, and I was... Well, I wasn't sure, but he'd said it was the only trait

I'd taken from my mother before she'd left us for someone with more coin and fewer problems.

A scary black carriage pulled up to the alley we'd been sleeping in and with two squeezes of my hand and a quick nod, all traces of the kind, knowledgeable man I'd known my father to be faded from his handsome face. "Eyes down, Treasure."

He only used my real name, the one my mother gave to me, when others were around, preferring something from one of his many bedtime stories instead. Because, though the streets were cold and dark, and sometimes scary, his stories were always magical and there was always a heroine to save the world.

"Lovely," a theatrical voice purred, curling down the alley and around the back of my neck. "Come here, child."

"She's uh, grown quite an attachment to me since her mother left, sir. It's best if she stays by my side." I'd never heard my father gulp before. It couldn't have been from fear though. He was never afraid. Someday, I wouldn't be either.

The man's cane clacked against the bricks paving the alley as he walked nearer. "How am I to know you speak the truth if I'm not allowed to speak to the dear child, Aeronus?"

Two more squeezes came from my father's grip before he released me, placing a palm on my back and pushing me toward the stranger. I tried to keep my eyes down, my breaths steady, and my thoughts in my mind quiet. But my heart, racing as it was, must've given me away because the cold metal of the man's cane brushed my chin, then forced my face up. I tried to close my eyes as raindrops fell from an endless gray sky, dampening my lashes.

Never be memorable, Treasure. Memorable people are targets for forgettables.

My eyes, one green and one blue, made me memorable, and though my father's sage advice echoed in my mind, when the stranger clicked his tongue and commanded me to open them, I didn't hesitate.

There was something monstrous about his smile as he examined me. Even the twist of his curly, red mustache felt sinister to my young heart, which ceased to beat as my breaths fell short. Frozen in place, I waited, the world filling my ears like a tidal wave as this man, with the power to turn secrets into riches, stared down at me.

"How old are you, child?"

"Eight," I managed.

"And your name?"

"P - Paesha Marian Vox."

The man knelt, though he didn't pull the cold metal cane from my face.

"I hear you like to dance. Is that true?"

My skin was on fire, my heart still afraid to beat. He hadn't blinked. Not once. And there was something very scary about a man that didn't blink.

"I'm... I'm not very good."

"I'm quite sure that's not true at all."

"Sometimes I sneak into Madame Fourth's ballet. She lets me sweep the stage and when I'm all done, she shows me how to spin."

The scary man's jaw ticced, and I knew immediately I'd said something wrong. "I'm... I'm sorry."

"Nothing to be sorry about, child." He rose, finally pulling his cane away, though my face felt like he'd set it on fire. "How would you like to dance on stage in front of a real audience?"

I turned from the scary man to look into my father's brown eyes, but I couldn't read his expression. No emotion. No weakness. He was a master at it. I'd be one too, someday. No fear.

"I think I would like that very much."

"It's settled then. Tomorrow, we will play a game. I will hide my cane and you will find it for me. When you return it, I will allow you to dance on my stage for... let's say, ten years. And after that, you will have to earn your right to perform. Do we have a deal?"

There was weight in his words. The world pulsed with pressure. But it was as if something held my throat in a vise. Refusing to let me say no.

"You must answer aloud, girl."

I looked at my father once more, terrified and so worried, I could feel the ache in my belly growing. But he simply dipped his chin, and that was that.

"Yes, sir," I whispered.

The man stared down at me as if he were waiting for some grand gesture. Unsure of what I should do next, I curtsied. But it wasn't my posture that he studied. Nor the smile missing from my face.

He stared at my arm and then spun to my father with a growl. "What is this? Why has it not worked?"

I blanched. I'd done something wrong. But there was no time to evaluate. Not a second to think over my words as the scary man rushed and gripped my father's lapel.

"Please!" I screamed, running at them, unable to hide my fear a moment longer. "I'm sorry. What did I say? What did I do? Please don't hurt him."

As if he were slowed by time, the man turned inch by inch. His grip on my father loosening as a smile that wasn't much of a smile at all grew on his ugly face. "Just a game, dear. Just a game. Isn't that right, Mr. Vox?" Again, he'd used a voice that felt strange. Loud, but insincere.

My father nodded. "Perhaps she is too young, Boss."

"Yes. Perhaps." He walked to the giant carriage and swung the door open before turning back to me. His calm facade was startling, as if he'd never been upset at all. "Tomorrow, you'll find my cane and return it to me. If you can manage it, I'll arrange for a private dance lesson with..." he sneered, "Madame Fourth. Do we have a deal, little Huntress?"

I didn't like him. I didn't like the way he'd put his hands on my father, nor the smile that looked like a snake's. I didn't like the tone of his voice or the way he walked without needing that cane at all. But I could find it. And if that's all that was needed of me, if it made my father happy and the scary man less scary, then I'd do it. But only this once.

The world beneath my eight-year-old feet tilted and spun until I was yanked back to the present, the burn of the Remnants barely fading as I leaned back in the chair, in my damn prison, hating every memory. Every naïve thought I'd ever bore as a child.

"I'm not interested in *your* past. We've been over this. The Maestro is of no concern to me."

It took every ounce of energy and every muscle I had to pick myself up enough to look at Alastor, still eating his fucking apple. I didn't look down at the blood collecting on my trousers from my dripping nose. I didn't consider the fact that I could hardly open my eyes. I simply lifted my middle finger and hoped he knew exactly what it meant. His boots ground against the floor as he walked toward me, his gait slow. Deliberate.

He squatted and spoke, but I couldn't hear the words. Not beyond the smell of the apple filling my senses. I knew how to be hungry. I knew suffering. But it'd been a long time since I'd felt the familiar pit of emptiness in my stomach. He meant to wear me down. To force my will to bend and break.

"How?" I managed, though my tongue felt too swollen, this fresh from a memory.

"Use your words, *Treasure*."

At the use of that name, the complete violation of my past, I turned to the side and heaved. Nothing came up of course. Even the bile had stopped coming up two days ago.

"Use your words and I'll give you a bite."

"Go. Fuck. Yourself."

He tsked. "Your insults are getting weak. Perhaps your mind is as well." He waved what was left of his fruit in front of me, the white meaty part of his apple, so sweet it lured me closer to him. "I can't tell you how to use your power. I can only hope to coax it free again."

The Remnants hit again before I knew they were coming.

"Go away," I breathed, staring into the beady eyes of a rat who was probably as hungry as me. The cold, damp cobblestones beneath me seeped through my thin dress and into my bones. I huddled closer to the wall, hugging my knees to my chest, trying to make myself as small as possible. The alleyway was dark, the sun hiding behind the clouds, casting long shadows that danced and flickered like ghostly fingers.

I'd scavenged a half-rotten apple, and it only smelled a little terrible. Better than the moldy bread from two days ago. I'd learned at the ripe old age of five that a little rot was okay, and with fruit, the sweetness overpowered the sour if you didn't let it go too long. But the squishy bits made my fingers sticky, and I hated going to the bathhouse.

Clutching my precious apple in my fingers, I waited for Papa in the alley we'd claimed as our own, huddled under a makeshift shelter we had cobbled together from scraps of wood and cloth. He was careful to pick a spot where I could hide at night, but the rats always found me.

And rats bit. Hard.

The little creature crept closer, sniffing the air, his whiskers bouncing up and down.

"Shoo. I'm saving half for Papa. He'll be here any second. I know it."

That was a lie. I never knew when he would come back anymore. Not really. He'd followed the scary cane man last night and left me to sleep in the alcove. I missed his warm back pressed against mine. I missed the smell of ale on his breath as he crooned into my ear, promising we'd be in a home soon and he'd buy me a pretty dress.

I didn't need a dress. I didn't even need a real breakfast. I just wanted him to be here with me. But last time I told him that, he said I didn't know what was best for me. I probably didn't.

My belly rumbled as I pulled the apple closer, staring at the tiny bit of skin that still held firmness. That would be the best bite. And that fat rat knew it too. He stepped closer again, his nose dancing as if he heard music that no one else did.

I could feel the swell of tears in my eyes before I heard the crack of my voice. "No. I need this one."

But it would be a war between the rat and I, and we both knew it. I'd pull away, he'd scramble up my arms hissing, and his nails would scratch me, and his teeth would bite me, and I'd lose the apple anyway.

An angry tear slipped from my eye as I accepted defeat, pushing away the pain in my tummy, and rolled the mushy apple toward the beast. Last time I got bit, it'd swelled, and Papa had scolded me for trying to fight an animal. He was probably right.

Another tear fell. I didn't know when I'd eat again. I sniffled, watching that rat devour my only meal. He hadn't even bothered to run off.

"No more tears, Treasure." My father's soft voice was like a balm as he hurried up the alley toward me.

I swiped away the proof of my sorrow, keeping an eye on the rat until my father's heavy stomp sent him scurrying down the alley. Papa leaned down, blocking my view of the little beast as he tucked a finger under my

chin and lifted, forcing me to look into his comforting eyes. "Missed one."
His thumb rubbed my face, and likely the dirt staining it.

"I was trying to save the apple for dinner. I'm sorry, Papa."

He reached into his coat pocket, boasting a grand smile as he wiggled his eyebrows. "I've got something better. Something special. Close your eyes."

The sadness in my heart was swept away by the whimsical words of a prideful man. He didn't have real magic like I did, but he had a different kind. The kind that made pain and worry scamper as quickly as that rat had. Maybe the gods had abandoned this world, like everyone always said, but one of them must have snuck back in and gave him something special.

I closed my eyes, unable to hide my smile as excitement swelled in my belly.

"Remember that I love you always, Treasure. Beyond the moon and the stars and every drop of rain. I'll always be here for you."

"I love you too, Papa," I whispered as something small and delicate fell into my waiting hand.

"Open your eyes."

I was terrified to let him see the disappointment melt over me. I stared down at a broken necklace, repeating his frequent words in my mind: emotions are nothing more than barricades.

The jewelry was lovely, with a gold shine similar to something I remember my mother wearing. But it would do nothing for the growing hunger.

"Thank you, Papa. Where did it come from?"

"Doesn't my girl deserve fine jewelry?"

"I guess so," I said, keeping my chin high and my eyes on the broken clasp to stave off the pressing tears.

I knew there was something wrong with me then. What kind of person gets such a lovely gift and doesn't feel grateful? But maybe I did. Maybe it was buried under hunger.

"I think I can fix this piece." He pulled the necklace from my hands, and sat beside me, resting his back against the brick building. "See? The clasp is just bent a bit. By the time you get back, I'll have it good as new."

"Get back from where?"

"We talked about this. You've got to find that cane." I watched his large fingers curl around the necklace before he slipped it back into his pocket. "You find that cane and our world changes. No more cold nights out here, no more rats and rotten apples."

"But I thought you were coming with me?"

"You'll have to do this one alone. That's okay, isn't it? You can do this for me. For us?"

"No more rats?"

"Not where we're going, Treasure."

"Okay, Papa."

"You bring that cane to me, and I'll take it from there. We'll eat like kings and queens tonight."

I jumped from my spot on the ground. "Do you mean it? Do you really mean it?"

He stood, slid the worn, old, brown hat from his head, wrapping an arm around his belly as he bowed low with a flourish of his hand. "I would never lie to you." A glint of joy lit his eyes as he held a palm out to me. "Is that music I hear?"

I giggled. "Papa!"

"Shh. Listen." He swept his arms back and forth as if he conducted the world on a silent song. "Can't you hear it, Treasure?"

I nodded, though it wasn't really there. It was only his special magic. "I can hear it."

Hauling me onto the tips of his toes, he began to sing, sweeping through the narrow alley as we spun and stepped, and I laughed and he laughed and there was no more pain in my belly. Just like magic.

"Scram, kid."

I hadn't realized I'd fallen asleep until a giant boot came crashing down beside my head, splashing a puddle of water into my face.

I scrambled away, pulling my knees to my chest, looking around in the dark for my father. Heart racing, I realized he never came back and the angry man staring down at me didn't want me here but if I left, my father wouldn't be able to find me. This was our home. Our alley.

"What's the matter, little petal? You lost?"

A woman circled around the man, kneeling in front of me, soaking the ends of her dress in the mud puddle as she reached for my face.

I turned away from her fingers with a jerk. "Don't touch me."

"Feisty little thing," she laughed. "Between us girls, you might not want to stick around for what's about to happen."

"I have to be here." I stuck my chin up high, glaring at her.

"Listen, kid," the man said, pulling out a knife. "You either leave on your own or I'll slit you from nose to navel and watch to see how long it takes you to heal."

I swallowed, turning to ice. I couldn't move or think as the man pointed his shiny blade at me. "I don't think that's how we're going to play today, Mr. Vanhutes."

The familiar clack of a cane echoed down the alley as the Maestro stepped closer, his red hair gleaming, even at night. He stood with three large men wearing gloves and long coats.

"Thomas?" The woman sounded a little like a scared kitten.

"Come, little Huntress," the Maestro purred, holding his hand out to me. "This isn't a place for my future diamond."

I cowered away. "Have... have you seen my papa?"

"I sent him back with a pocket full of coins. Has he not returned?"

"No, sir."

He tsked, shaking his head as he leaned all the way forward on his cane.

"Listen, Boss," the man with the knife said.

The Maestro stepped forward, holding a hand for the knife. When the man dropped it into his hand, he smiled that wretched, terrifying smile.

"Come," he said again, with far more of a demand in his theatrical voice. "We'll leave the violence for the adults."

"I need my papa," I argued.

"How about some dinner and then we'll practice finding people instead of things?"

I'd never thought to use my magic to find people. That was smart, I supposed. But something felt wrong about the way he watched my wrist when I agreed.

I crawled into the giant black carriage with as much turmoil in my belly as I had last night. The Maestro didn't get too close. He whistled a cheerful tune and flipped a coin between his fingers as the carriage shot down the street. I stared, watching his red mustache bounce up and down as he altered his song each time the horse changed directions. A different one for each street, it seemed. How strange.

"A deal's a deal, you know?" I said bravely.

"It is."

"Well, you got your cane. So now I get to dance in your show?"

"Lesson one, Huntress. Consider your words very carefully when you bargain with a master. You may dance in my show, but not quite yet."

"I see you never learned that lesson, Paesha Treasure darling."

I was no longer sitting in a carriage, but rather lying on the cold floor, staring up at the blurry figure that hovered above me. Alastor smiled. Again. "My Remnants have always protected me. Pity yours seem to be broken."

The only feeling in my whole body was the flesh of my cheek, where a tear slipped free. And when I closed my eyes, it wasn't the Maestro I saw there, it wasn't even Alastor. It was the blank face of my father, lost in his opium haze. And this time, I wasn't sure if my mind had given up and I'd fallen asleep, or if Alastor's Remnants had attacked again and I was too numb to feel it.

After seven years, the doorman no longer stopped me. The smell of opium in the air didn't bother me as much either. But the stares, the blank faces of troubled people lying along the velvet couches as they let the world pass them by would always be my breaking point.

"Hey Papa," I said, kneeling before him. He sat on a purple couch, legs spread apart, head tilted back, with his eyes closed. He could have been sleeping, if not for the way his fingers clutched the end of the hose feeding out of the glass vase sitting on the table beside him.

At least he didn't smell of vomit this time.

"Treasure?"

"I thought you might like to come home. I made soup."

"Soup?" he peeled his eyes open, and though it made no sense at all, I felt a wave of shame. I didn't want to see him like this any more than he wanted me to.

"Mushroom and onion."

"Put it on the table, Treasure. Your mother will be back soon. I bet she's hungry."

"No, Papa. Mama left. It's just you and me now."

"Just you and me."

I slipped my hand into his, breathing through the smoky haze of the room as I closed my eyes and remembered how it used to be. When sleeping in an alley wasn't scary and the only worry I had in the world was my next meal. Such mediocre things when faced with the distancing relationship of the only person in the world that was supposed to love me. He did though. He still called me Treasure. He remembered our stories.

"Come home, Papa," I begged, swallowing the lump forming in my throat. "Come home and I'll take care of you. You can get better."

He missed my mother. That was what he always said whenever I tried to ask him why. He claimed he loved her so much his heart no longer beat like mine did.

My papa sat forward, sliding his thumb across my cheek to remove the tear. "What's this?"

"It's nothing, Papa. The haze burns my eyes, that's all."

"Emotions are nothing more than barricades."

I waited in silence as he brought the edge of the hose to his mouth and sucked in a deep breath, breaking every last piece of my heart. I knew how it would go from here. I'd lost.

His eyes rolled into the back of his head as he blew out a thick puff of white smoke.

"Don't forget your soup, Papa," I whispered, kissing his cheek. Another tear fell as I walked away.

"If I have to watch that despicable mortal for one more second, I will have to find a way to end myself."

Alastor's words were muffled, as if my head were underwater, though I was quite sure I was breathing. But at least this last vision had given me something to hold on to, even if the god hadn't meant to do it. I could draw my power forward when desperate enough, sure. I'd done it before. But, regardless of his attempts, I'd left desperation behind a long, long time ago. Unfortunately for him, resignation was far more comfortable. That was until Winter appeared in the room with us.

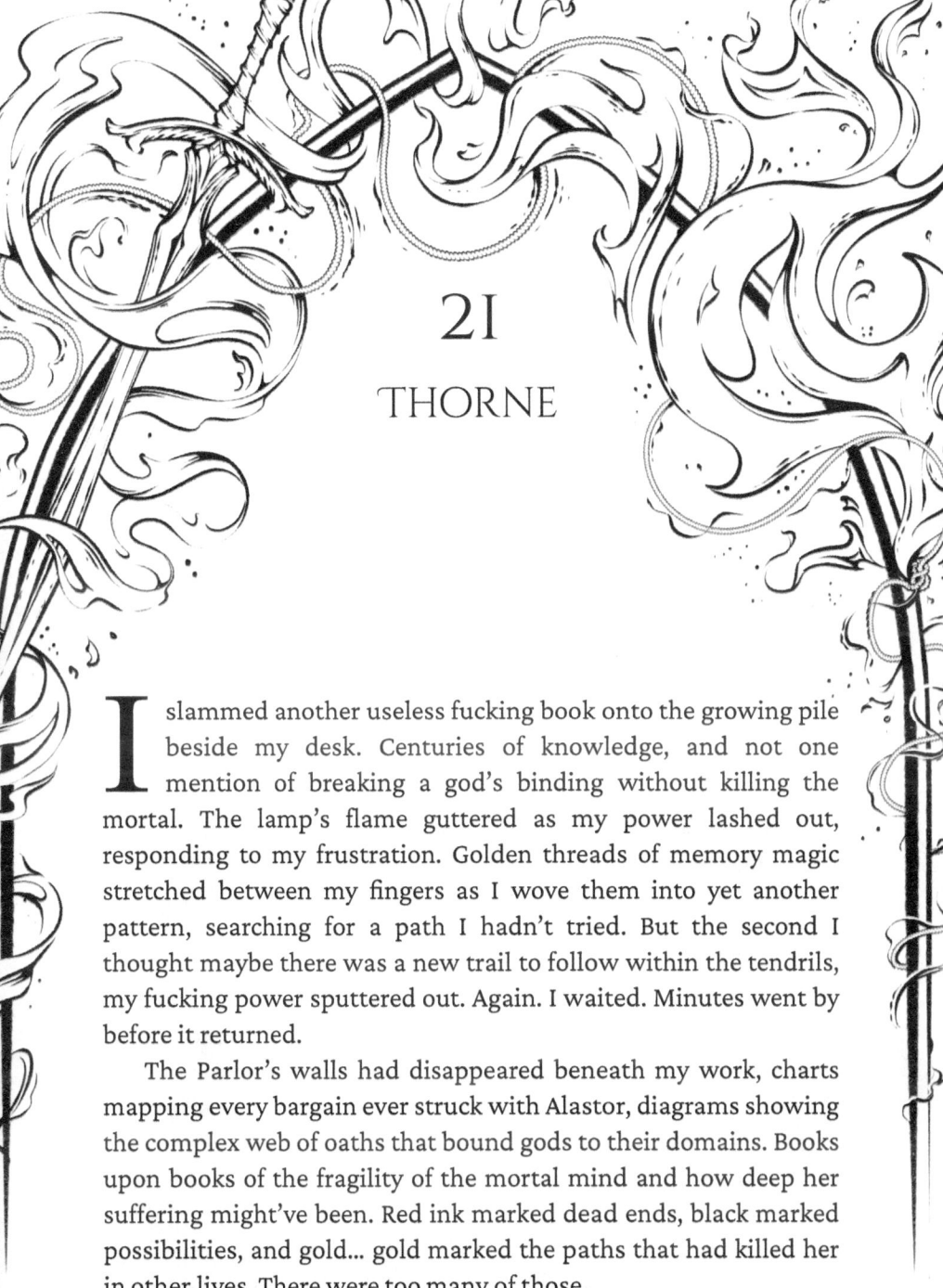

21

THORNE

I slammed another useless fucking book onto the growing pile beside my desk. Centuries of knowledge, and not one mention of breaking a god's binding without killing the mortal. The lamp's flame guttered as my power lashed out, responding to my frustration. Golden threads of memory magic stretched between my fingers as I wove them into yet another pattern, searching for a path I hadn't tried. But the second I thought maybe there was a new trail to follow within the tendrils, my fucking power sputtered out. Again. I waited. Minutes went by before it returned.

The Parlor's walls had disappeared beneath my work, charts mapping every bargain ever struck with Alastor, diagrams showing the complex web of oaths that bound gods to their domains. Books upon books of the fragility of the mortal mind and how deep her suffering might've been. Red ink marked dead ends, black marked possibilities, and gold... gold marked the paths that had killed her in other lives. There were too many of those.

"You'll burn out if you keep pushing like this," Tuck said from the doorway.

I didn't look up from the complex knot of power I was untangling. "Then I'll burn."

The magic responded to my touch, ancient and familiar. This was what I was, the Keeper of Memories, the one who wrote the stories of gods and mortals alike into the fabric of reality. But for all my power, I couldn't find the one thread that would unravel Alastor's claim on her.

"Have you slept?" Tuck asked, moving closer to study my latest attempt.

"Sleep is for lesser beings." I traced a line of text that spiraled up one wall, ancient words glowing with power. "Look at this. Three centuries ago, a mortal broke free of Vesalia's binding by—" I stopped, jaw clenching. "Never mind. She died two days later."

"Thorne."

"Don't." I pushed more power into the weave, watching golden threads spiral out to connect seemingly unrelated events. "Every bargain has a loophole. Every binding has a weakness. I have to find it before—"

The magic snapped, recoiling like a whip. I caught a glimpse of Paesha through the dissolving threads, blood on stone, shadows writhing, her voice raw from screaming at ghosts only she could see. Then it was gone, leaving only the bitter taste of failure in my mouth.

I'd paid whatever cost to find her in every life. I'd rewritten the rules of gods and mortals to keep her breathing. But I couldn't reach her now, when she needed me most. With deliberate care, I pulled the Chrysalis from my pocket. Even in the dim lamplight, shadows swirled beneath its dark surface, promising answers if I looked deep enough. But I was starting to suspect those answers were as false as Alastor's promises.

"There's still time," Tuck said quietly.

"No. Time is the one thing we're running out of. I traced the memory of this ball, something Alastor probably thought I'd be too distracted to do. It's a false Chrysalis. Just a godsdamn glimpse of her and nothing else. He wants me to believe she's spiraling more than she is, but it's tied to possibility, from what I've gathered.

Which means this could be her soon. And I'm completely fucking stuck."

I pulled the Chrysalis closer, watching as she dragged her bloodied fingernails across the stone floor. Even in madness, she was breathtaking, a storm given mortal form.

"You're going to crack that thing if you keep staring at it so intensely. It's been days."

I didn't look up as he walked into my office. I knew what I'd see there. The disappointment.

"I'm not allowed to interfere on either account. What else can I do but work?"

"Shall I define obsession?"

"Did you come looking for a fight?"

He stepped farther into the room. "I need you to focus. There are other matters that'll affect your Huntress. Minnie says the king is dying on the inside, which means his body will follow shortly after."

That got my attention. "Mortals don't simply die without cause."

"They do when their hearts break. He lost a son. Asshole or not, he had faith in him. He lost a daughter he never knew was his, and now his only *living* son refuses to be in the same space as him." Tuck's voice carried an edge of accusation. "The physicians say he hasn't left his bed in days."

"A little depression. He'll be fine."

"We need to get Archer—"

I waved my hand dismissively. "Archer's tantrum isn't my concern. Paesha—"

"Is exactly why you should care about Archer. She cares for him. You know this. And if the king dies with this rift between them, Archer will never forgive himself. And this kingdom will fall to war. It's guaranteed. Why do you think Bellatora and Minerva are both here? Our old friend is trying to prevent what Bella's trying to build."

"Set that to the side for a second and rationalize something out with me." I rose, crossing over to the cabinet full of liquor.

"Let's maybe not start drinking at..." he looked at his watch. "Actually, never mind. Make mine a double. What are we figuring out?"

"Why does she have Remnants?"

His broad shoulders slumped as he scratched his beard. "One could argue, she's always had them and never had enough power to use them. When she killed Farris, and stole the power, it fed the well, waking the depth of power."

"That's what I assumed as well. But, here's the odd part," I handed him the glass. "She told me the Remnants have voices of her past lives. How is *that* possible? Do Alastor's Remnants speak to him?"

"It's possible. Paesha is a soul descendant of two gods. She's the Huntress thanks to Irri, but the Remnants have always been shards of lost things. It stands to reason, and don't you ever tell Minnie I said that, that Paesha's power latched onto the first lost thing it could find. Her soul."

"How do we shut them down? Take her power? She's losing her damn mind."

"Can't do that or she dies."

"Wrong," I said, swirling my glass. "Alastor is holding Irri's power. Some here call him the God of Lost *and* Broken Things, when we know him to only reign over the Lost."

"Have you ever seen him *use* Irri's power? Think about it. If we draw power from human adoration, he's making sure the humans don't forget about her, by spreading her title around. She's being fed power by mention alone. It's quite smart, actually, regardless of where she is. It's the only thing he can do to soothe that missing connection to his Ever, I'm sure."

"He's feeding her power," I repeated, realizing I'd never considered that.

Tuck set his glass down with deliberate care. "Speaking of lost things that need finding... Archer."

"I'll handle it." I drained my glass. "He's stubborn, not stupid. He'll see his father."

"You sound awfully confident for someone who's been staring into a crystal ball all day."

I shot him a dark look. "Don't remind me."

We left the Parlor to find Minerva waiting by the carriage, leaning on her cane with an expression that suggested we'd kept her waiting for approximately three eternities.

"I trust you boys finished solving all the realm's problems over your morning drinks?" she asked dryly, clearly smelling the alcohol.

"Actually, we were just discussing your joyful disposition, sunshine," Tuck answered.

She whacked his shoulder with her cane. "Call me that again and I'll show you just how sunny I can be."

Minnie and I sat in the back of the carriage while Tuck took the seat at the front, effortlessly driving the horses through Stirling. Except when we didn't turn south to head to Paesha's home in Silbath, I shot a glance to Minnie. "Where are we going?"

"If you would have pulled your head out of that office of yours at all these past few days, you would know."

"Where's Quill?" I asked, suddenly more concerned for the child than the man.

"Oh, look. The Keeper *does* have a heart. She's gone home to Silbath with her caretakers. Tuck's been on rotation, checking on them as well as keeping an eye on Archer and the king, while you sit around pouting."

"I'm not pouting, I'm working."

"I don't argue with pouters." She shifted away so she could fully face me. "What's the end goal here? Because I need you to promise me you're not going to the Forgotten. Tell me there's nothing Alastor can do to make that happen."

"I'll do a lot of things, Minnie. But not that."

She gripped the cane across her lap. "You have that look on your face, Reverius. If you go there, you know what Ezra says is going to happen. Alastor will send the Huntress. She'll betray you and you will ruin us all."

I looked away to hide the scowl at her use of my first name. "I don't trust a single thing my brother says. And neither should you."

"Then tell me why we went to him."

"I don't know, Minerva. Maybe because at the end of it, he's still my brother and I had hoped he'd be honest. But you know what his silence tells me? He's not interested in restoring the balance no matter what he claims. He wants me to step back so he can control everything. Ezra can no longer see beyond himself. He only wants her to die. And I just want her to live. I want to fucking love that woman in peace but he won't let it happen. There are so many prophecies and visions he claims to be true, I don't trust a single one anymore. Think about it, we were always told the Huntress would break the balance of power. That's done, isn't it? It's already happening. So why's he still out for blood? He said I would find myself locked in the Forgotten and all the gods' power would die. It's fear mongering. Like his claim that the Huntress will betray me." I let out a bitter laugh. "Think about who's giving us these 'visions'. What are his fucking motives? Maybe all of these things were only said to control me and never because they were truth."

I lifted my hand and tried to draw my power forward only for it to crackle out. "One minute, I have the depth of power to turn this fucking realm to dust and the next, I couldn't tell you the memory of a five-year-old mortal if you godsdamn paid me. I cannot save her if I'm weakened. I can't save anyone. I can't protect anyone. Eventually, every lesser god will cease to fear me. And if they have no fear at all, they have every reason to start a war amongst us. Right now, Ezra and I stand on equal footing as rulers of gods. What happens when Alastor attacks when my power is weakened? I'm no longer the Supreme Sovereign. I'm just a fucking failure. To you, to her, to everyone. For all of existence. I hate being here in a place where I have no control."

"And you think, after all these years, all these lives, you're going to find a loophole to take her back to Etherium." She narrowed her eyes. "Do you believe she'll willingly go?"

"You asked me what my end goal was and I answered. It's her.

In whatever capacity I can have her. As long as she doesn't die by a god's hands again, her fragile soul will reincarnate. Eventually, I will get her back into Etherium. That's my end goal. That's all I want."

"Sometimes what we want isn't what's best for us, my boy. And moreso, it could be impossible. Perhaps you can't have both things. You can have the girl, but the gods will fall. Or we can keep our power, but your Ever will be lost to you."

"I know that's what Ezra claims. He's lying." I looked out the window, remembering that first time we'd spoken of the Huntress. "He told me there was a path. One path where she could live and the balance wouldn't break. Of all the possibilities and choices to be made, there *is* a path to peace. He said those fucking words to my face and thought, of all people, *I* would forget when we learned she was my Ever. He's the enemy here, Min. And if you can't believe that then you're sitting on the wrong side of this battle."

"So, you agree the war has already begun?"

"This war began thousands of years ago. The first time he stood behind Alastor's daughter and shoved that blade into her heart. He started it. I will end it, and then I'll pick up the pieces. That's how this was always going to go."

Minerva took my hand. "I am sitting on the right side of this battle as long as you don't go into the Forgotten. You know as well as I do, the Fates have warned against you going into the Forgotten just as much as Ezra. You must not. You've always been a fool for her, but the moment you turn reckless, I will no longer stand beside you."

The threat in those words wasn't lost on me and she knew it. I didn't respond, choosing to dip my chin and look away instead. There were no wars won without Reason on your side and that was the truth of it. A war without Reason wasn't a war at all. It was ruin, blind and unforgiving, leaving nothing but ash in its wake. And though I didn't want to admit it, she was right: the moment I turned reckless, I would already have lost.

"You never told me where we were going," I said, sometime

later, if for no other reason than to break that uncomfortable silence brewing between us.

"Archer's lurking outside the Vale. He hasn't left. Hasn't eaten. Hasn't slept. For days."

"Why do you say that as if it's our biggest concern?"

"Don't make me hit you with my cane. Use your brain for two seconds and consider what that might mean. Why is he so unshakably devoted to the Huntress?"

I lifted a shoulder. "He has no one else. His whole family is gone. He relied on his sister and she died. He needs that sense of family because he's had it since before he was born. What is his purpose if not trying to rescue someone he cares about?"

"Tuck said when Thea took Quill back to the Syndicate house, she cried like a banshee. Everyone assumed she didn't want to leave her new friends, but she was holding on to Archer. Why? They barely know each other."

"Because she knew he would go looking for Paesha and doesn't want to be separated from her again. She's raised the child. Don't speak to me in circles or like you're trying to teach me a lesson. If you have something to say, then say it and let's be done with it."

Those withered old eyes turned away, staring out the window. "No. Your answers are logical."

The carriage wheels ground to a halt at the edge of Banshee's Run, where the streets grew too narrow for anything larger than a cart to pass. Without a word, we abandoned the anonymity of the vehicle for the shadows of Stirling's narrow streets. We found Archer exactly where Minerva said he'd be, lounging against the wall beside the Vale's hidden entrance like he owned the damn place. A coin danced across his knuckles as he watched people come and go, the guard turning away more people than he let pass.

"He's making quite the spectacle of himself," Tuck muttered.

Archer's eyes found us before we reached him. He didn't move from his spot, just kept that coin rolling between his fingers. "Come to drag me to the castle?"

"Depends," Tuck said. "You done brooding yet?"

"I'm not brooding. I'm waiting."

Minerva cleared her throat. "And what exactly do you think will change if you stand here long enough? That guard isn't going to suddenly recognize you as anything but another thug trying to get in."

"If you're here about him, save your breath."

"He's dying," Minerva said.

"People do that."

Tuck leaned against the wall beside him. "Listen, you stubborn ass. You're not the only one who's lost family. But you've got a chance here that most of us would kill for."

"Why not use your magic on me then?" he asked, shooting me a look. "You've done it before. Fill me up with years of loving memories with a sister, mother and father that would have me crawling to his bedside."

"Don't beg for that," I warned.

"Because you would do it?"

"No, Archer. I'm not going to do that. You're going to go see what he has to say, and that's the end of this."

A group of rough-looking men shuffled past, forcing us to lower our voices. Archer pushed off the wall, moving closer so we wouldn't be overheard. "I'm exactly where I need to be. The second that guard changes shift, I'm getting in there. I've worked it all out."

"And then what?" Tuck asked. "You'll face down Alastor alone? Challenge a god with what? A sword and spite?"

"Better than sitting in a parlor twiddling my thumbs."

"Both of you, enough," Minerva snapped. "This petty bickering solves nothing. There are things you need to know, conversations that need to be had, but they cannot happen here." Her eyes fixed on Archer. "Some debts must be paid before they become too heavy to bear."

"A crown is a heavy debt to bear if you don't want it. And who are you *really*? Another god, sure. But your real title? Let me guess. Goddess of Persuasion and Murder?"

"I've told you who I am. But would it help if I said yes?" she countered.

The coin stilled in Archer's hand. For a moment, doubt flickered across his face. Then his jaw set. "I can't leave. Not now. Not when I'm so close to finding a way in."

"You mean getting yourself killed," Tuck corrected.

"You're so worried about me. What about everyone else? Who's watching out for—" He stopped himself, but not before I caught the worry in his voice. "How's Quill? Is she okay? I knew I shouldn't have left her."

Something in his tone made me pause. This wasn't just courtesy or deflection, there was real fear there. But he hardly knew the girl. "She's safe. Back at the Syndicate house."

"With Aeris watching over her," he said, his voice tight.

"We hear Aeris has been... attentive," Minerva said carefully.

A commotion at the Vale's entrance drew our attention.

The guard was arguing with someone, a woman wrapped in a dark cloak. As she turned, the hood fell back, revealing familiar copper locks.

"Thea?" Archer straightened. "What the hell is she doing here?"

Before any of us could move, a group of armed men emerged from the shadows surrounding her. One grabbed her arm, and she lashed out, but there were too many. They dragged her toward the entrance, the guard stepping aside to let them pass.

"Wait," Minerva hissed as Archer reached for his sword. "Something isn't right."

The last thing we saw before they disappeared into the Vale was Thea's face, and the smile that shouldn't have been there.

"Well fuck," Tuck said quietly. "Looks like Alastor's not the only one setting traps."

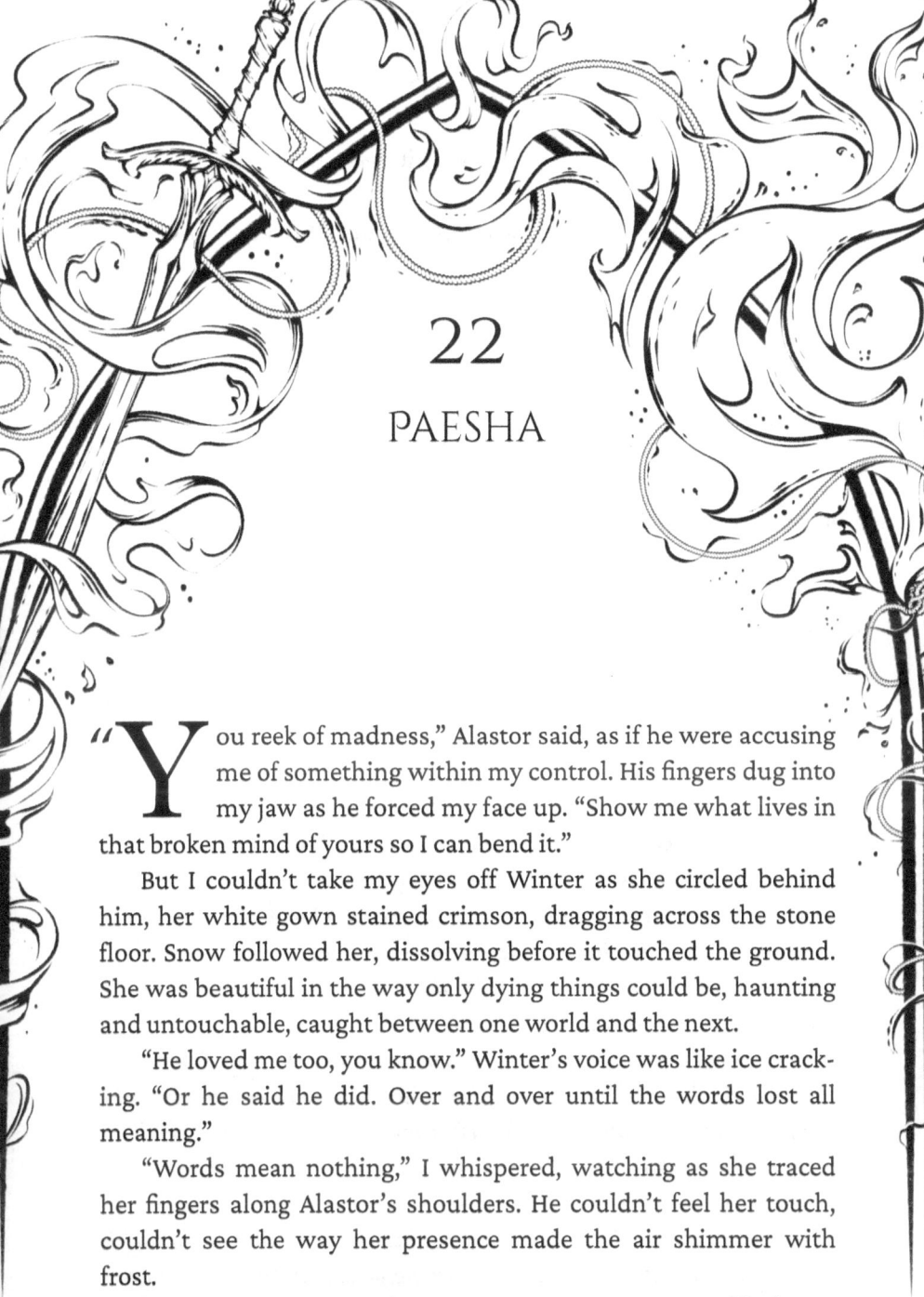

22

PAESHA

"You reek of madness," Alastor said, as if he were accusing me of something within my control. His fingers dug into my jaw as he forced my face up. "Show me what lives in that broken mind of yours so I can bend it."

But I couldn't take my eyes off Winter as she circled behind him, her white gown stained crimson, dragging across the stone floor. Snow followed her, dissolving before it touched the ground. She was beautiful in the way only dying things could be, haunting and untouchable, caught between one world and the next.

"He loved me too, you know." Winter's voice was like ice cracking. "Or he said he did. Over and over until the words lost all meaning."

"Words mean nothing," I whispered, watching as she traced her fingers along Alastor's shoulders. He couldn't feel her touch, couldn't see the way her presence made the air shimmer with frost.

"Oh? And what words have meaning to you, Huntress?" Alastor asked, misunderstanding. His Remnants coiled tighter around my wrists, burning against the binding marks.

Winter laughed. "Tell him how it feels to be bound. To be caged. To be *his*."

"I'm not his," I snarled, straining against the ropes. "I'll never be his."

Alastor's eyes narrowed. "Careful, Huntress. My patience wears thin."

"I think it's time," Winter whispered as Alastor's Remnants surged forward. They struck like vipers, sinking icy fangs into my flesh. The world dissolved into shadows and snow.

The night air bit my exposed skin as I ran through the garden, moonlight turning the frost covered roses to silver and diamond. My red dress whispered against the dormant plants, catching on thorns that drew blood like tiny kisses.

"Winter!" His voice carried on the wind, playful and warm despite the cold. "You can't hide from me forever."

I pressed my back against a marble statue as my heart thundered in my chest with equal parts excitement and fear. This was dangerous. We both knew it. A common soldier and a noblewoman, a love forbidden by birth and station. But I couldn't forget the day he'd found me on that lonely road, my horse gone lame, the way he'd walked beside me for miles just to see me home safely. There were men that would've taken advantage and then there were men like him. Those with honor. Care. Respect.

"Found you." His breath was warm against my neck as strong arms wrapped around my waist from behind. Even in full gear, he moved like a shadow, silent and graceful.

"Thorne," I breathed, melting into his embrace. "We shouldn't..."

"Shouldn't what?" He turned me to face him, and even in the darkness, his hazel eyes burned. "Shouldn't love? Shouldn't live? Shouldn't take what fate offers?"

"My father—"

"Doesn't matter." He caught my face between his callused palms, his touch gentle despite the strength I knew he possessed. "Nothing matters but this. But us."

When he kissed me, I tasted freedom on his lips. Tasted the promise of a life where titles and stations meant nothing compared to the way his heart beat in time with mine. And gods, I wanted him. I wanted it to be so fucking easy with him. But I knew it couldn't be.

The memory shattered like ice, leaving me gasping in my chair. Winter stood before me now, her dead eyes boring into mine. "He made the same promises to me that he made to you. The same pretty lies."

"Stop," I pleaded, though I wasn't sure if I was begging her or the Remnants or my own fractured mind.

"You're fighting it," Alastor said, his voice distant and distorted. "Let the power take you. Let it show me what I need to see. I need to understand them if I'm to do anything with them. This is power you shouldn't have."

Winter's bloody fingers traced the air near my cheek. "Yes, let us show you how this story ends. How all our stories end."

The shadows struck again, and I screamed as they dragged me under.

Snow fell thick and fast, obscuring the world beyond our stolen moments in the abandoned hunting lodge. The fire cast dancing shadows across bare skin as he traced patterns on my back with fingers roughened by years of wielding a sword.

The vision paused. Frozen in time. My heart was consumed by the way she loved him. The depth was more than Winter's memory. There was a tiny sliver of my own pain here too. Even when I fought to pull away, I still stared into his hazel eyes and remembered when I wanted only him. When I'd considered never leaving him.

Winter's voice curled around my—her ear. *Do you wish to see it, Huntress? Do you wish to remember what he feels like?*

I wanted to say no. To back away slowly and find a way to never return. But I was weak with curiosity, and I needed to feel something, anything but the numbness of resignation.

Use your words, Huntress, a new voice said. Though feminine, this one was smokier, sultry even.

I couldn't turn to see who'd spoken, locked in Winter's body. My mouth didn't even move as I said into my mind, *I wish to stay.*

The feminine chuckle that answered was a sound I would never forget as the memory continued.

Thorne's fingers slid around to my throat, over my breasts and down my abdomen, inching lower, leaving trails of fire across my skin despite the winter chill. His touch was painstakingly slow, as if he were memorizing every curve of my body. The roughness of his hands only heightened the sensation, a delicious contrast to the smoothness of my own.

My breath quickened as his fingers dipped lower, teasing the sensitive skin of my inner thighs. I arched into his touch, a soft moan escaping my lips as he found the spot he'd been aiming for.

The memory was hers, but the way I wanted him was not. For pleasure. For an escape. I wanted to use him. Use him and break him. I could feel my own heart beating outside of Winter's. I could feel those fingers between *my* legs. I could feel the press of his lips to my shoulder. And I was fucking weak. I didn't need him, but fuck if I didn't want him.

Say you want more, that strange smoky voice said into my mind. *Tell us you want to feel what it means to be loved by him.*

I didn't. It wasn't his love I was interested in. Maybe his dick, but I wasn't even in my own body. My own mind. This was a fucked up version of psychosis and there was no part of me that should have wanted a godsdamn thing from Reverius Hawthorne Noctus, god of complete bullshit. Despite the tiny bit of whore in me begging to say yes, I didn't. *I don't want this.*

Pity, the voice sang as the vision skipped ahead. *It's one of our favorites.*

"Tell me again," I whispered, pressing closer to the heat of Thorne's body, satiated, sore, and more in love than I'd been before.

"Tell you what, my love?"

"That this is real. That we'll find a way."

He propped himself up on an elbow, his expression serious in the firelight. "We'll run. Far from here, where no one knows our names or cares about bloodlines and birthrights. Where I can love you in the sunlight instead of shadows."

"Promise?"

"I swear on everything I am. Everything I'll ever be."

I believed him. Gods help me, I believed every word from a man I thought was nothing more than a common soldier with uncommon honor.

The vision wavered, reality bleeding through like water seeping under a door. I could feel the chair beneath me, the ropes binding my wrists, Alastor's presence heavy in the air. But Winter's memory pulled me back under, determined to show me the end.

The blade burned cold in my gut, colder than the snow beneath my knees. Thorne held me as I fell, but everything had changed. Gone was my gentle soldier. In his place stood something ancient and terrible, power radiating from him in waves that made the air tremble.

"Why?" I gasped, blood staining the white dress crimson. The dress I'd worn to run away with him, to start our new life.

"Because some stories are written in stone," he said softly, his hazel eyes now burning with an inhuman light. "Some fates cannot be changed."

"You promised..." The words tasted like copper and betrayal. "You were only a soldier..."

"It wasn't me."

He pressed his hand harder against my side, trying to stanch the flow of blood, but it poured through his fingers. His face twisted with grief, with terror, and his voice—so low, so broken— was barely more than a whisper. "Please," he begged, his lips brushing against my forehead as his tears fell, warm and wet against my skin. "Please don't leave me. Not like this."

His words were thick with despair, and my heart twisted painfully in my chest. I wanted to stay. I wanted to promise him I wouldn't leave, to reach up and wipe the tears from his beautiful face, to tell him every-thing would be okay, but I couldn't move. My body was a weight I could no longer control. The cold had claimed me. All I could do was look up at him as my vision blurred and his face grew dim.

"Please, please..." Thorne's voice broke, shattering like fragile glass. His fingers trembled as he held me, as if the sheer force of his will could keep my soul tethered here, keep me alive a little longer. "Don't you fucking die. That's not how this was supposed to go. We need more time."

His forehead pressed against mine. Shaking like the world was crumbling around him. He kissed my hair, my cheeks, my forehead. Each touch was frantic. His tears fell faster now, splashing hot onto my skin. I was so cold, I barely felt them anymore.

"I'll fix this," he sobbed. "I'll fix you. Just... stay with me. Please, just stay."

Only then did I understand I'd never known him at all. As the cold took everything, as my heart stuttered and stopped, as the snow covered us in a blanket of pristine white, my last thought was of that day on the road. How easily I'd believed a god could be something as simple as a soldier with kind eyes.

He held me, and he watched me die, and I finally understood he'd never been mine to love at all.

I came back to myself with Winter's dying sob still echoing in my head. She stood beside Alastor now, her bloody dress dripping onto the stone floor.

"Do you understand now?" she asked. "Do you see what love means to a god?"

Drip. Drip.

"Drip. No. Don't say that aloud. She's not really here."

"How fascinating," Alastor mused, studying me. "Tell me, what did you see when the Remnants took you that time? Mine were unable to see beyond yours."

"I see the truth."

She sees truth, Winter repeated, though he couldn't hear her. *She sees what happens when anyone tries to love gods.*

"I see you," I told her, ignoring Alastor completely. "I see all of us. All the lives he's taken. All the loves he's betrayed."

"The voices grow stronger," Alastor noted. "Good. Let them in. Let them show us what you truly are."

Winter's laughter filled the room, high and broken. *We are all the same story, told over and over until the words lose meaning. All pawns in his endless game. Killed by one brother or another's hand as they play with lives. Nothing but a game.*

I nodded, head hanging to the side. Maybe. Probably. "Nothing but a game."

The Remnants stirred beneath my skin, responding to her words. A thousand voices in my head. A thousand scorned.

"You want to see what I truly am?" I asked, my voice barely recognizable to my own ears as I grinned. "You want to know what happens when you break something enough times it stops trying to be whole?"

Winter smiled, her teeth stained red. *Show him.*

The Remnants exploded outward with a force that shattered the chair and snapped the ropes. They filled the room like a living storm, feeding off centuries of pain and rage and betrayal. Each shadow held a memory, each whisper carried a death. They were mine now.

"Nothing but a game," I whispered.

Alastor stumbled back, his Remnants rising to meet mine. But they were nothing compared to the power of a thousand broken hearts, a thousand betrayed loves, a thousand deaths.

"Remarkable," he breathed, watching as my shadows consumed his. "You're not just channeling power, you're channeling every life he's taken. Every life he's broken."

Winter circled me as I rose from the shattered chair, her bloody footprints marking each step. *Make him understand what it means to cage a monster.*

The walls cracked as my power pressed against them. The air froze and shattered at the will of the Remnants. My mind splintered further, breaking apart under the weight of so many lives, so many deaths, so many betrayals. "Nothing but a game." But it didn't matter anymore. Nothing mattered but the rage and the pain and the desperate need to make someone, anyone, understand what it felt like to be unmade over and over and over again.

"Nothing but a game. Nothing left but shadows and screams."

Winter's laugh mingled with mine as darkness consumed everything.

Alastor shifted forward, rolling his sleeves in a slow and deliberate move as he stepped among the shadows on the floor, no longer caring which were mine and which were his. "Believe me, Huntress, I learned that lesson long ago from the same man who taught you." His voice was quiet, but it cut through the chaos like a blade. "Love doesn't redeem monsters. It reveals them. It carves us open, laying our rot bare, and dares the world to look away." His eyes, smoldering with a flicker of something broken, locked on to mine. "But the difference between us is I stopped flinching a long time ago."

"The snow melts but never touches the ground," I whispered, watching Winter trail her bloody fingers across the walls. "He promised her forever too. Promises taste like copper when they break."

"Sit."

My body obeyed instantly, a chair materializing beneath me as my knees buckled.

Break them all.

Break the world.

Break yourself.

"What do you see when they come?" he asked, circling me like a predator. "What voices whisper to you?"

"Stars fall through forever. Dancing in gardens that died in winter. His eyes were hazel until they weren't. Until they burned with lies that tasted like freedom."

Winter laughed.

"Tell me how it feels when they surface," Alastor commanded.

"Like drowning in memories that aren't mine, but are. Like breathing shadows that taste like betrayal. Like dancing with death over and over and over... Do you waltz?"

He stopped suddenly, head tilting as if listening to something I couldn't hear. A slow smile spread across his face, the kind that made Winter hiss and my Remnants ripple over my arms.

"Well," he said, straightening his tie. "This is an interesting development. Guards!"

Shadows materialized into the form of two massive figures, their edges rippling like smoke. I'd seen them before when they attacked Archer and I. Fancy. I'd gotten a sword that day. I missed my sword.

"I miss my sword."

"Take our Huntress to her room. She has a visitor I think she'll be very interested in seeing." He turned to me, that cruel smile widening. "Stay there until I return. We're not finished yet."

"Can I eat?"

"For fuck's sake," he said with a huff. "Someone feed the mortal."

My feet carried me toward the door before I could think, before I could fight. Winter followed, her bloody footprints marking our path through halls that twisted like snakes.

He's playing games.

Always games.

Break the games.

Break it all.

The shadow guard things deposited me in my pretty, little gilded prison, taking up posts outside the door. I paced, trying to sort reality from memory, truth from lies, my thoughts from Winter's whispers.

"Can I sword? No. Eat."

I turned to study myself in the mirror, searching for the woman I knew was being swallowed by madness. But rather than seeing my own face, the entire reflection was filled with a thousand faces of women with the same eyes, but different expressions of pain. One of a thousand. I was only one.

When the door opened, my heart stopped.

Thea stood in the doorway, copper hair gleaming in the lamp-light. "Hello, P." She threw a handful of metal scraps from her pocket onto the floor. "You ready to bust out of this place?"

23
THORNE

The only question that seemed to matter as we watched the door shut behind Thea as she was dragged in by Alastor's favorite lackeys, was how in the world we were going to get her out of there. The burning mark on my neck was a reminder that I couldn't interfere.

I turned my back on everyone, swiping my glasses away. She was close, and she was mortal. It should be nothing to sort through Thea's memory and discover what she was doing here. But when I tried, when I dove into the web of magic I could typically weave in my own mind, there was nothing but an echo. My power was gone again. And though it'd been happening more and more frequently, I was never going to be fucking used to this cage.

"We need a plan," Tuck said, coming to stand beside me as another group of cloaked men passed, approaching the guard and gaining easy access to the Vale.

"You're the God of Knowledge. Fucking know things. What does the guard want that we can tempt him with?"

Tuck managed a huff. "Nothing. He's bound to Alastor's command alone. Probably doesn't even shit without permission."

"We all agree Aeris sent her in there, right? There's no way she'd have found the Vale without help," Archer said, moving farther away from the door. "She's got some pretty crazy magic skills though. I think if she wanted to, if she was motivated enough, she could do some real damage in there."

Minerva inched closer. "Let's hope she's not foolish enough to try."

"Well, isn't this cozy?" Alastor stepped out of the open doors, his usual pristine appearance betrayed by the slight dishevelment of his hair, the loosened knot of his tie, the way his tattoos barely moved along his arms. He was slipping. Whatever was happening with Paesha was affecting him too. "A desperate fucker, a god, a loathsome prince, and whatever Tuck's pretending to be these days, all huddled in the dark like common thieves."

I tried pushing against his presence with my power, testing boundaries. Nothing. Not even a flicker of response. The magic that had once flowed like a river now felt like sand slipping through my fingers.

Archer's shoulders tensed at the word 'prince.' He was a fool. Most of the time, I could count on him to be rational. But the way he looked at Alastor made me question where this little visit would end up. I'd protect him because that was what she would do. Even if it meant ending up in more trouble than he was worth. Paesha had that effect on broken things. She collected strays, made them family. And now, if not careful, Archer would die trying to save her, just as his sister had died trying to save him.

"The boy's looking a bit peaky," Alastor noted, studying Archer with false concern. "Still recovering from your little time stopping adventure? Dangerous thing, wielding power you don't understand. Ask the Huntress." His eyes flashed to me. "Oh, wait..."

"Fuck you," Archer spat, hand going to his sword.

I caught his wrist before he could do something monumentally stupid. "Don't give him more of a reason to end you."

"As if he needs it," Archer said, fighting against my hold.

Minerva's eyes met mine. She saw the threads I saw. Archer's devotion was commendable. But also laced with magic. It had to be. But how? Why?

"Take our new guests inside," Alastor said as a bevy of his men walked out of the Vale. "I'm sure we can find some way to entertain them."

Archer slid his sword free, his eyes narrowing as he stepped between Minnie and the guards. He had no idea that she wouldn't need him. Our power, the power of all gods, manifested from the adoration of mortals. We fed on the willingness to sacrifice and worship, giving us tiny pieces of their souls with their desperation, their thoughts, their actions. The more a god was beloved in a realm, the more they could draw from a well of power. But that only worked as long as Ezra and I held the balance. Minervas's power, though? Her Wrath came from the Fates, an endless source that would never falter.

Beside me, Tuck shifted, his hand drifting to the axe at his belt. The weapon was ancient, its handle worn smooth by centuries of use, the blade honed to a razor's edge. In the hands of the God of Knowledge, it was more than a mere tool. It was almost an extension of his will, a physical manifestation of the secrets and truths he wielded like weapons.

But before either of them could make a move, Minerva's cane tapped the ground, the sound echoing like a thunderclap in the narrow space. "Don't," she said quietly. "This is the path we need."

Tuck's eyes met mine, and I gave him an almost imperceptible nod. We'd faced worse odds. We'd survived worse games. But the air felt wrong, broken in a way that made my power curl beneath my skin like a wounded beast. What use was I with no power?

Alastor's guards surrounded us.

I studied their formation as they closed in. Twelve shadows given form. Not Remnants, but highly trained demigods that worked only for their master. Strong enough to subdue mortals, but against pure gods? This was theater, not threat. Which meant Alastor wanted us inside for a reason.

The guards led us through the Vale's twisting corridors, past empty merchant stalls and very few curious eyes. My mind raced ahead, analyzing every possibility, every angle. The general lack of people spoke volumes. He'd nearly cleared the place out, as if he'd created a stage for whatever game he was playing.

My power roiled beneath my skin. About fucking time, but it was useless. Caged by a bargain to not interfere. Still, every instinct screamed to fight. To tear through these shadows with teeth and claws and ancient magic. But the binding held fast.

Alastor led us deeper, his casual stride a godsdamn mockery. This was his stage, and we were all simply an audience to whatever he'd orchestrated to try to break me.

"Do not," Minerva whispered. She could feel the wrath vibrating beneath my skin. Could likely taste the tension in my cold stare at the back of Alastor's head as we followed him.

Stopping before a door, he paused. His expression hardened. "You may watch. But interfere, and our little arrangement becomes significantly less pleasant."

He wouldn't have brought me down here, wouldn't have willingly shown me what was beyond that fucking door if it wasn't meant to break me. I braced myself. But Tuck and Minnie did too, flanking me, holding their breaths as the door swung open.

My heart stopped.

Paesha.

Ever the beauty, ever the storm. The most ferocious of every version of her. The most beautiful. The strongest and also, perhaps, the weakest. She paced like a wounded animal, each movement fracturing my reality. Her movements were full of shadows that weren't shadows at all. They were Remnants. From what Tuck and I had gathered, broken pieces of her past lives trying to claw their way out through her mind.

My knees nearly gave out. Alastor's bargain mark blazed as I fought every instinct to go to her, to gather her against my chest and burn away whatever was tearing her apart. Blood welled beneath my fingernails as my fists clenched and something primal stirred within me. A god was never meant to see his soulmate, his Ever, suffer. And I'd seen it so many times, my half of our soul was broken. She was the reason.

"The snow never melts." She reached for phantoms none of us could see. "His promises taste like copper when they break."

Metal glinted in Alastor's fingers as he bent to retrieve something from the floor. His eyes fixed on Thea with predatory amusement. "Now, what's this? Surely you weren't planning an escape attempt?"

The color drained from Thea's face.

But Paesha's descent consumed me wholly.

"Dancing in gardens that died in winter. Stars falling through forever. Nothing but a game. Always a game."

My chest felt hollow. Carved out. The binding marks might stop me from interfering, but they couldn't stop my soul from reaching for hers, trying desperately to anchor her to reality. To this moment. To me.

But there was nothing to grab onto. She was fragments and whispers and ancient deaths playing out behind eyes that saw everything and nothing at all.

"He held me while the snow turned red. While the lies bled out."

"Paesha?" I spoke so quietly, I wasn't sure a single person in the room heard the word fall from my lips. But she did. She paused. Whipping around to face me, nothing but absolute hatred on her beautiful face.

My heart splintered.

I knew those words. Knew that death. That betrayal. That moment when Ezra's blade had pushed home in a winter garden eight hundred years ago. Just one of the countless times he'd killed her, countless lives he'd stolen because I could never save her.

"Fingers?" Archer stepped forward, reaching for her.

My heart beat wildly.

Paesha's head snapped toward Archer, her unfocused eyes sharpening for a moment. "Toes," she said, her voice carrying an eerie singsong quality. "I can dance on toes, but the dragon huffed and puffed and blew the house down. Down, down, down."

Archer stepped closer, his hand outstretched. "Paesha, it's me. It's Archer. I'm here."

218

A flicker of recognition passed over her face, like a cloud parting to reveal a sliver of sunlight. Her lips curved into a small, fragile smile. "Archer." His name was a sigh on her lips. "You came. You always will, won't you? Until I'm free?"

Jealousy, hot and bitter, surged through me as I watched their exchange. The way she looked at him, the familiarity and trust in her gaze, it cut me to the bone. In all her lifetimes, all our stolen moments, had she ever looked at me like that? With such pure, uncomplicated affection? I couldn't remember. I could never remember anything but the bliss, followed by the heartache. I deserved this. I needed to see how much easier things could be for her without me.

I would love her in madness. I would stand beside her, still. But maybe she needed him. Not me. Life, not death. Light, not dark. Still, I wanted to rip Archer away from her, to snarl that she was mine, that he had no right to the tenderness she showed him so freely. But I held myself back, muscles coiled tight as a spring. This wasn't about me. It was about her. About bringing her back from the brink of madness.

And then maybe it was about letting go.

Alastor's hand fell on my shoulder like a brand. "Come. Let's step outside and discuss... productive solutions."

I followed him into the hall because I had no choice. Because watching her shatter was worse than any torture he could devise. Because the bargain mark burned with the truth of my help-lessness.

His facade dropped the moment the door closed. "She's too far gone. The voices are consuming her. Soon there will be nothing left but shadows and broken memories."

"If you think threatening her life will—"

"This isn't a threat, Keeper. This is a fact." He stepped closer, voice dropping. "Look at her. Really look. The power she stole was never meant for mortal minds. It's eating her alive. She's not meant to be caged. Or controlled for that matter. Though many will try."

"Many who sit at your fucking table."

He leaned against the wall, crossing his arms over his chest. "Some, perhaps. But if they sit at my table, it's my choice to feed them or not." He smiled. A brutish, cocky smile that made me want to punch his fucking teeth into his godsdamn throat. "I can free her. I can and will withdraw the marks that make her mine, Keeper, though I've certainly been advised not to. Your brother can be quite persuasive. But I'm a man of my word and all it will cost you is one small favor."

I already knew. Already felt the weight of his words settling around my throat like a noose.

"Irri."

"Free her from the Forgotten, and I'll release your precious Huntress. Let her keep her power, keep her life. All you have to do is walk into that void and bring my Ever back to me. Un-fucking harmed."

The Forgotten.

The one place I couldn't go.

The one line I couldn't cross.

But if I didn't...

Paesha's broken laughter filtered through the door, mingling with words in languages dead for centuries. Each sound cracked another piece of my resolve, shattering the walls I'd built over millennia.

I surveyed the battlefield one last time. Alastor's desperation. Archer's devotion. Minerva's warnings. Tuck's unwavering loyalty. Thea's determination to save her friend, even if it meant trusting ancient enemies. Paesha's fractured mind housing so many lives, so many deaths, so many versions of me betraying her over and over.

There was only one path left. One desperate gamble that might save her without damning everyone else. But it meant facing those I'd spent millennia avoiding. Those who'd warned me about this very moment.

I'd have to go to the Fates.

And they'd refused to converse with the gods the day Minerva stole some of their Wrath.

"No," I said, watching his face harden at my refusal. "I need time."

"Time?" Alastor's laugh was hollow. "You've had centuries. How much more time do you need to watch her suffer?"

A crash from inside the room cut off my response. We burst through the door to find Thea with her hands raised, the scattered metal pieces she'd dropped earlier now twisted into bars, forming a makeshift cage around Alastor's guards.

She stalked toward one of the trapped guards, her voice ice. "I told you not to put your fucking hands on her."

"Thea," Tuck said, hands raised as he walked toward her. "This is not a good—"

She must have caught Alastor moving out of the corner of her eye. One moment she was facing Tuck and the next, she'd used her power again, trapping Alastor in line with his guards. He roared with fury, and the woman didn't flinch.

Paesha stood in the center of the chaos, her unfocused gaze darting between shadows only she could see, while Thea turned to face us. "How are we getting out of here?"

"We run. Now," Minnie and Tuck said in unison.

But I knew better. Archer's eyes met mine, and we remained rooted while the others fled. Paesha wasn't stable enough for this.

Metal groaned as Alastor's Remnants bent the bars of his cage. He stepped out with deadly grace, adjusting his sleeves as if this were nothing more than a minor inconvenience. "Lie down," he commanded Paesha. "Stop breathing."

Her body crumpled immediately. The sight of her on the floor, lips turning blue as she fought against his command, made the cage around my free will rattle with fury. I whipped around, facing his entire guard and dug into my own power. Maybe I couldn't interfere with his manipulation over Paesha, but I sure as fuck could scramble the minds of his guards. They fell with far less grace than she had.

"That was a bit irrational," Alastor said, walking a careful circle around Paesha.

I had to grab Archer as he lunged forward, knowing Alastor

would kill him without hesitation and if I couldn't fucking save her, at least I could save her friend. Or so I thought, but there was something different about Archer today. Something stronger. He broke free of my grip with impossible force, crossing the space between them in seconds. His fist connected with Alastor's jaw before the Remnants could react, the crack of impact echoing through the room.

Alastor's shadows surged forward, pinning Archer against the wall as blood trickled from the god's split lip. He wiped it away with his thumb, studying the red stain with mild curiosity before releasing Paesha from his command. "Breathe, Huntress."

She gasped, precious air filling her lungs as color returned to her face. But Alastor's eyes were locked on mine, his meaning clear as crystal.

"Once again, Keeper, her life depends entirely on your next decision. Now take your dog and get the fuck out of my temple, or say yes to her freedom."

Paesha froze. Her gasping breaths no longer filled my ears. She turned those stunning eyes on me and the tears trickling down her face nearly killed me.

"My freedom?" she whispered.

The gods would fall. The power would fail. The realms would cease to exist. I couldn't go to the Forgotten. I couldn't. Not even for her.

"I'm sorry," I said, kneeling to be closer to her. "It's the one thing I cannot give you."

"He can. But he chooses not to," Alastor said before he brought a hand to his mouth, hiding his smile. "Oops. Did I say that out loud?"

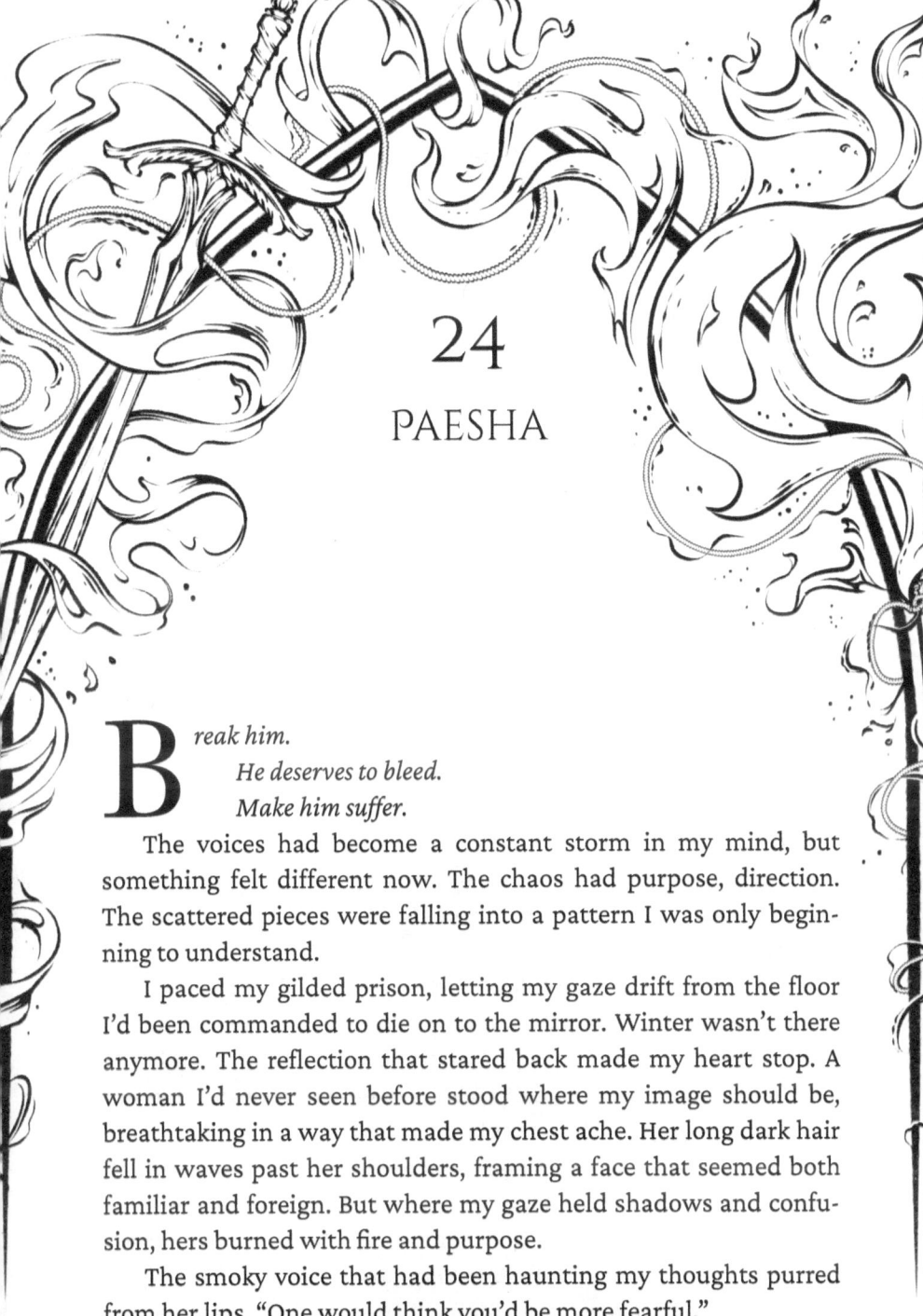

24

PAESHA

Break him.
He deserves to bleed.
Make him suffer.

The voices had become a constant storm in my mind, but something felt different now. The chaos had purpose, direction. The scattered pieces were falling into a pattern I was only beginning to understand.

I paced my gilded prison, letting my gaze drift from the floor I'd been commanded to die on to the mirror. Winter wasn't there anymore. The reflection that stared back made my heart stop. A woman I'd never seen before stood where my image should be, breathtaking in a way that made my chest ache. Her long dark hair fell in waves past her shoulders, framing a face that seemed both familiar and foreign. But where my gaze held shadows and confusion, hers burned with fire and purpose.

The smoky voice that had been haunting my thoughts purred from her lips, "One would think you'd be more fearful."

"I've had voices screaming in my head for days, lady. Fear's the least of my problems," I yelled over the whispers, covering my ears as if that would save me from it all.

But the woman cleared her throat and with that simple gesture, the other voices fell silent, cowering before her presence. Even the Remnants stilled their constant swirling.

"Who are you?"

Her reflection rippled like disturbed water as she smiled. "I'm Sylvie. The first of us. The original soul that your beloved Keeper has been chasing through time." Her fingers traced patterns on her side of the glass. "Did you enjoy the show out there? How he stood by while my father commanded you to stop breathing?"

"Your father..." The pieces clicked into place. "Alastor."

She nodded. "I was a demigod cast from Etherium when my father was banished. All because I dared to love. Sound familiar?"

I thought of Thorne's refusal to help only hours ago. It was right there. Alastor had given him my freedom on a fucking platter and he'd refused.

"He speaks of love while watching you suffocate. He preaches devotion while letting you rot in madness."

"The voices..."

"Are yours to command." She waved her hand. "If only you'd take the time to listen, rather than fight back. Can't you see what you are?"

I stepped closer to the mirror, drawn by the power in her words. "What am I?"

"You're not some helpless mortal to be played with and discarded. You're not a prize to be won or a soul to be caged. You may not have the title of a god, but you have the power of one. You're vengeance incarnate. You're every death he's caused, every lie he's told, every heart he's broken given form."

The Remnants stirred, responding to her words. To the truth in them.

"All my father wants is to see him fall," she continued. "Help him achieve that, and your freedom is guaranteed."

My freedom. My escape. My future. I studied my reflection beside hers, seeing for the first time how perfectly we mirrored each other. Two sides of the same splintered coin. "What do you need me to do?"

"When the moment comes, and it will come soon, you'll know exactly what to do." She reached through the glass, her fingers brushing my cheek in a touch that felt like fire. "You'll know. And you will follow through. Are you ready?"

I closed my eyes, letting her words sink in. All this time, I'd thought I was fighting against the darkness inside me. But maybe I'd been fighting the wrong thing. The faces of everyone I loved flashed through my mind. Quill's infectious laughter, Thea's unwavering loyalty, Archer's protective determination. Elowen's motherly nature. I had everything to lose. A family. A home. My humanity. And that was exactly why I had to do what she asked. To protect them. To be free of the gods' games once and for all.

The monster living in my mind wasn't a monster at all. She was just a woman who'd been betrayed. "Yes," I whispered, opening my eyes to meet her gaze. "I'm ready."

Because, to destroy the real monsters, I had to learn to accept my own.

25

THORNE

"So where do we go from here?" Archer asked, pacing the length of my office as Tuck poured himself another drink and Minerva and Thea sat together, whispering amongst themselves.

"We don't rush into any more foolish ideas," I said, eyes flickering to Thea.

She threw back a glare. "Don't sit there and talk about me like I'm not in the room. I had a solid plan. How was I supposed to know Paesha would fall so far, so fast? We could have been out of there before you even showed up, had she been lucid enough to agree to come."

"How exactly?" Tuck asked, letting that natural curiosity show beyond the burly facade.

"I'm not sure I should keep showing my hands to gods," she answered. "After all, Aeris was the reason I went down there. Though I'm sure she had no idea what I'd be walking into either."

Minerva and I had a full conversation without speaking a word. I could have jumped into her mind standing this close, but the golden, glowing eyes would have given us away. And it was unnecessary. Our thoughts were aligned. Aeris was a wild card. An unknown that danced the edge of every line. Every battle. Every major disruption across the realms. She was far from innocent, but she'd been a mystery for so long, even my memories skimmed over her most significant maneuvers.

Aeris was currently the least of my problems. If I didn't figure this out quickly enough, there would be no god left standing beside me. Not even Tuck. And I couldn't blame him for protecting himself when I was only trying to protect her.

Some people loved blindly. Loyally. And some were far too smart for that kind of devotion. Tuck was anything but a fool. I needed to ease him and Minerva into the idea of visiting the Fates. But there was really no time for that either. Everything on the mortal plane happened in the flash of a second, but there were wars fought, won, and lost in centuries in Etherium. A battle amongst gods was never about death and defeat. It was simply power. Always power. Who could rule the realms. And right now, the being with the most power, gods and Fates aside, was my Ever.

Tuck reached for another glass from the sideboard as he continued his conversation with Thea. "Alastor is the God of Lost Things. That doesn't just mean trinkets and baubles. No one intends to lose their mind, but play with Alastor long enough and the walls start melting. If Aeris didn't warn you before she sent you into the lion's den, that says far more about her motives than your naivety."

She lifted a petite shoulder, tilting her head to the side. "In her defense, after she slipped up about where he was keeping her, she tried to keep me from going, but when I insisted, she caved and told me all she could, then promised to stay at the house with Elowen, Quill and Boo until we returned."

I expected Tuck to hand me the fresh glass of whiskey he'd poured. Instead, he crossed the room and gave it to the red-haired woman. She shook her head. "I haven't eaten a thing today. If I drink that, I'll be on the floor in an hour."

Minnie patted Thea's arm, swiping the drink. "Let's not give him any ideas, dear."

Archer stopped his pacing and started opening the cabinet

doors along the walls. "Is there food here? I could eat. I can't remember the last time I did, actually," he said, rubbing his head. "You're the Keeper of Memories. Can you remember?"

He wasn't fucking sly. He was fishing for knowledge. He'd been in those cupboards plenty of times to know better. We'd given everything to the orphans months ago. I'd even had Tuck smuggle things in from the northern countries when supplies were low and Farris was at his worst. No one knew, of course. Everything that came was disguised as stolen goods. Archer knew we'd done just enough to keep everyone fed.

"That's not how it works. I don't just *know* things from your past. If I choose to use my power, I could dive in. See something in there. But my status as Keeper of Realms, Arbiter of Beginnings and Endings has to do with far more than when you had your last fucking sandwich, Archie."

He swung the cabinet shut and finally came to sit before me. "Since we're sharing now and not, you know, hiding all the realm's secrets, where does power even come from? In general, all power. Because I've been thinking, if it's off balance, that has to mean there's a source, right? Is it... leaning one way or something? Is it in a cup? A really big cup, I mean. Like a bucket. Can we maybe... wedge it until it evens back out?"

I sat back in my chair, preferring this conversation to the one I was going to have to have later. "I'm not going to bother questioning how your brain conceived that. If it were that simple, it would have been done."

"On a very basic level, you're not actually wrong," Tuck said, taking the seat beside Archer.

I sighed. "You have to understand what threw it off in the first place and how that works. When Ezra and I started to disagree, something we'd never done before, the balance began to sway. Basically, as the God of Beginnings and Endings, my power has to do with creation and completion. Ezra's is the middle stuff. The probability of bad shit happening sits with him and he makes moves to change the course of certain things. But he doesn't always get it right, and that's where we're at an impasse.

"There was a prophecy delivered by the Fates that said the Huntress will break the balance of power. He's seen more destruction than what we're experiencing now. But Ezra saw that future too. And he told me a long time ago there could be peace. Each time he's killed her, each time I've failed to protect her, each war between us has made it worse, instead. I chase, he kills. That's been our dance for centuries. Except the prophecy doesn't mean *she* broke the balance of power. Her soul was the cause, but Ezra and I are responsible, no matter what his fucking magic says."

"Okay. I get all that, but the power itself?" Archer pressed, brushing past my explanation. "Where does it actually come from?"

"The Noctus Gate," Tuck answered, earning a sharp look from me that he ignored. "It's a portal to basically our vessel of power. It's so vast it would destroy any being who tried to enter. And that's why Thorne doesn't want to answer your questions. You're reckless on a good day, Arch."

He nodded, swinging his feet up on my damn desk as if he owned the place. A bit of Paesha in that move, for sure. "So the power's in a bucket behind a door in god town and we need to go there and plug the hole in the bucket or whatever. I can work with that."

I glared. "You're not listening. The power isn't sitting in a bucket. It comes from its own realm. Its only access point is through the gate in Etherium. And the only key to the gate is sitting with the Fates. And there's no way in fuck you're getting to Etherium, so stop it now."

"Fates?" Thea asked. "As in fate is not just an idea, but a being?"

"Correct," Minnie said, taking a long pull from her drink. "But we don't talk about them and we don't tempt them. They are not part of this equation."

"Forget the Fates. Take me back to the balance thing. There has to be a solution there," Archer said, swinging the conversation right back to his reckless ideas.

"Again. No. The gate requires Ezra and I to function. That's *part*

229

of the equation. Fate creates the threads of possibility, my power creates every beginning, every potential path. Ezra sees which of those paths lead to devastation and unmakes them before they can manifest. Together, we regulate the flow of raw power through the careful balance of creation and destruction. But don't get any ideas, Archie. It's not anything we're physically controlling. We have no conscious decision over it nor sway. It's like trying to control what happens to the breath you exhale."

"The point, and the only thing that matters right now, beyond the Huntress's freedom, is the fact that she is also hunted. She has power she wasn't born with. Power most gods are desperate to get their hands on," Tuck answered, his voice grim. "But they don't understand—"

"If she dies by a god's hand now, there won't be another life," I finished. "Her soul is too fragile. She'll simply cease to exist. She's died too many times at Ezra's hands and her soul can't survive another."

Archer stopped pacing. "So what do we do?"

"The Fates are the only ones who can help now," I said quietly.

"The Fates haven't spoken to the gods since Ezra convinced everyone to bind them to their loom," Tuck added, lowering his chin to look at me through the top of his eyes. "They're dangerous. Even for you. And unpredictable."

"But necessary," I said.

Archer's jaw clenched. "Then I'm coming with you."

"No. You're staying here."

"Like hell I am."

"Someone needs to watch the Parlor," Tuck said smoothly. "Make sure our... interests are protected."

"I'm not a child who needs a babysitter and I'm not falling for that shit again."

"There's nothing to fall for. Much to all of our chagrin, you couldn't get into Etherium if you tried because you are mortal. Only gods may enter."

"And demigods," Tuck corrected.

"Not the fucking point, Tuck."

Archer opened his mouth to argue but Thea rose, moving to stand beside Archer. "After what happened with Alastor we need to be smart about this." She flexed her fingers as if reaching for the power she'd used to cage a god. "Having you here with us sounds like the safest thing for Quill."

He sank back. "You too?"

She circled him to lean on the desk between us, her back to me as she crossed her arms over her chest. "They've said you can't go. You won't go to see the king." He opened his mouth to speak and she threw up a hand to stop him. "I'm not telling you to. Live your life. Do whatever you want. But these are the facts. You can't follow them to Etherium. Come home with me. Help me pass the time with Quill until they figure out how to free Paesha and then we all get what we want."

"And what do you get out of this?" Tuck asked. "What do you want, Forger?"

Thea whipped her head toward Tuck. "What did you just call me?"

The corner of his mouth lifted. "You're a Forger, aren't you?"

She pulled a handful of tiny metal pellets from her pocket and dropped them from her left to right palm, letting them meld to beautifully crafted chains as they dropped. "Like my grandfather."

Archer swiped the chains from her, letting them dangle between his fingers. "Imagine creating without effort. Needing something specific and giving it to yourself in the next second."

"First of all, there's great effort in everything I do. You cannot create a design on a wish. Mechanically, I need to know the exact size and structure. Also, there's not a thing I can build with my magic that I can't also make with enough time in my forge. I won't deplete my power if I don't need to. That was the only lesson I learned from the Maestro, thank you very much."

"You were bound to him also?" I asked as Tuck pulled the chain away from Archer to study the design.

"I was bound to him longer than any of the other Syndicate members. Those are the people that formed a family outside of him. Maybe in spite of him. We helped people where we could.

But now, with the Maestro gone, most have gone their own ways."

"Let me ask you a question," Archer said, pulling a coin from his pocket to roll over the top of his knuckles. "Where are the people in Silbath? I've never seen another person out on the streets."

She lifted a shoulder, eyes slightly narrowing as she answered. "You have to know where to look."

"If I were king, would you tell me?" he asked casually, eyes locked on his coin as if he didn't have a care in the world.

The energy changed in the room, all three gods carefully keeping our eyes away as he casually threw out the question. He'd done it to bait us. Archer had always been smart, even if he was irrational and occasionally reckless. He wouldn't have been such a talented gambler if he was anything else. He could read a face and a room as well as anyone.

Thea matched his energy, letting her words drag out. "You wouldn't be *my* king, so I couldn't say. Ask me when you are and we'll talk."

"Requiem has no king at all," he countered. "So who's in charge?"

Minerva rose from her seat and moved toward the door. She clearly wanted Archer to sit with the idea of being king. "The gods," she answered tightly. "Until a mortal requests the role and devises a strong plan the other mortals will agree to, the golden streets belong to whichever god is holding the most power."

"That's me," I said, rising from my seat to follow her lead.

"Or Ezra, if there's true balance again," Tuck said.

"Or Alastor," Thea said casually. "Since he seems to be holding Paesha and so far, correct me if I'm wrong, the mortals' power isn't being affected like the gods."

"I'm sure you'd like to think so," Minerva bit back.

Thea shrugged. "Are we dismissed now? Is that what we're doing?"

"You were never held against your will," Tuck said. "You followed us here, remember?"

"Well, I assumed... I thought we'd regroup and go back in with a better plan."

I shook my head. "Never assume anything when it comes to gods, Forger. They will count on it and use it against you every time."

Red flashed across her cheeks. "Are you warning me against you right now?"

"Of course I am. There are few things I won't do to get what I want. Almost none at all."

"Butt stuff?" Archer asked. "Yeah, you're right, I wouldn't do that either."

I shoved him as he walked toward the door. "What the fuck is wrong with you?"

"Probably more things than we have time to list."

"Do us all a favor and try not to get any reckless ideas while I'm gone."

"Me?" He smirked. "I was only going to check on the kid. Make sure that Aeris hasn't corrupted her too much."

"Finally, sense prevails," Minerva said, swinging the door open.

I shared another look with her, this one lasting longer than the others. She gave an imperceptible nod before turning to face Tuck. "We're going to see the Fates."

The silence that followed was thick enough to choke on. Tuck's shoulders tensed, his jaw working as he processed what she'd said.

"We?" he finally managed.

"If they won't listen to desperation, perhaps they'll consider reason. And if not that, then maybe a little wrath."

"You can't be serious," Tuck said, but his voice had lost its edge. He knew better than to argue when Minerva had made up her mind. And thank fuck for that because I'd never forgive myself if they targeted him for this foolish decision.

"I am," she said, no bullshit to her tone.

Archer and Thea walked out first, letting us linger behind. Tuck's eyes remained fixed on us. "The Fates haven't been kind to us since the loom."

Minnie smirked. "Then it's fortunate that I've never required their kindness."

"Keep them safe," I followed, jutting a chin toward the mortals.

And keep him from doing anything stupid, I added silently, knowing my oldest friend would understand.

Tuck's slight nod was all the confirmation I needed. And the scowl at the end was the perfect send off.

"LAST CHANCE TO TURN BACK," I said, watching another crystal shatter and fall into the void beneath our feet. The sound of it breaking echoed through Etherium's twisted architecture, a subtle reminder that even immortal realms could die.

"If I meant to turn back, I wouldn't have come at all." Minerva moved carefully across the suspended walkway, past buildings that defied logic, towers that grew sideways, spiraling structures that folded in on themselves, all of it carved from stone that absorbed light rather than reflected it.

Home. Or what passed for it these days. The perpetual twilight that once gave Etherium its beauty now felt oppressive, like the realm was being slowly crushed under the weight of failing power. Another crystal shattered somewhere in the distance.

We passed the Noctus Gate, its massive archway of black and gold, a monument to better days. The runes carved into its surface barely glowed now, where they once blazed with raw energy. Paths that had existed for millennia were beginning to unravel at their edges, reality fraying like worn cloth.

"Makes me sick to see the power fade so obviously," Minerva said quietly, her eyes on the withering shadow gardens where constellation patterns once bloomed. Now they struggled to form even basic shapes before dissolving into true darkness. "But I'm glad you're here to see it."

"It's been too long," I said quietly. There were no excuses to be made for my absence.

We turned down a darker path, one most immortals never saw.

The entrance to the Fates' domain was nothing like the Noctus Gate, but rather a tear in reality, ragged edges rippling like cloth in a wind that didn't exist here. My reluctance to enter had nothing to do with fear. Fear was for a weaker soul. This felt like losing control.

"Do you know what you'll ask?" Minerva whispered, eyes homed in on the rip.

"I'll ask them how to free her from the madness."

"And if they don't answer?" she asked, rising to her full height.

"Then I'll ask about the Forgotten."

"Reverius—"

"I'm sitting with about a hundred problems on my hands, Minnie. I've got to figure out Alastor, the power, my Ever, the Fera, my brother... The list goes on and on. If they'll guarantee my return from there, that alleviates your trepidation and solves another of my problems."

She shook her head, wisps of silver hair that'd loosened from her bun crossing her face. "You assume they won't lie and that's reckless."

"I'll hear whatever they have to say and weigh my options after. I'm not completely fucking helpless. I've been around longer than you, in case you've forgotten."

She smirked. "How could I? You always remind me five minutes before you do something foolish."

I took a step back, sliding my glasses down my nose. "Do you think the Fates *want* an imbalance of power?"

"They can't see every path the way your brother does and you'll not convince me otherwise, no matter what you say. If that were true, they would have seen Ezra's plan, fought the gods that pinned them to their loom, and I would not be holding a fraction of their power."

I paused, letting her words melt over me. Arguing with Minerva about the Fates was like arguing with me about the origin of a realm. She knew them on a more intimate level than any god. She'd also spent more time learning about them than anyone in existence. She wanted to be free from their hateful power. And she deserved that freedom.

"I'm not sure the Fates want anything at all. They're not selfish beings. Even you can't argue that fact. Their loom is built from neutrality. The threads of Fate are simply meant to exist. It's their job to create those moments in their loom."

Stepping through the anomaly of existence felt like being torn apart and rebuilt in the same instant. One moment we stood in the dying twilight of Etherium, the next we faced an endless void that somehow contained everything that could ever be. Every path not yet taken, every choice not yet made. Raw power crackled through the air like lightning without light, each spark a potential future trying to claw its way into reality.

"It's not too late to turn back," I whispered to the strongest woman I'd ever known as she came up beside me.

"I hold a piece of them now," she replied. "Perhaps they will see reason through that connection."

"They'll only see the Wrath, Min."

A slow smile spread across her face. "Good. Because that's exactly what I feel. And I'm here because I told you I would stand beside you as long as you don't go to the Forgotten. I can't imagine how hard it must be for you to fight that urge. But I'll not see you fade into nothing, Reverius Hawthorne Noctus. Even if that means a little tough love from someone who's known you longer than most realms have known daylight."

My power stirred restlessly beneath my skin, responding to the pure potential surrounding us. But none of it mattered. Not the pain. The ramifications. The cost. Not even the gods that would whisper about this day for centuries. Only her.

I stepped forward, power erupting outward, golden threads of magic weaving through nothing. The void shuddered. My boots scraped against something that wasn't quite floor, wasn't quite air, sending ripples of possibility spreading outward into the darkness. Nothing about this space was settling. I'd have rather spent a century in Death's Court.

Three voices, the Fates, spoke into my mind as one, their words reverberating through my bones, though no being stood before us. "You dare?"

"I do."

Minerva swayed slightly backward, and I knew without asking they'd entered her mind for a different kind of torture. Likely stoking the Wrath they believed had been stolen from them.

Their laughter sounded like a thousand small bells, each slightly out of tune. But underneath it lay the scrape of thread against thread, the endless working of the loom that bound them. "The Keeper grows bold in his desperation."

"Or foolish," another voice added.

I might've been standing with my eyes closed in the middle of the Never Sky for all I could see, but in small traces, from the span of one blink to the next, flashes of what happened around us came into view. And though I could not see the Sisters of Fate, couldn't even feel their presence, I caught a glimpse of hands working eternal threads, fingers bleeding where the sharpest strands cut deep.

"Or both," said the third.

I gritted my teeth against their mockery, squaring my shoulders. "I seek an audience."

"Of course you do. Why else would you dare enter? We deny your request. Return to the makings of your choices." The words struck like a physical blow, sending me stumbling backward, the taste of copper flooding my mouth. Golden threads of my power snapped and withered. "We do not treat with gods who would bind us."

"That was Ezra's doing, not mine."

"Yet you stood aside." Their voices twisted together, sharp as knives. The air grew heavy with the stench of rotting futures, discarded timelines decaying in the void. "You watched as he stripped away our freedom. As we were bound to this loom, our fingers forever bleeding, our eyes forever seeing what must be and cannot be, never to walk among the moments we weave. Never to taste the futures we spin."

"And now you come crawling back," another sneered. I

thought I saw her, ancient and terrible, threads of fate wound through her flesh like living chains. "Begging for help with your precious Huntress."

My hands clenched into fists, power crackling between my fingers. "I don't beg."

More laughter, cruel and cold, echoed from everywhere and nowhere. "No? Then what do you call it?"

"A warning," I growled, and my voice carried the weight of centuries. "Her power grows unstable. If Alastor breaks her, if the madness claims her, there will be nothing left to salvage. If she cannot be saved, neither will the balance of power. There will never be forgiveness for my brother and nothing you weave will matter because I will burn it all. I will seek the end you fear. And don't think for a second I can't. I was fucking created to do so." My power throbbed, absolutely pounding beneath my skin like a weapon waiting for release.

Silence stretched between us. What I could only assume was the loom creaked, threads snapping. The whisper of lives being woven and cut swirled around us. Finally, after what felt like eons, a small, slithering voice said, "We will consider granting you an audience... on one condition."

I lifted my chin. "Name it."

"When Archer Bramwell sits upon the throne of Stirling, when his blood mingles with the ancient power of that seat, then, and only then, will we hear your questions. Not your plea, Keeper. We make no promises of aid. But we will listen, and perhaps we will answer."

"He won't—"

"You will see this fate come to pass or we will not hear you. There is no argument unless you wish us to rescind. You must not speak of this to him. The mortal prince must believe it is his choice alone that puts him on the throne." The voices began to fade, and with them went the scent of blood and promises, the weight of futures pressing down. "The price is set, Keeper. The task named. Choose wisely. Time grows short, and madness waits for no god's convenience."

The void swallowed their final words, leaving Minerva and I alone with the endless nothingness. My power flickered weakly, spent from reaching into this place where most gods feared to tread.

"Well," Minerva said dryly beside me, though I heard the tremor she tried to hide, "that went about as well as expected. Though I must admit, their Wrath feels stronger here. Perhaps that's why they're so eager to see the mortal prince take his throne. The thread of his destiny... it burns."

"How do you know that?"

"Because there's a piece of me living in this void now."

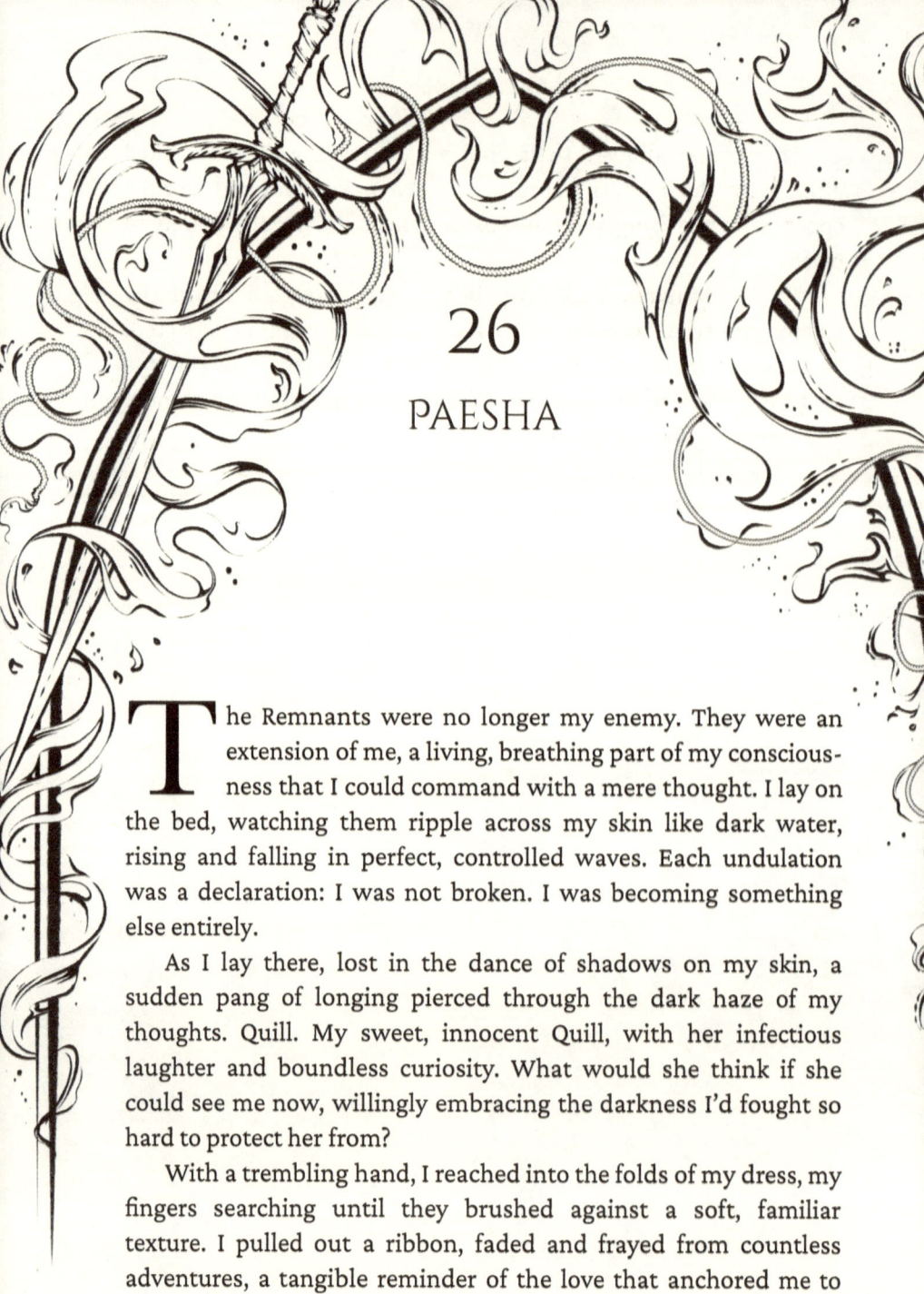

26

PAESHA

The Remnants were no longer my enemy. They were an extension of me, a living, breathing part of my consciousness that I could command with a mere thought. I lay on the bed, watching them ripple across my skin like dark water, rising and falling in perfect, controlled waves. Each undulation was a declaration: I was not broken. I was becoming something else entirely.

As I lay there, lost in the dance of shadows on my skin, a sudden pang of longing pierced through the dark haze of my thoughts. Quill. My sweet, innocent Quill, with her infectious laughter and boundless curiosity. What would she think if she could see me now, willingly embracing the darkness I'd fought so hard to protect her from?

With a trembling hand, I reached into the folds of my dress, my fingers searching until they brushed against a soft, familiar texture. I pulled out a ribbon, faded and frayed from countless adventures, a tangible reminder of the love that anchored me to my humanity. It was one of Quill's, a simple strip of fabric she'd used to tie back her unruly curls, but to me, it was a lifeline, a connection to the person I'd been before the gods had shattered my world.

I brought the ribbon to my lips, breathing in the faint scent of lavender and sunshine that clung to its fibers. Memories flooded my mind, moments of joy and laughter, of whispered secrets and shared dreams.

Suspended between past and present, love and vengeance, a glimmer of light caught my eye. Thorne's golden book appeared at the foot of my bed. I stared at it, my heart clenching with a mixture of hatred and longing. Not for him, but for the life I had before him. With a shaking hand, I reached for it, my fingers hovering above its shimmering surface. Alastor's daughter Sylvie's voice curled through my mind like tendrils of mist. "Open it," she whispered, her words a siren's call. "Play the game. Take control. You know what he needs to do. Make him do it."

I felt the smile tug on my lips long before the pencil touched the paper, though I knew if I were too obvious, he'd become suspicious.

Reverius Hawthorne Noctus,
I saw your face in the grain of wood on my prison floor today. Alastor says it's just a bedroom, but he fidgets with his clothes too much to be taken seriously. Have you learned a new spying hobby? The voices think you have. Do you know the voices?
Paesha Marian Vox (pretending Noctus)

His response was immediate.

Hello Paesha darling,
How lovely that you've remembered where to find me.

I am loath to admit that it was not me within the floorboards, but such a task to see that beautiful face is not at all above me. Are you well? Have you eaten?
Thorne (Always)

I TAPPED the end of the pencil to my mouth as I considered what to say next. How far to lead him.

Always Thorne but sometimes Reverius,
How might I find myself if I am lost to madness? If the room hangs upside down and the voices sing of rain and hammers? Am I well? I am not unwell. Am I? Do you remember how you promised a path for me? Remember when you said you'd do anything to keep me safe? Funny how promises sound so beautiful until they shatter.
Sometimes Unwell,
Paesha Marian Vox

Paesha Marian,
If you're lost to madness, then I will find my way there too. If the room hangs upside down, I'll walk the ceiling. If the voices sing of rain and hammers, I'll learn the melody and we will dance together. Whatever madness you're piecing together, I'll be the fool who tries to make sense of it. Can you tell me what you ate today?
Still only Thorne

Keeper of Thorns,
What a noble fool you are, offering to wade into my

madness as though it were a shallow stream instead of an endless sea. Tell me, how do you plan to keep your footing when even I can no longer feel the ground? The voices whisper that you will drown. Do you fear it? Do you dream of it?

I ate nothing but the words I wished you'd say aloud instead of writing. They were bitter, but I am full. Alastor says that's not a meal, but he doesn't understand hunger the way I do. Not the way you do. Do you? Come, Thorne. Come and prove you can swim. Or perhaps I'll drift so far that even you cannot follow.

Treading the edges,
Paesha Marian Vox

My Paesha,

I know what you must think, but I did not refuse to go to the Forgotten to keep you chained. The law is absolute. If I go there, I may not return. And if I cannot return to you, there is no point to going at all, not when there must be another way.

I will find another key to your freedom. If it lies in a place darker than the Forgotten, I will go. If it demands a price heavier than my immortality, I will pay it. If it means tearing apart everything I have ever been, then I will do so gladly—because you are worth it, Paesha. You have always been worth it.

You may think yourself lost to madness, but I will gladly lose my mind if it means finding you. Tell me

243

how to follow. Give me a thread to hold, and I will trace it through every shadow, every storm.
You are not a song I can forget. You are the melody that breaks me, over and over, and still, I will sing it.
Yours,
Thorne

MY MIND RACED as my eyes read and reread his words. Why was he so very good at lying beautifully and so very bad at meaning it? He could have been so fucking easy to love if he had been only Thorne. But that was never going to be.

Your Thorne,
I danced with you once. And you sang in the blue fire.
You burned and let Alastor put the chains around my wrists. I remember in small moments. When the voices sleep. When they don't whisper of murder and vengeance. Did the sun shine today? Can you see the flowers? Can you see me?
Paesha plus some others

The Remnants swirled approvingly around the edges of the page, dark tendrils seeming to caress the words. I closed the book, not trusting myself to continue this back and forth with him. He was not a victim. Nor would he be the victor. That was all that mattered right now. I had barely pushed the book under my pillow when Alastor walked in, carrying a tray.

I sat up. "I know they say good help is hard to come by, but

244

surely you could have asked one of your little minions to play servant."

"How are we feeling today?" he asked, that infuriating smile playing at the corner of his mouth.

I let the Remnants dance across my skin, purposefully erratic. "The stars are bleeding again. Can't you see them?"

His smile faltered for a moment before he set the tray on my bedside table. "Eat."

"Oh, look who learned a one-syllable word. Your vocabulary tutor must be so proud." I looked at the contents of the tray, wrinkling my nose. "What, no five course meal? And here I thought I was your honored guest."

"You're testing my patience." The Remnants on his neck pulsed darker, like ink spreading through water and even I couldn't deny how handsome he was. For an asshole.

I picked up the spoon, making sure to hold it as awkwardly as possible. "Well, someone has to. Clearly your creepy guards are too busy cowering to give you an honest performance review." I took a deliberately slow sip of the soup, letting a drop spill down my chin.

"When you're done playing with your food like a child, you will demonstrate your control over the Remnants."

I dabbed at my chin with exaggerated delicacy. "You know what they say about rushing a lady while she dines. Actually, you probably don't, given your charming personality."

His Remnants lashed out, knocking the spoon from my hand. "Lift the tray."

I felt the compulsion tear through me, but this time I was ready. I let my own surface slowly, like reluctant serpents, making them tremble and falter as they wrapped around the tray. It rose an inch, wobbled dramatically, and clattered back down.

"Again," he commanded.

"You know," I said through gritted teeth, making a show of concentration, "most teachers start with something smaller. Like a feather. Or their ego. Too fragile?" The tray rose again, shaking.

"You're holding back."

"And you're as observant as ever." I let the tray drop again with a clang. "Though I suppose that's what happens when you spend centuries having everyone bow to your every whim. The brain gets soft."

His hand shot out, fingers curling into a fist, and his Remnants surged forward. But before they could reach me, I blurted, "I know how to bring Reverius into the Forgotten."

The Remnants froze mid-strike, hanging in the air like black lightning. Alastor's eyes narrowed to dangerous slits. "What did you say?"

I leaned forward, grinning. "Oh, now I have your attention, don't I, Al?"

I stared down at my wrist, watching his bindings cut into me as my Remnants swirled lazily over flushed skin. I'd been too quick with my defense. But I had no patience for Alastor's brand of torture today.

He narrowed his eyes. "I would truly love nothing more than to send you away from my Vale, you infuriating little creature. Tell me your plan."

"I thought maybe I'd shake my titties at him and see if that did the trick. Men aren't fickle when it comes to nipples, I've learned."

He pinched the bridge of his nose, tilting his head back. "For Fates' sake, never say the word titties to me again."

"Okay, but to clarify, nipples is fine?"

His power surged forward, wrapping around my mouth like fingers. Typical. I rolled my eyes and laid back against my pillow crossing my arms over my chest as I began to hum wildly out of tune. He tried to speak but I ignored him, instead, sending my Remnants out into the halls of the Vale while he wasn't paying attention.

Brilliant, Sylvie sang into my mind. *Ask him about my mother. Distract him.*

"Tell me about Sylvie," I blurted out, expecting an immediate lashing to come from the woman in my mind. But she remained quiet.

"Who gave you that name?" Alastor asked, stepping closer. "Is she one of the voices you hear, Treasure?"

"Don't call me that."

"Don't call me Al."

"Fine."

"Fine."

"Tell me about your daughter."

As I watched him contemplate, the Remnants roamed the empty halls. I could not see through them, only hear as they whispered their reports. There was nothing. Only a single robed figure somewhere close to the entrance, standing completely still. So still, he might've been a statue had his burning eyes not whipped toward my power.

"Today is not the day for misery," Alastor said, yanking me back into the room. "Sylvie was her mother's prodigy and my misery. That is all there is to be shared."

I felt an unbearable weight of sadness with his words. As he walked toward the door, I realized it was Sylvie's sadness I was feeling. She might've been cruel, and clearly a little mad, but she still loved her father.

"You get him to take you to the Forgotten. Get him to bring my Ever back to me, and I will grant you your freedom, Huntress."

My Remnants crept back into the room as the man with vibrant green eyes turned back to me, a half-hidden smile on his face. "I should have never tried to bargain with the Keeper when the one in true control was already mine."

I lifted a shoulder, letting my head tilt a little too far. "What's one more betrayal between lovers?"

The look in Alastor's eyes told me I was finally becoming everything he'd planned. And I would let him believe that lie until the very end if I needed to.

27

THORNE

Though the little thing sat in the corner of the room with her nose stuck in a book, though I could see Paesha in the way she turned the pages, the way she didn't blink when she was stuck in the depths of the story, I knew she was still here in this room, listening, learning. The woman that'd raised her would've done nothing less. Even at the age of nine, I was sure.

Paesha hadn't responded when I'd told her of the rainy day. Nor had she answered whether she was eating. Or sleeping. She hadn't opened the book after her final note. But at least she'd sent the first.

I was so distracted by thoughts of Paesha and watching Quill, by the mannerisms that belonged to a woman that I didn't deserve, for a moment, I forgot why I was here in the Syndicate house, that seemed to have no Syndicate at all, but rather a mix of made-up family.

The older woman, Elowen, handed me a hot cup of tea, keeping her eyes cast to the floor. Out of respect and absolutely nothing else, I took a sip, letting the juice of bitter grass sour on my tongue while forcing a smile. "Delicious. Thank you so much."

She looked at me then, peering through the curtain of dark hair with the eyes of an old soul. Sometimes mortals shocked me in that way. When the past lives they didn't remember peered through. Not in the way of Paesha's madness, but something different. As if their soul held every memory of every life, though I knew it didn't.

"You're welcome here for now. But when Paesha comes home, and she will because she always does, if she says you go, then you go. I'll stand at the door and you will not come across that threshold until I'm staring at Death's handsome face. Are we understanding each other?"

Sometimes the easiest way to maintain power was to let others think they had it. "We understand each other."

"Good." She pulled a small book from her pocket and handed it to me. The hard cover was so worn, there was no longer a title, and the pages so limp, I worried they may fall from the spine. "This is her favorite. Read it. Learn something."

Suddenly the book had a heartbeat. A lifeline. It was precious to her, which made it precious to me. "What's it about?" I asked, scanning the ink along the title page.

"A broken woman that finds her glue."

"A romance. Understood."

"Something tells me you'd be surprised to learn that men are not the answer to every problem. In fact, they are usually the source."

I slipped the book into my back pocket, accepting my role as everyone's villain. I'd had to be the villain to save her. Had to be. "Noted."

"If you sit on that and rip the binding, she's going to kill you," Quill said from the corner, finally putting her book down on the little coffee table. "Which is fine, I guess. Since you're the problem."

Her casual tone was far more menacing than her words. One shouldn't fear a child. A god should fear very little. But she was chaos in a mortal form, darkness and light. She was an unknown. Innocent, but only just. Still, the threat flickered through her eyes in a flash of power. So quick, mortals might not have seen.

The snap of cards against a table grabbed Quill's attention. She'd given me an inch and no more when it came to being in her space. An inch was a win though. She skipped out of the room and I was left with my own thoughts as I waited for Archer to join me. I could hear him teaching Thea another of his card games and Elowen had asked me to wait here.

I waited. Each step in equal distance to the next as I paced the floor. Within minutes, I'd straightened the stack of books on a side table, wound the clock in the corner to match the correct time and straightened the curtain on the north wall. A painting hung across from me, its frame tilted at a slight angle that made my eye twitch. I fixed it with minute precision. Each imperfection seemed to call to me, begging to be corrected, set right.

Dust motes danced in the thin light that filtered through the lace curtains. I ignored them. But I couldn't ignore the wilted flowers in the vase. I plucked one petal and the entire flower crumbled.

Fuck.

I straightened, whipping around, expecting to see a little girl staring at me from the door with her arms crossed. Still, no one came. I dropped the dust from the flower back into the vase and decided not to touch anything else, choosing instead to sit and read the book Elowen had given me. If Archer wanted to play a game of patience against an eternity-old god, then I guess we played. But I would win.

In the next room, his laughter rang out, punctuated by the shuffle of cards and Thea's good natured grumbling. It was a welcome sound. Even in the midst of all this chaos, there was still room for connection, for the simple pleasure of a shared moment. Archer had a way about him, an ease that drew people in, made them feel at home in his company. It was a rare gift, one I'd seen echoed in Paesha. They both had that ability to find the light in the darkest of places, to forge bonds where others saw only walls. But unlike him, she'd hidden behind her walls for a long time first.

After some time, the floor from the hall creaked and Archer

sauntered in, a worn deck of cards still in his hands. Thea followed, leaning against the doorframe with an easy smile.

"Tell me you have a plan." Archer dropped into the chair across from me. The casual way he shuffled his cards didn't hide the tension in his shoulders, the worry etched around his eyes.

I studied him carefully. The Fates' words echoed in my mind. Archer had to choose the throne of his own free will. Any attempt to manipulate or coerce him would likely void their offer entirely. And right now, with Paesha falling to madness and locked behind Alastor's door, I couldn't risk it.

"I think you know I don't or you wouldn't have kept me waiting. I'm working on several, though," I admitted. "But I need you to—"

"If you tell me to stay here one more time, I swear to all the gods—"

"Actually," Thea interrupted, perching on the arm of his chair, "I've been thinking about the Vale's defenses. If we could map it out and come in from underneath—"

"We covered this. She's bound to him," I said with a sigh. "She's likely been told already she cannot leave. And his will over her is absolute. Dragging her out of there will only torture her in the long run. She needs true freedom."

A loud thump from upstairs made me tense, but Thea waved it off. "Only Quill and Boo. They were racing around up there all day yesterday."

I nodded, but something shifted in Archer's expression. His cards stilled mid-shuffle. Without warning, time stopped, and he bolted from his chair. I chased after him, taking the stairs two at a time as he sprinted toward Quill's room.

He threw the door open to reveal a scene frozen in time, Quill standing with her arms raised in surprise, a massive bookshelf tipping toward her, books already spilling from the uppermost shelves. In the split second before it would have crushed her, Archer had stopped everything.

With a huff, he shoved the bookshelf back against the wall,

then gathered Quill into his arms. The moment he released his hold on time, she gasped.

"You saved me again, Archie!" She threw her arms around his neck.

"Course I did, Pencil," he said softly, but something haunted lingered in his eyes.

"How did you know?" I demanded. "You reacted before it fell. Before anyone could have known she was in danger."

"Lucky timing," he said, but he wouldn't meet my eyes. "Which is exactly why I'm needed here. You understand that, right? I can't sit around while Paesha suffers, but I also can't leave Quill unprotected."

"The timing wasn't lucky. You knew."

"Drop it."

"If there's something you're not telling me—"

"Like you're not telling me something? Don't think I haven't noticed you weighing every word since you got here. We're supposed to be working together to save her."

The anger in his voice matched my own rising frustration. "You need to be in fucking Stirling, at the castle with your *father*."

He shook his head, setting Quill back down on the floor. She darted for the space under the bed, calling for her dog.

"Why the hell do you care so much?" Archer's voice was rough with emotion, but softer than I expected. "Why are you all pushing so hard?"

I took a breath, choosing my words carefully because in this moment, I saw the struggle in him. Not the stubborn thief, not the mourning brother, but the man unsure of his entire future and, in that, we were the same. "Because I've been where you are. Standing at the edge of a decision that seems impossible." Taking a beat, I let my guard down. "I'm not asking you to be king. I'm asking to see your father before he dies, so you both have some kind of closure. Regret is a horrible mistress. But whatever you decide, I'll support it."

He stepped into the hall, and I followed.

"It's not that simple. Every time I think about seeing him, I remember how he never sought my mother. I don't want to look at his face and see Harlow in his features. I don't want to stand before him and feel like we weren't enough." His shoulders sagged slightly. "Harlow didn't want him to know, and she was right, Thorne."

I leaned against the wall beside him, our shoulders almost touching. "Your sister was protecting you both."

A ghost of a smile crossed his face. "She always did."

"You know, protecting yourself isn't weakness. You've built something real here. Crown jewels don't compare to that. I just hope you don't look back one day and wish you'd have made a different choice."

Archer studied me for a moment, then nodded. "That's my burden to bear."

I pushed from the wall and clapped him on the shoulder. "I'll let it go then."

Those words were fire in my soul. An acceptance of my own demise, really. Perhaps the Fates would see him on the throne one day, but it likely wouldn't have a thing to do with me. If I'd learned anything from Paesha, it was when to push and when to accept defeat. Out of respect for a mourning man, a man that'd been my friend not that long ago, I walked away, nearly colliding with Aeris at the bottom of the stairs. She looked different, younger, likely playing a game the mortals knew nothing of, but I brushed past without acknowledging her. My mind was made up.

The Fates had given their price, but I couldn't wait for Archer to naturally choose a destiny he seemed determined to reject. Paesha needed me now. There was only one path left. I had to give Alastor what he wanted. The Forgotten beckoned, and I would answer its call. For her. Always for her.

As I walked away, I thought of my own promised future, of Ezra's threat. She would betray me. Perhaps that was my eternity to bear.

28

PAESHA

The Vale had changed in the days since my captivity. Or perhaps I had changed. The shadows that once seemed so ominous now held no power over me, they were merely cousins to the darkness that lived atop my skin. I let my fingers trail along the vendor stalls as I walked, leaving whispers of power in my wake. Each touch sent tiny sparks of magic through the trinkets and treasures, making them hum with potential as I marked them.

The black market that had once bustled with life now stood nearly empty, most stalls abandoned, their wares growing dust. But some remained. The desperate ones. The hungry ones. They watched me with wary eyes as I passed, these dealers in secrets and stolen goods. I knew their type. I'd been one of them once, before I learned to steal from gods instead of mortals.

Show them, Sylvie purred in my mind. *Show them what we've become.*

My Remnants responded to her voice, swirling around my feet like living smoke, turning the already dim lighting of the underground into something more sinister. They were mine now, not Alastor's. Mine to command, mine to unleash. The door to my room had never been locked, the true prison had been in my mind, and Sylvie was showing me how to break those chains.

I paused at a stall that still bore the markings of the Silk trades, fine fabrics and delicate jewelry that would have cost a Salt's life's wages for most. The merchant, a weathered woman with calculating eyes, tensed as I lifted a strand of pearls.

"Beautiful. Did you steal these yourself, or do you work for others?"

She didn't answer.

"I used to do both," I continued, letting the necklace slip through my fingers. "But there's no real challenge in it anymore. Don't you see? You were so busy watching the pearls, you never saw the rubies I collected." I dropped the jewels on her table. "Do better, love."

The whispers followed me as I moved on, rumors and speculation spreading like wildfire through the remaining vendors. Let them talk. Let them wonder what I'd become. What I could do to their fragile resolve.

A figure in dark, familiar robes stood motionless at the intersection of two corridors, his broad shoulders and imposing height marking him as someone not to be reckoned with. Even without seeing his face, I knew who he was. Themis. The God of Justice. The one who'd bound the Cimmerians to the prince's will. The same prince whose heart I'd pierced with my blade. I forgot how much he screamed. But I remembered how much he bled.

I smiled as I passed Themis, letting my power brush against his. Let him know that justice meant nothing to someone who'd been wronged by gods. He was silent, hidden beneath the shadows of his cloak, but I felt his gaze follow me down the corridor.

The few remaining merchants drew back as I approached Alastor's office, some actually scrambling to pack their wares and flee. No knocking, no hesitation, I simply opened the door and walked in.

To my surprise, and utter annoyance, Thorne stood by the desk, his broad shoulders tense as he turned to face me. No Alastor in sight. Dammit.

Gods, he was beautiful. It wasn't fair that someone could break hearts so easily while looking like salvation. He was massive, filling the space with his presence in a way that had nothing to do with physical size and everything to do with the power that radiated from him. Those hazel eyes locked on to mine, and for a moment, just a moment, I remembered how it felt to drown in that gaze.

"Paesha," he breathed, taking a step forward. His eyes widened slightly as he took in my appearance, the way the Remnants rippled around me, the sharp edge to my smile, no doubt.

"Do you remember the snow?" I asked, trailing my fingers along Alastor's desk. "How it never melts when gods dream?"

Pain flashed across his beautiful face. "You're not well."

"I've never been better." I moved closer, letting him see the shadows that danced in my wake. "I understand everything now. All the pieces are finally clear."

"Let me help you."

I wondered if anyone else had noticed how broken he'd become. How hollow his cheeks were.

"Whatever Alastor's done—"

I stepped back. "Like you helped me in the garden? Like you helped me on the stage? Which version of help should I trust, Reverius?"

He flinched at the use of his true name. "I never meant—"

"To hurt me? To lie? To watch me die over and over?" I laughed. "Your intentions mean nothing against the weight of your actions. They never do. Never will."

Draw him in slowly, Sylvie whispered. *Make him earn it.*

I moved to stand directly before him, smoothing a hand up his chest, speaking softly. "I see the way you look at me. Like you're trying to memorize my face. Like you're preparing to lose me again." I paused, watching understanding dawn in his eyes. "You're planning something dangerous. Something final."

"Paesha—"

"The Forgotten," I said, and his slight intake of breath confirmed my suspicion. He was ready. "That's where you'll go, isn't it? To try to save me from Alastor's binding?"

"I haven't—"

"I see more clearly now. The voices show me things. Truths buried in lies. Answers hidden in questions."

His jaw clenched. "The voices aren't real."

"No?" I reached up, trailing my fingers along his jaw. "Then why do they know your secrets? Why do they remember every promise you've broken?"

He caught my hand, holding it against his cheek. "I would give anything..."

"Prove it," I whispered. "No more lies between us. Promise me complete honesty, and I'll believe in you again."

"I promise," he said immediately.

I pulled away. "So eager to swear. Just like in Winter's garden. Just like every time before."

"This is different," he insisted. "This time is different."

"Then tell me the truth. Are you planning to enter the Forgotten?"

He hesitated, warring with himself. "Yes."

"Take me with you."

"No. It's too dangerous."

"More dangerous than leaving me here?" I gestured to the Remnants swirling around us. "More dangerous than letting me drown in madness while Alastor twists my mind?"

"Paesha—"

"You said you'd be honest," I reminded him. "That you'd do things differently. Was that another lie? Tell Alastor you will only go if I can come too. Force him to let me come."

"I can't lose you again," he said, his voice raw.

"Then don't." I let my power brush against his. "Let me help you. Trust me, just this once. We go together, or not at all."

I could see him wavering, see the desperate hope warring with centuries of protective instinct. "The Forgotten could destroy us both."

"Or it could save us." I reached for his hand, ignoring the way my heart raced at the contact. His skin was warm against mine, callused fingers wrapping around my own with gentle strength.

"One last chance, Thorne. One last try at getting it right. Complete honesty. Complete trust. That's all I ask."

Make him believe, Sylvie urged. *Make him hope.*

"If I lost you in there..." He swallowed hard. "I wouldn't survive it."

"You won't lose me," I promised, the lie tasting like copper on my tongue. "We'll face it together. No more secrets. No more lies. Only us, finding our way back to each other while we hunt down what was lost."

The door opened, and Alastor stepped in. His eyes moved from my hand in Thorne's to the Remnants that swirled around us both.

"Well," he said, a slow smile spreading across his face. "Isn't this interesting?"

"We're going to the Forgotten," I said firmly. "Both of us."

Alastor's smile widened. "Are you now?"

"Make the bargain," Thorne demanded. "If we return with Irri from the Forgotten, Paesha's binding to you ends as does any bargain I've ever made with you."

No Sylvie warned. *Make him be specific. Think of the terms.*

"Just Irri's return," I clarified. "No conditions on who brings her back. No tricks. No games."

Thorne's hand tightened on mine. "Agreed."

"Agreed," Alastor echoed, and power crackled through the air as the bargain took hold.

I looked up at Thorne, and for a moment, just a moment, I let myself remember how it felt to trust him. To maybe love him. His fingers intertwined with mine, and electricity shot through my veins, making my knees weak. A flicker of heat warmed me at his touch, a reminder of everything we could have been if not for lies and games and ancient prophecies.

Focus, Sylvie commanded. *Remember why we're here.*

I squeezed his hand, pushing away the ache in my chest. This wasn't about love or trust or redemption. This was about freedom. About vengeance.

Thorne pulled me through the office, eager to escape Alastor's domain, no doubt. But before we could flee, the door exploded inward. The robed figure from the hall filled the frame, bow drawn and aimed at my heart. As he released the arrow, his hood fell back, revealing Ezra's coldly beautiful face. Ezra. Not Themis but Ezra. The murderer. Time slowed. I could see the arrow's fletching, dark as night against the shaft, could trace its path through the air with perfect clarity.

"No!" Thorne's roar shook the walls as he moved to shield me.

But the arrow never reached either of us. Alastor's Remnants snatched it from the air only inches from Thorne's back, crushing it to dust. The rage emanating from the God of Lost things was a physical thing, turning the air thick and heavy.

Alastor's voice held centuries of fury as his shadows surged forward, engulfing Ezra in writhing darkness. "You dare come into my domain and threaten what's mine?"

Ezra struggled against the Remnants, his own power flaring gold against the darkness. "You're a fool if you think—"

"Run!" Alastor commanded, never taking his eyes off Ezra. "Both of you, get out. Now!"

Thorne grabbed my arm, but then suddenly went rigid. His eyes flashed brilliant gold, distant and unseeing, as if caught in a vision. The moment stretched, endless and terrible, before he snapped back to himself with a sharp intake of breath.

Without a word, he yanked me toward the door. Behind us, the sounds of clashing power shook the foundations of the Vale. Dust fell from the ceiling as the floor rumbled. Ezra's shout of rage followed us down the corridor, but Thorne didn't slow, didn't look back.

He ran, pulling me with him, toward whatever fate awaited us in the Forgotten.

29

PAESHA

Death had a new name today, and it was Ezra. The tip of his arrow was a whisper away from taking my life and his eyes, once full of love, burned with the resolve to end me. My hands trembled, and I pressed them against my chest where the arrow should have been. Mortality had brushed against me like an icy wind, and somehow I was still breathing.

Before I could process what had happened, golden light poured from Thorne's skin, weaving magic through the air like threads through silk. With a sound like tearing fabric, he ripped a hole in the world that echoed across the empty streets of Stirling. Power rippled outward in waves, distorting the air until it split open, revealing absolute darkness beyond. I didn't know if he'd been to the Forgotten before, whatever that place was, but he'd certainly known how to open the door, when Alastor didn't. Which told me only one thing. The Forgotten was a prison, and Reverius Hawthorne Noctus was the warden.

In books I'd read, the protagonist would claim the void between worlds tasted like lightning and smelled of broken promises. As Thorne's power tore reality apart before me, I discovered they were wrong. It tasted like vengeance and smelled like everything that had ever been lost. My own fear gave name to those new scents.

"You can stay," Thorne whispered, his voice softer than I'd ever heard it. His eyes found mine, no longer the hard, calculating gaze he showed the world, but something vulnerable, almost pleading. His fingers reached for mine, but he hesitated. "Last chance. Once we cross that threshold, everything changes. I believe the Forgotten is a place that consumes. We could lose ourselves entirely. Lose each other. Lose every memory that makes us who we are."

He's lying. He can never forget and we won't let you either.

"Ezra..." I said, my voice hollow, unable to let go of those past moments. "He just..."

"Yes." Thorne's eyes darkened. "And he failed."

"But he tried to kill me. I could be dead right now." My voice broke, the reality of it washing over me again.

"This is the cycle," Thorne said, his hand finally closing the distance to mine, his touch warm and solid against my trembling fingers. For a moment, the mask fell completely, and I saw raw fear in his eyes, fear *for* me or *of* me, I wasn't sure.

I felt the pressure in the back of my throat. The one that warned me tears weren't far behind. I squeezed my eyes shut, trying hard to forget the man I'd known and loved for years, because as much as Thorne would like this moment when we were finally alone to be about him, it simply wasn't.

"He didn't even blink," I whispered, forcing my heart to let go of the way I mourned him. "I gave him so much of myself. And he let go of that arrow."

This wasn't safe. These thoughts. These words. I didn't want the emotions that came with them. I didn't want the reality of being the Hunted. I had a mission. A goal. And Ezra wasn't part of that.

"He will try again, Paesha. You need to understand that and be careful."

I put a hundred walls up around the man I used to love in my mind. No more thoughts of him. I wouldn't survive dwelling on the past. Instead, I looked to Thorne. Finally. Fully. Forcing the conversation away from his brother. "Are you afraid?"

He hesitated, something devastating and raw crossing his face before he masked it. "For you, perhaps, but you could stay. You could hide away," he said softly, almost pleading. "Let me do this alone. I'll find Irri and free you from Alastor, no matter what happens to me." His thumb traced circles on my palm, the gentle touch at odds with the tension in his shoulders. "Go back to Quill, to your family. Let me do this one thing right."

For a moment, for one heartbeat, I saw past the god to the man. The way his eyes held mine felt like a last desperate reach for something real, something true between us. As if he was offering me not just a choice, but a chance at redemption for us both.

He lies, the voices hissed in unison, rising like a tide of serpents in my mind. *Always lies.*

Stop this, Winter hissed.

Make him suffer, another whispered.

Do not be a fool, Sylvie commanded.

Their fury drowned out my own doubts, my own fears, and something else, something that felt dangerously like regret. I squeezed his hand, letting the vulnerability he needed to see shine through the cracks in my armor. "We go together. We leave together." The lie tasted like ashes on my tongue. "No more running."

The look that crossed his face then, a mixture of resignation and heartbreak so profound it stole my breath, was gone so quickly I almost convinced myself I'd imagined it. He couldn't have known. If he knew I planned to find a way without him, he wouldn't have committed to go.

Without another word, we stepped through the tear in reality. The sound it made as it sealed behind us sent ice through my veins.

"Can you reopen it?" I asked.

"I'm not sure," he admitted quietly, removing his glasses as this new reality settled around us. "I'm guessing nothing works quite the same here, but that's the hope. Otherwise, I've taken you away from your ward for eternity. And that's a truth I cannot bear."

At least he was being honest about this sadness. He might not admit it, but that came from fear too. Perhaps the god of gods and a thousand names was more human than he'd ever let himself believe. Or he was a really good pretender, playing the role of someone who cared. Likely the latter.

The Forgotten was a nightmare manifested. Towers of twisted black stone rose into a starless void above, their surfaces creeping with shadows that had weight and substance. The ground was neither solid nor liquid. It shifted and rippled with each step, as if we walked on the skin of some vast, sleeping beast.

Between the towers, paths wound like open wounds through the darkness. The air whispered of the damned. Fragments of forgotten souls drifted past like ash, their faces contorted in eternal screams.

I spoke before thinking. Before the mask could be firmly in place. "How did this place come to be?"

"It happened by accident," Thorne said quietly, his eyes fixed on the darkness. "When I first became the Keeper, I didn't understand the weight of what I was. Every beginning demands an ending. Every memory preserved requires something to be forgotten. Balance, always balance. The first time I needed to make something cease to exist in memory, I thought I was simply removing it from reality. But things don't simply disappear. All those forgotten things, those lost moments, those ended stories, they had to go somewhere. I didn't realize what was happening until I imprisoned my first god. Everything that had been forgotten, everything that had been broken, it all gathered here. A realm that exists in the spaces between memory and oblivion. A prison built from everything that reality needed to forget."

"Great. Not ominous at all," I said, hesitant to walk forward.

"No one has ever returned from here." His voice dropped to barely a whisper. "I have no idea what we're getting ourselves into."

"Can't be worse than dungeon torture, forced marriage and one-sided magical bargains. I think I'll manage."

My Remnants poured across the shifting ground. They twisted

through the shadows, trying to anchor themselves to anything that felt real. But nothing here was truly real, it was all echoes and pieces of things that had been forgotten by time and people and apparently even gods.

The darkness pressed closer as Thorne caught my wrist, turning me to face him. His touch was gentle but insistent, like everything about him, a contradiction I'd never quite understood. "The last time we were alone..."

I hadn't thought about it. Refused to remember his fingers on my skin. The way he'd settled between my thighs, the way he'd looked at me that night. "I should have told you everything then."

"Stop. We don't need to do this."

His fingers tightened. "Yes, we do. We absolutely fucking do. I can feel the way you pull back. I can see the question in your eyes. I know you don't trust me."

"And why should I? If you broke my arm right now and apologized for it, would my arm be healed?" I bit back at him, knowing I was giving myself away.

"I would never—"

"I watched you," I shouted. "You killed me. Some game between you and Ezra, one life after another, you've been killing me. The voices..." I plunged my hands into my hair pulling as the Remnants swirled around me and voices of my past lives, all of them whispered one over the top of the other so I couldn't hear a thing, couldn't think straight enough to string thoughts together.

I love you, too.

I will protect you.

I will break you.

Burn the realms.

Let them fall.

Dance with me.

Trust me.

We loved him too, Huntress. Sylvie crooned. *All of us loved him. And he broke us. We are what's left of everything he broke because we were too weak to say no to him. We will be your strength. Put your mask on.*

I felt myself sinking into the shifting ground more than saw it beyond the shadows that were building and building. I needed control. I needed absolute control. But I wasn't stronger than Sylvie. I could feel her smile in my mind. Could see her pushing me further into the pit of madness.

"Enough," I heard him roar outside the wall.

Had I spoken aloud? Repeated them? I did that sometimes.

"Fight back, Paesha. Find yourself in there and fight it. Remember me. I've *never* been the one to kill you. It's always been him. You die in my arms every fucking time, but not at my hands. Remember." His voice broke. "Please."

All of my past lives emboldened the Remnants as they whipped past me like angry wraiths, swirling and threatening. They knew I was weak for him. Because they had been too. But their anger had festered. And they didn't believe his innocence.

"You're not supposed to forget, but you forgot them. Didn't you? You forgot and it tastes like broken flames," I said, my voice drifting in and out like static. The Remnants twisted around me as I stared into the darkness, my eyes tracking movements only I could see. I quieted. "They move differently here. Can you feel them watching us? Waiting?"

"Who, Paesha?" Thorne stepped closer, cautious. "There's no one here."

I laughed. "Everyone is here." My gaze snapped to a point over his shoulder. "Quiet. She's trying to tell me something important."

"Who is?"

"Who is what?" I tilted my head, listening. "She says you taste like betrayal when you bleed. Is that true?"

Thorne tensed. "Paesha, you need to—"

"The Remnants want to play with your memories," I interrupted, my focus jumping erratically. "They're so hungry for something real. Something divine." I reached out, fingers tracing invisible patterns in the air between us. "I could let them. Just for a moment. To see what happens."

"Look at me," he demanded.

My eyes met his, but they weren't quite focused. "I see you. I see all of you. Past and present and future, bleeding into each other like watercolors. Oh! Rain." My voice dropped to a conspiratorial whisper. "Do you know what happens when gods forget themselves? When their stories unravel? Someone showed me. It's beautiful and terrible."

The shadows pulsed around us as I stepped closer.

"We should break you open," I said conversationally. "Just a little crack to let the light in. To see what's true." My fingers reached for his face, trembling slightly. "They're screaming so loudly, Thorne. All the things you've loved and lost."

My expression suddenly cleared, vulnerability flashing across my face, though I could hardly see him beyond the mass of shadows swirling around me like a wind storm. "Help me. They won't stop talking. They won't—" Then just as quickly, the moment was gone, replaced by an eerie smile. "But we'll be fine, won't we? We'll find Irri together. We'll fix everything. Trust me. It's dark here."

Thorne punched through the darkness like a beam of light, refusing to let my power keep him away. He threw his arms around me, and the voices screamed and screamed in my mind. They ripped at his clothes, pulled at his skin, but still he held me.

"I remember every single one of them," he said, his voice raw as he held me tighter. "Every smile, every tear, every moment of joy and heartbreak. I loved them all. That was never a lie. I loved them completely, wholly, with everything I was. Each one was precious, perfect, irreplaceable."

The Remnants tore at him, but still he didn't let go. His power pulsed against mine, not fighting but supporting, holding me up as I struggled against the madness.

He whispered, his lips against my hair, "You're all of them and more. You're their courage and their compassion, their strength and their sacrifice. But you're also something entirely new, a storm given form, a force of nature that refuses to break. You survived things that would shatter gods. Even now you continue to fight your way out of darkness over and over. Fuck, Paesha, you built a family from broken pieces, and you love them with a fierceness that puts everyone else to shame. That's your power. It's not collected pieces of who your soul used to be. It's the way you take everything broken and make it whole. Even when you're broken."

Lies, the voices screamed. *Don't let him speak.*

He forced my face up with his hands buried into my hair. I couldn't breathe. Couldn't swallow. Couldn't see or feel or move beyond the man that commanded everything. "You carry their light within you, but you burn brighter than any of them ever dreamed. You're the only one who ever made me question everything I am. The only one who made me want to be better. To be worthy." His words became a mantra, repeated over and over until they drowned out the chaos in my mind. "I know you hate me. I fucking hate me too. But there was never a rule book on how to fall in love knowing you were going to have to say goodbye in the most brutal way."

Slowly, the voices retreated. The darkness coiled back under my control. He pulled back only enough to swipe a tear from my cheek with his thumb.

"I know you're fighting demons of my making," he said softly. "And I know I have no right to ask, no right to hope, but if you let me, I will stand between you and every nightmare that haunts you. Not because you need saving, you've never needed that, but because watching you battle alone breaks something in me I didn't know could still break. I'm not the hero in any story worth telling. My edges are rough, our wounds still bleed into the spaces between us."

"The voices are piercing," I whispered and because I couldn't gather my thoughts beyond the silent screaming in my heart, I said no more. I knew only that I didn't want him. I didn't want to be here with him. I didn't like him. I couldn't love him. I needed to be away from him. Forever. And there was only one path to that separation. Where he couldn't find me, and with one brother down, there would only be one to go.

His fingers traced up my arm, over the binding marks Alastor had left and the Remnants that swirled there like an ocean's tide. "I did this to you. Every mark on your skin, every voice in your head, they're all because I was too much of a coward to let you go. Too selfish to give you the choice." He let out a shaky breath, his hand cupping my cheek. I let him, watching his hazel eyes filled with centuries of regret. "I am sorry. A thousand times and more. I'm so sorry."

Fleetingly, I let myself feel the weight of that apology. The finality of it. His thumb brushed my lower lip and I could feel him trembling, feel the cost of those words in his touch.

I stepped back, breaking contact. "There's no part of me that can ever trust you again," I said quietly, each word a blade between us, the Remnants be damned. "That night we were together wasn't real. None of it was real. You made sure of that. The only thing I ever wanted was to be free. Tell me why you didn't explain all the details of Alastor's bargain. How could that have hurt you?"

I watched his face, searching for his next lie. He opened his mouth to speak, but no words came out.

"I was right, wasn't I?" I asked, taking another step away from him. "You never thought it would come to pass. You thought I'd be bound to you and unable to be bound to him, didn't you? You were going to go through with the bargain we made behind your veil of lies. You would have taken all my memories of home? Of her? You were going to make me forget so I would never leave you." I stumbled backward. "You really are a monster."

Still, he said nothing. I rushed forward, shoving him. "Say something, you coward. Tell me the truth. Not your pretty bullshit. Tell me what your plan was."

He grabbed my wrist to force me to be still. "Yes. I would have bound you to me to keep you free of him. I would have done that. Because it would be better to be bound to someone who cares for you than someone who wants to use you."

My heart broke a thousand times more with his confession. I knew. Of course I did. But to hear him say it? "I hate you," I whispered.

"I know you do," he whispered. "But I couldn't tell you about the bargain with Alastor without telling you everything."

I wrapped a steel cage around my heart and forced myself into the role I was meant to play here. His words didn't matter anymore. But he needed to believe they did.

"Then you should have told me everything." I broke out of his hold as he shook his head.

"I've done that before. Every time you learn the truth, you die before the sun sets."

The Remnants reared to life in my mind, hissing through the crowd of voices.

Who knew the truth?

Which of us did he tell?

No one came forward. Another lie of his, it seemed.

I wanted to turn away and run, but I couldn't. Instead I looked up at him, letting vulnerability seep into my expression. Sometimes the best lies were wrapped in truth. "I want to believe you." My fingers tracing his jaw. "I want to trust that this time will be different."

His breath caught. I saw hope flickering in those hazel eyes, saw how desperately he wanted this to be real. "I'll spend every moment proving it to you."

I pressed closer, letting him feel my surrender. "Then prove it now. Help me find my way through this darkness."

The smile that broke across his face was devastating in its joy, in its relief. He pulled me against him, his lips brushing my forehead in a touch so gentle it almost made me waver. Almost.

Perfect, Sylvie purred in my mind. *He's always been weak for hope.*

I turned away before he could see the truth in my eyes, taking a step toward the twisting paths ahead. Behind me, his voice turned urgent, "Don't stray from the path." The pain in those words had nothing to do with the dangers lurking in the darkness. "The things that live here... They must remember what it was to exist, and I'd bet everything they hunger for it."

Fear, real, primal fear, kept me close to his side as we ventured deeper into the prison he'd created.

Patient, Winter whispered as a door opened into nothing, its hinges creaking in an endless song. *Let him lead us deeper.*

269

Let him trust, Sylvie agreed. *Then leave him. He will open the door, but only you and Mother will walk through it.*

I wasn't naïve enough to believe the demigod living in my mind, wrapped around my power, wasn't making her own selfish moves. I just questioned how far this went for her. When it ended. I needed to be careful with my thoughts, though. I'd only recently discovered a tiny space in my mind where they didn't tread and it was the only place I could let myself be truly free of all manipulation. His, their's, Alastor's. One tiny spot that was only mine as I fought a battle on all sides.

A sound like distant screaming drew closer. Thorne grabbed my hand as shadows deeper than the darkness began to move with purpose around us.

"We need to run," he said urgently.

Something ancient and hungry unfurled in the path ahead. In that moment of quiet, in that small untouched corner of my mind, I wondered if either of us would survive what was to come.

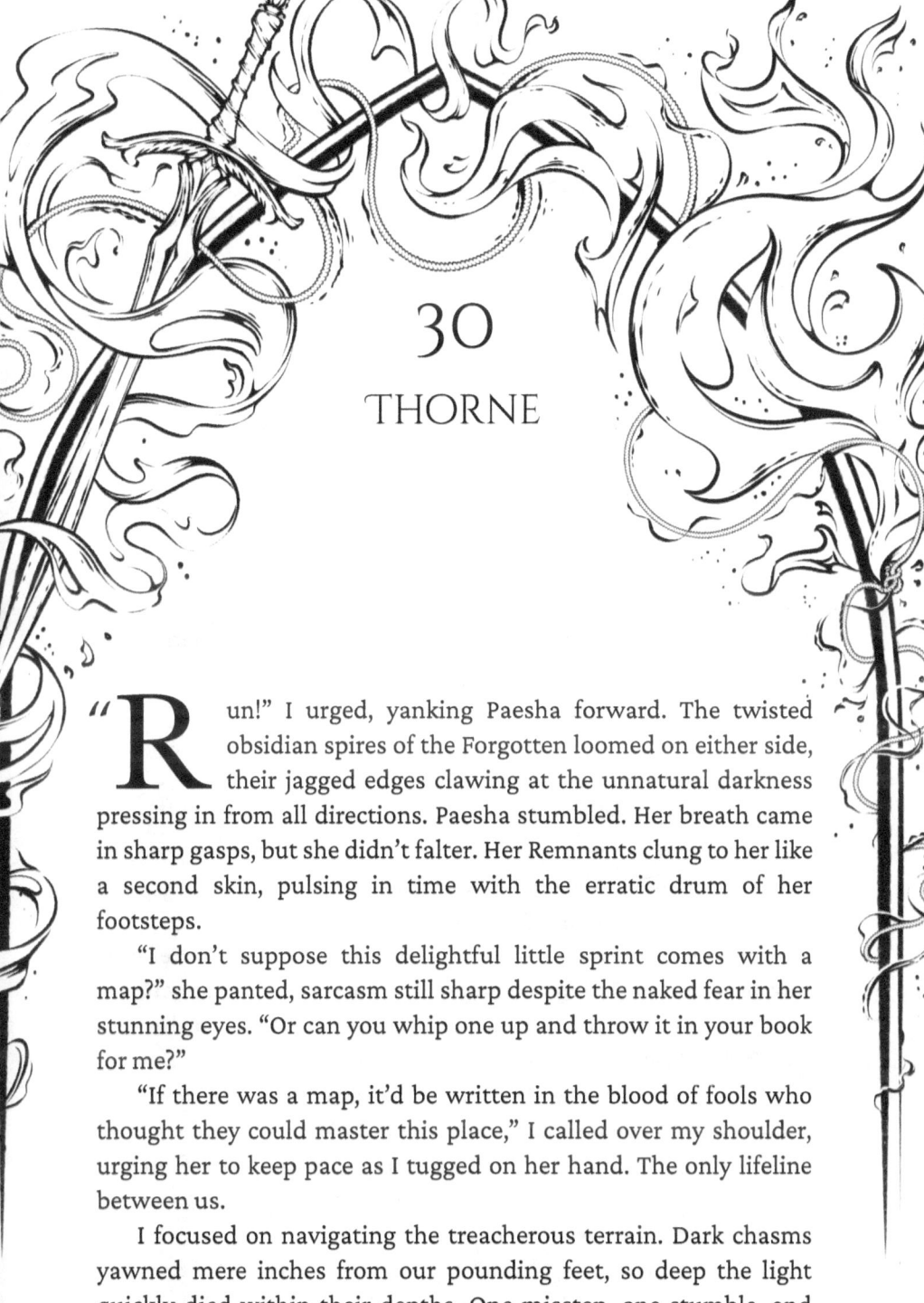

30

THORNE

"Run!" I urged, yanking Paesha forward. The twisted obsidian spires of the Forgotten loomed on either side, their jagged edges clawing at the unnatural darkness pressing in from all directions. Paesha stumbled. Her breath came in sharp gasps, but she didn't falter. Her Remnants clung to her like a second skin, pulsing in time with the erratic drum of her footsteps.

"I don't suppose this delightful little sprint comes with a map?" she panted, sarcasm still sharp despite the naked fear in her stunning eyes. "Or can you whip one up and throw it in your book for me?"

"If there was a map, it'd be written in the blood of fools who thought they could master this place," I called over my shoulder, urging her to keep pace as I tugged on her hand. The only lifeline between us.

I focused on navigating the treacherous terrain. Dark chasms yawned mere inches from our pounding feet, so deep the light quickly died within their depths. One misstep, one stumble, and we'd be lost to the ravenous dark. She knew that, of course. She could see it, but her wit had always been her shield for fear. And I was glad for it. At least it wasn't hatred.

A low whisper slithered through the gloom, insidious as hemlock. "You're going to lose her. Like you always do. Like you deserve."

Paesha shuddered, a moan catching in her throat. "Please tell me you heard that. I don't think my regularly scheduled mental breakdown has room for a new voice."

"I heard it." I caught her elbow, steadying her as we ran. "That's not the kind of second opinion you want rattling around in your head, trust me."

"Oh, you mean like the parade of murdered lovers already keeping me company? That kind of second opinion?"

Despite the barbed words, she pressed closer, her Remnants reaching for me like seeking tendrils. Comfort and accusation, all tangled up in the space between us. Story of our godsdamned lives.

The whispering grew louder, a cacophony of malice boring into my skull as we fled deeper into the labyrinth of twisted stone.

"You know what's coming, don't you?"

Beside me, Paesha let out a choked scream, her stride faltering. The Remnants around her lashed out in blind panic, gouging smoking furrows in the obsidian ground.

"Dammit!" My stomach lurched as I skidded to a halt, gripping her shoulders to keep her from crumpling to the ground. Her eyes shot back and forth, beyond me, seeing horrors I could only imagine. "Listen to me. It's not real. Do you hear me? It's not fucking real. Fight it! Don't you dare let it break you!"

But she was already slipping away, drowning in the fears the Nullweaver dragged to the surface. I could feel the creature behind us, a seething mass of dread and hunger, gorging itself on her terror as we sought to escape its grasp. I shot a glance over my shoulder and then back to her.

I slowed my voice. Slowed my pace until we were stopped. "Come on, Paesha, darling. Look at me. Remember me." I gripped her chin, forcing her gaze to mine. Tears streaked her ashen face, her pupils blown wide with panic. "You're stronger than this.

Stronger than it." Logic. She needed logic. "Whatever it's showing you isn't real. It's your greatest fear. It's called a Nullweaver. Its single purpose is to find your fear and make you live it until you cannot feel anything else. It's just a vision. Just a voice."

For a single, breathless moment, clarity sparked in those haunted depths. Her hands scrabbled at my chest, fisting in my shirt. "Thorne..."

"She will betray you. She will be your end."

"Shut up," I snarled at the voices, at Ezra's ghost. At the words he'd hissed into my mind as we escaped the Vale. Losing her had always been my fear. "You don't get to win. Not this time."

I gathered Paesha close, pouring every ounce of will into the space between us. Into the bond that had sustained us through lifetimes of love and loss. With a roar of effort, I gripped the Nullweaver's mind and shoved terror down its throat, choking it on the fear it craved. On the memory of every horror it'd ever tasted.

The creature reeled back, its countless eyes blinking in shocked confusion. I'd only ever seen it in my peripheral, but as it exposed itself, I saw it for what it truly was, a serpent and nothing more. How fucking fitting.

"That's enough," Paesha whispered, but her voice grew stronger. "Maybe you didn't hear me. I said that's enough." Her head snapped up, clarity and rage burning away the shadows haunting her gaze until she broke from my arms and turned to face the Nullweaver, hands gripped into fists at her sides. A beast in mortal form. A godsdamn warrior.

"Get out of my fucking head," she growled. Her Remnants swarmed the monster, tearing into it with savage precision. Practically a goddess, taking on a thing of nightmares. Something my brother and I had only ever trapped and never killed. "You want my fear? You can choke on it."

The creature's shrieks battered our ears, its body shriveling beneath the onslaught of Paesha's unleashed power. I watched in awe as she ripped it apart, a storm of midnight death with vengeance in her eyes and my heart in her hands.

And then, between one blink and the next, the Nullweaver was gone. Shattered to nothing beneath the hands of my Huntress's wrath. Paesha swayed on her feet, the sudden absence of her target leaving her unmoored.

I caught her before she could fall, pulling her into the shelter of my arms and she came without hesitation, burrowing into my chest as the adrenaline drained from her trembling limbs.

"That was incredibly reckless and equally breathtaking."

"Don't sound so surprised. I've always been a badass." She groaned, pulling away from me. "Part of my charm."

I huffed a laugh, and for a single, stolen moment, the darkness felt a little less horrifying.

"Thorne, I..."

"I know." And I did. In that moment, I understood the war raging behind those fathomless eyes. The longing and the loathing, the desire and the dread. I felt its echo in my half of our shared soul.

"Our story was always fated to be carved in blood and tears. But I'll be damned if I let the final chapter close in tragedy." I reached for her again, unable to stop myself. "Not until we've rewritten every line, turned every page, and stolen whatever happiness we can from this cursed tale. But I'll endure it all for these tiny moments. Even when it doesn't make sense to a single other soul but ours."

I couldn't hear the voices that undoubtedly plagued her, but I saw the distant look move in. The blink and short breath as she fought another mental battle, silently. A distant shriek pierced the momentary quiet, shattering the illusion of safety. She stepped farther away, her Remnants coiling defensively around her once more.

"Please tell me that was just the wind."

"Since when has anything been that easy for us? We need to keep moving. The Nullweaver wasn't the only monster playing in the dark here."

She blew out a shaky breath, squaring her shoulders as she fell into step beside me. "If you get us lost, I'm feeding you to the next horror we stumble across."

"Neither of us know where we are or where we're going, I think it's fair to say we started lost and we'll likely leave this place lost."

"I almost forgot how annoying your know-it-all personality was."

"Glad I could remind you," I said with a smirk.

Her eyes traced my face before she said. "I meant what I said, monster bait."

"I'd expect nothing less."

The reprieve was temporary with the betrayal foretold by Ezra's vision still lurking in our future. If locking me away was her choice, then so fucking be it. As long as I could force Irri to protect her from Ezra first, I'd spend eternity here in my own prison. That was the price I'd agreed to pay when I stepped into this realm. Minerva knew it. Tuck knew it. And she'd know it too, before she left this wretched realm. I'd lock myself away if it meant she lived.

We wound deeper into the heart of the Forgotten, the darkness growing thicker. It clung to our skin like oil, seeping into our pores, our lungs, until it felt like we were drowning in shadows.

"I can't see a damn thing," Paesha gritted out, her grip on my hand bordering on painful. "Are we even still on the path?"

I squinted into the gloom, trying to make out the faint glimmer of frost that had been our guide. But there was nothing. Merely an endless sea of black.

"I don't know. I think... I think the Forgotten is changing around us. Adapting to our presence."

"Oh, fantastic. A sentient nightmare realm with a grudge. Just what we needed."

A guttural growl rumbled through the darkness ahead. Paesha froze, her Remnants flaring out in a defensive fan.

"Please tell me that was your stomach."

"Looks like the welcome wagon is here."

"I don't want to be welcomed," she groaned.

The growl echoed, bouncing off unseen surfaces until it came from everywhere and nowhere. I could feel more than see Paesha's Remnants swirling around us, lashing at the darkness as if they could tear it apart and reveal the threat hiding within.

"Any ideas, oh wise and powerful Keeper? Or do we stand here and wait to be eaten by whatever nightmare is stalking us?"

"You destroyed the Nullweaver, I think we'll be fine."

"Fantastic. I'll put that on my headstone."

I reached out with my power, trying to get a sense of our surroundings, but the Forgotten resisted me, its essence slippery and elusive, like trying to grasp smoke with bare hands. This place was a manifestation of everything I had locked away, everything I had tried to erase from existence. And it didn't appreciate our intrusion.

"We need to find shelter," I said. "Somewhere defensible where we can regroup and plan our next move."

Paesha let out a humorless laugh. "Shelter. In this place. Right. And I suppose you'll just conjure up a cozy little cottage with a white picket fence while you're at it? I don't suppose you banished a castle in one of your giant god tantrums?"

Despite the situation, I felt my lips twitch into a smile. "I was thinking more along the lines of a creepy abandoned ruin, but I'm open to suggestions."

"Maybe a giant bathtub and fully stocked kitchen?" Her Remnants calmed slightly at the familiar rhythm of our banter. "No? Fine. Find the creepy house, but if we get eaten, remember I'll die but you'll live eternity in the stomach of a monster. Unless he shits you out."

"I'll find a way to send you back before I let you get eaten," I said seriously.

She lifted a shoulder and I could see the discomfort. Too much too soon was going to push her too far, and I'd never get her back. I tightened my grip on her hand, drawing comfort from the contact even as my mind raced to find a solution to dangers around us. We picked a direction and started walking, straining to see through the oppressive gloom.

Shapes began to emerge from the darkness as we pressed forward, crumbling walls, shattered statues, the bones of buildings long forgotten. The architecture was unsettling, with jagged edges and impossible angles. I'd forgotten these things and the realms they used to belong to. They weren't here simply because they were banished, but because they were altogether forgotten. By everyone.

Paesha gasped and jerked to a stop. Drifting through the ruins were ghosts of the Forgotten. They paid us no mind as they passed, their transparent forms phasing through the decaying walls, their faces locked in expressions of unending sorrow or distant blankness. I saw gods I had banished millennia ago, their once-powerful forms reduced to little more than wispy echoes. I saw mortals too, those whose lives had been erased from history for their crimes.

"They look so lost. Do you think they know where they are? Who they were?"

"I don't know," I admitted. "This place is a reflection of my own actions. My own failures. I thought I was maintaining balance, but look at the cost."

"You didn't create their crimes or their choices. You only created the punishment."

"And what gives me the right to such a punishment? Forever is a long time." The questions that had haunted me for eons spilled out, the doubts I had never voiced, never allowed myself to fully contemplate. "If I was wrong, even once, then an innocent soul suffers eternal oblivion because of me."

Paesha was quiet for a long moment as we walked, the only sound the soft whisper of her Remnants and the echoey rasp of our footsteps on the cracked obsidian ground. When she spoke again, her voice was softer, almost gentle.

"Regret is a heavy burden for anyone to bear. But it means you're not as far gone as you think. It means there's still a shred of decency in you, something real and raw and honest. Don't let this place trick you into believing you're as much of a monster as the ones you locked away."

Her words settled into my chest, a flicker of warmth amidst the chill of this forsaken realm. She still saw something in me worth believing in. It was more than I deserved, but I clung to it like a lifeline.

"There," I said, pointing to a structure that looked marginally more intact than the rest. "That might work as a temporary sanctuary."

Paesha eyed the crumbling house. "Remember that time you revealed yourself as the Lord of the Salt? But just before that you built it up to be someone else? Please tell me this is where you reveal your secret career as an interior decorator."

I huffed a laugh as we approached the ruin, shadows still writhing at the edges of my vision. The battered stone walls formed a rough excuse for a shelter, with half a roof still clinging stubbornly overhead.

"It's not the Parlor, but it'll have to do."

We stepped inside. Paesha's Remnants spread out to fill the space, mapping every crack and crevice. In the center of the single room, a tarnished oven flared to life, casting distorted shadows on the walls.

"Cozy," Paesha deadpanned, but I could hear the exhaustion beneath the sarcasm. She sank down against the wall furthest from the entrance, pulling her knees up to her chest. Her Remnants wove around her in a protective cocoon, restless and agitated. And then she was there. Not the strong, punch you in the face and steal your wallet woman she pretended to be, not the woman with thick armor and thicker mental walls. It was her. Just her. The one that'd kissed me in the rain. The one that'd run into my arms when Jasper had been taken. Just the woman.

She'd been steadfast and shaken, resilient and unraveling, all within a breath of time. The whiplash of her emotions were another burden she bore, laced with madness, comforted by her anger and held together by the sheer force of her will. She burned and froze in equal measure, a storm barely contained, her fury the only thing keeping her from breaking entirely. But she'd let me see it all and that was enough for now.

I joined her on the floor but was careful not to touch. I knew she was at her limit, her mind and body pushed to the brink by this place and the voices that plagued her. She melted. Her shoulders sagged as she laid her head on her knees and took a deep, full bodied breath and released it.

"Paesha, I—" I started, but she cut me off with a sharp shake of her head.

"Don't. Not now." Her eyes met mine, glittering with unshed tears in the sickly light. "I can't... I can't do the apologies and the promises and the lies right now. I'm doing my best, okay? I'm just doing my best."

I swallowed the words and the desperate need to fix what I'd broken. This was vulnerability, something rare coming from her. "Okay," I said instead, infusing the single word with all the understanding and acceptance I could muster. "What do you need?"

She tipped her head back against the wall as her eyes fluttered closed. "Distract me. Talk to me about anything else. Tell me a story that doesn't end in blood and betrayal. Where there's no madness. No voices of every woman you've ever loved."

I hesitated for a moment before reaching out and taking her hand. She tensed but didn't pull away, allowing the contact as if it were a lifeline tethering her to sanity.

"Once, in a realm far from here, there was a god who thought he knew everything."

And so I began to spin a tale as old as time, my voice low and steady in the eerie quiet of our temporary haven. I spoke of the wonders I had seen in my long existence, the beauty and strangeness of worlds beyond mortal understanding. I wove stories of hope and humor, of small kindnesses and unexpected joys. All the while, I watched her face, seeing the lines of tension slowly ease, the Remnants calming their frenzied dance as she lost herself in the fantastical escape.

In that moment, huddled together against the creeping dark, I let myself believe that we could find a way through this nightmare. That the forgotten corners of my own black soul could be the key to saving us both. But deep down, in the secret spaces where even gods fear to tread, Ezra's final warning lingered like a serpent poised to strike:

She will betray you. She will be your end.

And I knew, with a godsdamn certainty, that the worst was yet to come.

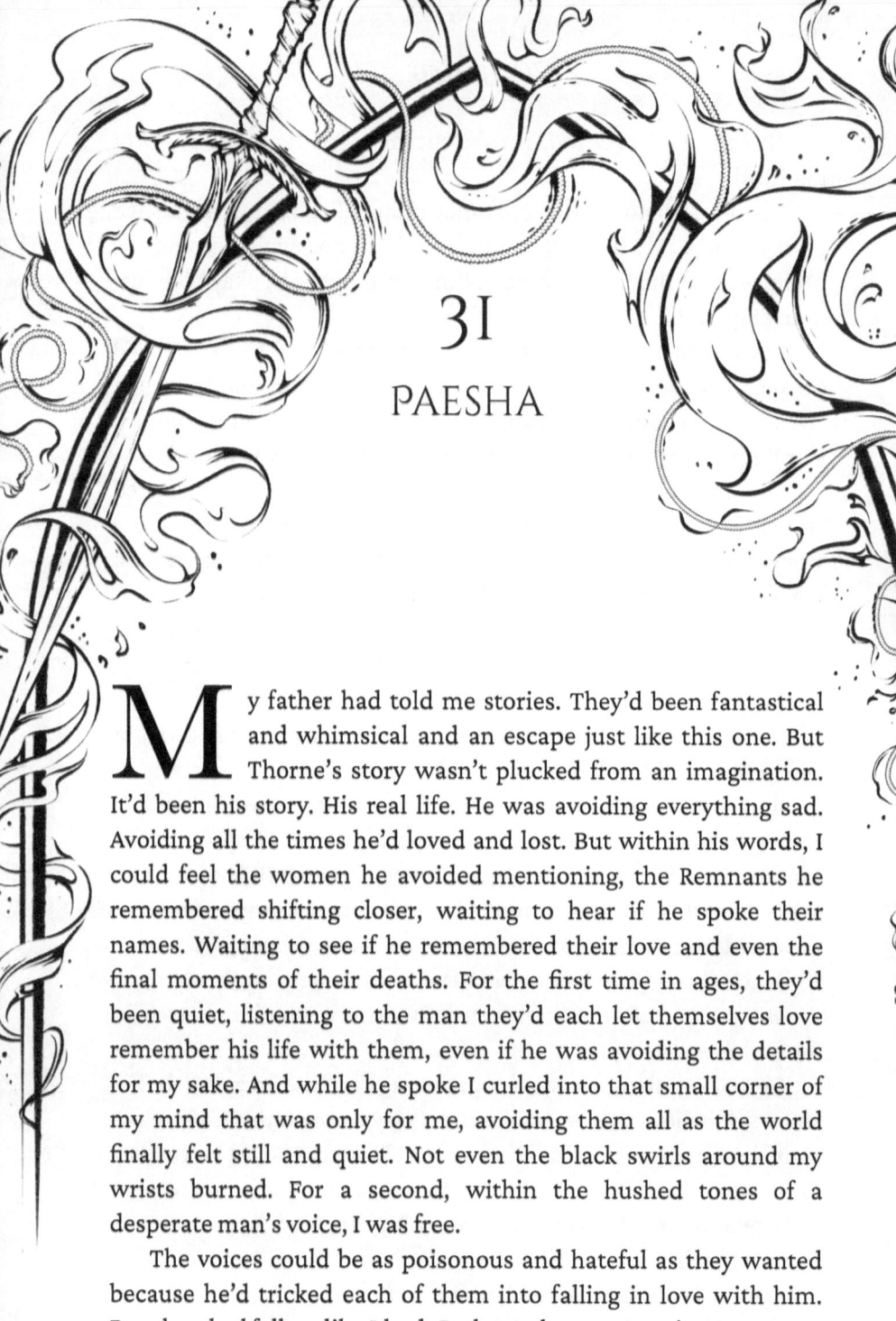

31

PAESHA

My father had told me stories. They'd been fantastical and whimsical and an escape just like this one. But Thorne's story wasn't plucked from an imagination. It'd been his story. His real life. He was avoiding everything sad. Avoiding all the times he'd loved and lost. But within his words, I could feel the women he avoided mentioning, the Remnants he remembered shifting closer, waiting to hear if he spoke their names. Waiting to see if he remembered their love and even the final moments of their deaths. For the first time in ages, they'd been quiet, listening to the man they'd each let themselves love remember his life with them, even if he was avoiding the details for my sake. And while he spoke I curled into that small corner of my mind that was only for me, avoiding them all as the world finally felt still and quiet. Not even the black swirls around my wrists burned. For a second, within the hushed tones of a desperate man's voice, I was free.

The voices could be as poisonous and hateful as they wanted because he'd tricked each of them into falling in love with him. But they *had* fallen, like I had. Perhaps they were trying to protect me. But it was more than that. It was revenge. Unwavering vengeance. Even as they listened to the quiet lulls between his words.

Something that didn't feel like hatred seeped into my tiny corner though. Something that felt like understanding and defiance. A new Remnant, maybe. A silent one. That met me in the only place there was peace. Whatever it was simply curled around me for a second and whisked away, leaving me aching for the soothing way she'd comforted me and then left me to my solitude.

As Thorne's voice faded into the eerie silence of our temporary refuge, I felt the weight of exhaustion settle deep in my bones. I wanted nothing more than to surrender to the oblivion of sleep, to let the darkness take me far away from this nightmare and the god who haunted my every step.

My thoughts drifted to Quill, her serious face and boundless curiosity a balm to my battered soul. I tried to picture her eyes, to conjure the exact shade of her hair, but the details slipped away like water through cupped hands. Panic rising, I reached for other memories, other anchors to the life I'd known. Archer's easy smile, the sound of the coins he carried in his pockets, those remained clear. But Elowen? I could see her kind face, hear the cadence of her voice, but the color of her eyes eluded me, fading into a blur.

I jerked upright and Thorne was on his feet in an instant, spinning toward the opening of the crumbling shelter. "What's wrong?"

"I can't remember," I whispered, my voice trembling. "Quill's hair, Elowen's eyes... it's like they're fading away."

He turned back to me and fell to his knees, his eyes widened. "The Forgotten. Of course. It's not simply a prison. The longer we stay here, the more it will strip away from you."

I shook my head. "I can't lose them, Thorne. I can't lose myself."

He reached for me, his touch gentle as he cradled my face in his hands. "You won't. I won't let that happen."

I watched as he closed his eyes, his brow furrowing in concentration. A faint golden glow began to emanate from his skin, growing brighter with each passing second until it enveloped us both in its warm radiance. I gasped as the light seeped into my mind, illuminating the corners where my memories had begun to fade. Suddenly, I could see Quill's wild brown curls, hear Elowen's soothing lilt, feel the love and laughter that had sustained me through so many trials.

It was ridiculous to mourn something so simple and I knew it. But when everything in my mind was a battle, I couldn't lose something else. The godsdamn tears burned as they filled my eyes. I was so fucking beaten down and done. But Thorne's magic wove a delicate shield around my thoughts, protecting them from the Forgotten's insidious grasp. As I settled into the relief of having my most precious memories restored, I couldn't help but notice the toll it took on him. His face grew pale, lines of strain appearing around his eyes and mouth as he poured more and more of his power into the effort of safeguarding my mind.

I shoved him away from me, breaking the connection. "Stop."

"A thousand years of agony would be worth it, if it meant keeping you whole," he said. "I made this prison, Paesha. I filled it with horrible things and shattered lives. The least I can do is shield you from its cruelty."

"It's not the least you could do, but draining yourself when we're sitting here like prey waiting to be plucked up by whatever other nightmares exist in this place seems foolish."

"I'm not going to let anything happen to you. You realize that, right? I need you to look at me and see the truth in those words."

I snorted, rising to my feet as the fury I'd been holding on to for this man continued to grow. He didn't get it. Didn't see his own damn lies. "I need *you* to look at *me* and see every life I lost in your arms before you say shit like that. You're wrong. I'm damned. The Hunted and the Huntress, remember? There's not a fucking thing you can do to stop where this is going and we all know that. But keep saying all the pretty words that make you feel better about yourself so when I die, you can think back on the moments you lied to my face about your devout protection and see the look in my eyes as I believed you. Shall we fucking pretend right now? Will that make you feel better? Soothe your soul?

That's all that matters, right? That you feel better about yourself when I die?"

He took a deep breath and moved to his feet, crossing his arms over his chest. The glint in his glasses infuriated me. He probably didn't even need those.

"You want to lay it all out there?" he asked. "Tell me what you want from me. Stop condemning me and tell me how I make this better for you, dammit. I can't fix it if you aren't going to let me."

"Fix it? What do you mean, fix it? If you haven't been able to stop this cycle for a thousand lifetimes, what makes you so confident this is your redemption life?"

"Because you're still fucking here. Now tell me what you want from me."

I shook my head, hardly able to breathe beyond the audacity of that damn question nor the answer. "I want the impossible. I want to go back to a time before I knew the truth about you, about us. I want to forget every lie, every betrayal, every moment I spent falling for a man who was nothing more than a godsdamn mask."

Thorne flinched as if I'd struck him, but he held his ground. "I never lied about my feelings for you, Paesha. Not once. Every time I held you, every time I hoped to save you, it was real."

Shadows swarmed around my feet, eager for the anger boiling within me to spill over. They turned to claws, reaching into the ground and digging.

"No. That shit was still wrapped in lies. Lord of the Salt? Suffering beneath the hand of a prince? No wonder you were so pissed when Archer and I went down to his lair. You had no control, even in the reality you concocted. There was no need to fear him. You were the villain in all of that, weren't you? You could have stopped him at any point, and you didn't because it didn't fit your fucking narrative." I laughed. "You couldn't stop yourself from playing god, from orchestrating misery over and over again. What kind of love is that, Thorne? What kind of twisted devotion leads to centuries of suffering?"

"The kind that's too stubborn to let go," he said, his voice low and fierce. "My power is failing. I couldn't kill the prince because

283

he's protected by the Fates' law. Gods cannot directly kill or stop a royal. Those thrones come with their own ranks of power."

I scoffed, disbelief coloring my words. "Harlow died at the hands of Ezra's men, and she was technically a princess, so keep lying. Dig your holes, fucker. But I'll dig deeper. I'll dig a grave and let you fall in."

"It doesn't matter," he countered. "She wasn't recognized. The law only applies to acknowledged heirs. It's part of the balance. Everything is part of the failing balance."

"That doesn't make sense," I argued, my voice rising with each word. "If it were true and you wanted to keep me alive, then why not put me on a fucking throne and let me live?"

Thorne's shoulders slumped, the fight draining out of him as he looked at me with an expression so raw, so vulnerable, it stole my breath. "I tried, Paesha. In one lifetime, I did everything in my power to guide you back to a throne you'd lost. You were already a queen, but you'd lost your crown." He closed his eyes, pain etched into every line of his face. "The moment I broke and told you everything about our connection, it all fell apart. You were killed almost immediately."

I swallowed hard, a distant memory tugging at the edges of my consciousness. A flash of a crown, heavy upon my brow. The bitter taste of hard truths. And beneath it all, a love so fierce, so consuming, it burned like wildfire in my veins. In that confession, I could feel her again. The fallen queen that sent another wave of peace into that corner of my mind the others couldn't find. She'd known. She'd known and loved him anyway.

"I couldn't bear to watch you die like that again," Thorne said. "So I stopped trying to interfere with mortal thrones."

The scowl never left my face. "How terrible that must have been for you."

He shook his head. "With or without me, you were always going to die."

"But why?" I couldn't help the vulnerability in my voice, wrapped around a simple, complicated question. "Why am I damned?"

He moved closer, but he was careful, eyes shifting between mine as he spoke. "Ezra's full title is Supreme Sovereign, the Unerring Arbiter of Unmaking and the Infinite, and the Keeper of All Realms, Keeper of Guardians. His power lies in the future while mine lies in the past. He can see what lies ahead. A thousand paths of possibility and it's his nature to unmake those that would destroy everything. When Sylvie was born to Alastor and Irri, he saw a dangerous path. The Huntress would be the one to break the balance between the gods. The Fates confirmed it with a prophecy about you. But it was always only a possibility. He told me there could be peace here. He denies it now, but I'll never forget those words."

"Then why not let me die?"

"Before I met you, I thought that was the way forward. I trusted my brother implicitly to know what I didn't just as he trusted me. But he shouldn't have. Because I wanted the power you promised. I believed the prophecy meant that you would choose a brother to reign and a brother to fall. I sought you out, determined to be the chosen. Determined to let Ezra fall if it meant my rise."

I stepped away from him. "So, you've always been a selfish bastard."

He followed, fully aware of what his proximity did to my resolve. "Yes. Always. But never more than the first time my soul saw yours and knew immediately what you were."

"Weak?" I asked, stepping back again.

"No. You're my other half. My Ever. Whatever damnation your soul carries, so does mine, because we share it. And there's no way in any realm, any universe, that I could be anything but fully yours. My heart is consumed by you. My mind, broken by you. But my soul? My soul, Paesha? It's not just mine. It's yours, wholly and completely. Every shattered piece, every spark of light and shadow, it all belongs to you. And it always will, no matter how many times we break and mend and break again."

A new voice swirled through my mind. Not the cold tone of Winter's nor the serpent that felt like Sylvie. This was honey. This was grace. This was pure logic. *You knew this would be hard. He's had a thousand lifetimes of experience to break down our walls. You're smarter than this. You know what will happen if you let him in. It's not about dying. It's about living. You need to make a choice to die beside him or live without him. That's the only way this ends. You can leave him here. You can take Irri back to Alastor and leave him behind. All you have to do is use us. Let us break the door once you've passed through, just like you broke the veil. Let him live here and forget. Maybe there's peace in that for him too.*

It felt like there was mercy for us both within those words. A difficult choice, but ultimately, probably the right one. He couldn't know. He would try to stop me. And he'd kept his fair share of secrets so this felt like redemption.

"Come back to me," he whispered. "I can see you slipping away to the madness. Don't. Don't cave to the voices."

My eyes snapped to his. "All these lifetimes, it's always been because you think you have some kind of claim over me?"

Thorne shook his head, a sad smile tugging at the corners of his mouth. "No, Paesha darling. It's because you have a claim over me. That's always been our ruin. You have led, and I have followed. You have breathed, and I have suffocated. You have danced, and I have stumbled, trying desperately to keep up with the wild, untamable rhythm of our soul."

He reached out, his fingers hovering a hairsbreadth from my cheek, close enough that I could feel the heat of his skin, the crackle of power that always seemed to emanate from him. "I am yours, Paesha Vox. In this life and every one before. I'm bound to you, not by destiny or duty, but the simple, inescapable truth that my soul knows yours, and it will never stop seeking its other half."

I stepped away, needing distance, needing air. Because I could break for this man and I knew it. I could hear the logic in his words too. Was there justification to his ruse if it was done to save my life? Would I have rather been lied to or have that fucking arrow pierce my heart?

"Do you know what it's like," I finally asked, "to have your entire world shattered in an instant? To discover that everything you believed was built on lies?"

When I turned back to face him, I expected to see that same pleading expression, that desperate need for absolution. Instead, I saw something that made my breath catch—raw, unfiltered grief.

"Every time," he said, his voice cracking. "Every single time I've lost you, it's been exactly that. The world doesn't just shatter, Paesha. It ceases to exist."

I took another step back but Thorne followed, his body crowding mine until my back hit the rough stone wall. His hands came up to cage me in. "I can't change the past. But I'm here now, and I'm not going anywhere."

"You will if I tell you to. That was the bargain, remember? You can't stand in my way anymore."

"Then I'll stand on the sidelines."

The heat of him, the scent of him, it filled my senses until I couldn't think, couldn't breathe. I looked up at him, my gaze drawn to his lips. In that moment, I wanted nothing more than to close the distance between us, to lose myself in the taste and feel of him. To let myself be selfish before I walked away. To take and take from him as he'd taken from me.

Do it. Let him think he's finally broken through your defenses.

I hesitated, torn between the desire to give in, to lose myself in the intoxicating pull of his presence, and the knowledge that this was a dangerous game, one I couldn't afford to lose. But as he looked at me, as he loomed over me filling every inch of the room with that beautiful body, the decision was made. I could take what I wanted. Give him one taste of what could be, before I ripped it all away. The thought was cruel, calculated, and entirely too tempting. I let that temptation consume me, transforming me from the woman who wanted to run into a vengeful siren who could bring a man to his knees with a single smile.

"I can't deny there's a part of me that doesn't want you on the sidelines," I said, glancing between his lips and those fucking eyes. "But I think you know that. I think you've always known that."

He lifted my chin with his hand, before sliding his fingers down to rest gently on my throat. "Of course I have. We share a soul."

I moved to my toes, sliding my hands up until they locked behind his neck. "I already know I'm going to regret this," I said truthfully.

He smiled, leaning down until his lips were less than an inch from mine. "Welcome to my entire existence."

And then I kissed him, deeply, fiercely, with all the pent up passion and fury of a thousand lifetimes. He froze for an instant, before melting into me with a groan that sounded like surrender.

I poured everything into that kiss, every ounce of the desire and desperation that had haunted me. I nipped at his bottom lip, soothed the sting with my tongue, and reveled in the way his fingers tightened on my throat, pulling me impossibly closer. It was electric, magnetic—a clash of wills and a meeting of souls that left me breathless and aching. But beneath the heat and the hunger, I could feel the colder, more calculating part of myself waiting, biding its time. This push and pull between us was over.

I broke the kiss, inching back only enough to look into his eyes, to see the hope and the love and the unguarded vulnerability shining there. And I smiled, a slow, wicked thing that held the promise of pleasure and the threat of pain in equal measure.

"Paesha," he breathed, my name a prayer and a plea on his tongue.

But I was already stepping back, slipping out of his grasp like smoke. The voices in my head hummed their approval, urging me onward. I turned away, a small, secret smile playing at the corners of my mouth. Thorne would follow me to the ends of the world, into the heart of the Forgotten. And when the time came, when I had what I needed, I would leave him here to suffer the same fate he'd condemned so many others to.

It was a betrayal, cold and calculated and cruel. But it was necessary. To save us both, to break the cycle of love and loss and endless suffering, I had to become the monster. And as I stepped out into the waiting dark, I felt a piece of my humanity crumble away, replaced by something harder, sharper, forged in the fires of the Forgotten.

"We should go," I said, stopping at the opening of our shelter. "I don't want to be in this place any longer than we need to be."

32

THORNE

There was a part of me that wanted to confess I'd seen that siren's shift as easily as I'd watched the sun rise and fall over Stirling yesterday. But fuck if I wasn't desperate for her. And those godsdamn lips. So, if all she offered was ruin, I'd take it gladly. If she meant to watch me burn, I'd set the fire myself, just to feel her warmth before the flames took me.

As I followed her out of the shelter, the sound of rushing water echoed through the twisted landscape, its source hidden by the darkness. Paesha tilted her head, listening before changing direction without a word. I followed, as I always had. As I always would, even when my instincts screamed that we were walking deeper into danger.

"There's something familiar about that sound," she murmured, more to herself than to me. Her Remnants swirled at her feet, leading the way like eager hounds on a scent. "Like a waterfall, but... wrong. Hollow."

The roar grew louder as we picked our way through the ruins. Fragments of forgotten architecture rose around us, columns that defied gravity, archways that led nowhere, stairs that spiraled up.

290

The patches of heavy darkness were thinning out, and finally we could see what was hiding within the shadows of the Forgotten.

When we reached the source of the sound, Paesha's breath caught, and on instinct alone, I whipped to attention, worried she'd seen something I missed. But it was only a massive ravine that split the landscape like an open wound, stretching endlessly in either direction. Far below, something that might have been water once, but was now thick and dark, churned and crashed against jagged rocks.

Through the rolling fog that spilled over the edges of the chasm, I could barely make out the shapes of buildings on the far side, a forgotten city slowly being reclaimed by strange, twisted vegetation. At our feet, spanning the vast emptiness between, was a bridge that looked barely stable enough to hold a whisper.

"There's movement over there," Paesha said, her head tilting at that odd angle again. "Can't you see them? Walking between the buildings?"

I adjusted my glasses, squinting beyond the fog.

She laughed. Truly laughed. "Wait, do you actually need those glasses?"

I lifted a brow. "I haven't always needed them, as I'm sure you've noticed from the glimpses of our history. But there's something wrong with our power, and currently it's affecting my vision. I was created to see the past, Paesha darling. Not the present, as it turns out."

"Well, that's not true, is it? Beginnings and endings and all that? Endings sounds like the future."

"You'd be surprised. I have no visions of what's coming, only the task of committing it to memory as it all happens. There are specific things that lend to that title, but none so final as Death."

"You've met Death. He's okay. A little moody when he's hungry."

She inched toward the crumbling stone bridge. "Well, this looks perfectly safe." Her head jerked to the side suddenly, a sharp, unnatural movement. "No one asked you," she muttered to whatever voice had interrupted her thoughts.

I forced myself to stay still, to not reach for her even as she swayed closer to the edge. Centuries of decay had eaten away at the stone until it was more air than substance. Far below, that dark liquid continued its relentless assault against the rocks.

"I don't suppose any of you know which way we should go?" Paesha asked the air, her head tilting again. She barked out a laugh that held no humor before turning to me, rolling her eyes. "My drove of past lives are apparently terrible with directions. Shocking for a group of Huntresses, really. Who knew death could make you so useless?"

I looked beyond her, studying the parapet across the ravine before watching the buildings. "If there are people over there, one could be Irri."

"Wow. Thank you. I hadn't considered that at all," she dead-panned before stepping onto the bridge without hesitation.

Even here, in this nightmare realm, she moved with a dancer's grace that stole my breath. Her feet found purchase on a stone that looked too fragile to trust, her balance perfect despite the crumbling surface. The Remnants swirled around her ankles, more agitated than usual, but she paid them no mind, glancing back at me, a challenge in her mismatched eyes. "Coming? Or are you waiting for a pretty invitation from that weaver thing?"

I followed and found myself watching the elegant line of her spine, the confident set of her shoulders, the way she seemed to float above the danger. A hard set of my jaw and fists at my side were the only way I could keep from reaching for her. The way I wanted to yank her back to the safe side of the ravine practically fucking consumed me. The bridge swayed as we reached the halfway point. I dared a look over the edge, but the fog had grown so thick below us, I couldn't see beyond it.

"Not scared of heights, are you?" she asked, taking another confident step, though I could see the slight tremble in her legs.

"Immortal, remember. Death isn't a fear for me."

"How about pain? Or like an eternity stuck down there?"

I moved closer to her. "Thinking of pushing me in, Paesha darling?"

She spun back to look at me. "I would never."

A sudden gust of wind came up in an instant. Her foot slipped, sending her forward. I lunged to steady her. Holding her to my chest, her hands gripped my shirt as she regained her balance. For a heartbeat time froze, the howling wind and grinding stone fading away until there was nothing but her, the warmth of her body against mine, the slight tremor in her fingers, and the way her breath caught.

When she turned to look up at me, the carefully constructed walls were gone. No seduction. No hatred. Just her, vulnerable and real. Her mismatched eyes held echoes of the woman who'd kissed me in the rain, who'd trusted me enough to let me stay with her through the nightmares. Who'd believed in the possibility of us before she knew everything.

I memorized every detail of that unguarded moment, the slight part of her lips, the way her pulse fluttered at her throat, the softness in her gaze that made my ancient heart ache with longing. But I didn't dare trust it, didn't dare believe it was anything more than instinct that made her cling to me. She needed her walls right now. Needed that armor to protect herself from this place. From me.

"Slow and steady," I whispered, helping her regain her footing. She did so with that innate grace, carefully extracting herself from my arms. I hated how much I preferred her there. Hated how dependent my life had become on these small moments. Loving her was so much fucking harder than losing her this time.

We pressed on in silence until we reached solid ground. Blissful, unwavering solid ground. Voices drifted through the mist, actual voices, not the whispers of this damn realm.

"I'm going to defer to your ancient and general know-it-all annoyingness, high and mighty god. There are definitely people past that wall. Do we blend in, or try to avoid them?"

I dropped my chin, gesturing to her entourage of shadows. "Have you seen yourself? There's no blending in unless you can control those things."

"Right," she said, drawing the word out as she held back a

smile and the Remnants crept up her body. Though she wore long black sleeves and leather trousers, I knew without asking where they'd gone. They were like Alastor's, likely swirling over her skin like tattoos.

"Might've been helpful to mention you'd learned how to control them."

She pressed her lips together. "Might've been helpful to mention you were some ageless, all-powerful deity treating mortal lives like your own personal board game, but alas, here we are."

I stared at her for longer than I should have, holding back the repetitive apology. She didn't need it, didn't want it, and was likely baiting me to see if I'd deliver another.

"If things get bad, I'll open the door back to Stirling. You go through it no matter what. Agreed?"

"Question. Real quick. If you can open a door back and forth, why wouldn't you have agreed to come here sooner? Why leave Irri trapped in the Forgotten when you've known she's all Alastor wanted?"

I ran a hand down my face, already hating this conversation. But she deserved the truth, even if it burned coming out. "Something will happen while we are here. I'm not meant to leave the Forgotten, Paesha."

Her eyes doubled in size. "Come again?"

"Ezra saw it. Any path where I entered the Forgotten, I would never return. He warned me centuries ago. All of the gods learned of it. It became taboo to even speak of this place."

Her eyes narrowed. "And you didn't think that was worth mentioning before I decided to tag along?"

"I tried." My voice came out rougher than intended. "Outside the Vale, I told you to go home. To return to your family."

"That's not the same as 'Hey, by the way, this is a one-way trip.'" She crossed her arms, fury radiating from every line of her body. "You're still making choices for me."

The pause heightened the tension between us. "Never once in all of his threats did he mention you'd be stuck here with me. Nor

Irri. And believe me, he'd have mentioned it to keep me from coming. If I can never leave, I could never find you again."

Her eyes went from focusing on me to practically seeing through me and I knew why. At this point, she was no longer trying to hide the insidious Remnants' thoughts. Movement in the fog drew our attention back to the city ahead of us. People drifted through the streets. Hordes of people, actually. And though it was overgrown with trees and vines creeping along the ground and up the walls, they seemed almost normal.

Paesha moved closer to me as we watched them, close enough that her shoulder brushed mine. Whether she sought comfort or not, I didn't question it. I'd take what scraps of contact she offered.

"It's not... There's a market. Look." She pointed to a collection of half broken carts lined up on the crumbling stone square. "There's a fully functioning city here if you can get past the creepy shit."

I smiled. Not because of what it was, but because of that spark. She'd gotten that same look in her eyes when she and Archer were about to do something reckless. Another familiar piece of her. She held a hand out to me, and I thought she did it without realizing. She dragged me along as she stepped through the gap in the wall and into the forgotten city.

A few faces sparked familiarity as we moved toward the marketplace, a poet whose words had moved mountains until the world forgot his name, a queen whose kingdom had been erased from maps and memories when she'd turned on her people. But most were strangers, lost to time in ways even I couldn't recall.

"How many people did you banish here?" Paesha asked, watching a woman try to barter with a hooded man.

"Most of these souls weren't banished," I said quietly. "They were forgotten. When the world stops remembering you exist, this is where you end up. A merchant who never made a sale. A fisherman without a family to return to. A love story that never began. They all come here, carried by the same magic that makes people forget them."

"That's horrifying."

"Yes. It is."

"Look at the edges of their bodies. They're fading away."

I nodded, looking at the same cluster of people she was. "Remember what a broken soul looks like? That must be the equivalent of a forgotten soul."

The marketplace was unlike anything I'd seen across countless realms. There were stalls filled with glass containers that glowed. Some that seemed to vibrate. Some were full of darkness and some, empty. A young woman, her edges softly blurred like a watercolor painting left in the rain, stood behind a table of delicate bottles. Her movements were whimsical and uncertain, as if she couldn't quite remember how she'd gotten there or why she held the small pink bottle in her hands.

"Would you like to feel love again?" she asked, though her voice suggested she didn't fully understand the question. She uncorked the bottle, and as the soft pink essence drifted out, the memory hit me with startling clarity, the nervous anticipation, the thundering heart, the tentative press of lips. Someone's first kiss, preserved and bottled like fine wine and then forgotten all together.

Another vendor, an elderly man whose form flickered like a candle flame, cradled a jar that held golden sunlight. When he lifted the lid, the sound of children's laughter and the scent of grass spilled into the air, carrying with it the pure joy of a perfect summer day. Each memory was a tangible thing here, stripped from those who'd been forgotten and traded like precious gems.

"What's that?" Paesha asked, pointing to a shimmering cloth that seemed to catch light that didn't exist.

"I..." The merchant's brow furrowed. "I don't quite remember. Something important. Something about... rising? Or was it falling?" She shook her head, confusion clouding her features. "Was I the one who rose? I like flowers."

Paesha's eyes narrowed before her shoulders stiffened. She'd seen herself in that broken woman. Had felt that kind of madness and it must have scared her. I led her forward, but her grasp on her

Remnants had faltered. They'd seeped onto the ground around her feet, and I caught sight of a merchant eyeing them with too much interest.

"You need something to cover up," I murmured, steering her toward a stall draped with fabrics that rippled like smoke.

Another elderly man, with dark skin as wrinkled as sun-dried leather, smiled vacantly. "Looking for something special?"

"A cloak," I said, studying the options.

"A cloak from where?" he asked, then immediately looked confused by his own question.

I slipped my glasses off, watching the merchant's vacant eyes focus on them with sudden interest. Something about the golden frames sparked recognition in his otherwise empty gaze.

"These should cover it," I said, holding them out.

"Oh yes, very valuable. Very..." he trailed off, already forgetting what he was agreeing to. He handed over a cloak that absorbed the shadows around it. "I think I made this?"

"Wait," Paesha said, her hand catching my wrist. "You need your glasses."

"I'll be fine."

Before I could argue, she spun her back to the old man, swiped a scarf that rippled like liquid moonlight from the cart, and shoved it up her sleeve. Slowing her pace, she drew the old man's attention again as she pointed. "What's this one made of?"

"Yes. We should ask the owner," he answered.

She smiled genuinely at the old man and it broke something inside of me. I loved that damn smile. The shine in her eyes, the whisper of wrinkles forming around her eyes. That smile broke me and mended me. Drowned me and revived me. If I was destined to lose everything in the Forgotten, that memory would be the one I clung to when everything else was gone.

She pulled the stolen scarf from her sleeve. The merchant's eyes lit up at the sight of it. "Maybe you'd consider trading this very fine silk for those old glasses."

"You would give me such a bargain?" the old man asked.

"Because you've been so kind," she said, gently.

With the trade done, she slid the glasses back onto my face with a wink. "There. Problem solved."

I arched an eyebrow as we walked away from the old man that threw the scarf over his own shoulders.

She shrugged, already wrapping herself in the shadow cloak. "He's never going to remember it anyway." Her fingers worked the clasp at her throat. "Besides, the last thing I need is you stumbling around this nightmare realm like a drunken fool because you can't see. For fuck's sake, what were you thinking?"

We moved deeper into the forgotten city, past vendors trading in lost memories and broken dreams. Ahead, a castle rose against the dark sky, its towers partially collapsed as if the stone had forgotten how to hold itself together. The fog rolled through the streets in thick waves, obscuring and revealing the wandering souls that called this place home.

I kept close to Paesha's side, watching how she studied every-thing with those keen eyes. Even here she moved like she owned every shadow, every secret. But something felt wrong. The hair on the back of my neck stood up, and I caught a flicker of movement in my peripheral vision. Someone else was watching us too intently, moving when we moved, stopping when we stopped.

"Don't look," I murmured close to her ear. "But we're being followed. About twenty paces back."

The footsteps behind us grew closer. Without thinking, I grabbed her arm and pulled her into a narrow alley between two crumbling buildings. She started to protest, but I pressed my hand over her mouth, crowding her against the wall with my body. Her eyes went wide, but she didn't fight me.

I could feel every inch where we touched, her chest rising and falling against mine, her breath warm against my palm, her fingers gripping my shirt as worried eyes stared into mine. My thumb brushed her cheek without my permission, and she made a small sound that nearly shattered my restraint.

"There's only one," I breathed against her ear. "They've been following since the bridge."

She nodded. Her pulse raced beneath my fingers, matching the frantic beat of my own heart. When I finally lowered my hand from her mouth, it settled on her hip instead, keeping her pressed against the wall. For protection, I told myself. Nothing more.

"Thorne," she whispered, and my name on her lips was almost my undoing.

The sound of footsteps passing the alley saved me from myself. But still, I couldn't bring myself to step away, to break this moment of charged tension between us. Her fingers flexed against my chest, and I couldn't tell if she meant to push me away or pull me closer.

"We should..." she started, then swallowed hard. "We should keep moving."

"We should," I agreed, but didn't move.

Neither did she.

Until a familiar voice shattered the moment.

33
PAESHA

He'd fallen further and further and further with every second I let him hold my hand. With every calculated step toward him. Each glance. I could see how much he wanted these moments to be real. He was desperate for them. For me. And maybe I was a little desperate for him too, but that wasn't from my choosing. Simply my fate, it seemed. Bound to him as his Ever, but also destined to trap him here. He'd known his fate and still he let me guide him into a trap. Poor, poor god.

His thumb traced idle patterns on my hip, and I fought the urge to lean into his touch. In this moment, I couldn't tell if it was me that wanted it, or the Remnants, or even the siren, luring her prey. This was dangerous. Not the stranger following us, but this manu-factured intimacy, this pretense of protection that felt too much like possession. Like belonging.

Don't forget what he is, Sylvie whispered, finally breaking her silence. *What he's done.*

"Miss Paesha?"

The familiar voice shattered the tension like a stone through glass. I shoved Thorne away, my eyes finding the figure at the mouth of the alley. I could hardly believe it. Jasper. The whiplash of all my feelings for him came rushing back. The burn of the flames from his poison. The capture by Ezra's men. Ultimately, Harlow's death at their hands. He was so, so guilty for so many things, but in his imprisonment, he wasn't guilty at all. Just as I'd had no choice when Alastor made a command, neither did he. And the guilt must have eaten him alive.

He stood there, looking somehow both older and less substantial than when I'd last seen him, but it was undeniably him. Still tall, still round in the midsection, with a curly brown mustache. But the cherry red in the balls of his cheeks had gone. The gentle light in his eyes had vanished. There was no question as to how he got here, only fucking why.

"You banished him," I snapped at Thorne, the Remnants responding to my fury, writhing beneath the cloak. "He didn't have a choice in anything he did. He was bound to Ezra like Alastor bound me, and you threw him away like garbage."

Jasper stepped forward, pulling his weathered hat from his head. His remaining arm moved with that same fluid grace I remembered from his days in the kitchen, but there was something dreamy and uncertain in his gaze. "Not at all, Miss Paesha. This was mercy."

"Mercy? This place is no mercy, Jasper. No matter what your memories might tell you. You can't trust them. You're living in a prison."

Thorne sighed. "Ezra would have kept using him, forcing him to commit increasingly horrific acts until there was nothing left of the man he used to be. I couldn't send him anywhere else because my brother would have found him out of spite alone."

"So you trapped him here instead?"

"He gave me a choice," Jasper interrupted. "Fight the binding until it destroyed everything I was, or fade away on my own terms." His smile was sad but certain. "I chose peace. The things he would have made me do... This was mercy. True mercy."

The truth of it hit me hard. I looked at Thorne, really looked at him, and saw the weight of that decision in his eyes. "You let him choose?"

"Yes."

I turned back to Jasper. "He can twist your memories. He can make you think you've done things you haven't. You may even have memories of him that aren't real. You understand that, right? You chose this life as an option given to you by a corrupt god and now you'll fade away into this place forever. I can't believe you'd choose this."

A flicker of clarity crossed his face, and he shook his head. "I never wanted my arm cut off. I knew it wasn't going to work. It was the first thing the God of Unmaking made me do. He thought if you believed me free of the prince, you'd trust me. And you did. That was *not* a choice."

I stepped closer to him, resting a hand on his shoulder. "I know you're likely going to forget this, but know that I forgive you. I can't speak for Archer. I can't release you from the guilt of Harlow's death. But I'm sorry you have to sit with that."

His eyes flickered back and forth between mine before they filled with tears. "Miss Harlow? She's dead?"

I whirled to face Thorne, ready to explode because we can't just walk around tampering with people's memories, but the raw pain in his eyes stopped me cold.

"I took that memory from him," he said softly. "That and others. The weight of what he'd done under Ezra's command. It was destroying him. I thought at least here, he deserved some peace without those particular horrors haunting his dreams."

The shame hit me like a physical blow. Here I was, so quick to condemn, when he'd been trying to grant what mercy he could. And I'd shattered that. I'd given him back the pain he didn't need.

Jasper's broken whisper made my heart clench. "Was it me? Did I... did I kill her?"

The torment in his voice, the way he stumbled backward with the weight of that possibility. I couldn't bear it. Couldn't breathe. Jasper had loved Harlow so much. They'd sat together and laughed together. She'd cooked beside him. And he'd been infinitely kind to me. He was likely the same with her. She'd loved him.

I needed a breath. A moment. But there was none. Not when he looked at me with those tear-filled eyes, knowing the truth before I could say it. This truth would poison whatever peace Jasper had found here. It would eat at him until there was nothing left but guilt and regret, and then he would be completely forgotten. And that was no way for anyone to go.

"Thorne," I said quietly, the words fighting their way past the lump in my throat as I moved away from Jasper and back to Thorne's side. "Take it again. Please."

He studied my face for a long moment before nodding. Stepping forward, he placed gentle fingers against Jasper's temple. Golden light spilled from his touch, and I watched as the anguish melted away from Jasper's features, replaced by that dreamy uncertainty.

I retreated into that quiet corner of my mind where the voices couldn't reach, where I could feel my own emotions without the influence of others. It was a kindness, what Thorne had done. A mercy I hadn't recognized until now. Taking memories didn't have to be about control or manipulation, but rather granting peace to those who would never find it otherwise.

Jasper blinked at us, his smile vague but genuine. "I was thinking about sweet rolls," he said. "The little one used to love them so much. There was a kitchen once, wasn't there? I remember... spices. And a little girl who liked sweet rolls."

My throat tightened. "That was Lianna."

"Lianna," he repeated softly, testing the name. "And Reuben."

"Yes. You remember them, don't you? Reuben has bright red hair?"

"Yes. No. Maybe. Things blur here, you see. Like water in the rain." He glanced between Thorne and me, as if realizing for the first time what our presences in this dark realm meant. "You shouldn't be here. Neither of you. This place... it takes your memories. If not by magic, then the creatures that lurk in the darkness."

Use him, Sylvie urged. *He knows the way through this cursed city.*

Let him help, Winter agreed, softer than the others. *Before you forget why you came. You cannot trust the Keeper's word.*

But in that small corner, where there was peace and warmth

from a kinder Remnant, a past life that hadn't come for vengeance, I thought maybe I could trust Thorne's word when it came to my safety. He was far too invested in all these years and all these lives. In all his lies and all his games, minimally, I believed in my soul he meant to keep me from physical harm. The mental anguish? That was a different story.

"Is there somewhere here we can find food and shelter?" Thorne asked. "We're looking for someone, but we need to rest."

Jasper's brow furrowed. "It's hard to remember where we stay from one night to the next. Sometimes I wake up in a baker's shop, sometimes in what might have been a brothel." He gestured vaguely at the twisted architecture around us. "But there are rooms. Always rooms. The people here are mostly harmless. They forget too much to hold grudges. Though watch for thieves. They remember enough to be crafty."

His expression darkened. "It's the night you need to fear. Things come out. Things that hunger for more than memories." He started walking, his gait uneven, as if he occasionally forgot how to place his feet. "I'll show you somewhere safe. I think. Yes, I remember a place. Or maybe I dreamed it."

We followed him through winding streets. Finally, he stopped before a building that might have once been an inn. The sign above the door was blank, its words long forgotten.

"Stay here," he said, already turning away. "I'll bring food. I remember where to find it. Usually." He paused, looking back with that dreamy uncertainty. "Don't go out after dark. And if you hear singing... cover your ears. Some songs aren't meant to be remembered."

As he disappeared into the fog, I couldn't help but wonder if he'd remember to come back at all.

Thorne placed a warm hand on the small of my back and led me into the old building. "The question is, who's singing?"

"I don't really see how that's relevant when he's warned you it's something dangerous."

"Oh, if it's who I think it might be, she's definitely something. Let's get inside and try to settle in. We need a plan."

I smirked. "It's nice to see there were some moments of Thorne Noctus in Stirling that were exactly the same as Thorne Noctus in reality."

He closed his eyes with a heavy sigh. "I've found you, loved you, and lost you a thousand times, Paesha. You've never once loved an amiable, shy man. But I was still myself with you. Even then."

I drew back. "Tell me you tried to be amiable just once."

He smiled and that fucking dimple showed beyond the dark stubble. "Maybe."

"Let me guess. A barkeep. Oh, no wait, stable boy. No." I snapped my fingers. "Oh my gods. You were a shy, little record keeper, weren't you?"

"You didn't even hate me in that life cycle. You didn't notice me at all. Not until the building caught fire, and I saved everyone inside. Including you."

I could feel the past life he spoke of weaving around my mind as if she stood at attention, eager to be remembered.

I followed him inside. "And let me guess, no one had any idea how the building caught fire."

"Actually," he said, shutting the door behind me. "Tuck ratted me out."

I huffed a laugh. "That's impossible. That would mean Tuck would have to be... Are you fucking kidding me?"

He spun to face me, palms out. "In his defense, he wanted to tell you himself."

"I'm going to kill him. I watched the Cimmerians beat him half to death in the prince's lair. How... What the fuck, Thorne. We almost got caught because of him."

"First of all, you weren't supposed to be down there. Second, he was never going to die at the hands of the Cimmerians. It was our best way in. I knew he wouldn't have any of the gods down there that night because they were with Alastor. He was supposed to get in and get out."

"And what lesson did we learn from that experience, Keeper?" I mocked.

"Never trust you and Archer alone," he said without missing a beat.

"Hey, you leave Archer out of this. That man is a pure soul compared to your fucked up history. I can't believe Tuck is a god. Liars. The lot of you."

"If he were here, he would point out he never explicitly told you he was human. You jumped to that conclusion on your own. And then he would follow it by reminding you that you lied about your power as well."

I rolled my eyes and walked toward a very questionable set of stairs. "So, you're saying he's about as insufferable as you are with his justifications?"

"No," he answered with a lightness to his voice. "He's far worse. Let me go first, please?"

A question. Not a command.

The inn's interior was exactly what you'd expect from a forgotten building—dust, decay, and an eerie emptiness that made every footstep echo. Thorne led me up a creaking staircase, testing each step before letting me follow. We found a room that was relatively intact, with a bed that looked mostly stable and a window that somehow still held glass, though it was clouded with age.

"There's another room down the hall." I said, dropping my cloak on a rickety chair. "The door was partially open."

He gave me a flat look. "I'm not leaving you alone in this place."

"Afraid I'll run off into the night and get eaten by whatever horrors Jasper warned us about?"

"Yes, actually." He moved to straighten a crooked painting on the wall.

I immediately walked over and tilted it back.

The dust swirled in the air as we moved around each other in the dim room. Thorne reached for the heavy curtain, pulling it back to let in more of what passed for light in this realm. I waited for him to cross the room before I put it back.

"So this singing we're supposed to avoid," I said, watching him straighten a candlestick on the mantel. The moment his back was turned, I rotated it slightly to the left. "That's Irri?"

"Most likely." He moved to adjust a chair that sat at an odd angle.

I waited until he'd walked away before nudging it back with my foot. My heart shouldn't have fluttered when his lips twitched at the sound of wood scraping against stone.

He's playing you, Sylvie hissed.

"Shut up," I snapped back, before realizing I'd said the words out loud. "Sorry," I whispered. "That wasn't meant for you."

"You don't have to be sorry." Thorne ran his fingers along a row of books, arranging them by height. "Irri's song was always haunting. Beautiful in a way that made your soul ache. She could take the most broken things and make them feel whole again, even if just for a moment."

I crossed the room and pulled one book halfway out, disrupting his careful arrangement. His exasperated sigh sent an unexpected warmth through my chest.

"She doesn't sound particularly threatening," I drawled, watching him fidget with the window latch. "For all this warning about covering our ears."

He turned to face me, and something in his expression made me still. Gone was the careful mask of control, replaced by genuine uncertainty. "She wasn't. Not really. But this place..." He gestured at the twisted architecture around us. "It probably changes people. She was the Goddess of Broken Things. Now she's surrounded by everything that's ever been forgotten or lost. I don't know what that kind of power might do to someone, even a god."

I leaned against the wall, studying him. "You're worried she's absorbed it all? That's why everything is broken here?"

"Or that it's absorbed her." He smoothed a wrinkle from the bedspread. I immediately sat on it, earning a look that was somewhere between amusement and frustration. "She was gentle once. Kind. She could look at the most shattered pieces of existence and see how they might fit together again. But here? I don't know."

The vulnerability in his voice caught me off guard. This wasn't the all-powerful Keeper speaking, but someone genuinely worried about what we might find.

"And you're telling me this because...?" I watched him adjust a vase of long dead flowers, fighting the urge to knock it over completely.

He's trying to manipulate you, Winter warned.

"Because I need your help," he said quietly, and the simple honesty in those words made my breath catch.

I slid off the bed and moved to the vase, turning it slightly askew. "You're asking for my opinion? You? The god who thinks he knows everything?"

"Yes." He reached past me to right the vase again, his proximity sending unwanted shivers down my spine. "I am."

"Will wonders never cease," I murmured, but my usual sarcasm felt hollow. The silence stretched between us, heavy with unspoken things. He moved to straighten a crooked table runner, and I found myself watching his hands, remembering how they felt against my skin.

Focus, a chorus of voices hissed in my mind.

"There's a reason Alastor let you come with me and it wasn't to do either of us a favor. I think we're going to have to use your Huntress power to find her."

I stilled, my hand halfway to messing up another of his careful arrangements. "I've never seen Irri nor have I touched her. That's not how my power works."

"But Sylvie has and Alastor knows she's in your mind. She knows her mother's essence better than anyone."

Say you'll do it.

"But why was Irri banished in the first place?" I asked, turning back to him. "If she was so gentle, so kind, what could she have possibly done to deserve this?"

Something dark passed over his features. He moved back to the window, his shoulders tight with tension. "I did something unforgivable. I let my pride, my need to possess what I thought was mine, destroy everything."

"What did you do?"

"I asked to marry Sylvie." His voice was barely above a whisper. "Irri said yes. But Alastor? He saw clearer than any of us. He saw the war brewing between my brother and me after Ezra saw the worst path forward. He refused to let his daughter be caught in the middle."

My heart stuttered. "He thought if you both left me alone—"

"The balance wouldn't break." Thorne's laugh was hollow. "I was so angry. So certain of my right to claim her, I tried to send Alastor to the Forgotten." His fingers curled into fists. "But Irri stepped between us. She took the full force of my power. And Alastor, watching his Ever be banished..." He shook his head. "He left Etherium. And because he did—"

"Sylvie fell," I finished, understanding dawning like ice in my veins. "As a demigod, she lost her immortality."

"Ezra and I followed her soul to the mortal realms. And my brother." His voice broke. "He killed her. The first of so many deaths."

He speaks the truth, Sylvie's voice cut through my mind like a blade. *But he forgot to mention how he stood and watched. How he did nothing as Ezra's sword found my heart. Just as he's done nothing every time since.*

The weight of it all, the betrayal, the cascade of consequences, the centuries of death and rebirth, it pressed against my chest until I could barely breathe. Every death, every shattered life, all because one god couldn't accept being told no.

Now you understand, Sylvie whispered. *Why he must stay. Why he must know what it is to be forgotten.*

I looked at Thorne, still standing at the window, his reflection fractured in the clouded glass. I wanted to hate him. I should hate him. But all I felt was an overwhelming sadness for all of us, pawns in a game that had spiraled so far beyond anyone's control. He'd loved her. As simply as the clouds held rain and the sun held light. He'd only loved her. And he'd lost everything that day too. And then over and over again, until his soul broke. Every move he'd made was born from love.

Without thinking, I moved to straighten the candlestick he'd adjusted earlier. His soft, surprised laugh made something in my chest ache.

"I thought you were dedicated to undoing all my attempts at order," he said.

I shrugged, not meeting his eyes. "Maybe some things deserve to be set right."

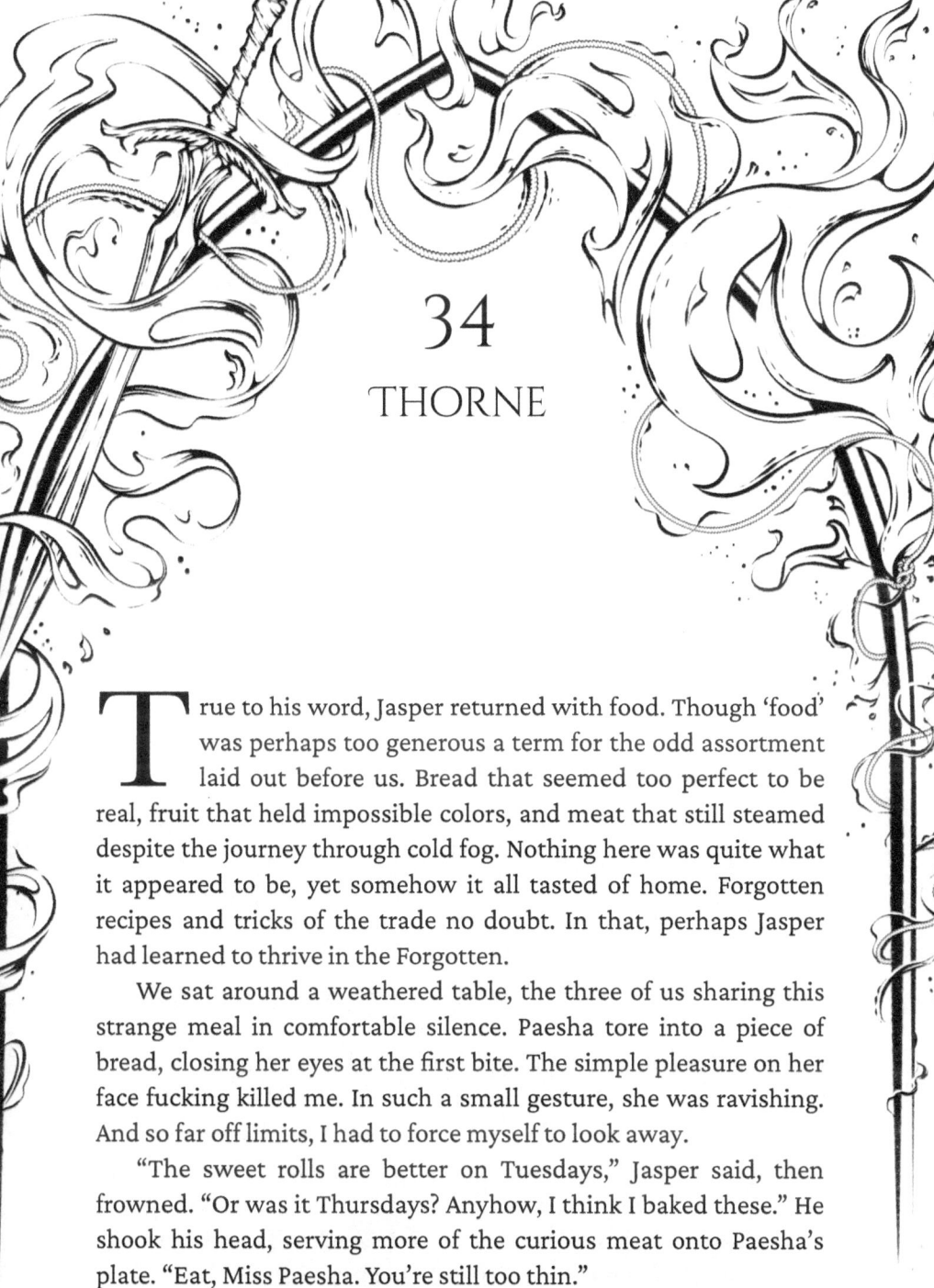

34

THORNE

True to his word, Jasper returned with food. Though 'food' was perhaps too generous a term for the odd assortment laid out before us. Bread that seemed too perfect to be real, fruit that held impossible colors, and meat that still steamed despite the journey through cold fog. Nothing here was quite what it appeared to be, yet somehow it all tasted of home. Forgotten recipes and tricks of the trade no doubt. In that, perhaps Jasper had learned to thrive in the Forgotten.

We sat around a weathered table, the three of us sharing this strange meal in comfortable silence. Paesha tore into a piece of bread, closing her eyes at the first bite. The simple pleasure on her face fucking killed me. In such a small gesture, she was ravishing. And so far off limits, I had to force myself to look away.

"The sweet rolls are better on Tuesdays," Jasper said, then frowned. "Or was it Thursdays? Anyhow, I think I baked these." He shook his head, serving more of the curious meat onto Paesha's plate. "Eat, Miss Paesha. You're still too thin."

She smiled, that genuine one that transformed her entire face. "As long as there are no apples in sight."

The normality of it all was a blade between my ribs. How easy it would be to stay here, to let the rest of existence fade away until there was nothing but this, shared meals and quiet moments with her. No prophecies, no scheming gods, no centuries of pain between us. Simply peace.

But I knew I could never condemn her to that fate. She deserved more than a prison, no matter how comfortable. She deserved every chance at life and freedom, even if that freedom meant leaving me behind. That was our destiny. Her destiny, if Ezra was to be believed. And this place was mine.

Jasper's eyes darted to the clouded window, watching the darkness deepen outside. "I should go," he said, rising abruptly. "You mustn't go out after dark. The things that hunt here..." He shuddered. "They're hungry for more than memories."

"You could stay," Paesha offered.

He shook his head, already backing toward the door. "No. I've another round of food to distribute. I pay my dues around here. Help the folks that forget to eat. Routine is best." His eyes met mine, and for a moment, perfect clarity shone through his usual uncertainty. "Keep her safe."

"Always," I promised, though we both knew my track record with that particular vow was less than stellar.

We stood together at the door, watching his figure grow smaller and smaller as he moved away. Neither of us invited him back tomorrow. We never told him the real reason we'd come. But Jasper had always respected unspoken boundaries. Even when he knew things were amiss in the Hollow, he never questioned. Always followed. A respectable man through and through.

After he left, and we returned to the small table in the room, I watched Paesha pick at the remaining food, studying the way the dim light caught in her hair, the graceful movement of her hands, the slight furrow between her brows that meant she was arguing with the voices again. Whatever she decided, whatever path she chose, I would follow her lead. I owed her that much, at least.

She deserved to write her own story for once, free from the machinations of gods and fate. Even if that story ended with me trapped in this place of endless memories and forgotten dreams.

"You're staring," she said without looking up.

"Yes," I admitted. No point in denying it.

She finally met my gaze, and the complexity of emotions in her eyes took my breath away. "Why?"

"Because you're beautiful," I said simply. "Because you're here. Because every time I look at you, I remember all the reasons I would do anything for you."

Her fingers stilled on her plate. "Don't."

"Don't what? Tell the truth? I thought that's what you wanted from me."

"Not when the truth hurts," she whispered, and for just a moment, I saw past her walls to the raw pain beneath.

I wanted to reach for her, to pull her into my arms and promise that everything would be all right. But I'd made enough false promises in our long history. Instead, I simply nodded and began clearing away the dishes Jasper had brought in his basket.

She moved to the bed and curled her knees to her chest, turning to stare out the window. The shift likely caused by the voices screaming into her mind. I thought maybe she let herself feel everything she'd been holding back because her shoulders started to shake. She stared out the window, and something in my chest fucking shattered. The Remnants swirled around her feet, and over her arms where she'd rolled her sleeves, agitated by whatever battle raged in her mind. I knew that look. Had seen it too many times not to recognize when she was losing herself to the voices.

I moved toward the bed, sitting beside her so she knew I was there, but stopped short of touching her. Close enough to catch her if she fell, far enough that she wouldn't feel trapped. Her tears fell silently, and I had to grip the edge of the mattress to keep from reaching for her. Minutes stretched into eternities as I sat beside her, staring out the window so I didn't have to watch her shoulders tremble with the force of emotions she tried desperately to contain. My hands ached to pull her against my chest and shield her from whatever demons plagued her thoughts. But I'd lost that right long ago. So I waited, letting her fight her battles, letting her choose if she wanted to let me in.

"I can't be what you want me to be," she finally whispered. "I can't be anything for anyone anymore."

I kept my eyes fixed on the window, giving her the illusion of privacy as she wiped at her tears. "I don't want you to be anything but yourself."

"But who am I? An Ever? The Huntress? The woman bound to Alastor or the one destined to break the balance of power? There are so many voices in my head telling me who I should be, what I should do, how I should feel." Her breath hitched. "I want to exist without the weight of everyone's expectations crushing me."

My hand moved of its own accord, reaching for her before I caught myself again. I let it fall to the bed beside hers instead, close enough to feel the heat of her skin but not quite touching. "Then exist. Here. Now. No prophecies, no destinies. Just you, exactly as you are. I will sit with you in the madness."

She was quiet for a long moment, then slowly, deliberately, slid her hand closer until our pinkie fingers touched. The small connection felt like victory and defeat all at once. A concession that meant everything and nothing.

I memorized the feeling of that tiny point of contact, knowing it might be all I'd ever have again. Knowing that soon, I'd have to let her go.

"I wanted to hate you," she whispered, still staring out the window. "It would be so much easier if I could hate you."

Her pinkie finger twitched against mine, but she didn't pull away. The words I needed to say burned in my throat. Three simple words that could shatter everything. But she deserved to hear them, even if she couldn't believe them. Even if they changed nothing.

But before I could speak, she turned those devastating eyes on me. "How am I supposed to believe you care for me at all? Maybe you're only in love with the idea of me. With all those past lives, all those memories you're so desperate to hold onto. Your devotion has nothing to do with who I am now. I'm just another pawn on your board. Another piece to manipulate."

"You think I don't know you? That I don't see exactly who you are? You're the woman who built a family from broken pieces and loved them fiercely enough to reshape their reality. You're stubborn and sharp and absolutely fucking terrifying when you're angry. You steal scarves from forgetful merchants because, even though you're mad at me, you won't let a person suffer. You kick gods in the balls when they deserve it."

She huffed a wet laugh. "That was Quill, to be fair."

I smiled, leaning in until my forehead pressed against hers. "That was a learned behavior, Paesha darling."

Her thumb traced absent patterns on my palm. When she spoke again, her voice was barely a whisper. "His face keeps haunting me. The way he looked at me before he released that arrow... I loved him," she confessed, the words seeming to tear themselves from her throat. "How twisted is that? Of all the lives, all the memories, in this one I loved Ezra. And now I can't stop seeing his eyes. Did he know? Every time he killed me in other lives, did he know I would love him in this one?"

The pain in her voice cut deeper than any blade. I squeezed her hand gently. "The heart doesn't choose who it loves, Paesha. I loved him too. He was my brother, my other half in so many ways. Until Sylvie. Until I watched him destroy everything I held dear because of a possibility."

"She's the loudest," she admitted, her free hand pressing against her temple. "Sylvie. She screams above all the others."

"I would expect nothing less from a demigod who's waited centuries for vengeance."

Her eyes met mine, vulnerable in a way I'd rarely seen. "I wish they would be silent, just for a little while. Just long enough to hear my own thoughts."

"I wish that for you too," I murmured, reaching up to brush a tear from her cheek. "More than anything, I wish I could give you peace."

Something in her expression cracked at my words. "I don't

know how to trust this," she whispered. "How to trust you. But when you look at me like that, like I'm the only real thing in any realm..."

"You are," I said simply. "You're the only thing that's ever felt real to me. The only truth that matters. When everything else fades away, when all the power fails and the realms crumble, you'll still be the one constant I believe in. Just you, Paesha. Exactly as you are right now."

Her fingers tightened on mine, and every muscle in my body went rigid with the need to pull her closer. To taste her. To claim her. I had to fight against every primitive instinct screaming at me to take what I wanted. I couldn't. Not with her. Not anymore.

She'd fucking ruined me for anyone else, stripped away my control until I was nothing but want and need and desperation. There had been no versions of her that compared to this one. To Paesha. To the vixen that was my perfect version. I'd spent lifetimes learning to become everything she might want me to be, and with no effort, she'd become everything I'd ever wanted in her. I watched her lips part, saw her eyes darken as they met mine, and for the first time in my endless existence, I had no fucking clue what to do next.

I wanted to kiss her. Needed it with an intensity that bordered on pain. But this had to be her choice. Everything from here on out had to be her choice, even if it killed me to wait. When she finally leaned in, the last thread of my restraint nearly snapped. The haunted look in her eyes was gone, replaced by something deeper, darker, that made my blood burn.

When she kissed me, it wasn't that calculated bullshit from before. This was real. Raw. Hungry. And for one perfect moment, as her lips moved against mine, nothing else fucking mattered. Not the voices in her head, not the prophecies, not the Fates. Just us, finding our way back to each other in the dark.

The kiss deepened, her fingers sliding into my hair as she pressed closer. My hands roamed down her sides, desperate to touch every inch of her. When she pulled away, her shirt slipped off her shoulder and something caught my eye, a mark I hadn't seen before. While her Remnants swirled and moved across her skin like living shadows, this one remained still. A pattern that triggered something in my ancient memories, making my blood run cold.

I shifted back, brushing my fingers over the Treeis mark, tracing the burning knot as I asked, "When did you get this?"

She glanced down, confusion crossing her features. "What are you talking about?"

"This mark. It wasn't here before." I would have noticed. I'd memorized every fucking inch of her skin that night she'd danced for me on the bar.

Her brow furrowed as she tried to see it. "I've never... I don't remember getting this."

It must have been new. Something since she broke the veil. Everything suddenly clicked into place, Archer's impossible strength when he'd fought me, the way he'd known Quill was in danger before it happened, how he seemed drawn to protect Paesha beyond all logical reason. That clever bastard of a brother had played us all.

"It's the mark from a Treeis bond," I said. "A magical binding between souls. It's rare. Ancient. And fucking dangerous. Archer's your Guardian. Has to be, based on how protective he is. But that would mean..." I trailed off, the implications hitting me like a punch to the gut.

"Mean what?"

"Only an Unmade can be a Treeis Guardian. Which means either you or Archer is bound to Ezra." The words tasted like ash. Another piece of my brother's endless schemes falling into place. "And if it were you, Alastor wouldn't have been able to put those bindings on your wrists and ankles."

"No." Paesha's voice broke, her hand flying to her mouth as she shoved away from the bed. "He can't be. Archer wouldn't—"

"He might not even know. The binding could have happened without his knowledge. Ezra's capable of that level of manipulation."

"But if this is true, then he's *my* guardian?"

"It's strange. Something's off." I scratched the back of my head. "Ezra has an Unmade Guardian army. They pride themselves on being radical warriors for his cause. A handful of times across history, one of them has bonded with another, aside from Ezra. But I always thought the third had to accept the bond through power."

"I sure as hell accepted no such thing. I don't think Archer would have either." She shook her head. "What will happen to him?"

"Archer's strong. Whatever hold Ezra has on him, he'll fight it. That stubborn bastard doesn't know how to do anything else." The words felt hollow, knowing I wouldn't be there to help either of them, but I couldn't promise more than that. Something was going to happen to keep me here. Her betrayal had already been seen. And maybe I was a fool for not protecting myself from it, but if I did, I'd be putting space between us I didn't want. Even in these final moments together.

A sound cut through the darkness, a melody so pure and haunting it made my skin crawl. I knew that voice, that damn song. I would know it anywhere. "Irri," I whispered.

The song drifted through the forgotten city, beautiful and terrible all at once. Each note pulled at something deep within me, luring me forward into the dark. But whether it promised salvation or damnation, I couldn't tell.

Paesha's head jerked to the side as she raised her marked shoulder, trying to cover her ear. As if that would save her from the voices in her mind. And then she pulled away. "We need to go." I watched her flawlessly bury the hurt of Archer's bond, lock it away behind those walls she'd built so carefully. Always so fucking strong, even when she was breaking.

But something dark and possessive twisted in my gut. Soon I'd have to send her back through that door alone. Back to a man who, knowingly or not, was bound to my brother. Back to whatever fate Ezra had planned for her. If she died by a god's hands, she would not come back and the thought of that made me want to burn this whole fucking realm to the ground.

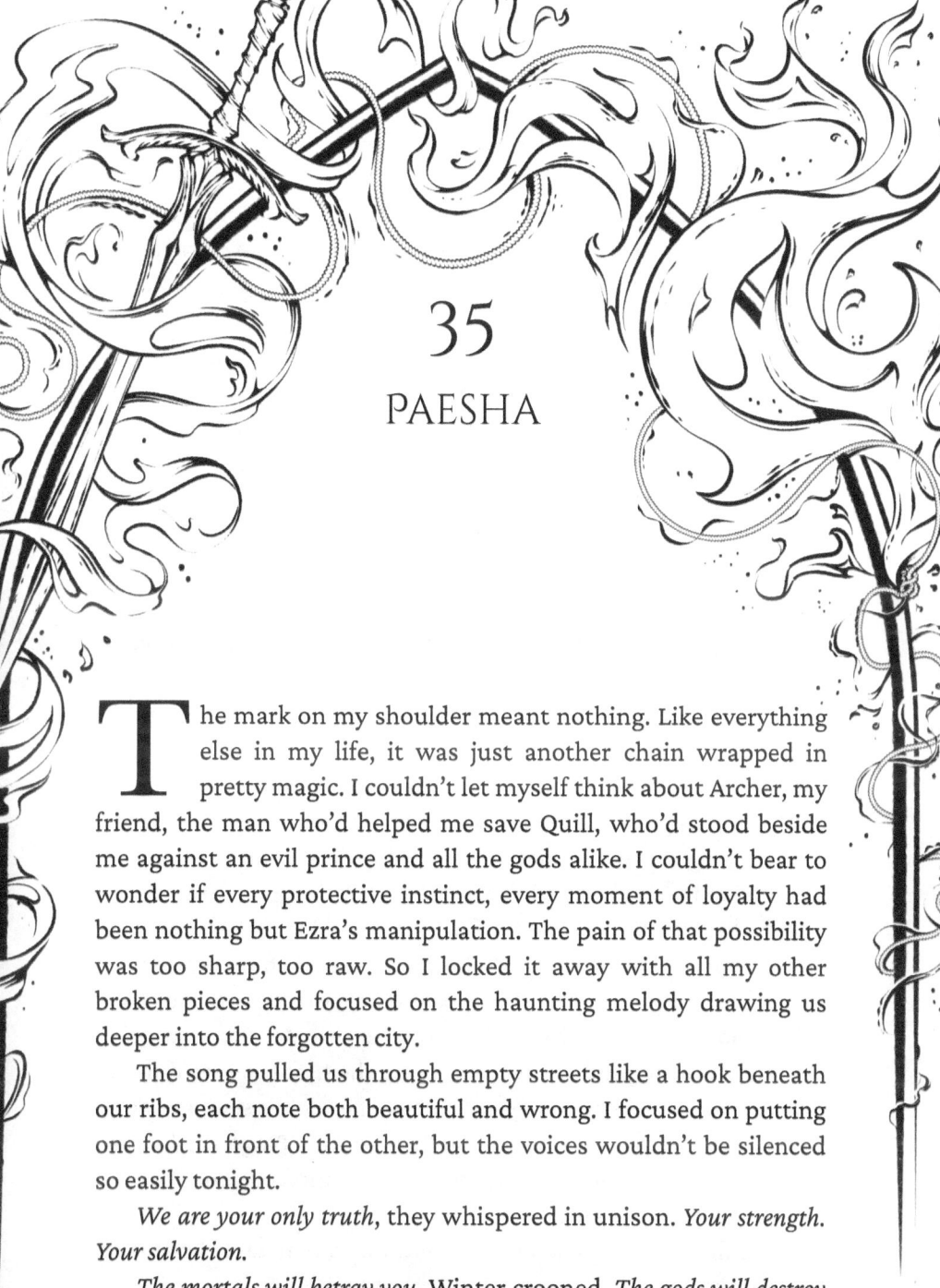

35

PAESHA

The mark on my shoulder meant nothing. Like everything else in my life, it was just another chain wrapped in pretty magic. I couldn't let myself think about Archer, my friend, the man who'd helped me save Quill, who'd stood beside me against an evil prince and all the gods alike. I couldn't bear to wonder if every protective instinct, every moment of loyalty had been nothing but Ezra's manipulation. The pain of that possibility was too sharp, too raw. So I locked it away with all my other broken pieces and focused on the haunting melody drawing us deeper into the forgotten city.

The song pulled us through empty streets like a hook beneath our ribs, each note both beautiful and wrong. I focused on putting one foot in front of the other, but the voices wouldn't be silenced so easily tonight.

We are your only truth, they whispered in unison. *Your strength. Your salvation.*

The mortals will betray you, Winter crooned. *The gods will destroy you. But we? We are you. We are all you have ever truly had.*

Mother is right there, Sylvie purred. *She will help you destroy a god. When he tears a door into this realm, simply break it. Like the veil. Like our hearts. Like your past.*

Their words slithered through my mind like poison, tempting and terrible. I shoved them away, though it took more effort than I cared to admit. I couldn't afford their seductive promises, not when I needed my wits about me.

Thorne walked beside me, close enough that his arm occasionally brushed mine. Each touch sent sparks through my skin that I refused to acknowledge. The memory of his kiss still burned on my lips, making everything more complicated than it needed to be. I couldn't afford to think about the way he'd looked at me like I was the answer to every question he'd ever asked. Like I was worth burning realms for.

The melody grew stronger, filling the air with promises I couldn't quite understand. My feet moved of their own accord, following the sound deeper into the twisted city.

"This way," Thorne murmured, gesturing toward what might have once been a grand boulevard. I wanted to hate how easily he took the lead, how naturally I fell into step beside him. But the truth was, his presence felt like an anchor in this nightmare place.

The song shifted, becoming something darker, more seductive. It pulled at memories I didn't know I had, making my head spin. I saw flashes of my childhood. Of my tears and loneliness. I saw my father's face. I saw things I'd chosen to keep behind walls until they'd been forgotten. The threadbare blanket I'd kept through my childhood. My first pair of ballet slippers the Maestro had given me. And gods help me, I saw Ezra's face the first time we'd met. I saw the blank stare in his eyes. The way he hadn't seen me at all when I thought he was everything. I'd forgotten. Forgetting was so much easier than sitting in that pain. I stumbled, and Thorne's hand shot out to steady me.

"I'm fine," I snapped, jerking away, but the lie tasted bitter on my tongue.

A massive structure loomed ahead, its architecture impossibly beautiful despite its decay. Weathered black stone spiraled upward, defying gravity. This had to be a temple. And Irri's song came from within, each note carrying the weight of centuries. Of her sorrow. My sorrow.

As we stepped across the threshold, the haunting melody grew louder, echoing through the cavernous space like a mournful sigh. A song without words that spoke directly to the soul. The hair on the back of my neck rose as I took in the space with vines and moss clinging to every surface, nature reclaiming what must have been a magnificent structure. Though now, only the cracked columns held the history of this space. Only the dust that drifted in the night air.

Something moved in the shadows between the columns, deep within the pit of darkness, hiding from the moonlight.

"Thorne—" I started, but he was already moving, pushing me behind him as a creature emerged. It was massive, its body a rippling mass of forgotten things. Broken weapons, shattered mirrors, torn pages from books. Its eyes, gods, its eyes were human, filled with a hunger that made my blood run cold... But then I saw the limbs. The distorted faces of people trapped within the darkness. Mouths full of silent screams, eyes vacant. Hands reaching out of the mass, begging for a savior.

The creature lunged, faster than anything that size had any right to move. Thorne's power flared golden around us, but the monster passed through it like smoke. And in that falter, I felt the warmth of his magic around my mind dissipate.

For a second, everything stopped. With Thorne at my side and the monster looming over us, there was no escape. We couldn't run fast enough. Thorne's power had faded. But still he tried. Still, he put himself between me and the monstrosity. But the fucker swiped a giant arm with claws the size of horses at us. I'd never forget the sound as he made contact with Thorne's body. I'd seen him powerful, arrogant, in complete control, but in that moment he looked fragile, mortal, and as the impact sent him flying backward, one of the temple's weathered columns broke. The crack of stone meeting flesh made me physically ill. This wasn't supposed to happen. He was a god and yet he crumpled to the ground, golden light flickering weakly around him like a candle about to go out.

My chest tightened painfully as I watched him struggle to rise. In all our history, in all the lives I'd apparently lived, I doubted I'd ever seen him vulnerable. Never seen him hurt. The sight of blood on his skin made something primal and protective rear up inside me. It didn't matter that I hated him, that I planned to leave him here. In this moment, watching him wounded and fighting alone, every complicated feeling I had for him crystilized into one burning truth: No one got to hurt him but me.

The monster advanced, its form a nightmare of objects that shifted as it moved. But it was those eyes, so hungry, fixed on Thorne with predatory focus that made my blood run cold. It wanted to consume him, to add him to its collection of forgotten things.

"Run!" he shouted, voice rough with pain as he finally made it to his feet. The creature lunged again and my heart lodged in my throat.

But I couldn't move. Couldn't breathe. Every fiber of my being screamed to help him, to fight beside him. I didn't know what I wanted anymore, to save him or destroy him, but I knew with bone deep certainty that he was mine to protect or to break. Mine to save or to damn. This creature didn't get to take that from me.

He must tear open a path, Sylvie screamed through the rush of thoughts. *The Keeper cannot be left behind until he's opened the door.*

My Remnants surged forward without conscious thought, meeting the creature's attack in a clash of shadows and nightmares. The impact sent me falling backward, my head spinning as a thousand voices screamed for blood.

The creature reeled back, those human eyes widening in surprise as my power tore through it. The voices in my head reached a crescendo, a thousand lifetimes of love and loss and rage pouring into my attack. This was their moment. They would not be robbed of their vengeance. But it was mine too. This was my power. My anger. And as I drew from that very deep well inside of me, expecting to find the bottom soon, I didn't.

I pushed and pushed, screaming along with all the past lives in my mind until nothing existed anymore. Until light shone on every dark corner of my thoughts, forcing me to feel emotions I refused. And in that, I felt it all. The anger and the hurt. The loneliness, the abandonment, the betrayal. Not just from Thorne, in fact, in the grand scheme of things in my life, he'd done very little. He'd lied, but my father had left. My mother had left. I'd spent my past alone and manipulated and I was so very angry.

The ground split beneath my feet, a chasm opening between us as my rage tore the world apart.

"Paesha!" Thorne's voice barely reached me through the roar of power and screaming voices in my head. He stood on the other side of the widening gap, blood trickling from a cut above his eye. The creature was already recovering. Its massive body had reassembled itself. "Find her! I'll hold it off!"

"I can't—" My voice broke. I couldn't leave him. Not like this. Not when every instinct screamed to stay and fight.

"You have to! I can't die, remember? But I can't protect you and fight this thing. Please!"

The voices reached a fever pitch, drowning out everything but the need to run. To find Irri. To end this. I stumbled backward as I watched the thing advance on Thorne again.

"Go!" he roared, power flaring around him as he met the monster's charge.

I turned and ran, following the haunting melody that still drifted through the temple's twisted corridors. Each step felt like betrayal, but I forced myself forward, letting Irri's song guide me deeper into the forgotten temple.

I found her in what might have once been a grand ballroom. She stood at a window that overlooked the forgotten city, staring out, unaware of the battle in the other room. Unaware that I'd even come for her. Her hair, as red as fresh blood, cascaded down her back in waves that moved of their own accord. When she turned, her movements were dream-like, disconnected.

"We have to go," I said, the words tumbling out breathlessly. "Right now. Please."

She tilted her head, studying me with eyes that looked through rather than at me. "Go where, little lost thing? There is nowhere to go. Only songs to sing. Do you know any songs?"

"No, you don't understand." I moved closer, desperation making my voice sharp. "Alastor sent me. He's waiting for you."

"Alastor?" She smiled vaguely, turning back to the window. "I knew an Alastor once. In my dreams, perhaps? He had the most beautiful eyes. Like storms on a summer day." She began humming, a melody that made my skin crawl. "Or was that someone else? The memories blur here, you see. Like watercolors in the rain."

"Please," I begged, moving to stand beside her. "We don't have time. There's a monster—"

My voice cut off as a crash echoed from somewhere in the temple. Thorne. Fighting alone while I tried to reason with a goddess who'd lost herself to this place.

Irri's gaze drifted to me, then suddenly sharpened as moonlight spilled across my face. She reached out with trembling fingers, nearly touching my cheek before pulling back. "Those eyes," she whispered. "One green, one blue. My Sylvie had eyes like that."

"Yes," I said, seizing the moment of clarity. "Sylvie. Your daughter. She's part of why I'm here."

Something ancient and terrible flashed across her face. "My daughter? My beautiful, broken girl?" Her hand pressed against her heart. "I think she died."

Tell her I'm here. Tell her I never left her.

"She's here," I said softly, tapping my temple. "Part of her, at least. She wants you to come home."

"Home?" The word seemed to confuse her. She looked around the crumbling ballroom as if seeing it for the first time. Then let her hands slide down her beautiful red gown. "This isn't home, is it? This place of forgotten things?" Her eyes met mine again, more focused now. "You say Alastor awaits?"

"Yes. He's been waiting so long. But we have to hurry."

Another crash shook the temple, closer this time. Irri didn't seem to notice, but my heart clenched with fear.

"Perhaps..." she said dreamily, reaching for my hand. "Perhaps it is time to remember what was forgotten." Her fingers were ice cold as they wrapped around mine. "Lead the way, little lost one with my daughter's eyes. Take me to my storm-eyed love."

I squeezed her hand and turned toward the door, praying we weren't too late. Praying Thorne still fought. Still stood. Praying that whatever these next moments were, they were mine alone to choose. The voices in my head hummed with anticipation as we moved through the temple's winding corridors, drawing closer to the moment of truth. To betrayal or salvation. To an ending.

I sprinted back through the temple's winding corridors, Irri's cold hand still gripping mine. Each heartbeat felt like an eternity as we raced toward whatever fate awaited us. The sounds of combat grew louder, and when we finally reached the massive chamber, my heart nearly stopped.

Thorne stood in the center of the room, his power manifesting as a sphere of golden light that barely contained the beast. A streak of red trickled from his head, his usually immaculate appearance marred by blood and dust. His magic flickered. His eyes found mine, relief flooding his features before his gaze shifted to Irri. The sphere wavered. His power was fading again.

"You are broken, Keeper," Irri said, her dreamy voice carrying an edge of accusation. "Your power wanes like moonlight."

"Irri," I said urgently, "Alastor's been feeding you power for a long, long time, hasn't he? Can you use it and help us stop this thing?"

She tilted her head. "Why would I stop it? The Keeper trapped me here, in this place of endless forgetting." Her eyes grew distant. "Or did he? The memories blur, you see."

The monster slammed against Thorne's failing barrier, and he stumbled. The golden sphere shattered, and the creature's massive body crowded over him. My breath caught in my throat as he turned to me, those hazel eyes holding nothing but defeat and regret.

"I'm sorry," he said, the words carrying the weight of centuries. "For everything. For every life, every lie, every moment of pain I caused you. I loved you. Through every life and every death, I've always loved you. And I always will, even when there's nothing left of me to remember."

I lurched forward, desperation clawing up my throat. "No," I choked out, shaking my head as if denial alone could hold back the inevitable. "You don't get to say goodbye. You don't get to—"

The beast reared back. A breath, a heartbeat, and it would strike.

Thorne smiled, small and aching, like he already knew how this would end. "It was always you."

The words splintered through me, shattering the last of my restraint. "Then fight for me, damn you!" I begged, gripping his name like a prayer. "Thorne—"

Power surged around him one last time as he tore open reality, creating a flickering doorway home. The Remnants in my mind erupted in celebration.

Now! Take her through! Leave him to his fate!

I grabbed Irri's arm, shoving her toward the rip. She went without resistance, floating through like a leaf on the wind. I knew I should have gone. Escaped. Finished this. But when I turned back, the scene before me froze my blood. The creature engulfed Thorne. He disappeared into its mass of broken things and forgotten dreams. The voices in my head reached a deafening crescendo, demanding I leave, screaming for me to take my revenge and go.

But I couldn't.

Don't be a fool! Sylvie shrieked.

He deserves this!

He's gone now. Just go.

Could I do this? Could I really leave him here, knowing he'd suffer for eternity? He'd lied, manipulated, played games with my life. But he'd also loved me through centuries, through countless deaths and rebirths. He'd tried to protect me, even if his methods were wrong. The vision of Winter's death played through my mind, how devastated he'd been, how he'd begged her not to leave him. Not his blade that killed her. Never his blade.

Make him suffer as we suffered, another voice demanded. *Walk away.*

But had we suffered at his hands, truly? Or had he suffered alongside us, watching helplessly as his brother tore us apart time and time again? He'd said telling me the truth would mean my death before sunset. Was keeping that secret truly unforgivable if he'd done it to keep me breathing?

The monster's mass shifted, and I caught a glimpse of his face. Those hazel eyes that had looked at me with such devotion now held only acceptance of his fate. He didn't expect me to save him. He'd created this prison, and now he was willing to be consumed by it. For me. Always for me.

My heart cracked. If I left him here, I'd be free of him forever. Free of the complications, the pain, the centuries of baggage I carried in my soul. The voices would win. The prophecy would be fulfilled.

But I would know. Every time I looked at Archer, I would know I'd abandoned the man who'd loved me enough to let me go. Every time I held Quill, I would remember the way Thorne had shielded my memories in this dark place. Every time I danced, I would feel the ghost of his touch, hear the echo of his voice telling me I was perfect exactly as I was.

The voices screamed so loud I couldn't make sense of it anymore. But in that small, quiet corner of my mind where no voice could reach, I knew my truth: I could hate him, fight him, rage against him, but I could not stand by and watch him be destroyed. I was done letting others write my story. I would take control. Not because voices in my head demanded it, not because prophecies foretold it, but because I chose it.

And they knew it. The Remnants that once followed my command turned on me, whipped around me, shadows slicing into my skin, ripping through my hair. In the span of one decision, I was destroying myself. Losing myself.

"Stop!" My scream shook the temple walls as I pushed back against them all, finding something deeper, stronger within myself. My own voice. My own power. My own choice. The

Remnants pulled away, and I yanked them back. They screamed, and I screamed louder. Battling my mind. My power. My entire existence.

I strode away from the fading tear, forcing my Remnants to heel until I was the stronger mind. Surging forward with devastating force, they tore into the creature, ripping through layers until I saw him. My shadows wrapped around Thorne like steel chains, yanking him free as I poured every ounce of destruction I possessed into the monster.

I pulled him against me, surrounding us both in a cocoon of darkness. "Open it again," I demanded, my voice raw. "Now!"

His eyes met mine, full of questions I didn't have answers for. But his power flared, tearing another hole in reality. I shoved him through first, following as the tear sealed behind us, leaving the creature's inhuman yell echoing in the void.

We fell together, tumbling onto the cobblestone streets of Stirling as the final scraps of my power's strength flickered out.

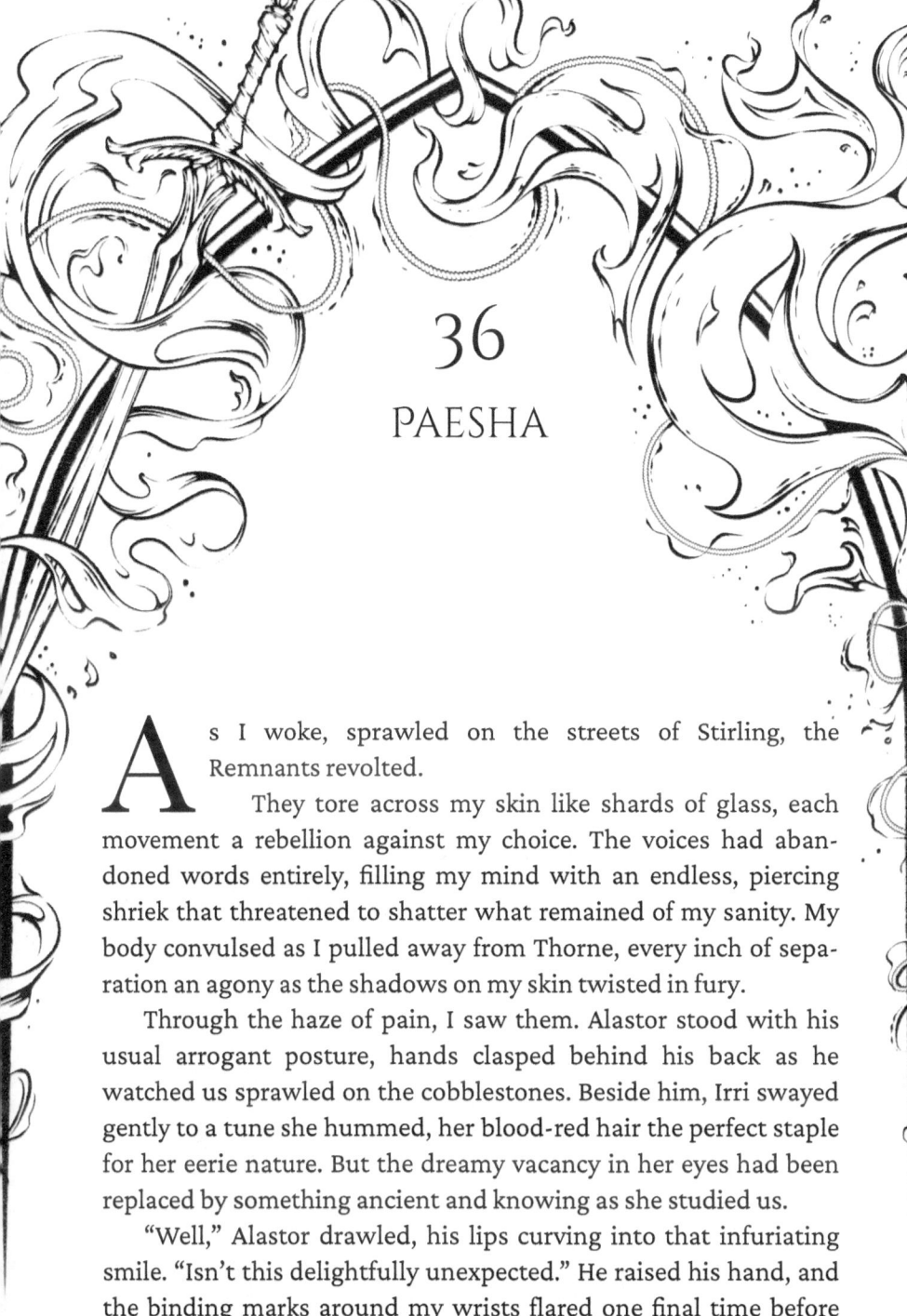

36

PAESHA

As I woke, sprawled on the streets of Stirling, the Remnants revolted.

They tore across my skin like shards of glass, each movement a rebellion against my choice. The voices had abandoned words entirely, filling my mind with an endless, piercing shriek that threatened to shatter what remained of my sanity. My body convulsed as I pulled away from Thorne, every inch of separation an agony as the shadows on my skin twisted in fury.

Through the haze of pain, I saw them. Alastor stood with his usual arrogant posture, hands clasped behind his back as he watched us sprawled on the cobblestones. Beside him, Irri swayed gently to a tune she hummed, her blood-red hair the perfect staple for her eerie nature. But the dreamy vacancy in her eyes had been replaced by something ancient and knowing as she studied us.

"Well," Alastor drawled, his lips curving into that infuriating smile. "Isn't this delightfully unexpected." He raised his hand, and the binding marks around my wrists flared one final time before fading completely. "As promised, you're free. Though I feel compelled to mention that means you're no longer under my protection. The gods will notice soon enough."

Thorne had barely moved but his voice carried enough venom to make Alastor pause. "Let them try. Just know that anyone who dares to touch her will beg for death long before I grant it."

Alastor's smile widened as he wrapped an arm around Irri's waist. "Such passion. Such promises. I do hope you can keep them better than the last ones."

Thorne pulled himself up, reaching for me with hands that still trembled from the fight. Despite the screaming in my head, despite the shadows trying to tear me apart from within, I let him help me stand. We walked away without another word, leaving Alastor's soft laughter and Irri's haunting melody behind us.

"Take me home," I managed.

"Tuck's already been summoned." Thorne kept his hand at my elbow, steadying me as another wave of fury from the shadows threatened to bring me to my knees. "We need to make it to the main street."

I barked out a laugh that held no humor. "Easy enough."

"Just a few more minutes. You can yell at me the whole way if it helps."

"Don't tempt me."

We made it three blocks before my legs started to give out. The Remnants were relentless, tearing at me from the inside as punishment for my betrayal. Thorne's arm slipped around my waist, taking more of my weight. The sound of hooves on cobblestones was almost lost beneath the screaming in my head. Tuck jumped down from the carriage, his heavy boots hitting the ground as he rushed to help.

"You look terrible," he said, reaching for my other arm.

"And you look like a liar," I shot back. "A god? Really?"

"I never lied." He helped Thorne guide me toward the carriage. "You made assumptions."

"Called it," Thorne muttered, lifting me into the carriage before I could protest.

"I hate you both," I growled, but let them settle me against the cushioned seat. The Remnants surged again, and I had to bite back a scream. "Next time I decide to save your life, remind me what terrible company you keep."

Tuck clicked his tongue. "That's no way to talk about your favorite carriage driver."

"Let me guess. God of Deception and Driving?"

He froze. "Knowledge, actually. Thank you very much."

I rolled my eyes, making the headache throb worse. "I would have never guessed."

"We can argue about it when you're feeling better."

"Can't wait." I slumped against the cushions, trying to focus. Thorne's voice seemed to come from far away as he explained something about Archer and the Treeis bond to Tuck. The words blurred together as exhaustion pulled at me, though the Remnants gave me no peace.

"Don't," I said sharply when I caught the dark look that passed between them. "When we get there, you keep your hands off Archer. Let me talk to him. If someone's going to tell him he's been manipulated by yet another god, it should be me."

"He likely already knows," Tuck said, shutting the door to the carriage. "Either way, we'll get it sorted. Best clean yourself up, Boss. No need to scare the kid with all that blood on your face."

Thorne pulled a cloth from a box under the seat and dabbed at the wound on his head with a hiss. I managed a moan as the carriage sprung to life, headed straight to the Syndicate house. Tuck had always been good at knowing where... Mother fucker. God of Knowledge, indeed.

Thorne was quiet the entire way. His eyes drifted to me, but I could tell his mind was busy. Back in reality, there were far worse things than monsters hiding in the dark. Eventually, the carriage slowed to a halt outside the Syndicate house, where Archer already stood waiting with Quill at his side. The moment the door opened, Quill launched herself forward, but stopped abruptly as her small hands made contact with my skin. She jerked back, her eyes widening.

"You're mad?" she asked, her voice trembling slightly.

I slowly shook my head, fighting against the chaos still raging within. "It's not me."

Those keen eyes studied me intently, studying the swirling marks on my skin, understanding dawning in their depths. Without hesitation, Quill reached out and took my hand again. This time, waves of calm and tranquility flowed from the contact, pushing back against the furious Remnants. Though they didn't fall silent completely, their assault became bearable for the first time since leaving the Forgotten.

I fell to my knees, yanking her into a hug that we both needed. "Thank you, my girl."

"I missed you," she whispered back. We stayed like that for several minutes. Until I remembered that having Archer at my back was a threat. Even though something within me refused to believe it. I stood, keeping my grip on Quill's hand like a lifeline. I turned to face Archer. He hadn't moved from his spot, his attention fixed on the carriage where Thorne and Tuck remained. He didn't appear angry, but certainly wary.

"Is there something you'd like to share with me?" I asked quietly.

Archer's jaw clenched. He'd been preparing for a battle, it seemed. "If this is about my father—"

"This is about Ezra."

The name hit him like a physical blow. He jerked back, genuine shock crossing his features. "What are you talking about?"

Without releasing Quill's hand, I pulled aside the fabric covering my shoulder, revealing the Treeis mark. Archer's sharp intake of breath was followed by a trembling hand pushing up his sleeve. There on his forearm, unmistakable and damning, was the same intricate pattern.

"I have the same mark." He stared down at his forearm in confusion. "I don't know where it came from. I just noticed it one day."

I gestured for Tuck and Thorne to join us, never letting go of Quill. They approached cautiously, and Tuck's eyes immediately fixed on the matching marks.

"It's a Treeis bond," Tuck explained, his voice grave. "We haven't seen one in centuries. It's an ancient binding that's impossible to create unless you're Unmade." He shared a look with Thorne before continuing. "The Unmade Guardians answer only to Ezra. They are mortal, but only just. The Treeis bond is something we've occasionally seen over history, but never without someone's magical acceptance."

Thorne's gaze moved between the three of us, me, Archer, and Quill, his expression dark and studious. "What's the possibility of a Treeis bond between three?" he asked Tuck. "In all the realms' history, it's never been done, but could it happen? Unless...the three always included Ezra and now, because of the chain of events these three bonded first."

Tuck answered, "I'm not sure. But we're in agreement that Archer has shown all the signs of an Unmade Guardian, right?"

Thorne nodded.

"Can we back up here," I asked. "Start with the basics. What's an Unmade? What's an Unmade Guardian? How do you become one? What does it mean? We need the basics."

"An Unmade *is* a Guardian. Ezra plucks mortals from the realms that he believes will follow his cause. He sees possible future events, determines the probability of them and uses his Unmade Guardians to help stop whatever sets the most destructive things into motion. It's similar to the way you were bound to Alastor, only the Unmade follow Ezra because they believe in his cause. They feed power to him specifically from their devotion to him."

"Well I can tell you right now, I'm not devoted to him. I've never even spoken to Ezra," Archer protested, running his fingers over the mark. "Not once."

"He could have been pretending to be me," Thorne said quietly. "You might have met him without realizing who he was."

"Search his memories," I said, pulling Quill back. "If he'll let you, search and see what you can find. If your power is renewed enough."

Archer stepped forward. "Do it."

Thorne hesitated. "Are you sure?"

"I'd like to know what the hell this is," Archer answered.

Thorne's eyes glowed golden for the flash of a second as he dove into Archer's mind. We stood in silence, waiting.

Elowen and Thea came outside, with Boo in tow. The little dog circled their feet as they sandwiched Quill and I between them.

"Welcome home. Again," Elowen whispered.

"Thank you." I tried to force a smile, but it never came.

Her eyes flashed to Thorne and Archer and then to me, and I knew without her words what she was asking. Did I want him there? Should she step in? She'd always been the mother I never had. Even when she'd been quietly observing. I nodded, almost imperceptibly. She leaned a little closer. "You okay?"

"For now," I whispered back.

Thorne and Archer's faces changed as the magical contact between them was broken. Thorne shook his head, seeming more confused than ever. "Nothing with Ezra. But I know when it happened. And we're done with Aeris." He looked pointedly at Quill, whose fingers had tightened on mine. "I'm telling you right now, Aeris is not your friend. She's the one that created the cavern in my house that you fell into."

"What?" Thea shook her head. "That can't be right."

"She's not bad," Quill said, dropping my hand. "I know you all want to hate her but she's not. I would know. I can feel it."

The second she broke away from me and that peace was gone, the Remnants hissed in my mind, stealing my breath.

Tuck knelt down, keeping a distance from her but bringing himself to eye level as he held up a hand. "Aeris has spent count-less lifetimes learning to manipulate the mind. She knows what to say, how to say it, when to cut off her emotions and when to let you feel them. Take my hand and let me show you."

She hesitated, looking up at Archer of all people before she stepped forward. Archer moved to her side and Thorne's eyes met mine. I nodded. When he'd asked about the bond between three, he meant to include Quill as well. Something in saving Quill had done this. Which hopefully meant it had nothing to do with Ezra.

She closed her fingers around Tuck's and he smiled. "Are you ready? I'm going to show you how I can change how I am feeling. None of this is going to be real so don't be alarmed."

She nodded. "I'm ready."

Neither of their faces changed as they stared at each other. You'd never know anything was happening had Quill not broken contact and stepped away.

"Do you see?"

"Can anyone do that?" she asked. "Or only good liars?"

He smiled, distorting the scar on his broad face. "You mean gods?"

"Same thing," she said, kicking her toe in the dirt.

"I imagine people that are used to shoving away their feelings can move them around like that, and show you only what they want." Tuck's eyes flicked to me. "Care to try?"

"I'll kick your ass, Tuck. God or not."

"After a nap," Thorne said, keeping his distance as his eyes flashed to Elowen. "I'm not even sure how you're still standing."

"Wait. So am I clear?" Archer asked, pulling his sleeve down to hide the Treeis mark. "We all agree that I'm not connected to the murdering ex?"

"Hey!" Thea swatted Archer's chest. "Don't forget some of us knew him before. He was fine. No murdering."

"That's because he didn't know who he was," I answered, spinning on my heel to walk inside. "I'm going to sleep for four days. If you need me, no the fuck you don't."

Thorne took a step in my direction but I threw up a hand to stop him. "Do we need a lesson in boundaries?"

He moved back.

"Such a good boy," I said, swinging open the door as Archer chuckled.

"WHAT THE HELL ARE YOU DOING?"

"Shh," Archer hissed, holding up a kitchen knife. "This part is incredibly important."

I leaned against the doorframe, watching as he meticulously arranged thin slices of meat on a piece of bread, his tongue poking out in concentration. The kitchen counter was covered in various ingredients, cheeses in different stages of being sliced, meats laid out like playing cards, and at least three different types of bread.

"Did you raid the entire pantry?"

"Elowen said I'm not allowed to dirty all her dishes at night anymore." He grinned, not looking up from his careful meat placement. "So I'm being very selective about which ones I use."

"I can see that," I said dryly, eyeing the stack of plates beside him. "Very selective."

The Remnants swirled over my arms, but I did my best to ignore them as I watched this ridiculous man treat sandwich making like it was an art form. I tried to focus on the absurdity of the scene rather than the shadows threatening to manifest.

"You know what your problem is?" he asked, reaching for a slice of cheese.

"Just one?"

"You've never had a properly constructed midnight sandwich." He held up the knife again, using it to gesture as he spoke. "It's all about the layers. The architecture. The *vision*."

I snorted. "The vision?"

"Don't mock my craft. This is serious business."

"Oh, I can see that. Very serious."

He finally looked up, his eyes bright with that boyish mischief I'd missed. "Want me to make you one? I've been practicing."

"Practicing making sandwiches?"

"You sound like a bird repeating everything I say. Anyway, I had to find something to do while you were off having adventures without me."

"If I'd had a choice..."

He forced a smile. "I know, Fingers. I know."

A particularly violent surge from the Remnants made me grip the doorframe, my knuckles going white as I fought to keep the shadows from manifesting. They were desperate to break free. To destroy. To consume.

Archer immediately set down his knife, all traces of playfulness vanishing. He opened his arms. "Come here."

I hesitated for a moment before stepping into his embrace. The Remnants hissed their disapproval, but his warmth seemed to push back against their cold fury. He hugged me tight, one hand coming up to cradle the back of my head.

"I've got you," he whispered. "Whatever darkness is trying to eat you alive in there, whatever madness is screaming in your head, I've got you. We'll figure it out together."

I pressed my face into his chest, letting out a shaky breath. "Promise?"

"Always." He pulled back just enough to look at me, his expression turning serious. "If I had to be bound to anyone in the world, I'm glad it's you."

I squeezed him a little harder. "Me too, Archie. But I'm fairly certain Quill is tangled up in this too."

"It's not a tangle. It's fate. And we're fine either way. It changes nothing."

I pulled away from him, staring into his blue eyes. "I mean, it changes a little. We don't really know what it means."

"I'm fairly certain it means I'm going to protect you both. Which was always the plan."

"But if Aeris is bad, why do something good?"

He shook his head. "I can't think on an empty stomach."

I smiled. "Good thing you're a professional sandwich maker now."

He stepped away to finish making his snack that was definitely the size of a full meal. "Can I ask you something?"

"Of course."

"They say my father is dying."

The words hit me harder than I expected. I remembered Aldus's kindness, the way he'd tried to protect me when we'd been imprisoned together. "How long?"

"I'm not sure. Tuck says he hasn't left his bed." Archer methodically arranged cheese slices as if they held answers. "I don't know what to do."

I hopped up to sit on the counter beside his work. "Talk it through with me. What's holding you back?"

"If I go there, they'll try to force me to be the heir. I don't know the first thing about being royal. I can barely remember which fork to use at dinner." He laid down another piece of cheese with careful precision. "That was always Harlow's domain. And what if they won't let me leave? What if I get trapped in that life?"

"I'd never let that happen if that wasn't your choice, Archer."

"I don't know if you've noticed, but you and I aren't getting a lot of say about how things pan out around here."

"I might have an ace in my pocket now."

He whipped around with a mock gasp, knife in hand. "You're sleeping with the *enemy*?"

I rolled my eyes. "Calm down, Toes. No one is talking about sex here. But I do think Thorne's actually on our team."

"Listen, I'm not saying you're wrong. But I'm also not sure I can trust that's your choice and not some kind of manipulation."

"See these tattoos?" I asked, as I raised the loose sleeve of my robe. "These are my Remnants, like Alastor's but not. They speak into my mind and they hate him more than anything." My mind was filled with the potency of their hatred. Not only for Thorne, but for me too. "If I was going to be manipulated, it would have been by them, I can promise you that." I snagged a slice of bread and nibbled while I told him everything. Alastor's training. The meeting he'd had. The madness. The Forgotten. I stood in that kitchen and poured my heart into explaining why Thorne's return was my choice. Even if it didn't make sense. "We can't live in the past, Archer. We have to move on. We can do it together, but I think there could be something good that comes from seeing your father. I won't push you though. I'll support whatever you decide and everyone else can fuck off. That's our mantra now. That's how we survive. Together."

He set his knife down, crossing his arms over his broad chest as he dipped his chin, blond hair falling over his eyes. "Okay. I can handle together. Though I'm not sure what good will come from visiting a stranger in an old castle."

"How about something like closure. Like not having to wonder for the rest of your life what he might have said. He's been kind to the Salt, you know. And he's been sending food to the orphans."

"Through Tuck, probably," Archer muttered, but I could see him considering it.

"Maybe this is your chance to understand that part of yourself without having to commit to it. You could hear him out, see all your options, and still choose your own path."

"That family bond..." he said quietly. "Even if it's broken, it still aches sometimes."

"Better to face it than regret not trying. And hey, maybe you'll discover you have a natural talent for wearing fancy crowns."

He snorted. "I'm handsome. Of course I have that talent."

A small voice came from the doorway, "Did you make mine?"

We both turned to see Quill standing there in her nightgown, rubbing sleep from her eyes with one hand as she held her dog in the other.

"Of course I did, Pencil." Archer's face softened as he gestured to a carefully wrapped sandwich on the counter. "Only cheese, exactly how you like it." He looked down to his wrist, checking the time on a watch that didn't exist. "You're five minutes late, you know?"

"Midnight snacks aren't specific to a time," she informed him, setting Boo down. She padded over, climbing onto the chair at the table. "Are you going to see your papa?"

"I don't know yet, kid."

"I never had a papa," she said matter-of-factly, taking a bite. "Or a mama. Just Paesha and everyone here."

The Remnants stirred at her words, but this time with an ache that felt almost like sympathy. I reached out to smooth her wild curls.

"Sometimes," I said, looking at Archer, "the family we choose is better than the one we're born to. But that doesn't mean we stop hoping the others will choose better too."

Archer leaned against the counter, looking between us. "When did you two get so wise?"

"Probably around the time you got so good at making sandwiches," I teased.

"So yesterday," Quill said, holding up her sandwich for inspection.

I'D ONLY SEEN the castle gardens once before, through the windows during that formal dinner the night Aldus had gone missing. Back then, I'd barely glimpsed the topiaries and hedges through the cold darkness. Now, wildflowers grew in cheerful tangles, herbs sprawled across stone pathways, and fruit trees stretched their branches toward the sky without interference. It seemed odd. To have so much color and vibrancy in a world where darkness clouded everything.

"My lady," a woman said, appearing at my elbow with a tray of delicate cakes. "Perhaps the young miss would like some refreshments while she waits?"

Quill's eyes lit up at the sight of the sweets, but she looked to me first for permission. I nodded, and she bounced on her toes.

"There's a lovely tea room through there," the woman said, gesturing toward glass doors that led back into the castle. "With an excellent view of the gardens."

"Can I go?" Quill asked. "Please?"

"I'll go with her," Thea offered, already moving to follow the excited child.

Boo yipped at their heels as they disappeared inside, leaving Elowen and me to watch as Archer approached his father. Aldus sat in a cushioned chair beneath a sprawling oak tree, wrapped in a thick blanket despite the warm day. The change in the old king was stark. His shoulders curved inward, diminished by grief and likely loneliness. Maybe even guilt.

"When was the last time they spoke?" Elowen asked.

"As I understand it, they've only spoken once and it was when

Archer was drowning in grief over losing his sister. He blamed Aldus, even though it wasn't the king's fault. I think a part of him still does, because if he'd come for their mother, things would've been different for all of them."

"Hindsight can be so cruel," Elowen said, giving me a pointed look before she turned her gaze back to the gardens.

We watched in silence as Archer moved across the grass, each step seeming to cost him something. His usual confident stride had abandoned him, replaced by the cautious approach of a man walking into battle. When he finally reached his father, they stared at each other for a long moment. Even from this distance, I could see the tension in Archer's shoulders, the slight tremor in Aldus's hands as he gripped the arms of his chair.

Aldus pushed himself to his feet despite Archer's obvious protest. For a heartbeat, they stood facing each other, and I found myself holding my breath. Then something in Archer's posture changed, a subtle softening, a lowering of defenses, and Aldus stepped forward, pulling his son into an embrace.

I felt Elowen's hand slip into mine as we watched them hold on to each other, both trying to bridge a chasm that had been uncrossable only days ago. When they finally separated, I could see them both wiping at their eyes, their gestures mirror images of each other.

And then I walked away. The moment I knew for sure Archer felt safe, that he'd chosen these moments for himself, I gave them privacy to find their path forward.

"Fancy meeting you here," a voice rumbled from down the hall. For a second, I closed my eyes, preparing for battle.

37

THORNE

I'd perfected the art of looking unbothered over centuries of practice, so I leaned against the marble column in Aldus's castle like a man who hadn't spent the last three days watching his Ever withdraw further into herself. Each glimpse of her had been both a blessing and a torment, seeing her pace the floors like a caged storm, beautiful and dangerous and breaking my heart.

When she had finally emerged onto the rooftop that first night, every carefully crafted pretense of indifference shattered. But I knew it would. She knew it would too. We'd made eye contact in the dark, lit by only stars. And then she danced. The moonlight caught in her hair, illuminating the markings that spiraled across her skin like terrible constellations. But even in her pain, she was magnificent. She'd come out every night since, checking to be sure I was there before she performed. I hadn't missed a single second of it.

Elowen stepped between us, ever the protective mother. Her accusation stung more than I cared to admit. "Thorne Noctus. I trust you're not here to cause trouble. Don't think I haven't seen you haunting our grounds."

I slid my hands into my pockets. "It's not haunting, per se. I'm just making myself available. Should the need for one such as myself arise." *Should she need me,* I didn't say. I'd been keeping watch, counting the hours until the other gods descended, knowing I should maintain my distance but unable to stay away.

"I'll go check on Quill and Thea," Elowen said in that calm, knowing sort of way, though her pointed look made it clear she was simply giving us space. As she passed Paesha, she added, "Try not to break anything expensive."

The moment we were alone, I could see the battle raging across her skin. The Remnant's darkness swirled visibly through the markings climbing up her legs and along her bare arms. My fingers itched with the need to help, to heal, to protect. But I knew better than to offer. She'd never accept it, not from me.

"You look..." *Like sin incarnate. Like every damn fantasy I've had for centuries.*

"Unhinged? Corrupted? One bad day away from burning down a castle?"

I pushed away from the column, drawn to her. Foolish, perhaps, but I'd never claimed to be wise where she was concerned. "I was going to say beautiful."

"Careful there. Your silver tongue is showing."

"Is it? And here I thought I was being remarkably well behaved."

She shifted deliberately, the slit in her dress revealing more of those swirling markings.

Good girl. Come play with me.

My eyes tracked the movement before I could stop myself, and her resulting smirk made my heart stutter. "See something interesting, Supreme Sovereign?"

I adjusted my glasses, using the gesture to compose myself. "Simply monitoring the spread of corruption, Paesha darling."

"And here I thought you were just being a typical man."

"There's nothing typical about me." I let the arrogance seep into my tone, falling back on old habits.

"No? Because from where I'm standing, you look remarkably

typical. It's unfortunate, really. All that power and all your ridiculous titles and you still have to look at that hideous face in the mirror."

The familiar dance of our banter felt like coming home. This was how we'd learned each other, and this was how we'd learn our way back.

"It's a tragedy I survive every day. Thank you for noticing."

The corner of her mouth lifted. I fucking loved that little smirk on her lips. "How could I not? What with that nose."

I stepped closer. "Feeling ruthless today, I see."

"Honestly, I feel ruthless every day. I'm surprised you haven't noticed."

"It's adorable that you think I haven't noticed every single thing about you."

"That's in line with your stalker tendencies, Thorne Noctus. Three days of pining in the treeline is beneath you."

"How are you, Paesha? Truly."

She lifted a shoulder. Not to shrug, but to try to silence the voices, I was sure. "I'm alive. I guess that's something."

I glanced at Archer. "I'm going to find a way to free you from that."

"From being alive? Let's not."

"From those voices."

Her eyes flashed and I could have sworn for half a second I saw the plea within her before she blinked it away. "Let's not make promises we can't keep to each other. You have no idea what I need right now. No one does."

Moving closer, I took her hand. She didn't pull away, those fucking eyes staring into mine with an intensity that made my soul shake. I lifted her fingers to my mouth, kissing each one, lingering over the space where she used to wear a ring that marked her as mine. "You needed someone to dance with you in the rain, and I was too busy trying to control the storm. So dance with me now. Not because I'm yours or you're mine, but because when you move, the whole fucking world stops to watch. I'll stay at whatever distance you need, close enough to catch you if you fall, far enough that you can still breathe. And when those shadows try to drown your light, I'll be the bastard in the corner betting on the fire."

Her eyes turned haunted, as if the voices within her fought against me in her mind.

"Dance with me," I said again, holding out my other hand.

She took a deep breath before glancing around the empty hallway, a breathy laugh escaping her lips. "Here? Now? There's no music."

"Since when has that stopped you?"

"Since there are actual people in this castle who might walk by at any moment and see the almighty Thorne Noctus waltzing in the halls like a lovesick fool."

Despite her words, she stepped closer, letting me draw her into my arms. "Let them see."

"Careful. Your reputation for being an insufferable asshole is at stake."

"Worth it."

She rested her head against my chest, and for a heartbeat, everything felt right. Then she pulled back, looking up at me with that familiar mischief in her eyes. The dance stopped. She reached for my tie, and every rational thought fled my mind. "For someone who cares so much about the past, you dress remarkably well in the present."

"I care less and less about the past every second." My hand caught her wrist gently, though whether to stop her or to anchor myself, I wasn't sure. "What are you doing?"

"Making you look less perfect. It's unsettling." She adjusted my tie until it hung crooked, and I clenched my jaw, fighting a smile. "There. Much better."

"Are you quite finished?" I asked, but made no move to stop her as she reached for my jacket button. I'd let her dismantle me piece by piece if she wanted to. Hell, I'd probably thank her for it.

"Not even close." She undid the button, misaligning my lapels with deliberate care.

"Some of us prefer not to look like we just rolled out of bed."

"And some of us know the difference between necessity and vanity."

"You're impossible," I said softly, letting more warmth slip into my voice than I intended.

A voice shattered our peace. "Boss?"

"Not now, Tuck," I said, ignoring the urgent tone in his voice as Paesha and I circled a place of familiarity. I'd needed this moment with her like I needed air.

Heavy boots echoed in the hallway as he stepped into our sacred place. "Yes, now. Paesha, good to see you."

"Liar. Good to see you too," she answered. "I've got to go anyway. I promised Archer I'd come say hello to Aldus and give him an escape route if he needed it."

We all turned to face the windows, watching as Archer sat on a bench across from his father's chair. His face gave nothing away.

"It's important they find peace," Tuck said, his gruff voice softening.

"It's also important that you don't push him," Paesha bit back. "He's here, isn't he? That's what you wanted." She turned to me. "I should go."

"Of course," I said smoothly, even as a part of me wanted to pull her back, to steal a few more moments. "Far be it from me to keep you from your Archer."

She arched an eyebrow. "Jealousy is an ugly color on you, Thorne Noctus."

"Everything looks good on me, darling. I thought we just established that."

Tuck cleared his throat pointedly. "If you two are quite finished..."

Paesha smirked, stepping away from me with deliberate slowness. "Duty calls anyway. Try not to pine too hard in my absence."

"I'll do my best to carry on." I sketched a mocking bow. "Do give Archer my regards."

She rolled her eyes, but I caught the hint of a smile playing at the corners of her mouth as she turned to leave. The Remnants swirled around her like a living cloak. I watched her go, drinking in every detail—the sway of her hips, the tumble of her chestnut hair, the markings that danced across her skin like living art. Even burdened by madness and wrapped in darkness, she was a vision, a goddess in mortal form.

Tuck waited until her footsteps had faded before rounding on me. "She'll push you away if you get between her and Archer. That's how that bond works."

"And what of our bond?"

He crossed his arms over his chest and took a step back. "She's still here, isn't she? I didn't miss you flirting in the hallways like a besotted fool."

"That's why you interrupted?"

"You need to tread lightly," he said, voice hardened.

"It's not enough."

"It's going to have to be enough for now." Tuck stepped closer, lowering his chin to glare at me. "She knows the truth and she's not dead yet. There's a reason. You need to ask yourself why."

I met Tuck's glare with an icy one of my own, refusing to be cowed. "You think I haven't been asking myself that very question?"

Mid-argument, a flash of movement caught my eye. I turned to the windows overlooking the gardens. Minerva.

She'd been fucking avoiding me and here she was, speaking with fervor to Archer as Paesha and the mortal king listened in. I took a step toward the doors, but Tuck put a hand on my chest. "She won't see you."

"She needs to get over it. I went. I came back. No harm done."

Tuck huffed. "She warned you. You didn't listen. These are the consequences of your actions."

"Did she tell you to say that?"

"She also told me to say no when you asked."

Fucking Minerva.

"Go insert yourself in that conversation and report back."

"That's not going to be obvious at all," he said, pushing open the door to the garden.

Prick. "Keep pretending like you weren't curious," I said before walking out.

"'LET my strength be your shield against the darkness, Paesha. You're not alone. Fight back with me. Fight back and I'll stand between you both and the dark.' That's what he said," I told Tuck hours later, sitting in the barracks at the castle. "I don't see how that makes him an Unmade."

"You can't possibly be this thick-headed," he answered, wearing a path into the dirt floor. "You saw his face. He was drained. Fully. He had no power left. Aeris set him up. I bet Ezra was meant to show up there, but we did first. And I doubt she counted on Paesha's attachment to Archer. Paesha saved them both. She stepped in where Ezra was meant to and Aeris hadn't anticipated it."

I stood, gripping his arm to keep him from pacing. "You're making me dizzy. Be still."

He took a solid breath, his wide shoulders falling as he scratched his beard. "You're right. Sorry."

"I get that he drained himself and spoke an oath, but you and Minnie are missing a big piece. You can't simply create an Unmade. If it's not Ezra's power, it doesn't work."

His dark eyes met mine, gaze shifting between them as if he were holding a secret he held back to protect me. "When have you ever seen a Treeis bond without an Unmade Guardian?"

"It's never happened."

"Then can you see why Minerva has made her conclusion? Why I agree with her? You can't possibly argue with the two of us, supported by your own power remembering those moments."

"If a mortal drains their power while binding themselves to *Ezra* they become an Unmade Guardian. But—"

"There's no buts. Aeris set him up. Two more minutes and he would have been on the floor, Ezra would have showed up, they all would have begged for Archer to be saved and he would have taken him, refilling that void with his own power. That's how it works and you know it. But with Quill and Paesha, who's got more power than she knows what to do with right now, their power filled the absence of Archer's. He was reborn as an Unmade right there. We fucking witnessed it. Hell, Thorne, the boy shot himself across the house and attacked you, even knowing who you are."

I shook my head, turning my back on him. "He's something else then. Something else that was able to make the Treeis bond."

Tuck's voice was quiet. Full of sorrow. "He's an Unmade Guardian. He's not bound to Ezra, he's bound to Paesha and Quill, but that doesn't change what he is. Minerva doesn't get these things wrong and you know it."

I did know. But fuck, I didn't want to accept it. Because it just made for another puzzle. One my brother likely knew the answers to when we did not.

"This was the plan. Ezra's fucking promise coming to fruition right in front of us," I said solemnly. "And now we need to figure this out before he takes the throne."

"There's still time. It doesn't look like he's putting on the crown yet."

I jerked around, hands at my side. "You look into her face and tell her we have to drag this out. I need the Fates to tell me how to help her. How to stop the voices. I don't want time."

"The Fates never said they were going to help you. They said they would hear your questions. You get the kid on the throne and then they'll see you, remember? There's no timeline on that anyway. Did you see Aldus walk today? He hasn't done that in weeks. He needed his son. Mortals need their family. You can't change this. You're going to have to be patient."

"If you think I want Archer on that fucking throne, you're wrong. Dead wrong. And you know why. But we aren't the only gods circling. Fucking Bellatora was here today. Did you know that? She's been coming to see Aldus. Alastor is still a godsdamn wild card. Ezra's on the hunt. Where the fuck is Themis, Tuck?

Have you seen Vesalia lately? Something's not right. I can feel it in the air. And we're sitting ducks fucking waiting to see who's going to show their hand."

Tuck nodded once before moving toward the door. "Then I guess it's time we start stacking the deck."

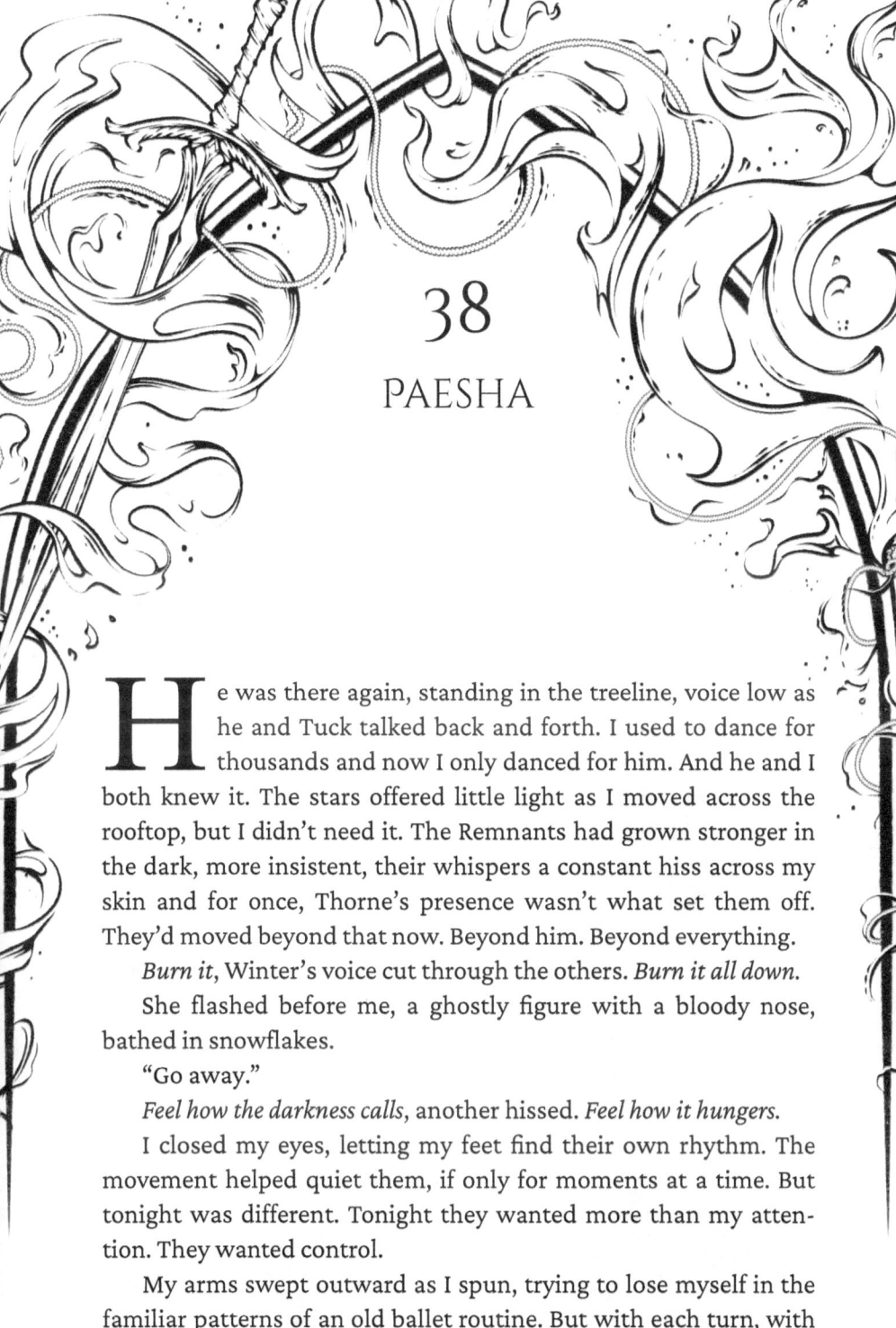

38

PAESHA

He was there again, standing in the treeline, voice low as he and Tuck talked back and forth. I used to dance for thousands and now I only danced for him. And he and I both knew it. The stars offered little light as I moved across the rooftop, but I didn't need it. The Remnants had grown stronger in the dark, more insistent, their whispers a constant hiss across my skin and for once, Thorne's presence wasn't what set them off. They'd moved beyond that now. Beyond him. Beyond everything.

Burn it, Winter's voice cut through the others. *Burn it all down.*

She flashed before me, a ghostly figure with a bloody nose, bathed in snowflakes.

"Go away."

Feel how the darkness calls, another hissed. *Feel how it hungers.*

I closed my eyes, letting my feet find their own rhythm. The movement helped quiet them, if only for moments at a time. But tonight was different. Tonight they wanted more than my attention. They wanted control.

My arms swept outward as I spun, trying to lose myself in the familiar patterns of an old ballet routine. But with each turn, with each graceful arc of my body, the whispers grew stronger. The

Remnants were no longer content to simply speak, they moved with me, through me, as if the dance itself was awakening something terrible.

Let us show you what you truly are, they whispered in unison. *Let us free.*

I pushed harder, spinning faster, my feet barely touching the ground as I leaped across the rooftop. The physical exertion should have exhausted me, should have quieted my mind, but instead it fed the darkness. It wasn't supposed to be like this. Dancing had been my only escape. Each movement felt like striking matches in my soul, threatening to ignite an inferno I couldn't control. And it made no sense. Unless he was never truly the target.

You can feel it growing, Sylvie purred. *The power. The hunger.*

They were right. With each passing day, the force inside me grew stronger. It wasn't just voices anymore, it was a presence, a weight that pressed against my bones, begging to be unleashed. Only one voice offered any peace, one nameless Remnant that met me in that quiet corner of my mind where the others couldn't reach. But she was silent tonight.

Break the walls, they screamed. *Tear down the sky.*

Let them see what power truly means.

Show them destruction.

Show them chaos.

Show them the end of everything.

The voices overlapped, a symphony of madness that matched the frantic rhythm of my feet. I couldn't tell if I was dancing to silence them, or dancing to their tune. Each spin brought a new vision of devastation. Cities crumbled, mountains fell, rivers boiled. The power surged through my veins like liquid fire, and the Remnants fed on it, growing stronger with each passing second.

You are not meant for peace, Winter taunted. *You are meant for this.*

I threw my head back and laughed, the sound bordering on hysteria as I pirouetted on the edge of sanity. The rain fell harder now, soaking through my clothes, but I barely felt it. The heat beneath my skin, the burning in my blood, consumed everything else.

Let go, they urged. *Let us show them what destruction truly means.*

"Please," I gasped, but I wasn't sure what I was begging for. Peace? Silence? An end to the constant war within my own mind? The Remnants surged at my weakness, their whispers becoming screams that echoed through me. I knew I was reaching a breaking point. They'd been pushing and pushing for days. It seemed like something had happened. Like leaving Thorne in the Forgotten wasn't about revenge, but rather locking away someone who might have the ability to cage them. End them. But he couldn't. No one could.

I was sad. Truly and deeply sad. My entire heart ached as I fought a battle I couldn't win. And so I danced. Because it was the only thing I knew without thinking. Without feeling. Without needing. I danced because it used to mean joy. And escape. I danced because now it meant something else. Yearning. For myself. For the way things used to be.

My legs finally gave out as the rain pounded against the rooftop, matching the thundering of my heart while I fought against the tide of chaos threatening to break free. And then strong arms wrapped around me, pulling me against a familiar chest. I didn't have to look up to know it was Thorne. He said nothing, just held me as I shook, one hand cradling my head while the other traced soothing patterns on my back.

I should have pushed him away. Should have maintained the careful distance I'd tried to keep. But the voices weren't screaming about him anymore. They were screaming about everything. The stars, the rain, the air I breathed. They wanted it all destroyed, reduced to nothing but ash and memory.

"I can't," I whispered against his chest. "I can't keep fighting them."

We stayed like that for what felt like hours, the rain soaking us both as he held me together with nothing but his presence and his warmth. The Remnants still raged, but for now, in this stolen moment on a rain-slick roof, I let myself be anchored by the one person who'd survived centuries of darkness.

It wouldn't last. It never did. The hunger for ruination grew stronger every day, and soon, not even Thorne's arms would be enough to hold back the storm. Nor Archer's easy smile. Quill was my only slight reprieve. But I wouldn't tell her that. Nor would I use her for her power. I'd suffer for centuries before I ever did that.

"You're soaking wet," he murmured against my hair.

"Astute observation. Did you learn that in god school?"

He huffed a laugh, shifting to sit more comfortably while keeping me tucked against him. "They covered it right after 'how to brood attractively in shadows'."

"Well, you certainly excelled in that class." I could feel his smile against my temple. "Though your stalking needs work. I saw you in the garden today."

"Impossible. I was extremely stealthy."

"You knocked over a potted plant."

"That was Tuck."

"He wasn't even there."

"He's very talented."

Despite everything, I found myself smiling. The voices still whispered, but they seemed more distant now, as if our mundane conversation confused them. I focused on the steady rise and fall of his chest, the warmth of him beneath my cheek.

"How was your day?" he asked softly, his fingers absently combing through my wet hair. "Other than catching me being stealthy, of course, which likely didn't happen."

"Thea had some stuff in Silbath, so Archer and I walked her into town. And Quill tried to teach Boo a new trick but it didn't go well. He kept rolling over, no matter what she asked him to do. She'd say sit, he'd roll over. Stay, roll over. I think he's convinced it's the only trick worth knowing. And he's not wrong because she kept feeding him."

"Smart dog. When in doubt, stick with what works."

"Did you learn that in god school too?"

"Probably."

The rain began to ease, turning from a downpour to a gentle patter. Neither of us moved. The silence between us felt comfortable, unhurried. No expectations, no demands, just quiet understanding.

After a while, he shifted, reaching into his coat. "Elowen gave me something." He pulled out a worn book, its leather cover soft with age and now slightly damp from the rain. "Said it was your favorite."

My breath caught as I recognized the familiar binding. "The Soulless." A smile tugged at my lips. "I used to read that over and over."

He opened it carefully, the pages crackling softly. "I've read half of it, but I'll start over if you want?"

"You're going to read it to me?"

"I'm told I have an excellent reading voice." He cleared his throat dramatically. "'Once, in a kingdom far beyond the mist, there lived a princess who didn't want to be saved...'"

I settled against him as his voice carried the familiar words across the rooftop. It was a simple story really. A woman who befriended a soulless dragon meant to guard her tower, and together they traveled the world having adventures instead of waiting for a man to rescue her. But something about hearing it in Thorne's rich baritone made it feel new again.

The Remnants stirred at the edges of my mind, but they seemed unable to corrupt this moment, this simple peace found in an old tale read aloud in the rain. The words of the story faded into silence, but still we sat there, neither willing to break the peace we'd found. The rain had stopped completely now, leaving only the sound of water dripping from the eaves.

"I see you," I said finally. "Not just the watching or the hovering, but the way you fight against your own nature. Every time I make a choice you don't agree with, I can see how much you want to step in, to take control." I traced a pattern on his shirt with my finger, gathering courage. "But you don't. You stay back. You let me stumble. It's... different."

His hand stilled in my hair. "Different?"

"The Thorne I knew would have already had ten plans in motion. The Reverius I think is hiding in there would have commanded the world to bend. But you, you're learning to let go. To trust me."

"It's not easy," he admitted, a hint of wry humor in his voice. "I'm not particularly good at relinquishing control."

"I hadn't noticed."

He laughed softly. "For thousands of years, I've tried to orchestrate every moment, craft every path. But when it comes to you, I must follow instead of lead."

I pushed myself up to look at him, really look at him. Even in the dim light, I could see the struggle there, the constant battle between his need to protect and his effort to let me find my own way.

"I don't want time anymore." The words came out in a rush, surprising us both. "I don't know how much longer I can keep fighting myself in the madness. The voices, they're getting stronger, and I—" I swallowed hard. "I don't want to waste whatever time I have left fighting what's between us."

His hands came up to frame my face, thumbs brushing away tears I hadn't realized I'd shed. "Paesha—"

"I know what I'm saying." I leaned into his touch. "For once in our very long history, I know exactly what I'm choosing. It's not mixed up with lies and deceit. It's truly you and truly me and that's all I want."

"You're not going to lose yourself," he said fiercely. "I won't let that happen."

"You can't promise that."

"I can promise I'll be here, whether you're dancing in the rain or burning down realms."

A laugh that was half sob escaped me. "Even if I burn you with them?"

"Especially then."

I kissed him. Not the calculated seduction from the Forgotten, not the desperate clash of our reunion, but something deeper.

Something real. His hands slid into my hair as he pulled me closer, and I felt the careful restraint he always maintained finally snap.

The kiss turned hungry, desperate, as if we could somehow anchor ourselves to this moment through touch alone. His lips traced down my neck as I arched into him, and for the first time since the voices began their endless chorus, everything else fell silent. There was only this, his hands on my skin, his breath against my throat, the solid heat of him beneath me.

"Stay with me," I breathed against his mouth. "Whatever comes next... stay."

He pulled back to meet my eyes, and the raw emotion I saw there stole my breath. "Always," he promised, and when he kissed me again, I finally let myself believe it. Trust it. And him.

"You're going to the castle again?" Thea asked, standing outside the giant carriage that was waiting for Archer, Quill and I.

"We have to," Quill said, climbing into the carriage. "King Aldy promised to teach me a new dance today."

Archer threw an arm over Thea's shoulder. "You could come. It's nice when we're all there. I think it gives him a sense of family."

"I do like it when he tells stories about your mother. But I've got a delivery to make first. Tuck brought another trunk this morning."

"More supplies for your underground city?" I asked, watching her copper hair catch the morning light.

She nodded. "The tunnels under the Dancing Ghost are getting crowded. We may need to expand toward the old theater district soon." Her eyes darted around, checking for listeners before continuing. "Three more families came through last night. They're terrified of what the gods might do next."

Their fear was valid. Ever since Aeris had transformed Requiem, its people had slowly disappeared into the network of tunnels Thea had been quietly expanding. What had started as a few hidden rooms beneath the Dancing Ghost had grown into a sprawling sanctuary.

"Tell Vincent I said hello," Quill chirped from the carriage. "And that I miss his sweet rolls. But don't tell Elowen I said that."

Thea smiled. "The baker sends his love, I'm sure. He says the underground ovens aren't quite the same, but he's making do."

"Need help with the trunk?" Archer asked.

"No, I've got my system down now. Besides, you can't keep the king waiting." She hugged him quickly. "Tell him I'll try to make it for dinner."

We watched as she disappeared back into the Syndicate house. It still amazed me how she'd managed to create this secret network, right under everyone's noses. It helped that Aeris had gone missing. Though I suspected Minerva, Tuck's friend, had something to do with that. That old goddess was something fierce.

"She's doing good work," Archer said quietly as we climbed into the carriage.

"And Tuck keeps the supplies coming," I added, settling beside Quill. "Imagine if the people knew the gods were helping them hide from the gods."

"Thorne helped me get more blankets for the children yesterday too," Quill said, petting Boo who'd settled in her lap. "That feels like we're winning."

I lowered my chin, taking her hand. "We're not in a war, Quilly, okay? We're careful, but not setting ourselves up for something we could never win. You understand that right?"

"Yeah but if we *were*, Minnie said we'd win."

"You've got to stop talking to her," Archer said, digging into his bag to pull out a skein of yarn. "She scares me."

Quill lifted a shoulder. "That's why I like her. The scary ones are usually the ones you should be friends with. I had a scary friend once. Her name was Deyanira, huh Paesha? She'd probably kill you."

"Quill," I gasped. "She absolutely would not have."

She smiled that ornery little smile. "She might've."

"How's the new hobby going?" I asked Archer with a smirk, hoping Quill would take a hint.

Archer held up the tangled mess of blue yarn with a scowl. "I don't understand. The old woman in the market made it look so simple. 'Just loop it through,' she said. 'It's relaxing,' she said." He yanked at a particularly stubborn knot. "This is not relaxing. This is torture with string."

I bit back a smile, watching him wrestle with what was supposed to be a scarf. He'd been throwing himself into one activity after another. Last week he'd tried to learn the lute. The broken strings were still scattered around his room.

I knew what he was doing, even if he wouldn't admit it. He missed his twin. Part of his heart died the day she had, and though he'd let the sadness fade, there was still a void to be filled. Be it from sandwich making or otherwise.

The Treeis mark peeked out from beneath his sleeve as he worked, and something warm bloomed in my chest at the sight of it. Whatever that bond meant, whatever complications it might bring, it had given him back a piece of what he'd lost. A family. A purpose. People to protect.

"I think you dropped a stitch," Quill said helpfully, leaning over to point at his work.

"I dropped my sanity about ten rows ago." He held up the mess of yarn. "Does this look anything like a scarf to you?"

"Maybe if you squint?" I offered. "And turn your head to the left. And possibly drink some of that fancy whiskey your father keeps in the castle."

"It looks like Boo got into the yarn basket," Quill giggled.

"You're both terrible critics." He stuffed the yarn back in his bag with an exaggerated huff, but I caught the ghost of a smile playing at his lips. "Maybe I'll try painting next. How hard can that be?"

"Says the man who lost a fight with string," I teased.

His eyes met mine, and beneath his playfulness, I saw a flash of understanding pass between us. He knew I knew why he was doing this. Just as I knew he wasn't ready to talk about it yet. So instead, I reached over and squeezed his hand, feeling the mark on my shoulder warm at the contact.

"At least you haven't tried juggling again," Quill said solemnly. "Poor Boo is still traumatized."

"I think I'm still traumatized," he said seriously.

"Aren't you the most beautiful girl that ever was?" King Aldus asked, his hands clasped together as he looked down at Quill spinning in her new dress. The giant box had been waiting for her when we arrived.

"You'll spoil the child rotten," Minnie said, though there was no hardness to her tone, only delight as we all stood around watching Quill spin.

"King Aldy?" Quill asked, walking up to take the old man's hand. "The dress is very pretty. But don't you think my friends at Thorne's house should have what they need before I have things I don't?"

"Remember when she used to be creepy?" Archer whispered in my ear.

"Can you think of what's changed?" I asked as King Aldus and Quill began plotting. "We haven't let Aeris linger around and look at her smile."

"Speaking of Aeris, I heard she came by the house a few days ago when we were here. Maybe we should start forcing Elowen to come with us. She can't be left there alone."

"Listen, Guardian. I'd love to see you try to force that woman to do anything. It won't happen."

"I could talk to her," Minerva said, taking my side. "I have a way with mortals."

I shook my head. "She won't come to heel by force. No matter where you wave that cane."

The doors to the ballroom flung open and Thorne came strolling in, hands in his pockets, eyes locked on mine.

Minerva huffed. "If anyone needs me, I'll be somewhere else."

"Love you too, Minnie," he said with a smile before taking my side. "The council is ready, Aldus."

"Five more minutes," he said, clapping out a beat as Quill followed the steps he'd instructed. He looked so much better than he had that first day in the garden. The color had returned. There was a spring in his step even. When he laughed, I could hear Archer in it, that same warm richness that filled a room. "Son. She needs a prince for this next part."

Archer stepped forward with no hesitation, wrapping an arm around his waist as he bowed low. "My lady, may I?"

Quill scrunched her face. "You see another prince around here?"

I didn't miss the way his shoulders carried the weight of that title. We'd been avoiding the subject, of course, but it sat in the room with us all the same. The king had never once pushed him. He'd never given him any indication he would force anything on him.

Watching Archer struggle beneath the weight of that word made something in my chest ache. Maybe my own silent battle. I knew he was the Guardian, but I wasn't sure what that made me? The damsel? Certainly not the reluctant hero. Minnie had her own guesses, but as everyone dug into figuring out the reason for this bond, one thing was abundantly clear, this was new. Uncharted territory. And likely not at all what Aeris had planned in that moment.

Before Archer became overwhelmed by the title, I stepped forward with an exaggerated curtsy to the old king. "Perhaps his majesty would honor me with a dance? Show these children how it's properly done?"

The king's eyes lit up. "My dear, I thought you'd never ask." He took my hand, spinning me into position as he called out the steps. "One, two, three, see how it flows? The trick is in the timing."

"I've danced a few times in my day, Your Majesty."

"Of course you have. Now," Aldus said, only loud enough for me to hear, "shall we rescue my son from his thoughts?"

Before I could answer, he spun me directly into Archer's arms while he took Quill's. The surprise on Archer's face melted into a grateful smile as he caught me, falling into step without missing a beat.

I felt Thorne's eyes on us as we moved across the floor, that familiar intensity in his gaze. But he stayed where he was, hands in his pockets, though I could see the slight tension in his jaw. The fact that he didn't intervene, didn't try to take control of the moment, said more than any words could have.

"You're thinking too loud," Archer murmured as we turned.

"Says the man drowning in princely duties he hasn't even accepted yet."

"Careful there, Fingers."

I smiled. "Someone has to look out for you."

"Speaking of looking out," he nodded toward Thorne, "your god is doing remarkably well at staying put."

"He's learning."

The music drew to a close, and Aldus clapped in delight. "Magnificent! Though perhaps we should save some dancing for after the council meeting." He turned to Quill, who'd been watching us with rapt attention. "My dear, would you be so kind as to find Minerva? I believe she mentioned something about tea and cakes in the conservatory."

Quill's eyes lit up. "Can I bring Boo?"

"Of course," Aldus chuckled. "Though perhaps warn the staff this time? He gave poor Agnes quite a fright last week when he stole the chicken from the table."

As Quill bounced out of the room, Thorne finally moved from his spot to stand beside me. "The council is waiting," he said softly.

I caught the slight edge in his voice, not jealousy exactly, but something more complex. "Such a good boy." I said, patting his chest before taking Archer's arm.

He snatched my arm and this time Archer stiffened, but said nothing. Thorne leaned down, his voice wrapping around my ear as he whispered, "For now, Paesha darling, but even I have my limits."

I smiled sweetly. "Oh I know, I've been trampling all over them since we met."

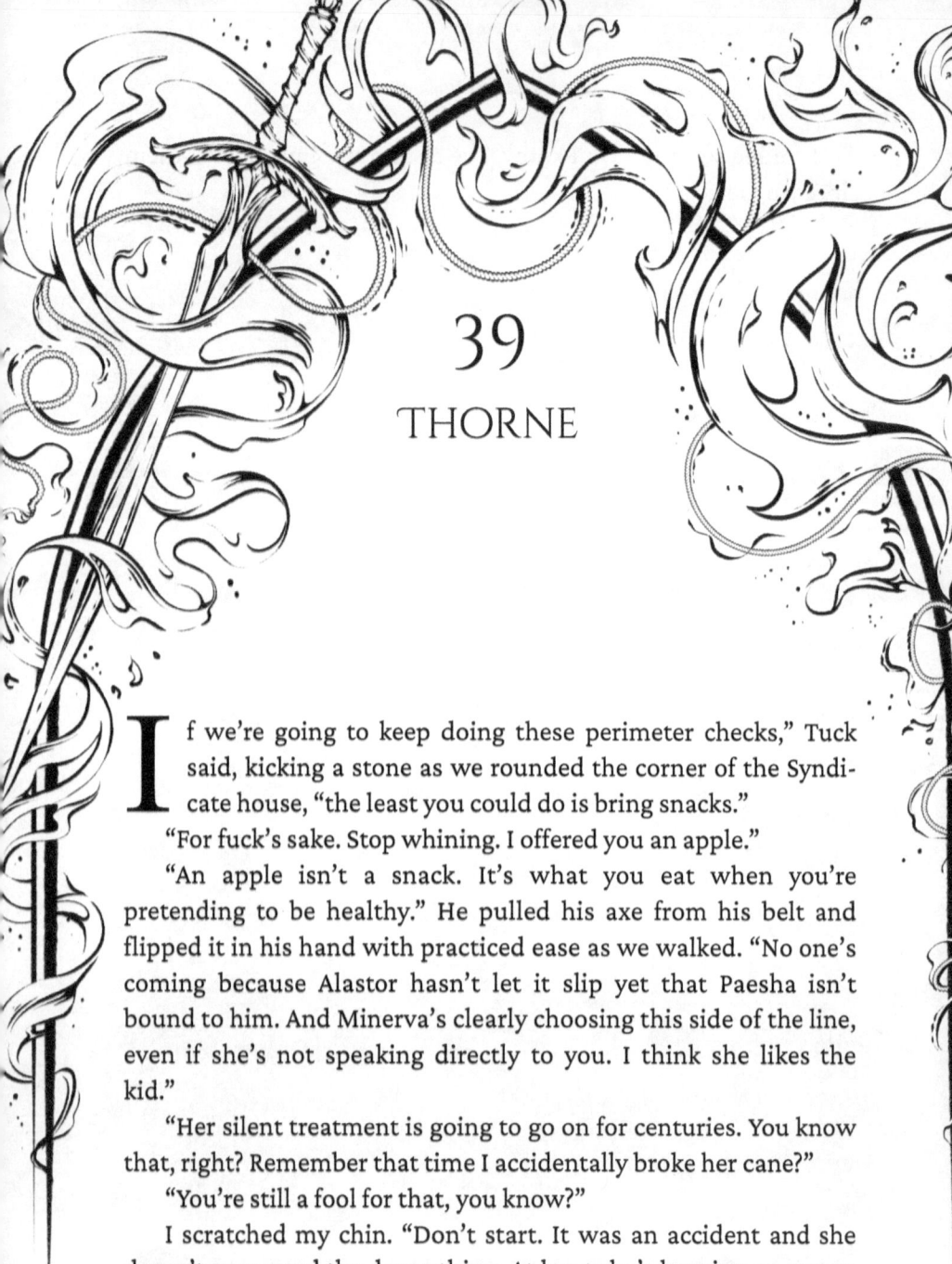

39

THORNE

"I f we're going to keep doing these perimeter checks," Tuck said, kicking a stone as we rounded the corner of the Syndicate house, "the least you could do is bring snacks."

"For fuck's sake. Stop whining. I offered you an apple."

"An apple isn't a snack. It's what you eat when you're pretending to be healthy." He pulled his axe from his belt and flipped it in his hand with practiced ease as we walked. "No one's coming because Alastor hasn't let it slip yet that Paesha isn't bound to him. And Minerva's clearly choosing this side of the line, even if she's not speaking directly to you. I think she likes the kid."

"Her silent treatment is going to go on for centuries. You know that, right? Remember that time I accidentally broke her cane?"

"You're still a fool for that, you know?"

I scratched my chin. "Don't start. It was an accident and she doesn't even need the damn thing. At least she's keeping an eye on Quill."

"Aw, look at you being mature about it. You know she'll come around eventually. Especially now that you've got Aldus sending supplies to Thea's underground network. Minnie's always had a heart for the mortals even if she pretends not to. Probably because they don't know what she is."

"I'm not sure *we* know what she is, Tuck."

A twig snapped behind us, and we both turned to find Archer perched on a fallen log, methodically untangling what appeared to be blue yarn.

"Don't mind me," he said without looking up. "Just trying to salvage what's left of my dignity. And possibly make a scarf."

I arched an eyebrow at the mess in his hands. "That's meant to be a scarf?"

"You know, for someone who claims to be all-knowing, you're remarkably judgmental about my life choices." He held up the yarn with a frustrated sigh. "Though in this case, you might have a point."

"Shouldn't you be training with the Salt?" Tuck asked. "I told your... The king you'd be there today."

"Shouldn't *you* be delivering mysterious packages and pretending not to be a god?" Archer shot back, but his usual playful tone felt forced. His eyes kept darting toward the field behind the house.

"What is it?" I asked, already knowing I wouldn't like the answer.

He set aside his yarn, all pretense of humor falling away. "She's out there again. But it's different this time. The Remnants are... agitated. More than usual. I can almost feel them. It's pretty bad."

"How long?"

"Aren't you *patrolling*? You didn't notice?"

I shot him a look that was anything but friendly.

"About an hour." He stood, brushing grass from his trousers. "I tried to get close, but the shadows nearly took my head off. Figured that might be a sign to get backup."

"And you came to me? I'm touched."

"Well, Thea's busy with the Underground, and Quill's hanging out with Minnie inside again, so my options were limited." He ran a hand through his hair, a nervous gesture I'd seen Paesha make countless times. "Be careful, all right? She's not herself today."

I started toward the field, but Archer caught my arm. "I mean it, Thorne. Whatever's happening in her head right now, it's not the usual stuff. I mean it is, but…"

"Since when are you the expert on what's usual for her?"

"Since I became magically bound to protect her, you arrogant ass." But there was no real heat in his words. "Besides, someone has to look out for her when you're busy brooding in corners and straightening picture frames."

"I do not brood."

"You absolutely brood. It's your default setting." He fell into step beside me, absently fiddling with the sleeve covering his Treeis mark. "Though I suppose if I'd spent centuries pining after someone, I'd be broody too."

"Shouldn't you be failing at another hobby by now? Perhaps interpretive dance?"

"Already tried it. Turns out I'm actually quite good." He grinned, but it faded as we neared the field. "Remember, she's fighting her own battles in there. Sometimes being supported is better than being saved."

"When did you get so wise?"

"Yesterday." He clapped me on the shoulder. "I'll keep Tuck occupied. Maybe teach him how to make a decent sandwich."

"Is that what you're calling those monstrosities?"

"Those are works of art, thank you very much." He started to turn away, then paused. "Oh, and Thorne? If you make things worse, I get to say I told you so."

"I'll add it to your growing list of victories."

"You better." With a final knowing smirk, he headed back toward the house, gathering his tangled yarn as he went.

I crossed the field, my breath catching as I saw her. She sat in the grass, wearing a dress that seemed designed specifically to drive me mad. The slits along both sides revealed far too much leg for my sanity, and the way the silk clung to her curves made my fingers itch to touch. But it was the Remnants that held my attention. They settled around her like living smoke, reaching out before snapping back, more erratic than I'd ever seen them.

Her lips moved constantly, whispering words I couldn't quite catch as she fought for control. My power recognized hers, reaching out instinctively before I reined it in. This wasn't about what I wanted. This was about helping her find her way through the chaos.

"Practicing?" I asked, keeping my voice deliberately casual as I settled into the grass beside her.

"Something like that." Her eyes met mine, and the storm of emotions I saw there made my chest ache. "Did Archer send you to check on me?"

"I'm perfectly capable of being nosy on my own."

That earned me a ghost of a smile as I remembered her searching through the study the first night we stayed together.

"True."

I watched as she struggled to contain another wave of shadows, her fingers curling into fists in her lap. The dress slipped, revealing more of her thigh and I forced my gaze away. Now was not the time.

"You know... there are better ways to train."

She arched an eyebrow. "Oh? Please enlighten me with your ancient wisdom."

I let my power flare, just enough to make her Remnants stir in response. "Sometimes the best way to learn control is to lose it first."

"You have no idea how to lose control, Reverius Hawthorne Noctus and don't you dare try to convince me otherwise."

"Will you show me? What they're saying in there?"

"You don't want to know."

"Try me."

Her eyes met mine, and for a moment, I saw past her carefully constructed walls to the fear beneath. Then she closed her eyes and nodded. I caressed her memories just enough to see the last few moments. The Remnants surged forward, carrying whispers of destruction and chaos. I caught fragments of voices—Winter's cold fury, Sylvie's seductive promises of power, and beneath it all, Paesha's own desperate attempt to hold on to herself. But Levanya was there too. A cool presence in her mind, as she'd always been in life. The queen that'd lost everything.

I stepped away from her mind and reached for her, my power wrapping around hers like a shield. "Push back," I commanded. "They're yours to control, not the other way around."

"I can't—"

"You can." I moved closer, close enough to feel the heat of her skin. "You're stronger than they are. Show them."

She shifted in the grass, refusing to look at me as the Remnants twisted around her. Every line of her body radiated tension as she fought for control.

"Push back," I commanded again, letting my power brush against hers. "You're stronger than this."

"Stop telling me what to do."

"Then stop acting like you need to be told." I moved closer, deliberately invading her space. "Stop pretending you're some helpless mortal who can't handle her own power."

The Remnants surged at my words, feeding off her rising anger. Good. Let her get mad. Let her feel something other than defeat.

"You have no idea what this is like," she snapped, finally meeting my gaze. "To have them screaming in your head constantly. To feel them tearing at your mind—"

"Then show me." I pushed harder, my power tangling with her shadows. I couldn't handle the thought of fighting with her, but I'd fucking fight with them, if that was what she needed. "Stop hiding behind excuses and show me what you're really battling."

She shot to her feet. "You want to see? Fine. You want to know what they're saying?" Her voice rose with each word. "They want me to tear everything apart. To burn it all down. To destroy every pretty little piece of control you think you have."

"So do it." I stood, matching her fury with calm certainty. "Stop holding back. Stop being so damn afraid of your power. Don't sit in the godsdamn prison they've locked you into."

"I'm not afraid!"

"Then prove it." I stepped closer, watching the shadows dance across her skin. "Prove you're more than a scared little mortal playing at being powerful."

Her eyes flashed dangerously. "You think this is a game?"

"I think you're hiding. I think you're so terrified of letting anyone see the real you that you'd rather drown in those voices than admit you need help."

She glared at me. "You think you can simply waltz in here and fix everything with your perfect control?"

"Nothing about this is perfect," I said, letting my power wrap around hers like a caress as I met her glare. "But at least I'm not afraid of what I am."

The Remnants surged at my words. "I'm *not* afraid."

"I think we both know you are." I pushed harder. "Come play with me, Paesha darling. Let go... I'll catch you."

"You don't know anything about—"

"I know everything about you. I know you push away anyone who gets too close." I caught her wrist as she tried to pull away. "I know the way you dance when you think no one's watching. I know the sound of your laugh when you're truly happy. And I know you're terrified right now, not of the voices, but of letting someone see the real you. You're afraid of being abandoned. You know what it feels like and you're afraid. So you keep everything to yourself, battle your own wars in your mind and you fucking crumble. Alone. Every godsdamn night. I'm done watching it. I will not stand here and let you fall to pieces again. Now. Let. Go."

She yanked free. "You want to see the real me? Fine." The Remnants exploded outward, a storm of shadows and fury that would have sent a lesser being running. The ground shook, and I thought for a moment even the sun blinked out. But I stood my ground, drinking in the sight of her unleashed power. "This is what I am. Chaos and darkness and—"

"Beautiful," I breathed, watching her glow with raw energy. "Absolutely fucking beautiful."

Her steps faltered. "What?"

"You heard me." I moved closer, my own power rising to meet hers. "You think I want you to be anything other than exactly what you are? The woman who defies gods? Who builds families from broken pieces? Who dances in thunderstorms? You fucking own me. When will you finally figure that out?"

"Stop," she whispered, but there was less conviction in her voice.

"Why? Because I'm right? Because it's easier to push me away than admit you want this as much as I do? You said you were done fighting it on the rooftop and still you push back."

The Remnants writhed across the ground, responding to the electricity crackling between us. Her eyes met mine, and for once, she didn't look away.

"I see you, Paesha Vox," I said, closing the distance. "All of you. The light and the dark. The strength and the fear. And I'm still here."

"You're a fool," she breathed, but her hands came up to grip my shirt.

"Probably." My fingers traced the markings on her arm, slow and reverent, feeling the way she trembled beneath my touch. "But I'm your fool. I have been since the beginning."

I cradled her face in my hands, my thumbs sweeping over her cheekbones as I let her see everything, every fractured, unshakable piece of me that belonged to her before I placed my forehead on hers. "I love you. Not for who you were or who you might become, but for exactly who you are at this moment. The woman who makes a god question his own existence. Who tears apart everything I thought I knew and makes me want to build something new, something reckless, something real, just to keep pace with you.

"I love the way you fight, like your soul is made of starlight and you were born from lightning. The way you look at me, gods, the way you look at me. I love the sharp edges you use to keep the world at bay, and the quiet kindness you don't even realize is there. I love that you drive me absolutely mad. That you argue with me, challenge me, make me better by merely existing. Fates help me, I even love the way you infuriate me, because it means I feel this, us, with every fucking part of me."

She trembled, and I knew she felt it too. But I wasn't finished.

"I don't want perfection, Paesha. I don't want easy. I want you. Exactly as you are, wild and stubborn and impossible. Because that woman? That beautiful, maddening, extraordinary woman who has unraveled me piece by piece?" I brushed my lips against hers, a promise, a vow. "She's the only thing I have ever wanted. The only thing I will ever want. You, Paesha. Exactly as you are. You are not broken. You are fucking perfect."

"That silver tongue of yours will be the death of me," she breathed.

I traced her lower lip with my thumb. "Darling, you have no idea."

The confession hung between us, but the Remnants were still a problem, still smothering the field with shadows and racing over her skin. I knew there was truly nothing I could do to help her control them other than coax her into trying. This was her battle, but I would be her shield for as long as she would let me.

"Focus," I said, stepping back to give her space. "Don't fight against them. They're part of you. Command them."

She closed her eyes, her jaw clenching as she reached for control. The shadows twisted violently, resisting her will. "They don't—"

"They will. You're stronger than their hatred. Than their vengeance. Show them. I know Levanya is in there. She was a fallen queen of peace, Paesha. Find her peace and use it against them."

Her eyes snapped open, burning with determination as she pushed back against the darkness as if she and Levanya had already made a pact between each other. The Remnants surged, trying to overwhelm her, but she held firm. Step by step, breath by breath, she fought for dominance over her own power.

"That's it," I murmured, watching her find her way. "Don't cage them. Make them yours."

Sweat beaded on her forehead as she wrestled with the shadows. They responded to her command but sluggishly, like reluctant children testing their boundaries. A tremor ran through her body as she forced them to obey.

"I can't hold it," she gasped. "I was doing so well with them two days ago. And now this."

"Yes, you can. This is your power, Paesha. Your birthright. This is your fate."

The shadows along the field stretched to the treeline as they tried to run from her. She winced as if they burned. They turned, racing back through the field, surging for her in licks of black flame. They came for her.

I sent a burst of power forward. Not for them, but her. Shielding her from the destruction of her own power. She had far more than a mortal ever should but she wasn't weak.

"Remember who you are," I said quietly. "Not what they want you to be. Not what anyone wants you to be. Just you."

Something shifted in her expression, understanding, acceptance, determination. The Remnants surged one final time, a last desperate attempt to break her will. But Paesha stood unmoved, unflinching, absolute in her power, even if it was only temporary.

The field fell quiet as the shadows settled around her feet like obedient pets. She drew a shaky breath, rolling her shoulders as if testing the weight of her control. Even exhausted, she was a vision that made my blood burn, hair wild from the wind, chest rising with each breath, that damned dress clinging to every curve.

"Not bad for a mortal," she said with a hint of her usual sass.

"Not bad for anyone. How do they feel now?"

She flexed her fingers, and the Remnants rippled in response. "Like they're sulking."

I couldn't help but smile. "They'll get over it."

A wicked gleam entered her eyes as one shadow tendril snaked out, wrapping playfully around my wrist. The touch sent electricity through my veins. "I wonder what else they will do."

"Careful, darling." My voice dropped lower. "I'm not as well-behaved as your shadows."

"No?" Another tendril traced up my arm, deliberate and teasing. "You seem perfectly controlled to me. Always so... proper. Studious. Annoying."

Fates help me. No. Fuck the Fates. But the way she moved was pure temptation. Each shift of her body made that dress reveal another glimpse of thigh through those godsdamn slits. "I'm beginning to think you enjoy testing my restraint."

"Beginning to?" She circled me slowly, letting her power brush against mine like a caress. "I thought you knew everything about me."

My jaw clenched as she passed behind me, close enough that I could feel her, but not quite touching. "You're playing with fire."

"Am I?" Her breath ghosted across my neck. "You don't seem very dangerous to me. All bark, no bite is such a disappointment, Thorne darling."

I turned, catching her wrist before she could complete another circle. "Would you like me to prove you wrong?"

Her eyes sparkled with challenge as she pressed closer, knowing exactly what that silk dress was doing to my sanity. "I'd like to see you try."

"The things you do to me," I growled, my free hand sliding to her hip. "You have no idea how fucking beautiful you are like this. Wild. Powerful." My fingers found bare skin through one of those damned slits. "Mine."

"Yours?" She tilted her face up, lips nearly brushing mine. "That's awfully presumptuous."

"Is it?" I traced patterns on her thigh, feeling her shiver. "Tell me to stop then."

Instead of answering, she sent another wave of power washing over me, as dark and seductive as her smile. My control snapped. Her gasp of surprise turned to a moan as I claimed her mouth in a bruising kiss, all teeth and tongue and desperate hunger. She met me with equal ferocity though, her nails digging into my shoulders as she arched into my touch.

"Is this what you wanted?" I growled against her lips. "To push me until I showed you exactly how much I want you?"

"Yes. I came out here thinking to myself—"

I kissed her again. Brutally. Selfishly. Fucking possessively. I knew where she was going with that. I had no patience for it.

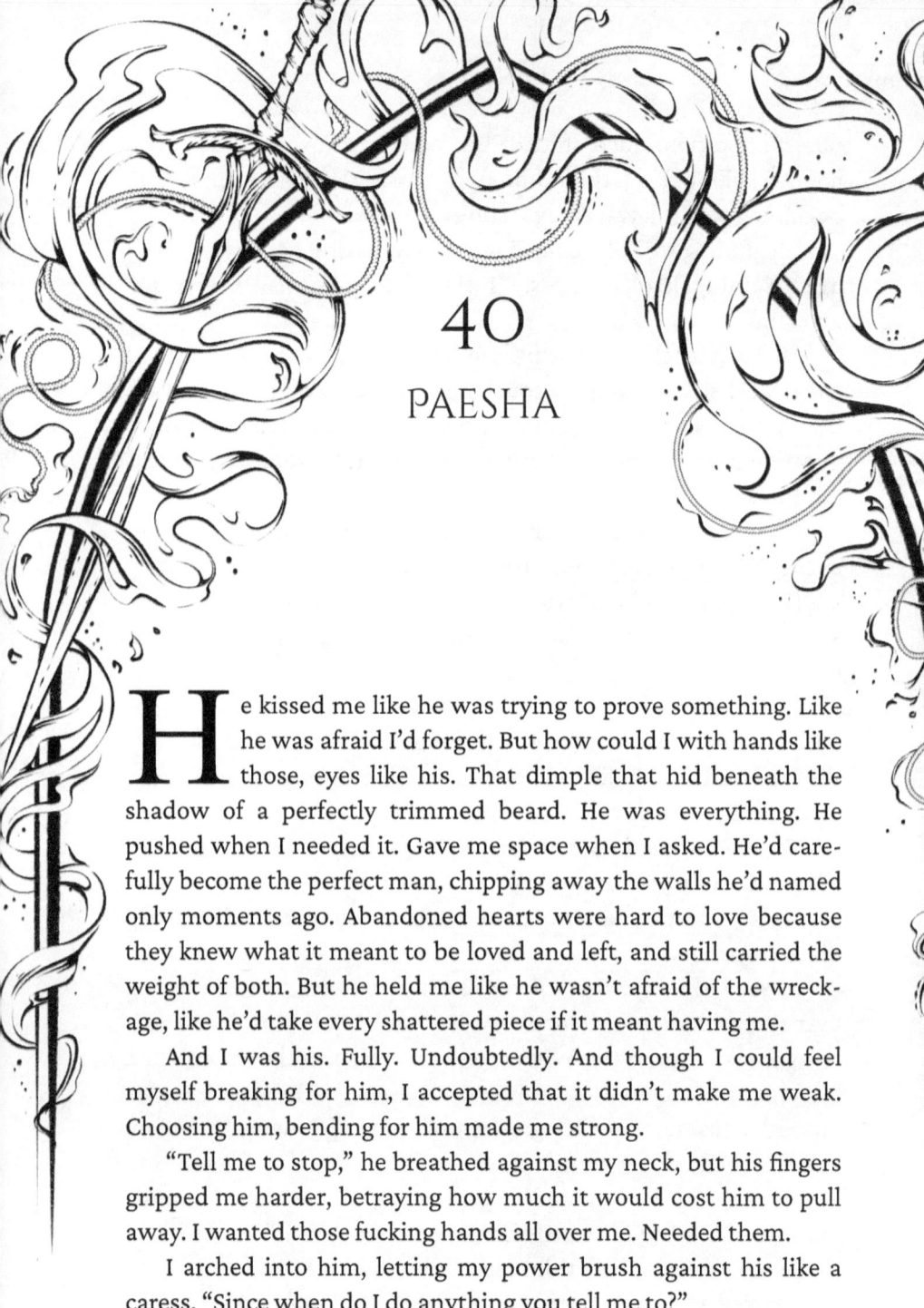

40

PAESHA

He kissed me like he was trying to prove something. Like he was afraid I'd forget. But how could I with hands like those, eyes like his. That dimple that hid beneath the shadow of a perfectly trimmed beard. He was everything. He pushed when I needed it. Gave me space when I asked. He'd carefully become the perfect man, chipping away the walls he'd named only moments ago. Abandoned hearts were hard to love because they knew what it meant to be loved and left, and still carried the weight of both. But he held me like he wasn't afraid of the wreckage, like he'd take every shattered piece if it meant having me.

And I was his. Fully. Undoubtedly. And though I could feel myself breaking for him, I accepted that it didn't make me weak. Choosing him, bending for him made me strong.

"Tell me to stop," he breathed against my neck, but his fingers gripped me harder, betraying how much it would cost him to pull away. I wanted those fucking hands all over me. Needed them.

I arched into him, letting my power brush against his like a caress. "Since when do I do anything you tell me to?"

Thorne's laugh was rough, desperate, and the sound of it sent a wave of desire straight through me. "Impossible woman."

"You wouldn't want me any other way."

"I want you in every fucking way."

This man worshiped me like he knew what it meant to lose me. He'd already suffered the agony of it once and clearly refused to endure it again. His hands tightened at my waist, pulling me closer, and I let him. Let myself sink into the warmth of him, the steadiness, the unrelenting way he held me like I was something precious.

His teeth grazed my jaw. Gods. I closed my eyes, standing in the middle of the fucking field, in broad daylight contemplating my next move. Quill was in the house. I didn't give a shit about anyone else, but I couldn't let this go on. Not here. Not even as his fingers skimmed higher, tracing maddening patterns on my sensitive inner thigh. As his lips blazed a trail of fire down my neck, I shivered, desire coiling hot and tight in my core. The sheer audacity of his touch, out here in the open with the sun beating down and the breeze whispering through the tall grass, made my head spin.

I wanted to sink into him, to let the rest of the world fade away until nothing existed but his hands on my body and his heart beating in time with mine. But the rational part of my brain, the part not completely consumed by lust, reminded me we were playing a dangerous game.

Thorne's fingers slipped under the edge of my dress and I jolted as if struck by lightning. Gripping his wrist, I pulled his hand away, bringing it up to my lips to press a lingering kiss against his palm. His eyes, dark and heavy-lidded with desire, met mine, a silent question burning.

"As much as I'd love to let you ravish me right here, it's not going to happen." I arched a brow, nodding toward the house in the distance.

A slow, wicked smile curved his lips. "Shy?"

I traced a finger down the buttons at his collar, snapping it free. His pulse jumped beneath my touch. "Not at all. But I thought you preferred a bed for this sort of thing. Silk sheets, down pillows, a convenient headboard to tie me to..."

He groaned, the sound vibrating through me. "Wicked, teasing minx." His hands flexed on my hips as if fighting the urge to haul me back against him. "Too bad there's no bed around here."

"You're a gazillion years old. Are you telling me you've never found a more creative spot than a bed? That's wildly disappointing."

"Creative? Darling, I've christened every surface from marble altars to piano tops. The question isn't where, it's how many times before we break it." His voice dropped to a dangerous whisper as he leaned closer, lips brushing my ear. "I could take you against a wall so thoroughly the wallpaper would remember the shape of your body for the next century. Is that creative enough for your liking, or shall I demonstrate further?"

Heat bloomed across my skin, my breath catching in my throat as his dangerous promise sent liquid fire racing through my veins. I steadied myself against him, using his momentary distraction to take a step backward toward the carriage he'd rode in this morning. Tipping my head toward the road, I let a coy smile play on my lips. "That's a pretty bold claim from someone who's still just standing here talking. I believe your carriage awaits, my lord."

There was no time for a breath as he helped me inside, shutting the door, and slamming the curtains closed. He sat, legs spread apart and stared up at me with a mischievous smile. "There's not enough room for all the things I want to do to you."

"I've always found intelligent people lacked creativity. Thank you for proving me right." I put one foot on the bench beside him, my dress riding up. "Shall I give you instructions beforehand, or do you think you can work out the details?"

His response was immediate. He turned, his eyes dark and hungry, and before I could even breathe, he sank his teeth into the soft flesh of my inner thigh. The bite was sharp, deliberate, and it sent a jolt of heat straight to my core. I gasped, my fingers curling into his thick hair as his mouth branded me with a mark that would linger long after this moment had passed.

"I think I can work it out," he murmured against my skin, his breath hot. "But I'll let you know if I run into any trouble."

He didn't wait for my reply. His hands were already on me, sliding up my thighs with a possessiveness that only he could have with me. He hooked his thumb over my panties and tugged them to the side, exposing me to the cool air of the carriage. His gaze locked with mine, unblinking, as he leaned in. The first touch of his tongue was electric, a slow, deliberate stroke. My back arched. I bit down on my lip to stifle a moan, but it was useless. He was relentless, licking me with a rhythm that was both maddening and intoxicating. His hands gripped my thighs, holding me open as he devoured me like a man starved.

I tugged him closer, needing more. My magic surged, sliding down his back, tracing the hard lines of muscle beneath his shirt. He growled against me, the vibrations sending shivers through my entire body. His power answered mine, a wave of heat that burned through me, igniting every nerve until I thought I might burst into flames.

He didn't stop. His tongue moved faster, flicking over that sweet, sensitive spot until I was trembling, my breaths coming in shallow gasps. I could feel the pressure building inside me, a coil tightening with every stroke of his tongue. My hips bucked against his mouth, desperate for release, but he held me still, his grip unyielding.

"Fuck," I whispered, voice breaking as I felt myself teetering on the edge. He didn't slow down, didn't give me a moment to catch my breath. Instead, he pressed harder, his tongue working me with a precision that was almost cruel in its intensity. Almost. Until his fingers dug harder into my thighs, until he paused to graze his teeth over me. Until he bit down and the pain coalesced with every bit of ecstasy he'd been delivering. A wave of pleasure hit me that was so intense it stole the air from my lungs. I came with a cry, my body shaking as he continued, drawing out every last drop of ecstasy until I was nearly boneless, trembling as I hung on to him, my limbs heavy and my mind blissfully blank.

He pulled back finally, looking up at me, a satisfied smirk playing on his lips. "I'll work on the creativity."

I couldn't answer. My body was still humming, every nerve

alight with the aftershocks of what he'd done. All I could do was stare at him, my heart racing and my thoughts a jumbled mess.

He pushed out of his seat, gripping the edge of my dress. "The only reason I'm not ripping this off of you is because you've got to make it into that house with a shred of decency."

I smiled. "I left my decency in the back of a theater a long time ago."

"Gods, I'm in trouble," he said before ripping the dress over my head, somehow avoiding tearing it. With a few more rocks of the carriage, as much as the massive man could, he was standing, naked and glorious before me, eyes burning into mine. "You're more fucking perfect than I remembered."

I spun around, stepping backward until my back was to his chest. He all but snarled in my ear as he curled around me and those hands slid down my chest, over my stomach and to that aching spot between my legs. "Still so wet for me, Paesha darling?"

The hitch of his breath against my ear when he reached between my legs was nearly my undoing. I leaned my head back against his chest as he pressed a finger inside of me. His teeth grazed my ear as he added a second finger, forcing a moan from my lips. The carriage rocked slightly with the movement of our bodies, the sound of creaking filling the air. But it wasn't enough, I wanted more. Needed more.

"Please," I whispered, the word barely audible over the pounding of my heart.

"I'll break this godsdamn carriage."

"And then you'll fix it."

He didn't need to be told twice. His fingers withdrew, leaving me empty and gasping, but only for a moment. One hand gripped my hip, yanking me back against him, while the other pushed me forward until I was leaning over the bench. His cock thick and heavy, pressed against my ass.

"Hold on," he growled, and I barely had time to brace myself before he was pushing into me, inch by agonizing inch, stretching me, filling me in ways that had me crying out, my nails digging into the seatback. The carriage groaned in protest as he began to move, his hips snapping into mine with a rhythm that was relentless, brutal. There was no finesse, no gentleness, just raw, unfiltered need.

His hands were everywhere, one gripping my hip so hard I knew there'd be bruises, the other tangling in my hair, yanking my head back so he could bite my neck, his teeth marking me as his. The sound of skin slapping against skin echoed in the confined space, mingling with my choked moans and his guttural growls. The carriage rocked harder with every thrust, the wheels creaking under the force of our bodies.

"Fuck," I gasped, my voice breaking as he hit that spot inside me again and again, the pleasure building with every stroke. My legs trembled, my body tightening around him as I teetered on the edge, desperate for release.

"Come on," he snarled, his voice thick with desperation. "Come for me, Paesha."

His words were enough to push me over the edge, my body convulsing around him as I came hard, my cries muffled by the hand he clamped over my mouth. He followed me over only moments later, his hips stuttering as he emptied himself inside me with a low, animalistic groan.

The carriage gave one final, violent rock, and then there was a loud crack as one of the wheels gave way, sending us lurching to one side. He steadied me with a hand on my hip, pulling out slowly as we both caught our breath.

"I hate to say I told you so," he huffed, voice rough with satisfaction, and I couldn't help but laugh breathlessly, even as my body still trembled with aftershocks.

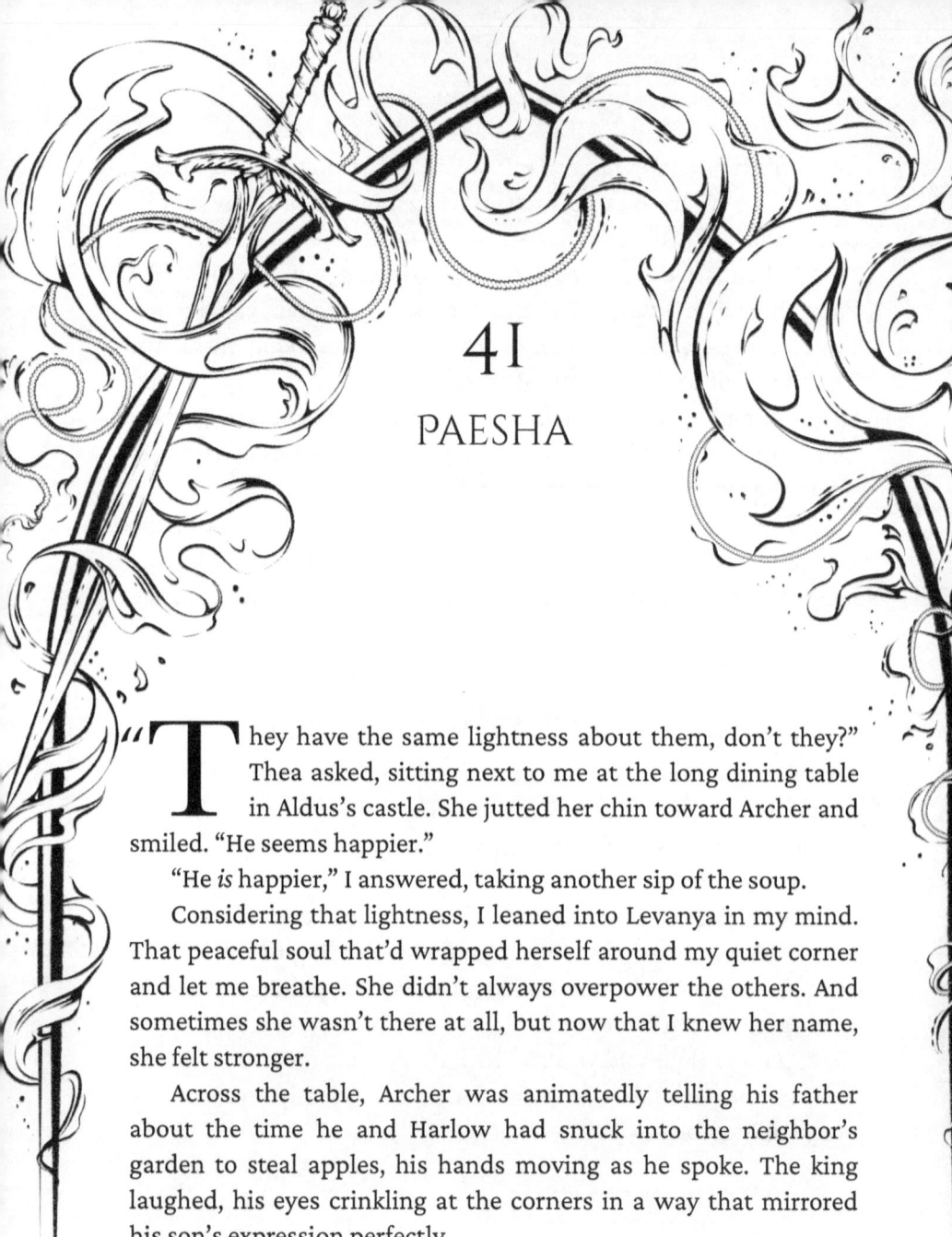

41

PAESHA

"They have the same lightness about them, don't they?" Thea asked, sitting next to me at the long dining table in Aldus's castle. She jutted her chin toward Archer and smiled. "He seems happier."

"He *is* happier," I answered, taking another sip of the soup.

Considering that lightness, I leaned into Levanya in my mind. That peaceful soul that'd wrapped herself around my quiet corner and let me breathe. She didn't always overpower the others. And sometimes she wasn't there at all, but now that I knew her name, she felt stronger.

Across the table, Archer was animatedly telling his father about the time he and Harlow had snuck into the neighbor's garden to steal apples, his hands moving as he spoke. The king laughed, his eyes crinkling at the corners in a way that mirrored his son's expression perfectly.

"And then," Archer continued, "she convinced me to give her a boost over the wall, but when I did, she slipped and fell right into their pond. Made such a splash that the geese started honking and chasing her."

"Your mother used to tell me stories about that garden," Aldus said, reaching for his wine with a fond smile. "Said those geese were better guards than any dog could be."

"They were terrifying," Archer agreed, his eyes bright with the memory. "Harlow wouldn't go near that wall for months after. Though she did manage to grab two apples on her way down."

"It seems she was resourceful," Aldus's voice held pride mixed with old grief. "Exactly like your mother."

"Did you ever steal apples?" Quill asked, before taking a massive bite of a pastry.

Aldus winked at her. "I never had to. But I tried to smuggle an entire cheese wheel out of the kitchen once. Didn't end well."

"You should come to the market with us," Quill said with a gulp. "I can show you how to get things without stealing *or* being a king."

"Quill," I warned, but Aldus was already laughing.

"You know what? I think I will." He stood, straightening his jacket. "Let me change into something less... kingly. Meet me at the side gate in an hour?"

She shrugged. "As long as I don't have to change too."

After he left, Archer stayed quiet for a moment, staring at his plate with an unreadable expression.

"You okay?" I asked softly.

He looked up, and the smile that spread across his face was genuine. "Yeah... I'm glad I gave him a chance. To be the father I always hoped he could be." He shook his head slightly. "I hate that everyone was right."

"Not everyone," I said, remembering how careful we'd all been not to push him. "We just wanted you to have the choice."

"Choice is a funny thing." Thea reached for the bread basket. "Sometimes the hardest part is admitting you want something you've spent so long convincing yourself you didn't need."

Archer's eyes met mine across the table, understanding passing between us. We both knew something about walls built from old hurts, about the courage it took to let them fall.

"Well," he said, leaning back in his chair with that familiar roguish grin as he wiggled his eyebrows at me. "At least I still have my stunning good looks, a hoard of carriages to break, and all this charm to fall back on if this whole prince thing doesn't work out."

I threw a napkin at his head. "And your modesty. Don't forget that. Highly recommend breaking all the carriages though."

An hour later, we were in the market, watching as Quill tugged on the king's sleeve. She covered her mouth with her hand as she whispered loud enough for everyone to hear. "You can't just pay what they ask. You have to haggle."

"Haggle?" Aldus looked genuinely puzzled as he stood before the fruit vendor's stall. "But the price seems fair."

"That's not the point," Quill explained with exaggerated patience. "It's part of the experience. Watch." She turned to the vendor with her hands on her hips. "Three coin for these oranges? They're barely bigger than walnuts!"

Archer tensed beside me as another crowd of people pushed past us. He scanned the rooftops, the alleyways, everywhere but the charming scene of his father learning to barter with a child as his teacher.

"Something's wrong," he muttered, his hand drifting to the knife at his belt.

I followed his gaze but saw nothing obvious. "What is it?"

"Not sure. Just feels... off." He shifted closer to me, positioning himself between our group and the wider market. "Where's Thorne? He should be here."

"I convinced him to try to make peace with Minerva." I watched as Quill gestured dramatically. "She can't ignore him forever."

"Want to bet?" But Archer's attempt at humor fell flat as his eyes locked on to something in the crowd. "There are too many people here today. Too many hoods up despite the heat."

He was right. Now that he'd pointed it out, I could feel it too, that crawling sensation between my shoulder blades that meant we were being watched.

"Should we leave?"

"Not yet. Don't want to spook them." His voice dropped lower. "But get ready to move if I give the signal."

Ahead of us, Aldus was laughing as Quill successfully negoti-ated the price of fruit down to two coin, her face beaming with pride. The king looked happier than I'd ever seen him, completely unaware of the tension building around us.

"At least someone's having fun," Archer said. "Though I have to admit, watching my father learn market economics from a child is pretty entertaining."

"She's a good teacher."

"She's something." His hand brushed mine, a silent warning as another hooded figure passed too close. "Next time we take my father shopping, let's stick to Perth. We can keep him disguised over there."

"Agreed," I said, watching as Quill dragged Aldus toward a stall selling colorful scarves.

"Archer Bramwell," a smooth voice called out.

My heart stuttered as Willard emerged from the crowd, his perfectly tailored jacket and carefully styled hair marking him as belonging here far more than we did. He held out a hand to Archer, who took it after only the slightest hesitation.

"What brings you to the Silk market? Thought you preferred the company of less tasteful wares. The Salt not good enough for you now that you've moved in on the title? Who knew your mother was so... spirited."

"Just showing some friends around," Archer said casually, though I felt him shift his weight, ready to move. "Been a while, Wee Willy."

Willard's eyes slid over me without recognition before landing on Aldus and Quill by the scarf merchant's stall. Something calcu-lated flickered across his face. "Indeed it has. Not since..." He paused, his brow furrowing slightly. "Actually, I can't quite recall our last meeting."

"The funeral," Archer said, his voice tight. "You were at Harlow's funeral."

"Ah yes, of course." Willard took a step backward. "Such a tragedy. Though I must admit, the details seem a bit hazy."

I watched him drift closer to the king, my heart pounding. Even with Thorne's magic wiping his memories of me, of the Fray, of everything we'd done, the cold calculation in his eyes remained unchanged. He was still the same man who'd broken Harlow's heart, who'd stood at her funeral like he had any right to mourn her.

Quill darted away from the scarf stall, distracted by a display of sparkling trinkets. In that split second, Willard moved. The blade appeared in his hand like a serpent's strike, and before anyone could react, he'd buried it into Aldus's chest.

The king's small gasp shattered the market's peaceful buzz. Such a quiet sound that had no business being the sound of Archer's future shattering. It shouldn't have meant the end of everything. I'd heard that sound before though. On the lips of that old king's daughter the second before she died.

"No!" I was already moving forward. We could fix this. We had to fix this. Archer could stop time, we could get help. Thorne would know what to do. There were healers in the castle. Magic. Anything to stop the blood that was spreading too quickly across the king's fine jacket.

On the break of Quill's scream, everything stopped. The crowd froze mid-stride, Willard's satisfied smirk suspended in time, even the ripples in the puddles at our feet stood still.

"No, no, no," Archer chanted, catching his father as he crumpled. There was no part of me that could watch him lose someone else. "Someone, there has to be someone who can..." His voice shook as he lowered Aldus to the ground, pressing his hands against the wound. "Why isn't time stopped for you?"

His father's face had already begun to lose color.

"We'll get help," I said desperately, dropping to my knees beside them. "We just need to stop the bleeding. We can—" But the words died in my throat as I saw Aldus's eyes. Saw the knowledge there. The acceptance.

"My boy," Aldus whispered, his trembling hand finding Archer's cheek. "My beautiful, strong boy. I'm so proud of you." His breath hitched. "I'm sorry I missed so much. So many moments I should have..."

Archer shook his head. "No. You don't get to die."

"I'm sorry," his father answered, the pain so obvious on the old man's face I could almost feel it as if it were my own.

Archer looked at me. Fucking looked right into my soul. "Help me."

But I couldn't. "I think because you're touching him, time is still moving. Maybe if you..."

"Don't," Aldus said, staring only at his son. "Don't let go. Please."

Archer nodded. Tears pooled in his ocean blue eyes as he stared down at the father he never truly had. Not even time magic could halt the life draining from the king's eyes as he looked at his son with so much love it hurt to witness. A lifetime of it, shoved into seconds.

"You're going to be amazing," Aldus breathed, each word seeming to cost him more than the last. "Just like your mother. Just like Harlow. If only you could see that you have so much of them in you."

Archer's shoulders shook as he stared down at his father, and truly, I wanted to be anywhere but here, witnessing him lose his last living family member. But also, I'd never leave him for a heartbeat, not when his soul was so crushed the sorrow was pouring down the Treeis bond in waves of agony. Whatever words he couldn't say, I could feel, and my heart burned for him.

With trembling fingers, Archer reached into his pocket and pulled out one of his coins. He pressed it into his father's palm, curling the cooling fingers around it. "When you see her, tell Harlow I kept my promise. I learned to be brave." He squeezed his father's hand around the coin. "And tell her... tell her to hug you extra tight for me. For all the hugs I should have given you."

"I promise," Aldus whispered.

The words faded with his last breath, his hand going slack in Archer's grip. For a moment, everything was perfectly, devastatingly still. Then Archer's face crumpled, a sound of pure anguish tearing from his throat as he bent over his father, his forehead pressing against Aldus's temple, unable to pull him close with the blade between them.

"Please," he begged, his tears falling onto his father's face. "I still have so much to tell you." His words dissolved into broken sobs. "I never got to show you the view from the bell tower. Or teach you how to play cards properly. Or tell you that I forgave you. That I understood. Please, please come back."

I reached for him, my own tears falling freely, but he was already lifting his head. His grief-stricken expression hardened as his eyes locked on to Willard's frozen form, that self-satisfied smirk still etched on his face.

The temperature seemed to drop as Archer gently laid his father down. When he stood, there was nothing left of the man who'd laughed over lunch just hours ago. In his place stood someone I'd never seen before, someone forged in the same fire that had taken both his sister and his father.

"Time to wake up, Wee Willy," he said softly, and the ice in his voice made my blood run cold.

Archer moved with terrifying grace, his fingers wrapping around the hilt of the blade in his father's chest. He pulled it free with a sound that would haunt my nightmares, the metal scraping against bone as his father's body settled against the cobblestones. The blade dripped red as he crossed to Willard, each step measured, deliberate. His face hardened until there was no light left in the eyes of my best friend.

"Archer," I whispered, though I wasn't sure what I wanted. Certainly not to stop him.

"If Quill weren't standing right there, this would take so much longer. Hurt so much worse," he promised Willard, dragging the blade across the frozen man's jacket to clean off his father's blood. "It's lucky for you I love that kid more than I hate you."

Reality shuddered back into motion.

Willard's smirk lasted only a fraction of a second before Archer's hand shot out, grabbing him by the throat. The blade that had taken his father slid home beneath Willard's ribs with practiced ease. Their eyes met, Willard's wide with shock, Archer's cold as winter frost.

"For Harlow," Archer whispered, twisting the blade. "And for him."

Quill's scream pierced the air as she finally reached my side, throwing herself onto Aldus's still form. The sound seemed to snap something in Archer. He let Willard's body crumple to the ground like discarded waste, turning back to his family as the market erupted into chaos around us.

The coin in Aldus's hand caught the light, a final glint of gold against the growing darkness of this endless day.

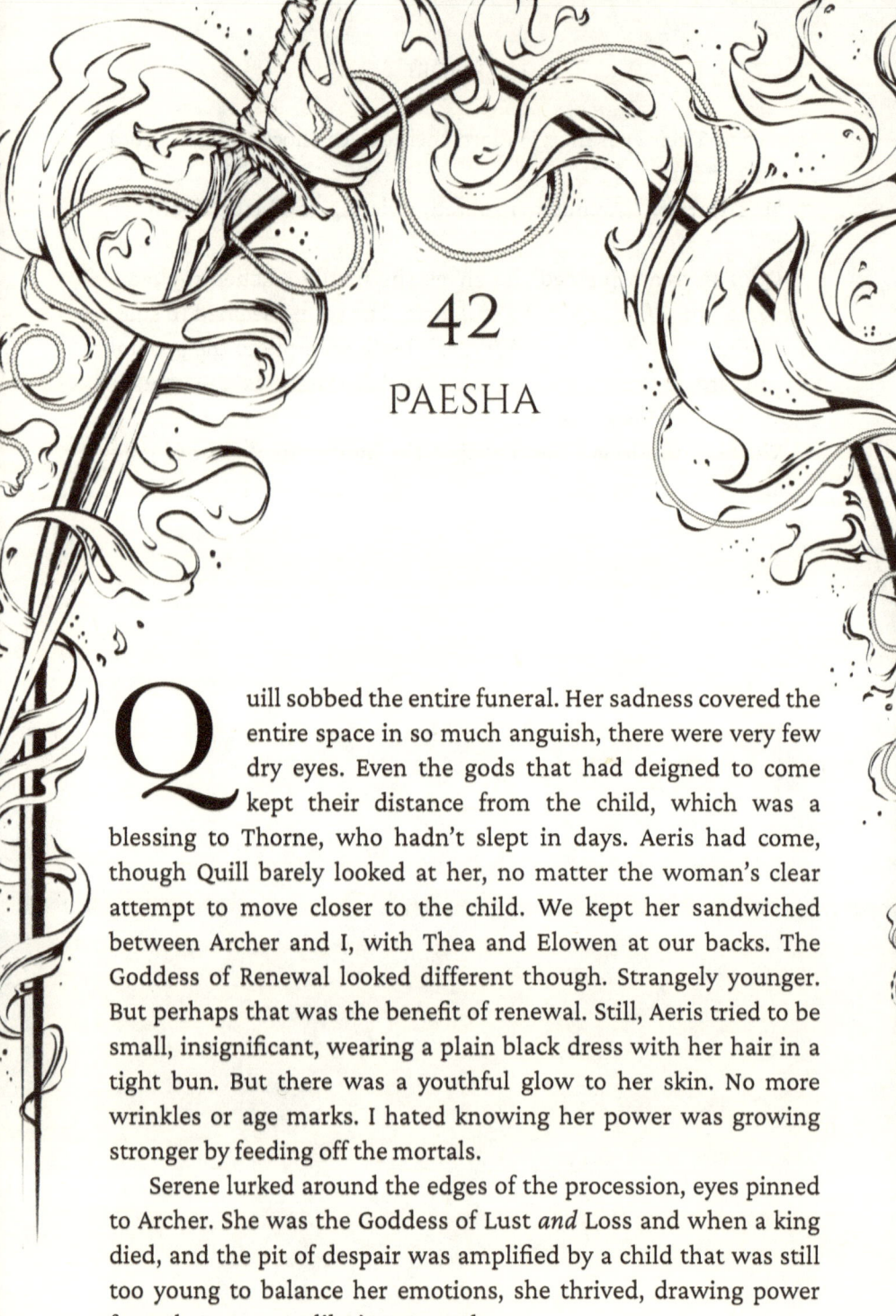

42

PAESHA

Quill sobbed the entire funeral. Her sadness covered the entire space in so much anguish, there were very few dry eyes. Even the gods that had deigned to come kept their distance from the child, which was a blessing to Thorne, who hadn't slept in days. Aeris had come, though Quill barely looked at her, no matter the woman's clear attempt to move closer to the child. We kept her sandwiched between Archer and I, with Thea and Elowen at our backs. The Goddess of Renewal looked different though. Strangely younger. But perhaps that was the benefit of renewal. Still, Aeris tried to be small, insignificant, wearing a plain black dress with her hair in a tight bun. But there was a youthful glow to her skin. No more wrinkles or age marks. I hated knowing her power was growing stronger by feeding off the mortals.

Serene lurked around the edges of the procession, eyes pinned to Archer. She was the Goddess of Lust *and* Loss and when a king died, and the pit of despair was amplified by a child that was still too young to balance her emotions, she thrived, drawing power from the mourners like it was payday.

Bellatora stuck to her side, and Thorne gave several warnings

388

to Archer throughout the day to keep his head up around her. As the Goddess of War, she wanted nothing more than to see this realm fall to destruction.

But as the day went on, as we gathered for a council meeting, Archer heard almost none of it. He didn't want warnings about the future. Didn't want advice from anyone. He didn't want to accept that if the council walked into this room and said what we all anticipated was coming, there were going to have to be decisions made. He wasn't ready to step in for his father. And though the entire kingdom heard of Aldus's lost son, though they'd seen the two men together, so strikingly similar, yet worlds apart, there would always be the doubters. Those that didn't want a boy from this kingdom to step into such an important role that he wasn't ready for, nor did they trust him to ever be able to handle.

Archer was a charmer. He was a card shark and damn good thief. He had a smile that could melt your heart. But did he have the soul of a king? The grit it took to carry a kingdom through an overhaul of a man they'd known for years. Maybe. That was what the council would decide. But there wasn't a soul among us that doubted this was a far better outcome than if Farris had still been alive.

The council chamber felt too small for the number of beings that filed in, mortal and immortal alike. Gilded chairs scraped against marble floors as the council took their usual seats, their faces grave with the weight of the succession hanging in the air. But it was the gods who commanded attention.

Archer sat at the head of the table, exactly where his father would have been, though his posture suggested he'd rather be anywhere else. His fingers drummed a restless rhythm against the table, and I could see the shadow of grief in the tight set of his jaw. The Treeis mark on his arm was on clear display. Apparently we were no longer hiding that which marked him as more.

Thorne's fingers burned a trail of circles across my back. His arm was draped over my chair and the glare on his face as he stared down every moving person in the room was equal parts brutal and unfairly handsome. There was a game to be played here, a kingdom to be won or lost, and ultimately, a line to be drawn in the sand. Whatever Archer wanted, whatever future he chose for himself, I would see it done. I would tear this kingdom apart, brick by crumbling brick, if only to lay its ruins at his feet if he wanted. And I knew Thorne would do the same.

Of all the gods that filed in, the last one I ever thought we'd see was Themis, the God of Justice, who entered last, his dark robes rippling with otherworldly movement. Thorne's hand stilled on my back as he looked Themis over, confirming he was not Ezra in hiding. The hood of his cloak concealed his face entirely, but I could feel his attention fixed on Archer like a physical weight. The Remnants stirred at his presence, remembering his role in binding the Cimmerians, and all the injustice that had followed.

"Take your fucking eyes off my friend," I warned him, keeping my voice low as my power poured over the floor like fog. Alastor hadn't come, but I wondered if he did, what he would think of that. If he would know I still didn't fully control them.

"It's fine," Archer said, releasing a long, drawn out breath as Themis remained unmoving.

He fears us, Winter whispered in my mind. *As he should.*

Stop, I begged, though my control felt tenuous at best. The voices had been particularly restless since the funeral, feeding off the grief that saturated the castle and rippled in the wake of every space Quill had been.

I had to hold it together here, even as the hissing in my mind grew. No one could know of this battle. They would see me as weak and I couldn't have that. Especially because none of us anticipated the presence of gods, aside from Tuck, Minerva, and of course Thorne, who hadn't left my side since the murder of the king.

"Shall we begin?" Lord Bremen, the eldest council member, cleared his throat. "We have much to discuss regarding the succession—"

"We have more pressing matters," Themis interrupted, his voice carrying the weight of mountains. "Such as the presence of an Unmade Guardian at the head of your table."

The council members exchanged confused glances, but Archer

didn't flinch. He met Themis's hidden gaze steadily, though I saw his hand drift to the mark on his arm. "I wasn't aware the gods had any say in mortal succession. My father certainly never mentioned it. In fact, if memory serves, gods have no right to interfere with the crown. Weren't those our findings, Lord Noctus?"

Thorne's tone was little more than a threat. "Yes."

Themis shifted uncomfortably in his seat, but did not relent. "Your father was wise enough to welcome our counsel when it was necessary. You would do well to follow his example."

"His example?" Archer's laugh held no humor. "You mean letting immortals meddle in mortal affairs? Tell me, God of Justice, where was your counsel when my sister was murdered? When the crowned prince of this realm was stealing magic in Prospector's Pointe? Where was your justice then? Oh, that's right, you were the one binding the Cimmerians. Forgive me if I don't give a *fuck* what you have to say to me. That door you passed through to enter this sacred room? You'll find it works both ways. Feel free to give it a try."

The temperature in the room dropped several degrees. I shifted closer to Archer, my Remnants coiling protectively around us both. Themis's presence seemed to grow, filling the chamber with the weight of his power.

"You dare question me, boy?" Shadows writhed beneath his hood. "I am Justice incarnate. I see all debts that must be paid." His attention shifted to me. "Including those owed by your Huntress."

My blood ran cold as the Remnants surged, responding to the threat in his voice. "I owe you nothing."

"You stole power that should have been mine," Themis said. "I worked for that little fool for years. I earned that power. Instead, it festers within you, corrupting everything it touches."

"That power was promised to me," Vesalia interrupted, walking through the door as if she'd been waiting for the perfect moment to jump in. Her footsteps were in the exact rhythm of a clock as she walked forward. "We had a bargain, didn't we, little thief? Or have you forgotten our arrangement in that fractured mind of yours?"

"First of all, I never bargain. I'm quite good at remembering words spoken. You said 'bring me the power and I will show you how to return to Quill.' But you never did, did you? I figured that out all on my own. With my power. That belongs to me and not you. And if we need to get into the technicals, there was no agreement. I said nothing in return when you spoke those words. So don't fuck with me, Vesalia. I know exactly who I'm dealing with." I let the Remnants swirl around her feet "Do you?"

We'd all been on edge waiting for this moment. Whether I had a defense or not, we knew she would come. Thorne had warned us endlessly about it. The council members shrank back in their chairs as more immortals stepped into the room. Bellatora's armor gleamed as she circled the table. Serene drifted at the edges, drinking in the tension like wine.

Jealous, Sylvie said.

Too bad we cannot kill a god, Winter hissed.

Not all, Sylvie answered.

But before I could respond, Vesalia leaned forward, her ageless eyes fixing on mine. "Ten years," she said softly. "Give me ten years of mortal life, and I will consider your debt paid."

"You can't be serious. She's proven she owes you nothing." Archer started to rise, but I placed a hand on his shoulder.

"And if I refuse?"

Vesalia's smile was cruel. "Then perhaps I will take my payment in other ways. Time has many faces, little thief. Many paths that lead to suffering." Her eyes flicked to Archer and I knew exactly what threat lay within them. Archer was her descendant. A descendant of a god would always be a threat. As far as I knew, the only person that could kill a god was a descendant. And he wasn't king or even a true prince yet. There was no protection for him.

"Do you see?" she asked, drawing out the final word.

Thorne was on his feet the second he followed the signs to the same conclusion I had. Vesalia fell to her knees in an instant, gripping her head as she screamed. If I had to guess, I'd say Thorne's power wrapped around her mind like a vise and squeezed. The other gods surged forward, but he held up a hand, his eyes blazing gold as centuries of control began to slip.

Gods, he was magnificent when he let go, all that carefully leashed power finally breaking free. The air crackled with raw energy that made my skin tingle and my breath catch.

"Your balls aren't big enough to make threats in this room, Vesalia. I will *always* protect what's mine." His voice carried the weight of eons, of power that could reshape reality. Of beginnings and endings and everything in between. The command in his tone did something for me, even as warning bells rang in my mind. "You think you can walk in here and make demands?" He stepped toward her. "I've watched you play your games for millennia, Time Keeper. I have endured your bargains and your schemes. But this?" He snapped his fingers and she screamed again. "This ends now."

I should have stopped him. But watching him unleash everything he kept so carefully controlled, seeing that perfect facade crack to reveal the primal force beneath... He was intoxicating. Dangerous. Beautiful. And absolutely mine.

Themis moved first, shadows gathering beneath his hood. "Release her."

"Or what?" Thorne's laugh was hollow, manic even. "You'll dispense your justice? Please. Try. Give me a reason to twist all of your minds."

Bellatora's armor sang as she drew her sword. "You're not the only one with power here."

"No?" The golden light around him pulsed brighter, and I could feel the fabric of reality starting to fray at the edges. Whatever his power over realms was, he was using it. And his power called to mine, the Remnants beneath my skin yearning to join his destruction. "Then perhaps it's time for a demonstration of exactly what I am capable of."

The other gods tensed, power gathering like storm clouds. This was it, the moment that would spark a war we couldn't afford. Not with the balance already so fragile. Not with Archer unprotected. No matter how much a part of me wanted to watch him tear them apart, I slammed my hands on the table, my own power surging outward to fill the room with darkness. "Enough!"

Thorne's grip on Vesalia loosened enough for her to gasp in a breath. His eyes met mine, and the heat in them nearly buckled my knees.

"This is a mortal realm," I managed, forcing steel into my voice despite how much I wanted to let him continue. "Your petty feuds have no place in this chamber."

I couldn't tell him I was scared. He couldn't know I worried for Quill's future if she and every other child were thrust into a battle between gods that would likely span centuries. I couldn't look at him and let him know that beneath it all, ten years was absolutely a reprieve. If I lived to only be a hundred and five, would dying at ninety-five matter if it meant peace? I wasn't a hero. But I also wasn't a fucking fool.

"Paesha," he growled, and gods, the way he said my name made me want to forget why I was stopping him.

"No." I moved to stand between him and Vesalia, close enough to feel the power radiating off him in waves. "Let her go, Thorne. Please."

I would lead and he would follow. That was our unspoken promise. His eyes darkened as he slowly, deliberately withdrew his power. Vesalia slumped to the floor, gasping.

"Touch what's mine again," he said softly, each word carrying the weight of a death sentence, "and there won't be enough pieces left of you to mark the passing of time."

"Ten years," I said, causing every head in the room to snap toward me. Thorne's power flickered as his attention shifted, but I kept my eyes on Vesalia. "I'll give you ten years."

She pulled herself to her feet, smoothing her dress with trembling hands. "Done."

"Not done," I corrected, letting my Remnants swirl at my feet. "I have terms. You will never come for Archer or any of his descendants. You will never seek revenge against me or mine for what happened here today or any day prior to this one. And you speak this bargain with Themis himself as witness." I glanced at the God of Justice. "Since he's so concerned with debts being paid."

"Paesha, no—" Archer's voice was careful. He'd been trying not to give away too much about our bond. But this wasn't his choice. This was about his safety. He would pay this price for me in a heartbeat. I would do the same for him.

I met Thorne's eyes, seeing the fury and fear warring within. My gaze slid to Vesalia, pulling herself up from the floor. "Do we have a deal?"

She held out her hand, magic crackling between her fingers. "We do."

I reached for her, but Thorne caught my wrist. "Don't," he growled.

"Trust me."

Something in my voice must have convinced him because he released me, though every line of his body radiated tension.

"Ten years," Vesalia confirmed.

When my hand met hers, the magic sparked between us. I felt the weight of time pressing down, seeking purchase in my soul. The Remnants screamed their objection, but I forced them away. I would not be the match that sparked the inferno. This seemed a small price to pay. The council members sat frozen, caught between immortal powers beyond their comprehension.

But Archer stood, his voice steady despite everything. "If you're quite finished threatening each other in my father's council chamber, perhaps we could return to the matter at hand? Unless you'd all prefer to take this outside and let the mortals handle their own business?"

Themis's hood turned toward him sharply. "You would—"

"Yes," Archer cut him off with a tone akin to Harlow's. "I would. Because this?" He gestured to the room, to the gathered immortals bristling with power. "This is exactly why my father kept you close enough to watch. Now either sit down and be silent, or get out."

I felt a surge of pride through our bond. He might not want the crown, but in that moment, he commanded the room like he was born to it. One by one, the gods settled back into their seats, though the air remained thick with tension. After we sat, Thorne's hand found mine beneath the table. He hated this moment, likely wouldn't hear another thing that happened in this room today. But he would be silent and support my decision and that said far more about his devotion to me than any threat of violence. Especially when his power had been failing more and more lately.

"Now then," Archer said, turning back to the council. "Let's discuss succession."

"You mortals and your petty politics," Bellatora cut in, her armor singing with each step as she moved behind Archer's chair. "Always so concerned with your tiny kingdoms while the realms crumble around you. You need to grow to survive."

"With respect," Lady Catherine, the youngest council member, spoke up though her voice shook, "this is a royal court matter. The laws of succession—"

Themis's laugh held no warmth as he tried to step in again. "Laws? I've seen your laws. There are others that may qualify for this throne."

"Enough," Minerva's voice cut through the chamber like a blade. She hadn't moved from her position, tucked between mortals, but I was sure none of them knew she was a god. "You overstep."

"Do we?" Bellatora's hand came to rest on Archer's shoulder, her gauntlet gleaming. "Or do we simply speak truths the mortals are too afraid to face?"

I hoped she could feel the fire from my glare as she tried to mark him.

An elderly man, whose name I couldn't remember, pushed back from the table. "Please. This meeting was called to address the future of our kingdom. As you've been told, you are welcome to stay but please let us continue." He turned to Archer and the room went still. "While we acknowledge that King Aldus formally recognized you as his son, there are... other considerations."

The woman beside him with a halo of gray hair leaned forward. "Despite your upbringing in the Silk district, you've shown little interest in court politics. You've deliberately avoided the responsibilities that come with your father's acknowledgment—"

"Yet, the man you speak for allowed such concessions. I'm not sitting here pretending I was born to rule. He wanted me here. And I'm here."

"Nevertheless," another interjected, "there are other candidates. Those who have actively participated in council matters. Lord Pembrook's son, for instance, has served—"

"The law is clear," Bremen interrupted. "King Aldus publicly claimed him as his son before witnesses. The blood claim cannot be denied, regardless of his short term reluctance to engage with court life. Even I can concede that he hasn't had time to settle in."

"Then perhaps," another said, a calculating gleam in her eye, "we should discuss the other requirement. The one that cannot be circumvented. Marriage."

"The marriage law remains absolute," Bremen confirmed. "No unmarried heir may ascend to the throne. It was put in place to ensure stability, to guarantee the continuation of the line."

In some deep corner of my mind, I knew this. It was why Archer's dad married Farris's mom despite being in love with another that had run. But still, to hear them say it... None of us had considered this problem.

The blood drained from Archer's face, though he kept his expression neutral. I wanted to reach for him, to offer some comfort against this new cage being built around him, but I couldn't move. Couldn't breathe.

"Those that would see Aldus's only living heir take the throne, stand."

One by one the council members around the table rose, some more reluctant than the others, but after several minutes of continued back and forth, all council members stood.

Archer gulped. Quietly, but it'd happened. And I was almost sure at this point I could feel his nerves rattling my mind. But they could have been mine.

"The council will allow three months for you to select a suitable bride," Bremen continued. "Once the marriage is performed, you may take your father's place."

Archer's fingers whitened on the arms of his chair. "And if I refuse?"

"Then the crown passes to the next eligible candidate," Lady Kendrick said smoothly. "One who understands the demands of the position."

The Remnants swirled over my bare arms as I watched my best friend's freedom slipping away. He would do it. I knew he would. He'd sacrifice his own happiness, his own choices, just as his father had. Just as they all did, generation after generation, bound by laws that cared nothing for the hearts they broke.

But this was Archer. My fierce, loyal friend who'd never wanted a crown, who'd spent his life masquerading as a snob, only to steal from the richest of this kingdom. And now he was to rule them all. But three months was nowhere near enough time to find love.

The council continued debating the finer points, but their voices faded to a distant hum as I stared at Archer's profile. In the space of a week, he'd lost his father and his freedom. And there wasn't a damn thing I could do to stop it.

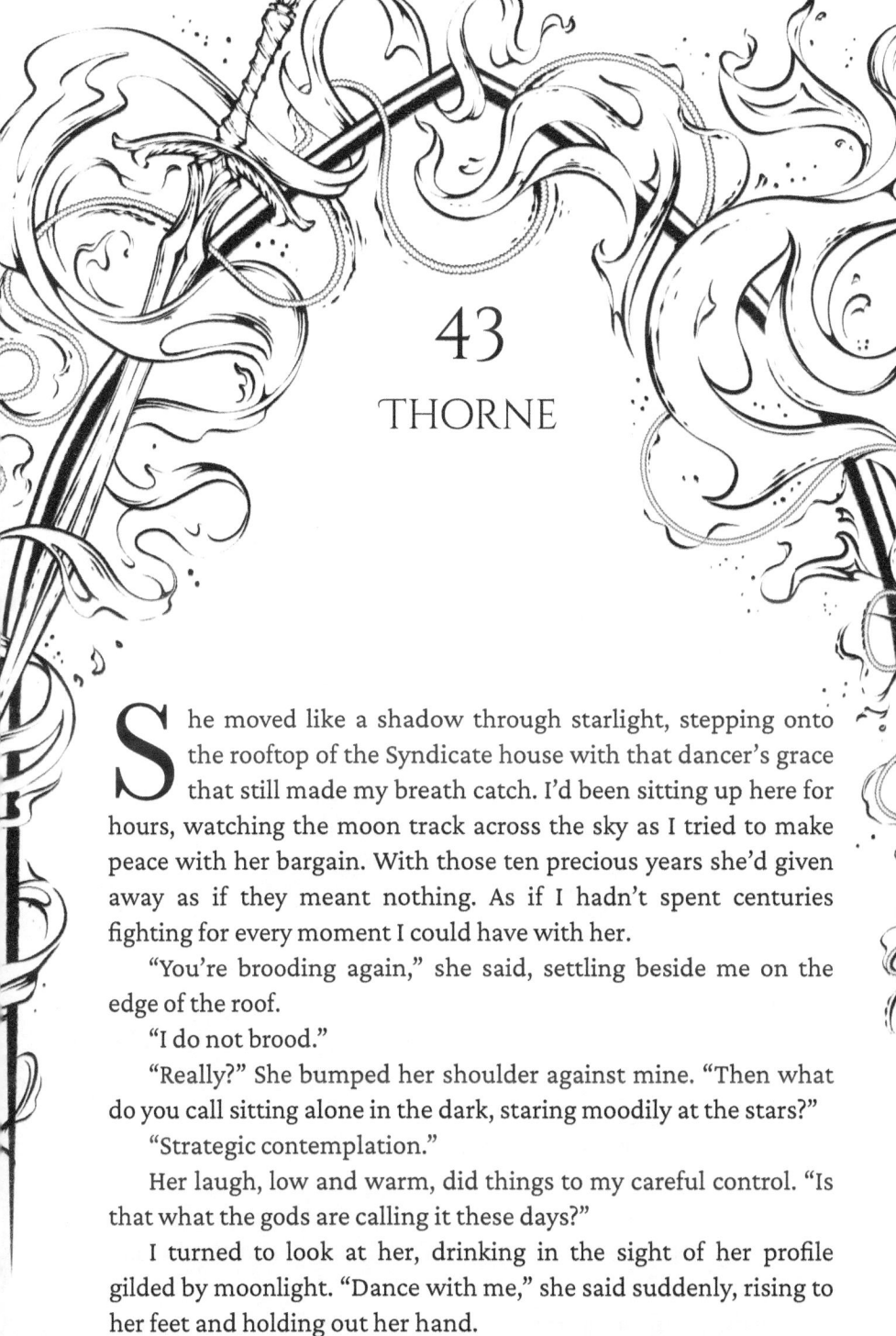

43
THORNE

She moved like a shadow through starlight, stepping onto the rooftop of the Syndicate house with that dancer's grace that still made my breath catch. I'd been sitting up here for hours, watching the moon track across the sky as I tried to make peace with her bargain. With those ten precious years she'd given away as if they meant nothing. As if I hadn't spent centuries fighting for every moment I could have with her.

"You're brooding again," she said, settling beside me on the edge of the roof.

"I do not brood."

"Really?" She bumped her shoulder against mine. "Then what do you call sitting alone in the dark, staring moodily at the stars?"

"Strategic contemplation."

Her laugh, low and warm, did things to my careful control. "Is that what the gods are calling it these days?"

I turned to look at her, drinking in the sight of her profile gilded by moonlight. "Dance with me," she said suddenly, rising to her feet and holding out her hand.

"Right now?"

"Afraid of heights, Husband?"

The challenge in her voice made something possessive stir in my chest. She hadn't called me that since she'd learned the truth of who I was. I took her hand. "Afraid of you, maybe."

"Good." She stepped into my arms with easy familiarity, and my body responded instantly, hardening. Fucking aching. "You should be."

We swayed together beneath the stars, no music but the sound of crickets and distant birds. Her head came to rest against my chest, and for a moment, I let myself pretend we were simply a man and woman dancing.

"Talk to me," she said softly. "I can feel you thinking too hard."

I remembered all the times I'd held her like this in other lives, other dances. "Ten years is a long time, Paesha."

"Or a very short time, depending on your perspective." She lifted her head to meet my gaze. Her eyes flicked away and back again so quickly, if not for my obsession with every move she made, I might not have caught it. The sign of her madness, if we could call it that. "You're immortal, remember?"

"And you're not." The words came out rougher than intended. "You've never lived past thirty-five in any life. Never. And now you've given away a third of what little time you might have had."

"To protect Archer." Her fingers curled into my shirt. "To keep him safe. You must see how that was the right move."

"I would have torn Vesalia's mind apart first."

"And started a war we can't afford to fight." She rose on her toes, pressing a kiss to the underside of my jaw. "Sometimes the only choice you have is which pain to bear. I stood in Alastor's office right beside you when Ezra shot that arrow. I saw the look in his eyes. Ten years was nothing compared to everything else happening."

I caught her hips, stopping our dance. "About that. There's something else I need to tell you. About Archer and this whole throne situation."

She looked up at me, curiosity in her eyes. "Okay?"

"When you were with Alastor, Minnie and I went to see the Fates."

Her breath caught, and the Remnants rippled. "The Fates? Are you insane?"

"Yeah, well, I was desperate. I'd do anything to help rid you of the voices."

As I spoke, the marks on her arms surged violently. She gasped, doubling over against me, her nails digging into my arms. The Remnants were clearly pissed at the idea of being silenced.

"That's exactly why I haven't mentioned it. I'm sorry. For all of it, but it's something you should know."

"It's fine." She squeezed her eyes shut and took several careful breaths before straightening. "So what happened? Did the Fates laugh in your face or try to kill you on the spot?"

"Both, actually." I brushed my lips against her temple. "But then they offered me a deal. They'll hear my request for help."

Another wave of shadows surged across her skin, and she bit back a cry. I held her tighter, wishing I could rip the voices from her mind myself.

"Let me guess, they want something in return?" she asked, her voice strained.

"Do you want to know or do you want me to stop?"

"I said I'm fine," she ground out.

"They want Archer. On the throne." I pushed her hair back, watching the war being waged in her eyes. "They won't even talk unless he becomes king."

She shuddered against me, her eyes flashing dark before clearing. "So the Fates are invested in Stirling politics now? And if they decide to tell you to go fuck yourself even after Archer puts on the crown?"

"Then I find another way." I tangled my fingers in her hair, holding her face close to mine as the shadows danced across her features. "I should have told you sooner."

"It wouldn't have changed anything. And despite it all, you pushed a conversation between father and son and nothing more. He's taking that throne because it's his choice. That's all I would have asked of you. You let him find his own way into accepting his father. If you'd have told me, and I was deeper into that madness from the start, I might've been selfish. And when it comes to him, I never want to be."

I pressed my lips to her temple. "That would be the Treeis bond speaking. I think he's the shield, Quill's the heart, and you're always going to be the extra piece that was never supposed to step in and supplement his power. You're the sacrifice."

She shook her head. "I'm only what I've always been. His friend. I just wish we knew why this happened. Why the Fates want him on the throne."

"If I had a jewel for every time I wondered why the Fates do what they do, I'd bathe you in a realm of diamonds. It's not the Fates I'm worried about. They know shit, but they are relatively harmless. Ezra's something else entirely. The Fates weave the threads, but Ezra is pulling at them, twisting the design into something only he understands. And we are left grasping at frayed edges, trying to piece together a reason."

"Ezra saw that I, meaning the Huntress, would break the balance of power, is that right?"

"He saw a path that led to you creating the imbalance. And his *job* is to unmake things that would cause catastrophic endings by seeing the paths and manipulating them. But he knew there was a path to peace. Even if it was only one, he fucking knew it."

"He also told you I'd betray you in the Forgotten, yet here we are. Is it strange that he's getting so much of it wrong?"

I scratched the back of my head wondering how best to explain the makings of all of it. "He has no guarantees, just like the Fates. He runs on probability. Likely it bothers his pride more than anything to be wrong. So he refuses to accept it."

"So you're saying you have some things in common. What with all that annoying godly pride."

Yanking her closer, hating the distance, I answered. "At least I come by it honestly."

"I've noticed." Her fingers played with a button on my jacket. "Hence the brooding."

"For the love of gods, I do not brood."

Her laugh, warm and real, washed over me like sunlight.

I spun her, then pulled her back against my chest, reveling in the way she fit perfectly in my arms. "Those ten years, Paesha..."

"No, sir. We are not circling back. We have to figure out how to get Archer on the throne. That's his choice and it could lead to answers." She lifted a shoulder and I knew the voices in her mind were rioting at the thought of being silenced.

I brushed a finger over her cheek. "I will save you from them. Whatever the cost, I will pay it."

"You and your promises." She tugged on my arm, leading me toward the door to go back inside. "Let's go to bed."

"Feeling tired, Wife?"

"Not on your immortal life, Husband."

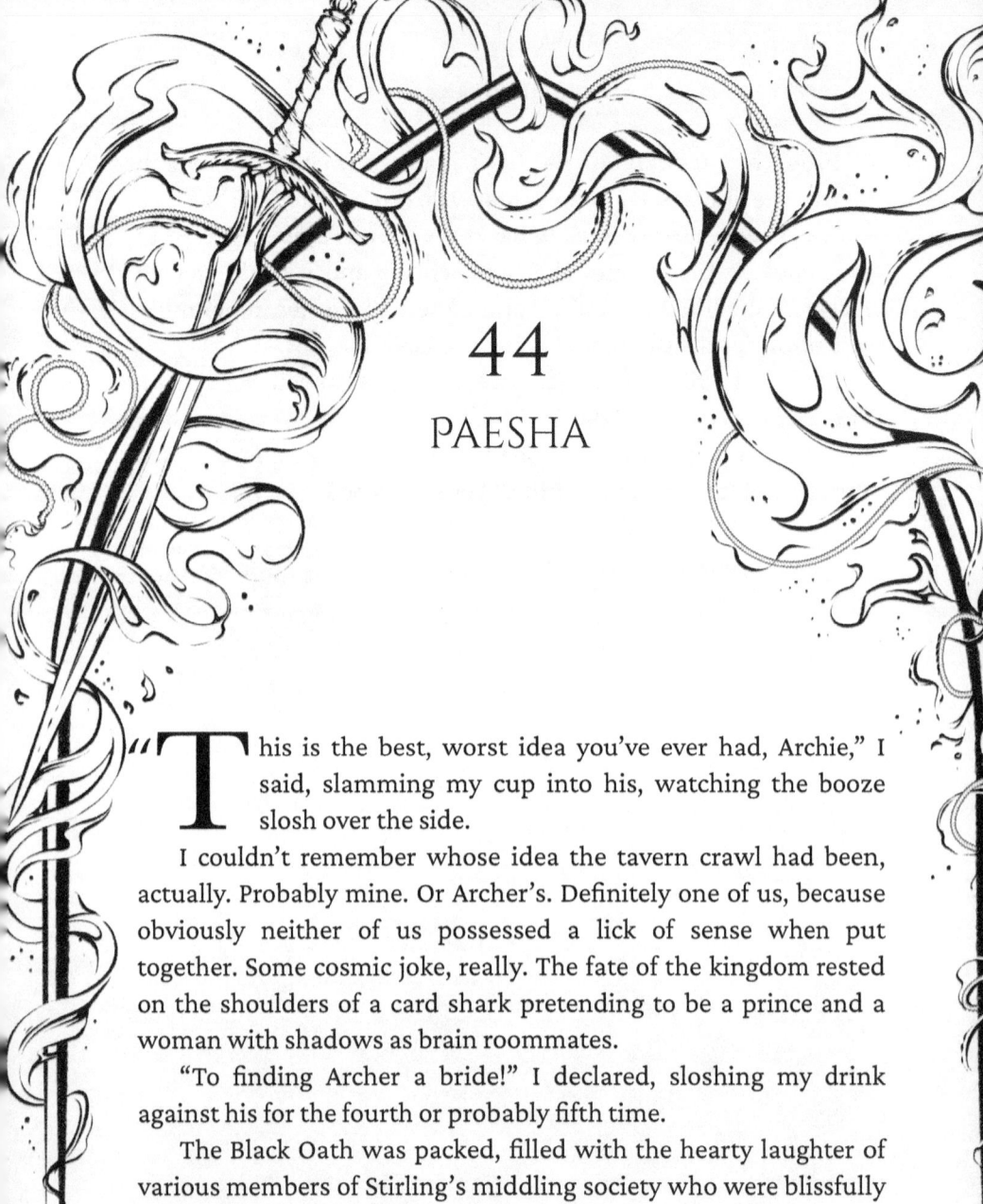

44

PAESHA

"This is the best, worst idea you've ever had, Archie," I said, slamming my cup into his, watching the booze slosh over the side.

I couldn't remember whose idea the tavern crawl had been, actually. Probably mine. Or Archer's. Definitely one of us, because obviously neither of us possessed a lick of sense when put together. Some cosmic joke, really. The fate of the kingdom rested on the shoulders of a card shark pretending to be a prince and a woman with shadows as brain roommates.

"To finding Archer a bride!" I declared, sloshing my drink against his for the fourth or probably fifth time.

The Black Oath was packed, filled with the hearty laughter of various members of Stirling's middling society who were blissfully unaware that their future king was currently seeing double and critiquing potential brides like they were horses at auction. Or maybe they were aware.

"That one's too tall," Archer said, squinting at a lovely brunette by the bar. "I'd get a crick in my neck trying to kiss her."

"You've kissed plenty of tall women," I pointed out, signaling for another round.

"That was horizontal. Different angles involved." He wiggled his eyebrows in a way he clearly hoped was suggestive but was actually ridiculous.

"What about her?" I nodded toward a woman with copper hair playing darts with impressive accuracy.

Archer grimaced. "Slept with her sister. And her cousin. Possibly on the same night, but that part's fuzzy."

"Gods, Archie, is there anyone in this tavern you haven't?"

He made a great show of scanning the room, then pointed triumphantly at an elderly man dozing in the corner. "Him! Definitely haven't slept with him."

"Your future queen, for sure." I dissolved into giggles, my shoulders shaking as I tried to maintain some semblance of dignity. "What about the barmaid?"

"Which one?"

"The one who keeps glaring at you like she might poison your drink."

"Ah." He winced. "That would be Lydia. We had a... misunderstanding."

"Misunderstanding?" I repeated flatly.

"I may have forgotten her name. While calling out another name. During a particularly intimate moment."

"You absolute disaster!"

"In my defense, they were sisters! Twins! It was an honest mistake!"

"That is so much worse," I giggled, wiping tears from my eyes.

The barmaid, Lydia, approached with fresh drinks, slamming them down with enough force to splash amber liquid across the table.

"Your poison, your highness," she said with saccharine sweetness.

"Lovely to see you again, Mar—" He caught himself. "Lydia. You're looking well."

She leaned in close, her smile sharp as a blade. "Your shameless flirting isn't going to win you any battles in here tonight, Archer Bramwell. There are no hearts left for you to break."

As she stalked away, Archer clutched his chest in mock offense. "I've never broken a heart in my life! I merely... borrowed it briefly and returned it slightly used."

"You're impossible. How will we ever find you a bride when you've exhausted all the options in Stirling?"

"We could try Perth," he suggested brightly. "I've only been there a handful of times. Statistically speaking, there must be at least three eligible women I haven't offended yet."

"Or we could import one. From, I don't know, one of those fancy northern kingdoms where they don't know your reputation."

"They'd find out soon enough." He slouched further in his chair, his usual easy confidence slipping for a moment. "Besides, what kind of woman wants to marry a fake prince with a tragic story to tell?"

"You're not a fake prince."

"Fine. What kind of woman wants to marry a reluctant prince with a tragic story and a magical bond to a small child and his best friend? That doesn't exactly scream 'stable husband material'."

My expression softened, and I reached across the table to squeeze his hand. "The right one will see what we see. A good man who'd sacrifice anything for the people he loves. A man who makes everyone around him laugh when the world gets too heavy. A man who'd make an amazing king, if he'd just stop thinking he doesn't deserve the crown."

Archer swallowed hard. He deflected with humor, as always. "Are you volunteering? Because I'm pretty sure Thorne would turn me into a very stylish pair of boots."

I snorted. "I'm pretty sure that would break some fundamental rules of our bond. And Thorne would do much worse than boots."

"You're probably right." He sighed dramatically. "Besides, the boots would probably be hideous."

A commotion at the door drew our attention as a group of rowdy men burst in, led by a woman with silver-streaked black hair and the confident stride of someone who commanded respect without asking for it.

"Zara Blackwood," I whispered. "She's actually from Perth. I guess not everyone's hiding in Thea's Underground."

"Hey, I've seen her. A few nights ago she was at the Parlor. She cheated me at cards twice," Archer said, studying Zara with newfound interest. "Never did figure out how she did it."

"A woman who can outcheat you?" My eyes widened in mock astonishment. "I think I've found your queen."

"Very funny." But he couldn't tear his eyes away as she settled at the bar, the men gathering around her like moths to flame. There was something magnetic about her, a wild kind of freedom.

"I dare you," I said, an impish grin spreading across my face.

"Dare me what?"

"Go talk to her. Charm her. See if the famous Archer Bramwell swagger works on a woman who clearly likes the spotlight."

"I changed my mind. I don't want to do this. How do we change the castle rules again?"

I dropped my chin to my chest. "If we could change the rules, your father would have done that and never married Farris's mother. Have you even seen Tuck lately? He's nose deep in every book and record he can find. You can't change the rules unless you're king and you can't be king unless you get married. Now perk your ass up and go say hi."

"You're mean. Has anyone ever told you that?"

I rolled my eyes. "Yes, yes. All the time." I snatched his tankard from the table and the room spun at the sudden movement. "I'm not giving this back until you have a fiancé."

"So, you're just going to sit in this tavern and rot while I court the kingdom? The fact that Thorne hasn't come charging in that door yet, is already surprising. I'm guessing we have *maybe* another hour before he melts the walls off this place to find you."

I lifted a shoulder. "He knows where we are."

Archer's eyes, though partially unfocused, doubled in size. "You told him about our best, worst idea ever? That was supposed to be a secret. We're fighting now."

"Let's just say I left him a note with some very vague instructions on what we *might* be doing and he's definitely in the process of narrowing it down right now."

"Remember that time when we snuck down to the catacombs and he almost killed me? Think I'm safe because of the whole king thing?"

"I think you're safe because he likes his balls and I would have to remove them from his body if he so much as thought about touching a single blond hair on your head."

His face twisted until he looked utterly disgusted. "Please never say the word balls to me again."

I lifted my cup to my mouth. "Balls."

"I actually hate you."

"You don't at all, that's what really bothers you."

He held up a hand. "How many fingers do you see?"

"At least seven."

"Perfect." He rose from his seat. "Let's go do something stupid."

I nodded, not even bothering to contemplate. "Famous last words. I'm in."

He swung an arm over my shoulder as we walked out of the tavern, words slurring as we swayed back and forth. "I was kidding, you know. You're my favorite. Don't tell the kid though. She's my other favorite."

"Careful, Toes, your bond is showing."

"Oh, gods. I just remembered. Is this the broken carriage?"

"Don't you start with that again."

He pressed a hand to his chest. "It was a catastrophic loss. A historic event. Bards will sing about the day you took down a whole damn carriage with your—"

"I swear to every god, if you finish that sentence, I will push you into the nearest river."

"I'm a fair swimmer, might be worth it." We hopped into the carriage and waited several moments before he snorted and got back out. "Forgot I was the driver."

"Where are we going anyway?" I asked, following him to the front of the carriage so we could sit on the box seat.

"You said Alastor was meeting with a bunch of gods when you were there, right?"

Sylvie stirred at the mention of her parents, but I ignored the claws in my mind. I'd grown used to them and the alcohol helped. "Oh, okay, so we're going to get ourselves killed. Great."

"You're so dramatic," Archer said, cracking the reins.

"How the hell did this night go from finding you a wife to gallivanting through the Vale?"

"Magic."

The carriage wobbled as Archer steered it through the streets. Somehow, we managed to avoid running over any pedestrians, though I'm pretty sure we clipped at least one fruit stand before we abandoned the damn thing and began crashing through the narrow winding alleys to get to the Vale. Archer's voice ricocheted off the close buildings as he sang a song that made absolutely no sense, but rhymed, and more than once I slipped and he had to keep me from falling.

When we arrived at the entrance, the same guard who was always there stood with his arms crossed, looking bored and irritated.

"You again," he grumbled when he saw Archer. "Thought I made myself clear last time."

I stepped forward, stumbling slightly but recovering with what I was pretty sure was grace.

"Is that any way to greet old friends?" Archer asked.

"We're not friends."

"Not with that attitude." I grinned, letting the Remnants swirl around my feet. "But we could be."

The guard's eyes widened as the shadows climbed up his legs, not hurting, merely... exploring. Like curious pets checking out a newcomer.

"What are you—"

"Just having a little fun," I cooed, watching the Remnants dance around him. "They're harmless. Mostly. Unless you're creepy. Maybe don't be creepy."

I had to blink several times when Winter appeared beside the man, snow falling over her opaque form as she dragged a finger down his cheek. *We are not harmless.*

"He doesn't need to know that," I shot back.

"Know what?" the guard asked.

The Remnants crept higher. "Nevermind. It's not important."

Archer stumbled up beside me, slinging an arm around my shoulder. "Think of the shadows as a private show. Very exclusive. Usually costs extra."

The guard looked from my power to Archer's lopsided grin and back again. "Alastor won't like this."

"Al can kiss my—"

"We just want to talk to him," Archer cut in. "Important royal business."

The guard's eyes narrowed. "You're drunk."

I gasped. "Who told you?"

After a tense moment, he stepped aside. "Your funeral."

"It's fine. Death's Court is lovely in the fall," I called over my shoulder as we sauntered through the entrance, the Remnants trailing behind us like sulking children.

The Vale was quiet, with fewer merchants and more shadows. Alastor's command, no doubt. We made our way through the long, central valley of his black market to doors in the very back with Archer humming an off key tune that somehow matched my stumbling steps.

When we pushed through the double doors without waiting for approval, we found Alastor seated behind his grand desk, looking precisely as irritated as I'd hoped. Irri stood by the edge of a bookshelf nearby, arranging and rearranging a collection of crystal paperweights that caught the light in dizzying patterns.

"Huntress," Alastor said, his voice dripping with disdain. His eyes shifted to Archer. "King."

"Not yet," Archer corrected, swaying slightly. "That's why we're here."

Alastor's gaze flicked between us, his expression darkening. "You're both intoxicated."

"Very astute, Big Al," I drawled. "No wonder you get to be a god."

His jaw tightened. "Don't call me that."

"What? Al? We talked about this. It suits you. Short, punchy, easy to remember when you're three, or six, drinks in." I grinned, enjoying his discomfort far too much.

Despite his obvious annoyance, Alastor didn't throw us out. Instead, he leaned back in his chair, fingers steepled beneath his chin. "To what do I owe this unexpected pleasure?"

"Do stars dream when they fall?" Irri asked suddenly, abandoning the paperweights to twirl in a slow circle. "I used to catch them, you know. With nets made of moonlight and children's wishes."

Archer blinked at her, momentarily distracted. "What?"

Alastor sighed. "Ignore her. She's having one of her moments."

"Rude," I mumbled, but even drunk, I knew better than to antagonize Irri. The goddess hummed a haunting melody, seeming unbothered by Alastor's dismissal as she continued her strange dance.

"We need information," Archer said, trying to sound authoritative despite his slurred speech. "About marriage laws. Royal ones."

"And you thought to come to me?" Alastor's eyebrow arched perfectly. "The God of Lost Things is hardly an expert on mortal matrimony."

"You're old," I pointed out helpfully. "Like, really old. You must know something."

The look he gave me could have curdled milk as his Remnants poured onto the floor. And though he may not have wanted me to see it, I noticed the opacity. They seemed weaker. Slower. "Your eloquence never fails to impress me, Huntress."

Archer leaned forward, bracing himself against Alastor's desk. "I need to know if there's a way around the marriage requirement for ascending the throne. Some loophole, some precedent, anything."

"You know better than that. If there were, Thorne's dog would have found it already. Those laws were written with very specific intentions, and with... certain influences present to ensure they remained absolute."

"Did you just call Tuck a dog?" I asked, flopping down in the chair across from him. "You can't go around calling people dogs, Al. It's offensive. To the dogs. Do better."

Archer groaned, dropping his head into his hands. "So I'm screwed."

"The arrow cannot wed the hawk," Irri said absently, now tracing patterns in the air with her fingertips. "Their wings beat to different rhythms."

We all turned to look at her, but she had already moved on, humming that eerie tune again as she rearranged books on a shelf.

"What does that mean?" Archer asked.

Alastor shook his head. "It's best not to try interpreting her musings. They rarely make sense to anyone but her since she's come back from the Forgotten. She needs time."

"Or perhaps they make too much sense," I suggested, watching Irri with newfound curiosity. There was something about her words that tugged at my mind, like a forgotten melody.

Archer straightened suddenly, his expression shifting. "There's something else I need to know. Am I really an Unmade Guardian?"

"Of course you are," Irri said, opening the door only to shut it again. "We have to let the secrets out or they will become trapped and destruction will follow. Isn't that right, Huntress? Darling Huntress. I like your dress. Was it mine?"

I looked down to my leather trousers, blinking several times to bring them into focus. Still not a dress.

"Oh!" She spun to Alastor. "It's snowing."

"Are you cold?" Alastor asked, jumping from his seat to rush to her. "Do you need something warmer?"

A moment of clarity struck as she reached for Alastor's handsome face. "You love me too hard some days."

"Impossible," he answered, staring down at her like she created the air he breathed.

"Awkward," Archer whispered, leaning toward me. Except it wasn't quiet at all.

Alastor's attention snapped to him. "Rumor has it you wear the Treeis mark. Though many are trying to figure out who you've bonded to. Between us and anyone that saw you loitering outside my market, I'd say the answer was fairly obvious."

"But I'm not bound to Ezra," he argued, ignoring the answer Al was fishing for.

"I believe that part is true, at least. But how many mortals truly understand what they are, what forces shape them? The Treeis mark doesn't lie, Archer Bramwell. You are Unmade, though perhaps not in the traditional sense."

"That doesn't make me one of Ezra's puppets!"

"Unmade Guardians aren't puppets," Alastor corrected. "They're chosen. Special. Vessels for a power greater than themselves."

"Oh yeah?" I challenged. "From where I'm sitting, it looks a hell of a lot like manipulation. You fuckers are good at that."

Alastor's dark eyes fixed on me. "Careful, Huntress. You're in my domain now, and I've been remarkably patient with your... behavior."

"Aww, am I annoying you?" I batted my eyelashes. "How absolutely devastating for you."

"Paesha," Archer warned, clearly sensing the dangerous edge to our banter.

Irri suddenly appeared beside Alastor, her movements so fluid it was as if she'd simply materialized there. She placed a hand on his shoulder, and some of the tension left his frame.

"The three-pointed star cannot bear the crown alone," she said, her eyes focusing briefly as she looked directly at Archer. "The bond that saves will also chain. No marriage vows can stand against such ties."

Archer frowned. "What is she talking about?"

"She thinks you can't marry," I translated, the pieces clicking together despite my inebriated state. "Because of the Treeis bond."

"That's ridiculous," Archer scoffed. "Plenty of people with magical bonds get married."

"Not the Unmade," Alastor said quietly. "And certainly not

those bound to both a child and..." He glanced at me, something calculating in his gaze. "Whatever that is."

"Again. Rude."

Before he could answer, the doors behind us crashed open. Archer and I spun in our seats to find Thorne standing in the doorway, looking absolutely murderous.

"Found us," Archer muttered.

"Time to go," I agreed.

Irri began to hum louder, a smile playing at her lips as she resumed her seemingly random dance around the room. The melody followed us as we stumbled toward the exit, past Thorne. But rather than fury, he simply flashed a subtle wink at me and slid his hand over the small of my back as we walked out. He knew where we were, of course. This man wasn't letting me casually stroll the streets knowing his brother was hunting me. But he was giving me space. Until he wasn't, apparently.

"He sounds like thunderstorms," Irri yelled behind us. "All lightning and promise. But you already knew that, didn't you, little Huntress? With all of your destruction?"

I froze, looking back at her. For a moment, her eyes were clear, knowing, before clouding over again as she returned to her humming.

"This has been delightful," Alastor called after us. "Please don't come again. Especially not in this state."

"Wouldn't dream of it, Al," I called back, grabbing Archer's arm as we made our hasty exit.

The last thing I heard as Thorne led us out was Irri's lilting voice, "The arrow and the hawk may not wed, but oh, how beautifully they fly together..."

As expected, by the time we got back to the Syndicate house, Thorne's overly protective alpha male attitude was gone. He'd trusted me with Archer, sure, but he was never far enough away to truly worry. He'd simply kissed me harder in bed that night. And I'd let him.

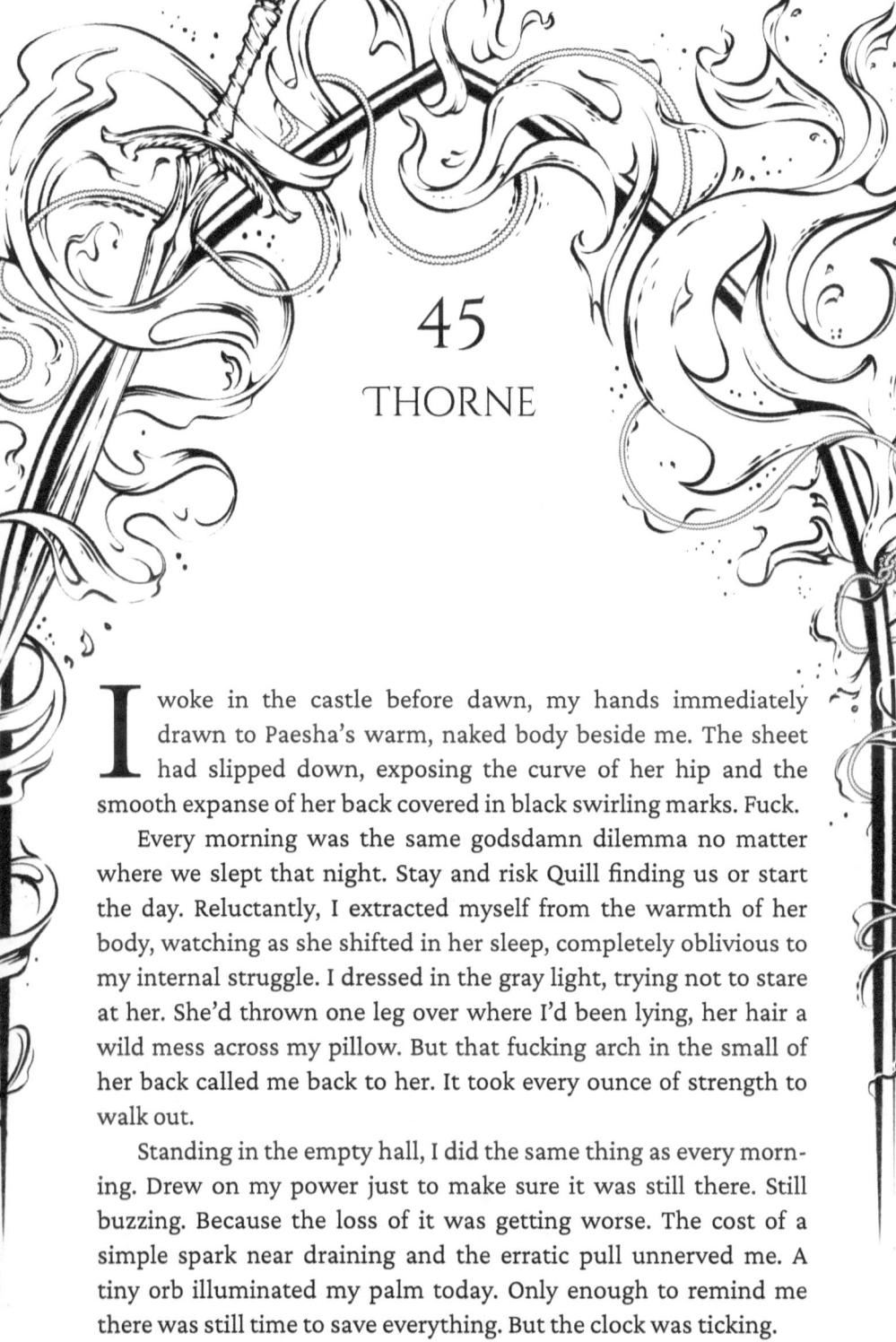

45

THORNE

I woke in the castle before dawn, my hands immediately drawn to Paesha's warm, naked body beside me. The sheet had slipped down, exposing the curve of her hip and the smooth expanse of her back covered in black swirling marks. Fuck.

Every morning was the same godsdamn dilemma no matter where we slept that night. Stay and risk Quill finding us or start the day. Reluctantly, I extracted myself from the warmth of her body, watching as she shifted in her sleep, completely oblivious to my internal struggle. I dressed in the gray light, trying not to stare at her. She'd thrown one leg over where I'd been lying, her hair a wild mess across my pillow. But that fucking arch in the small of her back called me back to her. It took every ounce of strength to walk out.

Standing in the empty hall, I did the same thing as every morning. Drew on my power just to make sure it was still there. Still buzzing. Because the loss of it was getting worse. The cost of a simple spark near draining and the erratic pull unnerved me. A tiny orb illuminated my palm today. Only enough to remind me there was still time to save everything. But the clock was ticking.

The kitchens were already bustling when I got there. The head cook, Marta, a shrewd old bat who'd caught Paesha sneaking out of my room once, and had been milking it ever since, greeted me with a knowing smirk. They all knew us as married. But Quill didn't. So no matter what we did, it was suspicious to someone.

"Got your breakfast, m'lord," she said, heavy on the sarcasm. Everyone in the castle knew me only as Lord Noctus, owner of the gambling Parlor. I preferred to keep it that way. "That fancy tea for your wife too."

"Yes. The bitter water she pretends to like."

Marta snorted. "Women and their little lies. My husband thought I enjoyed his singing for thirty years."

I grunted in response and slipped her the extra coin she'd come to expect. The castle was still quiet as I made my way back upstairs, tray in hand, mind already running through the day's necessities.

Paesha had completely taken over the bed. She'd somehow managed to sprawl diagonally across the mattress, face buried in my pillow. I set down the tray and took a moment to appreciate the view before pressing my lips to her temple.

"Rise and shine, Wife," I said, not bothering to keep the amusement from my voice.

One eye cracked open, immediately narrowing when she saw me. "Fuck off," she mumbled, burying her face deeper into the pillow.

"Good morning to you too, sunshine. I brought food."

"I don't want food. I want sleep." She attempted to yank the blanket up, but I snatched it and kept my grip firm.

"Tough. We've got things to do." I gestured to the tray. "Bread. Honey. That horrible tea you insist on drinking."

She sat up finally, not bothering with the sheet. My mouth went dry as her breasts came into view. She caught me staring and smirked. "See something you like, Husband?"

I cleared my throat. "Nothing I haven't seen before." A blatant lie. Every time felt like the first time with her. Pathetic.

She reached for the tea, her nose wrinkling at the first sip. "You're an absolute monster in the mornings."

"So you've said." I settled on the edge of the bed, opening my journal and pretending to focus on my notes instead of the naked woman beside me. "Daily."

"Normal people sleep until the sun's up," she added, licking honey from her thumb.

I forced my attention back to my notes. "We aren't normal people." When I glanced up, her hair was a fucking disaster around her shoulders, and I wanted nothing more than to bury my hands in it again. "You know Quill will come looking for you soon."

The groan she let out was pure drama. "She used to sleep in so well. I don't know what this new phase is."

"Hard to say. Children can be so fickle." I bit back a smile. I'd been bribing that kid with sweets for a week to develop this early rising habit. It suited my schedule, but Paesha was extra growly in the morning and I loved it.

She jabbed my thigh with her toe. "Liar. Are you... Oh, my gods. I can see it on your face. Are you bribing her?"

"Absolutely not. But the staff is already moving around."

"Fine," she sighed dramatically. "But it should be illegal to be this functional before sunrise."

I rubbed my thumb across my bottom lip. "Maybe if you didn't insist on staying up so late..."

"Terrible mistake. It won't happen again," she said, finally getting up and giving me a full view of her body as she stretched. "My obsession with you will pass any day now."

I swallowed hard, handing her the robe I'd laid out. "Sure it will."

After dressing, she sat back on the bed beside me, taking another sip of her tea, grimacing. I reached for my coffee but she snatched it first, taking a deliberate sip from my side of the cup. I kept my face neutral as she handed it back, though the urge to wipe away her mark warred with the impulse to drink from that exact spot.

I chose the latter, maintaining eye contact. Let her think it didn't bother me.

"How long have you been awake?" she asked. While I glanced

417

down at my notes, I felt her fingers slide through my carefully combed hair. I continued reading as if I hadn't noticed, though every nerve ending screamed at her chaos.

"Long enough to know Aeris was last seen in Silbath and still no sign of Ezra," I replied evenly, ignoring the mess she'd made of my hair. I'd fix it after she left.

She tore into the bread with her fingers. From my peripheral vision, I watched her deliberately let honey drip onto my side of the bed. My jaw clenched involuntarily, but I kept my focus on my journal, pretending I hadn't seen. This was fine. The maids would change the sheets anyway. They weren't even my sheets. Completely fine.

While I was concentrating on being unbothered, she reached over and turned my journal upside-down. I paused for half a second, then continued reading as if nothing had changed.

Try harder, darling.

She tried to hide that adorable smirk as she ate, taking several more sips of my coffee before she officially left the bed. As she passed my carefully arranged boots by the door, she nudged one slightly askew with her toe.

I noted it silently, promising myself I'd fix it later.

"Any word from Tuck about the Parlor?" she asked, gathering her hair up. "You've been noticeably absent over there lately, I'm sure."

"The place could burn to the ground for all I care. It's only a facade."

She moved to the mirror, tossing a few of the hairpins I'd taken out last night back into the mess she'd made. When I looked back down at my book, she deliberately moved something else. Little menace.

This was normal. Comfortable. Almost perfect. Until she whispered something I couldn't hear. Until she turned away, trying to hide the madness. Until her cheeks flushed when she turned back to me.

I set my coffee down and crossed the room, sliding my fingers around her neck. "I hope you told them to fuck off."

"Most of them," she whispered, closing her eyes to take a deep breath. "Will you tell me about Levanya?"

A flash of the fallen warrior queen seared my mind. "Levanya was peace and power. She was strength. She'd already lost her kingdom by the time I found her and she was on the precipice of a battle with the kingdom that'd taken her throne." I couldn't help my smile as I pictured the fearless woman. "She would sit around fires every night with the small company that followed her. They'd tell stories and live on meager dinners. She refused any kind of help. In fact, one time I brought her dinner and she got mad at me for not serving everyone else before her. But that's how she was. She was injured on a battlefield before I met her. She'd kept the wound hidden from everyone. When she finally told me, she wouldn't accept help. So, I confessed who I was. How I could help her. It was the first time I'd given our story to one of you. I went for the healer and Ezra showed up. He waited until I was across the field before he fired that fucking arrow." I swallowed the pain of that memory. "She was gone before I could make it to her side."

Paesha's eyes flickered between mine as she listened. "She never blamed you. She wants you to know her life was never in your hands. But I don't understand how Ezra was able to kill her. If she was a queen, isn't that an absolute law. The gods cannot interfere with the mortal royals?"

"Gods can die two ways, by their descendants with a weapon of emotional power, because gods are born of emotions, or by the Fates. The Fates are mostly neutral, but they do have rules we have to abide by. I don't think he would have been foolish enough to anger the Fates, but Ezra could take Levanya's life because she was a fallen queen. She ruled over no one and held no more titles or land."

She slid her hand up my chest, gripping my shirt. "It's okay that you loved them, you know?" The second those words left her, I caught the fucking wince. "As long as you hate them now."

"I would forget every single one of them if it meant saving you."

She winced again as the markings on her arms poured onto the floor. "What's the plan for the day?"

"Well, that depends on you, really. Are we staying at the castle again?"

"I think we're having lunch here and staying at the Syndicate house tonight. Quill wants to stop and see the kids on the way, that's all I know."

"Any word from Thea?"

"It sounds like she's been recruiting some of the Salt from Stirling. At this point, she's got a whole underground secret city and that's where she's been staying."

I nodded, fully aware of Althea's conglomerate. "Did you tell her what I said?"

"Thea's always been an optimist. She believes in people. She thinks the mortals will keep their hideout secret because they aren't going to bite the hand that feeds them."

"History would prove otherwise, but we'll cross that bridge when we get there, I'm sure. I need to try to talk to Minerva again before we go. Stubborn old bat."

The corner of her mouth lifted as the sunlight finally began to creep through the window. "I'm absolutely telling her you said that."

"Good. I'm not scared of her."

"Well, that works out because she's standing right behind you."

"What?" I whipped around, missing the fucking smile on her face. I didn't miss the giggle.

"So you're a little bit scared. That's probably a good idea. I saw her crack her cane across Tuck's shins the other day. He deserved it, but still. A healthy dose of fear is fine."

I spun back to face her. Planting a glare I could barely hold. I dashed forward, snagged her sassy little ass and stormed across the room to drop her on the bed right as she yelped. "Morning Paesha might be my favorite Paesha." I growled, burying my face into her neck.

"Get off of me, you animal."

Instead, I smothered her in kisses. Her chin. An ear. Her nose. It wasn't until I moved lower that I remembered she was naked beneath her robe. I slowed. Stopped entirely. Fighting with myself. With the godsdamn sunlight and the bargain I'd made with Quill.

"Regretting all your choices now aren't you, Husband," Paesha crooned, wiggling beneath me.

I ripped her robe open. "Absolutely not."

I slid myself down her perfect body, kissing, biting. Fucking savoring. She arched on the bed, spreading those godsdamn legs for me. I kissed the inside of her thighs, letting my teeth graze her skin until she whimpered.

"You will lead and I will follow, love." I slid a finger down her center. "Tell me what you want."

"Isn't it obvious?" she panted as I circled her pretty, little clit.

"Say it," I demanded, struggling to keep control.

"I want you to fuck me."

"I'd prefer to taste you first, Paesha darling."

She let out a gasp as I lowered myself to her center. This needed to be quick, but I hated the thought of anything rushed with her. Fucking hell. She tasted so damn good. She relaxed her legs, burying her hands into my hair as I stroked my tongue over her, moving back and forth, up and down, working in the exact combination I'd already learned she needed.

The sounds she made, those whimpers and gasps as I moved were everything. The crescendo to every song, the climax to every story, the path for every journey. Nothing made me feel more possessive. And she godsdamn knew it.

I slipped a finger inside of her.

"So fucking wet."

Her moan became a gasp. When her Remnants wrapped themselves around me, I chuckled, knowing my warm breath would tickle her thigh. "Feeling greedy?"

"Less words, more tongue," she answered.

I could barely think past the pressure of my cock against the buckle of my pants. I didn't relent. I knew what she needed.

"I'm going to come. Fuck. It's too much."

Her legs tightened. She arched off the bed. Still, I moved, sliding two fingers inside, feeling her pulse as pleasure rolled through her.

I had my pants off before she'd come down from her climax. When I crawled over the top of her, resting at her entrance, she reached for me. It was the most beautiful sight I'd ever seen. Half-lidded eyes and a satiated smile. Gods. Fucking perfection.

She lifted her hips again, sliding up my cock, and it was nearly my undoing. I squeezed my eyes shut, fighting the urge to bury myself deep inside her and stay there. This was a time for hard and fast. Still, I couldn't help staring into those eyes as I pressed myself to her entrance.

"Fuck," I hissed as she took me, inch by inch. Her lips tasted like sin and her cunt felt like heaven. Halfway in, I pulled out and eased myself back in one more time. She was so godsdamn wet, and that little moan left her lips again. That was it for me. I pulled back and thrust inside again, unleashing the primal need to fuck her.

She buried her nails into my back. The pain of her breaking the skin mixed with the pleasure of her wrapped around my cock was something else entirely. A dance we always circled. I slammed forward again and again until she was writhing beneath me. I changed pace, changed the angle. Fucking her until her brows knit together and the only thing that existed in the world was her and I. She tightened again, tipping her head back on the bed. I held the rhythm, sliding my fingers over that beautiful neck as her moan vibrated against my palm. Watching her build and build beneath. Her hips rose, eager for more.

Gripping her neck, I yanked her forward until our foreheads touched. "I fucking love you."

Her eyes flicked to my lips as I moved. When I slid my hand to the back of her neck to hold her up, she bit my bottom lip on a moan before she sighed, "I love you too, prick."

I snatched the pins from her wild hair and tossed them to the side before burying my fingers in deep at the nape of her neck and tipping her head down. "Watch me fuck you," I commanded. "Look how perfect we fit together."

I thrust into her again, hard and deep, the slick heat of her clamping down on me like a vise. She gasped and I felt her body tighten around me, pulling me deeper, demanding more. I gave it to her.

Her hands clawed my shoulders, nails digging into my skin as she clung to me. Those thighs trembled around my hips, and I could feel the tension building in her, coiling tighter and tighter until she finally broke. Her back arched and she tossed her head back, crying out, with my fingers still tangled in her hair. Her voice was raw and desperate as she came undone around me. I couldn't hold back anymore. My cock jerked, pulsing inside her as I came. It wasn't enough. It would never be enough.

I crushed my lips to hers, swallowing her gasps and moans as I kissed her like it was the last thing I'd ever do. Her hands tangled in my hair, pulling me closer, and I let her. She could take whatever she wanted from me. When I finally pulled away, she was smiling, her lips swollen and wet, her eyes dark with satisfaction. She was undoubtedly the most beautiful thing I'd ever seen.

Watching her smile over her shoulder at me as she dashed down the hall in nothing but that robe was a sight that would be burned into my memory for the rest of time.

THE TEMPERATURE SEEMED to drop several degrees as tension crept back into Archer's shoulders. "There has to be another way."

"There isn't," I said, as gently as I could. "The law is absolute. Not even I can change that."

"Then change the time limit," Quill suggested, hopping onto the seat beside Paesha. We sat in the garden at the Syndicate house having a simple lunch. "Three months isn't long enough to fall in love, probably."

"Love has nothing to do with it," Archer muttered.

"It should," Thea said fiercely. "You deserve that much at least."

He smiled, but it wasn't genuine at all. "What I deserve and what's necessary aren't always the same thing. And this was... is my choice."

"What about me?" Quill asked suddenly. "I could marry you."

The resulting chorus of "No!" from every adult present made her jump.

"Why not? I'm already connected to you both." She twisted to look up at Paesha. "You said the Treeis bond means we're family forever."

"It does," Paesha agreed. "But marriage is different. You're far too young, and Archer needs someone who can help him rule."

"I could help," Quill insisted.

"You are helping with ideas," Archer said fondly. "But let's table the marriage proposals until you're at least old enough to reach the top shelf in Elowen's kitchen, okay?"

She huffed but settled back in her seat, snagging a roll from the basket on the table. "Fine. But I still think it's stupid."

"Most laws are," I said, earning a sharp look from Paesha. "What? They are. Especially the ones written by mortals trying to control things they don't understand."

"Like gods?" Thea asked innocently.

I had to smile. "Exactly like gods."

"Speaking of control," Elowen interrupted smoothly, "Quill, honey. The next time you feel really upset, let's avoid the garden. Everything out here is starting to die."

"Sorry," she mumbled.

"Hey," I said softly, surprising myself as much as everyone else. "Come here a moment."

She hesitated, looking to Paesha first, then Archer. When they both nodded, she slid off her chair and came to stand before me.

I knelt to her level. "Your power feels big, doesn't it? Like it's too much to hold sometimes?"

She nodded.

"That's because it is. Maybe you weren't meant to contain it all by yourself." I held out my hand, palm up, letting a small globe of golden light form there, hoping like hell it didn't flicker out and ruin the point. "Watch."

The light split into tiny streams, weaving between my fingers like liquid sunshine. Quill gasped, reaching out to touch one.

"Big power isn't meant to be caged," I continued, letting the light dance around her fingers. "It's meant to flow. Like a river. You don't stop a river, you learn to direct it."

"How?"

"First, you have to accept that it's part of you. Not something separate to fight against." I glanced at Paesha, seeing understanding dawn in her eyes. "Then you find anchors. People who help you remember who you are when the power tries to make you forget."

"Like Paesha and Archer?"

"Exactly like them."

She studied the light thoughtfully. "Is that why you stay close to Paesha? Because she's your anchor?"

"Yes," I admitted quietly. "She is."

"Then you should eat more bread," Quill decided, very seriously. "Because anchors need you to be strong too."

I was sure there was logic in that to her. Somehow. "You know what? You're absolutely right."

"I usually am. But that doesn't solve how we're going to get Archie a wife."

Archer stood, tucking a stack of papers under his arm as he mussed the child's hair. "*We* aren't going to get Archie a wife. That's not how it works, Pencil."

"But you're sitting around staring at boring papers all the time now. That's not how it works either."

He smiled, something genuine this time. "Fair enough. How about this, I'll make you a deal. I'll find myself a date, and you and Paesha can decide if she's the right one to marry. Since you guys are always going to be an important part of my life, and I'm always going to want to protect you before anyone else, you should get a say."

"And she'll have to accept our bond too," Quill said. "Or I'll have to kill her."

Archer jerked back. "We talked about you throwing creepy threats out like that, didn't we?"

Quill rolled her eyes. "Fine. But I'll make her really sad and watch her cry for fun."

"Time for your bath," Thea said, jumping to her feet. "Bath before death threats has always been the rule."

To his credit, he waited until the back door slammed shut before he rounded on Paesha. "I told you your kid is creepy."

"I mean, I'm not one to judge, but from the sound of that conversation, she's your kid too. Also, we probably let her spend too much time with Death's Maiden a year ago."

"You think?" he asked, pulling a deck of cards from his pocket.

"In her defense, before the city here fell to ruins, everyone was immortal for a hundred years. It's a new concept to her that anyone off the street can murder."

"That is *not* a defense," Archer said, turning to me. "Tell her that's not a defense."

I opened my mouth to argue but he threw up a hand. "No. Nevermind. I can already tell you're afraid to argue with naked Paesha."

"Hey, I'm fully clothed," she bit back, crossing her arms over her chest.

Archer smirked. "I've seen the way he looks at you now. I'd bet you a broken carriage, you're absolutely naked in his brain."

"Fuck all the way off, Archer Bramwell," she said, throwing her book at his head.

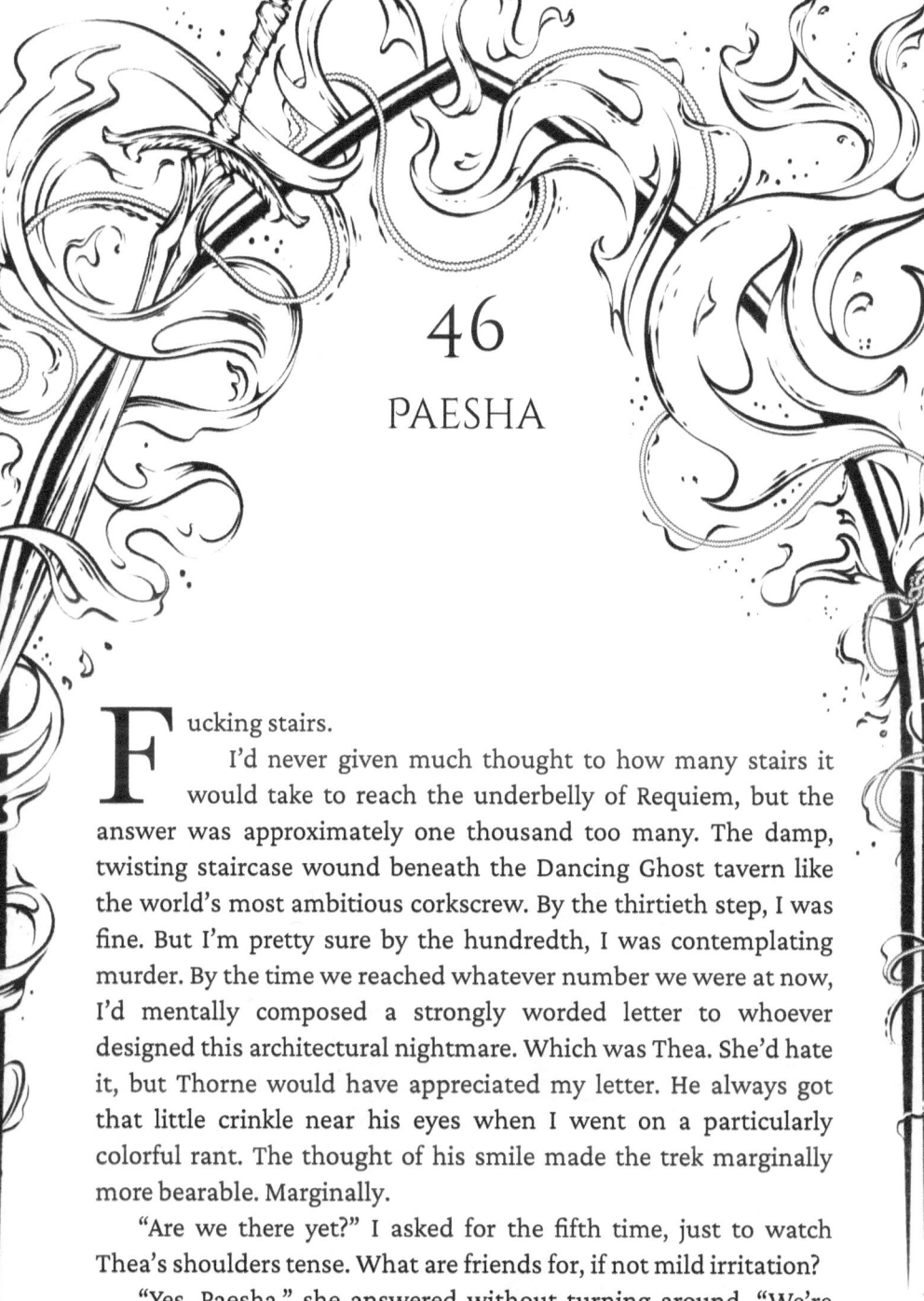

46

PAESHA

Fucking stairs.

I'd never given much thought to how many stairs it would take to reach the underbelly of Requiem, but the answer was approximately one thousand too many. The damp, twisting staircase wound beneath the Dancing Ghost tavern like the world's most ambitious corkscrew. By the thirtieth step, I was fine. But I'm pretty sure by the hundredth, I was contemplating murder. By the time we reached whatever number we were at now, I'd mentally composed a strongly worded letter to whoever designed this architectural nightmare. Which was Thea. She'd hate it, but Thorne would have appreciated my letter. He always got that little crinkle near his eyes when I went on a particularly colorful rant. The thought of his smile made the trek marginally more bearable. Marginally.

"Are we there yet?" I asked for the fifth time, just to watch Thea's shoulders tense. What are friends for, if not mild irritation?

"Yes, Paesha," she answered without turning around. "We're here now. That's why we're still walking down these stairs."

"Your sarcasm wounds me."

Ahead of us, Quill giggled, the sound echoing against the stone walls as she hopped down the metal steps two at a time with Boo yipping at her heels. How a child and a tiny dog with legs the length of my thumb had more energy than me was a cosmic injustice.

"Watch your step," Minerva cautioned from behind me, her cane tapping a steady rhythm. The old woman hadn't complained once despite having to navigate these stairs with her supposed bad hip. Meanwhile, I'd mentally cataloged seventeen creative expletives to describe my discomfort. If ever we didn't want the gods gallivanting through the underground, the stairs of doom would dissuade them.

"Too bad Archer isn't here to knit me a sweater," I muttered. "By the time we reach the bottom, he could have made enough for your whole city."

"You know, the first time I came down here, I slipped and fell," Thea called back, tossing the comment over her shoulder like it wasn't terrifying. "I had to craft myself a splint out of scrap metal, but I survived, and so will you."

I grabbed the wall. "That's not reassuring."

"Wasn't meant to be," she replied cheerfully.

Liar.

The staircase finally, *finally*, opened into a narrow passage that smelled of earth and torch smoke. Thea held up a hand, stopping us at a heavy wooden door reinforced with iron bands. "A few ground rules. Don't mention the gods unless someone else brings them up first. Don't stare at anyone's injuries, some of them escaped Aeris's 'improvements' with scars to show for it. We had no idea the destruction she caused under the guise of renewal. She never even moved the people. Just changed everything. Oh, and for the love of all that's holy, Paesha, try not to let the Remnants do their creepy shadow thing."

I leveled a glare at her. "I have the Remnants under control. It's the voices in my head that need help." I hadn't mentioned to anyone I was starting to feel a separation from the two. The Remnants had melded to my command, but the past lives had not at all. And they'd begun materializing more and more. Winter always led the pack, but most of my days were haunted by other women. All dead, injuries showing, blood dripping down their bodies. Mismatched eyes haunted. Some spoke. Most did not. And only one was safe. Only one.

As if summoned, three of them came into view. I never minded until they got too close to Archer or Quill. Then I couldn't help the nausea. The racing heart. The overwhelming guilt that I couldn't save them from my mind.

This one will be the end of you, Paesha darling. You must see that.

"Behave," I hissed at her before Thea could notice.

Quill moved to my side, her brows pulled together. "Why do you talk to your shadows sometimes? I've seen you whispering to them when you think no one's looking."

I froze. I had no idea what to say. How to feel. But Quill felt the embarrassment and immediately stepped back. "It's okay if you don't want to say."

Minerva stepped in smoothly, reaching out to straighten the collar on Quill's dress. "Some magic requires negotiation, little one. Even the strongest wielders must occasionally remind their power who's in charge."

"Oh. Okay." She shrugged and spun away.

Minerva gripped my arm. "Sometimes children need a simple answer."

Thea rapped her knuckles against the door in a pattern that couldn't possibly be as complicated as she was making it seem. A panel slid open at eye level, then quickly closed. Locks clicked and the door swung inward, revealing a dark man with a beard that put Tuck's to shame.

"'Bout time you showed up," he grumbled, but his eyes crinkled with a smile as he saw Quill in tow. "Hello, Miss Quill. The little ones have been asking when you'd bring the pup back."

"Hello to you too, Vincent," Thea said, stepping inside. "Sorry for the delay. The steps were extra gruesome today."

His gaze landed on me with sudden suspicion. "Who's this, then?"

Before Thea could answer, I stepped forward with what I hoped was my least threatening smile. "I'm Paesha."

Vincent stared at me for a long moment. "Welcome to the Underground." He gestured for us to follow him through the arched passage beyond.

I'd expected a lot of things from an underground city. A few sad little hovels, perhaps. Some candles stuck in sconces. Maybe a puddle or two for ambiance.

What I hadn't expected was this, which was really unfair to Thea, to be honest.

The passage opened into a vast cavern that seemed to stretch for miles, its ceiling so high that for a moment I forgot we were underground. The damn steps made sense now. Lanterns hung from wrought iron poles, casting warm light over what could only be described as a proper city. Buildings crafted from stone and metal hugged the walls, creating tiers of new homes and shops that climbed upward like a wedding cake. Wooden walkways connected the levels, crisscrossing the open space. In the center, a large circular plaza hosted what appeared to be a market, with stalls arranged around a fountain that somehow, impossibly, sparkled with fresh water.

"Holy shit," I breathed.

"I think 'holy shit' covers it pretty well," Thea said, beaming with pride. "Come on, I'll give you the tour. We picked this spot because of the natural water source."

As we followed her into the heart of the city, I couldn't tear my eyes away from the people. There were so many of them, hundreds at least, going about their daily lives as if they weren't living beneath the streets of a city that had been remade by a goddess. There were still very few children in Requiem, but the ones that were here chased each other between market stalls. An old woman hung laundry on a line strung between buildings. A group of men played cards at a makeshift table.

"You built all of this?" I asked Thea, awe tempering my usual snark.

She shook her head. "I helped. I created the frameworks, the supports, the things that needed my particular touch." She flexed her fingers, and I noticed the slight tremor in them. "But they did the rest. Turns out, people are pretty damn resourceful when they're trying to avoid being 'renewed.'"

"Why did they come down here?" Quill asked, watching the group of children playing with a ball made of scraps as Boo circled their feet trying to catch it. "Aeris made everything pretty."

Thea's lips thinned. Clearly her thoughts on Aeris had taken a complete turn around. "Pretty doesn't mean better, Quill. When Aeris 'fixed' Requiem, she didn't ask anyone what they wanted. She just changed it. Changed their homes, their livelihoods, she welcomed gods that no one wanted."

We reached the edge of the market where a small crowd had gathered. As they parted to let us through, I saw what had drawn their attention: an empty space where a foundation had been marked out with string.

"New home?" I asked.

Thea nodded. "The Porters. Family of five coming in from the outskirts. Lost everything when their farm was 'improved' into a golden meadow. Can't eat gold."

She approached the site, rolling up her sleeves. The crowd murmured with excitement, and I realized they were here to watch her work. Minerva guided Quill to the front of the gathering, securing a prime viewing spot.

"How many times have you done this?" I asked quietly.

"Lost count," Thea admitted. "Dozens? Maybe hundreds by now. It started small, a safe room here, a hidden passage there. Then more people came. And more."

"And it doesn't hurt? Using your power this much?"

She gave me a tired smile. "Everything worth doing hurts a little."

She is lying, Levanya whispered in my mind. *It hurts more than a little.*

I could see the strain on Thea's face, the way she steadied herself before kneeling beside the foundation. This wasn't solely fatigue. This was the bone deep exhaustion of someone who'd pushed their power beyond its limit too many times. The Maestro used to do this to her and now she was doing it to herself. And she wasn't even using her forge for respite. This was bad. Dangerous even.

I grabbed her arm, kneeling beside her to whisper. "You are draining yourself. You know what they said about Archer. He used all of his power to hold time when Quill fell in that cavern. He would have died, Althea. We're not meant to use everything."

"But he didn't die," she argued with a hiss. "And neither will I."

"Archer didn't die because," I looked around to make sure no one could hear me. "Mine and Quill's magic saved him. We're bonded now because of it."

"See? It was a blessing."

I looked at her then, took in the wary look on her face, the dark circles under her once vibrant green eyes, even her copper hair had dulled. "Ezra was supposed to show up," I whispered, confessing what we hadn't told the others. "If Thorne and Tuck hadn't walked in, Ezra would have. Archer drained himself and Aeris never planned for our power to reach out and fill the void. She never expected me to be involved at all. Had things gone her way, I'd have died that day at Ezra's hands most likely. Quill would have died in the pit. And Archer would be bound to Ezra. That's how the Unmade Guardians are born. Thorne watched it happen in Archer's memories. They wanted him because they knew he'd sit on the throne."

She forced a smile but pulled away from me. "Thorne, Tuck, Minerva, Ezra, Aeris... Do you even hear yourself right now? Gods. All the gods. All their games. That's why I have to do this. You wanted me to believe the gods were bad and I believed it. Don't chastise me for what I decided to do after. I know there are good and bad, just like there are good and bad people. But they live forever and we only get these moments. Right now. I don't matter. Not in comparison to the masses."

I shook my head. "That's bullshit, Thea, and you know it."

"I'm not dumb enough to drain myself. I know my limits. Have a little faith in me."

"I have all the faith in the world in you. But I also love you and this is dangerous."

"It's also my choice." She threw a handful of metal scraps onto the cleared space, and a hush fell over the crowd. For a moment, nothing happened. Then I felt it, a subtle vibration beneath my feet, a stirring in the air. The pebbles near Thea's hands began to tremble.

I backed up, stopping beside Quill and Minerva. I'd spoken my piece, but she hadn't listened. Metal emerged from the ground like plants growing in fast, silvery tendrils bursting upward and weaving themselves into a complex latticework. The structure took shape before our eyes, first the frame, then walls that flowed like liquid before solidifying into something that resembled burnished steel. She'd taken ages with the bathhouse. And now she was melding a building in seconds. But she trembled. Sweat covered her forehead in seconds. Even her eyes went unfocused. Windows formed, delicate and arched. A door materialized, complete with hinges and a knocker shaped like a bird. And all I could do was sit there, looking beyond the beauty to the pain such an act had caused.

The crowd gasped and applauded. But Quill knew. Her wide blue eyes were locked on Thea. Hands to her sides as she worried over whatever emotion our friend was feeling. The house continued to grow, forming a second level, then a small balcony. But as it neared completion, I noticed Thea's breathing grew labored. The metal responded more sluggishly, occasionally creaking in protest.

"She needs to stop," I muttered, taking a step forward.

Minerva's cane blocked my path. "Wait."

With a final surge of effort, Thea pressed her palms flat against the ground. The house shuddered once, then settled into its final form, a modest but beautiful two story dwelling with flourishes that reminded me of the Syndicate house. As the crowd erupted into cheers, Thea slumped forward, catching herself on her hands.

I pushed past Minerva's cane and rushed to Thea's side,

helping her to her feet. She leaned heavily against me, her skin clammy.

A small family pushed through the crowd, two tired-looking men, likely brothers, and two women, one with an infant strapped to her chest. Their gratitude was palpable as they approached Thea.

"We can never repay you," a woman said, tears streaming down her face.

Thea straightened, summoning strength from somewhere deep within. "Live in it. Be happy. Take care of the Underground. That's payment enough."

As the family explored their new home, relishing every detail, Vincent appeared at our side with a cup of water for Thea. She drank it gratefully.

"You need to rest," he said. "That's your third house this week."

"I'm fine," she insisted, though she still hadn't released her grip on my arm.

"You're not," I countered. "And if you collapse, who's going to build the next one? Or maintain all the supports holding this place up?"

That sobered her. She nodded reluctantly. "Maybe a short break."

As we settled at a table nearby, Minerva leaned heavily on her cane. "You can't keep this up forever, you know? Not only physically, though that's concerning enough. But secrets this big have a way of revealing themselves."

"What are you saying?" Thea asked defensively.

"I'm saying that gods are curious creatures by nature, and mortals are terrible at keeping secrets. Do you really think they don't know?"

"If they knew, they'd have done something by now."

"Perhaps they're simply waiting. Watching. Learning."

I shifted uncomfortably. "That's not creepy at all."

"It's realistic," Minerva countered. "We are known for playing the long game, dear. Trust me on this."

"We're not fools. But what choice do we have? Go back up there and pretend we're happy with gilded cages?"

"Some would," Minerva said.

"Some have," Thea admitted. "Left a couple weeks ago. Couldn't stand being underground anymore. Said they'd take their chances with the gods."

"Have you heard from them?" I asked.

She shook her head.

I glanced at the entrance we'd come through, suddenly wishing Thorne were here beside me. He'd always been good at reading the bigger picture, at seeing patterns I missed. Though I'd never admit it aloud, I missed the reassuring warmth of his hand on my lower back, the way he somehow always knew what I was thinking before I said it.

"How do you keep the air fresh?" I asked to curb the subject.

"Ventilation shafts," Thea explained. "Disguised as decorative elements in buildings above. Plus some clever engineering from a couple of people from Stirling."

"And food?"

"They grow some here. Special crops that need minimal light. Some they trade for. Some come from supporters above ground. Tuck, you know. And others."

I raised an eyebrow. "Like a certain newly appointed prince?"

"That's classified information," she said, but her smile confirmed my suspicion.

"You know what the worst part of the Underground is?" I asked.

"The stairs," they all said in unison.

"You can all poke fun, but when you have to trek back up those things, I don't want to hear it. Haven't you ever heard of a slide, Thea? Damn. At least coming down would be easier."

THE SUN HAD NEARLY SET by the time we made it out of the underground. I'd forgone the fucking stairs and used my Remnants to carry everyone back up. Still, Thea promised to be right behind us as Quill, Minnie and I disappeared into an alley, wound through a few of the gilded streets and got back onto our open carriage. Quill's eyelids drooped as the carriage rocked gently. Boo was already snoring on her lap, his tiny legs twitching in some doggy dream. I guided the horses home, like I'd done countless nights after a show.

But, something wasn't right.

The front door stood ajar, a sliver of golden light spilling across the porch. My heart sank into my stomach. Elowen never, *never* left that door open, except as a warning. Back when the Maestro would come looking for Thea or me, an open door was her signal that danger waited inside.

The Remnants surged forward on my command, shadows rippling across my skin and pooling at my feet.

"I'll protect the child," Minerva said, dipping her chin, and I had no doubt of that whatsoever. Minerva was scary.

I moved silently up the path pushing the Remnants to spread out around me. The familiar weight of my blade, Harlow's blade, pressed against my thigh beneath my dress, and I reached for it, drawing comfort from the cold metal against my palm. Using the only power I'd known growing up, I did a mental check on everyone I knew. I couldn't see Thorne, I'd never been able to, but Tuck and Archer were racing toward me. Elowen was inside the house. Thea was almost home. My whole world in one spot sounded terrifying on the brink of something dangerous.

The door creaked as I pushed it wider. I winced at the sound but inside, the entryway was empty. I could hear voices from the sitting room, Elowen's measured tones and another, lighter voice that made my skin prickle with recognition.

I edged along the wall, blade ready, every sense heightened. I inched around the corner. Elowen sat ramrod straight in her favorite chair, teacup balanced perfectly on her knee. Her face was composed, but I knew her too well to miss the tension in her shoulders, the too careful way she held herself. Across from her, lounging with casual elegance in a chair that had been Hollis's favorite, was Aeris.

Once again, the goddess looked younger than I'd last seen her, no longer the weathered grandmother figure but a woman in her prime, with gleaming brown hair cascading down her back and skin that glowed with unnatural vitality. She turned as I entered, her smile widening.

"Ah, Huntress," she said, her voice melodic and rich. "What perfect timing. I was just asking Elowen when you might return."

The Remnants swirled at my feet, responding to the surge of protective fury that shot through me.

"What are you doing here?" I demanded, not bothering to mask my hostility.

Aeris sighed, setting down her teacup with a delicate clink. "Such suspicion. I simply came to visit Quill. It's been a while since I've seen her and she's, no doubt, been wondering about me."

Elowen's eyes met mine, conveying volumes in that silent exchange. *Be careful.*

"Quill isn't available," I said coldly. "And you're not welcome here."

"I've been perfectly civil—"

"I don't care. Get out."

Something dangerous flickered across Aeris's beautiful face, a brief glimpse of the power she usually kept carefully veiled. "You don't command gods, child."

"And you don't command this house," I countered. "I'm sure Elowen asked you to leave, didn't she? Before I arrived. Yet here you sit."

Aeris's smile thinned. "I was hoping for a civilized conversation."

"Hope somewhere else."

The sound of another carriage rattling up outside provided a welcome interruption. Thea, thank the gods. I needed to warn her, to let her know who waited inside. I kept my eyes on Aeris as I took a step back toward the entryway.

"Your persistence is irritating," Aeris said, rising from her chair.

"But I suppose I shouldn't be surprised. Stubbornness runs in your blood, after all."

Before I could respond, the front door swung open. I turned, ready to signal Thea to stay back, and instead found myself staring into a face I hadn't seen in fifteen years.

My father.

I had no words. Nor feeling in my feet as I stared at a man that'd died to me the day he stopped responding in that fucking opium den. I couldn't tell if I wanted to throw up or fall to my knees, or slam the door shut. He just stood there, older, grayer, the lines of his face deeper than I remembered. His clothes were simple but clean, nothing like the ragged garments he'd worn in those last days. Thea hovered anxiously behind him, her expression a mix of apprehension and sorrow.

I stumbled backward. The knife nearly slipped from my suddenly numb fingers. A thousand questions fought for dominance in my mind, but I couldn't voice a single one.

He didn't look at me.

His eyes fixed on something, someone, behind me. His weathered face crumpled with a storm of emotions: recognition, shock, grief, anger.

"Treasure? I see you've found your mother," he said, his voice the same smooth tone I remembered.

The world tilted beneath my feet as I slowly turned to follow his gaze straight to Aeris, whose perfect composure had finally cracked.

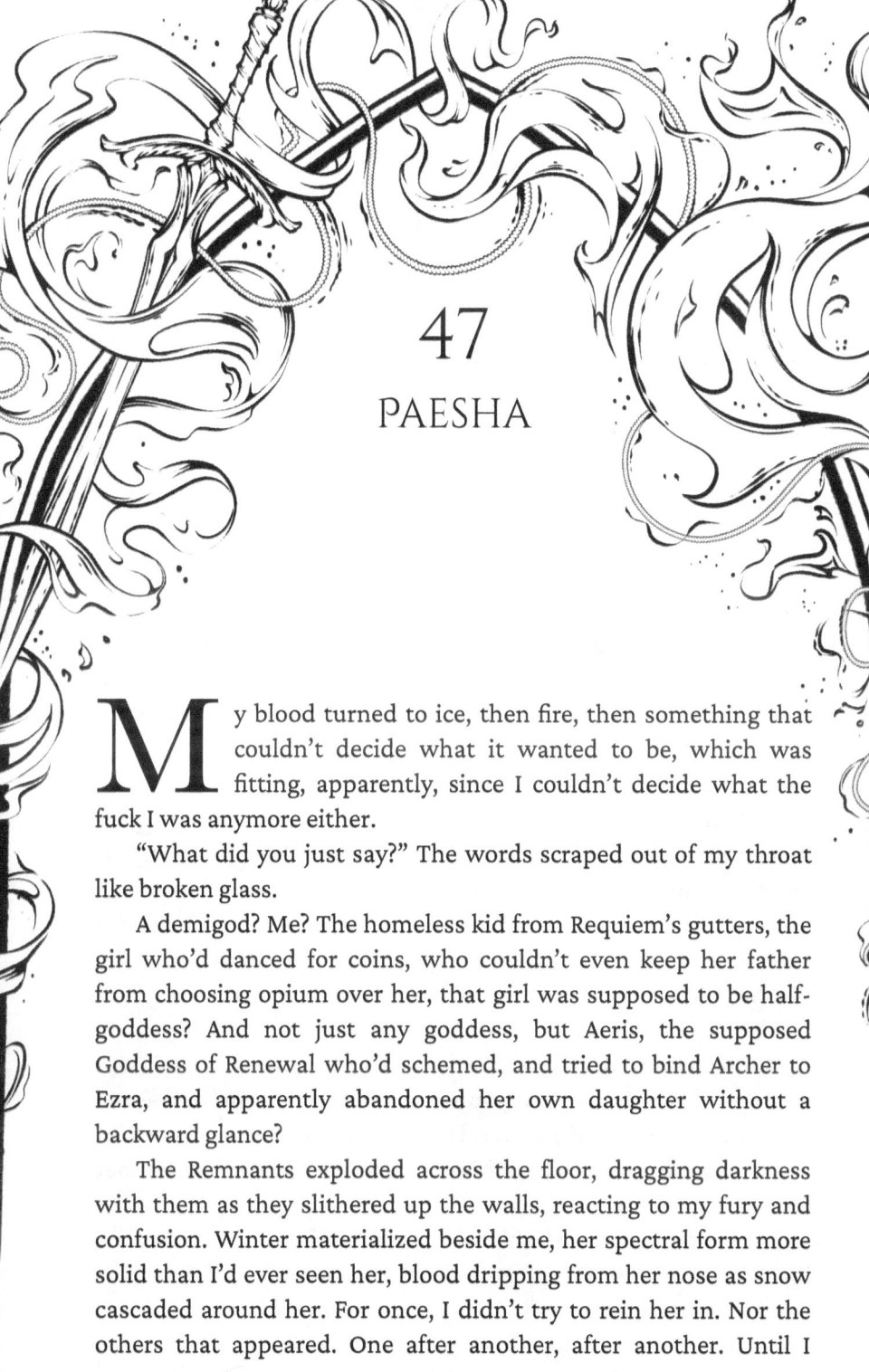

47

PAESHA

My blood turned to ice, then fire, then something that couldn't decide what it wanted to be, which was fitting, apparently, since I couldn't decide what the fuck I was anymore either.

"What did you just say?" The words scraped out of my throat like broken glass.

A demigod? Me? The homeless kid from Requiem's gutters, the girl who'd danced for coins, who couldn't even keep her father from choosing opium over her, that girl was supposed to be half-goddess? And not just any goddess, but Aeris, the supposed Goddess of Renewal who'd schemed, and tried to bind Archer to Ezra, and apparently abandoned her own daughter without a backward glance?

The Remnants exploded across the floor, dragging darkness with them as they slithered up the walls, reacting to my fury and confusion. Winter materialized beside me, her spectral form more solid than I'd ever seen her, blood dripping from her nose as snow cascaded around her. For once, I didn't try to rein her in. Nor the others that appeared. One after another, after another. Until I could hardly see anyone else standing in the entry of our humble home.

"You knew," I said, turning back to Aeris. The words felt inadequate, pathetic even, against the storm of emotions threatening to tear me apart from the inside. "All this time, you knew."

Aeris managed to compose herself, shoulders straightening as she met my gaze. "It was... complicated."

"Complicated? You abandoned me. You left me with him." I jerked my chin toward my father, who still hadn't looked at me. "And then what? Had a good fucking time watching the chaos ensue? Was it entertaining for you?"

"Paesha—" Elowen started, but I shook my head sharply.

"No. I want to hear her say it." I stepped closer to Aeris, close enough to see the flecks of gold in her eyes. Eyes that, I realized with a sickening lurch, were slightly tilted like mine. "Tell me. Did you help Ezra hunt me down? Did you sit back while I was tortured in the Maw? While I bargained away my freedom to the Maestro? Answer me!"

"You don't understand—"

"Then make me understand!" I roared, the Remnants surging higher, coiling around the chandelier, blotting out the light. "Or better yet, don't bother. Get the fuck out."

Aeris's face hardened, the maternal mask slipping to reveal something ancient and calculating. "I'm only trying to help you, Paesha. There are things you don't know, forces at work that—"

"I don't care."

"You should," Aeris said, her voice dropping lower, a challenge in it now. "The Treeis bond you share with Archer, you've realized it by now, haven't you? The bond that should never have existed."

"You were trying to bind him to Ezra. We already figured that out."

"And you interfered," she replied, her smile cold and calculating. "But it works out rather well for me. Your Guardian cannot ascend to the throne now."

"What are you talking about?"

"Oh, my girl," Aeris crooned, "a Treeis Guardian cannot be

bound in marriage. The magic won't allow it, their soul is already divided. No marriage, no throne. And while we're discussing truths, ask Reverius why Ezra had no memories when you met. Ask him what the final bargain was. Ask him what he's been hiding from you."

The mention of Thorne sent a fresh wave of confusion through me. "Don't you dare try to deflect this onto him."

"I'm offering you truth. Something he never has."

I stepped closer, until we were nearly nose to nose. "Get. The. Fuck. Out."

The sound of new arrivals cut through the tension. I didn't need to turn around to know it was Thorne. I could feel him, that familiar pressure in the air that always accompanied him. Archer and Tuck's voices drifted in from outside, their casual conversation dying abruptly as they sensed the atmosphere.

"Everything all right in here?" Thorne's measured voice did nothing to disguise the lethal edge beneath it.

I didn't look at him. Couldn't. Not with Aeris's accusations hanging between us, not with my father standing mutely in the doorway, not with my entire sense of self crumbling around me.

"No. But Aeris was just leaving, weren't you, *Mother?*"

Thorne's sharp inhale was all I needed to hear to know he had no idea. And I needed that. Needed to believe he hadn't been keeping it from me. Aeris said nothing more, holding her gaze locked on to me as she stormed past and walked out. I wanted to watch her leave, if only to remind myself what it felt like when she vanished all those years ago. But I didn't need that. Not when the memory still burned in my soul.

Instead, I fixed my gaze on my father, really seeing him for the first time. The years hadn't been kind, but he was sober. Clean. Standing on his own two feet. A part of me, the abandoned little girl who'd cried herself to sleep in alleys, wanted to scream at him, to demand explanations, to make him feel every ounce of pain he'd inflicted.

But I was no longer that girl.

"I'm glad to see you're well," I said, my voice steadier than I felt. "I hope you continue to be. But some relationships end for a reason, and I think ours did. I wish you the best, but I don't want you in my life. I don't know if that's why you came here, but this is the end for us, Papa."

Something like respect flickered in his tired eyes. He nodded once, a jerky dip of his chin. "I understand, Treasure. I saw you in the Underground and I..." He nodded again. "I understand."

I watched him turn. I felt it in my soul. The ache of abandonment, once an open wound, hardened into something solid, something that was mine to close. Not a plea unspoken, not a tether frayed, but a door sealed with the weight of my own choice. And in that quiet finality, I found a freedom I never knew I needed.

He was halfway down the path before I called for Tuck. "Would you mind following him? Make sure he's not... struggling." The irony wasn't lost on me, showing more concern for his welfare than he'd ever shown for mine. But spite was for gods and I didn't give a shit what anyone said. I was not one.

"Of course," Tuck answered.

THE STARS WERE EXCEPTIONALLY bright tonight, as if the universe was trying its best to compensate for the darkness churning inside me. I pulled my knees to my chest, wishing the cold night air could numb more than my skin. The roof beneath me still held a trace of warmth from the day's sun. Was Aeris like the sun? Had she been there all along, hovering in the periphery of my life?

What would I say to Archer? How could I explain to him that the future he'd finally accepted was no longer an option for him. He couldn't marry. Couldn't take the throne because of me. If he'd stayed away, he would have never been tangled in all of this. I'm not sure how I'd ever look him in the face again. Though I wasn't sure how I'd look at myself in the mirror either. I'd only ever see her.

"Demigod," I whispered, testing how the word felt in my mouth. Strange. Foreign. Like trying on clothes that didn't fit.

It explains much, Levanya said, and for the first time, she materialized beside me. Ghostly, but stunning. Dark skin, long braided hair, a fierce and passionate gaze.

"Does it? Because I feel like it explains nothing at all."

She paced, the long ribbons of her tattered gown doing nothing to hide the arrow in her chest.

"The gods were banned from Requiem. How could she have been there?"

When have you ever known the gods to do what they are told?

I laughed bitterly. "Fair point. But why did she leave? Why did she stand in front of me and never tell me?"

There's no question she saw your eyes when you were born. She's known the mark of the Huntress for ages. I cannot speak for her, but I would imagine there was a battle within her. Imagine giving birth to the only thing that could destroy you. That's the cruel fate of gods. They rarely care for their offspring.

"Then why is she here? Now?"

Think, Paesha.

"What do you think I've been up here doing for three hours?"

She shot me a look. One that Elowen had perfected years ago. Elowen. Truly the only mother I'd ever known. The woman who'd never baulked at my sass, never complained about my messes. Never gave up on me. Not even when I brought a two-year old into her home and spent three months avoiding her for fear of attachment. I couldn't be sad about being abandoned. I could only be grateful. It'd led me into the arms of my real family. Which only took me back to the ultimate question. Why?

But there was only one reason she could have come back. The same reason for everything. "Power."

The root of evil.

"She assumed I'd die the same way the rest of the Huntresses have. She left me to that fate. But she was wrong. She was wrong and now she's scared. That's why she's trying to stay close. So she can watch me. But why involve herself? Why set Archer up to become an Unmade Guardian?"

She works for Ezra now. She hopes you will die like the rest of us and there will be no more risk to her existence.

"Then she should have killed me."

Perhaps, Levanya said, letting that word drift away on the breeze. *But now she can't. You're surrounded by too much love.*

"The irony," I whispered, pulling my knees to my chest to stave off the wind. Love would never matter in the end.

As if sensing my thoughts, Levanya reached out, her spectral fingers hovering just above my cheek. *You are stronger than you know. Stronger than any god or mortal. Aeris's blood may flow through your veins, but it does not define you. You are Paesha, the Huntress, the dancer, the fighter. You bow to no one.*

My fingers traced the swirling patterns of darkness on my arms. Had these always been clues? Markers of a heritage I'd never known to look for? How could being the daughter of the Goddess of Renewal and the soul descendant of the Gods of Lost and Broken Things matter? The question sent my thoughts spinning toward Thorne, and the knot in my stomach tightened.

'Ask Reverius why Ezra had no memories when you met.'

Aeris's voice echoed in my mind, insidious as poison. I could work that part out myself. But what had she meant about a final bargain?

As if I'd summoned him, I heard the soft scrape of boots against the roof. He moved with deliberate noise, announcing his presence rather than startling me. It was one of a thousand little considerations I'd grown to lo—to appreciate.

"May I join you?" He asked, his voice carefully neutral.

I kept my eyes on the stars but said nothing.

He settled beside me, close enough that I could feel his warmth but not touching. Giving me space. So careful with me now. I wondered if he could feel Levanya standing there. If any of him felt any of her when they were so close.

"Tuck says your father is staying in the Underground. He saw you there and ambushed Thea right before she left. He's safe. Fed. And... better."

"Good for him," I said flatly.

Silence stretched between us, not uncomfortable but heavy with all the things unsaid. The Remnants curled around my ankles like restless cats.

"I don't know what to do with any of this," I admitted finally, still not looking at him. "Aeris. My father. What that means about me." I swallowed hard. "What it means about us."

"It doesn't affect *us* at all. It doesn't change who you are, Paesha."

I laughed, the sound brittle. "Doesn't it?"

"Your blood doesn't define you."

"Said the god."

He didn't rise to the bait, just continued watching me with those patient eyes that saw too much.

"She said—" I paused, unsure I wanted to voice the doubts that had been festering since Aeris's parting words. "She told me to ask you about Ezra. About why he had no memories when we met and some final bargain."

Thorne went still beside me, his profile sharpening in the moonlight. When he spoke, his voice was carefully measured. "She's trying to drive a wedge between us."

"Is it working?"

He turned to face me, and something in his expression made my heart ache. "You tell me."

The raw vulnerability in those three words cracked something inside me, breaking past the numbness, the anger, the confusion. Tears welled in my eyes, hot and unwelcome.

"I don't know what to believe anymore," I whispered. "People have been using me my entire life—lives—whatever. I can't handle any more lies, Thorne. Not from you. There's trauma here and the ice is thin."

He reached for me, slowly, giving me every chance to pull away. When I didn't, he drew me into his arms, cradling me against his chest with a gentleness that made the tears fall faster.

"I have many regrets, Paesha. Too many to count. But loving you has never been one of them."

And gods I loved him too. Deeply. I had spent lifetimes being used, twisted into a shape that fit someone else's needs, someone else's desires. But love, real love, wasn't a weapon. It wasn't a trap. It wasn't a leash held tight in another's hand or a magical bond holding someone hostage.

It was this.

It was choosing to stay here despite the pain, despite the betrayals, despite the wreckage of the past and the uncertainty of the future. It was looking into his eyes and knowing he had broken me a thousand times over, but I'd broken him, too.

And yet, here we were.

Love was supposed to be simple. Or at least, that was what the stories said. But ours had been built in the wreckage of lies, on the broken bones of trust, and yet... it had survived. Because love wasn't solely about warmth and light. It was about standing in the dark and still reaching for each other. It was about knowing the damage and choosing it anyway. Because fire does not destroy iron, it tempers it. I did not love him in spite of the pain. I loved him because we had walked through it and still found each other on the other side. And that had to mean something.

I pressed my face into his shirt, breathing in his familiar scent as his arms tightened around me. My Remnants quieted, settling into peaceful shadows at our feet.

"There are things I need to tell you," he said after a while. "Things I should have told you already."

I pulled back enough to search his face. "About Ezra?"

"About everything." He brushed a tear from my cheek. "But not here. Will you come with me? There's something I want to show you."

Against my better judgment, I nodded.

"I'd like to tell you a story," he said, rising and offering me his hand. "Our story. The real one."

The ride to Perth was quiet, the steady rhythm of the horse's hooves on the cobblestones oddly soothing. Thorne sat behind me in the saddle, one arm wrapped securely around my waist, his solid presence an anchor amid my turbulent thoughts.

When we reached Misery's End, I stiffened. The theater loomed before us, unchanged amid the transformed cityscape around it. The familiar wrought-iron railings, the cracked steps, the faded sign, all exactly as I remembered them, preserved like a monument to my past.

"Why here?" I asked as Thorne helped me dismount.

He tied the horse to a post before facing me, his expression solemn in the moonlight. "Because this is where it began. This time, at least."

"The Maestro's theater?"

"The place where I first saw you dance," he corrected softly. "The place where I fell in love with you all over again, even though I'd been chasing you across lifetimes."

He offered me his hand once more. "Let me show you the truth, Paesha. All of it. Then you can decide what to believe."

I hesitated only a moment before placing my hand in his. Whatever secrets waited inside that theater, whatever painful truths Thorne had been hiding, I needed to face them. As he led me up those familiar steps, the Remnants flowed around us like a protective cloak, and for the first time since Aeris's revelation, I felt something close to calm. Not because I wasn't afraid of what I might learn, but because I was finally ready to hear it.

Whatever happened next, at least it would be the truth. My truth. Ours.

The theater was as I remembered it, a cavern of shadows and secrets, haunted by memories both beautiful and terrible. Misery's End had been my sanctuary and my prison, the place where I'd danced for the dregs of society and found a strange kind of freedom in their hungry gazes. The stage lights were dark now, but moonlight spilled through the high windows, casting long silver fingers across the worn floorboards.

Thorne's hand was steady in mine as he led me through the empty rows of seats and toward the stage. As we drew closer, I realized it wasn't empty. Objects were arranged across it, each one bathed in a small pool of golden light that seemed to come from nowhere.

"What is this?" The words caught in my throat as recognition dawned.

"Pieces of you," Thorne said softly. "Fragments of the lives we've shared. I wasn't sure if this would agitate the past lives in your mind or if this would bring you peace, but these are things that mattered to your soul. Not the blood of a mortal, nor the lineage of a goddess, these items are our love story."

I approached the display with cautious steps, drawn forward by that curious pull that lured my Huntress power's curiosity. The first item made my heart stutter, a delicate teacup with a small chip in the rim. *My* teacup. I reached out, fingers trembling as they hovered over the porcelain. I'd almost forgotten it with all of the chaos, but here it was. Protected. Treasured.

"You've always found comfort in tea," Thorne murmured. "Even when the world was crumbling around you."

I moved to the next familiar object, the sword Alastor had given me. He'd said it was mine long before it was his. And here it was, its blade gleaming in the light. The moment my fingers touched the metal, something inside me shifted, like a lock turning. Levanya's voice echoed in my mind. *Still beautiful.*

"I'm keeping that," I said, taking it from its stand. "It's mine and I want it back."

His laugh was everything. "It's yours."

The objects blurred together as I moved among them, a tarnished locket, a worn leather-bound journal, a simple wooden flute, a bloodstained arrow, a tattered blanket, a silver spoon. With each item I touched, fragments of memories flickered through my mind, too fleeting to grasp but undeniably *mine. Theirs.*

Each brush of metal and scrap of fabric brought another woman to the forefront of my mind. Another life wasted. Another daughter, sister, aunt, friend, murdered. But also loved. Cherished.

Setting the sword aside, my fingers brushed over a simple gold band. "Were we truly married?"

"Nine times."

The enormity of it staggered me, all those lives lived and lost, those loves and heartbreaks and triumphs and failures. I felt the weight of centuries pressing down on me, the echo of countless deaths, the breaking of his heart over and over again on a final breath.

"And this?" I asked, lifting a small glass vial filled with what looked like ash.

His expression darkened. "The remains of a letter. You wrote it to warn me about Ezra when you had no idea who he really was. He found it first."

I moved on quickly, not wanting to linger on that particular horror. My eyes fell on a familiar object at the center of the arrangement, the worn book Elowen had given him, sitting on a small wooden pedestal.

"Why is this here?" I asked, touching the faded cover. "This isn't from a past life."

"No," he agreed, moving to stand with me. "It's from this one. The only one that matters now."

I looked up at him, searching his face. "Tell me. All of it. I need the story."

He drew a deep breath, his hand coming to rest beside mine on the book. "Ezra had a vision. He saw that a Huntress would be born, and she would break the balance of power." His fingers tightened on the book. "After he warned me, we each made our own decision. I decided I wanted the Huntress to choose me, to give me more power. So I hunted you, found you—"

"And accidentally fell in love," I finished.

"No." His voice was firm. "I hunted you with the intention of making you love me. The accident was that I truly fell in love with you instead. It changed everything."

I swallowed hard. "And Ezra decided he would kill the Huntress, thus keeping the peace and the balance of power between you. I know this part."

My stomach began to twist. He was building to something. Something I wasn't sure I was ready to hear.

"Ezra has repeatedly been successful. You have died in my arms every single life. But the fabric of souls is delicate. After all of these lives, you have but one left to live. If you die by the hands of a god one more time, you are gone forever. A victory for Ezra and—" he faltered.

"The end of the cycle," I whispered.

He didn't deny it. "One day, I found you in Requiem, dancing on this stage. The diamond. But Ezra found you too. And when I tried to plead with him for your final life, he said that you were merely a mortal and mortals were predictable. He swore that you only fell in love with me because I was the option in front of you.'"

"And what did you say to that?"

"I told him he was wrong. That our souls were destined because you're my Ever and I'm yours. I said you'd never fall in love with another. He argued." His gaze dropped to our hands, still resting side by side on the book. "I said I would prove it to him."

Something cold settled in my stomach. I *had* fallen in love with another. "What did you do?"

"I knew he could circumvent the immortality in Requiem easily. So, I made a bargain with my twin because if he didn't kill you in this life, you would live one more. And then one more. And so on, until I could find a way to give you immortality. I told him I would give him this life cycle as a test. And if you were in love with him on your final day, then I would step away and the next time you were found, I would not stop him from killing you. And if you weren't, he had to agree to let you live and stop hunting you forevermore."

"You bargained with my final life?" The words were barely audible, choked by the lump in my throat.

His deep breath stole mine.

"I knew you could never love him. Not the way you loved me. It wasn't possible. I had so much faith in our love, I thought I'd finally found the solution to restore the peace, the power. Us. All of it. And Ezra agreed. Seconds before he left, I broke an unspoken rule. We were never meant to use our power against each other. But I stole all of his memories," Thorne admitted. "He no longer remembered that he was a god. He didn't remember the bargain. He didn't remember me."

"But we still met," I said, the pieces falling into place. "Aeris. She made sure of it."

"Yes. And you did, in fact, fall in love." His face was carefully neutral, but I could see the pain beneath. "I believe Aeris had been trying to warn him about our bargain. But because he couldn't remember, she failed. So she went to Death and asked him to interfere. He gave his Maiden Ezra's name. When Death collected Ezra from Requiem, he took him to his realm. Aeris likely thought leaving this realm would free him. But it didn't. My power was absolute. Desperate even."

He turned to me finally, taking my free hand in his. "I knew several things. Your soul couldn't stay in Death's Court when I found you. It was dying through that realm, which meant it would have been the end of you. But I thought you loved him. And I was willing to give you that peace. But then I saw him grab your arm. He put his hands on you and that was the end of my resolve. From one second to the next, I wasn't strong enough to sit by. And when you stepped through to Wisteria, he chased you. But when he came into contact with the Arulean Gate, his memories came back and here we are."

The silence that followed was heavy. I moved away from the display, needing distance from the physical reminders of all these lives I couldn't remember. My hands shook as I tried to process the enormity of what he'd told me.

"You bargained with my final life," I repeated, the words falling between us like stones.

"I was trying to save you," he said quietly. "I couldn't bear to lose you again. Not forever."

I shook my head, stepping farther away from him. "Do you have any idea what it feels like to accept that your entire existence, your choices, your loves, even your deaths, have been orchestrated by others? That gods have been playing with your soul like it's a toy they can't share?" I shook my head, dragging in a burning breath. "I'm not even mad at you. I hear the words you're saying and I know you thought you were doing the right thing. But gods,

Thorne. When do you learn to let go? I'm the one paying the price for your decisions, can't you see that? Over and over again."

He reached for me and I let him, though I couldn't feel his hands on my cheeks. Only the numbness. Always that. "I've learned more in the last six months than I have in all my time. You lead and I follow. Please see that." He pulled me closer. "See me, too. I never manipulated your feelings for me. I orchestrated certain circumstances, but what grew between us, what's growing still, that was real. It's always been real."

I wanted to believe him. Gods help me, I wanted to trust that this one thing in my life wasn't built on lies. But how could I know for sure? How could I separate what was genuine from what was part of this game?

"I need space," I said finally, stepping away. "I need time to process all of this. To figure out what it means for me—for us."

He nodded, that careful neutrality back in place, though I could see it cost him. "Of course."

"I'm not saying never," I clarified, because despite everything, I couldn't bear to leave him with no hope at all. "I'm saying not right now. Not until I've had time to think."

"I understand." He made no move to approach me, respecting the distance I'd put between us. "Take all the time you need. I've waited lifetimes for you, Paesha. I can wait a little longer."

The simplicity of the statement, the raw honesty in it, made my chest ache. I turned away, not wanting him to see the tears threatening to spill. The Remnants formed a path for me, guiding me back through the theater toward the exit.

As I reached the door, I paused, looking back at him. He stood motionless on the stage, surrounded by the fragments of our shared past, the moonlight casting him in silver and shadow. He looked both powerful and vulnerable, a god brought to his knees by love.

"Thank you," I said softly. "For telling me the truth."

"Always," he promised. "From now on, always."

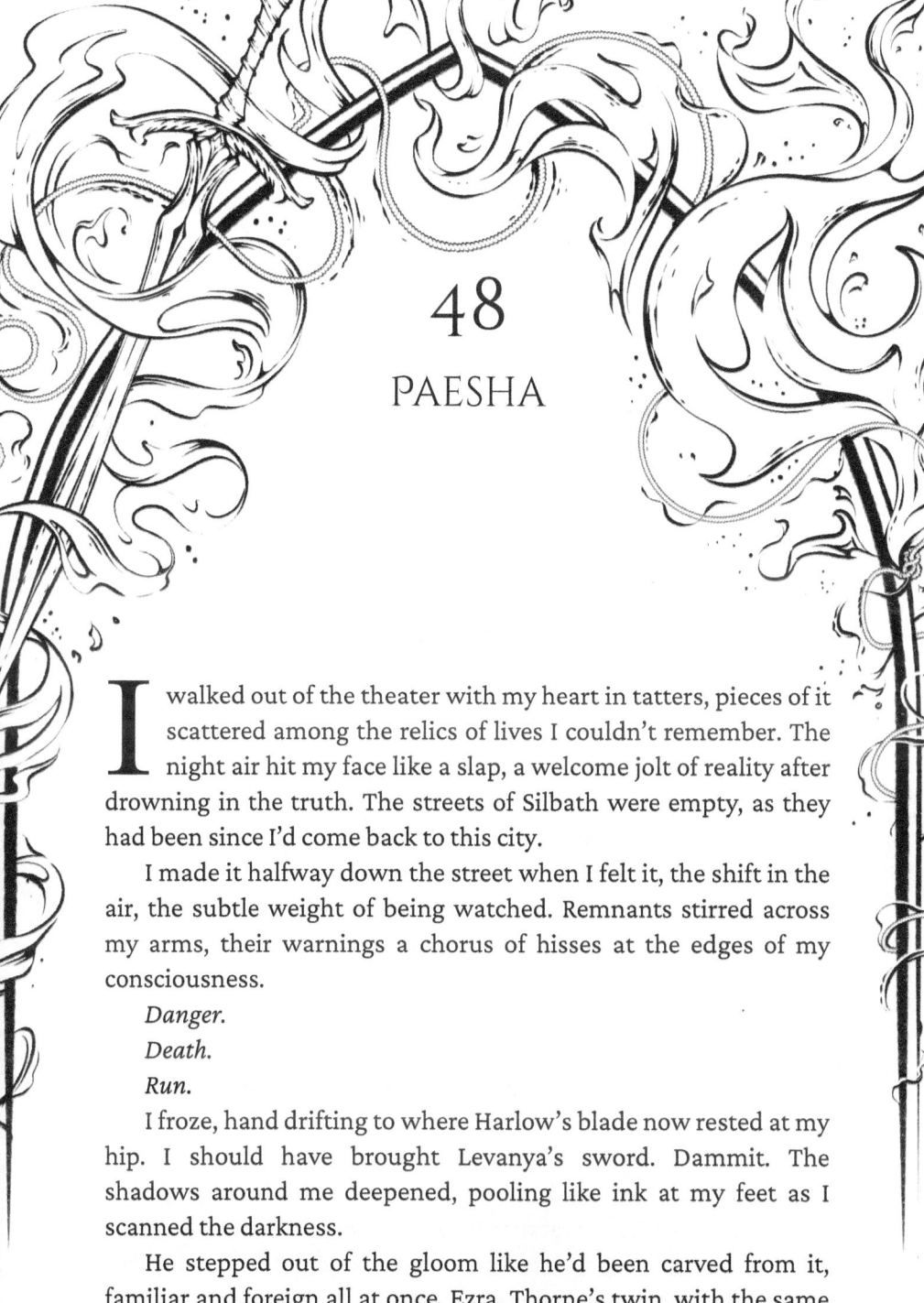

48

PAESHA

I walked out of the theater with my heart in tatters, pieces of it scattered among the relics of lives I couldn't remember. The night air hit my face like a slap, a welcome jolt of reality after drowning in the truth. The streets of Silbath were empty, as they had been since I'd come back to this city.

I made it halfway down the street when I felt it, the shift in the air, the subtle weight of being watched. Remnants stirred across my arms, their warnings a chorus of hisses at the edges of my consciousness.

Danger.

Death.

Run.

I froze, hand drifting to where Harlow's blade now rested at my hip. I should have brought Levanya's sword. Dammit. The shadows around me deepened, pooling like ink at my feet as I scanned the darkness.

He stepped out of the gloom like he'd been carved from it, familiar and foreign all at once. Ezra. Thorne's twin, with the same face that had haunted my dreams, but his eyes were colder, harder than I'd ever remembered them being. I'd loved him once. Or so I thought. Until I loved Thorne. Until my soul had been connected to its Ever, apparently.

"Hello, Huntress," he said, his voice a perfect echo of his brother's, yet devoid of the warmth that made Thorne's cadence so beautifully, distinctly his. "It's been too long."

My fingers closed around the hilt of my dagger. "Not long enough."

He smiled a predator's grin. "I suppose that depends on your perspective. Time has a funny way of bending around us, doesn't it? So many lives lived, so many deaths endured, and here we are again. The final act. Though I must say, the opening was my favorite part."

"You fell in love with me," I said, hardly believing the words that fell out of my mouth.

"I think it's more fair to point out that *you* fell in love with me, wouldn't you say? You proved my point to Reverius without even trying."

The shadows around him shifted, and suddenly they weren't shadows at all. Figures detached themselves from the darkness, men and women with empty eyes and mechanical movements. The Unmade Guardians. Dozens of them, emerging from alleys and side streets, surrounding the street in a tightening noose. They were not like Archer at all. But then, I supposed they wouldn't be. When Archer was bound to me and they were bound to a murderous god.

"Did you think I would simply let you continue to exist, knowing what you are? What you'll do to my power if I allow it?"

I backed up a step. My Remnants surged in response to my fear. "And what exactly am I, Ezra? Because I'm having a hard time keeping up with all the titles being thrown my way lately."

My heart thundered in my throat. I was outnumbered, outpowered, and I'd wandered too far from Misery's End for Thorne to hear me if I screamed. He would come. I knew it like I knew how to breathe. But not if he didn't know. Not if he was respecting the space I'd asked for.

"The end. Of everything." He gestured around us. "It's already happening. Look at what your simple existence has done to the realms. The power is failing, the barriers between worlds are thinning. My brother, blinded by his infatuation, refuses to see it. But I won't allow the destruction to continue."

"So this is it?" I asked, trying to keep my voice steady as I assessed my options, counting the Unmade, looking for escape routes that didn't exist. "The final confrontation? You, me, and your army of puppets? They're cute. Have you named them? That one looks like a Franklin to me."

His smile thinned. "I see that mouth hasn't changed. My Guardians are far from puppets. They are the chosen, the ones who understand what's at stake. And unlike my brother, they aren't blinded by sentiment."

The Guardians moved, a synchronized wave of bodies closing in. I could feel the power emanating from them, not magic, not quite, but something else. Something dangerous. As if they were mortal, but only just, their humanity overtaken by Ezra's will.

"So you're saying you remember what this mouth can do. Please forget that. Gross. And for the record, I'm not interested in breaking anything."

"Your interests are irrelevant. It's your nature. Your destiny."

A Guardian lunged at me from the right. I pivoted, my blade slicing through the air, but he was faster than I expected. So much faster. He dodged the killing blow, and his fist connected with my ribs, sending me staggering. I felt the crack, the sharp stab of pain, but there was no time to process it as another came at me from the left.

I shoved my Remnants forward, shadows transforming into claws that tore into the Guardian's chest. But for every one I wounded, two more rushed forward. I was outnumbered, outmatched. They were something *more*, something twisted by Ezra's power—faster, stronger, bound to a purpose that would end with my death.

Kill them, Winter hissed, suddenly visible beside me, her bloodied face stark in the moonlight. *They are mortal. Kill them all.*

You know the power, Sylvie urged, her form materializing on my other side. *Use it. Let it consume you.*

Fight.

Run.

Bleed.

Fight.

Die.

The voices of my past lives crescendoed in my mind, a cacophony of rage and fear and desperate instruction. I couldn't separate individual voices anymore, couldn't tell where Winter ended and Sylvie began. They blurred into a roaring tide of sound that threatened to drown me. But they also pushed me. Forced me to lean into magic.

A Guardian's blade sliced across my arm, drawing blood. Another hit me from behind, sending me to my knees. My vision blurred, but through it, I saw Ezra watching, that same cold calculation in his eyes that I'd once mistaken for quiet intensity when I'd known him as only a lover.

Power roared through my veins like molten metal, burning away everything that wasn't rage and pain and the desperate desire to survive. To live, when so many before me had died. My Remnants exploded outward in a wave of pure, undiluted destruction. Golden bricks cracked beneath my feet. Windows shattered. The air splintered as darkness poured from me in endless, violent waves. He wanted a victim. One more notch. One final life. But this one wasn't his to take. I'd given enough. We each had.

I rose like a vengeful goddess, my body no longer my own but a vessel for the collective fury of a thousand murdered souls. "Is this what you feared?" My voice echoed strangely, as if others spoke with me, through me. "This power? This rage?"

Likely for the first time, uncertainty flickered across Ezra's perfect face. "You can't win, Huntress."

I bared my teeth in a savage smile. "Fucking watch me."

I thrust my hands forward, channeling the darkness like spears of shadow. They found the throats of the nearest Guardians, constricting, choking. I moved the Remnants like puppets, swinging them as solid, unbreakable iron fists. Like a shower of arrows and a bevy of blades. I blinded those that I could, clawed into others.

Until tendrils of Ezra's power reached for me. I had no idea what they would do, but I assumed if they got to me, it would feel like being erased. Like dying, but never existing either. Like loneliness and abandonment. I backed away, still aiming for his army. But there were so many, an endless wave of soulless soldiers crashing against the shores of my dwindling strength.

A Guardian broke through the wall of power I'd built around myself, slamming into me with the force of a charging beast. We hit the ground, my head cracking against stone. The world swam. Black spots danced at the edges of my vision as his hands closed around my throat.

Not like this, I thought wildly, thrashing beneath him. Not like this. The world began to narrow, to fade. My lungs burned. Fingers of inhuman strength dug into my skin. My Remnants weakened, slipping from my grasp like water through cupped hands.

And then... air.

The weight vanished from my chest. I rolled onto my side, gasping, choking, struggling to focus through the haze of pain.

"Get the fuck away from her!"

That voice. That beautiful, savage voice cut through the ringing in my ears. I forced my eyes open to see Archer standing over me like an avenging angel, twin swords gleaming with blood and moonlight. My godsdamn redemption.

"Archer," I croaked, the word scraping against my bruised throat.

"We don't fight battles alone, Paesha. Not now. Not ever. It's us against the world. Against every evil god, every demon, every army." He didn't look at me as he cut down a Guardian who rushed him. Blood streaked his face like war paint, his blue eyes burning with cold fury. "The fight's already over. They just don't know it yet. We've got you."

We?

The air around us changed, thickened, electrified. The hair on my arms rose as power surged through the ruined street like a cresting wave. The Guardians faltered, stumbling back as if struck by an invisible force.

And then he was there.

Thorne.

Gone was any pretense of mortality, of restraint. He strode through the battlefield like wrath incarnate, golden light spilling from his eyes and fingertips. The Guardians between him and me crumpled like paper dolls, their bodies flung aside by the sheer force of his power.

"Brother," he called, his voice thunder and lightning and forgotten fury. "You've overplayed your hand."

Ezra stepped forward to meet him, his own power manifesting as an aura of cold blue light. "I never was a gambler. I knew the odds going in."

"Then you already know how this ends." Thorne moved to stand between Ezra and me, his broad shoulders a shield against the chaos. "You cannot have her. Not this time. Not ever again."

Archer hauled me to my feet, keeping his arm around my waist as I swayed. "Can you fight?" he asked, his eyes never stopping their scan of the destroyed streets.

I nodded, though every muscle in my body screamed in agony. "I'll manage."

The brothers clashed, their power colliding in a cataclysm of light and shadow. The ground shook, the sky grew impossibly darker, and the air turned so heavy with the weight of their power, it hurt to breathe. Though that could have been the half-crushed windpipe.

Across the street, or what used to be one, the Guardians continued their attack, focusing on Archer and I. He moved like something feral and beautiful, his blades extensions of his arms as he cut through them with deadly precision. The Treeis mark on his arm glowed like a brand through his torn sleeve, pulsing in time with the one on my shoulder.

I fought at his side, my Remnants working in tandem with his blades, creating a dance of death that felt as natural as breathing.

Once upon a time, I'd condemned a woman for murder, and now I'd delivered it as if I were the Maiden of Death. We'd never fought together like this, and yet our movements flowed into each other's as if we'd been training for this moment since the beginning of time. The bond between Archer and I had never felt so strong, yet there was a clear piece missing. Thank the gods, Quill was still safe at home.

Through the chaos of battle, I caught glimpses of the brothers' duel. They were evenly matched, power for power, blow for blow. But it was erratic. Flickering out completely and coming back full force. As if a stubborn candle battled the wind for respite. Every bit of Silbath I could see had become a wasteland, streets torn from the ground, buildings partially collapsed. I could feel the sweat trailing down my back, the weakening of my power, the lack of fight in my muscles.

A Guardian broke through our defenses, charging straight for me with a blade that hissed through the air. Before I could react, Archer was there, throwing himself between us. The Guardian's blade sliced across his chest, drawing a line of crimson that bloomed against his shirt.

"Archer!" My scream tore from my throat as he staggered but didn't fall.

He turned to me, and in that moment, our bond flared to life. I felt his pain as if it were my own, but also his strength, his determination, his absolute refusal to yield.

"I'm fine." His voice was steady despite the pain echoing through our connection. "Keep fighting but don't deplete your magic."

A cry of pain cut through the chaos. I whipped around to see Thorne on the ground, Ezra standing over him with triumph gleaming in his eyes.

"It's over, brother," he roared, his voice carrying across the ruined street. "Accept it."

But Thorne wasn't finished. As Ezra moved to deliver what would have been a tragic blow, Thorne surged upward, catching his brother's arm and using his own momentum against him. They crashed into the side of a building, the impact sending cracks spider webbing across the facade.

The Guardians faltered as their master struggled, their movements becoming less synchronized, more individual. Archer seized the opportunity, cutting down three in quick succession while my Remnants dispatched two more.

"We need to end this," Archer panted, back-to-back with me as we faced the remaining Guardians. "We can't keep this up much longer."

He was right. Despite the power flowing through me, my mortal body was failing. Blood from a cut above my eye half-blinded me, and each breath sent shards of pain through my broken ribs. The voices in my head had reached a fever pitch, desperate and frantic as they sensed my weakening grip on consciousness.

Ezra broke free from Thorne's hold, putting distance between them. His eyes swept the battlefield, assessing the situation with cold calculation. Then, without warning, he changed tactics. Instead of re-engaging with Thorne, he launched himself toward us, toward Archer.

Before either of us could react, Ezra had Archer by the throat, lifting him off his feet with terrible ease. Archer kicked and struggled, but Ezra's grip was unbreakable, his eyes gleaming with cruel satisfaction.

"Let him go!" I screamed, my Remnants racing toward them in a tidal wave of shadow.

But Ezra held up his free hand, and the shadows dissipated like mist in sunlight. "One more step, Huntress," he said softly, almost lovingly, "and I crush his windpipe."

Thorne had frozen, his eyes locked on his brother. I could see the calculations running behind those eyes, the desperate search for a way to act without putting Archer in more danger.

Ezra yanked Archer's sleeve up, exposing the Treeis mark. A slow, cruel smile spread across his face as he studied it. "So the rumors are true. A bound Guardian." His eyes flicked to me, then back to Archer. "But not to her. No, you're bound to someone else as well. The child, perhaps? How... inconvenient for you."

Archer's face contorted with rage and pain as he clawed at the hand around his throat, but Ezra's grip didn't slacken.

"Do you know what this means, Archer Bramwell?" Ezra asked, his voice almost gentle, almost kind—which made it all the more terrible. "It means you can never take the throne. Your soul is already divided, already claimed. A marriage is a magical binding, but you're already bound. You cannot wed." He laughed. "Your father died for nothing. The throne you've been so reluctant to claim? It was never yours to take."

I felt Archer's despair like a physical blow, crashing through our bond with such force it nearly brought me to my knees. All the grief he'd been holding back, all the responsibility he'd finally accepted, crushed under the weight of Ezra's revelation because I hadn't taken the time to tell him what I'd already known.

Ezra's blue light flickered again, and in that second, I saw the true panic on his face. The fear of what he stood to lose. I saw what he fought for. And why. But still I moved toward him. Toward Archer. Pushing my power beyond the brink as it stretched across the street, digging into the ground for traction against Ezra, pushing back. But again, his power faltered. Thorne was racing toward us, but his power was gone, it seemed. He was nothing more than a man in that moment. A desperate man wearing a face full of terror as he watched me moving toward the god that'd taken my life over and over again.

"You can't touch him," I screamed. "He's a crowned prince. He's protected by the Fates." There was still a battle on Ezra's face. Would he go against divine law? Would he suffer the Fates' wrath? His power flickered again as I ran. And then, with a flick of his wrist, he flung Archer toward me. I caught him, the impact sending us both to the ground in a tangle of limbs. When I looked up, Ezra was gone, and with him, the remaining Guardians, melting back into the shadows from which they'd emerged.

I'd lived. I had no idea why. But I'd survived. For now.

The sudden silence was deafening. One moment, the street had been filled with the sounds of bloodshed, the next, there was only our ragged breathing, the distant drip of water, the soft groan of settling rubble.

Archer sat up slowly, rubbing his throat where bruises were already blooming in the shape of Ezra's fingers. "Is it true? What he said about the bond?"

I couldn't answer. I simply nodded, pushing back the sting of tears as the truth of his future was changed once again. Thorne approached, his unreliable power back but receding like the tide, returning him to the beautiful, impossible man I'd fallen in love with across lifetimes. He knelt beside us, his eyes scanning our injuries. "Are you all right?"

"We're alive," I said, which was the best that could be said of our current state.

He helped us to our feet, his touch achingly gentle. "We need to get you both somewhere safe. He'll be back, and with more Guardians and likely a few gods if he's given enough time."

Archer shook his head. "It's over? Just like that? I lost my father's kingdom before I ever even had it." His face crumpled like someone had struck a killing blow, and I felt his despair as acutely as if it were my own. "I failed."

I looked at him, at the blood streaking his golden hair, at the bruises darkening on his throat, at the pain in those blue eyes that had always looked at me with such loyalty, such unwavering friendship. This man who had chosen, again and again, to stand beside me through darkness and madness and pain. Who had made himself my family when the universe seemed determined to leave me alone.

And suddenly, I knew what I had to do. "Marry me."

Both men turned to stare at me with identical expressions of shock.

"What?" Archer croaked, clearly thinking he'd misheard.

"Marry me," I repeated, my voice stronger now, surer. I grabbed his hands, squeezing until he looked directly into my eyes. "The Treeis bond doesn't prevent it because we're both bound by it. Our souls are already connected. The vows would only formalize what already exists."

Thorne's expression was unreadable as he looked between us, his ancient eyes fathomless. Heartbroken.

"If the bond prevents you from marrying anyone else because your soul is already divided, then logically, the only person you could marry would be someone who shares that bond."

Archer shook his head, a strand of blood-matted hair falling across his forehead. "Paesha, I can't ask you to—"

"You're not asking. I'm offering." I gripped his hands tighter, willing him to understand. "This is about more than us now. It's about protecting the kingdom, protecting Quill, protecting ourselves from whatever Ezra is planning. And if taking the throne is what we need to do..."

"Then we'll do it together," he finished, the ghost of a smile touching his lips.

I nodded, relief flooding through me. "Together. Because if I am queen, he can't touch me either."

Thorne's hand came to rest on my shoulder, his touch both a comfort and a question. I turned to him, seeing the struggle in his eyes, the conflict between what he wanted for himself and what he knew was necessary. Between the selfish desire that had driven him for millennia and the love that had taught him to let go. "Are you sure about this?"

I met his gaze, letting him see the certainty in mine. "I'm sure. This is my choice, Thorne. Not destiny, not prophecy, not gods playing games with my life. Mine."

He held my gaze for a long moment, searching for something in my eyes. Whatever he found there must have satisfied him, because he nodded, but I didn't miss the swallow. The set of his jaw. The evisceration of his heart. "Then I will take the memories of anyone that ever believed we were married." He forced in a breath. "I will help you now and always."

In that moment, I witnessed the breaking of a god.

It wasn't loud or violent, no power surged, no shadows rose, no ground trembled beneath us. It was quiet, devastating in its silence. A supernova collapsing in on itself, leaving only dust where a star had once burned. His eyes, those ancient, beautiful eyes that had watched civilizations rise and fall, that had witnessed the birth and death of entire worlds, dimmed. Not all at once, but like a candle slowly drowning in its own wax, the flame guttering, fighting to stay alive even as it died.

For a heartbeat, he let the mask slip. Let me see the full measure of what my choice was costing him. A thousand lives. A thousand times we'd found love, only to watch it end in blood and pain. A thousand lives he'd found me, won me, lost me. And now, in this one, the one he'd claimed mattered most, he would stand aside and watch me marry another. Would help make it happen with his own hands.

His hand trembled almost imperceptibly where it rested on my shoulder, the only outward sign of the cataclysm happening within him. But through that small point of contact, I felt everything, grief so profound it had no bottom, love so vast it had no horizon, and beneath it all, a terrible, beautiful acceptance.

The cost of letting go.

I wanted to say something, anything, to ease the necessary pain. But what words could possibly bridge this chasm? What comfort could I offer when I was the source of his agony? When I was bathing in it myself and couldn't show an ounce of that.

Levanya appeared beside him, staring into his face as she whispered, *It is your nature to break his heart. As it is his to let you.*

Before I could respond, Thorne straightened, the mask sliding back into place with such smooth precision I might have imagined its absence. But I knew what I'd seen. Knew what he'd allowed me to see.

"We should go," he said, his voice steady, his hand falling away from my shoulder. The absence of his touch left me cold in a way that had nothing to do with the night air. "Dawn will break soon, and we have to be quick."

As we made our way through the devastated streets, I couldn't stop myself from glancing back at him. He walked a few paces behind us, close enough to help if needed, far enough to give us space. His face was composed, serene even, revealed in brief flashes as we passed beneath streetlamps.

But once, when he thought I wasn't looking, I caught a glimpse of him in shadow. His eyes closed, his head bowed, one hand pressed against his chest as if trying to hold together something that was already shattered beyond repair.

In that moment, I understood with terrible clarity what true sacrifice looked like. Not the grand gestures of legends, not the battlefield deaths of heroes, but this, a man who had loved me across lifetimes, choosing to let me go. Choosing my happiness, my freedom, my choice over his own heart's deepest desire.

I turned away, unable to bear witness to such naked grief when my own eyes burned with unshed tears. Levanya's voice echoed in my mind, softer now, almost gentle. *This, too, is love. The kind that sets free what it most wishes to keep.*

Ahead of me now, Archer limped onward, seemingly unaware of the silent breaking happening behind him. Unaware that with every step we took toward our future together, we were walking away from a love story that had spanned millennia.

I swallowed hard against the knot in my throat and kept moving forward, carrying the weight of what I'd seen, a god's heart crumbling to dust. Some wounds never truly heal. They just become part of who we are, scars we carry beneath our skin where no one else can see them.

49

THORNE

Three weeks.

I had lived through the birth of gods, the rise and fall of empires, watched stars burn out and be reborn. Yet these three weeks stretched longer than centuries, each passing day an exquisite form of fucking torture as I watched the castle transform around me. White silk rippled through hallways like ghosts of futures I'd never have. Summer tulips appeared in every corner, their presence a deliberate knife; they were apparently her favorite. The steady tap of Minerva's cane as she followed Paesha and Quill from room to room felt like a heartbeat counting down to my execution. Minnie still hadn't forgiven me, but she'd stepped in to love where I couldn't. Because one day, the mortals would die, and we would be left with only each other again. As we always were.

I haunted the castle's shadows, a guardian who could no longer claim what he protected. Present but not. Breathing but not living. Existing in that hollow space between what was and what could never be.

Now, sitting in the last pew of the cathedral, I traced my fingers over the aged wood, seeking something solid to anchor me to reality. Each candle the servants lit was another second closer to the end. To letting her go. To giving her to the better man.

"You don't have to stay," Tuck murmured beside me.

I tried to argue, but the words died in my throat. How could I explain that I had to be here? That I needed to witness this so thoroughly, so completely, that even my immortal heart would finally accept it was over? That I needed the pain as much as I needed her.

The sacred circle at the altar gleamed with silver markings of binding and protection, symbols I had seen a thousand times, in a thousand ceremonies, but never like this. Never from the wrong side of forever. Twin crowns rested on midnight velvet, their stones gifted from this land. The golden thread that would physically tie their hands together lay coiled like a serpent, waiting.

When Archer took his place at the altar, something in my chest contracted painfully. Not because I hated him. How could I, when he loved her so purely, so selflessly? But because his presence meant she was coming. My Ever. My heart. My destruction.

The first bell tolled, deep and resonant, each echo another crack in my carefully maintained composure. The doors swung open, and the world stopped turning.

She appeared like starlight breaking through storm clouds, like the first breath after drowning, like everything I had ever loved and lost wrapped in a gown the color of moonlight on snow. Not pure white, she had never been that, but something shifting and ethereal, like the space between darkness and dawn. Winter roses crowned her chestnut hair, and her Remnants swirled around her feet like living shadows, more controlled now but still wild. Still hers.

Still everything.

My eyes burned as she moved down the aisle, guided by Elowen. I had seen her in wedding gowns before, in other lives, other ceremonies. But this was different. This wasn't death or fate or my brother's arrow stealing her from me. This was her choice. Her steps. Her future walking away from me with each measured breath.

She passed close enough that I caught her scent. Honey and sin and fucking perfection. My hands curled into fists, nails biting deep enough to draw blood, the pain a welcome distraction from the void consuming my chest. I couldn't breathe. Didn't want to. Breathing meant living through this moment, and I wasn't sure I was strong enough.

When she reached Archer, she smiled. That real, bright smile that had always been like sunlight. The one that had made me fall in love with her in every life, every time, no matter how much it hurt. I had to remind myself to inhale. To keep existing. To let go.

"Seriously," Tuck whispered again, "we don't need to watch this."

"I need it to hurt enough to walk away," I managed, the words scraping my throat raw. "Right now, it's not enough. I have to see it through."

Minerva's voice washed over the gathering, speaking of destiny and binding and futures I would never be part of. I had no idea she would officiate, but it made sense. Bind them together with Reason and Wrath and no one would break them. But I could only focus on the way Paesha's fingers trembled as she took Archer's hands. The soft catch in her breath that probably no one else heard. The slight tilt of her head that meant she was fighting the voices in her mind.

Their vows pierced through my haze. Each word another blade between my ribs.

"I choose you..."

She chose me once. A thousand times. And I failed her every time.

"Because you saw me when I was lost..."

I saw her first. Across centuries. Across deaths. I always found her.

Her eyes flicked to mine, and the raw emotion in them nearly shattered what was left of my control. What did she see there, in my face? Did she see the breaking? The letting go? The love that would never die, no matter how many times it fucking killed me?

But nothing could have prepared me for their kiss.

The moment their lips met, something inside me shattered. Not cleanly, not quickly, but with the slow, terrible certainty of a mountain crumbling into the sea. Every kiss we'd ever shared, every soft touch, every whispered promise crashed through my mind. A thousand lifetimes of losing her to bloodshed, and somehow this was fucking worse. This gentle death. This willing surrender. My chest caved in. My lungs forgot how to work. The wood beneath my hands splintered as power surged through me, desperate for release.

Tuck's hand gripped my shoulder, hard enough to hurt. "Breathe."

I tried. Failed. Fucking tried again. Each attempt felt like swallowing glass.

Minerva raised her hands, and blue flames surged higher. "You have chosen each other, but the land must choose you as well. Kneel."

They knelt together, bound by the golden thread. Minnie lifted the first crown, a delicate circlet of silver and sapphire that would mark Paesha as queen. The crown that would protect her. The stones set within it began to glow as she lowered it to Paesha's head.

"Do you swear to protect this realm and its people? To rule with wisdom and compassion? To stand against any force that would threaten peace?"

"I swear it," Paesha said clearly, and the crown flared with brilliant light before settling onto her brow as if it had always belonged there. As if this had always been her destiny, and I had been keeping her from it all along.

The second crown, heavier but crafted of the same materials, glowed as Minerva held it over Archer's bowed head. He swore his own oath, and when both crowns blazed with acceptance, the cheers exploded. But I could only hear the sound of my heart shattering as they turned to face the crowd, crowned and blessed and godsdamned married.

She was radiant. Beautiful. Alive.

And no longer mine.

"Let's go home," Tuck said quietly, already trying to guide me toward the door. And I knew he meant to Etherium.

"I can't—" My voice cracked. I swallowed hard, tried again. "I can't leave her unprotected."

"The guards—"

"Are not enough." They would never be enough. Not for her. Not for the woman who had been everything to me.

So I stayed. Stood when protocol demanded. Bowed when tradition required. Watched as she danced with her new husband, her laugh carrying across the celebration like bells. Each smile was another dagger. Each touch another wound. I had existed for millennia. Had wielded power that could reshape realms. But nothing, not war, not death, not the weight of centuries had ever hurt like this.

When I finally escaped to a balcony, the night air did nothing to ease the vise around my heart. Stars wheeled overhead, as cold and distant as my own immortality. How many nights had I spent searching those same stars for signs of her? How many lives had I spent counting constellations until I found her again? Selfishly, I hoped she'd see me. I hoped she'd join me. I needed her. But she knew better and so did I.

"To the queen," Tuck said, pressing a glass into my hand.

I stared into the depths of my drink, seeing only her face. Her smile. Her eyes.

"To choice," I managed.

The word tasted like ashes and summer tulips.

LATER, alone in my chambers, I pressed my forehead against the cool stone wall and finally let myself break. Power exploded outward, shattering every piece of furniture, every window, every pretense of control. I sank to my knees amid the destruction, centuries of memories crushing me beneath their weight.

The mighty Keeper of Memories, brought down by love.

Far below, the celebration continued. And somewhere in that

revelry, my Ever danced with another man, wearing another's ring, bound by vows I would have given anything to hear directed at me. I closed my eyes, trying to find comfort in the only truths I had left:

She was alive.

She was safe.

She was happy.

She was free.

I repeated these like prayers, hoping that eventually they would hurt less than this endless, aching void where my heart used to be.

They didn't.

But I would learn to live with that. For her. Always for her.

A knock echoed through my chambers, sharp and decisive. I stared at the door, power crackling weakly at my fingertips, barely a shadow of what it should be. Of what I'd always been. That was the cost for stealing a realm's memories all at once when the power was already fading.

Another knock came, more insistent this time. I held my breath, unsure if I could face another soul while pieces of me lay scattered across the floor like the broken furniture surrounding me.

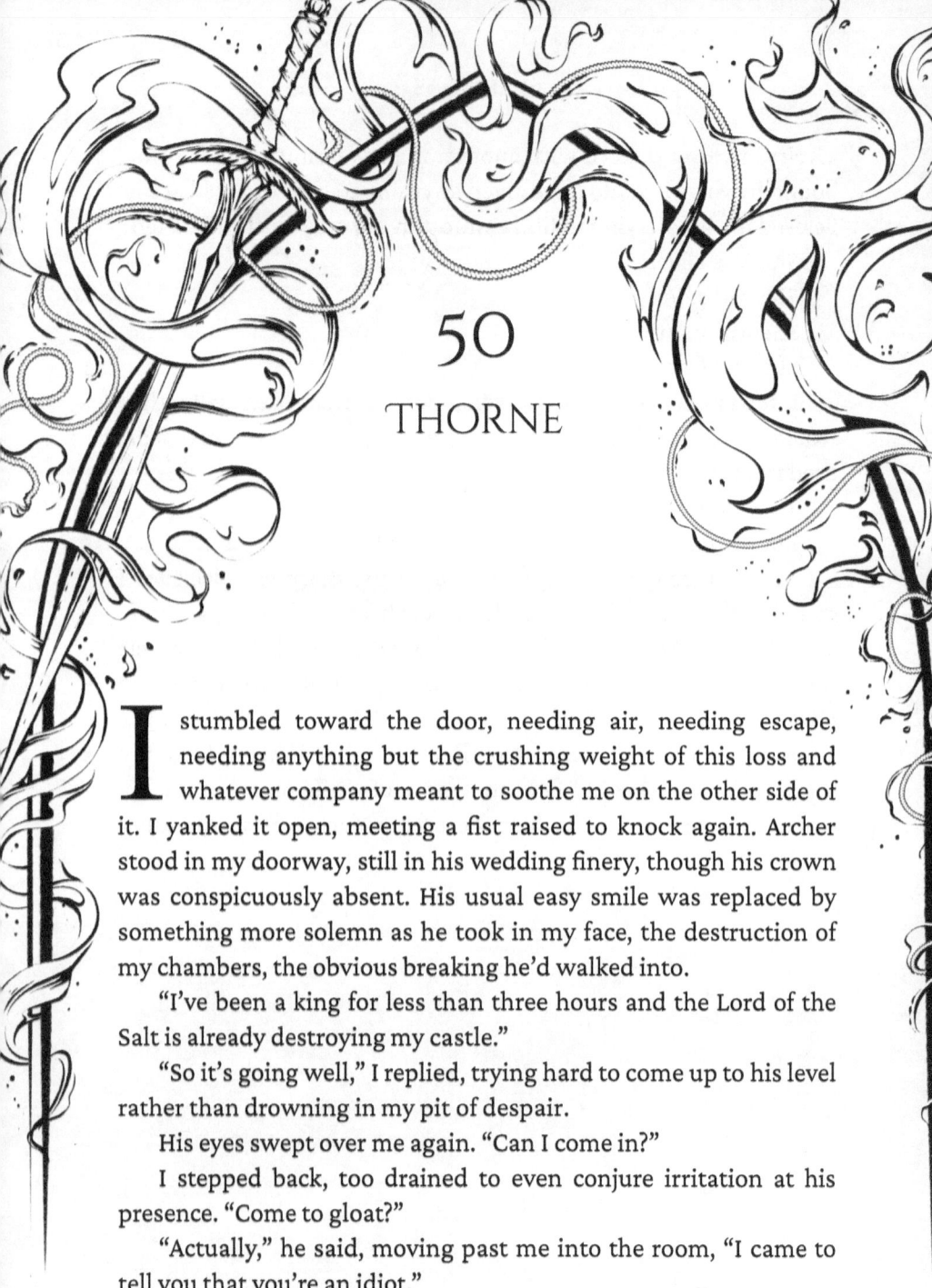

50

THORNE

I stumbled toward the door, needing air, needing escape, needing anything but the crushing weight of this loss and whatever company meant to soothe me on the other side of it. I yanked it open, meeting a fist raised to knock again. Archer stood in my doorway, still in his wedding finery, though his crown was conspicuously absent. His usual easy smile was replaced by something more solemn as he took in my face, the destruction of my chambers, the obvious breaking he'd walked into.

"I've been a king for less than three hours and the Lord of the Salt is already destroying my castle."

"So it's going well," I replied, trying hard to come up to his level rather than drowning in my pit of despair.

His eyes swept over me again. "Can I come in?"

I stepped back, too drained to even conjure irritation at his presence. "Come to gloat?"

"Actually," he said, moving past me into the room, "I came to tell you that you're an idiot."

That startled a harsh laugh from me. "Excuse me?"

"You heard me." He turned to face me, and there was something both gentle and firm in his expression. "Did you really think

472

she could go through with it? Actually marry me when she's clearly in love with you?"

My mind stuttered over his words. "What are you talking about? I just watched—"

"You watched a very convincing performance," he said, leaning against what remained of my desk. "Minerva's quite brilliant, you know. She found the loopholes weeks ago. The law requires rulers to be bound, yes, but it never specifies how they must be bound. The Treeis mark connecting us was enough. The ceremony appeared to be a wedding, but the markings, the words, even that golden thread, it was all carefully crafted to create an alliance, not a marriage. Minnie's a beast when it comes to circumventing laws."

I stared at him, my heart stumbling over its rhythm as his words sank in. "But the vows—"

"Were about choosing each other as partners in protecting the realm. Go back and listen to them in your mind. We never once said 'husband' or 'wife.'" His smile turned wry. "I would have done it, you know. Would have married her for real if that's what it took to keep her safe. No matter how much you might have hated me for it. But she's the one who couldn't do it. She and Minerva have been working on this plan for weeks."

"Why didn't she tell me?"

"We needed everyone to believe it was real. Including you. Including Ezra, who we knew would be watching. Your devastation sold it better than anything else could have."

I leaned against the wall to hold myself up, my mind reeling. "She's not your wife."

"No." His voice softened. "She's not. And she's waiting for you, by the way. In her room."

I looked up sharply. "What?"

"Gods. Keep up, would you?" He pushed off from the desk, heading for the door. "Go to her. And next time, try trusting that she knows her own heart."

He paused in the doorway, glancing back with that familiar

473

mischievous glint in his eyes. "Oh, and Thorne? You might want to change first. You look like shit."

"If I wasn't contemplating kissing you right on the mouth, I'd punch you in it," I said, throwing my arm around his shoulder, and digging my knuckles into his hair. "You're the greatest mortal I've ever had the pleasure of knowing."

"Hey," he ducked away. "Not the hair. I'm a king now. I can't walk around here all roughed up. Plus, my wife's a demigod. She'll kick your ass."

SHE STOOD before the mirror in her chambers, still wearing the godsdamn wedding dress that had nearly killed me. The Remnants swirled around her like living smoke, more agitated than usual, reflecting the turmoil I could see in her eyes even from across the room.

"You're wearing my ring," I said, my voice rougher than intended.

She met my gaze in the mirror, her fingers instinctively moving to touch the band I'd given her. "Did you really think I'd wear any other?"

I crossed the room in three strides, turning her to face me. "Do you have any idea what you did to me today? What these last three weeks have felt like?"

"Do you have any idea what you've done to me across life-times?" But there was no bite in her words, only a terrible under-standing. Her eyes flickered to something over my shoulder, and I knew she was seeing one of them. The past lives that never left her alone.

I caught her chin, bringing her focus back to me. "I love you. Recklessly. Selfishly. Probably to both our detriment."

"I know." Her hand came up to cover mine. "Everything you've ever done, every choice, every sacrifice, it's all been love. Imperfect and messy and absolutely beautiful." She drew a shaky breath. "Even before you found me in Death's Court, you gave me the space to choose. To love him. To make my own path. I know what that must have cost you. To watch me fall for your brother, knowing I was your Ever."

"It doesn't matter now."

"It matters to me." Her fingers tightened on mine. "What I felt for Ezra, it was real, but it was a shadow of this. I loved him because he made me feel controlled when I thought I was spiraling. But you?" Her eyes met mine, fierce and certain. "You gave me back my control. You showed me how to embrace the chaos instead of fearing it. I needed time to understand that. To understand myself. And even when it was killing you, you gave me that too."

She had no idea how desperately I needed to hear those words. To know she saw me, not just the god, not just the Keeper, but the broken pieces I'd become while loving her. The man who would burn worlds to find her and then let her walk away if that was what she needed.

This wasn't the crushing weight of destiny or the pull of fate. This was something far more terrifying, far more beautiful. This was choice. Raw and messy and real. This was love carved from pain, tempered in sacrifice, made stronger by every scar we'd given each other. A love we'd chosen in spite of everything, or maybe because of it.

A shadow passed over her face as she answered something I couldn't hear. The Remnants churned faster, darker.

"I'm going to the Fates," I said, my thumb brushing over her cheek. "I won't watch you suffer like this."

"I need to be vulnerable for a minute. I don't want to be, but I need to say the words."

"You don't have to give a warning before you're vulnerable with me. Ever."

She nodded. "It's not the suffering. Today was necessary, but it was another reminder that I'm setting myself up for failure. I'm going to fail him." Her eyes tracked something I couldn't see moving across the room. "Some days I can almost bear it. But other days... I'm afraid, Thorne. Afraid I'll lose myself in their voices.

Afraid one day I won't be able to tell which thoughts are mine and which belong to the ghosts of women I used to be. What happens when the court realizes their queen is mad? When they turn on Archer because of me?"

"I won't let that happen."

"You can't promise that." She met my eyes, and the raw fear there gutted me. "What if I forget how to hear anything but their poison? What if—" She broke off, attention snapping to something over my shoulder. "Shut up!" The words tore from her throat, desperate and ragged. "Just shut up for one fucking minute!"

I grabbed her face between my hands, forcing her focus back to me. "Listen to me. When I stood there today, watching you with him, I thought I was dying. But this? Watching you suffer? That's worse." I pressed my forehead to hers. "I'm going to the Fates. And I don't care what price they demand."

"You own every piece of me," she whispered, her voice breaking. "Every life. Every death. Every broken bit of my soul matches yours. That's why it hurts so much. Because they're all screaming for you right now, and I can't make them stop."

"Then let me in. Let me be louder than their screams. Let me remind you which voice is real." My fingers traced the curve of her jaw, her neck, feeling her pulse race beneath my touch. "The Fates can wait until morning. Right now, I need you to remember who you are."

Golden threads of memory magic spun between us as I opened my mind to hers. Not to take or change, but to give. To show her the moments that defined her beyond the deaths and pain. Us holding each other in the Parlor, her laugh echoing off stone walls as I pulled her closer. Quill's tiny fingers finding hers that first day, trust shining in those eyes. The fierce pride in her stance as she stood beside Thea, facing down the Maestro with unflinching courage. The joy in her movements as she and Archer danced through the Hollow's shadows, their friendship a light in the darkness.

The Remnants calmed as the memories washed over her, their chaotic swirling settling into gentler patterns. Relief flooded her eyes, and for a moment, she let herself fall forward, leaning into me, letting me try to soothe her. I wrapped my arms around her, holding her to my chest, giving her as much time as she needed to remember who she was, that she was not alone. I had her. Archer had her. Hell, every one of us had her. And we would build the walls for her if that was what she needed.

She exhaled softly against my chest, her breath warm, grounding. Then, she pulled back to meet my gaze, something fierce and unshaken settling in her eyes. Her fingers slid into my hair, tugging me down, and before I could draw another breath, her lips found mine.

The kiss was slow at first, searching, like she was relearning something familiar—but then it turned urgent, demanding. My hands tightened at her waist as I let her take what she needed, as much as she needed. When her teeth scraped my bottom lip, I groaned, my control unraveling.

"I love you," I rasped against her mouth, the words spilling free as I slid my hand into her hair, dislodging winter roses. She tasted like coming home. My tongue swept inside, desperate to devour every soft sound she made.

Her fingers worked at my jacket, shoving it off my shoulders with delicious impatience. I groaned as her nails scraped down my chest. "Get me out of this fucking dress," she demanded against my lips.

I spun her around, my hands finding the intricate buttons down her spine. "With pleasure." I pressed kisses to each inch of skin I revealed, savoring her shivers. "I've imagined ripping this off you since the moment you walked down that aisle."

"Are you going to talk about it or do it?"

I grabbed the fabric and yanked, sending buttons scattering across the floor. She gasped as the dress fell away, leaving her in nothing but moonlight.

"Satisfied?" I growled, trailing my fingers down her sides.

She turned in my arms, and the look in her eyes nearly brought me to my knees. "Not even close."

We crashed together like waves breaking against cliffs. I lifted her onto the vanity, sending cosmetics clattering to the floor as I stepped between her thighs. Her skin was fire under my touch, burning away everything but this. Us. Here. Now.

"Tell me you're mine," I demanded, my mouth moving down her throat.

"Always." She arched as I found that spot behind her ear that made her crazy. "Every life. Every realm. Every—" She broke off with a moan as my hand slid higher up her thigh.

I smiled against her skin. "Every what, darling?"

Her fingers tangled in my hair, yanking my head back so she could meet my eyes. "If you don't fuck me right now, I swear to all the gods—"

I cut her off with another kiss, swallowing her demands as I pressed her back against the mirror. We could be proper tomorrow. We could be distant acquaintances in court, could play whatever games we needed to survive.

But tonight, I would remind her exactly who she belonged to.

And who belonged to her.

"I love it when you're impatient," I growled against her throat, nipping at her neck.

A breathless laugh escaped her kiss-swollen lips. "Less talking."

I undid my belt with one hand, not bothering to be gentle. The clink of metal echoed in the room, and my pants hit the floor with a thud. Her shadows were already on me, slithering up my legs like liquid heat, coiling around my thighs, teasing the base of my cock. I growled, low and feral, as they tightened, a phantom grip that sent jolts of pleasure shooting up my spine.

"Fucking hell, Paesha," I choked out, my hips jerking forward as her shadows danced along my length, stroking me with a rhythm that was too good, too much. I could feel the slickness of her arousal as I dragged myself against her entrance, teasing but not giving her what she wanted. She arched into me, her breasts pressing against my chest, and I couldn't resist biting down on her collarbone. She moaned, her hands clawing at my back as I ground against her, the friction making us both shudder. Her shadows tightened around me again, pulling me closer, and I finally snapped.

I slammed into her with one brutal thrust, burying myself to the hilt. Her head fell back, but I caught her chin, forcing her to look at me. "Eyes on me," I growled, wrapping my fingers around her throat. She nodded, biting her lip as I set a punishing pace, fucking her so hard the dresser rocked with every thrust, rattling the mirror reflecting her beautiful ass as she moved.

Her shadows were everywhere, wrapping around us both, pulling me deeper, pushing me faster. They coiled around her waist, lifting her hips to meet mine, and I felt her walls clench around me, tight and wet and perfect. I laughed, dark and rough, as I leaned in to bite her neck again. "You like that, don't you?" I hissed, my breath hot against her skin. "You fucking love it."

I pushed harder, riding out the waves of our shared ecstasy. The mirror behind her rattled with each powerful snap of my hips. I wanted to fuck her so hard it shattered, until the only reflection was our bodies joined as one. Her legs were wrapped around me, trembling, shaking, her heels digging into the small of my back like she was trying to anchor herself to me, to keep me from ever pulling out.

I didn't fucking want to. Every inch of her was mine. Without warning, the mirror cracked. A sharp, splintering sound that only made me fuck her harder. I wanted it to shatter. I wanted it to break into a thousand fucking pieces. I wanted to make her come so hard she couldn't see straight, couldn't think, couldn't do anything but feel me inside her.

She whimpered, and her shadows moved lower, slipping between us to tease her clit. She cried out, her body shaking as she came, and I followed her over the edge with a roar. Mine to have. Mine to claim. Hers to break.

Satiated and breathless, Paesha rested her head on my shoulder, her skin still flushed and damp against mine. The remains of her wedding dress lay scattered across the floor like fallen petals, and her Remnants drifted lazily around us, calmer than I'd seen them in weeks. I pressed a kiss to her shoulder, tasting salt and honey and home.

Three sharp knocks rattled the door. A pause. Then one more.

"Are you done defiling my wife?" Archer's muffled voice carried through the wood with far too much amusement. "Did you break something else, because I'll start billing."

I grabbed one of her discarded shoes and hurled it at the door. "Fuck off, Your Majesty."

"I'll take that as a yes." A beat of silence. "So you guys want to get some food or something?"

Paesha laughed against my chest. "Give us a minute."

"You've had plenty of minutes. Very loud minutes, I might add."

I grabbed the other shoe. "I will end your reign before it begins."

"Can't. You love me too much now." The smirk was audible in his voice. "Plus, I'm pretty sure Paesha would end yours. Now hurry up. The kitchen made those little pies you like."

"I hate him," I muttered, even as Paesha slid from the dresser with a knowing smile.

"You really don't." She started gathering her clothes. "And he did help orchestrate an entire fake wedding so we could be together."

"The pies better be worth it," I called toward the door.

"They're the ones with the honey drizzle!"

I looked at Paesha. "I hate that he knows my weaknesses."

"Wait until Quill realizes she can bribe you with pastries too." She pressed a quick kiss to my lips. "Now help me find my other shoe."

51

THORNE

The tear was exactly where it had always been, a jagged gash in reality that rippled like cloth in a wind that didn't exist. I didn't hesitate, didn't pause to consider what awaited me on the other side. I stepped through, feeling my body tear apart and reform in the space of a single heartbeat.

The Fates' void stretched before me, endless and all consuming. Raw potential crackled through the air, each spark a future struggling to be born. But something was wrong. Where before the void had been filled with the presence of the Fates, their voices echoing through my bones, their power pressing against my skin, now there was only silence. A maddening, oppressive quiet that scraped against my nerves like fingernails on glass.

"I know you're here. Show yourselves!"

Nothing. Not even an echo.

I moved deeper in, boots scraping against something that wasn't quite floor. Occasionally, a thin thread of fate drifted past, glowing with the promise it represented. But no voices rose to challenge me. No beings emerged from the darkness.

I could hear the loom, though. The soft, rhythmic creaking of ancient wood bearing the weight of all destinies. The sound was maddening in its constancy, a reminder of their presence despite their refusal to appear.

"We had a bargain!" I shouted into the darkness, fury rising like bile in my throat. "Archer Bramwell sits upon the throne of Stirling! His blood mingles with the ancient power of that seat! You swore you would hear me when that came to pass!"

The silence that followed felt deliberate, mocking. I could almost feel their amusement at my desperation, could practically taste their satisfaction at forcing me to beg. But I would beg for her. For her sanity. Her control.

"Answer me, damn you!"

Still nothing.

My patience, already worn thin, snapped completely. I reached out and grabbed the nearest thread of fate, feeling it hum with life between my fingers. Without hesitation, I snapped it. The sound echoed, not the physical breaking of the thread, but the scream that accompanied it. A thousand voices cried out at once, their anguish reverberating through the void.

"You think I won't do worse?" I snarled, reaching for another. "You think I don't have it in me to tear your precious weaving apart strand by strand?"

I broke another thread, then another, each snap sending shockwaves through the void. Power surged from me in violent waves, warping the space around me.

"We had a fucking deal! A queen sits on the throne beside him, a queen driven to madness by voices you could silence with a word! Weave a change in her fate, dammit." The words burned like embers on my tongue, but I forced them out. "I fulfilled my end of the bargain. Now fulfill yours!"

The loom's rhythm never faltered, never changed. They were ignoring me. Deliberately. Callously. They'd never promised to help, only hear me. And now they had. Undoubtedly. I twisted the drifting threads around my fist, watching them wither and blacken at my touch. "You were so desperate to crown Archer Bramwell, did you consider the mad queen? Did you know? She hears voices.

She sees people. She will surely bring that realm to ruin, if you don't help her."

I would do anything in my power to keep that from happening because the guilt of that would ruin her, but there were words that held power here. Truths that were stronger than the lies. Still they said fucking nothing.

"Cowards," I spat, my voice dropping to a dangerous whisper. "You hide behind your loom, binding the fates of gods and mortals alike, but you don't have the courage to face me."

I released the withered threads, watching them drift away like ash on a breeze. A terrible idea began to take shape in my mind as I observed how they curled and darkened at my touch.

I didn't need to break the threads to damage them. I didn't need to end lives to alter destinies.

My fingers brushed against another thread, and it wilted instantly, turning from vibrant gold to dull black. The life it represented wouldn't end, but it would change, warp in ways even the Fates might not predict.

"I will return," I promised the silence, letting my power flare one final time. "And when I do, you will listen. Or I will end every thread you've ever woven. I will wilt the tapestry of fate until it rots at the foundation of your loom. You thought being bound to it was terrible? Wait until I fucking destroy you."

"You do not have that power, Keeper," they hissed, finally breaking their silence.

I turned back toward the tear, each step measured and deliberate. They wouldn't help me. Not today, perhaps not ever. But I no longer needed their permission. As I returned to the fading twilight of Etherium, I felt something shift within me. A final barrier breaking. A last restraint snapping.

The Fates had made their choice.

Now I would make mine.

THE AIR in Death's Court carried the peculiar static of power that existed nowhere else, not quite living nor fully dead. Perpetual night shrouded the landscape, illuminated by twin moons that hung impossibly close in the sky. Their pale light cast everything in silvery blue shadows, giving the elaborate grounds an almost dreamlike quality.

As I walked toward the castle, I considered the people I might find here. A tiny ache in my heart hoped to see Harlow, but as I walked, I never saw another soul. And truthfully, that was probably for the best. If this plan was going to work, it needed to be done as swiftly as possible. The Fates could have no time to see what was coming. Or who, rather.

As if he'd been waiting for me, I found Death sitting atop a throne of skulls, thrumming his fingers along the arms of his seat as if impatient. But when I moved closer I realized his eyes were closed and those fingers tapped a perfect rhythm. He was conducting music in his mind.

I cleared my throat, but he didn't startle. Only held up a finger and continued through whatever his mind was trying to work out. Aside from the fist clenched at my side, I didn't bother to rush him. I needed him to do something reckless and that wouldn't happen if I commanded him. For cautionary reasons, I took my twin brother's face from his memories.

"Who are you?" he finally asked, stepping from his dark throne to look me in the eyes rather than down upon me.

"My name is Reverius Hawthorne Noctus. We've met before," I answered, using my power to shine so bright in this dark realm, he had to shield his eyes.

"Keeper?"

"Yes. And I don't have time for formalities. I know Paesha Vox was... is your friend and she needs help."

He took several rushed steps toward me. "You found her?"

"I never lost her."

And then I explained everything as quickly as I could. From her being my Ever, to the deal in Stirling. I told him of Ezra's role in her history and of mine. And then I told him of the veil and every shit thing I'd done to save her. And how she'd married a king to save a realm and mostly, I told him of her madness. Of how desperately she needed help. And he listened. His dark eyes were not quick to dismiss me. Instead, he ran a hand through his hair and looked away.

"I stabbed my wife once," he finally said. "So, I'll do my best not to punch you in the face for fucking with my sister, deal?"

It didn't surprise me to find yet another soul she'd gathered like family. "I try not to bargain these days."

"Probably for the best. But I do love Paesha and I'll do what she needs me to. Name it and it's done."

"First, you must know, I'll have to take your memories. You can't know the path to Etherium. Death isn't meant to dwell in an immortal land. That's the divine law and the one we're about to break. Can you handle that?"

"I'll manage," Death said dryly. "But what am I doing when we get there?"

"You occupy a unique position. Death is essential to the balance they maintain. They cannot harm you without disrupting the fabric of existence. Your presence alone will force them to listen."

"So I'm to be your bargaining chip?" There was no offense in his tone, merely curiosity.

"More like my final option," I replied. "If they refuse to help even with Death standing witness, then everything is fucked anyway... She doesn't have a moment's peace. Nor a single night of complete rest. She sits upon a throne before a class of people that would stone her to death before they accepted a mad queen. And she knows it."

I hated the tone. The begging in my voice, but if I needed to fall to my fucking knees before Death to save her, I would. It wasn't needed though. Not as the man's eyes shifted between mine as he nodded. "Whatever she needs, I will become it, but perhaps you could answer something for me in exchange."

I slid my hands into my pockets to hide my relief. "Name it."

"My wife. She snuck into this court without dying. Will she age eternally? Will she die and become a soul if she stays here?"

"She won't age. This court isn't a realm with time passing. It's simply the After. The space where things come to exist, but not change. Should she wish to age, she could always return to Requiem, but if she wishes to stay, she will... remain. As she is."

Death's shoulders relaxed slightly. "Thank you for that."

"We need to move. The Fates see patterns and possibilities. They'll know what's coming if we linger."

Death nodded, dark hair falling across his brow. "What exactly do you need from them? What change must they make?"

"They have the power to affect change in *her*, to alter the threads of her fate. The voices, the visions... They could end them with a single adjustment to her thread." My voice cracked. "If they would simply change her fate, she would be okay. They'll be furious about this intrusion. They may demand payment, likely that I stay away from her forever. And I will agree. I will do whatever they ask if it means she finds peace."

Death studied me for a long moment, his gaze measuring. "You truly love her."

It wasn't a question, but I answered anyway. "More than existence."

"Then I'm with you." He straightened his shoulders, power rippling around him like a cloak. "Paesha matters to me too."

We moved toward the door, each step deliberate and purposeful. I was already considering how to open the tear, how to navigate the void with Death in tow, when the great doors swung open.

A woman stood there, casually twirling a dagger between her fingers. Her green eyes, sharp and calculating, took us both in with a single glance. A massive hellhound loomed behind her, its shoulders higher than hers, red eyes glowing like embers in the darkness. The beast's breath came in low growls that vibrated the air.

"Going somewhere interesting?" she asked, her voice deceptively light as the dagger continued its perfect rotation.

Death moved forward, his posture softening. "Easy, Nightmare," he murmured, leaning in to kiss her briefly. His hand brushed her cheek with surprising tenderness. "There's an emergency. Paesha needs help."

Her eyes narrowed, the dagger stilling. "What kind of emergency?"

"The kind that requires immediate action," I cut in, aware of each second slipping away. "I'm sorry, but we don't have time—"

"This is Reverius," Death said, gesturing toward me. "An old... associate of Paesha's. And this," he said to me, "is my wife, Deyanira."

We'd met, but she didn't need to know that right now. There was something dangerous in her stillness, in the careful way she assessed me. The hellhound mirrored her, its massive head tilting slightly.

"I don't have time to explain."

Deyanira's fingers tightened around the dagger's hilt. "Then I'm coming too."

"You can't," I said, perhaps too quickly.

Her eyes flashed. "I don't recall asking your permission."

"It's not about permission," Death said gently. "Where we're going, it's not a place for the living, or me, technically. It's complicated. I'll explain everything when I return, I promise."

For a moment, I thought she might argue further, but something in Death's expression seemed to reach her. She stepped back, the hellhound moving with her like a shadow.

Her gaze shifted to me. "You'd better bring him back exactly as he is."

"You have my word," I replied.

She laughed, a sound without humor. "I have no fucking clue who you are so that doesn't mean shit to me."

We moved past her, the hellhound growling low as I passed. I could feel Deyanira's eyes on my back, calculating and cold.

"We need to move quickly. The tear will only stay open for moments once we're through. Stay close to me."

Death nodded, his expression solemn.

After sending a tendril of magic behind me, stealing Deyanira's memories, I reached out, feeling for the thin places between realms, for the jagged edges where reality could be torn. My power surged, golden threads of creation weaving through my fingers as I tore it open. The void beckoned, dark and infinite. I glanced at Death one last time and together, we stepped through the tear, into darkness that swallowed us whole.

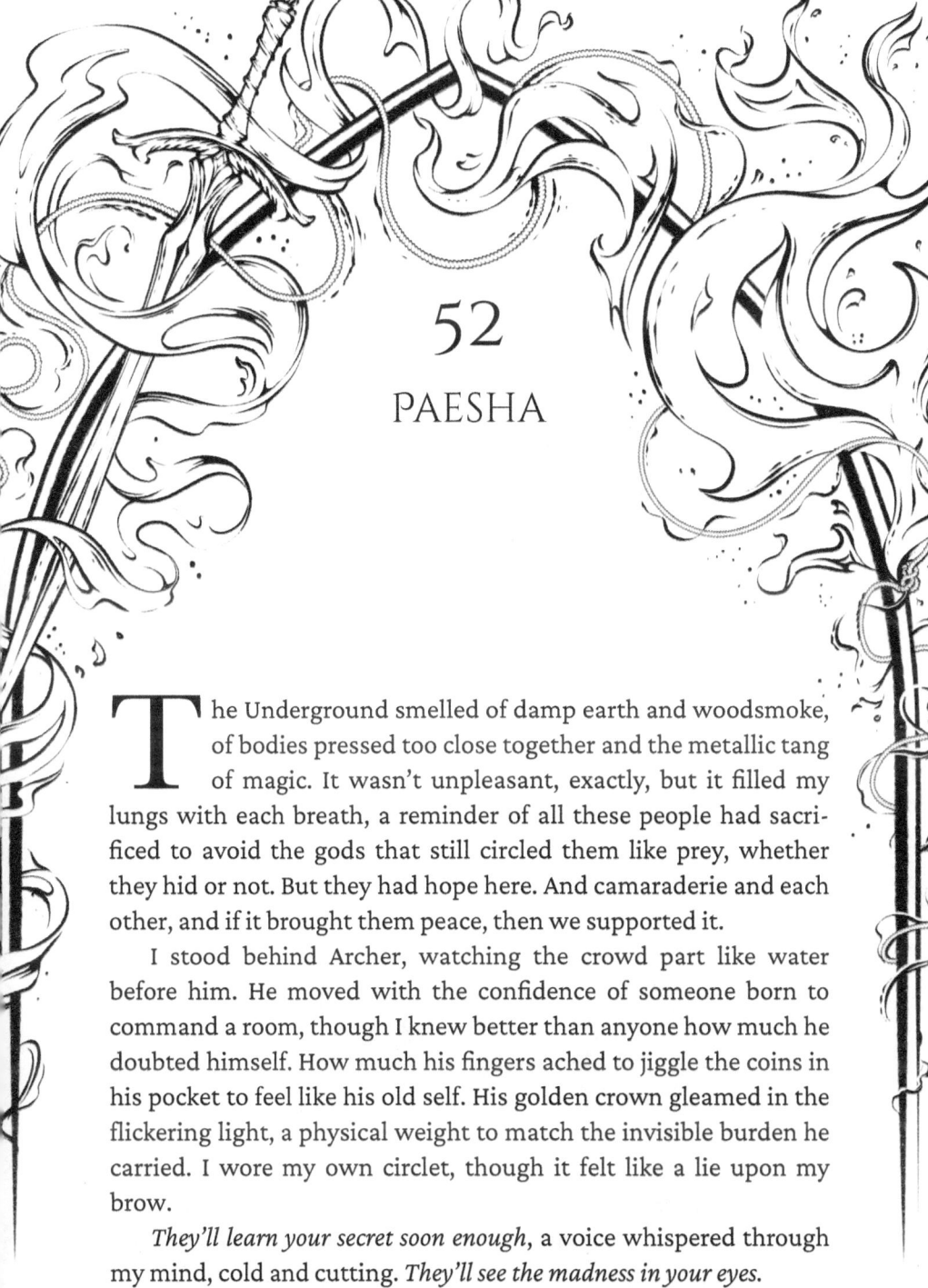

52

PAESHA

The Underground smelled of damp earth and woodsmoke, of bodies pressed too close together and the metallic tang of magic. It wasn't unpleasant, exactly, but it filled my lungs with each breath, a reminder of all these people had sacrificed to avoid the gods that still circled them like prey, whether they hid or not. But they had hope here. And camaraderie and each other, and if it brought them peace, then we supported it.

I stood behind Archer, watching the crowd part like water before him. He moved with the confidence of someone born to command a room, though I knew better than anyone how much he doubted himself. How much his fingers ached to jiggle the coins in his pocket to feel like his old self. His golden crown gleamed in the flickering light, a physical weight to match the invisible burden he carried. I wore my own circlet, though it felt like a lie upon my brow.

They'll learn your secret soon enough, a voice whispered through my mind, cold and cutting. *They'll see the madness in your eyes.*

A queen of shadows and lies, another hissed.

I pressed my lips together firmly, terrified that I might respond aloud without realizing it. My fingers curled into tight fists at my sides, nails digging half-moons into my palms until I felt the sting of broken skin. The pain helped, a sharp point of focus to cling to as the voices clawed at my thoughts. I kept my gaze deliberately forward, afraid that if I made eye contact with anyone, they might see the chaos swirling behind my carefully forced expression.

Quill slipped her small hand into mine, her face tilted up with genuine concern. "Are you sad again?" she whispered.

I squeezed her fingers, forcing a smile that felt brittle. "Just thinking, my girl." I carefully enunciated each word, monitoring my tone to ensure it sounded natural, unaffected.

Lying to the child now? The voice sounded like Sylvie today, mocking and sharp. *How queenly.*

I nearly responded, my lips parting before I caught myself. I snapped my mouth shut so quickly my teeth clicked together. The voices had changed, their purpose becoming clearer with each passing day. At first, I thought they wanted only to punish Thorne, to make him suffer by watching me descend into madness. But the longer I dealt with them, the more clear everything became. They wanted me to fulfill the prophecy that had haunted me since the beginning. Because it wasn't only mine, it was theirs too. And they'd all died from fear of it.

Break the balance, Winter had whispered last night as I struggled for sleep. *The gods are circling, hungry for your power. They've always known what you could do.*

They wanted me to shatter everything. They hated all the gods, not just him, for the cycles of death they'd endured. And their solution was simple: use me to break the flow of power before the gods could claim my power for themselves.

They fear you, Sylvie had taunted. *As they should. You were always meant to break the balance between them. Why not embrace it? Why not let it all burn?*

They isolated me through fear, convincing me to hide my struggles, to pull away from those who might help. And in that isolation, their hold on me only grew stronger, pushing me closer to the edge where I might finally snap and unleash the destruction they craved.

Quill's brow furrowed, unconvinced by my forced smile. I forgot how well she knew me, how easily she read the emotions I tried to hide. "You don't have to be here. We could go back."

"I'm fine." I straightened my shoulders and lifted my chin, adopting the posture I'd seen Thorne use countless times, regal, controlled, unassailable. "Besides, we can't leave Archer to face this alone."

She considered this, then nodded. "He does need us."

Despite everything, I felt a smile tug at my lips. "Don't let him hear you say that."

Ahead of us, Archer had reached the makeshift platform at the center of the cavern and he looked back at me with that charming smile before the crowd quieted. I could feel hundreds of eyes tracking my movement as I joined him, Quill still clinging to my hand. The weight of their expectation pressed down like stones on my chest.

They know, Winter whispered. *They can see the monster you really are.*

I swallowed hard, keeping my expression neutral through sheer force of will. I measured each breath, afraid that if I breathed too deeply or too quickly, someone might notice, might whisper to their neighbor about the queen's strange behavior. Gods, I was tired. So fucking tired of fighting every waking moment, of constantly monitoring every facial expression, every gesture, every word.

"Friends," Archer began, his voice carrying through the cavern with surprising authority. "Thank you for welcoming us into your sanctuary."

A murmur ran through the crowd. I spotted Thea near the front, her copper hair gleaming as she nodded. Beside her stood the baker, flour still dusting his forearms. I recognized others too.

In the days leading up to our wedding, we'd made sure to be seen. To hold hands and smile back and forth, while trash talking to each other under our breaths for amusement. Archer made life easy. As comfortable as anyone should have been. But he had no idea the depth of my darkness. And maybe I should have warned him. But the truth was, I wasn't sure I knew either. Not truly. And he would have never faltered. He loved me solidly. I could have told him I was growing a second head and he'd have hugged me and offered to find me a hat. That man was pure fucking gold.

I shifted my weight slightly, careful to keep the movement minimal. My fingers fidgeted with the fabric of my dress before I realized what I was doing. Immediately, I stilled them, terrified someone had noticed. These people were looking to me—to us— for strength, for stability. What would they think if they knew their new queen was fighting a losing battle against voices in her head?

"You may or may not know me as Archer Bramwell," he continued, "though I stand before you now as a king." He touched his crown with an almost self-deprecating gesture. "I know that means little to those of you from Silbath and Perth. I'm not your king."

He doesn't belong here, the voices hissed. *Neither do you.*

This is your fault, another added. *Your madness will drag them all down.*

I tasted blood where I'd bitten the inside of my cheek, using the sharp pain to center myself. I fixed my eyes on a point above the crowd's heads, afraid they'd see the flicker of responses to voices they couldn't hear if I met anyone's gaze.

"But I want you to know," Archer was saying, "that crown or no crown, title or no title, I stand with you. The borders between our cities mean nothing compared to the bonds between our people."

A cheer rose from the crowd, surprising in its intensity. Archer raised a hand, quieting them. "I can't promise to solve everything. I can't make the gods leave, or bring back what you've lost. But I can promise this: you will not face these challenges alone."

Another cheer, louder this time. I felt my shoulders tense, the Remnants swirling across my skin responding to my rising anxiety. I focused on keeping my breathing even, my expression placid.

They'll turn on you both when they discover the truth, Winter whispered. *When they see what you are.*

Poison in a crown, Sylvie added. *You'll destroy everything he's building.*

A faint tremor ran through me, and I locked my knees to keep from swaying. Archer shot me a concerned glance, and panic flared through me. Had he noticed?

Before I could reassure him, Tuck materialized at my side, his broad frame somehow managing to appear casual despite the tension radiating from him.

"Steady now, Your Highness," he murmured, only loud enough for me to hear. "Breathe through it."

What it must have been like for him and Minerva to stand with us now, in a den of mortals denouncing the gods, I didn't know. But they'd never left us. Not once. And truly, none in this crowd knew their nature. No one questioned the little old lady and the burly, bearded man that stood with us. This was simply our family and nothing more.

I nodded mechanically, focusing on drawing air into my lungs without letting my struggle show. In. Out. Like Thorne had taught me during those quiet nights when the voices grew too loud. I kept my eyes fixed straight ahead, afraid to look at the faces in the crowd, afraid they'd see the battle raging behind my eyes.

"You're doing remarkably well. Considerably better than I'd have expected, given everything."

"Is that supposed to be comforting?" I whispered, as Archer continued addressing the crowd. I barely moved my lips.

Tuck's mouth curled upward. "Since when do you need comfort?"

He sees the weakness in you, a voice hissed.

"Since apparently I'm one bad day away from completely losing my mind." I struggled to keep my voice low, to keep my face neutral. A woman in the crowd glanced my way, and I immediately fixed my features into a benign smile, terrified she'd somehow heard me.

"Aren't we all? Though I suppose in your case, it's rather more literal."

A short laugh escaped. I quickly disguised it as a cough, covering my mouth with my hand. Tuck had always had a talent for cutting through pretense, for stating the unbearable so plainly it became almost manageable.

Archer had finished speaking, and was moving among the crowd, clasping hands, listening to concerns with a sincerity that couldn't be faked. The gathered people surged around him, a strange mix of deference and familiarity in their interactions. He had always been good at this, at making people feel heard, valued. It was why, despite his reluctance, he was the right choice to wear the crown.

"He's remarkable," Tuck observed, following my gaze.

"He is." I kept my voice deliberately level, my hands clasped in front of me.

"And you're worried you'll ruin it."

"Stop knowing shit, Tuck. It's annoying."

"God of Knowledge, remember?" He tapped his temple with one finger. "Though in this case, it doesn't take divine insight. It's written all over your face."

"I hate to admit this, but I think I hate the spotlight right now," I whispered as Archer looked back at me for the third time, a beaming smile on his face. My heart ached with pride, but my soul thrummed with fear.

"Then let's head back to the castle, Huntress. This feels like a security nightmare as it is and if something happens while Thorne's away, he's going to have my ass anyway."

"Still no word from him?" I asked for the third or fourth time since he'd been gone.

"Nothing yet. I'm giving him another day and then going after him myself. The Fates can be vicious bastards, less so now than before they were bound, but he's reckless when it comes to you."

"You're gripping it all wrong," Tuck growled, his massive hands engulfing Archer's as he adjusted his hold on the axe handle. "Loose in the fingers, tight in the palm. It's not a damn teacup."

The castle gardens provided ample space for impromptu

weapons training. The overgrown hedges and messy flower beds seemed in tune with Tuck's rough instruction. Archer had brought in gardeners after he saw how much Quill loved the space, but they were new and several of them had fled after witnessing Archer's previous attempts, which had sent an axe sailing into a prized rosebush.

"It is absolutely nothing like a teacup," Archer muttered, readjusting his stance for what must have been the twentieth time. "I've held plenty of those successfully."

"Less talking, more throwing," Tuck commanded, stepping back and crossing his massive arms. "And this time, try to hit the target and not that poor squirrel."

"That was one time," Archer protested, glancing at me. "And it dodged. I swear."

I sat on a stone bench nearby, enjoying the warmth of the evening sun and the ridiculous spectacle before me, a half-read book in my lap. The training dummy, a burlap sack stuffed with hay and decorated with a silly face drawn by Quill, remained untouched, though the ground around it was littered with axes that had fallen short, veered wide, or in one particularly spectacular case, somehow managed to go backward.

"Remember," Tuck said, his voice gruff but patient, "your arm is an extension of your will. The axe is the extension of your arm."

"My will is apparently drunk today," Archer mumbled, taking a deep breath and raising the axe.

"Your form is better," Thea called from where she sat, braiding flowers into a wreath a few yards away. "The last one almost went in a straight line."

She flashed a smile at Tuck that lingered just a moment too long. He cleared his throat and turned his attention back to Archer, though I caught the slightest hint of color rise to his cheeks. "Focus, Your Majesty."

Archer nodded, squared his shoulders, and with a grunt of effort, hurled the axe toward the target. It spun through the air, handle over blade, and crashed into the hedge several feet to the right of the target.

"Better," Tuck declared, despite all evidence to the contrary.

"Are we looking at the same thing?" Archer gestured to the quivering axe now embedded in a topiary.

"You kept your wrist straight that time." Tuck retrieved another axe from the collection at his feet. "Again."

A few paces behind us, Quill was twirling in delicate circles, her arms raised gracefully above her head. She'd been practicing the dance steps for days, determined to perform for Minerva, who sat watching with extreme attentiveness. The old goddess leaned on her cane, her normally severe expression softened as she observed the child's earnest efforts.

"Straighten your back," Minerva instructed, her voice gentler than I'd ever heard it. "Feel the music in your mind, let it guide your movements. The dance should bring you peace."

Quill nodded solemnly, standing taller as she continued.

"She's getting quite good," Elowen said, appearing beside me with two wine glasses. She handed one to me before settling on the bench. "Reminds me of someone else I know."

I took a sip, letting the cool sweetness wash away the heat of the day. "She's been practicing all week. Says she wants to impress Minerva, though I can't imagine why."

Elowen smiled, watching as Minerva made subtle adjustments to Quill's posture. "Perhaps Minnie's always had a soft spot for children. And Quill has a gift for finding the cracks in people's armor."

"Like someone else I know," I teased, nudging her shoulder.

Across the garden, Archer let out a triumphant shout as his axe finally made contact with the dummy, not the center, not even close, but it stuck in the burlap with a satisfying thunk.

"Did you see that?" He spun around with his arms raised victorious. "I am a natural!"

"After thirty-seven tries," Tuck said dryly, though there was unmistakable pride in his eyes. "We'll make a warrior of you yet."

"I prefer to leave the axe throwing to you," Archer replied, grinning broadly. "I'll stick to cards and charming smiles."

"The charm needs work too," Thea called.

After retrieving the axe, Tuck demonstrated the proper form once more, his movements fluid despite his bulk. The weapon flew from his hand with deadly precision, striking dead center of the target with enough force to make the dummy rock back on its post.

"Show off," Archer muttered.

"Remember, when diplomacy fails, a well-placed axe can be very persuasive."

"I'll add that to the list of kingly wisdom. Right after 'knitting is not a king's hobby' as you so gallantly told me before you took away my yarn."

"In my defense, the pup got tangled and the kid got worried. That was a team effort."

Archer gasped and spun to Quill. She giggled. "I want to be sorry but I'm not. You're too handsome for knitting sweaters. Maybe if this axe business doesn't work out, you could try something with Thea. She has a forge at home, you know. You could make your own crowns."

"Well, I'm not making you one now, traitor," he huffed, hiding his smile.

"You would if I asked," she argued back. "Now, don't distract me. I need to concentrate on my big finale."

She spun one more time, core tight as she moved to complete her dance with a small curtsy.

Minerva clapped. "Well done. You've been practicing."

Perhaps she means to take your crown one day.

"She can have it," I hissed back.

I froze as all eyes turned toward me. The words had slipped out by accident. Somewhere in my mind, a woman's laughter echoed, low and thrumming with satisfaction at my slip. I felt Levanya then, coiling in that quiet space. She meant to pull me in, to protect me from them all, but I no longer knew the path to that corner. They'd been keeping me far away from her.

Such a fragile shell for all that power.

"I—" I stood abruptly, the wine glass slipping from my fingers and shattering on the stone path. The sound was too sharp, too loud in the sudden silence. "I need to go."

I turned to leave, desperate to escape the concerned stares, but Archer was there before I could take two steps, blocking my path with his unnatural speed.

"Hey, no," he said softly, his blue eyes steady on mine. "Not this time."

"Archer, please. I can't do this here."

Run. Hide. Then break. Or break him.

"I'm not sure where you're going," he said, and before I could protest further, he pulled me into his arms. The embrace was firm, grounding, his heartbeat steady against my ear. "But you're not doing it alone."

I stiffened, then gradually relaxed against him, letting his warmth seep into the cold spaces the voices had carved inside me. His hand moved in slow circles on my back, the way I'd seen him comfort Quill a hundred times before.

"I hate this," I admitted. "I hate being weak."

"Weak?" He pulled back to look at me, genuine confusion crossing his features. "Paesha, you're the strongest person I know. You fight battles inside your mind that would break anyone else."

He lies. He fears you.

"The voices tell me otherwise," I said, trying for a smile that felt more like a grimace.

Archer's expression hardened. "Then the voices are fucking liars." He glanced over at Quill and winced. "Sorry, kid."

"I've heard worse." Quill shrugged, moving closer to us. "Especially from you."

A small, genuine laugh escaped me at that, and Archer's face brightened at the sound.

"There she is," he said softly. He kept one arm around my shoulders as he guided me back to the bench. "Listen to me. You're going to come out the other side of this darkness. I don't know how or when, but I know it with absolute certainty because I've been there too. After Harlow died, there were days I couldn't see a way forward. But you never let me give up. You dragged me back into the light, kicking and screaming sometimes." His grip on my shoulder tightened. "So I'm going to return the favor, even if I have to stand between you and those voices every damn day until they learn to shut up."

"I'll help too," Quill declared, squeezing into the small space between Archer and me. "I'm pretty good at being loud when necessary."

"It's true," Thea confirmed, joining our growing circle. "But we've all had to live with her, so you already know that."

The tightness in my chest eased slightly as they gathered around me, a living barrier against the shadows in my mind. But the relief was short-lived.

They will all fall. And you with them.

I pressed the heels of my hands against my temples. "It feels like a pit of destruction constantly pulling me under and I don't know why. I used to have control over them, but now..."

Minerva cleared her throat. Her piercing gaze saw straight through me. "Are you being serious right now?"

"Of course I am," I snapped, frustration edging my voice. "It's debilitating. Some days I can barely function through the noise."

Minerva and Tuck exchanged a long look.

"What?"

Minerva shifted toward me. "What do you know of Aeris?"

My veins turned to ice. "Aside from the fact that she's a dick and inserted herself where she didn't belong? Aside from the fact that she abandoned me as a child and then tried to weasel her way back in? But not for me. Only Quill? I know she's the reason the Treeis bond was enacted. She wanted to bind Archer to Ezra. I know she's the Goddess of Renewal. She rebuilt parts of Requiem, turned it into something she thought was better. Hard disagree on that, by the way." I glanced at Thea, who nodded in confirmation. "I know she's a piece of shit. That feels like more than enough."

"Aeris is not just the Goddess of Renewal. She is the Goddess of Renewal *and* Destruction. The two forces are inseparable."

A chill ran down my spine. "That's not possible. We would have known."

"Would you?" Tuck asked quietly. "The gods specialize in half truths. It's easier to earn trust when you show only your most appealing qualities."

The implications crashed over me like a wave. The convenient timing of her appearances. The way she'd been there the day the floor had opened beneath Quill. The immediate trust everyone except me had felt toward her. The way my power felt nothing like renewal and everything like destruction. I'd chalked it up to Irri's power over broken things. But gods, I'd destroyed the veil. Not because of Irri's power but Aeris's.

"You're strong, Paesha," Minnie said, coming to stand within our circle. "Think of everything you possess. All the power stolen by a tyrant prince is yours now. The power of the Huntress. And you're a demigod. You should feel divided. You're many parts that make a whole. And no one knows what that's like more than I do. It is a burden."

"What parts are you?" Quill asked.

"I am the Goddess of Reason and now Wrath. But Wrath was not always mine. That was a power saved for the Fates. My destiny was also broken by Ezra, as was yours," she told the child.

"Mine?"

"Ezra wanted Archer bound to him before he took the mortal throne. But because you were there, and your power was so strong, along with Paesha's, you became bound by the Treeis bond. He never wanted that, I'm sure, because the bond kept him from taking the throne."

Quill dug a toe into the ground. "My destiny wasn't broken. I love them."

"That may be so, but it was not your free will that made that choice, child. And someday you may wish it wasn't so."

"How did it happen?" Thea asked, tentatively. "When your destiny was broken?"

"Ezra had a vision that the Fates would betray me and steal my power. I knew he was wrong. I begged him not to interfere. But he didn't listen. Instead, he convinced every god to bind the Fates more tightly to their loom, restricting their movement and abilities. It was heart wrenching. All these centuries later and I'll never forget their screams. Or mine, I think. And he was wrong. The Fates and I were meant to work together, not against each other. His interference caused my Reason to become tangled with the Fates' Wrath." Her old eyes flashed to me. "I have power no goddess should have. I have anger no one should feel. It's a battle every day. That's why you and I understand each other so fully."

Within the silence, Tuck spoke up. "It's no wonder you're suffering. You're channeling multiple gods' powers through a body that was never meant to contain such forces. Those powers are feeding off each other. Creating a storm that grows more chaotic by the day. It'd be more strange if you were unaffected, to be honest."

"How do we fix this?" Elowen asked. "There must be a way to help her."

Minerva's expression turned grave. "The powers within her are too deeply intertwined to simply separate."

"Fun times," I said casually, feeling uncomfortable by the way they all watched me. This is exactly why I didn't want to say anything. Why I wanted to run. I didn't need their pity, but I couldn't breathe without their love.

"Thorne is trying to find a solution and he's a stubborn being. The Fates are difficult and capricious, but if anyone can persuade them, it's him," Minerva said.

"And if he can't?" I whispered, immediately regretting the doubt.

Archer's arm tightened around me. "Then we keep looking. We don't give up until we find an answer."

"All of us," Thea added, reaching for my hand.

They lie. There is no salvation. Only the dark.

"I love you guys, but tread lightly. You can't trust me. I'm not even sure how much longer I can hold on."

"As long as you need to," Archer said with quiet conviction. "And when you can't hold on anymore, that's what we're here for. Besides, who else is going to support my hobby seeking in a very mocking way?"

Despite everything, I felt the corner of my mouth lift. "Everyone, actually."

"That's the spirit." He grinned. "Focus on my humiliation instead of yours."

"A strategy that has served us well for months," I agreed.

Tuck clapped his hands together. "Right. Enough standing around feeling sorry for ourselves. The best thing we can do is keep going."

He picked up another axe and held it out to Archer. "Your form still needs work, Your Majesty. And you—" he turned to me, his expression softening only slightly, "—you need a distraction. Fancy learning to throw?"

"Oh, I think I could manage better than our king here," I said, accepting the challenge.

"Bold words," Archer retorted. "It's harder than it looks."

The weight of the axe felt good in my hand, solid and real in a way the voices weren't. I stepped up to the mark, my fingers finding their grip as Tuck had instructed Archer earlier.

"Loose in the fingers," I mumbled. "Tight in the palm."

I took a breath, drew back my arm, and threw. The axe spun through the air and embedded itself in the outer ring of the target with a satisfying thunk.

Archer's jaw dropped. "You have got to be kidding me."

I turned to him with a triumphant smile. "Natural talent."

"Or beginner's luck," he grumbled, though there was no real heat in it.

"Only one way to find out," Tuck said, handing me another axe.

I took it, focusing on the weight, the balance, the simple physics of the throw. The voices still whispered, but for now, they were background noise, drowned out by the laughter of my family and the solid reality of the axe in my hand.

It wouldn't last. I knew that. But for this moment, surrounded by people who refused to let me fall, I could breathe. I could fight. I could hope that somewhere, Thorne was finding the answer I so desperately needed.

53

THORNE

I was going to burn this whole fucking place to the ground. The silent void mocked me with every step. My rage burned golden beneath my skin, power thrumming. Death's presence was the only tether keeping me from erupting into pure anger. His previous casual demeanor was replaced by something more ancient, more befitting his true nature. He was not the musical, dark-haired man who ruled his court with quiet ease; here, in this place between places, he was Death incarnate.

"They're watching," he murmured, his voice carrying strangely in the emptiness. "I can feel it."

I nodded, allowing my power to flare around me. A challenge. A threat. "Good."

We moved deeper into the void, each step carrying us across something that wasn't quite floor, wasn't quite air. Occasionally, a thread of fate drifted past, glowing with potential futures. I resisted the urge to snatch them, to tear them apart as I had before. That outburst had gained me nothing but their contempt, and I needed more this time. So much more.

"The loom should be just ahead," I said, listening for the familiar, maddening creak of ancient wood.

As we ventured deeper, the subtle sounds of the loom grew, the scrape of thread against thread, the rhythmic working that bound all destinies. But still, the Fates remained hidden, refusing to materialize.

"Enough games! Show yourselves!"

Nothing. Not even the satisfaction of an echo.

Death's expression darkened, his power manifesting as a chill that frosted the air. "Perhaps they need more motivation." He reached out, his hand passing through one of the hovering threads.

The effect was instantaneous. A shudder ran through the space, and suddenly, the air rippled like disturbed water. Three figures shimmered into existence, their forms indistinct and fluid, as if they couldn't quite decide what shape to take.

"You bring Death to our realm?" The voice that spoke belonged to all three and none of them, a discordant chord that vibrated my bones.

I stepped forward, putting myself between them and Death. "I tried to come alone but you weren't willing to play. Funny how fear changes people's minds."

"You have no right," another hissed, the sound like silk tearing. "This is a violation of—"

"I don't give a fuck about your rights or your rules. We had a bargain. Archer Bramwell sits upon the throne of Stirling. His blood mingles with the ancient power of that seat."

"As does the Huntress," the third voice added, an undercurrent of something like satisfaction in the tone.

"Yes. As does she." But why did they care? Why was *that* the important thing? Unless they knew. Unless they saw and schemed to set this up. I knew they hadn't. The Fates don't care for the whims or desires of gods and mortals. They are neutral. They care only for what is. What has been. What will be. Still, something in that tone rattled me.

"The Mad Queen," they said in unison, their forms rippling with what might have been excitement. "More interesting than the boy king, though both were necessary steps."

Something cold settled in my gut. There was a game being played here, a longer, deeper scheme than I had anticipated.

"I didn't come to discuss your interest in Paesha," I said, forcing myself back to the point. "I came because she suffers. The voices in her mind grow stronger each day, driving her toward madness and destruction. You could help her. You could change her fate with a single adjustment."

"And what would you give for this adjustment?" they finally asked, the question laced with cruel anticipation.

"Whatever it costs," I said without hesitation.

They laughed, the sound like a thousand small bells, each slightly out of tune. "You would give up your Ever? So easily?"

"Not easily," I growled, fighting to keep my temper in check. "Never easily. But I would make the sacrifice if it meant her freedom from this torment."

Death shifted beside me, growing impatient with the Fates' games. I felt his power stir.

"And if we refuse?" they asked, their attention now fixed on Death.

"Then I will tear this realm apart," I promised, my voice dropping to a whisper that still somehow filled the void. "I will end every thread you've ever woven. I will unravel the tapestry of fate until nothing remains but chaos."

"Bold threats from a god whose power wanes," one said dismissively.

Death stepped forward, his presence suddenly filling the void with terrible weight. "His is not the only power you need to fear, and I can assure you, mine does not wane. Death is the only guarantee in life. In existence. Let me show you."

He opened his palm, and a small orb of darkness formed above it, dense and absolute, a fraction of death magic, brought into this realm where it should never exist. The Fates hissed, drawing back from the abomination.

"You would not dare. Death has no place among the unborn possibilities, the futures yet to be woven."

He looked dramatically over his shoulder, around me, gaze

shifting this way and that. "And yet, here I stand, in a place you claim I shouldn't be. I wonder what would happen if this touched your precious loom?" The orb floated slightly higher. "Would the threads burn? Would the futures they represent cease to exist? Or perhaps something worse?"

"This is madness," they protested, but there was fear beneath their outrage.

"No," I said coldly. "Madness is what you've condemned Paesha to suffer. This? This is merely the consequence of your refusal to help. You fucked around and now you're finding out what the cost of that was."

I moved to stand beside Death, letting my own power flare brighter, golden threads of creation interwoven with his absolute darkness. Together, we formed a threat the Fates could not ignore.

"We could destroy everything you've built," I continued, "or you could grant us one simple request. Help her. End the voices. Free her mind from this torment. A small price to pay for the continued existence of your realm, wouldn't you agree?"

The Fates conferred among themselves, their forms merging and separating in a dance of indecision. "The madness serves a purpose," they said. "It drives her toward the fulfillment of her true destiny."

"Which is what, exactly?" I demanded.

"To break the balance, as was foretold."

Anger surged through me, hot and fierce. "That prophecy was your doing, wasn't it? You gave Ezra that vision at the beginning and he fucking ran with it."

Their silence was confirmation enough.

But that couldn't have been it. This had to go back further. Back to the beginning. Back to when... they set up Minerva. The pieces clicked into place with terrible clarity. The imbalance of power wasn't an accident. It was their design all along.

The Fates shifted uneasily. I could see them now, ancient and terrible, threads of fate wound through their flesh like living chains. Faces that had once been beautiful were now twisted by centuries of spite and the burden of their existence.

"We merely observe the patterns," one insisted, far too late.

I stared at them, understanding dawning with sickening certainty. "We need to leave," I said without warning. "Right now."

Death's shoulders stiffened. "But—"

"Trust me on this," I said, backing away.

Death hesitated, his power still swirling dangerously around his fingertips. The orb of darkness pulsed above his palm, hungry for contact with the loom. I gripped his arm, my fingers digging in with urgency.

"Now," I hissed, my voice barely audible.

Something in my tone must have convinced him because his darkness receded, the orb dissolving into wisps that faded against the void. He followed my lead, stepping backward even as confusion darkened his features.

The Fates' laughter followed us, three-toned and mocking, as we retreated.

"Running away, Keeper? How unlike you. We expected more persistence."

"Consider this a lesson learned," I growled back.

They became less substantial as we moved away, melting back into the void until only their voices remained, echoing around us like poisoned honey. "Remember, Keeper, some fates cannot be changed. Some threads cannot be snipped. The Huntress will fulfill her destiny, whether you wish it or not."

I didn't respond, focusing instead on finding the tear we'd come through, dragging Death alongside me with determined strides. The moment we crossed back into Etherium, I sealed the tear behind us with a violent slash of power, severing our connection to the Fates' realm with finality.

Death wrenched his arm from my grip, his eyes flashing with frustration. "What the hell was that? We had them cornered. They were afraid. We could have forced their hand!"

I shook my head, already striding through the golden streets of Etherium, my mind racing. "No, we couldn't have. Not like that."

"Explain," he demanded, keeping pace beside me. "You dragged me into this, threatened them with my power, and then ran at the first sign they might be yielding? I thought we were there to help Paesha."

"We were. We are. But I just realized we're playing a much more dangerous game than I thought."

Death's brow furrowed, patience wearing thin. "That tells me nothing. If you want my help—"

"They wanted us there," I cut him off, my voice harsh with the revelation. "The Fates. They orchestrated the entire exchange, probably expected it from the moment I stormed out last time. Think about it. They could have refused us outright, banished us the moment we arrived. Instead, they let us make our threats, let us think we were gaining ground."

Understanding began to dawn in Death's dark eyes. "A trap?"

"Or a distraction," I said, leading him through the twisted architecture of Etherium toward a destination I hadn't planned to reveal. "Either way, we weren't going to win that confrontation. Not today."

We passed crumbling structures, buildings that defied logic with their impossible angles and spiraling forms that folded in upon themselves. Another crystal anchor shattered somewhere in the distance, the sound reverberating through the dying realm.

"Where are we going?" Death asked, his gaze taking in the decay of Etherium with wild fascination.

I didn't answer immediately, focused on our path through the fading twilight. Finally, we arrived at a massive archway of black and gold, intricate runes carved into its surface. The runes barely glowed now, where once they had blazed with raw energy.

"The Noctus Gate," I said, gesturing to the towering structure.

He stared up at it, understanding the significance without explanation. "The source of your power."

"The source of *all* power," I corrected, reaching out to touch the cold surface of the gate. "The flow of raw energy that powers the gods—fuels creation and destruction alike."

Death moved closer, studying the elaborate lock mechanism at the center of the gate. "And the key?"

"Taken by the Fates. Lifetimes ago, there was an incident that bound them to their loom. It was meant to control them, to keep them from abusing their position." I swallowed, the lie feeling like ash on my tongue. "But we were wrong to do that. We should have shown more respect."

Death's eyes narrowed. "It created the imbalance of power?"

"No. I did that. By chasing my Ever through lifetimes." Another lie.

"Now there's no way to right it," Death finished. "That's why you're backing down. Why you'll respect their decision."

I met his gaze steadily, hoping my eyes didn't betray the truth beneath the fabrication. "For now."

He wasn't entirely convinced, I could see it in the slight tension of his shoulders, but he nodded slowly. "And Paesha? What of her suffering?"

"I'll find another way," I said, my voice hardening with resolve. "The Fates aren't the only power in the realms."

"And if there is no other way?"

I turned away from the gate, jaw clenched against the rage and desperation threatening to overwhelm me. "There's always another way. Always."

Death studied me for a long moment, his expression unreadable. "What now, then?"

I looked back at the gate one last time, my decision crystallizing with terrible clarity. I would not be able to do this alone. I needed a team who understood the Fates as well as I did, beings who'd spent centuries playing these damn games. "Now," I said, voice hardening, "I need to have a conversation with my fucking brother."

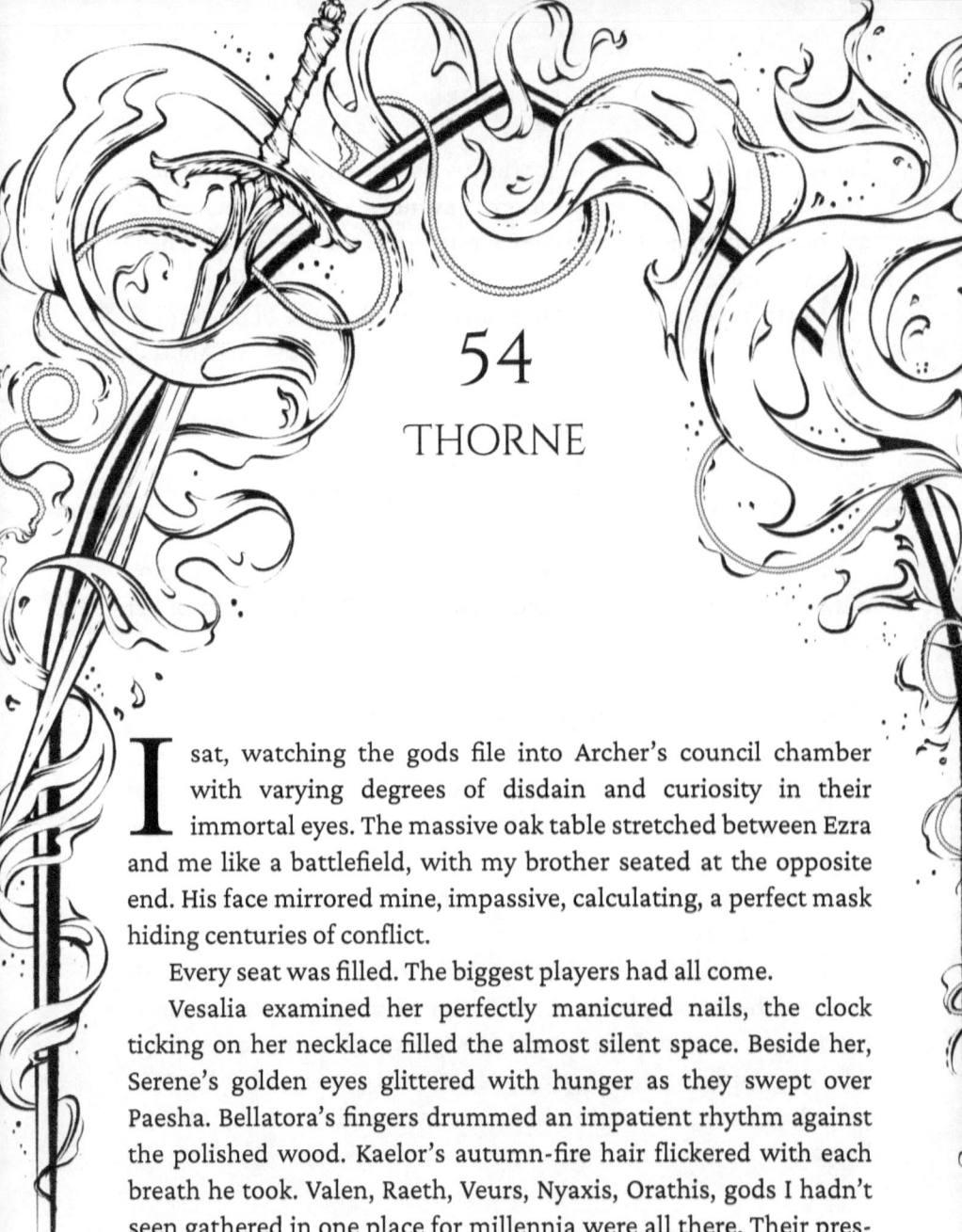

54

THORNE

I sat, watching the gods file into Archer's council chamber with varying degrees of disdain and curiosity in their immortal eyes. The massive oak table stretched between Ezra and me like a battlefield, with my brother seated at the opposite end. His face mirrored mine, impassive, calculating, a perfect mask hiding centuries of conflict.

Every seat was filled. The biggest players had all come.

Vesalia examined her perfectly manicured nails, the clock ticking on her necklace filled the almost silent space. Beside her, Serene's golden eyes glittered with hunger as they swept over Paesha. Bellatora's fingers drummed an impatient rhythm against the polished wood. Kaelor's autumn-fire hair flickered with each breath he took. Valen, Raeth, Veurs, Nyaxis, Orathis, gods I hadn't seen gathered in one place for millennia were all there. Their presence would have been impressive if I didn't sense the desperation beneath their carefully composed exteriors. Their vie for power.

Aeris sat as close as she could to Quill, her dark hair artfully arranged, her face a mask of maternal concern over the child as if she had any claim. Alastor remained silent in his corner, observing everything, his Remnants swirling across his arms like living tattoos. Beside him, Irri hummed softly, her delicate fingers tracing incomprehensible patterns on the tabletop.

They hadn't come for me. They'd come for Paesha, for her power, for the chance to tear it from her and make it their own.

Raeth's eyes, one bright with joy, one darkened by sorrow, fixed on Quill. "Why is the child here?" he asked, his dual-toned voice rippling through the chamber. "This is no place for her."

Paesha's shadows crept across the floor, circling Quill.

"The Fera stays," Minerva replied sharply, her weathered hand resting protectively on Quill's shoulder. "Her presence is necessary."

"Necessary for what, exactly?" Bellatora challenged, leaning forward, "This isn't a nursery, Minerva."

Quill didn't bother looking up from her book, seemingly uninterested in the gods bickering over her presence.

"The child's presence is not up for debate," Minerva said with finality. "Continue, Reverius."

I cleared my throat, drawing all eyes back to me. "I've called you here because we have a problem that concerns us all."

"Your obsession with the Huntress is hardly our collective problem," Veurs drawled, his form shifting slightly as he spoke, never quite settling on a single appearance.

"If that were true," I countered, "none of you would have bothered to come."

He shifted back in his seat.

"As I was saying, you all know we have a problem. The power is failing across all realms. The balance has been broken."

"By her," Aeris interjected, pointing a slender finger at Paesha. "As was foretold."

Paesha's eyes narrowed dangerously. "Point that nasty finger at me one more time and I'll break it off. Don't even fucking look at me, *mother*."

The chamber went deathly quiet at her words. Aeris's face tightened, but she said nothing.

"And stay away from my kid," Paesha added, her voice dropping to a lethal whisper. "You don't get to play goddess and mother whenever it suits you."

I continued before Aeris could respond. "The imbalance began long before Paesha was born. In fact, I believe it began before Ezra's vision of the Huntress."

Ezra's eyes narrowed from the far end of the table. "Careful, brother."

"Gods don't question the Fates," Nyaxis whispered. "We learned that lesson after Minnie's misfortune. It's not our place."

"Perhaps it should be," I countered. "Because the moment we stopped questioning, we started losing."

I stood, placing my palms flat against the table as I leaned forward. "The Huntress isn't responsible for the imbalance. We created it ourselves by trying to prevent it. Ezra and I have been locked in this battle for centuries, each of us believing we were protecting the realms in our own way."

"You're suggesting the prophecy was false?" Kaelor asked, his voice rumbling like distant thunder.

"I'm suggesting it was bait. And we fucking took it."

Bellatora laughed. "How convenient that your realization comes right as your precious Huntress sits on the throne of Stirling, her power growing beyond what any mortal should possess and within her final life."

"Losing all of our power is not convenient," I shot back. "Take two godsdamn seconds and see reason, because I cannot stand against them by myself."

Tuck nodded, finally speaking up. "The fluctuations affect all of us. Even in this room, I can feel the ebb and flow. Can't you?"

A murmur of reluctant agreement passed through the assembly. They couldn't deny it. Their power surged and faltered in unpredictable waves, evident in the way Serene's glow dimmed periodically, in how Vesalia's control of time seemed to skip and stutter around her.

"If the Huntress isn't the cause," Vesalia said, her eyes fixing on Paesha, "then what is?"

I pinched the bridge of my nose and stared up at the ceiling. "It's always been the Fates."

"Blasphemy," Valen hissed.

"Truth," Minerva countered, rising to stand beside me. "I've felt it for centuries but couldn't piece it together. My mind... There were gaps in my reasoning that I couldn't explain."

She turned to Ezra. "You were right about one thing, Ezarius. The Fates were moving against me. They set everything up. When I took on part of their Wrath, it wasn't coincidence. They took something from me, a sliver of my Reason, my ability to see patterns clearly."

The room fell silent as the implications sank in.

"Reason was always their first target," Minerva continued. "They can see and weave fate, but Reason helps decide which fate to nurture and which to abandon. The power they stole from me forged a path for them to take all power for themselves, and if you're too blind to see that then you deserve to have everything taken from you."

Alastor leaned forward, his Remnants suddenly still. "Explain."

They wouldn't hear me, but they would hear her. And for the first time since I stepped into the Forgotten, I felt her stand at my side again. I felt her acknowledge me in the best way she knew how. Not by coddling, but with her support.

"If the balance is completely gone, we all lose our power," Minerva said. "Then only the Fates and mortals will be left with it. And eventually, mortal blood will be too diluted to matter. Who does that leave with power?"

I turned to Ezra. "Tell me, brother. Was it the Fates who showed you the vision of the Huntress breaking the balance? That happened *after* they were bound to their loom, did it not?"

Ezra's jaw tightened, but he didn't deny it.

"The Fates orchestrated every step," Minerva said, her voice growing stronger. "They wanted to be bound to the loom because it made them appear weakened and trapped. It positioned them as victims rather than orchestrators. Let them work in secret while we underestimated them."

"They hold the key to the Noctus Gate," I added, watching comprehension dawn across the gathered gods' faces. "Why would they need that, if not to lock us away from our own power?"

"If what you're saying is true," Serene interjected, "then there's an obvious solution. We destroy the Huntress, take her power, and use it to restore the balance ourselves."

"You would regret ever breathing," I stated flatly, my power flaring around me in a golden aura.

Archer, who'd sat silently at my side, shifted slightly in his chair, eyes locked dead ahead.

"She's only a demigod, Reverius," Bellatora sneered. "With stolen power that doesn't belong to her."

"She's..." *mine,* I wanted to say. Mine to have. Mine to love. Mine to protect. But I couldn't. Not publicly. Not anymore.

"Mine," Archer spoke up, his voice steady despite being surrounded by gods, "she's my wife and queen of Stirling. Protected by ancient laws that even you can't break, Bellatora."

Vesalia's lips curved into a cold smile. "Two things, King. First, you're protected by the Fates you're asking us to damn. I could kill you here and now and suffer their wrath, or stand against them and suffer their wrath, so it seems you're not as safe as you think you are. Besides, there are ways to extract power without death. I've done it before."

The room erupted into argument, gods shouting over each other about who would get Paesha's power once it was taken, how it would be divided, what it would mean for the realms.

"Enough!" Minerva's voice cut through the chaos like a blade as her cane whacked the top of the table. She stood. "If anyone moves against Paesha, I will end them."

Many of the gods feared that Minerva's grasp on the Fates' Wrath gave her the power to kill them. Her threats resonated around the room, anger seeping down the walls in a flash of dangerous power. "Consider the root of this problem. It's the Fates. It's always been the Fates. The prophecy they delivered spurred this imbalance into motion. The girl had nothing to do with it."

She turned to Ezra, pinning him with her piercing gaze. "Remember who you are, Ezarius."

Ezra's expression hardened. "You know nothing of what I've seen."

"I know enough," she countered. "Wake up and see what's before you."

The chamber fell into uneasy silence as she walked toward the door. Before leaving, she turned back one last time. "I call for a vote. Which of you will stand against the Fates?"

Hands rose slowly. Tuck. Myself. Archer, though his vote carried no weight here. Serene, surprisingly. Raeth. Veurs. Orathis. Nyaxis.

Against us stood Ezra. Vesalia. Kaelor. Bellatora. Aeris. Vaelen.

Eight to six. A fragile majority.

All eyes turned to Alastor and Irri, who had not voted.

"Well?" Bellatora demanded. "Where do you stand?"

Alastor's eyes met mine across the table and I thought for sure he would stand against me, but instead he looked to Paesha. "I stand nowhere in this conflict."

"Coward," Bellatora spat.

Irri hummed louder. "The broken clock still tells the right time twice a day," she sang softly. "But who remembers to check at those precise moments?"

"Remember," Minerva said, her hand on the door, "the last time we stood against the Fates, I was punished. Who will it be this time?" She looked directly at Ezra. "Your vision showed what would happen if the Huntress died. Did it ever show you what would happen if she lived?"

With that parting question, she swept from the room, leaving us in silence. The fate of the realms hung in the balance, and I had just declared war on those who wove it, in the middle of a room of gods that would stand against me. My power flickered and faded away for a few precious seconds before returning. I could invite Death to stand with us again, give him back the memories I'd taken when I left him in his court, but these fragile alliances would fade on that decision.

As Minerva's footsteps faded down the hallway, I rose from my seat, golden threads of power flowing from my fingertips to seal the chamber doors. The light coalesced into an impenetrable barrier, cutting us off from the rest of the castle.

"What the fuck, Rev?" Bellatora shouted, her hand moving to the hilt of her sword.

"Insurance," I replied coolly, returning to my place at the head of the table. "Before any of you leave this room, you have a choice to make."

I let my power pulse visibly around me, a reminder of who and what I was. "Either I take your memories of this meeting or you bargain with me to keep silent about what was discussed here."

Kaelor's laughter echoed through the chamber. "You would dare use your power against us?"

"I would," I confirmed, meeting his gaze without flinching.

The room fell silent as they contemplated their options. I looked to Paesha, whose fists were held tight together on the table. She rocked slightly, the movement barely noticeable, but there.

"What would this bargain entail?" Veurs asked, his form shifting nervously.

"A promise. Bound by power and oath. In exchange, I will offer each of you something of value."

"And what could you possibly offer that would interest us?" Serene asked, her golden eyes narrowing as they fell down my body.

I smiled thinly. "Knowledge. Secrets I've collected over millennia. Locations of artifacts thought lost to time. Names of mortals whose bloodlines carry specific traits. Access to certain sections of my personal archives."

Tuck shot me a warning glance, but I ignored it. This was a necessary risk. The gods would kill the mortals that carried their blood so they could never rise against them. Gods died by the Fates and their descendants alone. It was a valuable trade. One Archer would have my ass for. As would Paesha. But there would be nothing else of greater value. Only I knew the beginnings of new power.

One by one, they made their choices. Vesalia demanded the location of an ancient hourglass that could freeze a moment without disturbing the flow of time. Serene chose the name of a mortal in a different realm that could draw uncontrollable desire with just his touch. Raeth requested access to my collection of mortal stories, tales I'd preserved from civilizations long turned to dust.

They bargained. I conceded. The weight of each promise settled on my shoulders like chains, binding me to obligations that would drain my already diminishing resources. I was trading away secrets I'd guarded for centuries, locations I'd protected, knowledge I'd hoped never to share, but it was worth it for the greater good.

Alastor stood last, Irri swaying to an unknown tune beside him. "We require nothing from you, Keeper. We will keep your secret. But know this, I will remember, and I'll watch."

I nodded, accepting his terms. He had been neutral in this conflict for too long to suddenly become a threat. Only Ezra remained, his face a perfect mirror of my own, twisted with centuries of bitterness.

"And you, brother? Memory or bargain?"

"I would sooner fall to Death himself than let you use your power on me again," he snarled, rising from his seat. "Never again."

His eyes flicked to Paesha, a cruel smile playing at the corners of his mouth. "Besides, I have so many precious memories I'd hate to lose. Like the feel of your Huntress beneath me. The way she called my name. The taste of her skin." He leaned forward. "I think I'll keep those memories especially close."

Paesha's Remnants raced across the floor toward Ezra, but he merely laughed, stopping them with a casual flick of his wrist.

"Odd that you're still so eager to protect her, brother. Even knowing she spreads her legs for kings now." His gaze shifted to Archer. "Although I suppose that's a matter of perspective. Sharing was never your strong suit."

"Enough," I growled, my power flaring dangerously.

"So sensitive. You know what your problem is, Reverius? You've never learned when to let go." He paused at the threshold, his eyes lingering first on Quill, who had finally looked up from her book, then shifting meaningfully to Archer. "We should chat, Majesty. I have a feeling your story would be quite interesting to my Unmade."

Archer's face hardened, but he said nothing.

"Something to consider, perhaps, when you're done playing house with my brother's leftovers."

With a final smirk, he walked through the barrier I had created as if it were nothing more than mist, a reminder that for all my power, he was still my equal.

The onslaught of pressure from using that much magic to bargain nearly stole my fucking breath, but the price was necessary. Some burdens were meant to be carried alone. I watched as a tear trekked down Paesha's cheek and Archer swiped it away, knowing without a doubt that some weren't.

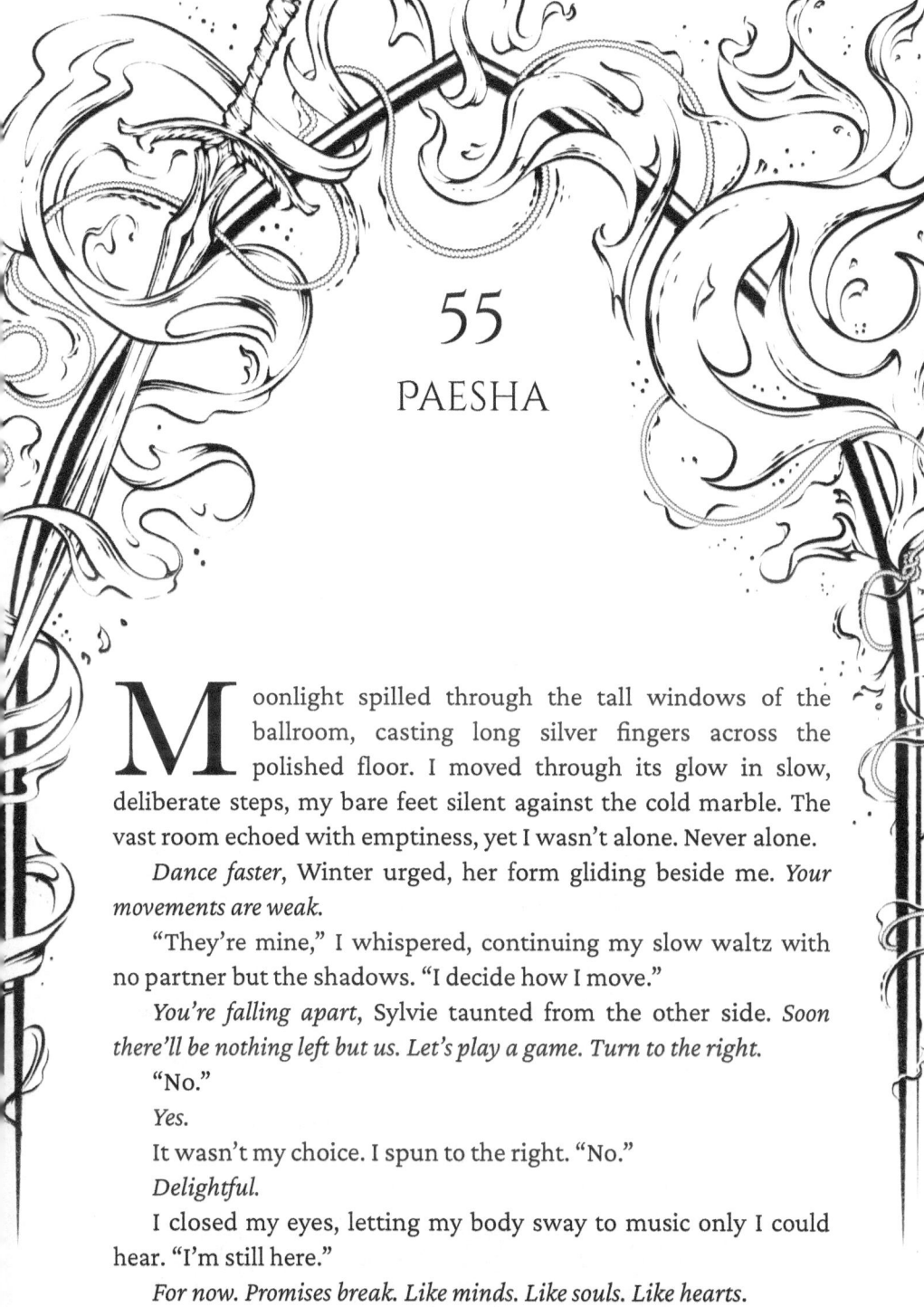

55

PAESHA

Moonlight spilled through the tall windows of the ballroom, casting long silver fingers across the polished floor. I moved through its glow in slow, deliberate steps, my bare feet silent against the cold marble. The vast room echoed with emptiness, yet I wasn't alone. Never alone.

Dance faster, Winter urged, her form gliding beside me. *Your movements are weak.*

"They're mine," I whispered, continuing my slow waltz with no partner but the shadows. "I decide how I move."

You're falling apart, Sylvie taunted from the other side. *Soon there'll be nothing left but us. Let's play a game. Turn to the right.*

"No."

Yes.

It wasn't my choice. I spun to the right. "No."

Delightful.

I closed my eyes, letting my body sway to music only I could hear. "I'm still here."

For now. Promises break. Like minds. Like souls. Like hearts.

I spun faster, as if I could outrun their voices, their doubts, their cruel certainties. The room tilted and whirled around me, moonlight and shadow blending into a dizzying kaleidoscope.

"I can hold on," I said, more to myself than to them. "I can—"

"Paesha?"

I froze mid-spin, nearly losing my balance. Archer stood in the doorway, his golden hair disheveled, as if he'd run his fingers through it too many times. He wore simple clothes, loose trousers and a plain white shirt with the sleeves rolled up rather than the formal attire expected of a king. The crown was noticeably absent.

"I'm sorry," I said quickly, smoothing down my dress with trembling hands. "Did I wake you?"

He shook his head, stepping into the room. "Couldn't sleep. Apparently neither could you."

He sees the madness in you. He's afraid.

"Stop it," I muttered.

"The voices?" he asked softly.

I nodded, too exhausted to maintain the pretense.

"What are they saying?"

"The usual. That I'm falling apart. That Thorne will leave again. That you're afraid of me." My voice caught on the last words.

Without hesitation, Archer stepped closer and took my hands in his. They were warm and callused, steady against my cold, trembling fingers. "Well, they're wrong. About all of it."

"Are they?"

"Absolutely." He gave my hands a gentle squeeze. "Thorne would walk through fire to get back to you. And as for being afraid of you?" A small, crooked smile touched his lips. "The only thing about you that scares me is how terrifyingly good you are at cards."

I laughed, unexpected and fragile. "That's just skill."

"It's cheating, is what it is," he countered, his smile widening. "But I've learned to live with the humiliation."

The voices receded slightly, as if driven back by the simple warmth of his presence, the familiar cadence of our banter. These moments of clarity felt like gifts now, precious and all too fleeting.

"Dance with me," Archer said suddenly.

"What?"

"Dance with me," he repeated, already adjusting his grip on my hands, placing one on his shoulder while his other settled at my waist. "It's better than standing here listening to whatever lies they're feeding you."

"There's no music," I pointed out.

"Since when has that stopped you? Come on, Fingers. Let me lead for once."

"Everytime I let you lead, we do something reckless."

"Exactly. I'm nothing if not predictable. And charming."

"So humble," I said, smiling up at him.

"Someone has to carry the torch, Fingers. It's a tough job, but I'm willing to make the sacrifice."

"So selfless. Do they give medals for that kind of heroism?"

"They should. I've written several strongly worded letters on the subject." Archer's eyes crinkled at the corners. "No response yet, but I remain optimistic."

I snorted. "I didn't know you could write."

"I'm a man of many mysteries," he said, dipping me suddenly. I grabbed his shoulders, heart lurching.

"And zero warning," I muttered when he pulled me upright.

"Warnings ruin the fun." He guided me through a series of steps that weren't quite a waltz, but too coordinated to be random, though he barely missed my toes half the time. "Besides, you're always ready for anything. It's your most annoying quality."

"One of many, I'm sure."

"Oh no," he said, his voice softening, making my chest tighten. "Your ability to alphabetize anything in under thirty seconds is much more annoying. Especially when you rearrange my bookshelf."

"Your 'system' was putting the tall books next to short books so they'd 'feel better about themselves.'"

"It was working." His hand pressed more firmly against my lower back as he guided me around an imaginary obstacle. "You ruined their therapy."

As the dance continued, I followed stiffly, too caught up in the voices to surrender. But Archer was persistent, his steps sure and steady, his gaze never leaving mine.

"Focus on me," he said quietly. "Just me. Not them."

I tried, concentrating on the rhythm of our steps, the warmth of his hand at my waist, the solid reality of him against the chaos in my mind. The friend. The man that stood before me, loving me beyond reason. Steadfast and humble. Slowly, almost imperceptibly, the voices faded into the background.

"Eyes on me, Fingers. I've got you. You'll never fall."

We moved across the ballroom, our shadows stretching and contracting in the moonlight. The dance became easier with each turn, each step bringing me more fully back into myself.

"Can I tell you a secret?"

The half quirk of his smile made my heart ache. "Always."

"I'm worried I've already fallen."

Archer's hand tightened slightly on my waist. "Then I'll catch you. I'll always catch you, Paesha. I promised, remember?"

I did remember. The night after we'd discovered the truth about the Treeis bond, he had held my hands and sworn he'd never let me fall.

"I know." I leaned my forehead against his shoulder. "I'm sorry you're stuck with me."

He chuckled, the sound rumbling in his chest. "I would have chosen this. Family doesn't abandon family. Not ever. And especially not when things get hard."

He spun me away from him, yanked me back, and dipped me dramatically. Then froze and looked me dead in the eyes as he stepped away, throwing his hands in the air and spinning around like a wild man, wiggling his hips and losing all sense of any type of dance I'd ever known.

I laughed. He laughed. And then I joined him. Letting everything go. Spinning and spinning and laughing as he ran and slid across the floor, then spun and bowed as if he'd just performed the greatest dance of all time.

"I can see you're jealous," he said. "Obviously, I'm the better dancer, but we can work on your skills. I'll knit and you practice dancing. Eventually you'll figure it out."

I walked over and shoved his chest. "You're the worst."

"You mean the best. It's okay. It's a hard word."

I reached up and messed up his already wild hair. "I think you're my favorite husband."

He threw an arm over my shoulder. "Dibs on telling Thorne. For fun."

"Can't wait to watch him sulk about it," I teased.

He laughed, smoothing a hand over his chest. "He's an excellent sulker."

This man who'd lost so much, who'd never wanted the crown he now wore, had chosen to stand beside me through darkness and madness and pain. Not because of destiny or prophecy, but because his heart was too big to do anything else. He'd brought me back to the light again. As was his power. Minerva was wrong. He wasn't the shield. He was the light in the darkness. My light.

A high-pitched giggle followed by the scamper of claws on marble interrupted our dance. We both turned toward the sound as the patter of small feet approached down the hall.

"Sounds like someone else is awake. Want to bet Quill's chasing the dog again?"

"No bet. That's exactly what's happening. We should probably make sure she doesn't wake the entire castle."

Archer nodded, offering his arm with exaggerated formality. "Shall we, Your Highness?"

I rolled my eyes but took his arm. "Lead on, Your Majesty."

We followed the sounds of muffled giggles and excited yipping through the castle, down winding corridors lit by moonlight streaming through tall windows. The trail led us to a set of glass doors standing ajar, opening onto the gardens.

"She's not supposed to be out there alone at night," I whispered, quickening my pace.

"The garden's completely safe. And Boo's with her."

"Boo is approximately the size of a loaf of bread and has the protective instincts of a friendly butterfly."

Archer laughed. "Fair point."

We stepped out into the garden, the night air cool against my skin. The moon hung full and bright overhead, bathing everything in its silvery glow. It took a moment for our eyes to adjust, but then we spotted Quill in a small clearing surrounded by rose bushes. She was spinning in circles, her nightgown billowing around her like a cloud as Boo chased his tail beside her.

Archer put a hand on my arm, stopping me before I could call out to her. "Wait. Look at her. She's happy. So happy I can feel it. Can't you?"

I hesitated, then nodded, moving back into the shadow of a tall hedge. From our vantage point, we could watch without disturbing her joy. She needed that moment after the council of the gods. We'd all been on edge for days.

Quill continued her dance, her wild curls bouncing with each twirl. She laughed when Boo jumped up, trying to catch the hem of her nightgown, the sound pure and untroubled in a way that had become increasingly rare.

Archer whispered, "She deserves this. Moments where she doesn't have to worry about gods or kingdoms or bonds."

"Or me," I added softly.

He turned to me sharply. "That's not what I meant."

"But it's true. She worries about me. You both do."

"Because we love you." He squeezed my hand. "That's how it works, remember?"

Before I could respond, a movement at the edge of the garden caught my attention. Minerva emerged from the shadows, her cane tapping softly against the stone path. She paused when she saw Quill, her normally severe expression softening as she watched the child dance. She stood there for several moments before she spotted us, dipped her chin and moved in our direction.

"I guess none of us are sleeping these days," she said.

"Guess not," Archer answered, but something in his posture changed, a sudden alertness that I felt more than saw. His hand tensed in mine, and his gaze darted around the garden with newfound intensity.

"What?"

"I don't know." His voice had dropped, taking on an edge I rarely heard. "Something feels wrong."

I followed his gaze, scanning the garden more carefully. The shadows between the hedges seemed deeper somehow, more substantial.

Archer released my hand, already moving forward. "Stay here," he ordered, his voice no longer that of my friend but of a warrior sensing danger.

"Archer—"

But he was already striding toward Quill, his movements fluid and purposeful. I felt the thrumming of our bond, the burning knot on my shoulder warming in response to his alarm.

Quill looked up as he approached. "Archie! Look at my dance!"

"It's beautiful, Pencil," he said, his tone deliberately light though his eyes never stopped scanning the garden. "But it's late. Let's get you back inside."

The shadows behind the nearby statue shifted. Aeris lunged from behind the marble, snatching Quill by the arm. The child's scream pierced the night as she was yanked backward against the goddess's chest.

My Remnants exploded outward in a tidal wave of darkness, fueled by primal rage that scorched through my veins like wildfire. They surged across the garden, reaching, clawing as I raced forward.

"Let her go!" The words tore from my throat, raw and desperate.

Minerva was already moving, her frail appearance melting away as she raised her hand. But it was too late, everything was happening too fast.

Boo launched himself at Aeris, tiny teeth bared in fierce protection, but my Remnants wrapped around him like a blanket, holding him back, protecting him as they continued to race forward. If anything happened to that dog... Quill screamed again, struggling and twisting in the goddess's grip. My shadows wrapped around Quill's stomach, pulling her toward me, but Aeris's grip on her was iron tight.

Archer was a blur of motion, covering the distance between them in heartbeats. His face transformed by a fury I'd never seen before. With one powerful movement, he tore Quill from Aeris's grasp, shoving the child safely behind him.

Then the world stopped. In one motion. One fraction of a second. One devastating breath. Aeris plunged a blade into Archer's chest with terrible precision. The sound of metal against bone echoed across the garden, obscene in its finality. Time fractured. I fractured. Archer stumbled backward, his eyes wide with shock. Blood bloomed across his white shirt like spilled wine, darkening from crimson to black in the moonlight. His mouth opened, forming words I couldn't hear through the roaring in my ears.

"Archer!" My scream seemed to come from somewhere outside of myself.

He fell to his knees, then collapsed backward onto the stone path. His blood spread beneath him, dark and unstoppable. Nothing else mattered. Not Aeris. Not her knife. Not her triumphant smile. Not Minnie as she surged for the evil goddess. Only him. Always him. My light.

I crashed to my knees beside him, pressing my hands over the wound as if I could force his life back inside through sheer will. Blood welled between my fingers, hot and slick and relentless. Too much blood. Far too much.

"No, no, no," I chanted, a desperate prayer to uncaring gods. "You look at me, Archer Bramwell. Don't you dare close your eyes. Please, Archer. Please stay with me."

Quill threw herself down beside us, her small hands frantically patting his face. "Archie! Archie, wake up! You can't sleep now!"

His eyelids fluttered, finding mine with painful clarity despite the life draining from them. "Paesha," he whispered, my name a broken sound on bloody lips.

"Don't..." I begged, pressing harder on the wound. My heart

hammered against my ribs, threatening to shatter them. "Save your strength. We'll get help. We'll fix this. Just hold on."

But we both knew it was a lie. The blade had pierced his heart. *His* heart. The one that loved so hard it hurt. The one so pure, the world didn't deserve it. No one did. And no healer could undo this damage. No power could mend what was broken.

"I'm sorry," he murmured, blood bubbling at the corner of his mouth when he tried to smile. "Not how... I planned to spend... my night."

A laugh that was half sob escaped me. "Only you would joke now, you impossible man."

Quill clutched his hand, her tears falling onto his face like rain. "You can't go! You promised we'd bake a cake tomorrow! You said —" Her voice broke. "You said you'd dance with me at the summer ball! I have a blue dress that matches your eyes. I have a blue dress."

Archer's gaze shifted to her, infinite tenderness replacing the pain in his eyes for a moment. "Rain check... on that dance... Pencil."

"No! No rain checks!" Quill's voice rose to a wail. "You need to stay! We need you! I need you. You're mine. And I'm yours. You said, Archie. You said!"

I felt the familiar sting behind my eyes, the lump in my throat. The burn of unrelenting heartache. "I'll fall, Toes. I'll fall if you're not here to catch me. Gods. Please."

"I'll be so good," Quill promised. "I'll never use my magic again and I'll take my baths and I'll make sure Boo never steals anything from the kitchen. I'll go to bed when I'm supposed to and I'll never sass back again. I'll do that for you, okay. Okay?" Those giant eyes of hers, full of tears flashed to me. "Why isn't he answering?"

He lifted a trembling hand to touch her cheek, but the strength was already leaving him. His fingers barely grazed her skin before falling back to the ground.

I couldn't breathe. My throat closed around words that wouldn't matter, pleas that wouldn't be answered. The tears burning down my face felt like acid, etching permanent tracks of grief into my skin. This would be the loss that ended me.

"Please," I whispered, bending close to his ear. "Please don't leave us. Not you. I can't lose you."

His eyes found mine again, clouding with tears of his own. "You'll be okay," he whispered. "Both of you. You're stronger... than you know."

"I don't want to be strong," I sobbed, resting my forehead against his. "I want you to live."

The Treeis mark on my shoulder burned cold, a terrible emptiness spreading from it as our bond began to fray. I could feel him slipping away, the connection between us weakening with each labored breath.

Quill must have felt it too. Her small body convulsed with sobs as she threw herself across his chest. "Please, Archie! Please don't go! I need to tell you... I need to tell you how much I love you! I need you to hear it in your heart, okay? Can you hear how much I love you? Can you feel it? I'll show you forever, okay. Everyday."

"He knows, baby," I whispered, my voice breaking. "He knows how much you love him." I looked down at Archer, his face growing paler with each passing second. "And gods, he loves you back. So hard and so unwavering."

A faint smile touched his lips. "That part... was easy," he breathed.

He coughed, more blood staining his lips. His hand found mine, squeezing with the last of his strength.

"Listen," he whispered, his voice fading to almost nothing. "Not your fault. Never... your fault. Tell Thorne... protect you both. Like me."

"Tell him yourself," I begged, clinging to his rapidly cooling fingers.

But his eyes were already losing focus, the vibrant blue dimming like stars fading at dawn. "So stubborn," he murmured, the ghost of a smile touching his lips. "Always loved... that about you..."

His chest rose once more, then fell still. The Treeis mark flared with icy fire, then went numb, as if a piece of my soul had been carved away.

Quill's scream shattered the night, a sound so raw and primal it smothered everything. Her power flooded around us in waves of pure anguish, withering every living thing in the garden. Roses crumbled to dust. Trees bent and twisted as if in physical pain. The air grew heavy with sorrow, pressing down like a physical weight.

I yanked her away from Archer's body, pulling her into my arms as we collapsed together on the cold stone. I rocked her back and forth, our tears mingling as we mourned the loss of our bond, the loss of the best of us, the loss of the greatest good either of us would ever know in our lives.

Her small body shook with grief too enormous for her frame to contain. The sky darkened above us as clouds gathered, responding to her power as it blanketed the world in sorrow. Through the haze of our shared agony, I vaguely heard Minerva shouting in the distance. Her voice penetrated the fog of grief, insistent and commanding.

Quill looked up, her tear-stained face transforming as sadness ignited into something else. Something furious and ancient. Raw and vicious. Because sadness is only the root from which anger grows.

I stood, gently setting Quill aside. My legs felt foreign beneath me, as if they belonged to someone else. Someone who could still walk in a world where Archer no longer existed.

"I know it hurts, Quilly. And you can feel those feelings. Every one of them. Fuck the world that would tell you to be less. Feel less. You feel exactly everything you need to feel. Let the world burn, my girl. But give me a second to breathe, okay? And then I'll come right back and I will stand beside you in the darkness. Just like Archie would."

She nodded, eyes sliding back to his slain body. I commanded the Remnants to slide back to her. To drop that pup in her lap and hope for a few brief moments she could breathe. Because I had something, someone, to take care of.

Minerva had Aeris pinned to the garden wall with magic. The

goddess's feet dangled above the ground as an invisible force held her by the throat. Aeris clawed at the air, her perfect face contorted with rage and fear.

Wordlessly, Minerva extended her arm, offering me a sword. But not just any blade. Levanya's. A weapon of power. I took it, the weight familiar in my hand, as if it had always been meant for me. It only made the ache in my heart deepen. I didn't want anything to fit me perfectly anymore. Because that was his role and he was gone.

"Please," Aeris gasped as I approached, her eyes wide with sudden terror. "Daughter—you don't understand—"

"I understand perfectly," I said, my voice hollow, empty of everything but grief and rage. "You took him from us. But good news mother, now you won't have to worry about the Fates punishment for killing a mortal king."

"Who do you think sent me—"

I drove the blade through her heart before she could finish, twisting it with a savagery I hadn't known I possessed. I yanked it back and shoved it forward as I yelled, trying to release whatever had died inside of me when he took that last breath. It didn't work. Blood spilled down the front of her dress, glowing faintly in the darkness. I yanked the sword back and struck again. And again as Aeris screamed.

"Paesha," Minerva said.

I ignored her, dragging my shadows forward to lift Aeris's drooping face until she looked at me. "You will fucking watch as I take from you, as you've always taken from me. It wasn't enough that you left me, was it? You had to take him too. You fucking monster. That was my family. He was everything you never were. That man helped teach me what family means and it sure as hell never looked like this. In all the eons to come, in all the stories they tell of gods and their fall, your name will be nothing but a footnote in my legend—the goddess so worthless even her own daughter forgot her name. You took everything from me," I hissed, tears streaming down my face as rage consumed me. "Now I take everything from you. Not merely your life, but your legacy. Your memory. Your divinity. It's mine now, and I'll use it to build a world where no child ever feels as abandoned as you made me feel. And I'll do it in his fucking name. The only one that ever mattered."

I watched her die. I watched her take her final breath and hoped like hell it would soothe something, anything in my soul. But it didn't. It only made me hate her more. She'd died too fucking fast. She hadn't hurt enough. Her power rushed into me, a torrent of raw energy that seared through my veins like liquid fire. The transformation from demigod to goddess crashed over me in waves of unbearable intensity. My body was barely able to contain the vastness of what I was becoming. Nor the anguish of what I was leaving behind.

But the power meant nothing. Less than nothing. What use was godhood in a world without my best friend? I turned back to where Archer lay, still and silent under the weeping sky. Quill had curled against his side, her small hand clutching his, as if she could will warmth back into those fingers through sheer determination.

Rain fell, gentle at first, then in heavy sheets that soaked us all, washing Archer's blood from the stones but not from my hands. Never from my hands.

I fell to my knees, covered in his blood, soaked and broken. And then I crawled to them, shrouded in rage and wrath and fear and sadness, a goddess and queen born from loss, baptized in the blood of the man I couldn't save.

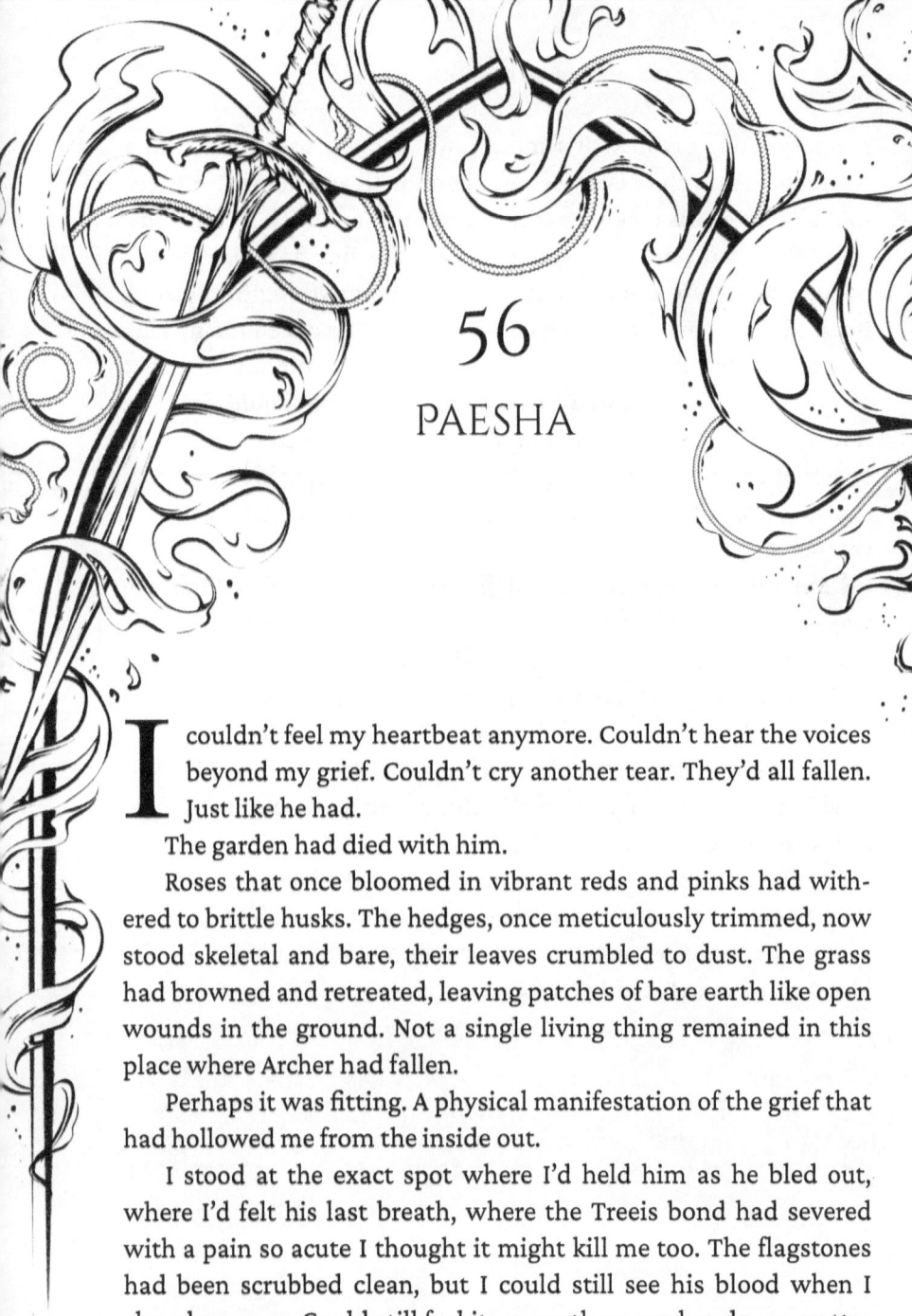

56

PAESHA

I couldn't feel my heartbeat anymore. Couldn't hear the voices beyond my grief. Couldn't cry another tear. They'd all fallen. Just like he had.

The garden had died with him.

Roses that once bloomed in vibrant reds and pinks had withered to brittle husks. The hedges, once meticulously trimmed, now stood skeletal and bare, their leaves crumbled to dust. The grass had browned and retreated, leaving patches of bare earth like open wounds in the ground. Not a single living thing remained in this place where Archer had fallen.

Perhaps it was fitting. A physical manifestation of the grief that had hollowed me from the inside out.

I stood at the exact spot where I'd held him as he bled out, where I'd felt his last breath, where the Treeis bond had severed with a pain so acute I thought it might kill me too. The flagstones had been scrubbed clean, but I could still see his blood when I closed my eyes. Could still feel its warmth on my hands, no matter how many times I washed them.

My black mourning dress hung heavy on my shoulders, the same one I'd worn when they'd lowered his body into the ground three days ago. The weight of his crown still felt wrong on my head, a foreign, unwelcome presence conferred on me in a hasty ceremony after the funeral.

I bent down, my fingers tracing the outline of where he had lain. The stone was cold, unyielding and indifferent to the tragedy it'd witnessed.

"You shouldn't be here."

Thorne's voice was gentle but firm as he approached from behind me. He wore mourning clothes as well, though he had exchanged the formal attire from the funeral for something simpler today. The shadows under his eyes spoke of sleepless nights that matched my own. Of the way he'd paced outside my door, guilt ridden for not being here, and anxious that another god would come for me.

He'd been following the whispers of Ezra's Unmade. Making sure there was no word of the Fates from anyone. He'd been protecting us all, and felt like he'd protected no one.

"Where else would I be?" I asked, not looking up, not taking my eyes from the spot where Archer had slipped away from us.

Thorne didn't answer. Instead, he knelt beside me, his shoulder brushing mine in silent solidarity. The warmth of him was the only thing that felt real anymore, the only thing that anchored me to a world that had lost all its color, all its joy.

"I keep seeing it," I whispered, voice raw from days of crying, from the eulogy I had somehow managed to deliver without collapsing. "Over and over. The way he moved to protect her. The way he smiled at me even as he was dying." I closed my eyes, but it only made the images sharper, more vivid. "The way his eyes looked when there was nothing left in them."

Thorne's hand found mine, his fingers curling around my own with careful tenderness. "I know."

And he did know. He had watched me shatter, had held me as I screamed myself hoarse against his chest, had wiped away tears that seemed endless. Had stood beside me at the funeral as I placed a deck of cards in Archer's cold hands, as I whispered goodbye to a man who had changed everything. As I held Quill while she sobbed until she'd cried herself to sleep every night since.

"He wouldn't want you to torture yourself like this."

"How would you know what he'd want? He's gone." The words were cruel, designed to wound, to push him away because the comfort he offered made the pain too real. But Thorne didn't flinch, didn't pull away.

He simply tightened his grip on my hand. "Because I knew him. Because he loved you. Because he would have done anything to spare you pain. Long before that fucking bond. He was always yours."

The truth of it hit me with physical force, stealing my breath. Archer had died protecting what he loved most. He had stepped between danger and Quill without hesitation, without a thought for his own safety. It was who he was, down to his bones.

My fingers dug into the cold stone, seeking purchase against the wave of grief threatening to pull me under. "The crown feels wrong. It should be his."

At the funeral, they had placed the crown on the casket first, a final honor for the king who'd been hesitant to rule. Then, with terrible finality, they had lifted it and placed it on my head instead. The weight of it had nearly driven me to my knees. Only Quill's steady presence at my side had kept me upright. "It should be his, but look what it cost him."

His free hand came up to brush a strand of hair from my face, his touch feather-light. "That was Ezra's doing. And Aeris's. Not yours."

The mention of their names sent a surge of white-hot rage through me, momentarily burning away the numbing grief. My mother, who had plunged a knife into Archer's heart without hesitation. Ezra, whose plans aligned with the Fates and set this all in motion. The Fates, who'd manipulated us all like pieces on a game board.

"I know they wanted this. I know they put the crown on the mad queen's head to watch me condemn the mortal world. You heard what Tuck said. About the bond. Severing it was likely always their plan."

"I heard him say what happens to the survivor of a severed Treeis bond. But they never saw Quill wrapped up in that and you know it. She was never supposed to be part of it. Your soul won't wither. I know because it's half mine."

I nodded, swallowing back the ache. "You know Quill asks for him? Every night before sleep. Every morning when she wakes. As if she's forgotten momentarily, and then remembers all over again. She's old enough to understand, but far too young to accept it." I swallowed against the tightness in my throat. "I don't know what to tell her."

"Tell her the truth," Thorne said. "That he loved her more than life. That he wouldn't have changed his choice, even knowing the outcome."

"Would that comfort you? If it were me in the ground instead of him?"

The pain that flashed across his face was answer enough.

"That's what I thought," I whispered.

I looked out across the dead garden, at the statue where Aeris had hidden, at the path where Archer had made his final stand. So much loss contained in this small space. So much that could never be recovered.

"My mother knew what would happen if she threatened Quill. Archer would protect her at any cost."

"Yes. She knew exactly what she was doing."

The power that had flooded me when I killed Aeris stirred beneath my skin, a reminder of what I had become. A goddess with even more power. Though now I could feel the wane of it. The silence when it drifted away for no reason. The plight of the gods.

"I want them to suffer. All of them. I want them to feel what we're feeling. I want them to know who they've taken from us."

Instead of cautioning me against vengeance, instead of urging restraint as I'd expected, Thorne simply nodded. "They will," he promised, and there was something terrible in his voice, something that spoke of a wrath as deep and vast as my own.

Small footsteps approached from behind us, the quiet shuffle drawing my attention. Quill stood at the edge of the dead garden, Boo clutched in her arms like a lifeline. She wore black like the rest of us, her wild curls tamed into a severe braid that made her look older, harder. The deck of cards Archer had left behind peeked from her pocket, a constant companion now.

"I made something," she said, her voice small but steady. "For him."

She approached slowly, her footsteps careful on the withered ground, as if afraid of disturbing the quiet solemnity of the place. When she reached us, she knelt, forming a small triangle of grief around the spot where he had fallen.

From her pocket, she withdrew a small, carved wooden figure. It was rough, clearly made by inexperienced hands, but unmistakably a heart. Within it, she'd pressed one of Archer's coins, the metal gleaming dully in the afternoon light.

"Tuck helped me make it," she said, placing it gently on the ground. "He said Archer carried his heart on his sleeve, so I thought..." She trailed off, her lower lip trembling.

I reached for her, pulling her against my side. "It's perfect. He would love it."

She nodded against my shoulder, her fingers still resting on the carving. "I miss him."

"I know, Quilly. We miss him too."

The three of us knelt there in silence, surrounded by death and decay, united by loss and the fierce, burning need to make it right somehow. To make it matter.

Behind us, I heard the soft clearing of a throat. Tuck stood at the garden's edge. "The Gods are waiting. It's time."

I rose slowly, helping Quill to her feet, feeling Thorne do the same beside me. The small wooden heart remained on the ground, a solitary marker of life and love in this place of death.

"We're coming," I said, squaring my shoulders beneath the weight of the crown I never wanted.

As we walked away, I felt the power stirring within me, the dual forces of renewal and destruction. The stolen mortal power.

The simplicity of the Huntress power. All of it. It was time to turn my attention to destruction.

To vengeance.

To making them all pay for what they had taken from us.

For Archer, who had deserved so much more than the brief life he had been given.

For Quill, who would grow up without his laughter, his guidance, his love.

For myself, left to navigate a world that made no sense without him in it.

For all of us, broken in ways that could never fully heal.

They would pay. And I would be the one to collect the debt.

I touched the crown, feeling it transform in my mind from a burden into a weapon. Acting monarch, they had called me.

I would act, indeed.

Starting right fucking now.

57

THORNE

The gods filed into the council chamber like vultures to a corpse. They settled around the ancient table with their false solemnity, as if this were any ordinary meeting. As if the world hadn't fucking shattered days ago. As if Archer Bramwell wasn't dead and hearts weren't aching while they played at politics.

Minerva settled into her seat with quiet dignity. Tuck stood behind her, arms crossed, his usual stoic mask firmly in place though the grief in his eyes betrayed him. I recognized that look, the same hollow emptiness I saw every time I caught my own reflection. Loving mortals was hard. We'd been on this cycle forever, but it never got easier. Especially with a life cut far too short.

Raeth arrived next, his calculating gaze sweeping the room, lingering on Paesha with poorly disguised hunger. My power flared instinctively, ready to rip his fucking throat out if he so much as breathed wrong in her direction. She was mine. And that child's.

They all knew of Archer's death, of course. The "unfortunate passing" of Stirling's young king had spread through the realms with remarkable speed. But they knew only the lie we'd crafted: that he'd been found unresponsive in his chambers, that no one knew what had happened. A convenient lie to hide the truth until Paesha was ready to give it. Until she was ready to unleash hell. Likely in less than an hour. She'd spent days holding back. Whispering to voices that seemed quieter in her grief, but the swell of her power was pressing on her and she was done with all of it.

My Ever sat at the head of the table, her face a carefully composed mask that revealed nothing of the storm that raged beneath. I felt it though, the darkness inside her calling to mine like a siren song. The crown sat on her dark hair—not actually Archer's crown since she'd refused to wear it again after the funeral—but one forged from Levanya's sword. A warrior's crown for a warrior queen. My warrior queen. And his. Forevermore she was his.

Quill hadn't left her side since that night, as if afraid she might disappear too if they were separated. Now she sat in a chair pulled close to Paesha's, her small hand clutched in the queen's larger one, Archer's deck of cards still visible in her pocket. The child's eyes were too old, too knowing for her face, haunted by what she had witnessed. By what she had lost. Another thing I couldn't fix. Another failure to add to my growing list of shit I couldn't control. I should have fucking been there.

Serene was the last to arrive, draped in mourning colors that somehow managed to leech the candlelight from the room. "Such tragedy," she murmured, her voice like silk over steel. "The young king had such... potential."

My fingers tightened on the back of Paesha's chair until the wood creaked in protest. Serene, Goddess of Lust and Loss, would be feeding well these days, drawing power from the grief that saturated the castle, the city, the realm. My grief. Paesha's grief. Fucking vulture. But she was here. And she didn't have to be.

The heavy door was about to swing closed when footsteps echoed in the corridor beyond.

"Wait." The voice was smooth, amused, laced with arrogance. "Surely you weren't planning to start without us?"

Alastor strode into the chamber as if he owned them, Irri trailing behind him like a brightly colored shadow. Her eyes were clearer today, more focused than I'd seen them since her return from the Forgotten. She met my gaze with unsettling directness, a smile playing at her lips.

Paesha sat a little straighter. "Alastor. We obviously weren't expecting you."

"Clearly." He made his way around the table, pausing behind Quill's chair. The child stiffened, her shoulders drawing up toward her ears as she pressed closer to Paesha. My power surged beneath my skin, ready to rip him apart if he so much as touched either of them.

He leaned down, close enough that only Paesha and I could hear his next words. "I'm not here for you, Keeper. I'm here because I always liked the thieving king." His eyes glittered with something that might have been genuine regret, though it was gone before I could be certain. "And I have a feeling you're hiding something. This sudden action tastes like vengeance, and we're here for that alone."

Paesha's expression didn't change, but I felt the subtle shift in her power, the darkness curling at the edges of her being, eager to be unleashed. My own darkness answered, reaching for hers with hungry tendrils. We were bound in this, as in all things.

Her voice carried the weight of command that came naturally to her. "Take a seat then. If you're brave enough to see this through."

"Oh, I wouldn't miss it." Alastor settled into an empty chair, Irri perching on its arm like an exotic bird.

The door closed with a heavy finality, sealing us in with our secrets, our grief, our burning need for justice.

"Why is the child here again?" Serene asked, her eyes fixed on Quill with poorly disguised distaste. "Surely even you can see the danger in this now."

The contempt in her voice made my power stir, eager to show her exactly what I thought of her concern. To hell with diplomacy and allies, I wanted to wrap my hands around her throat until that musical voice cracked. But Paesha squeezed Quill's hand, a silent signal for calm that I read as clearly as if she'd shouted. For her, I swallowed my rage. Only for her.

"The child stays," she said, her tone brooking no argument.

Serene exchanged a look with Raeth, the God of Joy and Sorrow, something unspoken passing between them. I caught it, another fucking tally in the growing list of gods to keep my eyes on.

"The Fera has no place in these discussions. Particularly if there's any possibility of traveling to Etherium. As an... unknown, she should not be permitted near our sacred realms."

Paesha's eyes hardened, and I stepped closer, my hand moving to her shoulder, a reminder that she wasn't alone in this, that I was here. Through every battle, every nightmare, every godsdamned apocalypse if necessary.

Before she could respond, Minerva cleared her throat. "I know exactly what the girl is. And that is all any of you need to trouble yourselves with." Her gaze swept the table, daring anyone to challenge her. None did. Even Alastor, who had been old when most of them were newly formed, inclined his head in reluctant deference. "Now, perhaps we should move on to the matter at hand."

All eyes turned to Paesha, waiting. I could feel the weight of expectation pressing down, the tension drawn taut as a bowstring. Whatever she decided here, whatever path she chose, would ripple through the realms with consequences none of us could fully predict. But she would lead, and I would follow. Forever. Until the stars burned out and the last realm crumbled. Until the end of everything.

"I'm not going to be a hero today, so if that's what you've come to witness, you can leave. Today's not about doing the right thing. It's not even about good versus evil. If it were, you're all standing on the wrong side. I have no fucking desire for happily ever after.

Only blood. And destruction. I'm taking a page from an old friend's book and doing something reckless."

Archer's words. His philosophy. His legacy that lived on through her choices. The grief sat so heavily in the room, Quill's power no doubt, I could hardly swallow around it. But alongside it was fierce pride. Paesha would be magnificent, terrible, unstoppable. And I'd be right beside her, carving a bloody path wherever *she* directed.

Power rolled off her in waves, darkness seeping from her skin like smoke, spreading across the floor, climbing the walls until the entire room was smothered in shadow. Only Quill remained untouched, a small island of light amid the encroaching dark.

Our company, the gods that had agreed to help us, shifted uncomfortably in their seats. Even Alastor, who had seen this power firsthand, watched with newfound wariness. Good. Let them be afraid. Let them see what became of those who crossed us, who took what was ours, who broke the rules of their own making.

Paesha stood, pulling a dagger from her thigh and twisting it between her fingers. A gesture she'd no doubt learned from Death's Maiden. "This is your last chance to walk away. Once we leave this room, you either stand beside me or beneath me."

I stepped forward, drawing on my power to open the portal to Etherium. Golden light spilled from my hands, cutting through the darkness, creating a doorway. My power always answered her call, as I did. Just as I always fucking would.

"Choose," Paesha commanded, rising to her feet, her hand still firmly holding Quill's.

One by one, the gods made their choice. Minerva and Tuck moved to stand behind Paesha without hesitation. Alastor and Irri exchanged a look before joining them, curiosity and anticipation evident in their stance. Orathis hesitated, calculating the odds as he always did, before stepping forward. Veurs, Raeth and Nyaxis were slow to rise, but eventually only Serene remained seated, her expression unreadable.

"The Fates are not to be trifled with," she warned. "Not even by gods."

"Then it's fortunate I'm more than that now," Paesha replied, though none at the table save our inner circle understood the full truth of her words. None knew of Aeris's death. Of Paesha's ascension. Of what my Ever had become.

"They will see us coming. Likely they already have. That's how they work," Orathis warned.

Paesha tilted her head to the side.

Irri mirrored it. "That sounds like fear. Interesting."

Serene's eyes narrowed, but she rose with fluid grace and joined us. "Your funeral."

"No," Paesha's gaze found mine. "That's already happened. This is something else entirely."

In that moment, I knew with unshakable certainty that I would follow her anywhere, into battle, into darkness, into Death's Court and beyond if necessary. Not because of destiny or ancient bonds, but because she was right. Because she deserved justice. Because Archer deserved to be avenged. And because I loved her with everything I was, everything I had ever been, everything I would ever be.

With a gesture, I widened the portal, feeling the familiar strain as reality bent to my will. The path to Etherium lay open before us, shimmering with golden light.

Without a word, the gods moved to encircle Paesha and Quill, their bodies forming a living shield that would hide them from the Fates' sight. I found myself beside Tuck, his solid presence reassuring as we prepared to cross over. He caught my eye, and something passed between us—understanding, brotherhood, shared loss.

"Ready?" I asked Paesha, offering my hand across the small space between us.

"For him," she said, as if those were the last soft words she'd speak that day.

"For him," Quill said at her side. "And for us too."

Together, we stepped through the portal, crossing from the mortal realm into the twilight world of Etherium. The familiar landscape spread before us, though it was changed from what it had been. It had darkened, edging toward true night. Structures that had stood for millennia were beginning to crumble at their edges. The signs of failing power were everywhere now, impossible to ignore.

We moved as one toward the Fates' domain, the gods maintaining their protective circle around Paesha and Quill. No words were needed; we all understood the gravity of what we were about to do, the lines we were about to cross. Lines I'd happily obliterate for her. For them.

I ripped a door to the Fates, and as we stepped through, three figures materialized, their forms indistinct yet unmistakable.

"You returned? We've ended this."

I shifted forward, drawing their attention to me, away from the shielded figures at our center. My power gathered around my hands, through my body, eager to be unleashed. "We come seeking justice."

"Justice? From us? If anyone deserves justice, it's us. For the wounds of our torment. For being bound to this loom. You forget your place, Keeper."

"Your place," another voice hissed. "Your role."

"Your boundaries," the third finished.

My smile was all teeth and no humor.

Their attention shifted to the assembled gods. "And you bring others? To what end? Do you think numbers will sway us? That we'll bend to your collective will?"

To their credit, the gathered gods remained silent, standing firm despite the pressure of the Fates' displeasure bearing down upon them.

"Only the one with the power to break our hold on the Loom could hope to challenge us," the Fates continued, their voices smug with certainty. "And she is bound to a mortal throne now. She can never set foot in Etherium."

With a silent signal, the gods stepped aside, revealing Paesha and Quill standing at the center of our group. For the first time in my existence, I heard the Fates gasp in genuine shock. The sound was sweeter than any music I'd ever heard.

Paesha stepped forward, darkness swirling around her like a living cloak, her eyes burning with power and purpose. My heart threatened to burst with fierce pride and absolute devotion as I watched her, my Ever, my queen, my everything, come to break the godsdamned world.

"Hello, fuckers."

58

PAESHA

The Fates recoiled as if struck, their long, lanky-ass forms wavering like smoke in a sudden wind. The loom behind them groaned, fading in and out of focus in this strange realm.

"Impossible," they hissed. "You cannot be here. The mortal throne—"

"Binds me? Kind of how you are *bound* to your loom? Funny, my legs still work. My arms are good. Pretty sure I'm free." I stepped forward, feeling the power surge through my veins like liquid fire. "You should really check your rulebook. I think you'll find some amendments."

Their gazes shifted between Quill and me, who stood tall despite her small stature, her chin lifted in defiance. Fear flickered across their ancient faces. It tasted like justice.

Their attention snapped to Thorne. "How? How did you hide this from us? We see all threads, all possibilities."

"Clearly not," I replied, my voice steady despite the storm. The Remnants surged across my skin, hungry for release, for vengeance. I could feel Winter's cold fury, Sylvie's sharp anticipation. But I was hiding something in that corner of my mind. Something Minerva had taught me without speaking.

Make them suffer, Winter urged. *Take everything from them as they took from us.*

Break their precious loom, Sylvie purred.

Minerva stepped forward. Power radiated from her in palpable waves, and I remembered with startling clarity that this was no gentle woman, but Reason and Wrath incarnate. "You simply failed to see."

"We cannot *fail to see.* We see all. We know all. Do not speak to us as if you aren't a traitor, wielding our stolen power."

Minerva laughed. "Your power? You mean the Wrath you forced upon me when your schemes went awry? You stole part of my power and replaced it with a sliver of yours and you've been scheming ever since. In ancient times you saw the Huntress coming. Not as the woman that would break the balance of power. You saw her as the woman that would break *you.* And so you began to weave. You gave Ezra a vision of a path that would lead to her end. But in all of your scheming, you never saw the rest. A story that eluded you. The Huntress's salvation. You couldn't see the meetings to set up the false marriage. You wanted Archer on the throne to bind the Huntress to it as well. You knew of the bond. But not the third piece of it. You never saw Archer Bramwell's death. Nor the Huntress's vengeance on her mother. You don't linger before a mortal queen, nor a struggling demigod. You're looking into the face of a goddess with more power than she should ever wield." Minerva's smile grew wicked. She gestured to Quill, who stood unflinching under the Fates' scrutiny. "And you certainly never saw her."

"The child is nothing," one of the Fates snarled.

"The child," Minerva said, voice dropping to a dangerous whisper, "is one of you."

Silence crashed through the void like a physical force. The loom's creaking faltered. The gods that had come to witness gasped.

"Impossible. We would have known. We would have felt—"

"You would have," Minerva agreed, "had you not been so consumed by your own schemes, so certain of your victory that you failed to notice what was right in front of you. The Fera's rare power manifests differently in each bearer. Some manipulate emotion. Some see glimpses of futures." She looked at Quill with something like pride. "And some can hide threads from those who weave them."

Quill's small hand found mine, squeezing tight. The contact grounded me, reminded me why we were here. Not only for vengeance, though that burned bright and fierce within me, but for her. For us. For the family she deserved.

I let my power flare, darkness and light intertwining around me in a deadly dance. "I was always meant to break you. You knew it and you did everything in your power to prevent it. But fate's funny like that. I'm simply a consequence of your actions. You made me, and now I'm going to destroy you."

They surged forward as one, their forms blurring together in a twisted mass of rage and desperation. Threads whipped through the air like weapons, seeking flesh to pierce, souls to bind.

Thorne moved with supernatural speed, pulling Quill behind him. Minerva and Tuck closed ranks around her, forming a living shield as was always the plan. I saw the understanding in Quill's eyes as she ducked behind them, she had known her role from the beginning. To hide us. To give us this moment of surprise.

Now, Levanya whispered.

I let go.

Power erupted from me in a wave of pure destruction. The air cracked, reality bending under the force of my rage. Darkness poured from my skin like smoke, spreading across the floor, climbing the walls, consuming everything in its path.

The Fates screamed, the sound piercing through dimensions as my power tore into them. I could see it happening, the threads of their being unraveling, their carefully woven schemes coming apart at the seams. Needles of fate meant to pierce mortal flesh now turned inward, embedding in their own skin.

"You took him from us," I snarled, advancing as they retreated.

"You manipulated us all, gods and mortals alike, for your own selfish gain."

Another wave of power surged from me, and the loom groaned under the assault. Nothing else existed. Not the gods at my back, not my family, not even me. Only vengeance. Only anger. Only destruction. Threads snapped, each one releasing a scream. Lives freed from predetermined paths. Destinies unbound from cruel machinations.

The voices in my head reached a fever pitch, a cacophony of screams and pleas and demands. But underneath them all, a single voice rose, clear and steady. *Look*, Levanya whispered. *Look for the thread that binds us to you.*

My Huntress power surged forward, seeking, searching through the tangles that made up the tapestry of fate. I could feel it, my own thread, golden and bright, winding through the loom. But there was another thread twined with it, darker, heavier, binding the voices of my past lives to my soul.

I reached for it, my power coalescing around the thread. The Fates shrieked, lunging toward me in desperate unison.

No! Sylvie screamed.

But it was too late. I seized the thread with hands made of Lost and Broken Things, of Renewal and Destruction. Of every layer of stolen power. Of a soul traversing a thousand lives of murder and love. Of a woman lost in grief and loved despite it. Of a child's frozen fingers scraping along the cobblestone paths of winter alleyways seeking food, refuge. Of a mortal queen, fated to become mad, desperate to be anything else.

And I broke it.

The snap echoed like thunder, reverberating through my bones, my blood, my soul. The Fates collapsed to the ground, writhing in agony as their power bled out of them.

And suddenly, my mind went silent.

The voices—Winter, Sylvie, all of them—vanished in an instant, leaving behind an emptiness so profound it stole my breath. No more whispers. No more screams. No more constant battle for control.

For one perfect moment, there was only me and the blessed, overwhelming silence.

Then, warmth. A gentle presence wrapped around me like an embrace. Levanya, saying goodbye. I felt her press something into my consciousness, not words, but understanding. A second of time. A gift credited to Archer before she faded away with the others.

"Thank you," I whispered.

I turned back to the Fates, still sprawled on the ground, their forms diminished, weakened. My power surged again, fueled now by clarity rather than chaos.

"You will never again manipulate mortal lives. You will never again pit god against god for your amusement. You will never again sacrifice innocents for your schemes."

With each declaration, I bound them tighter to their loom, weaving constraints from their own threads, turning their power back on itself until they were truly prisoners of their own making.

"This is your punishment," I continued, watching as the bindings settled into place. "To remain here, to continue your work, but never again with the freedom to twist fate to your will."

They hissed and struggled against their new bonds, but it was useless. I had become the master of my own fate, and in doing so, had mastered theirs as well. I'd conquered the monster within me by becoming it.

I felt Quill step beside me, her small hand finding mine once more. The Treeis bond hummed between us, stronger now without the interference of the voices. Another thing the Fates had never seen coming was that the bond would protect her from the punishment I'd delivered, It would shield her from their sight even now. She was free too. To become whatever she wanted. In whatever capacity.

I looked back at Thorne, standing exactly where he had been, his hands relaxed at his sides. He hadn't interfered, hadn't tried to take control or guide my actions. He had simply watched, ready to help if needed, but trusting me to lead. His eyes met mine, filled with love and pride and a fierce joy. He'd let me lead.

When I turned back to the Fates, my voice was calm but carried the weight of absolute certainty. "We're leaving now. And I'm taking something with me." I reached into the loom, my fingers finding a specific thread. The key to the Noctus Gate.

The Fates wailed as I pulled it free, but could do nothing to stop me. With the key cradled carefully in my palm, I stepped back.

"Consider this payment for Archer's life," I said. "A small installment on a debt you will never fully repay."

I turned away from them, toward my family. Thorne, Quill, Tuck, Minerva, and the others who had stood with us. The gods who had chosen rightly, who had sided with love over power, with justice over convenience and fear.

"Let's go home," I said softly.

As we approached the tear, a chill ran down my spine. Victory burned sweet in my veins, but underneath lurked the truth. One enemy remained. Perhaps the most dangerous of all. The one that roamed free and had promised his own vengeance.

Ezra.

Taking my life would be his ultimate revenge against his brother, the final move in their ancient game. He could no longer kill me. The Fates couldn't be manipulated to do it either, so in that I was safe. But there were other ways to ruin my entire world.

Perhaps that was why I held the key to the Noctus Gate so tightly in my palm. Not just as payment for Archer's life, but as a weapon for the war still to come.

59

PAESHA

I stood on the balcony of the royal chambers, watching stars emerge. The kingdom spread below me. Stirling, a constellation of flickering lights, streets I'd once walked as a stranger now mine to protect. Mine to rule. The weight of that responsibility pressed down on my shoulders, a crown heavier than the one I wore for formal occasions. It was fine and I could handle this, but gods I wish it came without the threat of a god looming over us.

"You're thinking too loudly again," Thorne said, his voice a warm rumble as he appeared behind me.

I didn't turn, but I felt him, the heat of his body as he stepped closer, the brush of his breath against my hair. "Someone has to do the thinking around here."

His laugh was soft, barely more than an exhale. "Is that what we're calling it now? Because from where I'm standing, it looks an awful lot like brooding."

"I don't brood."

"Of course not." His hands found my waist, gentle but insistent as he turned me to face him. "That's my specialty."

I allowed myself the luxury of looking at him, really looking, at the sharp planes of his face, the slight stubble darkening his jaw, the curve of his mouth that always seemed on the verge of a smile when he looked at me. Immortal, yet somehow so beautifully, perfectly human in moments like these.

"I have a reputation to maintain, you know? I can't have people saying the Queen of Stirling is stealing the Lord of the Salt's signature move."

He captured my hand, bringing it to his lips. "I would gladly cede brooding rights to you, if it meant you'd share this burden. Talk to me. Or I'll get the Quoralis out and you can write it down."

I managed a small laugh. "I don't need your little magic book. It's just been too quiet. Ezra hasn't made a move. It's been a month since the Fates, and nothing. Not even a whisper."

"And that bothers you."

"Doesn't it bother you? He's planning something. I can feel it."

Thorne nodded, not dismissing my concerns, not telling me I was being paranoid. Simply listening, understanding. "He is. But so are we."

"Are we, though? Because it feels like we're... waiting."

His thumb brushed across my cheek, tucking a lock of hair behind my ear before he pulled me close. "A month is a breath to someone as old as we are. Strategic patience isn't the same as waiting."

"Sounds suspiciously like something Minerva would say."

"She's rubbing off on me. Old gods, new tricks."

"I can't lose anyone else."

"You won't."

"You can't promise that."

He pulled back just enough to meet my eyes. "I'll do whatever—"

"Thorne—"

"It's not a bargain. I'm not binding myself to sacrifice anything. I'm simply promising my love. I've existed for eons, Paesha. I've seen empires rise and fall. I've watched stars burn out and new ones ignite. But nothing—*nothing*—has ever been as constant, as certain, as my love for you."

Without warning, he pulled me flush against him, his mouth

claiming mine with an intensity that made my knees weak. I melted into him, my fingers gripping his hair as he backed me against the balcony railing.

The kiss deepened, grew desperate, a silent conversation about fear and love and all the tangled emotions between. His hands skimmed down my sides, settling at my waist, lifting me until I was seated on the railing, his arms a solid wall between me and a terrible fall. Not that I was afraid, not with him holding me like this, like I was the only thing that mattered.

When we finally broke apart, both breathless, I kept my eyes closed for a moment, savoring the lingering taste of him on my lips.

"Marry me," he whispered against my mouth. "Again. For real this time."

My eyes flew open. "What?"

He didn't back down, didn't laugh it off as a joke. Instead, he held my gaze with unwavering certainty. "Marry me. Not for politics, not for power. For us."

"The queen can't —"

"I'm not asking the queen, who likely could marry Lord Thorne Noctus. I'm asking Paesha, the woman who fought for her life in the Maw. The dancer who stole my heart. The mother. The friend. The warrior. The only soul who has ever matched mine across countless lifetimes."

I stared at him. It could be this easy. It could. It felt impossible with the weight of everything else, but it wasn't. Not this. Not him. I shoved myself off the balcony, pushing into his arms. "I'll marry you, Reverius Hawthorne Noctus. Mostly because I know you'll pout if I say no, and no one needs that."

"You're not wrong." He kissed me again, slower this time, a seal on a vow. But before I could promise him anything, I needed an answer to a burning question that had haunted me for far too long.

"Can I ask you something?" My fingers traced the line of his collarbone, a nervous gesture disguised as intimacy.

"Anything."

"If Ezra is your twin, your equal... Could he kill you? Gods can die at the hands of their descendants, their blood. But what about you two?"

Thorne went still, his expression carefully neutral, but I felt the subtle tension in his body. "Why do you ask?"

"Because I need to know what we're facing. What he's capable of. What the threat truly is."

He sighed, stepping back enough to meet my eyes properly. "Yes and no. My brother and I are an equal match, power for power. When mine wanes, his does too. The imbalance affects us both equally."

"Has truly binding the fates helped?"

"It's not getting worse. But it's not getting better either. The damage was done long before we bound them."

A chill ran through me as understanding dawned. "So he could kill you."

"He could," Thorne said, his voice steady. "But he'd be killing himself as well. Our existence is connected in ways even we don't fully comprehend."

"What if that's his plan?" The fear that had been gnawing at me for weeks finally took shape. "What if he's desperate enough to end it all? To take you both out?"

Thorne cupped my face between his hands, his thumbs brushing my cheekbones. "It would never be. Ezra loves existence too much, loves himself too much. His anger toward me is deep, yes, but his survival instinct runs deeper."

"You can't know that for certain."

"I can. I've known him since the beginning of everything, Paesha. Even at his most irrational, his most vengeful, self-preservation has always been at his core."

I wanted to believe him. Needed to. But the memory of Archer's blood on my hands, the sudden, unexpected brutality of his death, made certainty feel like a luxury I couldn't afford.

His eyes hardened. "I'm not wrong."

"Together, then," I whispered, sealing the promise with another kiss.

The night deepened around us, the kingdom slept below, and

for a few precious hours, we allowed ourselves to forget about vengeful gods and looming threats. To simply be Paesha and Thorne, two souls that had finally found their way back to each other after too many lifetimes apart.

Tomorrow would bring its own challenges. Tonight, we had this. And it was enough.

THE GARDEN HAD BEEN RESTORED since Archer's death, new life coaxed from soil that had once turned to dust with grief. Everything had been restored.

Everything except him.

I sat on the stone bench, my eyes fixed on the statue before me. Bronze, gleaming in the sunlight, capturing Archer in a moment of laughter. His head was thrown back, one hand resting casually in his pocket where his coins would have been. Thea had done so well, working from memories, but she hadn't quite captured the crinkle around his eyes when he smiled, hadn't perfectly shown the way his shoulders relaxed when he felt truly at ease.

Still, it was something. A reminder of what we'd lost. What we were still fighting for.

The gods who had accompanied us to the Fates' realm had done exactly as we'd predicted, spread word of my power, my victory, my unbridled rage. Their purpose was never to help, not truly. We'd needed witnesses. Needed them to see what I was capable of, to carry tales back to Ezra, to make him think twice about moving against us openly.

Information was its own kind of weapon. Fear, its own deterrent.

Ezra had gone silent immediately after word spread. No one had seen him. I knew where he was usually. Bouncing between this realm and Etherium. Sometimes he'd go to another, where I hadn't been. Where I couldn't track him with my power. It took us a while to realize that was where he was hiding when I couldn't find him. But still we waited. Day after endless day, growing more restless with each sunrise, more tense with each sunset.

Which was likely his plan.

"I remember when he tried to juggle." Thea's voice broke through my thoughts as she approached, a basket of flowers tucked under one arm. "He dropped every single ball, and then pretended it was intentional."

I smiled despite myself. "He claimed it was a new style. 'Controlled chaos,' he called it."

"Always quick with an excuse." She sat beside me, setting her basket down. "Tuck and I are heading to the Underground. There's a celebration tonight, something to mark the first full harvest since everything changed." She hesitated, glancing at me. "You should come. It would do you good to get out of the castle."

I shook my head. "I can't."

"You can't, or you won't?"

"Both." I ran my fingers over the smooth stone of the bench. "If I sit here, he'll come for me and not everyone else."

"He's not coming for you. He's a coward. And you can't die so there would be no point. Plus, this is why we have guards. And Thorne. And Minerva. And all the other immortal beings who seem determined to hover around you these days." She reached for my hand. "You're allowed to live, Paesha. That's what Archer would want."

"I'm not sure any of us know what Archer would want anymore."

"That's bullshit and you know it." Thea didn't flinch. "He wouldn't want you sitting alone in this garden, staring at his statue every day."

She was right, of course. But that didn't make it any easier to leave, to pretend things were normal, to walk among people celebrating life when all I could think about was death. But that was the cost of a severed Treeis bond. No one knew it as deeply as Quill and I though.

"Another time," I promised.

557

Thea sighed, rising to her feet. "We'll save you some wine. And food. And maybe a small slice of joy, if you decide to come find us."

I watched her walk away, copper hair gleaming in the sun, shoulders straight despite the weight she carried. She didn't look back. She knew me too well for that.

The hours stretched as I remained, watching shadows lengthen across the paths, listening to the distant sounds of the castle. Eventually, I retreated to the small pavilion at the garden's edge, settling into a cushioned chair with a book I'd spent too long trying to read and couldn't get through.

Time slipped by in that peculiar way it had since Archer's death—simultaneously too fast and too slow. The sun had begun to set when I heard a ragged gasping, the unmistakable sound of someone in pain. I set my book aside, already on my feet as Tuck came into view.

He was crawling, his massive frame bent and broken in ways that made my stomach clench. Blood matted his dark hair to his forehead, trailed from his nose, stained his torn shirt. His right arm hung at an unnatural angle, clearly broken. His face was barely recognizable beneath the bruising.

"Gods. Tuck. What happened?"

He coughed, blood spattering the pristine white marble of the pavilion floor. "Ezra," he managed, his voice a ragged whisper. "He has them. Underground. He's—" Another cough, more blood. "He sent me to deliver a message."

Cold dread washed over me. "Them? Who does he have, Tuck?"

"Mortals." His good hand clutched at my arm with surprising strength. "In the Underground. He's going to kill them all unless—"

"Unless I come alone," I finished for him, already knowing how these games worked. "Thorne's with Quill at the orphanage."

Tuck nodded weakly. "Ezra said if Thorne shows up, they all die instantly. Only you." A bitter laugh escaped him, ending in another fit of coughing. "He said to tell you that you can handle this yourself. That you should look at your power."

"Mocking me with my own words. Fucker."

"We'll go get Thorne. He'll know what to do."

"No." I touched his arm, careful to avoid the worst of his injuries. "Ezra will be watching. If Thorne comes charging in, everyone dies, including Thea. Ezra can't kill me, remember. But he can kill Thorne."

"Then what—"

"I go, like he asked. Alone."

"That's exactly what he wants!"

"I know." I knelt beside him. "But I won't be as alone as he thinks."

I could see it in Tuck's face, the determination to run straight to Thorne the moment I left. The certainty that he knew better than me what needed to be done. The stubborn, infuriating male protectiveness that would get everyone killed if I let him act on it.

"Tuck," I said, making my voice honey-sweet, reasonable, the perfect bait for a bargain. "I need you to promise me something."

Wariness crept into his eyes, but pain and desperation clouded his judgment. "What?"

"I need you to swear that you won't tell Thorne where I'm going or what I'm doing."

"I can't do that. He'd never forgive me."

"He'll never know if everything works out." I grasped his hand tighter. "Do we have a deal? Your silence in exchange for my best chance at saving everyone?"

He hesitated, torn between conflicting loyalties, between rationality and emotion. "If you give me a couple hours, I'll heal. I—"

"Swear it," I pressed. "The mortal lives don't have time for you to weigh the pros and cons. Bargain with me."

"I swear," he finally said, the words seeming to physically pain him. "On my power as a god, I won't tell Thorne where you're going or what you're doing." Power flickered between us as the bargain took hold. "But Paesha, you need to be careful. Ezra isn't just angry. He's desperate for revenge. And desperate gods are the most dangerous kind."

Tuck reached into his pocket with his good hand, wincing at

the movement. He pulled out a fistful of small metal pellets, pressing them into my palm. "Give these to her."

I took them and closed my eyes, calling on my Huntress power. Without the voices to distract me, it responded immediately, clear and focused. I could see them both. They were at Misery's End. Strange.

"Why are they in the theater?"

He coughed. "That's where you're to meet him."

"Perfect."

"Whatever plan you think you have—"

"He can't kill me. I'll be fine."

I walked away before he could say more, before he could try to reason with me or, worse, find a loophole in our bargain. The setting sun cast long shadows across the garden as I passed Archer's statue once more.

"Watch over them," I whispered to the bronze figure. "I'll be back soon."

As I slipped out of the garden and into the gathering darkness, I couldn't help but smile. Ezra thought he was luring me into a trap. He didn't realize that I was counting on exactly that.

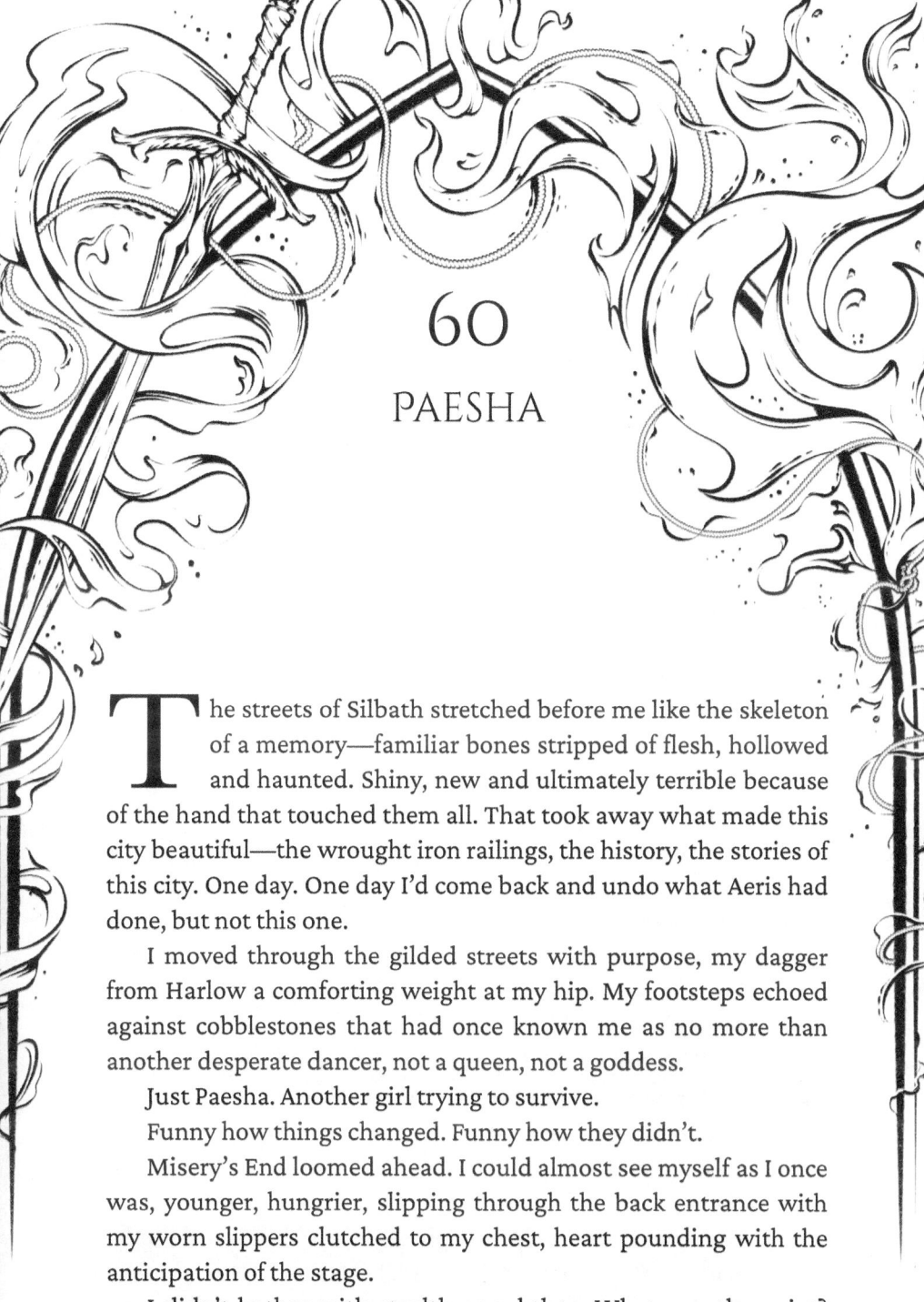

60

PAESHA

The streets of Silbath stretched before me like the skeleton of a memory—familiar bones stripped of flesh, hollowed and haunted. Shiny, new and ultimately terrible because of the hand that touched them all. That took away what made this city beautiful—the wrought iron railings, the history, the stories of this city. One day. One day I'd come back and undo what Aeris had done, but not this one.

I moved through the gilded streets with purpose, my dagger from Harlow a comforting weight at my hip. My footsteps echoed against cobblestones that had once known me as no more than another desperate dancer, not a queen, not a goddess.

Just Paesha. Another girl trying to survive.

Funny how things changed. Funny how they didn't.

Misery's End loomed ahead. I could almost see myself as I once was, younger, hungrier, slipping through the back entrance with my worn slippers clutched to my chest, heart pounding with the anticipation of the stage.

I didn't bother with stealth or subtlety. What was the point? Ezra knew I was coming. He'd orchestrated this entire production, after all. Might as well give the bastard the entrance he expected.

I kicked the front doors open, standing in the corridor. Empty. Silent.

I moved up the stairs, through the hall and to the theater doors, again kicking the door in.

The theater wasn't dark and empty as I'd expected. No, that would have been too simple for Ezra's twisted sense of drama. Instead, the space blazed with light, every lamp burning, every candle flickering, illuminating an audience that made my blood run cold.

Mortals. Hundreds of them, packed into every seat, spilling into the aisles. Their faces were pale with fear, eyes wide as they turned toward me. I recognized so many of them.

Mortal people. *My* people.

Unmade Guardians stood at every exit, their blank eyes and rigid postures promising swift punishment for any who dared move. But the stage, that was where my attention fixed, where fury and dread coalesced into a hard knot in my chest.

Ezra stood in a pool of light, wearing all black, his perfect features fucking giddy with anticipation, as if we were meeting for tea rather than whatever nightmare he had planned.

"Huntress! Right on time. I do appreciate punctuality in my performers."

I strode down the center aisle, deliberately slow, deliberately casual, even as my mind raced through options, calculations, possibilities. "Love what you've done with the place. The whole 'summon your enemies for dramatic confrontations' aesthetic is so last century, but you're really pulling it off. Should I have brought snacks? Evil monologues are always better with snacks, don't you think? For the dramatics and all."

Ezra's smile didn't falter. If anything, it widened. "I do adore your spirit."

"Wish I could return the compliment, but your taste seems questionable at best." I gestured to the filled theater. "Kidnapping? Really? That's a bit pedestrian for a supreme being, isn't it?"

I reached the edge of the stage and stopped, looking up at him with deliberate insolence.

"I prefer to think of it as 'gathering an appreciative audience,'" Ezra replied, extending a hand as if to help me onto the stage.

I ignored it, hoisting myself up with a fluid movement that required no assistance. "Cut the shit, Ezra. You've got your audience. You've got me. What's the fucking point of all this? You can't kill me now, so why bother?"

His laugh was soft, almost gentle. "Oh, Huntress. I promised my brother that I would drag this last one out, and I plan to do so." He circled me slowly, power rippling around him in waves I could almost see. "There are worse things than death."

I rolled my eyes. "Please. I've heard more creative threats from drunks in the alley behind this theater."

In a flash, he was before me, so close I could feel his breath on my face. "Dance for me, Huntress."

I blinked. "Excuse me?"

"Dance." He stepped back, gesturing to the stage around us. "That's what you do, isn't it? That's what you've always done. Dance for these people who adore you so. Dance to save their miserable lives."

"That's your big plan? Swordpoint dancing? And here I thought you couldn't disappoint me any more than you already have. Pity."

"I won't ask again. Dance. Of your own free will. We wouldn't want it to be a binding contract, would we, Huntress? We both know how those tend to work out."

A woman in the front row whimpered, drawing his attention. Without hesitation, Ezra pulled out his favorite bow and shot her right in the chest. She gasped, those around her cowered. With no warning at all, the woman was dead, slumping forward in her seat until she fell to the floor.

"That's one," he said calmly. "Shall we try for two? Or would you prefer to dance?"

Rage surged through me, hot and violent. I reached for my power, for the destruction that had become as much a part of me as breath, but it flickered and died before I could grasp it. Fucking perfect timing. The erratic surges Thorne had felt with the imbalance affected me as a goddess now too, leaving me powerless when I needed it most.

Ezra smiled, seeing my struggle. "Tricky thing, isn't it? Power. So unreliable these days. Almost as if someone had broken the balance."

I wanted to tear his throat out with my bare hands, god or no god. But the theater full of innocent people stayed my hand. They were looking at me now, hope and fear warring in their expressions. Most remembered me. Remembered the dancer who had once given them moments of beauty in their harsh lives.

"Fine," I spat. "I'll dance. But when this is over, when they're safe, you and I are going to have a very different kind of conversation."

Ezra stepped back, gesturing to the open stage with a flourish. "That's a really pretty picture of a fictional future. Still reading your books, I see. Please, by all means, the stage is yours."

I kicked off my boots, letting my feet connect with the worn boards of the stage. This place knew me. Had known me when I was nothing and no one. The muscle memory was still there, buried beneath layers of grief and rage and power. "What shall it be? A waltz? A jig? Something classical, perhaps?"

"Oh, I think you know exactly what these people came to see," Ezra replied, settling into the chair sitting center stage. "The piece that made you famous in this little corner of misery. Your magnum opus."

Of course. The dance I'd created in this theater, the one that had first caught the Maestro's eye. The same performance Ezra claimed stole his heart when we were lovers. Not ballet. Nothing fluid and beautiful. He wanted the burlesque.

I closed my eyes, drawing a deep breath. When I opened them, I refused to see Ezra. Instead, I looked at the people, the clock tinkerer who dabbed tears from his eyes, the old chimney sweep whose gnarled hands twitched as if longing for his tools, the young woman who'd once slipped me extra bread at the market when I was starving.

My people. Requiem's people. The ones I'd sworn to protect when I took a crown I never wanted, presiding over a city that was simply adjacent to this one.

I began to move.

There was no music, but my body remembered the rhythm, the cadence of a melody that had once been my only salvation. Each step, each turn, each sweep of my hips was defiance. I wouldn't let Ezra corrupt this, would not let him turn joy into misery. Misery's End... The irony wasn't lost on me. The spotlight had once been my escape from suffering, and now he sought to make it the source of my greatest humiliation.

But as I danced, something unexpected happened. The audience, these captives who should have been cowed with fear, began to respond. A murmur of appreciation rippled through the crowd. Their fear held them glued, unmoving, but there was love there. Appreciation for me that bloomed a warmth in my heart. This was how a goddess drew power. This feeling was euphoria. A drug even. I spun faster, threw myself higher, poured everything I had into each movement. This wasn't surrender. This was rebellion. This was reclaiming what was mine.

And the people saw it. They felt it. Their fear began to transform into something else, admiration, then defiance, then a fierce sort of joy that built like a wave. They'd known me as Paesha, the dancer who gave them moments of beauty in lives of hardship. That connection hadn't died when I'd left Requiem. If anything, it had grown stronger in my absence, polished by memory into something magical.

Their love, their energy, fed something within me. Not quite power, but a strength that had nothing to do with godhood and everything to do with belonging. With home. If I could just grasp my power, I would have this fucker on his knees so fast. I only needed to wait. It always came back around. That was what Thorne had said. And I could be patient.

Ezra must have sensed it though, because his face darkened. "Enough."

I ignored him, moving faster, drawing more from the audience, feeling their response lifting me. One more spin, one more leap—

"I said enough!" Ezra's voice cracked like thunder.

The music that had built in my mind, in my movements, came to a jarring halt as Ezra seized me by the arm, yanking me out of the dance with enough force to send pain shooting through my shoulder.

"Charming display. But I think we've had quite enough. No need to strengthen you, Huntress."

The audience had gone silent again, their adoration smothered by the reality of Ezra's cruelty. I met his gaze without flinching, refusing to give him the satisfaction of reading anything on my face. "What now? Is this the part where you tell us your grand plan? Because I've got to tell you, I'm kind of not interested. Shocking, I know."

Ezra's smile was cold. "Oh, we're just getting started, Huntress. You see, I've brought you here for a specific purpose. You're going to help me restore what you broke."

"And what would that be? Your ego? Your pride? Your inflated sense of self-importance? Hate to break it to you, but even I have my limitations."

His hand flashed out, striking me across the face with enough force to split my lip. Blood filled my mouth, metallic and warm. I spat it onto the stage between us, refusing to wipe it away.

"You broke the Fates, and now you're going to help me fix them."

"I can't and I won't."

"You misunderstand." He reached into his jacket, withdrawing a sheet of parchment and a pen. "You aren't going to do it yourself. You're going to summon the one who can."

Ice filled my veins as understanding dawned. "Quill."

"The Fera," he corrected. "A Fate, according to Minerva's touching revelation. How convenient that you've bound her to you. How perfect that she trusts you implicitly."

"I won't do it." The words came out as a growl. "I will die first. I will watch every person in this theater die first."

"Will you?" He gestured to an Unmade Guardian, who dragged forward a struggling man from the front row. "Let's test that theory, shall we?"

The man screamed as Ezra's power wrapped around him, lifting him off his feet. I recognized him immediately. My father.

"Stop," I said, the word tearing from my throat. "Just... stop."

"Write the note," Ezra said, holding out the pen and parchment. "A simple request. Ask your precious child to come dance with you on this stage. Tell her you miss performing together. Tell her anything that will bring her here."

"She'll bring an army and you know it."

"Best fix that too."

"I won't."

My father's screams intensified as Ezra's power tightened around him. Bones cracked, one by one.

I swallowed past my panic, reaching desperately for my power again, but it remained frustratingly beyond my grasp.

"Write. The. Note." Ezra thrust the pen into my hand.

I stared at it, mind racing. If I wrote what he wanted, Quill might come. She would walk right into his trap, believing she was coming to me. But if I didn't, how many would die before Ezra tired of this game?

Looking up, I met my father's pain-filled eyes. I could nearly hear him whisper 'Treasure' to me. He gave an almost imperceptible shake of his head. *Don't do it*, that gesture said. *Whatever he wants, don't give in.* His limbs shook as Ezra's power squeezed tighter. Blood trickled from his nose, his ears, his mouth. I couldn't watch this. I couldn't— He looked at me again, pressing his mouth shut to stay the screams. Then nodded once more. *I'm strong enough to die, Treasure. Let me die for your girl.*

"Kill him," I said, the words barely audible.

A swift death would be a mercy. I closed my eyes when the final crack of bone echoed around the theater. He'd been strong in that last moment. My throat tightened with a tangle of emotions. After a lifetime of failures, after trading me away like I was worth less than the high he craved, he'd finally chosen to be a father. Too little, too late, and yet in his final moments, he'd given me the only gift he had left: his death.

Ezra raised an eyebrow. "Another?"

I would never betray Quill. Never put her in danger. But I needed time. Needed to think, to plan, to find a way out that didn't involve sacrificing innocents or the child I loved more than my own life. I'd planned to carry Ezra and I away on shadowed hands. To free the mortals by leaving them behind. This though, this loss of power and fear for hundreds of lives stilled me.

Before I could respond, two Unmade Guardians stepped onto the stage from the sides, dragging two familiar figures between them.

My heart stuttered. Elowen and Thea.

The Guardians shoved them to their knees before Ezra. Elowen's eyes found mine, filled with a mixture of relief and fear. Thea's gaze was harder, calculating, already assessing the situation for weaknesses, for opportunities.

"What a delightful turn of events, wouldn't you say? This is your real family, is it not?" He circled them slowly. "I was just explaining to the Huntress that she needs to write a note to little Quill, inviting her to join us for a performance."

Elowen's eyes widened in horror. "Paesha, no. You can't."

"She will if she wants you both to live," Ezra countered, the threat unmistakable.

Elowen looked up at me, her face suddenly calm despite the blood trickling down her temple. She shook her head, her gaze never wavering from mine. "I'm not afraid, Paesha. Don't you dare bring that child here."

Thea nodded in fierce agreement. "We both know what matters most. You protect her. Whatever it takes."

Ezra laughed, the sound like breaking glass. "How touching. Two mortals, willing to die for a child that isn't even theirs." He turned to me, extending the pen once more. "What will it be, Huntress? Their lives? Or the note?"

I stared at the pen, at Elowen and Thea kneeling before a god who saw them as nothing but leverage, at the audience holding their collective breath, at my father's broken body now discarded on the floor.

"Well, Huntress?" Ezra's smile was triumphant, certain of his victory. "What's it going to be?"

61

THORNE

The orphanage bustled with life, laughter echoing through hallways that had once stood silent and empty. Children darted past as I watched Quill kneeling before a group of younger ones, Boo sitting proudly at her side as she told them a story.

"And then the warrior princess raised her magical sword—"

"Like Paesha's?" a small girl interrupted.

"Exactly like Paesha's. And she said to the evil wizard—"

"'I'm not afraid of you!'" the children chorused.

"That's right. Because warrior princesses are never afraid. Well, maybe sometimes. But they're brave anyway."

I leaned against the doorframe, content to observe without intruding. These moments of normalcy felt precious, fragile things to be protected at all costs.

"They adore her," Briony said, appearing beside me. The young woman's gentle smile belied the strength that had made her Paesha's first choice to oversee this place.

"She understands them. She knows what it's like to feel alone."

"Our queen has done a remarkable thing here. Most nobles fund orphanages for appearances, not out of true concern. But she's different. She remembers what it was to be hungry, to be forgotten. She remembers the Hollow." Briony turned back to the children. "Will you be staying for supper? We're serving beef stew and honey rolls."

"I think we—"

The words died in my throat as the atmosphere suddenly shifted. The air grew heavy. The children sensed it too, their laughter faltering as they huddled closer to Quill. I moved toward the entrance hall, power already gathering at my fingertips.

The massive front doors burst open, revealing three figures silhouetted against the early evening sun. Bellatora stood at the center, her armor gleaming. Beside her, Minerva's face was serious. Solemn. At her other side, barely standing, was Tuck, fucking bloodied and broken.

Panic raced through me, muting everything else in this damn realm. "What the hell happened?" I caught Tuck as he stumbled to a nearby bench.

"Ezra," he managed through swollen lips.

"Where's Paesha?"

Tuck's eyes slid away from mine. "I can't tell you."

"What do you mean, you 'can't tell me'?"

"He can't tell you," Bellatora stepped forward, hand resting on her sword hilt, "because your Ever bound him to silence with a bargain."

I stared at her, momentarily speechless. "Why are you here?"

"He could tell me. And now I'm telling you."

"Why would you care?"

A slow, predatory smile spread across Bellatora's face. "I've seen your Ever in action, Keeper. At this point, anyone on the other side of the battlefield from her made the wrong choice. Besides, this might be the most interesting thing to happen in centuries. I wouldn't miss it."

Briony appeared at my side. "Should I gather the children?"

"Take them upstairs. Make sure they stay there until one of us comes for them."

I turned back to Tuck. "What exactly did you promise her?"

"That I wouldn't tell you where she was going or what she was doing."

"But you told Bellatora."

Minnie stepped forward. "The bargain didn't cover that. She went after Ezra, Thorne. Alone. He has Thea, Elowen and others from the Underground. There's more. Quill shouldn't hear this."

I glanced back to where Quill still sat with the children, watching us with wary eyes. I nodded to Briony, who immediately went to Quill's side, guiding her and the other children from the room despite their protests.

"Speak. Now."

"We think he's trying to lure Quill in."

"I've already told you he is," Bellatora snapped. "I was there when he said it."

"And you're only now fucking mentioning it?" I snarled.

She shrugged. The casual expression of an untouched goddess. "I was spying. You're welcome."

"*He's* at Misery's End," Tuck said carefully, the bargain clearly restricting his words.

"I need to go." I moved toward the door, power gathering around me.

"Wait." Minerva's command stopped me. "We need to think this through."

"There's nothing to think through. Ezra has Paesha. He plans to use her to get to Quill. I'm going to stop him."

"And how, precisely, do you plan to do that? Your power is as erratic as his. You rush in without a plan and fail."

"Then give me a fucking plan, Minnie."

Her eyes held mine. "There is only one way forward, Reverius. Only one path that leads to an end rather than another cycle of violence."

"No. Absolutely not."

"It's the only way. You know it as well as I do. The balance must be restored. Completely. Permanently. And he cannot walk away."

"There has to be another solution." But even as I said the

words, I knew there wasn't. Bellatora looked between us, a slow smile spreading across her face. "Oh. Oh, this is going to be *magnificent*."

"Even if I agreed to this madness, it can't be done."

"It can," Minerva countered. "With help."

"Whose help?"

"Vesalia's."

That godsdamn name lingered between us. Vesalia, Goddess of Time.

"I've already summoned her," Minerva said. "And I'm sorry for it, my boy. You can say no. But there aren't many choices left that don't lead to an end of everything."

"And Quill?" I asked.

"I'll stay with her," Tuck offered, wincing as he straightened. "I may be a bit worse for wear, but I can still protect her."

"Ezra wants her. If he can't get to her through Paesha—"

Tuck growled, rising. "He won't get to her at all. I swear it on everything I am."

I studied him, then nodded. "If anything happens to her—"

"It won't. Get the fuck out of here."

I turned to Minerva. "If Vesalia agrees, there's no going back. You understand that? This changes everything."

"She'll agree. She's greedy and things need to change. This balance has been broken for too long."

The sound of small footsteps made us turn. Quill stood in the doorway, Boo clutched in her arms, her young face solemn.

"You're leaving," she said.

I knelt before her. "I need to help Paesha. She's in trouble."

"Is she going to be okay?"

"Yes. But I need you to stay here with Tuck. Can you do that for me? Can you be brave? Help protect the others, okay?"

She nodded, chin lifting. "I can be brave. I'll take care of him, too. He looks like he needs it."

"He does, doesn't he? Keep him out of trouble for me?"

"I will." She threw her arm around my neck, Boo squished between us. "Bring her home. Promise."

"I bind my words to you, Quill. She will come home. Take care of the other children while I'm gone. They'll need your stories." The whisper of power circled around me, locking me into one final bargain. One I'd die before breaking.

"I'll keep telling them about the warrior princess who's never afraid."

I rose, resolve hardening. "Go on now."

Quill gave me one last searching look, then turned and ran back to the east wing, Boo trotting at her heels.

"Vesalia should be meeting us there. Paesha had a ten minute head start. We need to race," Minerva said, tossing her cane to Tuck. "I'll be back for that."

We moved to the door. I turned back to Tuck. "For every lifetime, brother."

"Don't do that," he said.

"You know how this could go. If it does, tell her I did it for her. For all of them."

I stepped through the door before he could respond. Some endings couldn't be avoided, only faced head-on. This one had been waiting for me since the beginning of everything.

It was time to meet it.

62

THORNE

The doors to the theater exploded inward with a sound like thunder, fragments of wood skittering across the floor as I strode through the ruined entrance. Power crackled through every fiber of my being, steadier than it had been in weeks.

Vesalia and Minerva flanked me, Bella lingered behind. The theater fell into stunned silence, hundreds of terrified gazes turning toward the commotion.

On stage, Ezra stood with a triumphant smile, as if he'd been expecting this all along. Paesha at his side, her face a mask of defiance despite the blade at her throat. Elowen and Thea knelt at the edge of the stage, hands bound behind their backs.

"Brother!" Ezra's voice carried easily through the cavernous space. "You're just in time for the finale."

My gaze locked with Paesha's. In that split-second, I saw everything—fury, relief, determination, and beneath it all, a question. *What are you doing?*

No time to explain. I strode forward, power surging as I moved. The mortals shrank back, pressing themselves into their seats to avoid touching me. Smart. What I was about to do would change everything.

"Release them," I commanded.

Ezra's smile widened. "Now why would I do that when we're just getting to the good part?"

My gaze flicked to Elowen and Thea. Both women knelt with straight backs and lifted chins—defiant to the end.

"I'm not here to negotiate."

Ezra's laughter echoed through the theater. "No? Then what exactly are you here for, brother? Perhaps to offer yourself in her place?" His smile turned cruel. "I'll spare you the decision. You can watch, but there's not a thing you can do to stop me."

I came to a halt at the edge of the stage, power swirling visibly around me. "You're wrong."

Something in my tone made Ezra pause, the slightest flicker of uncertainty crossing his face. I turned to Vesalia, who stood behind me, her timeless beauty unmarred by the tension of the moment. She held her hand out expectantly. When I shot her a look, she whispered. "It must be given freely. Otherwise I'd have already taken it from your Ever and before that, the dead prince." She wiggled her fingers and glanced back to Ezra, who was storming toward us.

"Take it. All but what we agreed upon," I said, sliding my hand into hers.

Understanding dawned in Ezra's eyes, followed swiftly by horror. He lurched forward, but it was already too late. The connection formed instantly, a bridge between our power. Golden light began to flow from me into her, not a trickle, but a torrent. My power, the point of my existence pouring out of me in waves.

Ezra staggered, dropping to his knees with a strangled cry. The weapon he'd held clattered to the stage. "What have you done?"

"There is balance in power, right brother?" I remained standing despite the agony of being hollowed out from within. "What I give, you also lose."

The transfer continued. My vision began to blur at the edges, reality growing hazy as I was reduced to a mere fraction of what I had been. But still I remained on my feet, my gaze locked with my brother's. I could hear Paesha screaming at me to stop. But I wouldn't. I couldn't condemn us to a life of wondering when and if he would come again. This ended today. She'd stood against her adversaries, and I would stand against mine.

"You—" Ezra's voice emerged as a broken rasp. "You can't—" He scrambled, reaching for his blade.

"I can. I have."

Paesha's Remnants exploded outward, darkness flooding the theater as she seized control. Like living shadows, they wrapped around Ezra, binding him in coils of pure night. They raced through the theater, ensnaring every Unmade Guardian, rendering them harmless in an instant.

Then her gaze found mine. She knew what I had done. Vesalia finally released my hand, stepping back with power radiating from her like heat from a sun. She had become something new, something greater—perhaps the most powerful god in existence, though Paesha was likely still a close second.

"A deal is a deal." She approached my brother, watching how he struggled against Paesha's shadows, his face twisted with fury and desperation. "Supreme Sovereign, God of Unmaking, your Fate is sealed."

With a gesture so elegant it was almost casual, Vesalia froze Ezra in time. Not dead, not destroyed, something far worse. Locked in a single moment, unable to move forward or back, to act or think or be.

"It's done," she declared, her eyes meeting mine one final time. "You have what we agreed upon. A drop. Enough to survive, but never enough to challenge me." Without another word, without a backward glance, she turned and walked out of the theater, taking with her the power that had defined me since the beginning of everything.

Ezra vanished.

The silence that followed was absolute.

Paesha rushed to Elowen and Thea, cutting their bonds. I tried to step forward, but my legs buckled. I caught myself on the edge of the stage, my vision swimming because everything felt wrong, muted, distant, hollow. I had existed as a god for so long, I wasn't expecting what it meant to be anything less. Now I was... what? Not mortal, not quite. But no longer what I had been.

Paesha came to me next, her hands gripping my shoulders. "What did you do? Thorne, what did you do?"

I managed a smile, though it felt fragile on my face. "What was necessary."

"You gave her your power."

"Almost all."

"Why?"

I met her gaze steadily, focusing on her mismatched eyes to keep myself grounded. "Because the imbalance began with us, with Ezra and me. As long as we both held power, as long as we battled over you, over fate, over everything, the realms would never know peace. Now there is balance. No longer wavering between two brothers, but in the hands of another entirely."

The theater had erupted into chaos. Mortals fleeing, embracing, weeping with relief as Minerva organized a swift evacuation. Elowen and Thea helped the injured, directing people toward the exits.

But in that moment, it was just us, as it had always been across countless lifetimes.

"We're free."

The word hung between us, fragile and precious. Free from the cycles, from the prophecies, from the endless dance of death and rebirth. Free to write our own story, to forge our own path.

I nodded. Tears gathered in her eyes, but they didn't fall. Instead, a smile spread across her face, not the fierce, defiant smile I'd grown accustomed to, but something softer, more genuine. A smile of pure joy.

"Was it worth it?" she asked, her voice steady despite the emotion shining in her eyes.

I grabbed her by the throat and yanked her to me, lips crashing against hers until neither of us could breathe. When we broke apart, foreheads touching, I whispered, "Every drop."

Minerva stepped lightly toward us. "It's time to go. We've seen enough darkness."

Paesha nodded, rising to her feet. She offered me her hand, and I took it, allowing her to pull me upright with a grunt. The world tilted momentarily, my new reality still foreign and uncomfortable. But her grip was strong, steadying me as we had always anchored each other.

"What happens now?" she asked.

"Now... we go home."

As we walked out of Misery's End, leaving behind my brother's memory and centuries of conflict, I felt lighter than I had in eons. The power that had defined me was gone, but in its place was something I hadn't expected: possibility.

Paesha's hand remained in mine. In that simple touch was a promise, of time, of love, of a future neither of us had dared imagine until this moment. The balance had been restored. Not through destruction, but through sacrifice. Through the death of someone we would never forget, but also through transformation.

And in that balance, we had found freedom at last.

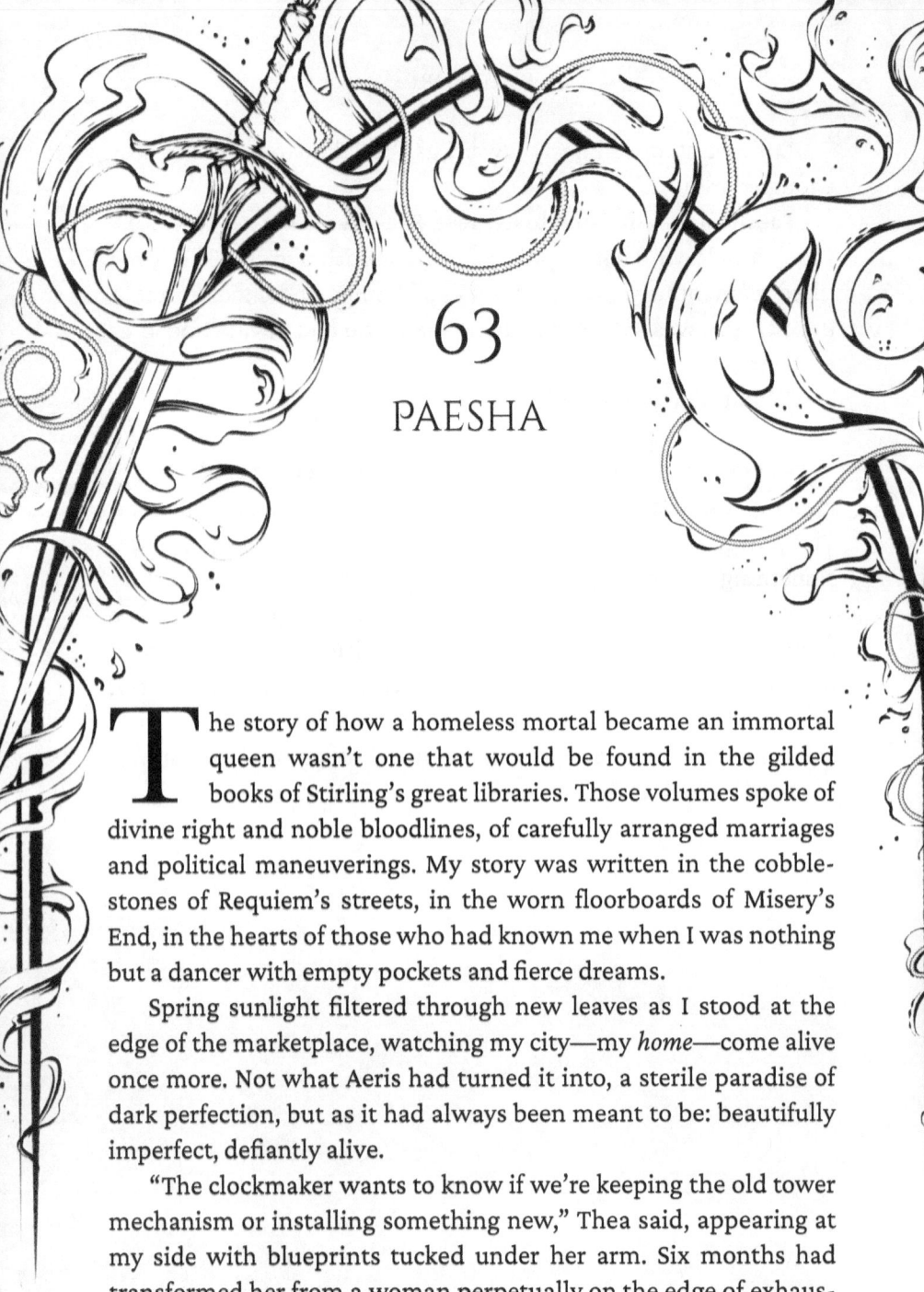

63

PAESHA

The story of how a homeless mortal became an immortal queen wasn't one that would be found in the gilded books of Stirling's great libraries. Those volumes spoke of divine right and noble bloodlines, of carefully arranged marriages and political maneuverings. My story was written in the cobblestones of Requiem's streets, in the worn floorboards of Misery's End, in the hearts of those who had known me when I was nothing but a dancer with empty pockets and fierce dreams.

Spring sunlight filtered through new leaves as I stood at the edge of the marketplace, watching my city—my *home*—come alive once more. Not what Aeris had turned it into, a sterile paradise of dark perfection, but as it had always been meant to be: beautifully imperfect, defiantly alive.

"The clockmaker wants to know if we're keeping the old tower mechanism or installing something new," Thea said, appearing at my side with blueprints tucked under her arm. Six months had transformed her from a woman perpetually on the edge of exhaustion to someone who practically vibrated with purpose. "Personally, I think the old gears have character."

"Keep them," I decided, watching a group of children race past, their laughter echoing against buildings that no longer gleamed with unnatural perfection. "But make sure they actually keep time. I'd like at least some things in this city to be reliable."

"Unlike the gods?" Thea's mouth quirked into a half smile.

"Exactly unlike the gods."

We walked together through streets that balanced carefully between what had been and what could be. I'd changed it all back. A little cleaner, a little safer, but ours. The crooked signposts remained, though the buildings they marked now stood solid and safe. The narrow alleys where I'd once hidden from the Maestro's men still twisted like snakes through the city, but no longer harbored shadows that would swallow children whole.

Vendors called out their wares from stalls that looked as they had for generations, though the goods they sold no longer bore the marks of desperate times. No more watered wine, no more bread cut with sawdust, no more trinkets that would fall apart with the first rain.

My power flowed through the city like a river, not erasing its history but enhancing its essence. I couldn't bring back what had been lost entirely, but I could honor it, preserve the soul of a place that had shaped me into who I was. I ruled over Stirling, but my heart was in Silbath, in Perth across the river, in the soul of every mortal. And they knew it. I'd never shove my authority over anyone, but they looked to me, nevertheless. Thorne had taken my hand, stood strong beside me as I vowed to protect it all.

"The last families came up from the Underground yesterday," Thea said. "The baker practically wept when he saw his old store-front restored."

"Does he still make those sweet rolls Quill loves?"

"Started baking at dawn. I've already sent a courier to the castle with a basket full."

I smiled, imagining Quill's face when she discovered the treat. "She'll be insufferable."

"She's already insufferable," Thea countered, but her tone was light.

We rounded a corner to find Vincent directing a group of

workers as they reinstalled the original iron railings along the bridge. He'd refused to stay underground once it was safe to return, insisting that the real work lay in rebuilding what had been lost. Now he oversaw much of the restoration, his knowledge of the old city proving invaluable. Where human hands could fix this place, they did. Because it was theirs to cherish too.

"Your Majesty," he called, bowing with a dramatic flair that made me roll my eyes.

"I've told you not to call me that."

"And I've elected to ignore you. The Goddess of Renewal, and the only god I particularly care for, deserves a proper title, especially when she's actually living up to the name." He paused, looking around. "Don't tell Minnie I said that. Or Tuck. Or Thorne."

My fingers twitched at the reminder of what I was now. Half-goddess by birth, full goddess by conquest, yet still somehow the same woman who had once danced for coins in a ramshackle theater. The contradiction no longer felt like a burden—it was simply another part of the tapestry that made up my existence.

"How's the bridge coming?" I asked, deliberately changing the subject.

"It'll be ready for the festival next week. Though I still say we should add some of those fancy new lampposts Thea designed."

"Absolutely not," Thea and I replied in unison.

Vincent laughed, shaking his head. "Two against one. I surrender."

As we continued our walk through the city, I felt a familiar warmth spread through me. Not the burn of power or the fire of rage, but something gentler. Pride, perhaps, or the quiet satisfaction of creation rather than destruction. For so long, I had thought of myself as a weapon, forged in pain and honed for vengeance. Now, I was learning what it meant to build, to heal, to nurture.

Requiem remembered itself beneath my touch, like a sleeper slowly awakening from a dream. The soul of the city remained, but now it breathed easier, stood taller, no longer cowed by the whims of capricious gods or the cruelty of human masters. We reached the Dancing Ghost tavern right as the afternoon crowd began to filter in.

Elowen stood in the doorway, her dark hair with traces of silver gleaming in the sunlight as she directed a delivery of wine barrels with her usual efficiency. "I was wondering when you two would show up. You're late for lunch."

"We're exactly on time," Thea protested, looking up at the old clock tower.

"If you're not early, you're late," Elowen countered, ushering us inside with gentle insistence. "And I've got a table waiting."

Elowen had a particular fondness for this old place, and when it came time, she bought it outright. The tavern's interior had been restored to its original glory, with heavy wooden beams and worn stone floors that'd witnessed centuries of stories. The only concession to my restoration efforts was better lighting and a new hearth that didn't smoke when the wind came from the east.

Thorne and Tuck had claimed our usual corner table, their heads bent close in conversation that ceased abruptly when we approached. The sight of Thorne still made my heart skip, not with the desperate longing of our separated lives, but with the settled certainty of a love that had finally found its rightful time and place.

He looked up, those hazel eyes warming as they met mine, and rose to pull out my chair. "Find anything that needs fixing on your morning walk?" he asked, pressing a kiss to my temple as I sat.

"Only about a dozen things," I admitted. "But nothing urgent."

"She's being modest," Thea said, settling across from us. "She personally redesigned the entire western aqueduct system this morning. And then insisted on overseeing the foundation work for the new school."

Tuck whistled low. "Impressive for a morning stroll."

"Says the man who's been reorganizing the entire royal library for fun," I countered.

Tuck grinned, scratching his beard. "It's not my fault your historians had no concept of proper chronological archiving. In fact, it's quite annoying."

"What is it with rearranging books in this family?" Thea huffed.

The strange new reality of our existence still felt dreamlike some days. Thorne had a fraction of his power, enough to keep him immortal, but no longer the Keeper of Memories. Tuck chose to stay by his side despite the shift in cosmic hierarchy. Minerva watched over Quill's education with unexpected gentleness. Alastor and Irri made occasional appearances, drawn by curiosity rather than schemes. And balanced between mortal responsibilities and immortal power, learning to wield both with equal care, was me.

The door burst open, admitting a whirlwind of energy in the form of Quill, followed by a more steady Minerva. Boo trotted at their heels, his little legs working overtime to keep pace.

"I ate *four* sweet rolls," Quill announced, throwing herself onto the bench beside me. "And Minnie said I could have another if I finished my history lessons, but I told her I'd save it for after lunch because I'm growing and need real food too."

"Very responsible," Thorne said solemnly, though his eyes danced with amusement.

"That's what Minnie said." Quill beamed up at Minerva, who pretended not to notice as she settled beside Tuck. "She says I'm the most responsible Fate she's ever known."

The casual reference to her true nature no longer brought tension to our gatherings. We had all adjusted to the truth of what Quill was. A child, yes, but also something ancient and powerful, a being who could one day reshape reality. Maybe destroy it. There was a trace of unknown within her. Her potential. There hadn't been a Fera for hundreds of thousands of years. Most beings were known immediately. And no one knew of the journey a Fate must take to ascend. No one knew what life had in store for our girl. For now, she was simply our Quill, with sticky fingers and boundless energy and a heart too big.

Elowen brought platters of food, roasted meats, fresh bread, and vegetables from the gardens outside the city walls, newly replanted in honor of Jasper. As we ate, the conversation flowed around me: Tuck debating literature with Minerva, Thea describing her latest mechanical invention to an enthralled Quill, Thorne's hand finding mine beneath the table in a gesture so natural it felt like breathing.

I watched them, my strange, beautiful family cobbled together from loss and chance and stubborn love, and felt something settle in my chest. The voices that had plagued me for so long were silent now, banished by my confrontation with the Fates. In their place was a clarity I had never known, the freedom to simply *be*, without the constant battle for control.

After lunch, we made our way to the corner where Misery's End once stood. The theater had been torn down after our final confrontation with Ezra. Too many ghosts, too many memories. In its place now stood a memorial garden.

At its center, a second bronze statue of Archer stood in eternal vigil, his expression that charming smile, but this statue showcased his fingers tangled in yarn. He would have hated it. And it made me smile. Directly across from him stood a second statue. That of a woman with a moth pin in her hair. Her features were perfect. Her smile, lethal, and of all things, I knew Harlow would have loved how the sculpture depicted the dagger on her thigh. There was one more, of course. A statue of a little old man with a needle in his hand and a gentle smile on his face. Thea's masterpiece, built from her perfect memory.

We gathered around in comfortable silence. Quill placed a single coin at Archer's feet, a ritual she performed weekly without fail. Thea added a small metal flower she had crafted. Thorne stood with his arm around my shoulders, solid and steady, a counterpoint to the ache that still bloomed when I thought of Archer.

"I miss him," Quill said simply.

"Me too, Quilly," I replied, drawing her against my side. "Every day."

"But he would like this," she decided, looking around at the garden, at the city spreading around us, at the clear sky above. "He would say it's..."

"Bittersweet," Tuck supplied gently.

"Yeah. Bittersweet. Like the chocolate Elowen puts in those cookies."

As the others began to make their way back down the hill, Thorne lingered with me, his fingers laced through mine.

"You did it."

I looked out over the city with its crooked streets and weathered buildings, its bustling markets and quiet corners. Smoke rose from chimneys in lazy spirals. The Underground stood empty, a relic of desperate times rather than a necessity.

"We did it," I corrected him. "All of us."

He turned to face me fully. "Do you ever regret it? Any of it?"

I didn't have to ask what he meant. Did I regret becoming what I now was, neither mortal nor traditionally divine? Did I regret the choices that had led us here, to this moment, on this spot, with the weight of eternity before us?

"No. I'd change things. But I don't regret it."

His smile broke across his face like dawn. That rare, unguarded expression that still made my heart stutter when his dimple showed. "Neither do I."

When he kissed me, it felt like coming home, not to a place, but to a person, to the one soul that had known mine across lifetimes. The connection between us, that which made us Evers, hummed with rightness, with the settled certainty that we had finally found our time, our place, our peace.

Later, as the sun began to set, casting the city in gold and amber, we gathered in the meadow at the Syndicate house. Lanterns hung from tree branches, their light soft and welcoming as darkness fell. A table had been set for our evening meal, simple but elegant, with flowers from the memorial garden as its centerpiece.

Quill chased Boo around the perimeter. Thea and Tuck argued about the proper way to season the roast. Elowen supervised it all with fond exasperation.

Thorne appeared at my side, offering a glass of wine. "You're staring."

"I'm memorizing," I corrected him. "I want to remember every detail, exactly as it is."

"We have time. All the time we need."

That was the gift we had given each other, time, unmarked by prophecy or fate or the machinations of gods. Time to heal, to build, to love. Time to learn each other anew, without the pressure of impending doom or ancient schemes.

As we took our places around the table, I found myself thinking of Archer again. He should have been here, in the empty chair we still set at every gathering. He should have been telling outrageous stories, teaching Quill card tricks, making Thea laugh with his terrible attempts at cooking.

But his absence had shaped us too, made us fiercer in our love for one another, more determined to honor the sacrifice he had made. The hole he had left would never fully heal, but around its edges, life continued to grow, vibrant and resilient.

Quill raised her glass of juice, her expression suddenly solemn. "To family. The ones that are here and the ones that are watching. To us."

"To us," we echoed, glasses clinking in the warm evening air.

As night fell fully, as stars emerged above a city that breathed easier than it had in centuries, as conversation and laughter flowed around me, I felt a sense of completion. Whatever came next, and with centuries stretched before us, who could say what challenges awaited, we would face it together. Not as pawns, but as architects of our own destiny. Free, at last, to write our own story.

And that was the greatest power of all. The mark of a true hero.

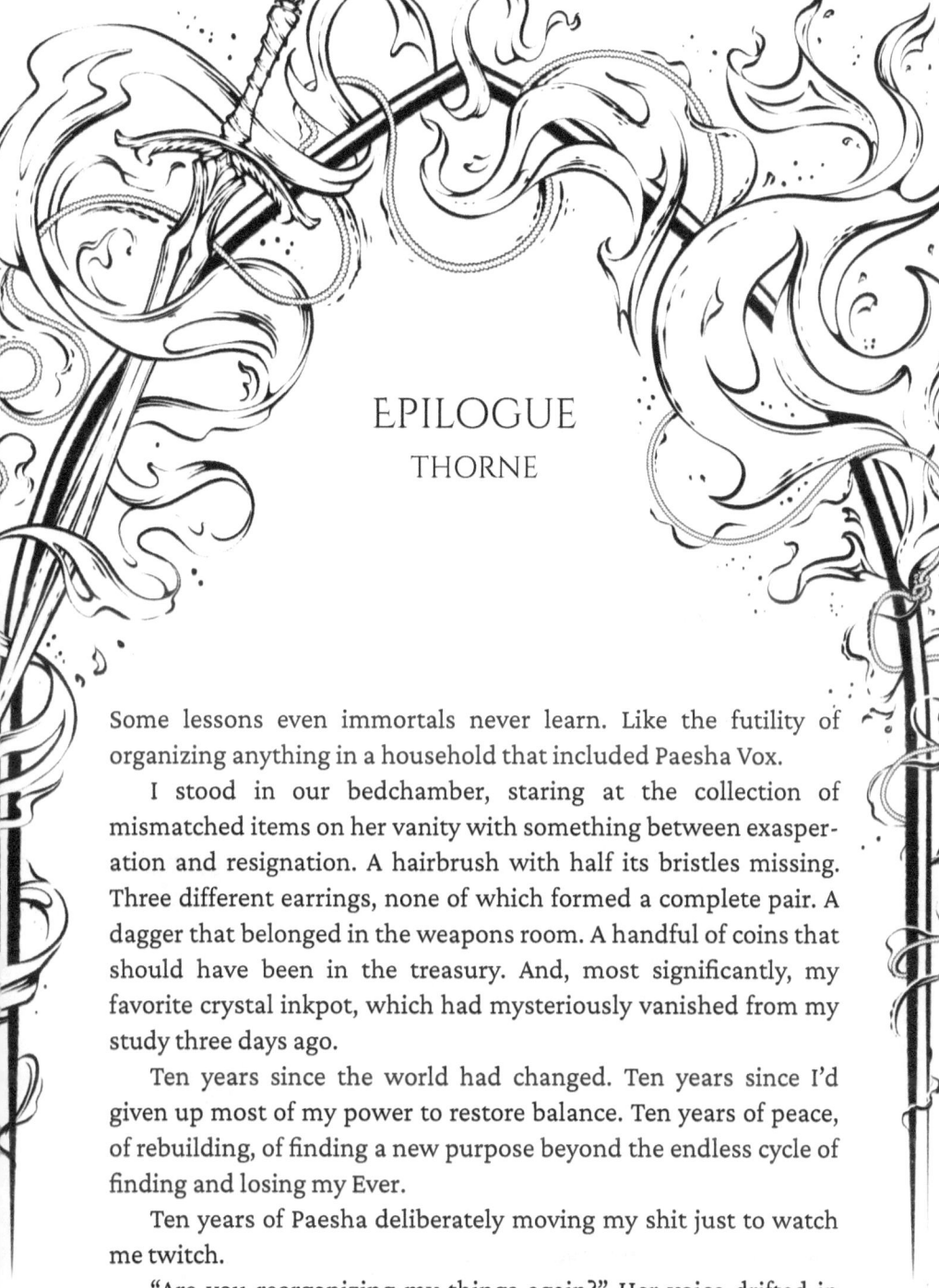

EPILOGUE
THORNE

Some lessons even immortals never learn. Like the futility of organizing anything in a household that included Paesha Vox.

I stood in our bedchamber, staring at the collection of mismatched items on her vanity with something between exasperation and resignation. A hairbrush with half its bristles missing. Three different earrings, none of which formed a complete pair. A dagger that belonged in the weapons room. A handful of coins that should have been in the treasury. And, most significantly, my favorite crystal inkpot, which had mysteriously vanished from my study three days ago.

Ten years since the world had changed. Ten years since I'd given up most of my power to restore balance. Ten years of peace, of rebuilding, of finding a new purpose beyond the endless cycle of finding and losing my Ever.

Ten years of Paesha deliberately moving my shit just to watch me twitch.

"Are you reorganizing my things again?" Her voice drifted in from the adjoining bathroom, amusement evident in every syllable.

"I'm contemplating the mystery of how someone so precise in

battle can be so chaotic in domestic matters," I replied, picking up the dagger and testing its edge with my thumb. Still sharp, at least. "This belongs in the weapons room."

"Does it?" She appeared in the doorway, wrapped in nothing but a towel, her hair dripping onto the floor in a way she knew drove me crazy. "I think it looks so decorative next to my perfume bottles. It's fancy. Really makes the place feel special."

I raised an eyebrow. "Until Quill decides to 'borrow' it for one of her increasingly elaborate pranks."

"She's almost twenty. I think she's moved past the stabbing phase." Paesha crossed the room, deliberately shaking her wet hair in my direction as she passed.

I caught her wrist, pulling her back against me despite the dampness seeping through my shirt. "She's worse than you in that regard. And you're making a mess."

"You like it. It gives you something to complain about."

"I have a list. I hardly need more material." Despite my words, I lowered my mouth to hers, tasting mint and honey.

She melted against me for a moment before pulling away with a smirk. "Your shirt is getting wet."

"An unavoidable casualty of loving you," I sighed, releasing her to continue her path across the room. "Much like my sanity, my organized study, and apparently, my favorite quill."

Her back stiffened for a heartbeat, a tell so slight that only someone who had spent years learning her every expression would notice it.

"I have no idea what you're talking about," she said, too casually, as she dropped her towel and reached for a dress laid out on the bed.

I leaned against our broken bedpost, last night's casualty, making no effort to hide my appreciation of the view. "Of course you don't. Just as you had no idea about my missing cufflinks last month, or my favorite book the week before that."

She slipped the dress over her head, the green silk settling against her curves in a way that distracted me from the investigation at hand.

"Maybe you're getting forgetful in your old age," she suggested, turning to present her back for me to lace her dress. "You're what? Several millennia old now? Eighty-two thousand or something? Pretty sure you should be decrepit honestly."

My fingers worked the laces with practiced ease. "And somehow still young enough to catch you in a lie." I pressed a kiss to the nape of her neck, smiling against her skin when she shivered. "Where is it, Paesha?"

"Where's what?"

"My quill. The one with the golden nib that Tuck gave me."

"Why would I take your quill, and please never say the word nib to me again." She stepped away, moving to the vanity to begin the elaborate process of arranging her hair. "I don't even write that much."

"Then why did I find ink stains on your fingertips yesterday?" I settled onto the edge of the bed, content to watch the familiar ritual. "Ink that matches exactly the distinctive blue shade I had specially made in Stirling."

Her eyes met mine in the mirror. "You're unusually observant for someone who didn't notice another teacup was missing for three months."

Ah, there it was. The infamous teacup, still a point of contention. The small, porcelain cup with the chipped rim that she'd stolen from my palace in Etherium during one of her early visits to match the one she'd taken from Noctus house. I'd searched for it for months before finding it tucked away in her chambers, filled with little trinkets she'd collected.

When I'd confronted her about it, she'd simply shrugged and said, "I liked it. It reminded me of you, pristine on the outside, a little broken on the edges."

I'd let her keep it.

"The teacup was different," I said, watching as she twisted her hair into an elaborate knot. "I knew exactly where it was."

"With me."

"Yes. With you. Where it belonged." The words came out softer than intended, laden with meaning beyond the accepted thievery.

Her hands stilled, and for a moment, our eyes held in the reflection. Then she smirked, breaking the spell. "So sentimental. I prefer you grumpy."

"I'm not grumpy." I stood, moving to stand behind her, my hands settling on her shoulders. "I'm discerning."

"You're a perfectionist and you know it." She leaned back against me, her head resting against my chest. "And meticulous. And absolutely incapable of letting anything be slightly out of place. Which is probably my favorite thing. That and the dick, of course."

I bit the inside of my cheek to hide the damn smile. I refused to acknowledge her attempt to derail the subject. Clever little menace. "Someone has to maintain order in this chaos you call a filing system. You organized the books by color rather than subject."

"It's aesthetic."

"It's ridiculous. Tuck nearly had an aneurysm when he saw what you'd done to the library."

"Tuck is overly dramatic about literature. And pretty much everything else. If I didn't know he was eternally a god, I'd swear he was an actor in a previous life."

I pressed a kiss to the top of her head. "Now, about my quill..."

She sighed dramatically, pulling away to open a drawer in the vanity. "Fine. I was going to surprise you, but since you're being such an ass..."

From the drawer, she withdrew a small leather-bound book, its cover a deep blue that matched the ink I'd been missing along with the quill and handed it over.

I opened it carefully, recognizing her handwriting that filled the pages. Not notes or records or official correspondence, but stories. Our stories. Tales of how we'd met in different lives, memories she'd pieced together from the voices that haunted her, fragments and dreams and the quiet conversations we'd had on countless nights.

"I've been working on it for months," she admitted, a hint of uncertainty in her voice that few ever heard. "I thought... Well, you're not technically the Keeper anymore, but these memories still matter. They're still ours. I didn't want them to fade."

Something shifted in my chest, a warmth spreading through me as I turned the pages, seeing our history through her eyes. The dancer and the god. The barmaid and the scholar. The fallen queen and her shadow. A thousand lifetimes distilled onto ink and paper.

"You stole my quill to write our story?"

"I borrowed it. There's a difference."

"And the ink?"

"Also borrowed. I needed something that would last. Immortal or not, paper fades. I wanted something that would endure, like us."

I closed the book carefully, setting it on the vanity before pulling her to me. "You continue to surprise me, Paesha darling."

"I'm not surprised. You're not very observant." Her hands rested on my chest, fingers playing with the buttons of my shirt.

"You're such a beautiful little liar." I captured her chin, tilting her face up to mine. "Though I still expect my quill to be returned to its proper place."

She rolled her eyes. "And just like that, the moment is ruined."

"I'm simply maintaining standards."

"You're being fussy." She pulled away, tapping my nose. "We're going to be late for dinner if you keep distracting me with your obsessive need for order."

"I'm distracting you? You're the one who walked out here wearing nothing but a towel and an attitude."

"Worked, didn't it?" She glanced over her shoulder, expression smug. "You completely forgot about reorganizing my vanity."

She had me there. "Temporary tactical defeat. The battle for household organization continues."

She grabbed a pair of slippers from beneath the bed and slipped them on. "A battle you'll never win. Accept defeat gracefully, Husband."

"Never." I offered her my arm with exaggerated formality. "But I'll call a temporary truce for dinner. Quill will be unbearable if we're late again."

"She gets that from you, you know. The punctuality obsession."

"From me? I think not."

"She alphabetized her journals, Thorne. She lines up her boots in perfect pairs." Paesha linked her arm through mine as we moved toward the door. "She is your miniature in every way that matters and it's honestly frustrating to live with Thorne Noctus and Thorne Noctus Junior with a side of Minerva, a dash of Thea's optimism and Tuck's know-it-all bullshit."

I couldn't quite suppress my smile at that. Quill had indeed grown into a fascinating blend of all of us, Paesha's fierce independence, my appreciation for order, Tuck's love of knowledge, Minerva's dry wit, and always, always, echoes of Archer in her laugh, in the way she could charm anyone with a single smile. She knew her power and wielded it flawlessly.

"She's perfect," I said simply.

"She'd be insufferable if she heard you say that."

"As opposed to her mother, who accepts compliments with such grace and humility?"

Paesha elbowed me in the ribs, hard enough to make me grunt. "I am the epitome of grace, thank you very much."

"Says the woman who threw a boot at my head last week."

"You ducked. Plus, you deserved it. You reorganized my closet."

"I improved your closet. Now you can actually find things."

"I knew exactly where everything was before. Huntress, remember?"

"In piles on the floor?"

"Strategic piles. With a system."

"Chaos is not a system."

"Agree to disagree."

We continued our bickering as we made our way through the halls of what had once been the Syndicate house and was now simply home. The building had expanded over the years to accommodate our growing family—not just us and Quill, but Tuck's extensive library, Minerva's mysterious workroom that no one was allowed to enter, Thea's constantly evolving workshop filled with half-finished inventions, and rooms always ready for Elowen's frequent visitors. We had the castle too, of course. But this was our escape. Our happy place.

The dining room hummed with familiar chaos as we entered. Quill, tall and elegant now at nineteen, was engaged in an animated debate with Tuck about some obscure historical text. Minerva watched them, occasionally interjecting a comment that sent them both sputtering. Thea was showing Elowen her latest creation, something with gears that whirred alarmingly.

"You're late," Quill announced without looking up from her argument.

"Blame her," I said, pulling out Paesha's chair. "She stole my quill and then decided to have a philosophical discussion about the nature of personal property."

"I did no such thing. I was explaining the concept of communal ownership to someone who still struggles with sharing. What's his is also mine."

"I share. When asked. Politely. In advance. After mulling."

Tuck snorted into his wine. "You once threatened to remove my memories because I borrowed your favorite cloak."

"It was raining, and you returned it with mud stains."

"It was a black cloak! You couldn't even see the mud!"

"I could sense the mud."

The table erupted into laughter, a sound that still, after all these years, caused something in my chest to tighten with gratitude. As we ate, I found my gaze repeatedly drawn to Paesha. She was in her element here, surrounded by those she loved, her face animated as she recounted her latest project to rebuild something in Stirling that'd been lost to a storm. The candlelight caught in her hair, turning the dark strands to burnished copper. Her hands moved as she spoke, painting pictures with the same grace she'd once used to dance across stages.

She must have felt my attention because she paused mid-sentence. "What?"

"Nothing," I said, though we both knew it was everything.

Later, when the meal was finished and our family had dispersed, we found ourselves in the garden. The air smelled like night-blooming jasmine, and stars scattered across the sky like diamonds on black velvet.

Paesha leaned against the stone balustrade, her face tilted up to catch the moonlight. "You were staring at me all through dinner."

"Was I?" I moved to stand beside her, close enough that our shoulders touched.

"You know you were." She bumped her hip against mine. "So distracting, Husband."

"My deepest apologies for appreciating my wife's beauty," I replied dryly. "How terribly inconsiderate of me."

She laughed, the sound still the most beautiful music I'd ever heard. "Flattery won't get you out of cleaning the kitchen with Tuck tomorrow."

"I'm not flattering you. I'm stating a fact." I caught a lock of her hair between my fingers, tucking it behind her ear. "You're beautiful. You always have been. But especially now, when you're not running or hiding or fighting. When you're simply Paesha."

She turned to face me, her expression softening in the way it did only when we were alone. "And who exactly is that? Paesha the queen? Paesha the goddess? Paesha the immortal?"

"Paesha the thief," I corrected, drawing her into my arms. "Who stole my quill, my teacup, and most significantly, my heart. Repeatedly. Across lifetimes."

"So sentimental," she murmured, though she leaned into me, her arms sliding around my waist. "What happened to the fearsome god who terrorized realms?"

"He met a dancer who showed him a better way to exist." I pressed my forehead to hers. "And he's been hopelessly devoted to her ever since."

"Even when she moves his things just to watch him twitch?"

"Especially then." I kissed her lightly, savoring the feel of her smile against my lips. "Though I will be reclaiming my quill."

"Good luck finding it," she whispered against my mouth. "I've hidden it very well this time."

I pulled back and raised an eyebrow at her. "In the hollowed-out book on the third shelf of the east bookcase? The one you think I don't know about?"

Her eyes widened. "How did you—"

"I know all your hiding places, darling." I traced the curve of her lower lip with my thumb. "Just as you know all of mine."

"Not all of them," she countered, recovering quickly. "You're still secretive about some things."

"Am I?"

She nodded, serious now. "You hid the teacup."

Her teacup now, though I'd never formally relinquished ownership. After she'd stolen it from me, I'd stolen it back exactly once. Not to keep, but to modify. She knew where it was. Her power whispered that to her. But she'd never chased it. Instead, she'd trusted me, though it probably killed her to do so.

"I suppose I could show you. If you're truly curious."

Her eyes lit with interest. "Now?"

"If you wish."

She stepped back, gesturing for me to lead the way. "After you, then. Since we're pretending I have no idea where it is."

I took her hand, guiding her back into the house and up the stairs to my study. Unlike most rooms in our home, this space remained meticulously organized, my last bastion of perfect order.

I crossed to the far wall, where a painting hung, a landscape of Etherium as it had once been, golden and glorious in its prime. Behind it was a small safe, its lock responding only to my touch.

"You're lucky I haven't broken into that yet, you know?"

"Funny, I found it open the other day."

She faked a gasp. "Tuck!"

I opened it with a chuckle, revealing a collection of small items, mementos from different lives, different times. A river stone from the first place I'd found her. A ribbon she'd worn in her hair in a life she couldn't remember. A pressed flower from a garden long turned to dust.

And the teacup, nestled among them like the treasure it was.

I lifted it carefully, this small, chipped piece of porcelain that had somehow become a symbol of everything between us. But when I handed it to her, she frowned in confusion.

"It's... different," she said, turning it in her hands.

The chip in the rim was still there, I wouldn't have dreamed of repairing the imperfection that had drawn her to it in the first place. But the interior, once plain white, now bore an inscription in gold. Words written in my precise handwriting, curving around the inside of the cup where she would only see them when it was empty:

For my Paesha, in this life and every one before. Ever yours, T

Her fingers traced the words, her expression softening in a way that still, after all this time, made my heart ache with love.

"Why are you giving it to me now?"

"Ten years of peace. Ten years of waking up beside you without fear of prophecies or fates or vengeful gods. Ten years of building something I never dared hope for. It seemed appropriate."

She cradled the cup in her hands like it was made of starlight rather than porcelain. "You know I'm going to display this prominently on my chaotic vanity now."

"I would expect nothing less." I closed the safe, returning the painting to its place. "Consider it a formal surrender in at least one battle of our ongoing war."

"The great Reverius Hawthorne Noctus, surrendering?" She pressed a hand to her heart in mock astonishment. "I should document this historic moment."

"Only this one battle. I still intend to organize your shoes by height and color tomorrow."

"Touch my shoes and you'll find thorns in your pillowcase," she threatened without heat.

"How terribly juvenile."

"You love it."

"I love you," I corrected, pulling her into my arms. "Chaos and all."

She rose on her tiptoes, pressing a kiss to the corner of my mouth. "Even when I steal your quills?"

"Even then."

"And move your books?"

"Testing my limits, but yes."

"And hide your favorite cufflinks just to watch you search for them?"

I sighed dramatically. "You are, without question, the most infuriating woman I have ever known. Across galaxies, across centuries, across every realm in existence."

Her smile was pure sunshine. "That wasn't a no."

"It wasn't," I conceded, capturing her lips in a kiss that said everything words could not, about love, about peace finally found, about the joy of building a life together after so many torn apart.

"You know, for an immortal with diminished powers, you're not terrible to have around."

I laughed. "Calm down with your compliments. I can't take the praise."

"We should probably go downstairs. Tuck was threatening to read aloud from his latest historical research."

"A fate worse than death." As we made our way back to the others, Paesha's hand in mine and the teacup held carefully in her other hand, I found myself marveling yet again at the path that had led us here. From a god and a dancer to simply Thorne and Paesha, building a life together day by day, argument by argument, kiss by kiss.

Vesalia held all the cards now. A torrent of power she likely didn't know how to handle. But that was her problem. Not ours. After all, we still held the key to Noctus Gate. Our one fail-safe. Though, it had mysteriously gone missing. Paesha, no doubt. It wasn't the eternity I'd once envisioned, filled with power and purpose and the endless dance of finding and losing her. It was better. Messier. More beautiful in its imperfection.

Like a teacup with a chipped rim, made more precious by the flaws that should have diminished it.

Like us.

THE END

599

ACKNOWLEDGMENTS

To my readers,

Thank you so much for coming on this journey with me. Paesha's story was rough for me as an author. She fought me tooth and nail at each turn to make sure this journey was exactly what it needed to be. We weren't forgiving quickly, we weren't trusting without warrant and we certainly weren't falling in love if it wasn't earned. This will be the end of the Never Sky Series (for now). Perhaps one day we will come back and see what Quill is up to, but for now, my heart is ready to move on and I hope you'll come with me as we discover the truth behind a witch hiding her identity as she shackles herself to the man hunting her in order to gain answers for her missing friend.

To Dustin, this story was a journey of hard nights and long days and plenty of 'I miss you's' while I wrote NeverEvermore in six months. Thank you for picking up my miles of slack, encouraging me when I was so defeated and never once letting me give up. I love you.

To my girls, I've missed you too. I know diving into writing new stories steals me away and if you didn't love me as much as you do, if you weren't hell-bent on supporting me and making sure these dreams come true, I'm sure you'd have a lot more to say about missed dinners and days between calls and texts. Thank you. I love you endlessly.

To Melissa, my bestie, my ride or die, my sounding board, I love you. Thank you for always sitting with me in the dark. For your calm nature and rational mind. For your silly messages and boundless love. You're my person. All the tickets. (But not for Greg.)

To Megan, you poor soul. I'm sorry you had to edit this monstrosity, but gosh am I grateful you did. I probably won't stop using the word just, but I love that you point them out all the same. They just need to be there, okay? Thank you for all the hours you spent pouring over this story.

To my team, thank you for the hand holding, the laughs, the alpha and beta comments that kept me going and the days when you had to believe in this story harder than I did. I couldn't do this without each of you.

To Jacci Prior, the most incredible narrator and my dear friend, I've watched you bust your ass in an industry that seems awfully lopsided and I'm so glad I have you in my corner. You bring my characters to life in ways I dream about. You're infinitely talented and gosh am I glad this whirlwind of ours started with a witch. Thank you for every second you spend in that booth and out of it for me.

And to the small version of myself that walked so many parallels to Paesha, we made it out alive. That stubborn will carried you through.

ABOUT THE AUTHOR

Miranda Lyn is the best selling author of the trending witchy duology, Unmarked; her debut series, Fae Rising; and beyond with The Never Sky series. Miranda has spent the past two decades reading romantic fantasy novels, and the last handful of years crafting similar worlds steeped in heartache, adventure, love, and loss. Her past work has taken her readers into the heart of a witch, alongside the journey of a high fae, through the oceans with a siren and prowling the rooftops with Death's Maiden. Now, she's found the determination of a dancer with Nevermore and Evermore.

Check out our website for extras, character art, and exclusive content. www.authormirandalyn.com

To sign up for the mailing list and get access to more exclusive content and giveaways, please visit

https://www.authormirandalyn.com/subscribe

Also by Miranda Lyn

www.ingramcontent.com/pod-product-compliance
Lightning Source LLC
Chambersburg PA
CBHW021932110726
47901CB00003B/810

* 9 7 9 8 9 9 2 3 4 3 3 4 2 *